SHIFTER SUSPENSE COLLECTION 1

ZOE CHANT

Copyright © 2021, 2022 by Zoe Chant

Cover by Marie Hodgkinson

All rights reserved.

No portion of this book may be reproduced in any form without written permission from the publisher or author, except as permitted by U.S. copyright law.

CONTENTS

Claimed by the Panther	1
CHAPTER 1	3
CHAPTER 2	13
CHAPTER 3	21
CHAPTER 4	37
CHAPTER 5	45
CHAPTER 6	59
CHAPTER 7	69
CHAPTER 8	77
CHAPTER 9	91
CHAPTER 10	103
CHAPTER 11	109
CHAPTER 12	125
CHAPTER 13	133
CHAPTER 14	141
CHAPTER 15	149
CHAPTER 16	155
CHAPTER 17	161

CHAPTER 18	165
CHAPTER 19	171
CHAPTER 20	177
CHAPTER 21	183
CHAPTER 22	199
EPILOGUE	209
EPILOGUE TWO	215
SAVED BY THE BILLIONAIRE LION SHIFTER	217
CHAPTER 1	219
CHAPTER 2	229
CHAPTER 3	237
CHAPTER 4	243
CHAPTER 5	253
CHAPTER 6	261
CHAPTER 7	277
CHAPTER 8	287
CHAPTER 9	297
CHAPTER 10	307
CHAPTER 11	313
CHAPTER 12	321
CHAPTER 13	327
CHAPTER 14	337
CHAPTER 15	345

CHAPTER 16	355
CHAPTER 17	363
CHAPTER 18	369
CHAPTER 19	383
CHAPTER 20	389
CHAPTER 21	399
CHAPTER 22	407
CHAPTER 23	417
CHAPTER 24	427
CHAPTER 25	439
CHAPTER 26	447
CHAPTER 27	463
CHAPTER 28	473
EPILOGUE	479
STEALING THE SNOW LEOPARD'S HEART	487
CHAPTER 1	489
CHAPTER 2	499
CHAPTER 3	511
CHAPTER 4	517
CHAPTER 5	527
CHAPTER 6	533
CHAPTER 7	541
CHAPTER 8	547

CHAPTER 9	555
CHAPTER 10	565
CHAPTER 11	571
CHAPTER 12	581
CHAPTER 13	595
CHAPTER 14	605
CHAPTER 15	621
CHAPTER 16	633
CHAPTER 17	643
CHAPTER 18	657
CHAPTER 19	661
CHAPTER 20	669
CHAPTER 21	673
CHAPTER 22	679
CHAPTER 23	687
CHAPTER 24	695
CHAPTER 25	703
CHAPTER 26	713
CHAPTER 27	719
EPILOGUE	733

CLAIMED BY THE PANTHER

SHIFTER SUSPENSE BOOK 1

Chapter 1

Irina

Irina Mathers tried not to catch sight of herself in the shop windows she was walking past.

The sound of her heels clacking on the sidewalk was bad enough. *Clack-clack, clack... clackclackclack* as she lost her balance, almost caught it, and almost lost it again.

This was a mistake, she thought, grabbing hold of a lamppost as her feet skidded under her for the tenth time. *Who decided high heels were appropriate footwear anywhere, let alone the middle of winter?*

She could be back in the mountains right now. She'd be just as cold and just as broke, but at least she'd be able to wear proper shoes without anyone sneering at her.

And she'd give up her one chance of making something of herself.

Irina looked up at the building in front of her. Light poured from the upstairs windows, but the street level was dark. Which meant it was as good as a mirror.

Irina took a deep breath. She was an artist, dammit. Couldn't she treat her body like one of her artworks? Not as literally as that one guy in her class had done, painting himself and rolling around on canvases, maybe, but surely there was something she could do to make her hair behave, or her face, or her... anything.

The face looking back at her from the window didn't fill her with confidence. The wind had slapped her cheeks red and her lips white. The dark shadows under her eyes were a nice contrast, at least. As for the rest of her...

She'd changed into her one good dress for the gallery opening, and her hair was still pinned back from her shift at the restaurant.

It could be worse.

Could be better, too.

The door slammed open. A young woman who managed somehow to be all angles and slinky at the same time stepped outside. Clare Farrell, Irina's roommate, was the reason she was here tonight. Clare had managed to sneak Irina's work into the opening when another artist had fallen out with the gallery owner.

From the look on her face as she stared at Irina, she was beginning to regret helping her out.

It's just Clare. You know she doesn't mean anything by it.

To cover her nerves, Irina rolled her eyes dramatically and pulled her winter coat closer around her plain dress.

"A 'hello' would be nice," she grumbled good-naturedly. "Can I come in? It's freezing out here."

Clare glared at her, sighed, and stepped aside so that Irina could scoot past her. "I was expecting you an hour ago! Where have you been?"

"My shift ran over, and I couldn't get away until my replacement showed up," Irina explained. "I promise I came as fast as I could."

She followed Clare up a flight of stairs to the gallery's back room and her heart sank slightly as she took in Clare's outfit.

How fancy is this event tonight? she thought, shaking off her coat.

Clare was wearing a slinky little black dress and pearls. Even her flyaway red hair was slicked back into a glossy up-do. Technically, Irina was wearing the same sort of outfit under her heavy winter coat as Clare was, but there was no way anything that fit over Irina's curves could ever be called a *little* black dress. And she could feel her dark curls escaping their thousand hairpins as she stood there in front of her best friend.

"No. No, no, no. You're not seriously wearing that tonight," Clare groaned as Irina hung up her coat. "No, God, Irina, don't do this to me! A black dress? *I'm* wearing a black dress, because I'm *staff*. You're—" She gestured up and down Irina's body then threw her head back and pressed the heels of her hands against her eyes. "I'm doomed. You're doomed. We're all doomed. Do you know who we're expecting tonight?"

"A pack of rich assholes who buy artwork by the square foot, and not because they appreciate our tortured artistic souls?"

"Hey. You sell even *one* square foot of art this evening, and your tortured soul has an apartment for another month. That's why we're here."

"I hadn't forgotten." Irina tried to avoid Clare's waving finger, but her friend followed her around.

"And you're not allowed to do your... thing." Clare's finger still waved perilously close to her nose, but her face betrayed real unease.

"My *thing?*"

"You know what I mean!" Clare's finger bent witchily. "Your *thing*. Where you stare at people and look straight into *their* tortured souls."

"Oh. That *thing*." Irina pushed her finger away. "Don't worry. I won't freak out the customers."

"Good."

Somewhere else in the building, an artistic wail of distress rose up. Clare growled under her breath and Irina took advantage of her brief distraction.

"I'll just disgust them with my horrible dress."

"Irina!" Clare shrieked. Then she raised both hands, hissed in a slow breath through her teeth, and smoothed her skirt. "You're doing this on purpose."

"Watch out. Next, I'll stare into your soul and see that you're really a little squeaky mouse on stilts."

Clare glared at her. "I'll bite you."

"With your mousy teeth?"

Irina laughed as her friend bared her perfectly non-mousy teeth at her and flung herself away out the door to deal with whoever was suffering from an artistic broken heart.

As soon as Clare was gone, her good mood fled, too. The laughter died in her throat. She ran her hands over her scalp and winced as another curl sprang free from her work-appropriate bun.

This always happened. So long as she had someone to bounce off, she could keep herself afloat. Leave her alone—to stare at herself in the mirrored darkness of a window or spruce herself up before a big night—and she sank.

There was a mirror in here, too. A huge one, wide and tall, meant for the sort of people who would enjoy looking in it.

"I look like I should be serving drinks tonight, not selling paintings," Irina whispered to herself. "What was I thinking? I'm a waitress, not a—a..."

The door swung open again. Clare fixed her with a determined stare, and her finger came up again. "*Don't* run away. I know I'm acting like a total bitch tonight, but—just stay. This could be your big break."

"I know!"

"Don't run off."

Irina took a deep breath. "I'm not going to—Clare, I'm *not* going to run off. Seriously. I know this is a great opportunity for me," she insisted, even though her tongue tripped over the words. "And I really appreciate you going to this much effort for my stupid paintings."

"They're *not* stupid. Creepy, yes. Stupid, no."

Creepy? But it was her portraits everyone said were creepy—the portraits she painted after she did her soul-staring *thing* and put more onto the canvas than people wanted to see. And she hadn't painted anyone's portrait in years. All the paintings Clare had sorted through to pick some for tonight had been landscapes.

Irina raised her hands in defeat. "Okay, yes, I swear not to say they're stupid *or* creepy in front of anyone who might buy them. Promise."

"Good." Clare disappeared partway around the door. "Remember. No running away and none of *this*." She circled her eyes with her finger, jabbed it at Irina again, and disappeared.

Irina bit her lip. She wanted to tell herself she was hurt that Clare would accuse her of wanting to run away. After all, wasn't this what she had always wanted? The opportunity to show her paintings in a real art gallery, as though she was a real artist and not just a college dropout who waited tables and painted when she could spare a few dollars for oils?

The problem was it was true. Irina had run away from every big change in her life so far, so why would Clare think she would do any different now? She lost momentum and sank, every time. She had dropped out of art school and run away home to the mountains. Then, when her Gran died, she'd run away back to the city. And then she'd spent the next few years yo-yoing back and forth. Sinking further every time.

She stared at the face in the mirror. Would it be easier if she could see in her own reflection what she saw in so many other faces? That hint of something *more*. She called Clare a homicidal mouse, but that was just for fun. She didn't really have something strange and inhuman looking out through her eyes.

Not like some people.

That was her *thing*. She saw too much. Things that weren't real. And she put them in her paintings. That strange, magical something *more*.

She knew it was just her imagination, but it had to be easier to be them, didn't it? To be more than just yourself.

If she had more than just herself behind her eyes, maybe she would stop running away.

Or maybe I'm crazy. Seeing things. She closed her eyes.

Anyway, she'd told Clare she wasn't going to run away. This time, things would be different. She was determined. Clare had fought tooth and nail to get her manager to accept a few of Irina's paintings into this exhibition, and she wasn't going to let her down.

Even if it had taken every inch of self-control she had to work herself up to actually showing up this evening, and it was only because she'd filled the last two days with back-to-back shifts that she hadn't had the time to panic and pull out.

After all, what's the worst that can happen? You spend the evening guzzling free champagne in the corner, while people who actually know about art look down their noses at your silly pictures?

When she opened her eyes again, she ignored everything except the bits of her reflection she could fix: her hair, her lipstick, and her customer-service smile. Then she went to find Clare.

When she did, she swept Clare into a quick hug. "Thanks for this, Clare. You're an angel. And I promise I'm not going to disappear on you."

Clare grumbled incoherently into Irina's collarbone. "Just don't change your mind when you see who RSVP'd."

Clare peeled herself out of the hug and smoothed her dress, not meeting Irina's eye as she asked: "Who? Who is it?"

But Clare was already halfway down the corridor and didn't hear her question—or didn't want to spoil the surprise. *Or scare me off, more likely.* Irina swore under her breath.

Clare's warning hadn't been enough. Irina gasped as she slipped through the door into the main gallery space.

The decor was almost painfully fashionable, the distressed bare-concrete, exposed-rebar look where you could tell every speck of rust had been lovingly buffed into place.

But that wasn't the most impressive thing about the space. Directly opposite the staff door, the exterior wall was one massive pane of glass, giving the impression that the room opened straight into the empty air outside the fifth story of the building. Snowflakes whirled like galaxies caught in the light.

It looked amazing, and Irina's heart sank. *Clare was right*, she realized glumly. *I'm going to stick out like a sore thumb here.*

There were only two ways you could face a room like this: either go in looking as fashionably trashed as the decor, or 180 degrees in the opposite direction, crisp and smart as a diamond in the rough.

Irina's outfit didn't fit either category. Not smart enough to contrast, and not casual enough to fit in. Just *shabby*.

Shit. What is this place?

The exhibition opening had already, well, opened, and the first of the guests were beginning to mill around, investigating the drinks and canapes with as much enthusiasm as the artworks.

Irina's breath caught in her throat. When Clare told her that she'd gotten Irina's paintings a spot in a new gallery exhibition, Irina had assumed she meant a small local gallery. When she'd joked about rich people buying art by the square foot, she'd meant *normal* rich people. This place was small, but from the look of the guests, it was the small that meant 'boutique and exclusive' rather than 'can't afford the rent on a bigger place.'

And as for the buyers...

Irina took a deep breath. *Too late to back out.* She might not be as perfectly turned-out as some of the guests here—or as fashionably untidy as the others—but, too bad. She was here now.

After all, those were *her* paintings on the wall.

Irina had done more than wait tables back in the Adirondacks. She had walked around the mountains and valleys, explored them—and painted what she had seen. The mountains, and the people.

She'd been visiting her grandmother out in the mountains since she was a little girl, and it never lost its magic, seeing people in the wilderness. There was something raw and vulnerable about the way people reacted to the impersonal power of the natural world. She'd seen people look at the mountains and see something close to God, and she'd seen people look and see how easily a rockfall or a river could sweep them away to nothing. And some people—the ones who had something *more* behind their eyes—found a connection that hit them like a boot between the eyes.

Those people, if they were lucky—or maybe unlucky—found a tall, fat woman with wild dark hair and creepy eyes staring at them from behind her sketchbook like she wanted to pull their soul out through their nostrils. She didn't put herself in her paintings. It was risky, really, even thinking about other people while she was painting. Sometimes too much got in even if she wasn't painting a portrait.

There was certainly nothing of herself in the paintings Clare had chosen for the exhibition. The burning summer tones and exuberant, harsh brushstrokes of her mountain landscapes were everything she wasn't. Powerful, assured, and a perfect fit for the gallery. The life she'd breathed onto the canvas confronted the stark surroundings, bringing the wilderness inside. And the contrast between the midsummer landscapes and the icy night outside…

Irina's heart lifted as she took in the sight. Clare was an angel. Somehow she'd wrangled things so that Irina's work was presented front and center. If even one of her paintings sold tonight, it could make her career.

Especially if whoever bought it was famous enough that everyone else wanted their own Irina Mathers original, too. She might joke about rich art-buyers, but that didn't mean she wouldn't roll around in their money if they threw it at her.

There were three of Irina's paintings on display. She gazed at the central one, a huge mountain landscape, and froze.

Oh no. Clare chose *that* one?

Why?

The canvas was wider across than Irina's arm-span, and almost as tall as she was. If the window across the far wall made you think you could step out into space, then this painting was like a portal into summer.

And Irina couldn't look at it without her stomach curling. The mountains were just as magnificent as in the other two canvases, the sky as endless, the roar of the wild almost audible—but this painting was full of a heavy, broken loneliness that left her wanting to weep. She'd painted it without knowing what it would turn out like, her mind full of one of the people with *something more* that she'd run into on the trails. His soul was there, on the canvas, and it hurt to look at.

Why? Irina wanted to scream. Why this one? How could Clare tell her not to do her *thing*, her creepy, soul-seeing *thing*, and then put *this painting* on her wall?

Heart thudding, Irina searched the crowd. A familiar face caught her eye. Tay, whose wail of despair had called Clare away earlier, gave her a shy wave. Tay had been in her class the one year Irina had managed to spend at art school, so Irina was familiar with both his dramatic cries of doom and how embarrassed he inevitably was after them.

Irina returned his wave and made her way across the room, scanning the gathered faces for Clare. One friendly face was great, but two would be even better. And—maybe it wasn't too late to take *that painting* down.

Chapter 2

Grant

"Is this the place?"

Grant stared up at the building. The contrast between the staid brickwork of the lower floors and the floor-to-ceiling, crystal clear fifth floor window was startling. It looked as though someone had sliced away the front wall to peer in at the inhabitants.

And as if that wasn't bad enough, it was starting to snow.

Grant's panther hated the snow. It hated the cold. It hated the city. Its emotions were separate from his own feelings, but still distinctly *there*, a constant, irritating itch.

He hated that he could feel them at all. He'd spent most of the last six months as a panther, trying to get it out of his system, but its instincts were still so close to the surface. If he had been in his panther form, he would have flattened his ears at the cold stuff and maybe even snarled at what his human brain knew were harmless white flakes.

Since he was in human form, he was spared the embarrassment of growling at *snow* in front of his old friend and new bodyguard, Lance MacInnis.

"This is it," Lance confirmed without glancing up. "You think she'll be here?"

Grant shrugged. "It's art, it's new, it's on a street I didn't know existed in a neighborhood that would make her mother scream—it's pure Frankie."

"And you're sure this is a good idea?"

Grant glared at the other man. "You clearly think not. Is that your official opinion?"

Lance snorted, his gray-green eyes fixed on the window above them. The young black man was solidly built beneath his well-tailored and fashionably styled suit, but the glasses he pulled from one pocket to perch on his nose gave a hint of incongruity to his appearance.

"My opinion as your bodyguard is that for a man of your demographic, gallery openings are a high-boredom, low-return investment of your time. And as your friend..." He peered at Grant over the top of his glasses. "There are *easier* ways for you to go about this, you know."

"I don't want to hear it." Grant's shoulders tensed.

"I'm just saying—if Mathis Delacourt isn't picking up the phone or checking in on Facebook, well, those are *human* ways to connect."

"This isn't up for discussion, Lance."

"Understood." The other man's face was professionally blank.

Are you in there, Frankie? And will you be able to give me some answers?

He was careful to keep the question to himself. The last thing he wanted was to reach out telepathically to another shifter. Even if it wasn't considered rude to broadcast telepathic messages before you actually saw a person, he was back in the city, now.

And in the city, he played human. No. He *was* human.

Grant's spine prickled, the same uneasy feeling that had been plaguing him for the last few weeks. He clenched his fist, trying to shake the sensation of wrongness.

His plan was so simple, it was hardly a plan. He would go in, find Frankie, and talk to her. And it was only natural that the talk would turn to her twin brother.

Yeah, and why I haven't heard a peep out of him since I got back from the jungle.

Up until a year ago, Mathis Delacourt had been Grant's closest friend. They had grown up together, two shifters causing endless trouble for themselves, each other, and their families. It had been a competitive friendship, but a close one. Grant had never been completely comfortable with his shifter nature, but without Mathis and his family, he never would have known the first thing about what being a shifter meant. Grant's mother was human and had been abandoned by his shifter father before Grant was even born.

Grant had always envied the family structure of the Delacourt pride. For lions, family was everything. For panthers—well. His father had abandoned his partner and unborn child. What else needed to be said? There was a reason Grant kept his animal and human lives separate.

Something had changed in the months before Grant left to exercise his panther. Mathis had seemed distracted. Grant himself had found it difficult to concentrate, his panther so restless it felt as though it was always about to burst through his skin, and now he could maybe admit to himself that he hadn't paid close enough attention to his friend. He'd stepped back and focused on his own needs, and Mathis had done the same.

By the time Grant came back into the country, Mathis had stepped back so far he'd vanished. All of Grant's calls and messages had gone unanswered.

Grant was a panther. They weren't pack animals—not like Mathis and his lion's pride. Not family-oriented. He didn't *need* to be around others to feel secure with his place in the world.

But, damn it, he did need his oldest friend to at least pick up the phone once in a while.

Tonight's mission might not unearth Mathis, but Grant was hoping that his friend's twin sister, Francine—Frankie—would find the lure of the art event too tempting to resist. Frankie and he might not have always gotten along, but surely she would at least give him some answers about why Mathis had ghosted him.

Time to find out, he told himself as he stepped out onto the street. Snowflakes settled on his shoulders as he hurried to the front door, his panther inwardly seething at the cold weather.

Lance fell into step beside him. He seemed completely at ease in the freezing weather—a side-effect of being a snow leopard shifter, Grant assumed, or maybe something to do with his military background. Whereas Grant's panther longed for the sticky heat of the jungle, Lance's feline form relished the ice and snow. Even in human form, Lance didn't seem to feel the cold.

Grant felt better the moment he stepped through the front door and into the warm embrace of central heating. By the time the elevator spat them out on the fifth floor, he was almost purring.

He took a moment to make sure that he wasn't. Satisfied, he glanced around the room.

The gallery was full of people. Grant took a slow breath as he looked around. He couldn't help it; even in his human form, he instinctively tried to identify the guests by scent as much as by sight.

Most of them were strangers, but one familiar scent made him turn his head to the end of the room.

Francine Delacourt was a statuesque platinum blonde, with skin as white as snow and iceberg-blue eyes. She looked a little like Marilyn Monroe, if Marilyn had been six feet tall and possessed all the warmth and kindness of a glacier.

Even when they were in human shape, lion shifters—like all predator shifters—had this aura of sheer *power* around them. Mathis used his in the ring, keeping his opponents on edge. Frankie used hers—or at least, so Grant had heard—to keep her company's board of directors in line. Right now, she seemed to be happily terrifying a circle of onlookers in front of some paintings of mountains.

"There's Frankie," he said, relieved his hunch had been correct. Then his shoulders slumped. He knew it was too much to hope for that Mathis would be here with his sister—the two might be twins, but they were far from inseparable—but some small part of him still grated at not finding his friend here. Frankie was holding court alone.

"You need me to come glare at her with you?"

Grant shook himself out of his restless thoughts and glanced at Lance. "This isn't a shakedown, Lance. I just want to talk to her. Go guard the canapes or something."

Lance snorted and moved away. Grant rubbed his forehead. This *wasn't* a shakedown—so why did he feel so strange? His skin was still prickling with the same sense of wrongness he'd felt earlier.

Or—was it wrongness? Or was it just *different*? A new, unsettling sensation. Something he couldn't identify. Something from his shifter side.

Someone's here. His panther bared its teeth inside him. If he'd been in the jungle still, he'd have slunk into the shadows, every sense alert as he waited for his instincts to zero in on what was wrong, on the watch for poachers or another predator.

In the city, though...

I'm in a crowded room, with my bodyguard behind me and a lioness shifter in front of me. What's the worst thing that could happen?

Frankie's white-gold hair shone like a flame at the far end of the room as Grant made his way toward her. He slipped easily through the crowd, people moving out of his way without even noticing they were doing it. Lions might ooze raw, visceral power, but panthers had their own effect on bystanders. Grant might not like it, but he had to admit it was useful.

He was only halfway there when Frankie turned around. The painting on the wall behind her was all burnished gold and umber, and her light face and hair stood out against it like a beacon. Her eyebrows drew together as she locked eyes with him, and a strange expression stole briefly over her face. She quickly smoothed it away, but the smile that replaced it looked strained.

She mouthed something, too quietly and too far away for Grant to hear it.

Frankie? he called out silently and saw her frown. She turned away and thrust her wine glass into the hand of the woman she'd been standing in front of. Grant could have sworn he saw her spine stiffen before she turned back.

It was so like Frankie to just hand her glass off to some poor human bystander. The woman wasn't one of waiters, with their expressions of mingled boredom and superiority. She was wearing a soft-looking black dress that hugged her generous curves and was almost as tall as Frankie. Unusual, for a human.

Grant raised his eyes to the woman's face, intending to give her an apologetic smile. Instead, he felt as though he'd been struck by lightning.

Next to Frankie's gleaming blonde hair and silver dress, this other woman should have faded into the background. Her dark curls haloed her face, and the dress that clung jealously to her curves was a matte black that seemed designed for blending in with shadows.

Instead, she was suddenly the only person in the room he could focus on.

Grant's eyes swept back up to her face, searching for—what? She wasn't even looking at him. Her eyes were cast down, looking at the half-empty wineglass Frankie had pushed on her. Her lips quirked, and she glanced up at Frankie's back—and past her, to him.

The strange feeling that had dogged Grant since they pulled up outside the gallery was swept away, replaced by a hot, thrumming need. It was a sexual need—*Oh, hell, is it sexual*, he thought, swallowing—but it was more than that, too. And it terrified him.

The woman's eyes were dark, a brown so deep they seemed almost black. When Grant looked into them, he was gripped by a need to protect so overwhelming that it was all he could do not to leap across the room and take her into his arms.

Go to her! his panther demanded. It wanted to break free, to make him shift and stalk through the room on four legs, tail lashing, a barely veiled threat aimed at anyone who would harm her. The scents of the room grew stronger as he came closer to shifting, his animal senses becoming sharper.

No, he told himself, and his panther, with all the self-control he could muster. *That is a bad idea. That is the WORST idea. What are you thinking?*

And this is the worst possible timing for—for this.

He knew what was happening. The thing he was most afraid of.

This woman, this *human* woman, was his mate. His soulmate.

He had spent the last six months letting his panther off the leash, in the hopes that that time in the wild would exhaust it. And now he felt as though he'd fallen into a trap from which there was no escape.

No. The situation wasn't the trap. His shifter nature was.

All shifters were meant to want to find their soulmate. It was a magic more powerful than their ability to shift, or their telepathic powers. True love; the sacred connection between two hearts. It was practically holy—and wholly inescapable.

Or it would be, until his panther tired of his soulmate like his father had his mother.

In one moment, as he stared at the dark-haired woman, Grant's heart was made whole and broke into a thousand pieces.

She was his soulmate. The one woman he would ever love.

The woman the creature in his soul would betray.

Chapter 3
Irina

The evening had gone to complete crap.

Clare refused to do anything about the painting. She called it a *conversation piece*. Said it was *striking*.

Like a knife to the gut, Irina wanted to say.

And then Francine Delacourt had turned up.

Sleek, gorgeous, and dripping with self-confidence, Francine Delacourt was a permanent fixture of the sort of *Top Thirty Under Thirty* listicles that seemed specifically designed to make everyone else feel like a pathetic under-achiever. Not only was she immensely wealthy, she was thickly built but had the confidence to wear her curves like a queen.

Irina wasn't sure which she envied more: Francine's money or her confidence.

Except the confidence probably comes at least a bit from the money, she reasoned. *If I could afford a dress like THAT, I would never have to worry about unsexy mono-boob ever again.*

She had the perfect opportunity to examine Francine's dress because the first thing the woman had done when she arrived was to stalk across to stand in front of Irina's paintings. Which would have been great, except...

Everyone knew about Francine Delacourt. Even Irina. She'd never met her, but she'd heard all the gossip about the ice queen of the art scene.

With a single word, Francine Delacourt could make an artist—or destroy their career forever.

Tonight, for God knows what reason, she had decided to terrorize the few people who had gathered to look at Irina's work.

Tay, bless him, had slunk away the moment the blonde woman had showed up. Irina didn't blame him. The last thing any artist wanted was to be next in Francine Delacourt's line of fire.

It was certainly the last thing *she* wanted.

You promised Clare you wouldn't run away, she told herself. *You promised.*

On the other hand... you made that promise based on the assumption that Francine Delacourt *wasn't going to turn up and rip you to shreds.*

And the door is only a few yards away...

The door might as well have been ten miles away. Irina couldn't have reached it if she tried. Francine was standing so close to her that Irina could count the diamond chips in her earrings, and Irina's feet were glued to the floor.

First, Francine stared at the paintings, her pale blue eyes expressionless. Then she swung her head around and stared directly at Irina.

It was like being caught in a spotlight. Irina felt like an ant trying to scurry away from a magnifying glass.

"Disappointing, isn't it?"

It wasn't actually a question. It might have been worded like one, but Francine's tone left no room for alternative views.

"Er," Irina said helplessly. "Yes?"

Francine waved one arm lazily, encompassing the entire room. "Look at them all. Two days ago, no one had even heard of this place. My idiot assistant makes one post on God knows what social media platform about the exhibition, and suddenly... lemmings. Desperate, squeaking lemmings."

Her mouth twisted, and Irina couldn't tell if it was in frustration or disgust. She still felt pinned in place and took a swig of wine to cover her nerves.

"Why are you here, then?" she blurted as soon as she finished swallowing, and immediately wished she'd just chugged the whole glass. *And lost the ability to talk. And passed out. And been taken away by an ambulance, never to be seen again.*

Francine's gaze grew even sharper, something Irina wouldn't have thought was possible.

"Certainly not for the artwork," she replied with a sniff. Her eyes slid sideways, and Irina sagged with relief that she was no longer under the spotlight.

Until she realized the other woman was now looking at the paintings. *Her* paintings.

"Are these yours?" Francine said, her voice expressionless.

"Yes," mumbled Irina, wishing a hole would appear in the floor under her feet. Across the room, Clare was staring at her wide-eyed, waving her hands in the universal gesture for 'Talk!'

But not, Irina noted, actually coming over to join the conversation herself.

"I, er," Irina stammered, glaring at Clare. *Come on. You can do this. Just... try to sound like you're meant to be here. Like you're not massively intimidated by everyone here, not just Francine.*

She cleared her throat. "Yes, I—er—I *summered* in the Adirondacks, and had a bit of free time to work on these. Clare—that is, the gallery manager—insisted I bring them with me back here, and..." Irina trailed off.

Summered? Is that something people still say? Or ever said?

Irina bit her lip and gave a shrug that she hoped looked casual and sophisticated, and not like she was a turtle trying to hide in its shell. Inside, she was groaning. *Can we rewind that and try again?*

Francine was still staring at the paintings with her ice-blue eyes. "The Adirondacks? I wonder…" She paused briefly, her perfect eyebrows drawing together. "Did you happen to meet…?"

Irina waited on tenterhooks for Francine to finish the sentence. She had the horrible feeling that she had fallen into some sort of art-world pop quiz. Any minute now, she would get something wrong, and Francine Delacourt and everyone else would know what a fake she was.

The pause lengthened into an even more uncomfortable silence. Francine was still staring at the painting, her eyes glassy.

"Did I meet…?" Irina repeated. "I mean, I met a lot of people, of course, it's very popular. Lots of outdoor activities. Lots of mountains." Her words echoed in her mind. *Lots of mountains? Are you serious right now?* "People also like the rivers." *Oh God. Stop. STOP.*

Thankfully, Francine was too distracted to notice Irina's babbling. She shook herself, as though she was waking up from a daydream and fixed her eyes on Irina again.

Irina promptly shut up.

Francine stared at her with the same intensity as she had just been inspecting the paintings. And Irina felt—*awful.*

Her heart was thudding in her ears, and her whole body was jittery with nervous energy. The last time she'd felt like this, she'd been clinging to a rope handrail ten feet above a stream, after a bridge she was crossing started to collapse. Irina had inched her way safely back to solid ground, but her body hadn't decided it was safe until she was back at the cottage that evening.

It was the same here. Nothing was wrong, nothing bad was happening—but Irina's body wasn't convinced.

What the hell? It's one thing to be nervous, but this is just… what's wrong with you? Even her tongue was frozen stiff. She felt… well, *terrified*, but wasn't that a bit over-the-top?

Finally, Francine broke her gaze, and said:

"Self-taught?"

Irina sagged with short-lived relief. Her palms were sweating from the intensity of—of whatever had just happened.

Oh, well. Here it goes, thought Irina miserably. *The tragic tales of the art-school dropout.*

She squared her shoulders. "Actually, I—"

She stopped as Francine held up one hand. "Wait."

Irina stared at the other woman's hand, mouth still open. She shut it with a *clack*. Francine Delacourt's hand was perfectly manicured, a sliver-thin gold ring her only jewelry. And she had stuck it palm-out in Irina's face to shut her up.

Worst of all, it had *worked*. Francine turned away, scanning the room, and Irina was left hanging.

Irina was already on edge from their strange, constantly shifting conversation, and now she felt her nerves flare into anger. *How dare she?*

Her anger sharpened. *Everything* sharpened. Thin lines of light appeared around Francine, limning her in shivering colors like the beginning of a migraine.

She was doing her *thing*.

She snapped her eyes shut. *I promised Clare!* And no matter how much of a snob Francine Delacourt was, going full freakazoid on her was *not* going to make Irina's career. *Break it forever into tiny pieces, more like.*

Irina felt sick. This was all going wrong. Clare and Tay had both vanished, and she didn't blame them, but...

Francine made a disgusted noise and thrust her wineglass into Irina's hand. She stared at it blankly. She had never felt so absolutely alone when surrounded by people. The sinking feeling caught her like a hook in her stomach, pulling her down. Making her want to run. She bit her lip and glanced around the gallery, desperate for a friendly face. No one was even looking in her direction, or if anyone was, it was only with short, furtive glances, as though afraid of attracting Francine's attention.

The only person who was facing Francine and Irina head-on was a man who must have just arrived. Irina didn't recognize him from her earlier scans of the room. And she knew she would have remembered him. He ticked all the boxes: tall, handsome, and well-built under his expensive-looking suit.

Francine was still directing her laser-glare elsewhere, so Irina let her own eyes linger longer on this newcomer than she usually would have. Or maybe it was just that she couldn't tear her eyes away from him.

Anyway, she reasoned with herself, *I must be practically invisible here, stuck behind Francine—so it's not like anyone's going to notice me staring, right?*

And, wow, was there a lot to stare at. The man had amazing cheekbones, and a sensuous jawline that looked all the better for a dark dusting of five-o'clock shadow. His black hair curled and was just long enough to swing flirtily over his eyes. And his eyes—his eyes were such an intense, vivid green that every other color in the room looked dull by comparison.

Irina closed her eyes and allowed herself one millisecond of a daydream in which this attractive stranger swept her off her feet and carted her off somewhere far, far away from Francine Delacourt.

She opened her eyes—and froze.

The handsome stranger was staring straight at her. For one moment, his eyes widened, as though he recognized her. But that wasn't possible. Irina knew she would remember if she had ever met him before.

And then he smiled, a slow, sensuous smile that was like the sun rising.

Irina's own lips began to curve in automatic response.

"*Excuse* me." Francine's voice hit Irina like a bucket of ice. In response, Irina snapped her eyes away from the handsome stranger. Francine was staring at her again, but somehow, her gaze didn't seem so terrifying this time.

"Yes?" Irina asked, wondering if Francine wanted her wineglass back. She gaped as Francine turned on her heel and stalked off.

Irina looked down at her full hands and gulped. *Did I miss something? What the hell just happened?*

She watched Francine's retreating back, as much to convince herself that the woman was actually leaving as anything else and saw that the other woman was striding directly towards the green-eyed man who had smiled at her.

Oh.

It wasn't me he was smiling at, at all, Irina thought, her heart sinking. He must have been smiling at Francine. That made a lot more sense.

She took a deep breath to calm herself down before looking down at her two wineglasses. The deep breath turned into an even deeper sigh.

So much for leaving waitressing behind.

And so much for being an artist.

Tears pricked at her eyes, and she blinked furiously. It wasn't just that Francine Delacourt had been so strangely terrifying—it was the fact that everyone in the room must have just seen her blow off Irina's work, guaranteeing that no one would bother to give her paintings so much as a second look. If the culture vultures at tonight's event were only here because they were following Francine's footsteps, they were hardly going to buy something their queen found no value in.

So where did that leave Irina? Standing by herself in the corner, holding two half-drunk glasses of wine.

She could drink the wine, she supposed. It couldn't possibly make her look *more* pathetic.

Irina clenched her jaw, willing herself not to cry. It wasn't like she should even really be upset. Her art had always been just something she did for fun. A hobby. Silly and pointless. Maybe she could have had a chance to make more of it years ago, but she lost that chance when she dropped out of art school. And, sure, it had been nice of Clare to think of Irina when she had a panic with a spare spot in the exhibition, but that was all her paintings were. A placeholder.

Irina squeezed her eyes shut. *If you're upset, it's your own fault for imagining this evening could lead to anything more.*

She had to get out of here. She had to get rid of these stupid glasses of stupid expensive wine, get her coat from out of the back, and—just *flee*.

Irina turned on her heel and almost walked straight into someone. Her eyes were swimming, and it took a moment for the dark splodge in front of her to resolve into a man wearing a charcoal-colored suit and silk shirt. The shirt was unbuttoned at the neck, right in line with Irina's eyes, revealing a triangle of bare, tanned skin.

"Hello," said a low voice, and Irina tore her eyes away from his neck. She looked up, and her world flipped upside down for the second time in as many minutes.

It was the handsome stranger, her pipe-dream knight in shining armor. Standing in front of her. *Right* in front of her.

Right. There.

Oh, hell, Irina thought, blinking furiously. He was so close she could have reached out and touched him.

Close enough to see that I'm ten seconds away from bawling my eyes out. God, how embarrassing.

"Sorry," she muttered, trying to dodge around him, but he laid a gentle hand on her elbow.

"Is everything all right?" His voice was low, quiet enough that no one could hear him but her.

"Oh, sure, fine," Irina blurted automatically.

"Are you sure about that? Most people aren't *fine* after an encounter with Frankie."

Irina had been about to push past him, but at that, she paused. The man was looking down at her, concern in his green eyes.

"I'm fine. Really," Irina insisted. She even managed to hoist a smile onto her face, although her mind felt like it was flying in a thousand directions at once. *Frankie?* "Do you know her? Because if you're worried about Ms. Delacourt terrorizing the guests, it's a bit late for me. You should probably go head her off before she picks her next victim."

Oh, good job, she thought bitterly. *Bitch about his friend right in front of him. You're so goddamn smooth.*

"The only person I'm worried about is you."

He sounded sincere. And he looked sincere, too, with no hint of sarcasm in his green eyes. Irina turned to face him in spite of herself. There was no way she was sticking around here to sob in the corner, but something about this man...

Maybe he had been smiling at her, after all. It hardly seemed possible, but—

He must have brushed right past Francine to come over here. The thought filled her with a sort of fierce glee. *Anyone* brushing off Francine Delacourt to speak to her instead would have been a miracle, but a man as good-looking as this?

It hardly seemed possible.

He was waiting for her to speak, his vivid green eyes on her. She remembered the careful catalogue she had been making of his various attributes before he caught her staring, and almost blushed before she considered what he must be seeing now.

Let's break it down, she thought, swallowing hard. *Wild hair, probably three-fourths fallen down by now. A dress that cost less than one of his designer socks. And no amount of foundation in the world can hide how blotchy I get when I'm about to cry...*

Now that he could see her up close, he was probably regretting coming within ten feet of her.

"Well, that's very sweet of you," she said at last. She held up the two sad, half-empty wineglasses and attempted another grin. *Let's both get out of this with as much of our dignity intact as we can manage.* "If you'll excuse me, I've got to..."

...Got to ditch these, slink out the back door, and spend the rest of the evening eating chocolate ice-cream in my PJs, waiting for Clare to come back to the apartment and put me on a guilt trip for running away.

Talk about pathetic. But what was the alternative? Hang around here until closing time, hoping Francine Delacourt didn't swing by for round two?

"I can help you with that, at the very least," the man murmured with a smile that made long dimples appear in the corners of his mouth, putting deeper shadows in his dark stubble. Before Irina knew what was happening, he lifted the glasses from her hands. His fingertips just brushed against hers, so softly she thought she might have imagined it.

Her surprise turned into indignation as a waiter almost immediately appeared and whisked the glasses away.

"Oh, *seriously*?" she burst out. "I was standing here holding those for how long, and you turn up and—pow!"

The man's mouth quirked. "Call it a knack."

"I *work* in hospitality. If there was a knack to catching a waiter's attention, you'd think I would know it," Irina grumbled. She knew she couldn't blame the waitperson, though. If there was a knack, it probably involved more "looking around for a nearby waiter" than "staring at your toes and sulking."

Not that this guy had been looking at anyone.

Except her.

In fact, he hadn't taken his eyes off her since he walked up to her.

Irina felt suddenly breathless. She smoothed her hands down her dress, trying to pull herself together.

"All right, Mr. Waitstaff-Magician," she said, hoping her face didn't betray her battling emotions. "I'm Irina. And what should I call you?"

His eyes widened slightly in surprise. "I—oh. Yes. Grant Diaz."

Irina held out her hand. "It's a pleasure to meet you, Grant Diaz. And your magical wineglass-disappearing powers." *And your Francine Delacourt-vanquishing powers.*

Grant took her hand in his. His hand dwarfed hers, but he didn't wring the bones of her hand together like some men did when shaking hands. His grip was firm but careful, and when he pulled his hand away, his fingertips brushed against hers and lingered.

"The pleasure is all mine."

Oh.

Irina felt unmoored, drifting in unfamiliar waters. Her mind was in a million places at once, and in its absence, her body took charge. She found herself reaching out, her fingers tangling with his, and sank into the green depths of Grant's eyes.

Had she really left those two half-glasses of wine undrunk? It usually took at least two glasses to make her feel this floaty.

"So, what brings you here tonight?"

Irina came back to Earth with a jolt and snatched her hand back. *What are you doing?* she berated herself, blushing furiously. Grant looked...

Disappointed?

Irina shook her head, which was full of images of lush jungles and deep mountain lakes reflecting the dark green of the trees. Oh no. Had she done it again, without even noticing?

She blinked. No creepy auras. She was safe.

It was a miracle that Grant Diaz even noticed her existence, and she was not going to ruin it by going all Sith Lord on him.

"What brings me here? Apart from the opportunity to act as Francine Delacourt's drinks table?" she joked, nodding over her shoulder to the paintings on the wall. "These, um, these are mine. My friend Clare knows the owner of this gallery and did me a favor. She must have thought they would fit in the, uh. The space available. On the walls."

She winced, but Grant didn't seem to notice that she was babbling.

"Beautiful," he said softly. But he wasn't looking at the paintings. His warm green eyes, edged with those decadently thick lashes, were still focused on her.

Irina caught her breath. She *couldn't* be imagining this. The lingering glances—and the lingering *touches*.

It was crazy. Men like this weren't interested in girls like her. Talk about being out of her league—Grant Diaz was playing an entirely different sport. He looked like he'd just walked off the cover of *World's Sexiest Men*. Not that there was such a magazine, but probably that was just because no one in the magazine business had seen Mr. Tall, Dark, and Delicious yet.

I'm babbling, Irina realized. *I'm babbling inside my own mind. God, he's so sexy.*

And I'm just standing here, staring at him. Come on! Stop it! Pull yourself together before he figures out what a complete weirdo you are.

"Um, and what brings you here?" she asked after approximately ten thousand years.

A fleeting frown passed over Grant's face, but cleared as fast as it appeared. "I was going to talk to—it's not important. Not as important as finding you. I mean, meeting you. I mean—it's very nice to meet you."

He closed his eyes, tipped his head back, and groaned. Irina bit back a laugh, a feeling like relief flooding through her body. *Maybe he's as nervous about flirting with me as I am with him. I just can't believe a guy like this is getting flustered over—well, over* me.

Even embarrassed, Grant looked amazing, and Irina couldn't help enjoying the view. Her fingers twitched to trace the line of his jaw and to feel the scratch of his stubble against her fingertips. It was even worse than holding onto his fingers earlier. She clasped her hands behind her back.

When Grant opened his eyes again, they flared as though he knew exactly what she had been thinking. Irina's heart fluttered.

"Find me here? You were looking for me?" She said it without thinking.

"I think—I've always been looking for you." A small crease formed between his eyebrows, and he looked suddenly very serious.

Irina giggled. "Oh, *nice*. I haven't heard anything that cheesy since high school."

Grant's smile returned, slightly crooked. "Sorry. That was terrible, wasn't it?"

"Awful."

He winced. "*And* I owe you a drink. Now that I think about it, the grand gesture of rescuing you from being Frankie's side-table doesn't work when I take away your glass, as well."

Irina paused with her mouth open. *Francine.*

Her eyes widened as an awful thought struck her. Grant didn't seem interested in the paintings, so he couldn't have come here to appreciate the art. He must have been hoping to catch up with someone. And hadn't Francine looked strangely shocked to see Grant? And even less pleased to see Irina eyeing him up...

Oh, shit. Is he her ex, or something?

She bit her lip. There was no way she could let this pass without knowing for sure.

"Um. Is she the person you actually came here to see?" *Oh, God. Just say it.* "Uh, you two aren't...?"

"God, no." Grant sounded so shocked by the idea that Irina knew he was telling the truth. "I'm good friends with her brother. Her twin, actually. I was hoping to see him here tonight."

Irina looked around. There was no one in the room tall or blond or terrifying enough to be related to Francine Delacourt, let alone be her twin.

"I guess we're both at a loose end, then."

Grant's answering smile sent a shiver down her spine. He opened his mouth, and she found herself leaning forward.

"Am I interrupting?" Francine Delacourt's voice cut through the air.

Irina spun around. Francine was standing over her shoulder, glaring daggers at Grant.

"I—yes?" Irina said and instantly regretted it. She gulped. Honesty was probably not the best policy in the face of someone who looked like she was one bad mood away from stomping you underfoot.

Francine's expression was icy, but it wasn't Irina she was looking at. Irina didn't envy Grant being on the other end of her laser-beam eyes.

Not that he seemed bothered by it.

Maybe he's built up an immunity after knowing her brother for so long.

Grant nodded a greeting to the other woman. "How are you, Frankie? And how's Mathis these days?"

Francine bared her teeth in something that wasn't quite a smile. Irina shuffled sideways, uncomfortable to have Francine hovering at her shoulder, and—not entirely accidentally—found herself standing at Grant's side.

"Mathis spent the summer traveling," Francine said slowly. "And Lance tells me you've been... in the mountains?"

"You know me. Six months of trees and rocks, then holing up here over winter." Grant cast a quick smile in Irina's direction, and she found herself smiling back.

"Hiking and hibernation?" Irina found herself saying. "If that's not the recipe for a perfect life, I don't know what is."

Francine's eyes sparked. "What would you know about it?" she practically barked.

Irina blinked. *Uh, what the hell?*

She gestured at the paintings on the wall beside them. Francine followed her gesture, eyes narrowing.

"The *disappointing* Adirondacks—remember?" The words came out a bit sharper than Irina had intended. Standing next to Grant must be giving her more courage to stand up for herself. She steadied her gaze on Francine, and the world went sharp again.

This time, she didn't fight it. *Let's see how you react to someone else freaking you out*, she growled silently.

The shivering lines around Francine brightened, but it was the other woman's eyes she focused on. There was something *more* behind them. Something not human. Not for the first time, Irina wondered if she really was crazy. She looked deeper—*Powerful muscles, a body made for hunting, bone-crunching teeth, the strength of the pack behind her, the scent of her prey in the wind—*

Grant shifted his weight, closing the distance between himself and Irina. The back of his hand brushed against her bare arm and the touch knocked her out of her trance.

She blinked. Francine was staring at her, her eyes flat and angry.

"I see." Francine's voice was quiet, but there was steel in it.

"I was hoping to catch up with Mathis now that I'm back in the city, but I'm having trouble getting hold of him," Grant said lightly.

Francine stared at him. "The last time I saw my brother, he was looking forward to seeing you," she hissed as she swept away.

"Well... great. Thanks," Grant said to her briskly retreating back. He rubbed his forehead with the back of his hand. "That woman gets more terrifying every time I see her."

Irina met his eyes and smiled. It was meant to be a chirpy smile, but it turned out a bit wobbly. "Terrifying is right."

Grant's eyes narrowed as he glanced in the direction Francine had disappeared, and his knuckles brushed against the back of Irina's hand again. The closeness of his body and the touch of his hand did more to make Irina feel better than anything he could have said. Somehow, just having him near her made her feel... safe. Protected.

The thought lit a warm spark inside her, and against her better instincts, she slipped her hand into his. Grant turned toward her.

"Even Frankie isn't usually that intense. If that's the way she was behaving before I came over—well, I'm sorry I didn't arrive sooner." He squeezed her hand.

Irina felt her cheeks go red. "True, well, unfortunately, I don't think I can forgive you for something that happened before you even knew I existed. On top of that... I'm still busy not forgiving you for stealing my drink."

She held her breath. Her mind might have been scattershot earlier, but now, every particle of her body was sharply focused. On his tall, strong body, so close to hers that she could feel the heat of it radiating toward her. On his hand holding on to hers.

And on his eyes. His gleaming, forest-green eyes, and the way he looked at her like she was someone special.

It had been a long time since anyone looked at her like that.

She held her breath and waited.

"Forget the drink," Grant said, and for a moment Irina's heart sank.

But only for a moment, because the next thing he said was: "Let me take you to dinner."

Chapter 4

Grant

Say yes. Say yes, he begged silently, staring into her dark eyes. He was looking into them so intently, he almost missed the blush that spread across her cheeks.

Then she raised her chin. "All right. I think dinner would *almost* make up for your vast and numerous errors."

Grant's panther purred in his chest. The noise was so loud in his mind that he had to take a moment to check that he wasn't making any sound out loud. His slip about "finding" Irina had been bad enough.

Irina. His panther had never reacted to anyone the way it did to her. He knew what it meant. *She feels it, too.* But she wouldn't know what it was.

If he went ahead with this, it would end with him destroying her.

But he also knew he didn't have a choice. He couldn't stop this. The need to be near her was more than physical—it tore at his soul.

That wouldn't have been reason enough, but he'd seen the hurt in Irina's eyes when Francine confronted her. For all her brave words, she thought she didn't belong here, and that un-belonging was an old hurt that Grant knew far too well. He would have left her, if the only danger was tearing his own soul apart. But it would hurt her.

There had to be a way to keep her safe. From everything. Including his own panther.

I am more than my panther. The words he lived his life by. The motto he'd stamped on his soul since he first shifted, and his mother told him the truth about his father. His strange, wild magical side—and how he had left her.

Could he be more than his panther now?

Lance, have the car brought around, he projected silently. He felt Lance's reaction as the other man received his telepathic message: the instinctual prick of the snow leopard's ears and the man's curiosity.

"So, I don't want to sound desperate, but…" Irina's hesitant tones instantly raised Grant's protective instincts, and he slid his hand from her elbow to settle against her lower back. Her spine felt stiff against his palm—no surprise, after a confrontation with Frankie.

"You're hungry?" he asked.

"I just think I'll enjoy dinner more if we leave before Francine's laser eyes leave me a pile of dust on the floor," she admitted with a grimace. "Sorry—I know she's your friend, but…"

Francine was still glaring at them both from the other side of the room, making no attempt to hide it. If Grant had been in panther form, his hackles would have gone up.

"I don't know what her problem is." He shrugged. "Knowing Frankie, it could be anything from her stock falling through the floor to someone looking at her the wrong way three days ago."

He looked down at Irina. She was tall, for a human woman. The top of her head was level with Grant's chin, and he imagined what it would be like to hold her closer, her head tucked under his jaw, the soft press of her curves against his body. He wanted to tell her that she had nothing to fear from Francine or from anyone else and that from now on he would do everything in his considerable power to keep her safe and happy.

And scare her off before you've even gone on a single date? Pull yourself together.

Instead, he lowered his voice. "She likes other people to be miserable when she is. Let's get out of range."

Irina's eyes shone up at him. "Now you're talking."

We're good to go, said Lance's voice in Grant's head.

"My car's right outside," Grant said out loud, "and I know this great little place downtown. Do you like Italian?"

"Sounds great," Irina replied, and looked around. "I should probably say goodbye to—oh, forget it. She's busy anyway." She gave a half-hearted wave to a red-headed woman who looked deep in conversation with an older couple farther down the room.

It was still freezing cold outside, and this time Grant's panther registered its displeasure not only for himself, but for Irina, as well.

Irina stopped dead on the sidewalk. "Oh, shoot. My coat—"

"—Is either right here, or we're about to be fleeing a charge of theft as well as Frankie's wrath," Grant interrupted as Lance stepped forward, a grey winter coat slung over one arm.

Irina looked at him uncertainly. "Oh—thanks, um...?"

"Lance MacInnis. My, uh, personal assistant."

"Uh-*huh*?" Irina's eyes were wide. "I mean, nice to meet you, Mr. MacInnis. I'm Irina." She glanced sideways at Grant, and he could almost hear her disbelief. He couldn't blame her. It was a rare person who would look at the seven-foot, heavily muscled black man and think 'Personal Assistant.' Even the spectacles did nothing to make him look like an office jockey.

Lance shook her hand, angling a crooked grin at Grant. "Someone's got to stop this guy from tripping over his own feet. A pleasure to meet you."

He held the door for Irina, then exchanged a look with Grant across the roof of the car.

You could have warned me this was a date night. Lance's voice was serious. *What's the plan, here?*

There's no plan.

Well, there needs to be. We'll discuss this later.

All right, Mom. Grant snorted and slipped into the back seat. In front, Lance lined up the rear-view mirror.

"Warm enough for you, ma'am?"

"It's lovely, thanks." The interior of the car was heated to tropical bliss, and Grant watched Irina relax back into her seat. "And—Irina is fine. Please." She raised her eyebrows at Grant.

"The only time he calls me 'sir' is if I'm in trouble," Grant said. "So, knock it off, Lance."

"Yes, sir." Lance replied, deadpan, and Irina giggled. "Where are we headed?"

"Moss's place," Grant replied, leaning back in his seat with a grin. "Let him know I'll have my usual table, will you?"

Lance activated the divider that shut off the front of the car from the passenger seats. Grant saw Irina relax as the partition went up.

Irina glanced sidelong at Grant. "So, how does this work? Is your PA joining us for dinner?"

Shit. I really should have left him at the gallery, shouldn't I?

"He'd better not," Grant said quickly. Irina's tone had been light, but it was the brittle sort of light that suggested she wasn't feeling entirely at ease.

Grant rubbed his forehead and then held his hand out to her. She took it, folding her fingers around his, and he gave her a crooked smile.

"To be honest, I'm not that used to having him around. He's only been working for me for a few weeks, so we haven't exactly arranged a protocol for what to do when I'm escaping boring social obligations in the company of beautiful women."

"Oh." Irina's eyes went wide. "So... this isn't something you do often?"

"On the contrary," said Grant, trying to infuse his voice with enough humor that his dead seriousness didn't come across too strongly. "In retrospect, it's embarrassing. We went over plans for every aspect of my life, except—er—dating."

Which was one hundred percent true, including the embarrassment. Grant had accepted Lance's offer to act as his bodyguard because as a fellow big cat shifter, Lance would be able to give him some insight on his panther's behavior and the specific difficulties a wealthy shifter might encounter.

Once Lance was on the job, they had covered strategies for keeping Grant's shifter nature secret in everyday life, plans for dealing with attempted kidnappings (Grant wasn't a huge fan of Lance's recommended first response, "turn into a massive big cat and bite the shit out of them"), and exercises to keep his panther under control. But Grant had delayed their discussions about what to do if he fell in love.

And now it was too late. He was hardly going to tell Lance to pull over and have an on-the-go meeting about strategies for handling a sudden crush on the most beautiful woman he'd even met.

So now, here he was. On a date, with a woman who made him feel as though his whole body was on fire with excitement. With a chaperone in the front seat.

A chaperone whose aunt was good friends with Grant's mother.

Oh, hell.

Grant bit the inside of his cheek. How would a normal, human man act in this situation?

He tried to see the situation from Irina's perspective. If she had heard of him, what would she know? Probably just that he was Grant Diaz, a rich boy grown into a rich man, who spent his twenties tagging along after the heir to the Delacourt fortune and had spent the first few years of his thirties fading out of the public eye.

So—what were his options? Reveal that he was rich; reveal *how* rich he was; reveal that most men as wealthy as he was employed at least one bodyguard to keep potential kidnappers off his back, and that he had a secret that let him swap out the bodyguard for a full-time personal assistant, whose main job it was to keep his other secrets safe?

He could already see that once he started talking, it would be all too easy to let it all spill out. Because he *wanted* to talk to her, more than anything. Wanted to open his heart to her.

And what troubled him most was that his panther wanted it, too. It was butting against him, purring and hissing by turns, as good as nudging him forward to tell her all his secrets.

He had to stop his panther's instincts from ruining this for him.

Grant ran his thumb over Irina's fingers, hoping it wasn't obvious he was stalling for time. "I—"

Irina giggled. "Poor Lance! Talk about being a third wheel. It reminds me of the time I accidentally gatecrashed one of Clare's dates…"

Her face fell. "Oh, damn. I did it. I ran away again."

She spoke quietly, as though half to herself. Grant felt as though he was missing something and squeezed her hand.

"Anyone who would blame you for running away from Frankie should be left in a room alone with her for five minutes and see how they feel."

"It's not that, it's—oh!" Irina looked like she was about to say something else when her coat, which was lying on the seat between them, started to buzz. She jumped and let go of Grant's hand to rifle through the pockets.

"Sorry. Sorry! It's probably my friend complaining about me leaving the event early, but if it's work I've got to take it—oh. No, it's my friend." She stared at the message, blushed, and clapped her hand over the screen.

"Is there a problem?"

"No, she's just—well, she's not upset about me leaving, which is good, but..." Irina met Grant's eyes and squirmed. "She saw us leave together, so now she's—oh, come *on*," she cried out as the phone buzzed again. "We already have a third wheel without Clare buzzing around my phone like an interfering bee, so I am turning this thing off." She jabbed the button until the noise stopped.

Grant grinned. "I'm not going to get anywhere asking what she said, am I?"

Irina glared at him. "Nope." She narrowed her eyes as the car drew to a stop. "And I think *that* is your cue to forget all about this. Are we here?"

Grant peered out the window. Snow—*ugh*—but, yes, the street outside was familiar. "This is the place."

Chapter 5

Irina

Irina dragged her eyes away from Grant long enough to look out the window. She didn't recognize the neighborhood, but all that meant was that it wasn't one of the half-dozen blocks she raced up and down each week to get to her various waitressing jobs. Here, the building facades were all worn stonework, with iron scrollwork in front of the windows. The only sign that they were parked outside a restaurant was a small plaque on the otherwise unassuming wooden door.

Irina was reaching for the door handle when Grant sprang out of the car and raced around to her side. He pulled open the door with a flourish and held out his hand to her.

"I hope you're hungry," he said, eyes gleaming.

"You know I am," Irina replied, thankful her stomach hadn't actually rumbled while they were driving. Grant helped her out of the car. As he shut the door behind her, she turned back.

"Wait—isn't Lance…?"

"He has some spreadsheets to work on." Grant grinned wickedly. "I hope you don't think I'll need a PA to help me wine and dine a beautiful woman?"

This time, she could *feel* the blush flood across her cheeks. Her face was so hot, she imagined the flurrying snowflakes vaporizing inches from her skin.

"I should hope not," she said primly.

Grant laughed, a full-throated sound that made Irina's knees weak. Then he stopped, and his gaze became strangely distant for a moment. "Lance has the rest of the evening off, actually."

"Oh, *really*." Irina did her best to sound cool, but knew she was grinning like a loon. "You're not just giving him the boot halfway through the evening?"

"Really." Grant made a show of checking his watch. "This is completely routine. No personal assistance required after eight-oh-five on a Friday evening. It's in his contract," he said gravely, leading her inside.

The restaurant was—well, if she didn't know it was a restaurant, she wouldn't have guessed it was one. It looked more like a beautifully preserved early twentieth-century family home.

But not quite. Oh, she could tell what they were trying to do, making guests feel cozy and comfortable with a side of "how Nana's house used to be." Kitchen-y, but not kitsch. Except Irina had yet to meet anyone's grandma who hung her pans and garlic plaits in the front hall, rather than tucked away in the *actual* kitchen.

Irina stifled a giggle as she imagined how her Gran would have reacted to someone hanging garlic beside the coat-hooks.

Her amusement faded as quickly as it had appeared. It was four years since Gran had died, but Irina still felt lost at the thought that the woman who raised her was gone.

"Is everything all right?" Grant's eyes almost seemed to glow in the low light inside the restaurant. Irina smiled back at him; she was surprised to find she'd stopped smiling to start with.

"I'm fine. This place is so cute!" she enthused. "And it smells *amazing* in here."

"Wait until you taste the food," Grant told her.

Irina decided she liked the place. The delicious smells of food definitely helped. But it wasn't the sort of place she had imagined a man like Grant bringing her to. From what she could see, the restaurant was homey, intimate, and *small*.

Irina had secretly thought that Grant seemed too large even for his car, lounging in the seat like a cat fitting itself into a favored shoebox. But that was nothing compared to seeing him navigate the spindly chairs and tables here.

Irina held her breath, expecting something to go crashing down at any moment. But Grant was surprisingly graceful for a man built on such powerful lines. Every time she thought they were headed for a bull-in-a-china-shop situation, he slipped through without disturbing so much as a doily.

"Grant! Jeez, you don't give much notice, do you?" A grinning man with light brown skin bounded out of a door at the back of the narrow dining room, bringing clouds of steam with him. Irina got a mouth-watering whiff of savory smells before the door swung shut behind him.

Grant put his hand on Irina's lower back, and she was so hungry by then that she couldn't honestly say whether that or the smell from the kitchens was more enticing.

"Irina, may I introduce Moss Taylor. Moss, this is Irina."

Strike that rubbish about the kitchen smells being more enticing. As Moss approached, Grant's arm slid further around her waist, his fingers spread wide as though he was trying to touch as much of her as possible. The gesture was strangely protective, and it sent a flood of heat through her. Grant had shed his suit jacket as they came in, and the silk shirt he was wearing under it was so fine she could almost see his biceps through it. And she could *definitely* feel them.

Irina pulled herself together enough to hold out one hand. "Pleased to meet you."

Moss waved apologetically. "No shaking, sorry, love. I've got to get back to the kitchen." He gave Grant an appraising look, then nodded towards a staircase at one side of the room. "Your table's ready. Settle yourself in."

Irina blinked as Moss disappeared in another puff of delectable steam. This time, her stomach gave a plaintive gurgle. Grant laughed.

"Come on. I'll show you up."

Upstairs, a short corridor led to a candle-lit courtyard. Green vines climbed up the stone walls that lined the four sides of the courtyard, and Irina was amazed to see potted plants with small flowers growing in them.

And it was *warm*.

"Wait—are we outside? Where's the snow?"

She looked up. Several stories up, the glint of glass gave away the courtyard's secret. Not a courtyard: a conservatory. If she squinted, she could just make out small drifts of snow at the very edges of the glass roof.

"Moss put in some sort of complicated heating and ventilation system that keeps it from getting too humid and damp in here," Grant explained as he led her to the only table in the conservatory, his warm hand on the small of her back. "And it keeps the snow from building up too much and coming in through the roof."

"I'm not sure whether I feel more secure knowing that, or not knowing that was even a possibility," Irina mused. "Oh—thanks!"

Grant had pulled a chair out for her and was waiting expectantly. She sat down, intensely aware of the tall, muscular man standing at her back.

His hands were still resting on the back of her chair. When she leaned back, her shoulders brushed against his fingers.

Irina licked her lips. If he kept his hands there—no, not held still—if he let his hands drift down, ghosting over her arms, around her stomach, while his mouth brushed against the back of her neck...

"Comfortable?"

"Um. Yes. Thank you." Irina banished the daydream with a brisk shake of her head. Grant sat down opposite her, moving as gracefully as ever. Irina met his eyes, remembered her vision, and quickly looked away.

"Do we order, or...?" she asked, trying to deflect attention before her blush returned.

Grant shook his head. "Moss doesn't believe in letting people choose what they eat. Allergies notwithstanding, of course." He looked stricken. "You don't have any food allergies, do you?"

"Nope, no allergies. If it's food, I'll eat it," she said, laughing.

"Well, don't feel bad about sending anything back to the kitchen, regardless. If Moss's psychic food-matching skills are on the blink, he'd prefer to know, rather than have someone not enjoy one of his meals."

"I'll keep that in mind," said Irina, knowing there was no way in hell she was going to send any dish back to the kitchen in a place like this. Hell, she'd spent most of the last summer eating beans and rice... and the last few days before pay day eating just rice, no beans. Anything would be better than that.

From her experience with clearing tables at nicer restaurants, Irina was expecting a sommelier to approach them with the night's wine list, but it was Moss who flung himself through the courtyard doors, wiping his hands on a cloth.

She must have looked confused because Moss winked at her and explained, "Got the girls to do prep while I go over the drinks with you. On the house if they mess it up."

Irina felt a light brush on her fingers and looked down to see that Grant's hand had stolen across the table to take hers. His eyes burned into hers then flicked back to Moss.

"You let them back into the kitchen? I thought they were dead to you after that drama last spring."

Moss shrugged. "Washing dishes and chopping produce is a good way to come back from the dead in this business. So! Tonight's wine list. I've got a few options for each of the dishes, depending on how you feel..."

He rattled off what sounded like a hundred options, from vineyards around the world. Irina hadn't even head of some of the varieties, and soon her head was spinning. With Grant sending burning glances her way, and the gentle touch of his fingers against hers, she was finding it hard to concentrate on the chef's detailed and enthusiastic descriptions of the various wines on offer.

She let Grant order and enjoyed listening to him spar with Moss in what was clearly a long-standing feud about wine choices. Irina told herself she would pay more attention when the actual meals came out—if nothing else, because Clare was sure to grill her about every aspect of the evening—but even before the appetizers arrived, she knew that was unlikely to happen.

When the first course arrived, ferried in by a pair of slender young men in matching silver waistcoats, all Irina could see was the strong curve of Grant's wrist as he deftly relieved them of the bottle of wine and poured her a glass. When the waiters vanished, all she noticed was how delicately he held his knife and fork. The way his Adam's apple bobbed as he swallowed. How his every move seemed at once powerful and intensely controlled.

At one point, he reached out to refill her glass, and the cuff of his shirt pulled back just a little over his wrist...

I want to paint him. Her fingers twitched with the need to hold a brush, her throat tight with the half-joy, half-terror of her wildest moments of inspiration. Painting Grant would be her Sistine Chapel. Her Mona Lisa. An intimacy that took her breath away just to think about it.

And it would destroy any hope she had of being close to him.

Her skin chilled. If she painted him, she wouldn't be able to stop herself from looking into his soul. And regardless whether he had something *more* to him or not—she hadn't dared look closely enough at him yet to know—she would see more of him than he wanted seen, and put it onto her canvas like an autopsy. And he would never want to see him again.

Better not to sink too deeply into those green eyes.

She watched his lips move instead, and only after they stopped, realized he had been speaking to her.

"Sorry, I missed that," she admitted, taking a quick sip of wine to cover the fact that she'd just been ogling her dinner partner instead of paying attention to what he was saying. The white wine burst onto her palate, complex and delicate all at once.

"It wasn't important," Grant demurred. There was an undeniably smug look on his face, like he knew exactly what she had been doing. "I was wondering if you enjoyed the scallops."

He *did* know exactly what she had been doing. Dammit.

Irina looked down. One lonely, white-fleshed scallop lay on her plate. She couldn't even remember eating the rest of them.

She couldn't even remember them *arriving*. Hadn't the waiters brought out breads to start with? She had a distinct—well, vague—memory of beautiful crusty, seedy rolls.

"I'm sure they were delicious," she said honestly. She speared the final scallop with her fork and popped it in her mouth. It *was* delicious. She wished she had paid more attention to the others.

Irina sighed. "I'm sorry. I'm not a very good dinner companion."

Grant raised one eyebrow with an apologetic smile. "Whereas I've been the perfect host, running my mouth about the wine list and not letting you get a word in edgeways."

"No, that was good, actually. You did a great job of covering up my utter lack of wine knowledge." Irina looked at her empty plate and sighed. "Please tell me that wasn't the last course, though? I didn't sleepwalk through the entire meal?"

She bit her lip and thought, *Sleepwalk. That's a nice euphemism for 'stared at your forearms.' All those months in the mountains must have left me totally desperate if I'm ignoring the best meal I've ever had to drool over a guy's arms.*

But his arms were so, so worth drooling over.

Irina shook herself. *Stop it! You're doing it again!* She raised her eyes to meet Grant's and saw him bite back a grin.

"You only—uh—*sleepwalked* through the first two courses, don't worry. The best is yet to come."

"I promise to pay more attention to the next dish," Irina joked.

"I don't know about that," Grant said, swirling the last of the wine in his glass. "I was rather enjoying the attention, myself."

His green eyes, dark in the low lighting of the courtyard, burned into Irina's with a warmth that filled her whole body. She dragged her gaze away. He ran one finger along the rim of his wineglass, and Irina's mouth went dry. The tantalizing, slow circles he was making on the glass... what would they feel like on her body?

It was all too easy to remember the soft touch of his fingers on her hand earlier. And to imagine them trailing up her wrist, to the crook of her arm, her shoulders... under her dress...

Grant leaned forward and whispered conspiratorially. "And I'm still enjoying it."

"Oh. Well. Um. That's good, because it doesn't look like I'm about to stop anytime soon," Irina admitted and then bit her lip, horrified at what she had said. A delighted smile spread across Grant's face, and he raised his glass.

"Here's to that."

"Cheers," Irina replied, biting her lip, and clinked her glass against his.

"So," Grant continued after they had both drunk, "Now that my voice has your attention..." He waited as Irina groaned and covered her face. "I think we should—and this isn't a euphemism—get to know each other better." He grinned his cat-like smile.

Irina peeked through her fingers. "And that's *not* a euphemism," she repeated. "All right. I suppose this dinner entitles you to know something about the strange woman you plucked from the jaws of certain doom. What do you want to know?"

"Oh—social security number, date of birth, paternal lineage through ten generations..." He laughed. "How about we start with your surname?"

"Mathers," Irina replied. "Irina Mathers." She reached across to shake his hand with mock formality.

"A pleasure to meet you," Grant drawled. "So, what brings you to the city? I can tell by your accent that you're not from around here."

"You got me." Irina took another sip of wine. "I grew up in—well, pretty much the opposite of New York. This tiny town out in the middle of nowhere, where the tallest building was the water tower. The sort of town that *has* a water tower, and it's such a defining feature, you take visitors to see it."

The waiters swept discreetly in again, replacing the empty plates with delicately arranged cuts of steak. Irina waited until they had gone, suddenly tongue-tied.

"I guess..." She stopped, not sure how to go on, and found herself staring intently at the triangular patch of skin under Grant's open collar.

He picked up on her stare and stretched luxuriously so that the fabric of his shirt stretched against his chest. Irina groaned, which only made him look more smug.

"Next time we dine out I'll wear a mask, so you can enjoy the meal properly," Grant announced with an air of benevolent self-sacrifice. "And a burlap sack. No, a canvas one. Burlap is so chafing."

"And canvas isn't?"

"Canvas is tolerable."

Irina laughed. Grant wasn't the first man she'd met who was well aware of how attractive he was, but somehow his method of constantly drawing attention to his good looks was more charming than off-putting. It didn't hurt that he actually was far better-looking than any of the meatheads whose idea of flirting was to flex their own muscles in front of a mirror.

"All right. Let me try again." Irina took a deep breath. *Try again... and try not to sound like a complete drop-kick loser. In other words, not like yourself.* "Like I said, grew up in the middle of nowhere."

Irina toyed with a morsel of steak, then speared it and popped it into her mouth. *Mmm. This is amazing. I so wish I hadn't missed the first courses!* She kept talking, only slightly distracted by the food.

"Where was I? Only child, born in—sorry, fast-forward—I was always interested in painting and art of all sorts, really, and I actually got this scholarship after high school." *Keep it cool.* "For a school here, actually. But my Gran got sick during freshman year, so I was back home again before I could blink. Then..."

She stopped. *Then I yo-yoed back and forth for the next four years. A few months back in the mountains over the tourist season, saving money to come back to the city and—what? Realize, time and time again, that I didn't fit here, either?*

What am I doing with my life?

"I don't know if you, uh, noticed my paintings..."

She glanced up in time to catch Grant's shamefaced wince. "Ah. Would it help if I said I was *very* distracted?"

Irina snorted. "Too busy stealing strange women's drinks? Anyway, my friend Clare—"

"—She of the texts I wasn't allowed to see—"

"—Yes, Clare of the terrible text messages. She got me the exhibition. Which was so kind of her, really, especially since..."

She paused and bit her lip. The words, *It's not like I'm a real artist or anything* were waiting on her tongue, ready to be said, but she couldn't make herself spit them out.

All those months of work. All those months *away* from work: hiking and climbing in the mountains around her grandmother's cottage. Hunting down the perfect scene, the perfect angle and light, and painting for so long every evening that the fumes made her dizzy. Letting her senses absorb everything about the world and put it on her canvases, even the *freaky stuff* she never let anyone see.

And all for—what? A dream she wasn't even brave enough to chase?

Everyone knew that no one made a living as an artist these days. Especially not girls from the middle of nowhere who'd dropped out of art school.

Especially not girls who didn't want to be artists, anyway. Irina *had* a job, and it was a pretty good one. Better than a lot of people had. Her waitressing paid the bills—well, most of them—and if it all fell through, she always had the cottage to go back to. How many other twenty-somethings could say the same?

Let Francine Delacourt sneer at her work. Irina didn't need any of it.

"Are you all right?"

Irina realized the smile had slid off her face while she was wrapped in her own thoughts. She pulled herself back together and flashed a grin at Grant. "Sorry. I was a million miles away."

"Back at your Gran's house in the mountains?"

Irina's smile wavered, but she pulled it up again. "My Gran passed away a few years ago, but, yes—back at her old cottage in the mountains. I worked on the paintings there over last summer."

"Well, here's to summer in the mountains." Grant raised his glass, but he was still watching Irina carefully. "Whether that's Bolivia, Irina's Gran's mountains, or wherever it is Mathis ended up."

Irina raised her glass as well. "To the middle of nowhere in the Adirondacks. And wherever your friend is."

"Probably punching a tree somewhere, if I know him." Grant laughed.

Irina relaxed, feeling safely back on solid ground.

"Well, that doesn't rule out the Adirondacks. Plenty of trees around there. I might have even seen him."

Her Gran's cottage was a few miles from the small town of Silverstream, tucked into a remote valley that nevertheless saw lots of visitors over the summer months. Irina racked her brains, trying to recall if she'd seen any tourists who might have harbored tree-assaulting plans.

"Does he look much like his sister? Same amazing hair?"

"He's tall and blond like her, but that's it." Grant shifted in his chair, as if he'd got pins and needles suddenly.

"What about the laser-beam eyes? I would remember seeing anyone with eyes like hers, I think." She bent her head to her plate and glanced up through her eyelashes at Grant. Yes, he was *definitely* looking uncomfortable.

He couldn't be jealous, could he? Of the remote possibility that she had gotten a glimpse of his friend, probably fried red by the sun and grimy with hiking?

The thought sent a thrill prickling down Irina's spine. She sat up a little straighter. Before she could stop herself, she felt herself lick her lips. *Damn her subconscious, giving away what he made her feel.*

"Is he into the outdoors? Well, I suppose he must be, if he likes punching trees." Irina raised one eyebrow at Grant. "And what about you? Did you punch many trees in—Bolivia, did you say?"

"I have more respect for trees than to punch them," he said gravely, but his eyes were sparkling. He leaned around the table, closing the distance between them, and bent his head to whisper in Irina's ear. "And I can think of better uses for my hands."

Irina had automatically leaned in to hear Grant better, and now she found herself frozen in place, her head bent close enough to Grant's face that she could feel his breath tickle her ear. Her skin broke out in goosebumps, every nerve in her body tingling, ready for more. More than just the touch of his breath.

If she turned her head...

"Do you know what?" Grant started speaking again before she could make a decision either way: stay where she was, or turn around and raise the stakes. His voice was a low rumble that seemed to reverberate in her very bones.

"Hmm?" Irina didn't trust herself to be able to make words. Was she trembling? Was she trembling so much that he would be able to tell? It wasn't like they were actually *touching*—yet...

"If I'm honest... I think you would be enjoying this meal more if you'd already had your fill of me."

Oh, my God.

Irina didn't stop to think. She felt as though electricity was dancing across her skin, and that if she looked down, she would see silver sparks leaping to cross the distance between her body and Grant's. Her lips ached to be touched, and Grant's face was so close to hers—

Screw it, Irina thought just before she closed the gap.

His lips were soft, a heart-melting contrast to the prickly stubble around them. Irina pressed her own lips against them, gently at first, until she felt Grant's tongue slip out to tease her lips and realized she couldn't hold back any longer. She gripped the table with both hands for balance and dove into the kiss, recklessly losing herself in sensation.

Somewhere very far away and very, very unimportant, she heard footsteps approach and beat a hasty retreat.

"Hmm," murmured Grant against her lips. "I think that was our dessert course."

Irina tried to catch her breath, but caught another kiss instead. By the time their lips parted again, she was gasping. Her face was stinging where Grant's stubble had scratched her skin, and her lips felt bruised and red.

She'd never kissed anyone on a first date before. At least, not like *that*.

She was still leaning too far forward, far enough that her chair was almost tipping over, but somehow her hands had moved from the table to press against Grant's broad shoulders. She could feel the swell of muscle under her palms and the hard line of his collarbone under one thumb. Grant's own arm was twined around her waist, holding her up.

The hell with it.

"Dessert?" she repeated, dazed. "If that means dinner's over... is it time to head home?"

Chapter 6

Grant

✶*Is the car still outside?* Grant projected wildly in what he assumed was Lance's general direction, the downstairs area of the restaurant. He'd told the other man to take the evening off, but hadn't been surprised when he sensed the snow leopard shifter still downstairs. An evening off eating one of Moss's dinners beat anything else.

Keys, he thought suddenly. *Shit. Keys?*

You have your own set in your pocket, came Lance's voice in his head, dryly amused. *Do you—*

Can't talk. Got to go.

She was in his arms—beautiful, glorious Irina was in his arms, and he couldn't waste any more time talking.

Kissing, though. He could waste time kissing.

He wrapped his arms more tightly around her, pulling her onto his lap. The pleased gasp she made as he held her close was almost infuriating. She turned him on so much, and every noise she made only reminded him how much closer he wanted to be to her. His cock was straining against his trousers. Could she feel it? Could she feel how badly he wanted to rip his clothes off and cover her body with his own?

"Your place or mine?" he growled into her mouth.

"Not mine. God no. Yours?" Irina turned pleading eyes to him. No force in the world could have made him refuse her.

Bring her home. His single-minded panther was insistent. And for once, stupid though it might be, Grant agreed with it.

"Follow me," he growled and stood up. For one delicious moment he held Irina's full weight against himself before he lowered her to the ground. He patted his pocket. Keys. Good. He took Irina's hand, and she gripped it tightly. "My place isn't far from here. I'll drive."

"Wait." Irina stopped at the top of the stairs. "Is—Lance—he's not coming with us, is he?"

"He's off duty," Grant growled, and the uncertain look on Irina's face disappeared.

"Good. Because..." She bit her lip on whatever she was about to say next.

"If you say *anything* involving the words 'personal assistance'..."

"I would *never*." She burst out laughing and then covered her mouth with one hand, as though shocked at herself.

They hurried down the stairs together, Grant acutely aware of how close Irina's body was to his as they navigated the narrow corridor.

He caught Lance's eye as they burst out into the main dining area and was shocked by the wave of adrenaline that hit him when he saw the other man looking across at him and his mate.

No, it's not the man, he realized immediately. *It's his leopard.*

This was the sort of thing he should have had Lance tell him about. A few moments ago, even the mere thought that Mathis might have crossed paths with Irina had unsettled his panther. And now it was seeing Lance as a competitor, too.

The icy night air hit him like a freight train as they hurried out into the street, and Grant automatically pulled Irina to him, shielding her from the cold wind. She looked up at him, her eyes so warm he almost forgot how cold it was.

"The car's just around the corner," he said, resisting the urge to tip her head further back and cover her face with kisses.

"And your apartment?"

"We'll be there before you know it."

He spoke too soon. The street had filled up while they were eating, and they soon found themselves in a sea of honking horns, angry shouts and idling engines. Grant started to growl deep in his throat, echoing the car engines...

...But not *his* car's engine, which was electric and silent.

He swallowed the growl, but not before Irina noticed it. She glanced sidelong at him, a smile dancing on her lips.

"Frustrated?" she murmured.

"Not at all," Grant replied with a groan.

"How about now?"

She reached over and slid one hand up his leg, her touch so light he could barely feel it. Grant groaned again, louder this time, and flung his head back against the headrest. Outside, the traffic was still at a crawl.

Irina sighed and settled back in her own seat—but her hand stayed where it was. "Would it be quicker to walk?" she wondered aloud.

Grant scowled out the window. They were only a few blocks away from his apartment building. But...

A few flakes of snow stuck to the windshield, and he fought back a full-body shudder. Only a few blocks... but a few blocks of icy winds. And snow. Snow that would stick, become *damp*, and slip down the back of his collar.

"The hell with that," he growled as he slung the car into reverse. The car's suspension took a hit as he backed up onto an empty patch of sidewalk to break out of the gridlocked sea of cars. A timely spin of the wheel brought them out on a side street.

His panther belonged in the jungle, in a world of damp heat with the warm smell of soil and growing things. But Grant? He belonged here. The concrete jungle. *His* jungle.

The car's electric engine didn't roar as he slipped in between two moving cars into the far lane, taking advantage of every break in the traffic. It was as quiet as he himself would have been, stalking through the hot, lush jungles of Bolivia.

Irina's grip on his leg tightened as he found an empty lane and picked up speed.

"Is this a shortcut?" she asked. "In the opposite direction to where we were headed before?"

"Shorter than being stuck in a gridlock? I sure hope so," Grant replied, eyes on the road. He eased around another corner, his mind playing out the options. Left here—no, the next block.

A map of the borough's streets and buildings flickered through Grant's mind. The next block would bring them to one of Frankie's hotels. He knew there had been road work outside the building. It stuck in his mind so clearly because he'd imagined Frankie's fury at the disturbance.

If he remembered correctly, the construction had only finished the day before. He hoped that most drivers wouldn't have heard about the completion and would still be avoiding the area.

One way to find out.

Grant hung another left, a new plan sparking in his mind. Irina was right. Who said they needed to drive all the way, after all?

Yes. The newly sealed road was smooth under the car's tires, and the Hotel Lyon gleamed like a golden spire in the snow. Irina was leaning forward, peering out in front of them. She gave Grant a questioning look.

"Is it just me, or are you driving in circles?"

"Strategic circles, I promise." Grant slowed down and eased into the parking level of the Hotel Lyon. The warden recognized him and waved him through; Grant coasted onto the automated parking.

"This is our stop," he announced.

"You live in a hotel?" Irina asked then covered her mouth. Sadly, with the hand that had previously been on Grant's leg. "Uh, no judgement meant, just—surprise."

"We can stay here if you'd prefer," Grant said quickly, "but my apartment isn't far. Honest. We're at least—oh, a few hundred yards closer now than we were at the restaurant." He grinned. "And it's a lovely walk. I promise."

Irina looked doubtful and shrugged. Before Grant could leap out and open the door for her, she turned the handle and stepped out.

Grant followed her, lightning-fast, and offered her his arm.

"Shall we?"

She took it, raising one dark eyebrow. "A romantic walk in the snow, when there's a whole hotel of warm, cozy rooms above us? Why not?"

She was right. The master suites of the Hotel Lyon *were* warm. All of Frankie's hotels were perfectly appointed.

But something inside Grant rebelled at the idea of spending his first night with Irina in a rented room. He wanted to take her home, to his bed, not to some temporary den.

Grant turned to lead Irina further into the building, avoiding both the elevator up to the hotel lobby and the way out to the street. She frowned, questions clear on her face, and Grant held her closer.

"Our choices aren't just traffic jams or cold, wet feet," he explained, lowering his mouth to her ear and feeling her shiver in his arms. "Let me show you how I managed to make it to the age of twenty-five in this city and still not know how to drive from one end of this block to the other…"

There was a plain metal door set into a dim corner in the back of the parking level. Grant tested the handle and grinned as it gave under his hand.

"Step one, complete," he said triumphantly. "Not that I didn't have an excellent save ready if that was locked."

"Of course not." Irina's eyes were wide. "So, you don't live in a hotel. You live... in a maintenance corridor?"

"The finest of all maintenance corridors!" Grant swept into the dingy hallway, and Irina laughed, spinning with him. "Come on—follow me..."

"Where are we going?"

He explained as they walked through the underbelly of the building, through the corridor to a storage area and past a startled security guard. Grant flashed a grin at the old man but slipped past him before the poor guy could figure out whether stopping people from breaking *out* was part of his job.

"I grew up in this neighborhood, and Mathis's family owned most of the block back then. So, we did what any young sh—uh, young kids would do. We explored. Ah—here we are."

He put his arm around Irina's shoulders just as they walked into a rush of cold air, stopping in front of a heavy metal grille. He'd never been entirely sure what this architectural quirk was for, although he and Mathis had exchanged theories. Since the grille was roughly door-shaped, the more likely of these theories (the ones not involving ninjas) was that it was something to do with ventilation or an emergency exit—if emergency exits were habitually left bolted shut.

Grant put his hands on the grille. The metal was cold under his fingers. "If I remember correctly—and if no one has fixed this in the last fifteen years..."

He glared at the door for a moment and then wedged his shoulder under a cross-bar. Sure, there was another exit farther along, but this way was more exciting.

He leaned his weight into the door the way he remembered and heaved.

Nothing happened.

Well, he thought ruefully, *This way* would *be more exciting... if we could actually get out here.*

He slid his eyes sideways towards Irina. There was no saving his dignity after that. He could lounge against the door as nonchalantly as he pleased; she wouldn't be fooled.

The corner of Irina's mouth tucked under in a badly concealed grin. "That worked when you were a kid, huh?"

"Every time," Grant admitted with a grimace. Irina's eyebrows rose, and he quickly added, "We always put it back afterwards! The trick to open it only works from this side. Or not at all, now."

Irina examined the door and then ran her eyes up and down Grant's body. An electric thrill followed her gaze.

Damn it, why did I bring her here? To show off? We could be in bed by now!

A very small, logical part of Grant's brain protested this—they'd more than likely still be in traffic, and nowhere near bed—but it didn't help with the heat that burned through him at Irina's glance. Not even the chilly air blowing through the grille could do that.

Irina leaned forward and prodded him in the chest. "How tall were you when you were a kid?"

"What?" Grant's mouth moved before his brain had caught up. "....Oh," he added, understanding dawning. He bent and wedged his shoulder about a foot below where he'd put it before. This time, when he put his weight into it, the whole grille, including the lock, popped off its hinges with a metallic *chunk.*

He stood and lifted the metal grille out of the way. "Can we pretend that worked properly the first time?"

"And ignore my incredible detective skills? Not on your life." Irina grinned as she stepped past him, wrapping her coat more closely around her body. Grant hated to see her cover her curves with the shapeless garment, but he hated the thought of her being cold even more.

Frankie always wears fancy clothes, he thought vaguely. *I should ask her for advice—something to buy for Irina.*

Something to buy for my mate.

Irina had skipped ahead, standing above him on the steps. She looked back at him over her shoulder, dark curls falling over her face.

Grant's heart twisted in his chest. Earlier today, he'd been a ball of stress, frustrated over his missing friend. He'd never dreamed his return to the city could turn out this—this *magical.*

He couldn't let his panther ruin this for him. How could he be this lucky, to find someone he connected with so quickly—and for her to be beautiful, and funny, and adventurous? For her to find this unconventional shortcut exciting, instead of irritating and unpleasant?

And it *was* unpleasant. Cold, windy and, if he remembered the alleyway above correctly, likely to be crammed with garbage. His eyes dropped down to Irina's feet. High heels. She'd navigated the underground levels well enough, but an alleyway full of rubbish? He couldn't ask that of her.

Not when the alternative was so enticing.

"What are you thinking?" Irina demanded, crossing her arms in front of her.

Grant leapt up the stairs to her, landing lightly at her side. "I'm thinking about you," he said softly. "About how you're probably very cold, and your feet are probably beginning to ache. And how I have an *excellent* solution to both of these problems."

"Oh, really?" Irina's dark eyes flashed up at him. "Does it involve standing around chatting in the cold?"

"Only temporarily." He stepped closer to her and inhaled, her scent filling his nostrils. The strongest smell was that of her clothes, the perfume from the detergent she used and the heavy smell of slightly damp wool from her coat. But under it—*Oooh.* That was *her.* And he wanted more of it.

He stepped closer again until he could lean forward and nuzzle his lips against her cheek. He felt her breath on his neck, a sharp gasp of expelled air, and then a softer hum of pleasure as he moved his lips down, brushing lightly against her jaw. He stopped to nibble her ear and her hum turned into a moan.

Grant pressed himself against her, pushing her against the wall of the stairwell as he wound his arms around her. She pressed back, and he went hard so fast it was almost painful. Irina's mouth found his, and he plunged into the kiss, hot and fierce. Her tongue traced one single, tantalizing line against his lower lip, and then she broke away.

"Is this your plan?" she gasped, breathless.

Grant grinned. He lowered his hands, stroking the generous curve of her ass through her coat, and lifted her up. She squealed and wrapped her legs around him for balance instinctively.

It was all Grant could do not to purr with satisfaction.

He looked into her flushed face, deep into her warm eyes, and pressed his forehead against hers.

"You won't wear out your feet like this," he said, softly, but unable to keep the rumble from his voice. "And do you feel... warmed up?"

Irina's eyes widened, but only for a second. She licked her lips, and her thighs tightened deliciously around Grant's waist. "Warm enough," she said, then paused. "Though I would prefer to be... warm... *indoors.*"

"Point taken." Grant secured his grip and leapt up the stairs three at a time. The alleyway above was as filthy as he had feared, and he moved through it as quickly as he could.

At the other end was another familiar door, wide open as Grant remembered it and spilling bright yellow light and uproarious noise into the night. Irina raised her head as he slipped inside.

"Is this a kitchen?" she whispered into his shoulder as he side-stepped past a gleaming stainless-steel bench. "Oh my God...!"

"Hey, you!"

"It *is* a kitchen," Grant admitted, speeding up. "Aha—I wonder if the chef remembers me…"

By the roar the chef gave, he did.

Irina was giggling wildly by the time Grant managed to dodge around a sous-chef and stunned server and escape through what he hoped was still the staff exit. The hot, steamy air cleared, and Grant looked around. Irina was collapsed against his shoulder, still laughing weakly.

"Almost there," he muttered into her wild curls, and made for the elevators.

CHAPTER 7

IRINA

Irina tucked her face into Grant's neck, completely incapable of wiping the silly grin from her face. Or even stopping the giggles that still burst out of her every time she thought she'd pushed them back.

Her head was spinning, and it had nothing to do with the wine she'd had at dinner. It was the dinner, and Grant's burning eyes, and his ridiculous show with the metal door, and—and all of it. Everything.

It was all *wonderful*.

And Grant himself was the best of all.

She peeked up, meaning to look around now they were out of the elevator, but found her face turning to his. One glimpse of pale carpet and creamy walls, and then *him*. She was close enough to his razor-sharp cheekbones that she could have kissed them. So she did.

Grant groaned, so deeply she could feel his chest reverberate against her breasts. The noise and the sensation sent a thrill of arousal directly between her legs. When she looked up again, it was straight into Grant's eyes. His pupils were so huge they almost blotted out the green entirely.

"One more minute," he begged. "My keys—"

Irina wriggled against a hard lump that was pressing into her upper thigh. She'd thought that it was too high up to be... well.

"Found them," she said, and slipped one hand from his shoulders to ease the keyring from his jacket pocket.

"Mmmph," he replied, his voice muffled by her lips. She kissed him hungrily, reveling in the contrast between the softness of his lips and the rough scratch of his stubble. Nimble fingers plucked the keys from her hand and a moment later she was pressed up against a door, her body rubbing even closer against Grant's, and then they were both tumbling inside.

For one breath-taking moment, Irina thought they would fall, but then Grant's entire body seemed to flex so that they stayed upright. She stared into his lust-blackened eyes and loosened her thighs' grip on his waist. Her body slid against his, slowly, slowly, until she felt the hard length of his cock.

Oh, it was *much* bigger than the lump his keys had made. But just as hard. Irina bit her lip and looked up at Grant through her eyelashes. He stared back, eyes hungry, but didn't pull her closer to him. There was a shade of uncertainty in his face.

"Do you—should we—?" he asked, and Irina shut him up with another kiss. There was only one question she wanted an answer to.

"Bedroom?"

Grant's face cleared. "God, yes."

"All right, then. You'll have to show me the way…" Irina broke off as Grant picked her up and launched into what was practically a sprint, with her in his arms. God, he was so *strong*.

She caught her breath as Grant pushed through another door and came to a stop. Irina dropped her head back and saw, upside-down, a massive bed towering with fluffy pillows and thick comforters.

One of Grant's hands slipped behind her neck. At the same time, his own head dipped forward, and as he pulled her slowly back upright, he pressed his lips to her breast, her collarbone, her neck…

By the time he reached her lips, Irina was dizzy with lust.

"Please," she murmured against his lips, "don't make me beg."

His mouth curved beneath hers. "As you wish."

She barely had time to register that he had changed his grip on her body before her back hit the pillowy bed. She raised herself up on her elbows, ready to hurl herself back up at the strong, powerful man standing at the end of the bed, but before she could move, he was on her.

Irina raised both hands to his chest, running her fingers across the hard planes of his pecs and up and over his shoulders. She pulled him against her, or herself against him—it didn't matter. All that was important was that her mouth found his. She ran one thumb across his jawline and felt as much as heard the moan that tore from his throat.

She tangled her hands in his hair, deepening the kiss. This was—this was just *kissing*, but it was so much better than any kiss she'd ever shared with anyone before. Grant's tongue flickered expertly against hers, teasing, *taunting*. And his teeth—

Irina moaned as Grant's teeth grazed her lower lip. He responded to her pleasure, nipping her lip lightly, and then soothed it with another lingering kiss.

She was breathless by the time their lips parted. Grant looked down at her, his eyes heavy-lidded and burning with need.

Irina wriggled, sinking deeper into the soft, enveloping bed. Grant's arms pressed down on either side of her, his biceps clear even through the fabric of his shirt. All that existed in the world were the clouds of bedding, the hot, heavy presence of Grant above her—and his eyes, burning into her own.

He shifted his weight onto one arm and slid the other under her, the pliant knit fabric of her dress catching under his fingers. Irina groaned in frustration. His touch was wonderful, it made her heart flutter, her pulse pound—but he was only touching her *dress*.

It wasn't enough. It wasn't *nearly* enough. She had felt his cock against her in the corridor, and even the thought of that now—oh, she wanted him so, so badly. She was wet already, every nerve in her body singing out for him to claim her.

She buried her face in Grant's neck, trailing kisses down to his collarbone. He gripped her hip, his fingers digging in as she scraped her teeth along his skin, the same way he had teased her.

"What did I say about making me beg?" she murmured, her tongue darting out to taste him. He held her tighter, both arms winding around her now, one hand sliding up her thigh and pushing her dress aside.

Irina gasped as Grant traced tantalizing circles on her stomach. He moved lower, slowly, so slowly she almost groaned, flexing her hips up to encourage him further down.

His breath tickled her ear. "Is this what you want?"

"*Yes,*" she gasped, and then: "Oh, God, *yes!*"

Grant's fingers slid under the waistband of her panty hose, under her panties, and brushed against her clit. Irina bit her lip as sensation coursed through her, not just between her legs, but everywhere, like lightning sparking across her skin. Her breathing grew ragged as he pushed one finger inside her slick folds, and then another. His thumb found her clit and circled slowly. Excruciatingly slowly. *Too* slowly.

And his fingers were wonderful, but they weren't what she really wanted.

She surged against him, pulling his face down to hers. "I want you inside me," she demanded, and the answering glint in his eyes made her whole body thrill. She clenched around his fingers—she was so close, *so close...*

Grant's fingers slid out of her, and she gasped at the loss. Then he was looking down at her, concern in his vivid green eyes.

"You said—" he began, and she didn't know whether to laugh or scream.

"I want you. Now. *Please,*" she gasped. "There—you've made me beg, now, *please*, Grant, I—"

He moved above her, his broad chest brushing against her breasts, his hard abs sliding over the curve of her stomach. She opened her legs to him, more than ready. Desperately ready.

Grant's eyes burnt into hers. She could feel his need. She could feel *him*, long and thick and hard between her legs, as ready for her as she was for him.

He slid his hand from behind her head and stroked her cheek with the backs of his fingers. His eyes glittered.

"You *tease*," Irina gasped, and caught his thumb between her teeth. "You—oh!"

Her words shuddered into a moan of white-hot pleasure as Grant's cock found her entrance and he thrust forward. He buried himself inside her, and she bit down, lost in sensation as her body adjusted to his size.

Oh, God, she thought, too breathless to speak out loud. He was *huge*. She hadn't looked, not really—just seen the bulge in his pants and felt him press against her through his clothes. She'd imagined he must be big, but this—she felt pinned to the bed. Anchored. Overwhelmed.

Wonderfully, gloriously overwhelmed.

Above her, Grant grunted slightly, and Irina realized she was still biting down on his thumb. *Hard.* She murmured something that she hoped sounded like an apology because she was pretty sure her tongue wasn't up to forming actual words. Not right now.

She gently kissed the pad of his thumb. And licked it. And heard Grant *groan*, this time, a low, heart-felt sound of pure longing he let go just as she felt him move inside her, pulling back and then thrusting back in. Every nerve in her body sang as she felt every inch of him, pushing deeper, faster, harder.

Irina wrapped her legs even more tightly around him, feeling the muscles of his waist flex under her thighs. Her body was sending her urgent signals, her desperate need reaching a breaking point. Gasping, she tilted her pelvis, and Grant's next thrust hit her g-spot so hard and fast she saw stars. Her orgasm tore through her like lightning, white-hot bursts of pleasure that flooded her entirely, body and mind, and left her trembling.

She opened her eyes and focused on Grant's face above her. There was a strange look of wonder in his eyes, but it only lasted for a moment before he buried his face in her shoulder. He came with a groan so deep she could feel it in her bones, and as he subsided inside her, she let her own eyes fall closed again.

Grant's weight pressed down on her, hot and sweaty and indescribably wonderful. Covered by him, his cock still pressed deep inside her, she felt entirely content. Safe, and happy, and as though she was exactly where she should be.

"Sorry about your thumb," she murmured lazily. Grant chuckled and ran his thumb over her bottom lip.

"I think I'll live," he reassured her.

She kissed it, just to be sure, and didn't complain when Grant rolled over, his other arm wrapped around her, so she rolled on top of him. She remembered, so vaguely it was like a half-forgotten bad dream, that she used to feel self-conscious about lying on top of her ex-boyfriends, worried that her extra height and weight would be too obvious in this position. But with Grant she wasn't worried at all.

Besides, given how he hauled you all the way up here, he can take it, she reasoned muzzily.

Lying on top of Grant was… *mmm*. So good it was taking away her words again. And he was still inside her. Still filling her, but without the same barely restrained urgency as before.

Without the same urgency… for now.

Irina wriggled, and her afterglow of arousal kindled new sparks. She looked down at her lover, letting her hair fall in curling waves around his face.

"Hmmm," she said, drawing the sound out and lowering her face until she was almost nose-to-nose with Grant. "I think that *almost* makes up for stealing my drink."

"Almost?" Grant's smile made her heart flip over, but she just managed to keep her cool.

"Almost." Irina bit her lip, not trusting herself to say anything more without breaking into giggles.

Luckily, Grant was suave enough for the both of them. He caught her face between his hands and kissed her passionately, his tongue teasing against her lips.

"I am so very sorry," he murmured against her lips, and then whispered into her ear: "Shall I try again?"

Chapter 8

Grant

Grant stretched luxuriously in his bed, enjoying the smooth feel of the linen sheets against his skin, the mountainous tangle of pillows and comforters—and the warmth. Mmm, yes, the warmth.

The warmth of not being the only person in the bed. Of sleeping alongside a beautiful woman, after a night of incredible love-making. He'd never felt this way with any of his previous girlfriends. It just felt so... right. As though he'd been waiting for it for—oh, for so long. His entire life. And now that he'd found her, it was the most amazing feeling in the world.

Irina made a soft mew of protest as he bundled her into his arms. Her hair was a wild mass of curls spread out across the pillows. He gently brushed a stray curl away from her face, and one chocolate-brown eye cracked open for a moment.

"Good morning, sweetheart," he murmured.

"Mmmph," she replied, and wriggled deeper under the duvet until nothing showed except her hair. Grant rolled on top of her, holding his weight on his elbows, and began to unwrap her. First, an ear appeared, and he bent down to gently nibble on it, feeling her squirm under him. Then her cheek—a kiss this time. Then his hands wandered lower, sneaking under the edges of the duvet to find the luscious, smooth curves of her breasts and belly.

Small, warm hands batted his away. "Nooo," Irina wailed softly. "'m 'sleep."

Grant leaned back on his haunches. He wanted to touch her, more than anything, wanted to wake her up with teasing strokes and kisses—but all cats knew better than to disturb another person's slumber.

Perhaps, though, there was another way he could tempt her out of bed...

Grant pulled on a pair of silk boxers and prowled into the kitchen. His panther was as sleepy as Irina, satiated and content, but even it perked up as he surveyed the contents of the fridge and pantry. Cooking breakfast might not be *hunting* exactly, but it still meant bringing food to his Irina.

The thought sent warmth flooding through his whole body.

My Irina. Mine. In my bed, in my home, in my life...

He plucked eggs and prosciutto from the fridge before he let his eyes linger over a selection of fresh herbs. He scooped all of it up and, half-distracted, carried it all over to the kitchen island.

Everything had happened so quickly, he had barely had the chance to think. Last night had been all instinct, giddy and joyful, driven by a single-minded, hot-blooded need to—to...

To claim our mate, his panther purred, and Grant's blood ran cold.

No. It can't be that. Not now. Not with her.

But he'd known that last night, hadn't he? He had known he was the poison that would irrevocably taint her life and had taken her anyway. Told himself he could protect her from his panther, as though they weren't one and the same. The wild creature whose fickle desires would destroy her—and him, the fool who went along with it.

No. He stepped back from the kitchen counter, his mind racing. He'd been attracted to Irina immediately, sure, but it wasn't just physical attraction he felt. He wanted to see her laugh, wanted to feed her and protect her and shower her with gifts. They had clicked, person to person.

It couldn't just be because of his panther. It *couldn't*.

He returned to the counter, chopping herbs almost frantically as his mind raced. He knew it had to happen eventually. His panther would find its mate and do its best to claim her. Grant had always promised himself he would be vigilant, ensuring he kept control so he didn't pull an unwary woman into that trap.

He hadn't considered the possibility that he would walk straight into it himself.

Irina. My mate. I am so, so sorry.

Grant swiped the chopped herbs into a bowl, broke in the eggs, and attacked them with a whisk.

What was he going to do now? He had to tell her—no, he couldn't. How could he live with himself, knowing he'd done that to her?

Oh, *hell*.

The full seriousness of what he had done washed over him in an icy wave.

This is what happens when you stop paying attention. When you lose control and break the most important promise you ever made.

He should never have brought Irina home with him. He should have run the moment he saw her, and instead he'd led them both straight into a trap.

Grant closed his eyes. Irina's face appeared before him, her eyes filled with tears, the way he had first seen her. She'd looked so lost and alone, and he'd moved on pure instinct to protect her.

No force in the world could have prevented him. Not even his own self-control.

Grant took a steadying breath and opened his eyes. Nothing in the world could have stopped him from protecting Irina last night, and nothing would stop him now. Except now, he had to protect her from himself.

From his panther.

Grant sighed and lit the stove. His hands moved automatically to cook breakfast as his mind tried to find a way through the maze in front of him.

Butter melted in the bottom of the pan. Grant scowled at it and then added another pat. *I should have thought about this months ago. I should have had a plan. Why did I waste so much time with Lance figuring out bullshit like PR and travel instead of the important things?*

He slowly drizzled the egg mixture into the pan, whisking as he went. He *knew* why he had avoided talking to Lance about this. He just had to admit it to himself.

He'd been afraid. He was still afraid. Secretly, Grant had hoped that he wouldn't be the first of his friends to find a mate. That Mathis, or Harley, or Moss, or hell, even Frankie, would find their beloveds first—and provide him with a good example of how a shifter male was meant to behave in that situation.

Because God knew he had no other good examples.

A quiet shuffling noise behind him pulled Grant out of his unhappy thoughts. Inside him, his panther began to purr.

Stop that.

"Good morning," he called out, looking over his shoulder. His stomach was twisting at how fast and strongly his panther had reacted, and he made sure he was smiling, so his discomfort wouldn't show on his face.

Irina was leaning against the doorframe, still wrapped in the comforter. Grant's heart thudded in his chest at the sight of her. She was so beautiful, with her rumpled hair spread over her shoulders and her feet peeking out of the bottom of the blanket.

Irina screwed up her face adorably and said,

"Mmmph?"

Grant's forced smile melted into a genuine grin. "The bathroom's back down the hall. First on your left."

"Mmmph."

That last one was probably a "thank you," Grant decided, watching Irina as she shuffled away again. His heart ached. If she knew the truth, she wouldn't be thanking him.

A few moments later, the sound of the shower turning on reached his ears, and he had to take a moment to get his thoughts back in line. He couldn't afford to be distracted. He couldn't think about the thick comforter falling to the bathroom floor, revealing Irina's soft, creamy skin. The marble tiles would be cool under her feet—cool enough to make goosebumps race across her skin? Or to make her nipples pebble, the soft pink darkening as they formed peaks. Her long, curly hair falling over her shoulders, smelling of... burning...

"Oh, dammit!" Grant cursed, snatching the pan off the heat. It was too late. His scrambled herby eggs were starting to smoke.

Hissing unhappily, he turned on the exhaust fan and dumped the burned mess out into the garbage.

What the hell are you doing? he berated himself and sighed. The pan was still sizzling slightly, and one glare at the stovetop told him he'd had the heat on far too high. And for too long. He reduced the flame and launched the pan at the sink, where it landed with a *clang*.

Grant cast a guilty look over his shoulder towards the closed door of the bathroom. There was no change to the steady rush of running water, so he could assume she hadn't heard. Or was still half-asleep enough not to notice the noise.

Irina, standing under the showerhead, hot water spraying down on her. He imagined her leaning back under the stream of water, eyes closed, water running in rivulets down her shoulders and between her breasts...

Grant groaned and knuckled his forehead. *Focus!* This was where things had gone wrong last night. He couldn't afford to lose his head again. He had to find a way out of this that wouldn't leave Irina hurt.

He needed to be *human*. And right now, he told himself firmly, that meant breakfast.

He opened the fridge again, letting the cool air wash over his bare skin. More eggs—right. And yogurt, sliced fruit—bread from the pantry...

He moved quickly, one ear pricked for noises from the bathroom. Fresh pan. Fresh whisk. Grant made a mental note to thank his housekeeper for keeping the kitchen well stocked, with utensils as well as food.

This time he managed to keep his focus. The fluffy scrambled eggs came off the heat perfectly golden and light, accompanied by thick slices of toasted sourdough and with slices of prosciutto to the side. Small serving bowls for the fruit salad and yogurt.

He debated briefly over whether to drizzle honey over the fruit salad but settled for placing it to the side. The mixed melons, dragon fruit and lychee were all perfectly ripe, despite being out of season on this side of the planet, so maybe Irina wouldn't think they needed extra sweetening.

Everything had to be perfect. What had he forgotten?

Coffee.

He had just finished blasting the beans through the grinder when the bathroom door opened, letting out a cloud of scented steam and a fresh-faced but tousled Irina. She was wrapped in his plush cotton dressing gown, almost as swamped within its folds as she had been by the comforter.

"Good morning," she said quietly, her lips curving into a shy smile. "Which is, honest, what I *meant* to say earlier, but..."

"...You're not very good at mornings?" Grant completed her sentence for her and gestured to the food arrayed on the island behind him. His voice trembled, just slightly, as he said, "Breakfast? We can eat here, or at the table, or..." He stopped himself just in time. *Back in bed? No. Bad idea.*

Irina groaned and closed her eyes. Grant bit the inside of his cheek as he waited for her to answer.

"Too many options. Here is fine." She padded forward on bare feet, just brushing past Grant. Before he knew what he was doing he reached out to her as she passed, slipping one hand under her damp hair and pushing it aside to lay a kiss on her neck. She hummed happily, almost a giggle, as the hairs on the back of Grant's neck rose.

Was that me, or my panther? How could I tell?

He took a careful step backwards. "Coffee?"

"Oh, *God*, yes. Please."

Grant pulled across a barstool for Irina. "I hope filter is okay."

"Perfect. Anything is fine. Dump the grinds straight in my mouth." She sat on the stool and leaned forward, elbows on the granite countertop. Grant could have looked at her forever, but forced himself to turn away. He filled the French press without spilling hot water on himself, somehow, and slid onto the stool beside her.

"This all looks amazing," Irina said, her eyes sweeping over the food—and then lingering on him. "You made all this just now? And I thought I was doing well figuring out how to turn the shower on."

"I'm sorry. I—shouldn't have woken you up so early." Grant winced, then passed her a plate of eggs and toast and pushed the fruit salad a little closer. And the honey. He waited until she took a bite, eyes closed, before picking up his own knife and fork.

"This is *amazing*." Irina moaned in pleasure and took another bite of eggs. "More than worth getting up at the early hour of..." She looked around the room for a clock. "Oh, hell, eleven o'clock? That's late even for *me*. But I, er, I guess I was up late..."

Despite himself, Grant caught her eye and remembered exactly what had kept them both up into the early hours of the morning. From the way her cheeks went red, she was remembering it, too.

But what are you remembering? Your own desire, or your panther's?

Irina chewed slowly, a line forming between her eyebrows, and Grant felt a tremor of unease. She swallowed and put down her knife and fork.

"Grant..."

"Is everything okay?"

He could *see* her shoulders tighten. "I just—oh, hell." She looked up, meeting his eyes. "Last night was amazing, and this is wonderful, but I want to be sure. I know I don't pick up on signals very easily when I've just woken up." She looked away, bit her lip, and looked back at him. "You didn't... expect me to disappear early, did you? I don't exactly have a lot of experience with one-night stands, you know."

Grant's panther jumped to its feet inside him, panicked. "Is that what you think this is?" he blurted out, and then covered his eyes with his hands. "Sorry. That came out wrong."

Irina was still watching him. "How should it have come out?" she asked cautiously.

Grant took a deep breath. *This is it. Your one chance to put things right.*

Wouldn't it be kinder to break it off now? To save you both heartache later on?

One look at Irina's anxious face, and he knew he couldn't. *There must be a way to fix this*, he reasoned with himself. *To have everything work out, despite the mate bond.*

He reached out and took her hand. "For a start, this isn't a one-night stand. At least, I don't want it to be."

And that's not even the half of it, he added silently, looking deep into her eyes. *I want to be with you forever. I want every morning to start like this, with you tousled and sleep-befuddled, and me tempting you out of bed with breakfast. And I want every day to end with me tempting you back into that bed.*

I just wish that all of me felt the same way.

Out loud, he added: "And I hope you feel the same."

Irina looked down at their intertwined hands, and the tension in her face eased. "Um. Yes," she muttered, her cheeks growing red. "I didn't think—I don't know. This is all so... different. *Good* different, I mean."

She looked up again and stared into Grant's face with a searching look in her eyes.

He didn't know what she was looking for, but he stared back at her, hoping with all his heart that she would find it.

"So," she said eventually, breaking the silence, "How about that coffee?"

After they had finished eating, Grant found himself searching for excuses to keep Irina around. He told himself it wasn't so that he could delay dealing with what would happen next.

Having her in his house felt so *right*. Whenever she looked around, taking in the luxury furniture and fittings, Grant had an overwhelming feeling of... rightness. As though all along, the penthouse had just been waiting for her to arrive, and now that she was here, everything had fallen into place.

Unfortunately, life wasn't that simple.

"Can you see my other shoe?"

Grant was tempted to say, no, he couldn't, and to kick the offending footwear further under the sofa. Instead, he fished it out and handed it to Irina. He caught her slight grimace as she looked at the spindly six-inch heels and hid his own smile as she quickly exchanged them for another pair of much more sensible-looking shoes, which had been stashed in her bag.

He even managed not to sigh as she put the sensible shoes on and slung her handbag over her shoulder.

They had already exchanged numbers, and schedules, and enough brief touches and kisses that Grant wanted nothing more than to drag her back to the bedroom.

"I'm working tonight," Irina had protested when he suggested they meet again for dinner that evening. "And I don't get my schedule for next week until Monday morning." She frowned, clearly frustrated. "I can see if someone else can take my shift, but we're really short-staffed at the moment."

"I understand," Grant said. At least, part of him did. He worried that the part of him that didn't might be his panther side. He—or it—wanted to keep her here, in the warmth and safety of his home—not let her go, out into the cold, and potentially not see her for days. *Days!*

She rubbed the strap of her bag as she gave him a hopeful smile. "I'll see if I can switch Monday out, at least."

Monday? But that's two days away!

"I'll see about making dinner reservations for us," Grant said, hoping his—or his panther's—impatience didn't show on his own face. "Anywhere in particular?"

Irina laughed. "Anywhere except..." she rattled off a list of restaurants, some of which Grant recognized. "...because if I negotiate Monday off and then make my workmates serve me dinner, they are going to be *pissed*."

"Understood." Grant pulled her to him for one last kiss. She was tall enough in her heels that he barely needed to bend down at all to capture her lips with his. "Until Monday, then."

"Until then." A smile hovered around Irina's lips. "Good luck tracking down your friend."

Right. Mathis.

As the door closed behind Irina, Grant tried to convince himself that he hadn't completely forgotten about his quest to pry Mathis out of wherever he was hiding the moment he'd set eyes on her.

Grant was clearing the remains of their breakfast away when he heard the front door open again. He spun around, hoping it would be Irina—and saw Lance striding through the door.

"Boss." Lance greeted him with a brief nod before he made an efficient survey of the room. His grey-green eyes, which always looked so startling against his dark skin, took in the dirty plates and coffee mugs, the burnt pan in the sink—and then flicked towards the bedroom.

Grant was almost certain that Lance couldn't see through the solid wood of the bedroom door, but that didn't stop him from staring pointedly at it, and then raising one suggestive eyebrow.

"Did you have a good night?"

"I don't think that's an appropriate question to ask your employer," Grant retorted, delaying the inevitable. He took a steadying breath. "She's—"

"Your mate." Lance's tone was matter-of-fact.

"How—" Grant's mouth twisted. What a question.

Lance gave him an incredulous look. "*How* do I know? Did you look in a mirror at all last night? Of course I know. Moss knows. His staff know. I'm sure Francine knows, from the way she was glaring at you both. Hell, everyone who saw you last night must know *something* was going on, even if they didn't understand what it was." He grabbed his phone out of his pocket and waved it at Grant. "I rerouted your calls through my phone after you two disappeared last night, and it's been ringing off the hook."

Grant paused. "Ringing? Who *calls* someone at a time like this?"

"All your friends' parents," said Lance flatly. "And my aunt. You'd better be giving me a bonus for *that* conversation, by the way."

"Oh." Grant leaned his elbows on the granite countertop and put his head in his hands. He took a deep breath. Speaking of difficult conversations... "Right. I need a plan."

There was a *click* as Lance set a tablet down on the countertop. "I have had some thoughts along those lines. Shifters mating with humans isn't that uncommon, and I've prepared several options for strategies going forward. From my research, most shifters reveal their true natures to non-shifter mates very early in the relationship, so I'm assuming you've told her—"

"No." Grant held up a hand to stop Lance. He pulled the tablet across and scrolled through a few pages. "I haven't told her. And these aren't going to work."

Lance was staring at him. "But you *have* to tell her."

"*No*," Grant growled again.

"Grant—" Lance sighed and pushed his reading glasses up his nose. "You hired me to advise you on keeping your shifter nature secret, fine. But you cannot keep it a secret from your mate. I know you weren't brought up in a shifter family, but—"

"Enough!" Grant slammed his hands on the countertop and stalked away. He rubbed his forehead, grimacing.

Not brought up in a shifter family? That was one way of putting it.

"All your—plans. They all involve telling Irina about the bond between us. I won't do that."

Lance's brow creased. "You're going to keep it from her? Obviously, it will be a difficult discussion, but she's your mate. You're meant to be together. Even if it's a shock, she'll see that it's meant to be."

"Really? Some man she met less than twenty-four hours ago tells her she's his soulmate, and she has to just go with it? I don't know what your *research* says, but I know for a fact it doesn't always work that way."

Not for shifters like me. Not for panthers.

Grant's heart was hammering. He stalked around the room, feeling trapped. As trapped as Irina now was.

"So, we need a new plan. All right." Lance's voice was steady and calm. Everything Grant wasn't. "You're not going to reveal your shifter nature to this woman. Not yet, or not at all?"

There was a hint of warning in his voice. Grant shook his head. "Later. I will, later."

"I'm glad to hear it." Lance's fingers flew over the tablet's screen. "Well, it will take some additional effort to keep your shifter activities discreet with a partner in the picture, but it won't be impossible. Do you have an end date in mind for your subterfuge, or...?"

Grant ground his teeth. Lance's professional attitude was infuriating, but he had to admit it was useful. It forced him to face up to what he was doing.

"I'll court her like a normal human. And then—if this does go anywhere, between us, as *humans*—then I'll tell her. But only then."

Lance snorted softly. "*If*? More like *when*."

"If," Grant insisted, and added silently: *And* if *I can love her. Truly love her, as a man, and not a faithless panther.*

Chapter 9

Irina

Irina set off down the street in a dream. Her body ached in a thousand good ways, and even though she hadn't ended up getting a lot of sleep, she felt completely relaxed and refreshed. All the little worries and stresses that had preyed on her mind since she returned from the mountains had been washed away by one night of incredible sex.

She snuggled into her coat. She supposed this was *technically* a walk of shame, but she was feeling anything but ashamed of going home with Grant the night before.

Irina inhaled slowly. She had showered off all traces of last night's fun, but it wasn't like she had brought a change of clothes to the party. Her skin smelled of the spicy-scented soap from Grant's shower, and her dress still held traces of *his* scent. It felt intimate. Erotic. She could still feel Grant's hands on her body, cradling her weight, sliding her dress up her thighs.

Even the memory of his tantalizing, spicy musk made her heart beat faster.

And he gave you his phone number, she thought, still amazed. *The best sex you've had in your life, with the hottest, most gorgeous man you've ever seen... and he wants you to keep in touch.*

She was so amazed that she wandered for several blocks before she realized she had no idea where she was.

And she was scheduled to work that evening.

"Damn," she said out loud, drawing a few stares from other pedestrians. She looked around, trying to find some landmark or street name that would help her orient herself. No luck. This neighborhood, wherever it was, might as well have been in another city for all Irina could tell.

Irina groaned and rifled through her bag for her phone. It was on the dumb end of smartphones, but she might be able to coax the map app open before the whole thing froze up.

Speaking of freezing up...

Irina selected the map app and stepped to the edge of the sidewalk so she wouldn't be in anyone else's way. While she waited for her phone to wake up, she rubbed her hands up and down her arms to warm them up. Even if the map app opened, it wouldn't be any good if her fingers were too cold to search for the closest subway station.

Traffic was slow this morning in whatever-neighborhood-this-was, so she wasn't paying any attention to the road and didn't hear the motorbike as it approached.

"Lady, look out!"

Irina looked up. A dark-skinned young woman with a cloud of brown hair was running toward her, hand outstretched. Suddenly, the rev of an engine roared through the air. Irina just had time to catch the look of shock in the other woman's eyes before something slammed into her from behind.

Irina screamed as she plunged forward, the engine roaring in her ears. A sharp yank on her shoulder pulled her around and she stumbled, trying desperately to keep her footing.

Her attacker was clad entirely in black leather, down to the leather glove tearing at the strap on her handbag. The pale morning light glinted off his full-face helmet.

"Hey—ow!" she cried out. Her bag was slung across her chest, and the biker was pulling on it so hard that the strap was beginning to cut into her neck. "Get off, you asshole!"

"Yeah, leave her alone!"

Irina ducked as a bag swung into her field of vision and smacked the biker in the face. It must have been heavier than it looked, because the biker jolted backward, losing his grip on Irina's bag.

Her rescuer, the woman who'd called out to warn her before, pirouetted unsteadily as the weight of her messenger bag spun her around. Irina grabbed her own bag with both hands and froze.

Her body was screaming at her to run, but her heart told her she couldn't leave the other woman alone. Not after she'd come to her help. And if this guy had been willing to run her down, what might he do to her?

She couldn't leave, but what *could* she do?

The other woman regained her balance and squared up against the biker, readying her bag for another swing. Irina's heart was beating so hard, she felt like she was about to choke.

"What's going on?" another voice called from farther down the street. Even with her eyes fixed on her attacker, Irina could tell that the sidewalk was beginning to fill with interested onlookers.

The biker leapt into movement, and for a moment Irina was terrified he was about to circle back and run her down. Instead, he swung the motorcycle around and roared off down the street.

Irina sagged with relief.

"Phew! What the hell was that about?" Irina's rescuer slung her bag back over her shoulder and dusted herself down. She looked across at Irina, frowning. "Are you all right? He didn't hurt you, did he?"

Irina took a deep breath and rubbed her neck. Her feet still felt rooted to the ground. If the guy had sped toward her instead of racing away, would she even have been able to move in time?

She looked down, taking stock and giving herself a moment to pull herself together. The top of her bag was open, but she didn't think anything had been taken. One of her high heels had fallen out, but her wallet was still there, and her phone was still in her hand.

"Uh, I'm fine, I think." *Ow*, she added silently as she dropped her phone into its pocket in her handbag. She had been holding onto it so tightly, its edges left little grooves in her palm.

"You sure?" The woman flexed her arm and winced. "I think my chiropractor is going to have a thing or two to say about my swinging technique." She patted Irina reassuringly on the arm, and then grimaced and stretched her shoulder again. "Well, I'm glad I was here, anyway. Are you sure you're okay?"

"I'm fine," Irina repeated quietly and shivered. It had happened so fast—the whole thing couldn't have taken more than a minute. "Just unlucky, I guess."

Irina bent down to retrieve her lost shoe. *Thank God I was wearing my work pumps instead of my stilettos,* she thought. *I'd have two broken ankles by now for sure.*

"Everything okay here?"

The crowd that had gathered during the confrontation was drawing closer. Irina closed her handbag and adjusted the strap over her shoulder. Now that the biker was gone, and nothing had happened, she felt more self-conscious than afraid.

"Thanks for—you know, going after that guy," she said awkwardly. "I—"

"Dr. Hope!" someone called out, and the woman's head snapped around. She waved at the newcomer and gave Irina an apologetic grin.

"Sorry—gotta run."

"I thought that was you!" A middle-aged woman with her arm in a cast came up and gave the woman—Dr. Hope—a one-armed hug. "I was just telling Danny, I said, that'll be the doctor..."

Irina let the crowd swallow her. Her rescuer was clearly well-known in the neighborhood, whatever neighborhood this was. A ten-year-old boy ran up and started re-enacting the confrontation with added *Biff!* and *Pow!* special effects, and it wasn't hard for Irina to slip unnoticed out the back of the crowd.

The apartment door swung open just as Irina reached for the handle. Clare stood with her arms folded on the other side, her nose held as high in the air as she could manage.

"And just *where* have you been, young lady?" she demanded, fixing Irina with a stern glare. The effect was undermined by her fluffy Hello Kitty dressing gown and the fact that her face fell as soon as she took in Irina's appearance. "Shit—are you okay?"

"I'm *fine*," Irina insisted.

"You look as though you saw a ghost," Clare exclaimed. "Are you feeling okay?" She paused. "How was your date?"

Irina closed her eyes and leaned against the wall. "Amazing. Wonderful. And then some asshole tried to sideswipe me and grab my purse when I was on my way back here…"

She broke off and let her head thud back onto the wall. "Dammit, he better not have bruised my neck."

Clare snorted. "Are we talking about Grant Diaz here, or…?"

"The mugger. Gross, Clare," Irina grumbled. She ducked around Clare and tossed her handbag through the open door into her bedroom. "Can I borrow your laptop? I need to check my schedule for next week, and my phone's had it."

"Go for it. Kitchen bench." Clare followed her into the "kitchen," which was really just the corner of their living area. The bench doubled as a dining table and study desk, when it wasn't home to a week's worth of takeout boxes.

Irina nudged a pizza box aside and found Clare's laptop. She nodded at the box as she waited for the computer to boot up. "Celebration pizza or misery pizza?"

"Celebration!" replied Clare chirpily. "The exhibition was fantastic, you'll never believe—aha, no changing the subject." She stood at the end of the bench, elbows on the countertop and chin in her hands. "*Talk.*"

"Mugger or date?"

Clare rolled her eyes. "Let's say… ten seconds on the mugger, because I'm a lovely person and care about your safety, and then the rest of the day on the date. Hey, don't look at me like that."

"Your priorities never fail to amaze me, Clare."

"Ten seconds!"

Irina gave Clare a brief, slightly edited version of her encounter with the crazy biker. She made it sound like the guy had just clipped past her, not rammed her head-on. After all, it wasn't like she was hurt or anything. She didn't want to make a big deal of it.

While she talked, she found the link for her work app and tapped in her login details. As always, she bit back a grumble of complaint as she waited for her account to load.

Irina had worked part-time for the same hospitality agency while she was studying before she had to go back home. Back then, the system had been simple: turn up at Ass O'Clock on Monday morning, squint at the schedule posted on the staffroom door, and copy down your shifts for the week.

By the time she came back to the city, the boss had gotten *technological*. And, *technically,* Irina supposed that the online scheduling system was a lot superior to the old bit-of-paper-on-the-door deal.

If you could afford a phone that could actually run it without freezing and dying, and if you didn't have to borrow your roommate's laptop every day to check that your schedule hadn't been changed at the last minute.

"... and Grant was, well, you know. He's really sweet and funny. We went to dinner at a restaurant run by a friend of his, and then, um. Back to his place."

Irina scanned her schedule for the next week, and her heart sank. Sure, she could tell Grant she was free for another date—if he didn't mind it being in the middle of the night or between the hours of three and four-thirty on Thursday afternoon. She groaned so loud she missed what Clare was saying.

"Sorry, what? I was busy regretting telling my manager I wanted extra shifts this month."

Clare prodded her in the shoulder. "I *said*, what was his place like?" She leaned closer. "What's it like to sleep in a billionaire's bedroom?"

"A—what?" Irina frowned. "What did you just say?"

Clare stared at her as though she'd just grown an extra head. "Oh, my God, Irina. *Grant Diaz*? His mother is *the* Mariana Diaz. The one who owns, like, half of every company you've ever heard of."

"Uh?" Irina racked her brain. *I've never heard of her. I've never heard of anyone. This is why I spent half the year in the mountains, where there is no one to know.*

"Irina, he is *mega rich*. Like, an actual billionaire. His mother raised him by herself, right, and he started working at the family business after college and made it *rain*." Clare ran over to the sofa and began sifting through old magazines. "I think there was a feature on him in one of these... but I can't believe you never heard of him! He was all over the internet last year. Especially after someone got a video of him getting out of a pool and Twitter went *nuts*. Come on, you can't tell me you haven't heard of him."

"Silverstream doesn't have Twitter," Irina said automatically.

"You mean *you* don't have Twitter. I've been to Silverstream, remember, I know that everyone else in the town lives in the twenty-first century. Did you ever even have the internet put on at the cottage?"

Irina shook her head absently. *A billionaire? Grant?*

"But he seemed so... normal," she said faintly.

"Oh, sweetie. Please tell me he has, like, a bath made out of pure gold. With diamond taps. As for his bed..." Clare squinted into the middle distance, lost in wild speculation. "I'm thinking either super space-age, like, oh, like hovers above the ground or something, *or*... some massive four-poster thing. Space or medieval. Am I right?"

Irina just stared at her. "It was... a bed? A normal, nice bed."

"Oh, you are *hopeless*. Okay. Dinner. Tell me at least that dinner was amazing. Where did you go?"

Irina was starting to feel like she was being interrogated. She pinched her lips together. "Um. I don't know? It was really nice, though, too."

Clare glared at her through her fingers. "Nice like the bed? Nice like Grant? That's all you've got?"

Irina racked her brains for any morsel of information that might satisfy her friend. "Um. The owner of the restaurant was a friend of his. Moss somebody?"

"Moss? You went to *Moss*?"

"No, Moss was the chef's name," Irina corrected her. Clare snorted.

"*And* the name of his restaurant. Holy shit, Irina. *No one* gets into Moss on a Friday night, that place has a twelve-month waiting list. And a waiting list for the waiting list, probably." She stared at Irina, her eyes like saucers. "Please tell me you at least paid attention to the menu."

Irina bit her lip and winced. "It's not my fault! I was distracted!"

Clare collapsed with a cry of despair. "And there I was, working the exhibition, thinking, *Sure, Irina might have run off and abandoned me, but at least I'll get some good gossip out of it*. So much for that!"

Irina shut the laptop. *And you were worried she'd be pissed that you turned tail in the middle of the event*, she told herself, and nudged Clare gently in the ribs as she headed for her bedroom. "So, make something up! A bed made out of a giant diamond, was that it?"

"I don't know, Irina, was it? Was it made out of a diamond?"

"Nope. It was emerald. To match his eyes." Irina stuck her tongue out and shut the door in Clare's despairing face. Alone in her room, she put her back against the door and took a deep breath.

Grant is a billionaire? I guessed he was well-off, but... holy shit.

A billionaire? Billionaires were people like Francine Delacourt: polished, remote, and so arrogantly confident in their massive, *literal* worth that they didn't bother treating normal people like Irina like, well. Like they were people, and not furniture.

Grant was confident. He moved through the world as though convinced that he belonged wherever he was, whether that was a fancy gallery opening or a grimy back alley. And polished, well, she didn't imagine that his five-o'clock shadow was ever allowed to make it to six-o'clock without a careful buzz. But remote? Arrogant?

Irina remembered how Grant had behaved around her. Smooth and suave and, yes, completely convinced of his own good looks. But he had been so—

She didn't want to use the word *considerate*. That sounded so dry and stuffy. He'd been... aware. Of her, and of himself, and the space he took up in the world. He was careful. As though he was watching himself watching her and was occasionally mortified by what he saw.

Irina realized she was smiling to herself. *Like when he introduced himself to you—that was adorable!* Sexy *adorable.*

She closed her eyes and brought up his face in her mind. The way his brow wrinkled in dismay when he flubbed his pick-up line. Even when he messed up, he was charming. One burning glance from those eyes, and she would forgive him any number of cheesy lines.

And now she wouldn't be able to see him for a week. *More* than a week. Her next evening off was nine days away. Monday. The most romantic night of the week. *Not.*

And she had to do laundry. And buy a new dress. And groceries. And a million other boring, mundane things before she saw him again.

Grant's emerald-green eyes disappeared in a puff of responsibilities.

Irina pushed herself off the door, sighing. Where was her bag, with her shoes? There—and her stockings, which went straight in the laundry basket.

Do billionaires do laundry? Oh, damn, I must have caught them on something. I bet billionaires don't have to fix runs in their stockings with nail polish.

Her hand hovered over her phone. The longing to call Grant hit her like—well, like a motorbike steered by a leather-clad maniac.

And if I call him now, I'll seem like the maniac.

She forced herself to plug the phone into the charger without unlocking it. Then, the moment she turned her back, it started to buzz.

The hairs on the back of Irina's neck prickled. *No way. It's gotta be work, or...*

Or him. The only people who ever called Irina were telemarketers. Or Clare. And Clare was still loudly despairing in the next room.

It's probably a telemarketer, Irina told herself, barely daring to look at the caller ID.

When she saw that it read *Grant Diaz*, all her breath rushed out and she sat heavily on the bed. She fumbled with the screen, accepting the call.

"Hello?" she said tentatively, almost in a whisper.

"Irina?"

Irina's shoulders relaxed as a tension she didn't know she'd been holding faded away. "I wasn't expecting you to call so soon," she admitted, then quickly added, "Um, I'm glad you did, though!"

"Is—is everything all right?"

Grant's voice was hesitant. Irina frowned.

"Yeah. I just got home, actually."

"Nothing's wrong? I thought..." he stopped, and Irina could almost see that adorable furrow form between his eyebrows and him rubbing it away with the back of his hand. He chuckled self-consciously. "Never mind. I'm being an idiot."

Irina flopped back, landing on a crumpled comforter that didn't hold a candle to the plush blankets and duvets on Grant's bed. She closed her eyes, focusing on his voice and the soft sound of his breathing, just audible through the phone.

"I checked my schedule," she said, figuring that was why he had called. "It's bad news, I'm afraid."

She explained about her double shifts, but not that she had been the one to request extra hours in the first place. Rent payments didn't exactly make for romantic pillow-talk.

"My next day off isn't until a week from Monday," she finished, trying not to sound disappointed. "I can talk to my manager then about the following week's schedule, but we're pretty low on staff at the moment, so no promises."

She waited for Grant's response. There was a tapping noise on the other end of the line, as though he was rapping his fingers on a table as he thought. Then the scrape of a chair.

"How much sleep would you be willing to give up on Sunday night? If I promise to make it worth your while."

Irina couldn't help the smile that spread across her face. With her eyes closed, she could almost imagine he was in the room with her. She covered her mouth with her free hand, feeling giddy and ridiculous.

"Oh, well, if you're going to make it worth my while," she replied, holding in a giggle.

"Dinner?"

"My shift finishes at ten."

"Dessert, then. And an adventure."

"You drive a hard bargain, Mr. Diaz." Irina tapped her fingers against her lips. She would have to mainline coffee all day to keep from falling asleep, but it would be worth it. "But I think I can make time for you in my schedule."

"When should I pick you up? And where from?"

Irina gave him her address and a time that would let her get out of her work clothes and into date mode. Afterwards, she stayed on the bed, staring up at the ceiling.

Sunday. Right now, that seemed like an eternity. And after last night's adventure, she couldn't wait to find out what he was planning for their second date.

No more running away, she told herself. *Not when you've got such a great guy to run towards.*

Chapter 10

Grant

Grant put down his phone and frowned. Lance looked up from his tablet.

"Everything all right, boss?"

"She's fine. I mean—everything's fine." Grant shifted uncomfortably as a cold shiver ran down his spine. The shiver was only an echo of what he had felt earlier: a sudden, bone-cold freeze that left his every nerve on edge. A feeling that something was very wrong.

His immediate instinct had been to find Irina. He couldn't have explained why—not least to her. Not even to Lance, who looked at him like he'd lost his mind.

He had held off for twenty agonizing minutes, unable to focus on anything except the lingering feeling of unease. And then, when he had finally decided enough was enough and called her, she was fine. Nothing was wrong.

"I'm imagining things," he said out loud.

Lance pushed his reading glasses further up his nose and peered at Grant through them. "Things like what?" he asked.

"Just... things."

"Hmmf. Call your mother," Lance advised, and returned his attention to his work.

His mother. Grant let the idea spin around his mind, just once, before batting it away.

It was technically a good idea. None of Grant's shifter friends were mated yet. Lance and Moss were constantly single. Harley was still more interested in his planes than any of the girlfriends he took up in them. Lance... well, he hadn't known Lance as long as he'd known the others, but he was pretty sure the snow leopard wasn't mated, either.

Mathis? Six months ago, Grant would have added him to the list, but he had to admit he had no idea. Maybe his old friend had found his mate and that was why he'd gone to ground. If that turned out to be the case, he'd have other things on his mind besides answering Grant's calls.

Grant stalked around the room, drumming out a beat on the kitchen countertop as he passed it.

His mother was traveling for work. Maybe that was a good thing. Grant couldn't imagine a situation in which seeing her in person before he figured out what to do with Irina would go well.

To Lance, it probably made sense for Grant to talk to his mother. Grant didn't know what the mating bond meant for a panther shifter; his mother would; therefore, he should talk to his mother. *What a plan.*

He could call Mathis's parents, but that wouldn't work, either. They were lions, pride animals. Grant needed to talk to someone who knew about panther shifters. And the only person Grant knew who fit that description was his mother.

Tap, tap, tap tap. Tap.

Unfortunately.

Rattle-tap.

How would his mother react to the news? He didn't need to guess.

Mariana Diaz wasn't a shifter. Until she was nineteen, she hadn't known there was such a thing. Then she'd met Grant's father.

He'd heard the story countless times growing up. A simplified version from his mom, with all the scandal and most of the pain edited out. But he'd picked up bits of the truth here and there, learned a lot about shifters in general from Mathis and the others, and pieced the story together eventually.

Until he was fifteen, Grant had only ever heard his father referred to as *That Man*, usually followed by a spit. Even after he found out his father's name, Grant found himself referring to him with the same epithet. And the same spit.

That Man had turned Mariana Diaz's life upside down. He was a panther who made grandiose claims about how he and Mariana were meant for one another. He took her on a whirlwind vacation around the world, introducing her to incredible places and experiences. He told her no one could know about his shifter secret, not her friends, not her family, no one. He made her feel special.

Six months later, he skulked out of their hotel room in the middle of the night.

He took Mariana's wallet and her passport and left her pregnant with a baby boy who turned into a tiny, black-fuzzed cub when he sneezed. A panther shifter.

So, how would Mariana Diaz react to the news that her panther-shifter son had fallen head over heels with a human woman? Probably not with the delight that Lance was imagining.

"Maybe later," he muttered. He shoved his phone into a pocket and jumped as it immediately started buzzing.

Frankie? he thought, seeing the name on the caller ID. *What does she want?*

He remembered how she had treated Irina the night before and bristled.

Whatever she wants, it can wait, he decided, and declined the call.

His circuit of the room took him back past the open-plan kitchen. *Tap-tap, taptaptap, ratta-tat. Tap.*

Across the room, Lance slammed his palms onto the desk. "Will you *stop?*"

Grant's fingers froze mid-tap. "What?" he said, innocently.

Lance slumped back in his chair. "Forget it. I need a break, anyway." He glared. "I'm going to get myself a drink. Try to restrain yourself from batting it off the side of the table."

Grant flung himself on the nearest sofa, instead. He listened to Lance padding around the kitchen, pouring himself a glass of water. *Bat it off the table?* Grant had more control over his cat-like impulses than *that*.

Most of the time.

Grant groaned. Screw water. He needed a beer.

"You might as well head home," he called out to Lance.

"Head home? You wish. Grant," Lance said, sitting down opposite him with a thump, "We need to talk."

Eyes closed, Grant bit back a groan. He could imagine just how the snow leopard was looking at him. Peering over the top of his glasses.

He glanced across to the other sofa. *Yep.*

Lance pushed his glasses up his nose. "I don't understand you. I know you didn't grow up in a shifter family, but you're good friends with other shifters. The Delacourts, Moss Taylor, the Ameses—I'm just going off the call log from last night here, by the way. They must have talked to you about the mate bond. Harley's parents' romance makes even my aunt sigh. So why are you acting like it's such a terrible thing?"

Grant sat up slowly. It was true. He'd had plenty of good examples of shifter relationships growing up. His mother had been diligent in making connections with the local shifter community, so Grant would learn about that side of himself.

But none of them were panthers. None of them came from homes broken by a panther shifter's disregard for his mate.

"I told you," he said out loud. "I'm done discussing that."

There was a *clink* as Lance set down his glass on the coffee table and settled back in the sofa. He pulled off his glasses and folded them into his shirt pocket.

"Very well. Then let's discuss what you're going to do next. Your *human* dating plan." He paused for Grant to interject, and when Grant remained silent, continued. "It sounds like everything went smoothly last night. Moss sent through the tab, and the apartment manager passed on a very polite note of complaint about residents who think it's appropriate to sprint through professional kitchens with strange women slung over their shoulders. What am I missing?" He paused. "Oh, yes. The traffic violations."

Grant drummed his fingers on the back of the sofa. "You've got a strange definition of everything going smoothly," he muttered.

Lance shrugged. "It worked out for you, didn't it? As for what you should do next... Gifts? Dinner? Er... Sexts?" He fiddled with his glasses again, and eventually slipped them back onto his nose. "You don't want to tell her you're a shifter—fine. She's human. Treat her like one. Lie to her, with casual, believable lies about how you're nothing but a rich guy who likes to travel a lot, and hope she falls deeply enough in love with that version of you that she forgives you when she learns the truth."

Grant leapt to his feet. "How *dare* you?" he snarled.

Lance didn't move. He looked up at Grant from the sofa, a patient expression on his face.

"I recommend not going all yowling-cat-man on her, either," he said calmly, and Grant realized that his fangs and teeth weren't just fighting to form: they had taken shape.

He stretched his jaw, willing his teeth to shrink back down to human size, and flexed his hands until the curved claws were replaced by short, smooth human fingernails.

"I'm sorry," he said, stunned. "That's never happened before. I usually have more control."

"I hope you get my point, Grant," Lance said, all seriousness now. He leaned forward, fixing Grant with his pale stare. "I understand the reasoning behind your decision—some of it, at least. You don't want to pressure her; that's admirable. But you have to be careful not to build your relationship on a lie."

Grant collapsed back onto the sofa, staring at his hands. "That's the trick, isn't it?" he said bitterly.

"Don't sound so put out. At least you're not cooling your heels in a cabin in the woods, or wherever it is that Mathis Delacourt's hauled himself off to after his last failed fling."

Grant looked up. "That's where he is?"

"Who knows? From what Frankie was saying last night, even she doesn't know where he is." Lance shrugged, and Grant remembered that the two men had never really gotten along. "Gone to lick his wounds somewhere is my guess. Anyway. Back to the topic at hand."

"Courting Irina. As a human." Grant sat back, staring at the ceiling.

"You can't do worse than Mathis."

Grant glared at Lance, who was quietly chuckling to himself.

Lance grinned and adjusted his glasses. "Show her a good time. Show her you're trustworthy, and that you'll look after her. Make her feel special. Does she like flowers? Chocolates? Jewelry?"

Gifts. Yes, Grant's panther purred. He remembered how happy Irina had looked, wrapped in his bed that morning, her skin caressed by Egyptian cotton. If he couldn't keep her in his bed all week, he could at least give her other comforts. Something to remember him by, when she couldn't be with him. Something to caress her skin when he wasn't there…

CHAPTER 11

IRINA

"You're *not* wearing that again."

Irina sighed and rolled her eyes. She'd raced home at the end of her shift and spent the last hour bouncing off the walls of the tiny apartment in a panic, showering, shaving, moisturizing, straightening her hair...

She hadn't seen Grant in a week, and there wasn't a minute of that time where he hadn't been on her mind. His eyes. His smile. The way the muscles in his arms flexed as he held her.

Those memories had done a lot to make her shifts more bearable. Every time she worried about getting an order wrong, or felt her shoulders ache as she hauled another pile of plates out back, she remembered Grant's smile, and somehow she didn't find it as difficult anymore. She had even talked back to the manager at that awful fish place when the guy tried to rip off her tips. And he'd backed down!

She felt like a new woman. And she *liked* it.

Half an hour, and she would see him again. Even just the thought of it made her shiver with anticipation—and fear.

What if he's changed his mind? What if he's decided I'm not worth the trouble?

In short, she was not in the mood for Clare's judgmental attitude about her wardrobe.

Their door buzzer had gone off a few minutes earlier. Clare had rushed off to deal with whatever the message was, and Irina had secretly hoped this meant she would have time to get dressed without any commentary. So much for that.

Clare was back, poking her head around Irina's bedroom door, and judging her outfit. *Dammit.*

"Give it a rest, Clare." Irina dropped the black knit dress back on her bed and glared at her friend. "It's the only nice dress I've got. I can't rock up to whatever fancy restaurant he's taking me to in jeans and a sweatshirt." *Or the mono-boob monstrosity,* she added silently. But it would be a cold day in hell before she forced herself into that dress again.

Still, the fact that she was stuck wearing the same dress she had worn on their last date stung more than she had expected. Irina had meant to find the time to go shopping and pick up a cheap outfit during the week, but her schedule—and bank account—hadn't played along. Even those extra tips had been immediately gobbled up by her share of the utilities bill.

She picked up the black knit dress and sighed.

"This will have to do. If I wear one of your pashminas with it, maybe he won't notice it's the same one. And if he does... well, it's got, you know, good memories attached to it."

Her cheeks burned as those memories flooded her mind. Not just the night itself, and that amazing breakfast with Grant sitting beside her in nothing but his underwear, either. She still got a thrill remembering heading home the morning after, wearing the same dress Grant had torn off her the night before, with his masculine scent and the memory of his touch lingering on her body.

She lifted the dress to her face and inhaled. She had washed it, of course, so it smelled like lavender. There wasn't a hint of Grant's spicy, intoxicating musk left.

Maybe we can change that tonight, she thought, and hid her grin in the fabric.

"Uh-huh," came Clare's voice from the door. "Sorry, do you and the dress want some privacy? Should I go?"

Without waiting for an answer, Clare swanned through the door. Irina noticed she was holding something big behind her back. As big as the grin spreading across her face.

"What have you got there?" Irina narrowed her eyes suspiciously. *Who was that at the door? I'm not expecting Grant for another half-hour.*

When Clare pulled out a garment box from behind her back, Irina's eyes widened in surprise. "Oh, Clare, you shouldn't have!"

"I didn't," Clare reassured her, her eyes sparkling. "That was Bolton from downstairs at the door just now. He said the courier must have left this behind his desk earlier, because it didn't fit in our mail slot, but he only found it now."

"A courier left it at his desk?" Irina stared at the box. She didn't recognize the designer's logo embossed on the front, but the box itself oozed luxury. It was cream-colored, with a raised linen texture, and looked completely out of place in Irina's messy room.

Clare pushed the box under her nose. "Open it!" she commanded, wagging the box back and forth. "Open i-i-i-it. No-o-o-ow."

"Wow," Irina breathed as she gently took the box. She felt as if she moved too quickly, it might disappear.

The box was lighter than she thought it would be, but it didn't explode or vanish or turn into mist. She pushed up the lid until she could feel it was about to come off.

"Three guesses who this is from," she murmured, glancing up at Clare.

Clare was practically bouncing up and down with anticipation. "Just open it!"

Irina took a deep breath and pushed the lid off. It slid to the floor, unnoticed, as she stared at what was inside.

"Oh, *wow*," she gasped.

"Wow is right."

Nestled on a cloudy cushion of tissue paper was a dress. Irina fumbled the box onto her bed and just barely hesitated before lifting the garment out. "Oh, this is—this is *too much*."

The dress was a rich forest green color, made of heavy, luxurious silk that seemed to glow in her hands. The fabric was cool to the touch, and even hanging from Clare's hands, it draped beautifully. She couldn't imagine what it would look like on.

Probably amazing. If it fits.

"I can't wear this," she babbled. "It's way too fancy. I..."

Even as she said it, Irina was looking for the zipper. There wasn't one. Instead, the whole dress fell open down the front, secured only by a few mother-of-pearl buttons and a wrap-around sash. She blushed as she thought of how easily the buttons and sash could fall away.

Her fingers itched to try the dress on, but her stomach twisted. Friday night had been a glorious, sexy adventure, and she was looking forward to dinner tonight, but this?

I'm not the sort of girl who gets sent dresses like this. She bit her lip before the words came out.

What is your problem? Why is this dress making you feel like your stomach is about to explode with butterflies?

It wasn't as though she regretted Friday night. She'd never had a one-night stand before, but everything had felt—well, so *right*. Grant was sexy and fun, and it had been far too long since Irina had let herself really cut loose and enjoy life.

But this... flowers would have been one thing. Chocolates. Thoughtful, but impersonal.

A dress was so much more personal. Grant had picked this out, chosen it with her in mind—chosen it with her *body* in mind. He'd probably imagined her wearing it. It was so *intimate*.

A tremble of anticipation went up Irina's spine at that thought, and her fingers tightened. She might not think she was the sort of women men sent fancy gifts to, but Grant clearly thought otherwise.

The dress shone in her hands, the silk whispering under her fingers. She couldn't help but feel as though it was promising so much more than just dinner and sex.

And if it was...

Irina shook herself. *Stop it. This is just... for fun, right? An adventure. Grant probably didn't want you embarrassing him again with your cheap clothing.*

"Well, I hope it fits," was all she said out loud.

"Can't be worse than the mono-boob monstrosity," Clare commented. "Do you need a hand with it?"

"No, thanks. I'm fine. Actually—can you grab your makeup bag? I think my face is going to need an upgrade to match this dress."

Irina waited until Clare had ducked out to the bathroom. She felt strangely self-conscious at the thought of putting on the dress in front of Clare.

She unhooked the tiny buttons one by one. Before she could change her mind, she quickly slipped out of her dressing gown and slipped the shimmering dress around her shoulders.

The fabric was so smooth it was cool to the touch, and the constricting tightness she was dreading as it inevitably turned out to be too small never materialized. The dress slid over her skin like—

Like silk! she thought, giggling with delight.

She kept her eyes closed as the dress settled around her and did up the buttons one by one. It felt amazing, and she didn't want to break the spell by opening her eyes. Not least because the top button was perilously far down her cleavage. She felt sexy and beautiful. She really didn't want to ruin the illusion by opening her eyes and seeing her bra spilling out of the neckline.

"Oh, my God, Irina! That is stunning!"

There was a heavy *thump* that Irina assumed was Clare's makeup bag landing on her bed, and a moment later she had to open her eyes as her friend grabbed her by the hands and forcibly spun her around.

"Ow—hey! Watch out!" Irina's eyes flew open, and she grabbed hold of Clare for support. Clare's eyes were gleaming. She grabbed the sash from Irina's unresisting hands and tied it in place, completing the ensemble.

"I *knew* it would look great on you. Look in the mirror!"

Reluctantly, Irina turned to face the long mirror on the wall beside her bedroom door. Her eyes widened.

It fit her perfectly. How, she didn't question. Whatever shop Grant had bought this from, their sales assistants must have some sort of remote dress-fitting magic powers.

Irina spun in front of the mirror, watching the skirt of the dress sway around her, feeling it brush against her bare legs. Magic was *definitely* involved here somehow.

She felt amazing. And she looked good in it. *Really* good. The neckline was far lower than anything she would normally wear, plunging deep to show her cleavage, but her breasts didn't bulge out the way she always worried about. The soft silk held close to her waist and hips and fell to skim just below her knees.

Irina imagined Grant at the boutique, running the dress through his hands, choosing something to flatter her curves rather than hide them. She could almost feel his hands on her already.

"Great," said Clare triumphantly. "Now let's do something about your make-up."

Thirty minutes later, Irina was feeling so primped and preened that she barely dared to move in case the whole illusion came tumbling down. Clare's handiwork was a few steps above her own smoky-eye attempts.

Her friend was as fierce with the make-up brush as Irina was with her paintbrush.

Clare had just set down her brushes when Irina's phone buzzed. As Irina dug through her handbag, Clare raced to the window and peered down into the street below.

"Talk about good timing," she said, smirking. "I think your ride's here, if your ride is six-foot-enormous with black hair and roses?"

"Oh, God." Irina grabbed her phone, dropped it, and stared up at Clare. "Do I look okay?"

Now it was Clare's turn to roll her eyes. "Shut up and get out there. And let me know if you plan on not coming home tonight this time, okay?"

"All right, *Mom*." Irina managed to grab hold of her phone and checked the notifications. One new message.

Grant: *I'm outside. Do you want me to come up?*

Up here? To mess central? Irina's fingers flew across the screen. *I'll come down. Two minutes!*

The butterflies in Irina's stomach felt more like wasps as she headed down to the street. She had exchanged a few text messages with Grant since Saturday morning, confirming that she was free Monday night and so on, but that was all.

If he didn't want to see you again, he wouldn't be taking you out to dinner, she told herself firmly. *He wouldn't have sent you this dress, for sure.*

She stopped with her hand on the front door. No matter how hard she tried, she still couldn't quite believe that Grant's interest in her was genuine. In fact, she'd spent at least an hour on Sunday worried that she'd imagined the whole thing. It just seemed so unreal.

Really, what are the chances? You're miserable, wishing you could be anywhere but standing in front of your stupid paintings with everyone judging them, and suddenly some handsome guy turns up and sweeps you off your feet? Literally?

And yet... it had happened. And this morning, when she tumbled into work and got her roster for the week, confirmed she still had the evening free, and texted Grant—he'd texted back almost immediately. As though he'd been waiting for her message. For *her*.

When she opened the door, the first thing she saw on the other side of it was Grant Diaz. All six-foot-enormous of him. And roses.

"Hello," he said, standing there holding out a bouquet of brilliant red roses. At the sight, all of the butterflies disappeared. "You look beautiful."

Irina's heart thudded as he handed her the bouquet and slipped one hand around her waist. With his other hand, he tucked a lock of her hair behind one ear. Then he leaned down and kissed her. Irina forgot all about the flowers and wound her arms around his neck.

His lips were soft, but the fire they ignited inside Irina burned out of control. She let herself melt into him, sliding her hands up his front to rest on his chest. When he pulled away, she caught hold of his lapels, holding him close to her.

He was as gorgeous as she remembered. Dark hair with a hint of a curl. Killer cheekbones, and those smoldering green eyes.

The suit under her hands fit him like a glove, and she couldn't help but remember how the last time she had seen him, he was wearing far, far less.

He bent his head, and she could feel his breath on her ear as he whispered:

"I did mean for you to keep the roses, you know."

"I—oh, hell, I am so sorry," Irina gasped, mortified. She knelt and snatched up the bouquet from where it had fallen on the steps. "They're lovely."

"And only slightly crushed." Grant took the bouquet, dusted it off, and tucked it under one arm. He offered the other to Irina, eyes lingering as she straightened up. "Do you like the dress?"

Irina took Grant's arm, fitting herself against his side. "Do I like the dress?" she mused aloud. "Well, I haven't dropped it on the ground yet, which puts it one up on the roses."

Grant's fingers tightened around her arm. "That's not fair," he complained, his voice rough. He glanced up at Irina's apartment building. "You tease. Unless you want to skip dinner…"

"My roommate is home," Irina said quickly.

Grant groaned deep in his throat. "Isn't it your turn to provide the third wheel?"

"Oh my God. I would never hear the end of it."

Irina started down the steps toward Grant's car, just in case he was being even slightly serious. Her and Clare's whole apartment was smaller than Grant's bedroom. When he imagined her housemate being a third wheel, he probably wasn't imagining paper-thin walls and piles of pizza boxes.

"And Lance is driving us tonight," Grant added, ruling out the alternative before Irina even dared to bring it up. He sighed, so dramatically that Irina laughed and dropped her head on his shoulder.

"Lance is driving us?" Irina winced. "Remind me never to apply for a job as a 'PA.'"

She stuck to Grant's side until they reached the car. Her coat was warm, but he was warmer, a comforting, solid bulk of pure masculinity that warmed her from the inside out. He opened the back door, and she climbed in, almost reluctant to let him go.

"Evening, Ms. Mathers."

"Oh—hello again, Lance," she said, seeing him in the driver's seat and immediately feeling awkward. "Did, uh, did you get home okay the other night?" She blushed furiously, acutely aware that she was why Lance had been left hanging on Friday night. *So why are you here tonight, too?*

Lance chuckled as Grant took the seat beside Irina. Grant looked from Irina, to the driver, and back. "Oh. Right. Irina, I wasn't entirely honest with you about Lance here the other night."

Irina looked sideways at Lance. "Uh...huh?"

"He's not my PA."

Irina's eyes traced the lines of muscle clearly visible through Lance's jacket. Shoulders, back, biceps—the guy had it all.

"I thought he was a bit beefy for a personal assistant," she joked. "But I figured he just hit the gym to keep up with you."

Grant's brow had furrowed when she mentioned Lance's muscles, but her sly compliment brought a smile back to his face. He relaxed back in the seat, eyes smoldering at Irina from under lowered lashes.

"He's my bodyguard," he admitted at last. "Because I am clearly incapable of looking after myself, as well as being disgustingly wealthy."

Lance groaned. "*This* is how you want to have this conversation? In the car?" He rested his head on the steering wheel. "With *me* here?"

Grant dismissed his complaints with a wave of his hand, his eyes still fixed on Irina's. She felt a flutter of excitement in her stomach—or was it nerves?

"I know you're wealthy," she admitted. "But—your bodyguard? Where was he on Friday night, then?"

"Yeah, boss? Where was I?" Lance abandoned his forehead-to-steering-wheel stance and swung the car out into the street.

Irina raised her eyebrows at Grant. "Well?"

"He was obeying orders," Grant grumbled, clearly put out at the two of them ganging up on him. "You were never in any danger, I promise. I know that city block like the back of my hand."

I know you grew up there, Irina thought even as she felt an immediate stab of guilt. *And I shouldn't know that. I should have waited for you to tell me.*

She hadn't been able to resist Googling Grant after everything Clare had said. What she found had answered a few of her questions, like how they had skipped out on dinner without anyone running after them with the bill.

And it had answered some questions she hadn't even thought to ask. Things she wouldn't have even considered her business until later in their relationship—if this turned out to be that sort of relationship, and not just a winter fling. When she found herself reading about how "America's Most Eligible Billionaire" had grown up all alone in the big city, the only child of a workaholic single mother, she'd closed the browser. It felt too much like invading his privacy.

Because it *was* invading his privacy.

She shook herself. Grant was staring at her, a strange expression on his face.

"I hope you brought a flashlight," said Lance from the front of the car.

"I—what?" Irina turned to Grant. "A flashlight? I thought we were going to dinner."

"We are. And no, flashlights won't be necessary." He glared at Lance over the back of the seat, looking so disgruntled that Irina had to stifle a giggle.

She might have remembered how handsome Grant was over the last few days, but it was these occasional moments of obvious displeasure that really charmed her. He was good at hiding it, but like just now, every now and then she would catch him with his nose clearly out of joint—and him clearly trying to hide the fact.

She tried to figure out what it reminded her of, and almost burst out laughing when she connected the dots. The peevish reactions to being slighted or surprised, and then the quick recovery and self-conscious *Who, me? Bothered? Pff!* Attitude—it was just like her Gran's old cat.

Well, didn't you think it was odd that you felt so comfortable with him, right away? Maybe you just subconsciously associated him with Snuggles!

The drive to the no-flashlight-needed mystery location was less exciting than Friday evening's dash from dinner to Grant's apartment building, and Irina was surprised when they stopped outside a run-down warehouse. She stared around for any sign of a restaurant—after all, Moss's restaurant had been well hidden—but couldn't see anything except brick walls and graffiti-tagged, abandoned shipping containers.

She raised her eyebrows at Grant. "Is this it? Looks a little..." *Abandoned? Creepy? Like we're here to do a hostage handover in some sort of bad spy movie?* "...um, empty," she said at last.

"I'm assured that it's much nicer inside." Grant took her hand, running his thumb lightly over her knuckles. "The fanciest warehouse you've ever seen."

"Oh, good," said Irina weakly. "That's reassuring. I'm very reassured."

Grant led her to what she'd assumed was a garage door, while Lance trailed behind them. The corrugated iron door was big enough to fit a truck through it, but it didn't look as though it had been opened for months. As they approached, a light went on behind it, the glow just visible between the bottom of the door and the concrete. As Irina watched, the golden glow extended up a crack in the corrugated door, and then across—and a smaller door, inset into the cargo door, opened to them.

Irina looked around for whoever had opened the door, but there was no one there. She and Grant stepped through into a room that was clean, tidy, and warmly lit—but completely empty, except for another door on the opposite wall. Irina turned around, wondering if she had missed something at the entrance, but all she saw was Lance following them in. She watched him scan the room, and then relax with his arms folded.

She wasn't about to let Grant off so lightly.

"You're *sure* this is a restaurant?" she teased.

"It's extremely fashionable."

"So fashionable it doesn't have staff? Or food? Their overheads must be super low."

Grant squeezed Irina's arm. "After you told me about your work at pop-up restaurants, I had a thought. This isn't exactly a pop-*up* place... it's a bit more underground than that."

"Uh-huh." Irina knew her eyes were wide as saucers, but she couldn't be bothered pretending not to be intrigued. Besides, Grant's enthusiasm was catching. "And when you say *underground...*"

"I mean in both the totally cool and hip sense, and that I hope you don't get claustrophobic." Grant's smile froze. "You—you don't get claustrophobic, do you?"

Irina laughed. "No, don't worry. I'm not going to scream and jump into your arms."

"Too bad." Grant slipped his arm out of hers and put it around her waist. She leaned into him automatically, feeling the warmth of his body against hers.

He was right. It *was* a pity. Especially given how much she had enjoyed jumping into his arms the other evening. And what that had led to...

She twined her fingers around Grant's and stood on her tiptoes, so she could whisper in his ear without Lance overhearing. His arm shifted slightly on her waist, supporting her against him, and—

Ding!

The door at the far end of the room slid open to reveal an old-fashioned elevator, complete with wrought-iron cage and, at last, someone who looked like he might be a member of staff. Irina caught Grant's eye, and the look of disappointment that flickered across his face, as she lowered herself to the floor.

"Welcome to Solitude," announced the newcomer, stepping smartly out of the elevator. He was wearing charcoal slacks with a crisp crease down the front and a silver-colored waistcoat over a shirt with silver buttons and matching cufflinks. His brown hair was slicked back from his forehead. Irina was delighted. He looked as though he had stepped straight out of the 1920s.

"Mr. Diaz, Ms. Mathers, and—guest?" His rehearsed speech faltered as he looked over Irina and Grant's shoulders to where Lance was still looming behind them. "Mr....?"

"I also answer to 'Miscellaneous' or 'Et Cetera,'" said Lance dryly.

The greeter recovered quickly. "Welcome, all. If you will please step this way, your adventure is about to begin." He stood aside and ushered the three of them into the lift, which creaked alarmingly as it took Grant's weight. Then it made exactly the same noise as Lance stepped in, and Irina realized it was all part of the experience. The *adventure*.

After all, hadn't Grant promised her an adventure?

"Are we going to be running through any more kitchens?" she murmured to Grant. "Damn, and here I am in my heels again. You'll have to carry me after all."

"Don't tempt me," he murmured back.

The elevator swooped downwards so smoothly Irina was convinced it was a modern one, made up to look antique. Just like the greeter. It spat them out in what looked like a subway station.

Maybe it *was* a subway station. Surely no one would go to the effort of recreating a whole underground subway station just for a restaurant shtick?

Either way, the thought of a secret restaurant hidden under New York's streets was exciting. Irina squeezed Grant's hand as the greeter led them on. At the far end of the "station," where Irina would have expected to find stairs leading back up to the street, was a wall with a door-sized hole knocked out of it.

Literally knocked out of it. Right through the shiny white tiles and the concrete behind them, to reveal a hidden room.

Irina's laugh was almost a cackle. "A secret room inside a secret subway station—inside an abandoned warehouse?" she gasped. "Oh, this is too good to be true!"

Behind her, Lance snorted. Grant looked so pleased it was bordering on smug. He'd hoped, based on their previous date, Irina would enjoy this outing since she'd seemed to have fun on their mad dash through similar—if less well-maintained—tunnels and alleyways on their first date.

"A lot of this was used by bootleggers, back in the 1920s. I'm pretty sure this hole in the wall is a genuine antique, even. You like it?"

"It's amazing." She stepped through the hole in the wall onto thick carpet. The walls of the secret room were papered with a pattern of birds, and a gas lamp glowed in one corner.

"It gets better," he promised, and Irina tossed her hair back with pretend mockery.

"Of course it does. There hasn't been any food yet," she said sternly before promptly ruining the act by giggling.

"Follow me, please, ma'am, sir," the maître d' requested as he directed Grant and Irina down a series of corridors. A winding staircase took them down a few levels.

"I guess they weren't kidding when they said this place was *underground*," Irina whispered in Grant's ear.

"What is this place—an old subway station?" Grant asked their guide, who smiled.

"Partially. Plus, various basements, old cellars … all structurally reinforced, of course."

CHAPTER 12

GRANT

Grant nodded. He wasn't entirely comfortable with the constrained surroundings, but Irina's interest in the place's aesthetics more than made up for it. The renovators had clearly been told to retain as much of the original ambience as possible: the three of them walked past walls of old stone and brickwork and even the occasional wooden strut. Irina exclaimed in delight as they stepped through an artistically smashed hole in one wall to find themselves walking on intricate mosaic tiles.

He took a deep breath. The air was as fresh down here as it had been on the street.

Fresher, even, he thought, thinking of the city's car-exhaust aroma. The architects might be laboring the point with all the "step into the past" design, but not at the expense of good ventilation, heating, and lighting.

He had been skeptical at first, when Solitude was recommended to him as a late-night date venue. A trek through the city's abandoned underground spaces sounded more like a school field trip than a romantic date. Now that he was here, though, he was glad he had decided to go for something more exciting than a regular dinner date.

He made a mental note to find out the name of the architect. One glance at Irina, looking around with her eyes shining, was enough to let him know how much she loved the decor.

"It's like a whole city under the city," Irina breathed.

The maître d' smiled at her. "New York's undercity isn't as extensive as, say, Rome's, but there's more *city* to this city than most people realize," he said, making the phrase sound not quite like something that had been drilled into the restaurant staff by management. Grant stifled a grin and leaned closer to Irina.

"Perhaps we should visit Rome next," he murmured.

She hesitated before replying, and Grant felt her uncertainty like a blow to the chest. He slipped an arm around her waist, as much to reassure himself as her—and felt, again, a brief pause before she let herself relax against him.

Her reticence only lasted a moment.

"Perhaps we should," she replied teasingly, looking up at him through her eyelashes.

He kissed her, a brief brush of his lips against his, but couldn't entirely fight back the icy memory of her hesitation.

I'm not lying to you, he wanted to say. *This isn't just a date. It's the biggest adventure of my life. I want to give you the world—and I need to know that you'll believe me when I say that.*

He bit back a sigh and pulled back. That was the problem. There was nothing stopping him from telling Irina that he loved her—that every particle in his body, every atom of his soul wanted to spend the rest of his life by her side.

The problem was that she wouldn't believe him. Not when they'd only known each other less than a week. How could she?

And if he revealed his true self to her—No. That wasn't an option. He would never pressure Irina to stay with him over her own wishes, simply because *he* needed *her*.

The maître d's polite voice pulled him out of his unhappy thoughts.

"...through here. Now, many of our guests find the darkness somewhat disorienting, so please take as much time as you need to seat yourselves.

You will find a silk rope just inside the door, which will lead you to your table."

Irina's eyes were sparkling. "Silk rope. Got it."

"To reflect the restaurant's concept of Solitude, servers will not make their presence known to you. Food will seem to appear on your table out of nowhere, and your dishes will be whisked away as though by magic."

Grant raised one eyebrow. The idea was an intriguing one, but he would be surprised if the wait staff managed to evade his heightened senses. "You have it all figured out," he remarked.

"If at any stage you do desire assistance to move around the restaurant, please simply raise your hand like so," the maître d' finished, demonstrating.

He asked if they had any questions, and when they both assured him he had covered everything, ushered them through to a small, dimly-lit atrium. Another door led through to the dining area itself. The maître d' excused himself, leaving Irina and Grant alone.

"I guess that last bit was code for 'If you need to use the bathroom...'" Irina suggested, eyeing up the door.

"Or 'If you spill your entire bowl of soup down your pants,'" Grant agreed.

Irina tossed her hair back. "Excuse me? If that happens, I expect to find myself immediately cleaned up and whisked into a fresh dress. As though by *magic*," she said, giggling.

Irina's skin glowed in the soft light, and Grant almost groaned as the movement of her hair sent a tantalizing waft of her scent toward him.

"The only person who's going to whisk you out of your clothes is me," he growled softly into her ear, and she gasped extremely satisfactorily. He ached to brush his lips against that soft skin, taste her, feel her tremble under his mouth again.

He pulled his eyes away and looked at the door. If he was this tempted when they had only been alone for less than a minute, then what would the rest of the evening be like, hidden away with her in a darkened room?

"Shall we go in?" he suggested as he opened the door.

Grinning, Irina slipped past him, close enough that he could feel the heat of her body, and then he pulled the door shut behind them both.

The room beyond was pitch black. Not the black of a moonless night or a darkened room, but the dense, heavy dark of underground caves where no light has ever reached.

Grant's panther stirred. Grant shared its discomfort. The hairs on the back of his neck rose. Panthers were predators of the night, stalking their prey in the pale light of the moon and stars—but even Grant's powerful night-vision couldn't penetrate the darkness here. It was as though someone had slipped a blindfold over his eyes.

Then he felt Irina's hand slip into his, small and warm. In the heavy darkness, her touch felt intimate, as though they were the only people in the world—and she had reached out for him. No hesitation.

There are other senses than sight, after all.

"Can you find the rope? I—oh, there it is," Irina whispered. She paused. "Why am I whispering?"

Grant turned his body toward her voice, and found her other hand with his own. She was holding onto a soft, braided rope, one end of which was fastened to the wall beside the door, the other stretching into the darkened room.

"Perhaps you're worried the darkness might hear you," he murmured throatily.

He felt her shiver and smelled the rush of her desire.

"You shouldn't have said that," she whispered back.

"Oh?" He leaned forward, so their bodies just touched.

"Mmm." He could hear the hidden laughter in her voice. "Because now I *am* worried about people hearing us. All those magical waiters..."

She slipped under his arms and tugged on the rope as she followed it farther into the room. "...I'm sure they're not paid enough to listen to *that*."

His disappointment at being rebuffed vanished—*Like magic—hah!*—as he realized she was as turned on by the situation as he was. He stalked after her, silken rope loose in his hand and a contented warmth filling his body.

She feels this, too. She wants you. Wants to be with you.

And if the only reason she pulled away was that she was worried the wait-staff might be hovering too near...

"Oh!"

Grant had been following the sound of Irina's footsteps and was as surprised as she was by the clatter of wood on stone.

"I think I found our table," she said, laughing. "Ow, my poor foot!"

"I'll kiss it better," Grant promised. "Later." He slipped through the darkness, zeroing in on her voice. "When the wait-staff have magicked themselves away."

Irina jumped at the sound of Grant's voice right behind her shoulder. She spun around, and Grant took advantage of her confusion to steal a sneaky kiss.

What with the darkness and her still moving, the kiss ended up on her ear.

Worth it, Grant thought smugly.

"Sneaky," Irina complained. "How come I'm the one crashing into furniture, and you're strolling around as easy as if you can see?"

Grant slid his hands down her sides. "See? I can't *see* anything." His hands roamed further. The dress she was wearing was modest, but the fabric was so thin he could feel her heat through it. Her breath sped up. "If I could, I would have been a bit more suave than to kiss you on the ear."

"Oh," Irina replied. "Like this?"

She pressed herself against him, standing on her toes. Grant's pulse thrummed in appreciation as her breasts slid up his chest, and he felt the soft caress of her breath on his neck. Her lips almost touched his... and then she planted a kiss on his chin.

"Hmm," she said, very seriously. "Yes, I can see the problem."

Her fingers wound into his hair. "I can think of another problem, too," she murmured.

"What?" Grant twined his arms around her. *The hell with the wait staff,* he told himself. *If they're so discreet, I'm sure they know how to discreetly close a door behind them...*

Irina's lips touched his ear. "I had to work through my break today, and if I don't eat anything soon, I'm going to pass out," she admitted.

"Oh, you cruel temptress," Grant groaned, and let her go. "Let's eat, then. *Fast.*"

He heard Irina laughing softly as they both fumbled at the table. Grant managed to pull Irina's chair out for her, and she managed to sit in it, but not without a near-collapse.

Grant knew that if he concentrated, he would be able to navigate the pitch-black room without too much trouble. He might not be able to see, but the various scents and sounds filling the air would be enough to let him build a picture of the space. That, though, would require him concentrating less on the invisible, sensuous woman across the table from him. The sounds of her breath, of her hair brushing against her shoulders, her fingers exploring the table setting, all made the rest of the room pale into insignificance.

As for her scent—cinnamon and cream, and below that, the intoxicating musk of her arousal...

Solitude. The restaurant was meant to make diners focus intently on the experience of being alone in the world with their dinner companions. And it was working. For Grant, nothing else existed in the universe except for Irina.

He found his own seat with minimal trouble. The small noises of Irina's explorations filled his ears.

"The furniture is heavy," she noted. "All the better for clumsy guests like yours truly to avoid sending everything in here flying, I suppose." There was a quiet *ting*. "Wine glasses... cutlery... oh!"

Even before Irina spoke, Grant had half-risen from his chair, every sense on high alert. *Someone else is in the room.*

There was a rush of air as one—no, two—figures moved smoothly through the pitch darkness, their footsteps almost completely silent.

Clink!

Grant relaxed back into his seat as the spicy aroma of pinot noir filled his nostrils. The servers worked quickly and efficiently, filling first Irina's glass and then his own. A moment later, the smell of wine was joined by that of their first course.

Chapter 13

Irina

Eating was... challenging.

Joking about spilling food down myself is one thing, Irina grumbled to herself, chasing a cloud-light puff of pastry around her plate. She groaned with frustration as her fingers slipped through a smear of something semi-liquid on the side of her plate. *Oh, hell. I'll be lucky if I get out of here without sauce all over my face.*

And all over this beautiful dress.

I hope that whatever I'm eating, it's green...

The food was delicious, even if eating it was an exercise in frustration. The meal was a finger-food degustation, multiple courses of delicious morsels. Every dish was designed so you could eat it with your hands, but Irina was so petrified of spilling food over herself that half the time, she was dropping her food before she even got it off the plate.

"Aha!" she cried out as she managed to spear the pastry on one finger. "Mmm. Delicious. Absolutely worth the effort. What was that, do you know?"

"Some sort of delicious... thing. Did yours have mousse inside?"

"No-o-o, but I swiped it through this, um..." Irina licked her fingers. "Relish?"

She hunted out another puff and popped it into her mouth, slightly less clumsily than the last time. "Umph! You could have said it was *mushroom* mousse."

"Was it? Mine was more pumpkin-y. Oh, here's the mushroom one."

Irina carefully explored the tabletop until her fingertips brushed up against her wineglass. She took a sip, enjoying the burst of flavor. It wasn't that she disliked mushrooms. She just didn't like to be surprised by them.

She tentatively poked at her plate. The pastry puffs had probably been arranged beautifully when the dish was brought out but had succumbed to Irina's clumsiness almost immediately. There were another two left, and—dammit—there was the relish again.

Irina sucked on her finger, glad Grant couldn't see the face she was making in the darkness.

"How was your day?"

Now she was *definitely* glad he couldn't see her face. "Oh, it was just fine," she said even as she winced again at the fake cheerfulness of her voice. She cleared her throat. "Sorry, I guess I forgot to turn off my customer service settings there."

"It was that bad?" Grant's voice sounded guarded.

Oh, great. What a conversation-starter. Irina bit her lips. "Well, you know. Any day where some asshole on a bike doesn't try to steal my purse is a good day in my books."

"*What?*" Grant's voice was a strained mixture of horror and outrage. Glass clinked in warning as he reached across the table, his hand finding Irina's with unerring accuracy. "Are you all right? What happened?"

Irina grimaced. *So much for lightening the atmosphere with a joke.*

"It's nothing, really. Some asshole clipped me when I was heading back from your place on Sunday." She lifted her free hand and rubbed her throat self-consciously. The bruise was hidden under Clare's pashmina, fading but still visible.

"I'm sorry. I should have sent you home in a car."

"*Sent* me *home?*" Irina hoped she sounded more amused than outraged, but she felt Grant's fingers stiffen under hers as she repeated his words. She squeezed his hand. "I don't think you can take responsibility for every bad driver in the city, Grant. Anyway, that's life, right? Back home, I would have been clotheslined by a branch. Here, I get clipped by a scooter."

Grant's grip relaxed, and he stroked the back of her hand. "I don't like to think of you hurt," he said softly. "If there's anything I can do…"

"Well… just don't freak out when you see my neck, okay?" Irina quickly explained the bruise on her neck. If Grant suspected that the story about the bruise and the story about a scooter "just clipping" her didn't quite match up, he didn't say anything. Just held on to her hand.

"How is your week going?" she asked after a few moments. "Did you catch up with your friend?"

"Mathis?" Grant was making lazy circles on the palm of her hand with his thumb. "No, actually. He's steadfastly ignoring me. Mind you, I haven't exactly been hunting him down. I suppose I was rather… distracted."

The scrape of chair legs told her he was standing up, and he lifted Irina's hand to his lips. He kissed each knuckle on her fingers before turning her hand over and nuzzling the underside of her wrist.

Irina licked her lips. Her skin tingled at his touch, hot and electric. And he was only touching her hand. Her wrist. She had so many other places she wanted him to touch…

"I don't think your plan is working very well," she murmured, her voice husky. Grant's answering chuckle sent shivers down her spine.

"No," he agreed, his own voice low and rough, sending her mind straight back to the bedroom. "Instead of being distracted by the sight of you, I'm imagining what you look like, sitting there. In that dress. Or *not* in that dress."

"I do like the dress," said Irina primly. "Perhaps I'll keep it on."

She felt Grant's laughter, hot against her wrist. He slid his fingers farther up her arm, to brush against the delicate skin inside her elbow.

Irina gasped. Her entire body felt flushed, her nipples hard and rubbing against her bra.

"What's the next course?"

"Dessert next, I think."

"Thank God," she replied, and he laughed out loud.

The invisible servers whisked around the table again, and now Irina blushed for a completely different reason.

"Er, not that the meal hasn't been delicious—my compliments to the chef..." she said weakly. The servers worked so swiftly and so quietly that the only way she could tell they were there was the occasional breeze of air against her bare arms from their movement.

Thank God for quick service, she said silently. *The sooner we are done here, the sooner we can get back to his apartment so I can rip his clothes off.*

She licked her lips at the thought. Then another thought struck her.

Aware of the presence of the wait staff still around her, Irina raised her arm as the maître d' had demonstrated. Someone paused and took her gently by the elbow.

"Irina?"

Grant was still holding on to her other hand and must have felt her movement. She could almost hear the concerned frown in his voice.

"I'll just be a minute. Don't want to hold us up after the meal," she explained, squeezing his fingers before she stepped away from the table.

This time, she actually did hear Grant chuckle.

"I'll be back soon," she promised, and stood up.

The server gently guided her across through the darkness. Despite the disconcerting black, and the several glasses of wine that had accompanied the meal, she managed not to trip over her own feet. Her heels clacked slightly on the floor as they moved into what she thought might be another room—at least, the air felt slightly different. A few moments later, her guide stopped.

"The bathroom is just through this door, ma'am. Please give your eyes a few moments to adjust. I'll wait here to take you back to the table."

This is so weird, Irina thought as she took a random stab in the dark and made contact with a doorknob. *Being escorted to the toilet! Who would've thought fine dining and kindergarten had so much in common? I guess we'll see when I get a look at myself in the mirror...*

She still wasn't convinced she had escaped any of the meal's delicious courses unscathed. At least she had the pashmina. If she had dropped any food on herself, she could always arrange the scarf over the stains. *Artistically.*

Because, she told herself, leaning on the doorknob, *I am an artist. Artiste.*

I am extremely fancy and sophisticated. Also, there is a man in the next room who wants to take me home and fuck my brains out.

She gave up pushing on the doorknob and pulled instead. *Ah. And maybe I am a* little *tipsy.*

The room on the other side was as dark as the one she had just left, but as Irina stood there, the impenetrable gloom lightened. Soon, there was enough light for her to make out a few shapes, then colors, then the room was suffused with a soft, white light that was easy enough to see by. Irina blinked a few times to check that her eyes had finished adjusting.

The first thing she looked at was the mirror.

Phew. I don't look like a kindergartner who smashed her face into her lunch, at least. Just a bit pink.

The facilities were simple but modern and comfortable. Irina used the toilet, spent a few self-conscious minutes fussing with her hair, and then paused with her hand on the doorknob.

Should I...?

Irina hadn't managed to make it to any clothes shops between Saturday and tonight's date. Grant's surprise gift had fixed the problem of what to wear, but underneath the flowing silk, Irina's underwear was more practical than sexy. Her bra and panties were beige, supportive, and the closest thing to lace on either of them was the size tag.

Irina sucked in her lower lip, thinking. There was nothing she could do about the bra. Maybe someone with a smaller cup size could have managed it, but Irina needed secure upholstering to keep everything in check.

But her panties... her boring, beige, granny-styled panties...

Wouldn't it be sexier to *not* be wearing them at all when they got back to Grant's place?

What had she said to him? She didn't want to hold them up after the meal? Going commando would save at least five seconds.

She had her purse with her, after all. She could just... slip them off and go back to finish the meal commando. Maybe she could even tease Grant with some hints about it, even though she wouldn't be able to *see* his reaction. Only imagine it. *Mmm.*

Then she remembered the server waiting on the other side of the bathroom door.

Nuh-uh.

Panties-free might be sexy, but panties-free and being guided around by some poor unsuspecting waiter? That was just gross.

The underwear stays on. For now.

The light in the bathroom didn't seem to be changing at all, so Irina assumed she was just meant to leave. She stepped through the door and back into darkness.

"I guess there's no point waiting for my eyes to adjust this time," she joked to the server who had guided her over.

There was no response.

"Hello?"

The darkness pressed in on Irina. Her voice sounded small, as though the darkness was a solid mass that muffled the noise she made.

"Is anyone there?"

Apparently not. *Well, damn. I guess I get to find my own way back to the table, after all.*

Irina tried to remember what direction she had come from. The bathroom door had been on her left, and it was behind her now, so...

She turned right, took a few careful steps, and stumbled as her foot hit something lying on the ground.

"What the hell?"

Of all the places to leave something in the middle of the floor, Irina thought, hopping backward. Whatever she'd walked into, it was heavy. She knelt down, intending to move whatever it was out of the way, and froze as her hands felt what was unmistakably someone's shoe.

And its owner was still wearing it.

"Oh, shit," Irina gasped, falling to her knees. She found the unconscious figure's shoulders and shook them, but the person didn't move. "Oh, my God." *Is this the waiter from before? Did he have a stroke or something? Oh, shit!*

She stumbled to her feet and opened her mouth to yell. There must be *someone* close enough to help. But her words choked in her throat as someone slammed their hand over her mouth and pulled her backward.

Off-balance, Irina screamed, but the hand muffled her voice. A second person, hidden in the shadows, grabbed her arms and tied her wrists together. She was hauled away down the corridor, still trying to scream, even though she knew no one would hear her.

CHAPTER 14

GRANT

She's been gone a long time.

Grant rapped his fingers on the table. They were the only part of him that moved. If he'd been in panther form, his tail would have been flicking from side to side, the rest of him as still as though he had been carved out of black marble.

He hated that he knew that. His panther was close to the surface. Too close. As though it sensed something he didn't.

Tap-tap, tap, tap-tap-tap.

Where was she?

And where, come to think of it, was everyone else?

The room was silent, apart from Grant's constant tapping, and empty. He froze. Silence spread out from the table like a liquid, filling the space. Grant had felt the presence of the wait staff every time they approached the table, from the moment they slipped through the doors at the far end of the room; but now, there was no one.

He strained his ears. His dull, human ears. Nothing. The hum of air conditioning, the distant throb of some sort of machinery—but no soft pad of footsteps, no whisper of breath.

No one at all.

Grant ignored the heavy feeling of worry in his stomach. He told himself to stop being so paranoid. Irina had gone to the bathroom. That was all. She was taking a long time, but that was what women did, wasn't it? Take a long time in the bathroom.

Tap, tap, tap.

His feeling of dread was growing, a cold ache that spread from his stomach, up his spine, to the hairs on the back of his neck. He tried to ignore it. Tap-tap, tap, tap-tap. It was the same feeling he'd had on Saturday before he called Irina. He had felt deep in his bones that something was wrong—that Irina was in danger. It was beyond his panther's instincts, beyond his human intuition—or maybe it was some combination of both. A knowledge that something was wrong.

But nothing *had* been wrong. Irina had sounded breathless when she answered his call, and a little surprised, but not afraid. She'd been fine.

Except...

The scooter. What had Irina said about the scooter? Someone had hit her. *Clipped* her, she said, but she also said they yanked on her handbag strap so hard she had a bruise on her neck.

She had told him not to freak out. Well, he was freaking out now.

Grant stilled his fingertips on the tabletop and stood, slowly. He only noticed the movement behind him when it was too late.

"Irina."

The word was a half-gasp, half-croak, wheezing out from a dry throat. Grant coughed, caught his breath, and coughed again. He rolled onto his hands and knees.

He was on the ground. Lying on the ground. When had that happened?

And *where was his mate?*

He steadied himself and sniffed the air. His senses weren't as sharp in his human form as they were for his panther, but maybe that was to his advantage here. His panther could sift through scents like a master sommelier, but the heavy fug of traffic fumes here in the city acted like a blanket over his nose. His human nose might be less attuned, but at least it could ignore the pollution.

The room was empty. He could smell the remains of their meal on the table, a few feet to his left.

There was no one else here. But even in human form, he could trace Irina's scent. He rolled to his feet and moved quickly, his footsteps as silent as a panther's paws.

He found the door the waiter had led Irina through. The waiter had closed it behind the two of them, but now it hung open. Grant pushed through.

Halfway down the corridor, the air grew thick with the sour smell of fear. And under it, the soft rasp of a man's breathing.

Grant clenched his jaw. He could smell the man lying on the floor—but there was no sign of Irina. Only the remnant smell of her terror.

He took a deep breath, fighting for control. His panther was wild inside him, teeth bared and roaring to be set free.

That won't help anything, he told it, but he could feel cold sweat forming on his forehead with the strain of keeping his panther in check. Soon, he wouldn't be able to control it.

He crept forward and knelt beside the unconscious man. Whatever had happened here, it was clear this unfortunate server had nothing to do with it. His breath and pulse were steady, but Grant couldn't rouse him.

A blow to the head? Grant felt around carefully and found a vicious lump behind the young man's ear. On a sudden thought, he felt at the base of his own skull.

So that was how they had got him. He hadn't even noticed the pain when he woke up. All his focus had been on Irina. He couldn't let the dull throb distract him now. Whatever injury he had, his shifter healing would deal with it.

He inhaled, mouth open. Irina's scent was stronger here. She had knelt where he was now and touched the unconscious man. Which meant that the server was attacked before her. Before she came out of the bathroom, maybe.

Whoever had taken her must have lain in wait here. They'd attacked the server before taking Irina.

Grant concentrated, trying to sift through the stifling scents of fear. He stalked forward slowly, tasting the air. Irina had been here, and then—

There. Two other men, their scents masked by—by what? Grant shook his head. Their scents were faint, as though days old, but whatever trick they had used to mask themselves was ruined by the overlap between their own scent and Irina's.

Grant broke into a run. The trail of mingled scents led him to a locked door at the far end of the corridor. Snarling, he slammed his shoulder into it and heard the crack of splintering wood. He backed up and charged again, bursting through the door in a hail of splinters and dust.

The room on the other side was dimly lit, a storeroom of some sort, with piles of crates and bottles stacked against the walls. A real storeroom or another fashionable fake? Grant couldn't tell and didn't care. He ran on.

Another door led to a dusty tunnel. A cracked pipe leaked water down the walls, making the floor slippery. Grant skidded but kept going, following the trail only he could sense.

The corridor ended in a steep flight of stairs. He raced up them three at a time. The landing at the top was only a few paces wide. He crashed through a barred double door with more brute strength than any human ever had and stopped, blinded by sudden light.

Grant blinked. After so long in the pitch black, it took even his shifter eyes a few moments to adjust.

He was standing in a loading bay. Harsh fluorescent lights floodlit the concrete flooring and heavy metal garage doors.

And nothing else. The bay was totally empty.

One of the doors was open, but beyond it was nothing but the cold dark of the night. Grant walked forward, fists clenched at his sides. Just beyond the open garage door, tire marks revealed where the getaway car had skidded before disappearing into the city streets.

No.

"No!" he screamed aloud, unable to hold back any longer. He sprinted outside, but it was no use. The car was long gone, its tang of oil and gas indistinguishable from the thousands of other vehicles that had used the road.

She's gone. And I can't track her. Grant groaned and fell to his knees on the icy ground. Something crinkled in his suit pocket. Paper.

The only thing that should have been in his pocket was his phone. Grant clapped one hand to the pocket. Back in the dining room, when he had felt that presence – had someone slipped past his defenses so well that they could place something in his pocket without him noticing?

That's impossible, he thought. But then he remembered the strange, muffled scents of Irina's kidnappers.

Whoever did this knows that I'm a shifter. And they came prepared.

Ice crept up his spine. Someone was targeting him, and they were using Irina as—what? Bait? Collateral?

His hand closed over the paper. He pulled it out, stomach clenched in dread at what he might be about to read.

He caught his breath as he scanned the paper. There were no demands. Just a set of coordinates and a short message:

Follow her, or lose her forever.

Grant's pulse thundered in his ears and the world swung around him. The words seemed to burn into his mind. *Lose her forever.*

He fumbled at his watch. It was a special model, a gift from his mother. All the bells and whistles, including a panic button. The watch would send an alert to Lance, letting him know Grant's location. The bodyguard would be here within moments.

As he lowered his hand, something else caught his eye. The time.

—But that can't be right. We only arrived at eleven. It can't have been five hours.

His watch read four in the morning. He could hear the city coming alive around him. Delivery trucks. Early commuters. His world had just been broken into pieces, but everyone else's spun on.

He'd lost five hours. And now, every second counted.

Grant tried to stand but stumbled. The dull throb in his head swelled to a pounding pain, like someone was driving a wedge into his skull. Worse than the pain, though, was the fuzziness the injury left in his mind.

It hadn't been so bad when he was focused on one simple task—following Irina's trail—but any thoughts more complex than *run and hunt* were like punching through cotton wool. He couldn't focus enough to form a plan of attack. Or defense. Or any sort of plan.

He stared helplessly at the single sheet of paper. The note was printed: no handwriting, not even a remnant scent of the writer to give him any clue who was behind Irina's abduction.

Dimly, he noted the purr of the car's engine as Lance spun around the corner into the front of the loading bay. He looked up as his bodyguard leapt from the car and knelt by his side.

"What happened?"

Grant explained the situation in a few words, his voice hollow.

"Someone left this in my pocket." Grant crushed the note in his hand, then desperately smoothed it out again. This could be his only way of finding his mate: he couldn't let his panther's anger risk destroying it.

Still kneeling on the concrete, he pulled out his phone and plugged the coordinates into a map app. They led to the middle of nowhere, a tiny patch of mountainside miles from the nearest road or town.

In the Adirondacks.

Grant smiled grimly. They may not have meant it, but this brief note told him more than just the coordinates. The location was hundreds of miles away. Whoever was behind this must know that he would be able to fly there; if they were taking Irina there, to get there before him they must have access to some kind of aircraft, as well.

Whoever had taken his mate had access to money. Which meant this might not be about separating Grant from his fortune.

And…

"The Adirondacks," said Grant slowly. "Why is that so familiar?"

He met Lance's eye and saw him work it out at the same moment the pieces clicked into place in his own mind.

"I'll call Harley," Grant said, his jaw stiff. "You drive."

CHAPTER 15

IRINA

Ow. That hurts.

Irina groaned. Her arm was twisted up behind her uncomfortably. *Both* arms were. Ow.

Did I fall asleep on it? On both of them? While sitting up?

Am I sitting up?

I feel like I'm sitting up.

"Mmmph?" she mumbled groggily.

Why am I sitting up?

For Irina, waking up was a daily ordeal. Other people seemed to make the transition from asleep to functional easily, but for Irina, it was like swimming upwards through cold molasses. Without any arms or legs.

Wriggling upwards through molasses. Like a very sleepy, grumpy worm.

It usually hurt less than this, though.

Irina groaned. She normally groaned a bit as she woke up, but this time, it was because she was waking up into a body that *ached*. Her shoulders weren't happy about her arms being twisted up behind her. Nor was her neck. Or her head. It felt like someone was playing drums on the inside of her skull.

She shook her head groggily and tried to roll over, but couldn't.

What the hell?

Irina lifted her head and opened her eyes. Or tried to, at least. They were strangely heavy, and her eyelids clung together, refusing to separate. Which was nothing new, except...

Except she wasn't lying down. She was sitting upright.

No wonder my neck hurts, she thought hazily. *God, I really need a stretch...*

She couldn't stand up.

She wasn't just sitting down. She was tied down.

"What the hell?" she mumbled and tried to move again. This time, she felt the straps binding her to the chair.

"*What the hell?*"

Her yell echoed in her ears. She struggled, confusion fighting with panic. It was pointless. She was strapped into a high-backed chair, thick tape crossing her torso and securing her ankles to the chair-legs. Her arms were stretched around the back of the chair, wrists tied together.

Irina gathered her strength and yanked at her arms again, twisting her wrists against each other. The strain sent pain lancing through her shoulders. In response, she slumped back, panting with exhaustion, as her head rang from the effort.

What the hell is going on here?

The last thing she remembered, she had been at the restaurant, finishing up her meal with Grant. No, wait—that wasn't the last thing.

Irina concentrated, sifting through memories that seemed as hazy as mirages. She remembered getting up to find the bathroom... the server's light touch on her elbow...

"Oh, God," she blurted unwillingly. *The server.* She'd found his body on the floor. And then—

And then she woke up here.

Her chest constricted as she pieced together the pieces. Someone had attacked the server at the restaurant, and then... kidnapped her.

The word rolled around Irina's head, not fitting in anywhere. Kidnapped? Her? A twenty-six-year-old nobody, an artist with no money, no valuables, no connections—

Oh, no.

A sick feeling spread through Irina's stomach. No connections? What about a freshly minted billionaire boyfriend, with enough money and valuables to fill any number of ransom demands?

Grant.

And her kidnappers thought that kidnapping her was their golden ticket to that wealth.

Irina's eyes stung as hot tears seeped out under her lashes. She wished she could believe that Grant would jump to her rescue, but she had to be honest with herself. They'd only known each other a few days.

She was on her own. The only question was how long she could convince her kidnappers that she was worth keeping alive.

No. That's not the only question.

There's also: What am I going to do to get out of here?

Irina gritted her teeth, fighting back the tears. She was on her own? Fine. That didn't mean she had to give up.

She closed her eyes. There was no point keeping them open—not when she couldn't see anything. She took another deep breath, held it, and let it out slowly.

Right. Okay. Here's what's going to happen. You can either panic... or figure out how to get the hell out of here.

Let's start by not *panicking. Great job. So, step one to getting out of here: figure out where* here *is.*

She concentrated on her surroundings. Wherever she had been brought, the place was as dark as the restaurant, but somehow, she knew she wasn't still cozied away under New York City's streets.

Irina took a deep, ragged breath and realized why. The air here didn't smell like it did at the restaurant, which had been climate-controlled to within an inch of its life.

No. The air here smelled... wet. And cold. She could feel it cling to her skin, as though it had been years since anything warm and alive had been here.

Wherever *here* was.

Now that she had noticed the cold, clinging air, other things started to leak into her awareness. The quiet, for one thing. Even in the restaurant, there had been a hum of distant machinery, the occasional rumble of traffic far above. Here, the silence seemed to press in. Except...

A soft trickling noise, so faint she couldn't be sure she wasn't imagining it.

Water? Am I near a pipeline of some sort? A sewer? Not that it smells like a sewer at all.

It smells like the outdoors.

She held her breath, concentrating fiercely, and heard something that made her heart freeze.

Breathing.

Someone else was in here with her.

"Inattentive little creature, aren't you?"

Irina's own breath hitched in her throat as she gulped back a scream. The voice was female, a passionless alto.

"Who are you?"

She thought the woman was behind her and twisted to look, eyes wide in the darkness. Suddenly, a bright light flared, blinding her. Eyes watering, Irina squinted into the light, trying to see whoever was on the other side.

"Who are you?" she repeated, trying to make the question sound like a demand. Her words echoed back from the walls, unanswered.

She couldn't see anything through the harsh light. The woman might as well have been invisible.

"Tch. As though you're in any position to ask questions." The woman's words echoed, just as Irina's had.

We must be in a large room, Irina thought. *Or...* She thought of the smell of cold, damp air, the feeling of old, bone-deep chill, and the sound of trickling water. *...underground? Are we in a cave of some sort? How long was I knocked out for?*

"Does that mean you have questions for me, then?" she spat out loud. "You didn't pick an especially nice location for an interview if you were hoping to charm me into talking."

Good one, Irina. Antagonize the psycho kidnapper.

The light was suddenly cut off as a dark figure lunged toward her. The woman slammed her hands on the back of the chair, either side of Irina's head. The chair rocked back, steel legs scraping on stone.

"Questions? *Questions?* I've only got one question for you, you evil bitch. *Where is he?*"

The blinding light haloed the woman's face, but for one brief moment Irina was able to see her features.

She was pale, white with fury but with dark shadows under her golden hazel eyes. And she was instantly recognizable, even with her face twisted with rage and hatred.

"Francine Delacourt?" Irina gasped.

Francine slapped Irina across the cheek so hard her head snapped sideways. Hissing with pain, Irina turned back to her attacker.

Francine was nothing but a silhouette against the harsh spotlight. Still, Irina could feel the other woman's eyes on her, burning with hatred.

"But you're rich," she blurted, too shocked to hold her tongue. "Why would you need to ransom me?"

There was a pause. Irina saw Francine's silhouetted hands flex, and hoped it was a trick of the light or her imagination that made them look like claws.

"I don't want any *ransom*," Francine said at last, her voice burning with barely controlled rage. "I want your boyfriend to tell me what he did with my brother's body."

She leaned closer. Irina's breath stopped as her eyes glinted icy gold. Terror made everything sharp, and behind the twin frozen suns of Francine's eyes, something wild and feline bared monstrous fangs.

Something more. And whatever that something was, it was terrifying.

"And he's going to tell me," Francine Delacourt hissed, "because if he doesn't, I'll make sure he never finds your corpse."

CHAPTER 16

GRANT

The helicopter roared through the air, shattering the majestic solitude of the mountains. Grant leaned out the open door, baring his teeth into the wind that whipped across his bare flesh. Out here, there was no smog of fumes to stifle his senses: he inhaled the scent of evergreen trees, small creatures, even the smell of mud under its light dusting of snow.

And overlaying it all, the unmistakable, acrid tang of another chopper's exhaust.

We're getting close.

"We're coming up on the coordinates," came Lance's voice through his headphones. He was sitting in the co-pilot seat, as comfortable as though he was sitting in a café on solid ground, not hovering hundreds of feet in the air with the helicopter doors open.

Next to him, a red-haired man in aviator glasses was seated at the controls. Harley Ames, whose love for speed had finally come in useful.

"You ready to go?"

"Ready," Grant confirmed, nodding firmly. "Harley, can you bring us around that ridge?"

Harley grunted in reply, and the chopper swung around. Grant spared a glance for his pilot as he readied himself to jump. To find Irina and save her from the person who had taken her from him.

Francine Delacourt.

It had only been a theory. A theory that made no sense. Francine was cold, and prickly, but she was their friend. Then Lance had called Harley and told him they needed his piloting skills for a last-minute flight. And Harley had asked, all innocence, *Oh, you're heading out to meet Frankie, too?* He'd seen her at the private airstrip outside of the city where he spent most of his time. With a bevy of bodyguards, and bulky luggage the size of a body bag.

Grant was still struggling to understand. Why would Francine do something like this? They were friends. Not close friends, maybe, but they had all grown up in the same circles. Different social strata, brought together by the fact that they were all young, bored shifters. Grant, Mathis, Harley, Lance—and Francine.

What happened?

Part of him didn't care. Part of him, a very big part, didn't care what reasons Francine might have for taking his mate away. He just wanted to find her, stop her, and get Irina back, and nothing else mattered.

But a small part of him—more human-shaped than panther-shaped, though there was plenty of human in the part of him that didn't care—that small part of him wondered what the hell was going on.

He scowled into the wind. In front of the chopper, the side of the mountain loomed dangerously close. Grant could see a few deceptively smooth-looking patches of snow from where he hung at the side of the chopper, but he knew any one of them could hide vicious rocks. The rugged crags that appeared when the wind from the chopper's blades blew the pines around was enough to put him off aiming for the ground.

He sighted along the helicopter's path, tensed, and flung himself into thin air. As icy wind tried to tear the breath from his lungs, he released his control on his panther.

By the time he reached the stand of pines, he was reaching for the branches with heavily clawed paws, not hands, his body three hundred pounds of pure, honed muscle under inky black fur.

He struck the closest tree with a crash, breaking through branch after branch until he landed on one that could bear his weight.

Grant's claws bit into the bark as he regained his balance. Then he bounded to the ground in an effortless leap. A moment later, another crash told him that his bodyguard was following close behind.

With his white-tufted fur and huge paws, Lance's snow leopard was far better suited to the sub-alpine climate than Grant' tropics-loving panther. The bulky mountain cat padded out of the trees, shaking a dusting of snow from its coat. If it wasn't for the pack strapped across its back, the cat might have seemed like it belonged here.

We're two clicks from the target, north-northeast. Lance's telepathic voice had the same warm baritone tones as his human voice, though with an underlying burr courtesy of his cat form. *There was nothing showing on the satellites, so my guess is we're after a cave of some sort.*

Grant bared his teeth and growled. *Out of the snow, and into the dark.*

It's not ideal, Lance agreed. He set off and Grant followed, every nerve on edge. *Not the worst hostage negotiation I've faced, but not the best, either.*

Hostage negotiation? Grant didn't bother to keep the snarl out of his voice, and Lance huffed back, the cat equivalent of a laugh.

Don't worry, Grant. The only thing we'll be negotiating is a path out of these mountains with your girl.

Snow began to fall as they skirted the mountain, heading for the coordinates from the note. After the third river crossing and second detour to avoid recent rock falls, Grant had to admit he was more of a city boy than he had thought. Lance, on the other hand, seemed to be navigating by some internal GPS. Here in the mountains, without his spectacles or the tablet that seemed constantly attached to his human hand, Lance looked every inch the predator.

At last, they reached the edge of a clearing. Lance dropped down into a crouch, and Grant followed suit. Under the trees, he could blend in with the shadows, but the clearing ahead of them was entirely open.

The pines thinned out, leaving nothing but brush for cover, and then no cover at all. In front of them, a creek bed full of snow led up to a deep, narrow crack in the mountainside. A cave?

Grant sniffed the air, opening his mouth slightly. The bitter air washed over his fangs, bringing with it a familiar scent. *Irina.*

She's in there, he told Lance.

Lance lowered his head. *Along with some machinery I can't make out... and Francine.*

The two felines exchanged a glance. Grant could feel the snarl on his own muzzle, but Lance's expression was blank, even for a cat.

Grant fought back a sudden rush of protective rage. *Stick with the plan, Lance. I know you get along with Francine better than any of the rest of us, but—*

She's crossed a line this time, Lance interrupted, with only a hint of unhappiness in his mental voice. *You can rely on me, boss. Now, are you going to shift?*

Grant was about to say *No,* but checked himself. He had to assume that Irina was safe. If she was safe, she would probably be conscious, and he couldn't risk her seeing him in his animal form. Grant concentrated, found his human shape, and began to shift.

The icy wind bit into his bare skin and he quickly changed into the spare set of clothing from the pack Lance had brought.

Try to act as though you came alone, Lance advised as Grant began the trek up to the cave mouth. *If you can keep Frankie's attention, I'll sneak in after you.*

The interior of the cave was so dark it looked as though it had been painted onto the rocks. The floor was uneven, cracked rock and fallen stones making a treacherous path into the pitch black.

Grant paused just outside the cave. He didn't know how deep this crack in the mountainside went, but that didn't matter. All that mattered was that his mate was somewhere inside. And nothing would stop him from bringing her home.

CHAPTER 17

IRINA

"What are you talking about? You're crazy!" Irina's blood was like ice in her veins. She thought she was going to throw up. "Your brother—Mathis? Is that who you're talking about?"

"As if you don't know," Francine spat.

"I *don't* know! Damn it!" Irina sucked in a ragged breath. Her mind was spinning. "Grant hasn't killed anyone. He told me he's been looking for Mathis ever since he got back from his vacation, he—"

"*Liar*!" Francine started pacing in front of Irina, her whole body coiled tight. Irina could see a muscle twitching in her neck. "I know everything. Mathis came out here to the mountains to meet his *friends*, and no one heard from him or Grant for six months. Until Grant came back. With *you*."

Her eyes had been fixed on Irina as she paced, pinning her to the chair as effectively as her bonds. Now Francine leapt forward, slamming her hands down onto Irina's bound arms.

"Did you think you were being *funny*? With your little *paintings*? Was that your sick idea of a joke?"

This close, Irina could see the hot, angry tears in the other woman's eyes.

"I don't know what you're talking about," she said again, her voice catching on a sob. "I—oh, God! Your teeth!"

Irina stared in horror as Francine's teeth lengthened and curved into fangs.

There was no aura. She wasn't using her power. But she wasn't imagining this, either. What she'd seen behind Francine's eyes, behind the eyes of so many strangers—it wasn't her imagination, or a delusion. It was real.

"What are you?" Irina gasped.

Francine stopped, and a strange look came into her eyes. Her lips curved back over her outsized fangs in something that wasn't quite a smile, and she straightened, covering her mouth with her hand. When she took it away, her teeth were normal-sized again, and hidden behind the thin line of her mouth.

"You don't know?" she asked, her voice tightly controlled. "He didn't tell you...?"

"Didn't tell me *what*?" Irina cried out. "I've only known him for a few days—you're talking like, like we're Bonnie and Clyde, or something, but I only met him that Friday night at the gallery!"

Francine's eyes bored into hers, their pale gold seeming to glow in the low light. Irina was somehow reminded of Grant, although his green eyes were warm and kind.

I wish you were here, she thought desperately. *Oh, God, Grant, what have I gotten myself into?*

After what seemed like an eternity, Francine looked away.

"You really don't have any idea," she said quietly. Her eyes flickered back to Irina, considering, and then away again. "You have no idea what he is. What *we* are."

"You're *crazy* is what you are," Irina muttered. She twisted her wrists back and forth, trying to free them from the thick tape while Francine's attention was elsewhere. Maybe she had imagined those teeth—fangs—whatever, but she sure as hell didn't want to stick around to find out for sure.

"I don't know which would be worse. If you're an innocent bystander in all of this or his unwitting accomplice. I thought your paintings were some sick in-joke between the two of you, about my brother, but—never mind," said Francine suddenly. Irina froze as she felt the woman's pale gold eyes on her again. "He'll come for you anyway. That much is clear, even if you don't understand why."

Francine was clearly mad. Grant couldn't have killed her brother. He *couldn't* have! He had been looking for Mathis that night when they first met. She was sure he would be horrified to learn that his friend was dead.

Unless that was another of Francine's delusions.

Either way, Grant wasn't coming for her. How could he be? Wherever Francine had taken her, it must be miles away from the city. There was no way that Grant would be able to find her.

If he was even looking for her. They had only known each other for a week, after all. They were only together for—for fun. A pointless, frivolous fling.

And even if he did really care for her... she had disappeared in the middle of dinner. What if he thought she had just left him?

Irina dropped her head, unable to stop the tears spilling down her cheeks. She couldn't even raise her hands to wipe them away.

"Ma'am."

Irina flinched as a strange man's voice cut through the air. She looked around wildly, and her eyes widened as a man wearing a night-vision mask peeled away from the shadows at the edge of the cave.

How long has he been there?

She shivered. The man was wearing combat fatigues and had a gun holstered at his hip. Suddenly, any plans she'd had to escape seemed like pipe dreams.

What he said next made her blood run cold.

"Ma'am, we're picking up movement from the entrance. He's here."

CHAPTER 18

GRANT

Grant stepped forward, just on the edge of the light. The megawatt fluorescent bulb that lit the cavern was so bright and so hot that the damp ground beneath it was hissing. It was hooked up to a freestanding cage, like a photographer's light, and he could hear a generator farther into the cave.

The hairs on Grant's arms rose, as though they were reaching for the heat from the fluorescent bulb. But the warmth of the light was nothing compared to the burning rage inside him.

"Get away from her," he growled.

His heart twisted at the sight of Irina, *his* Irina, sitting slumped in the chair she was tied to. She raised her head at the sound of his voice, and her wide eyes caught the light. They were bright with tears.

"Grant," she said urgently. "Grant, she thinks you killed her brother. That's what this is all about, she thinks you killed him. Tell her—"

Grant started forward, his body moving before his brain was in gear. If he hadn't been watching Irina so intently, he would have missed the moment her expression changed from surprise to shock.

"Look out!" she screamed.

He was already turning, following Irina's panicked gaze over his left shoulder, as the blow that would have shattered his skull came down and cracked into his shoulder instead. Pain blossomed, bone-deep, and Grant's panther rose up inside him.

He shifted without thinking, muscles bunching, sleek black fur bursting through his skin.

The man who had ambushed him was already swinging his weapon back for another blow. Grant ducked in under his arms, fangs bared. He struck the man dead in the chest with his paws, and they both hit the ground, tumbling back into the shadows. Grant flung himself onto all fours, crouching low in the darkness. Metal clinked on stone as his attacker grabbed his weapon—a baton? In the darkness, he couldn't tell, and he didn't have time to confirm. He bunched his muscles, ready to spring.

"Stop!"

Francine Delacourt's imperious tones rang through the air like a church bell. Grant froze despite himself, and so did the other man. They locked eyes.

Grant knew the effect his panther's glare had. Any predator's gaze was intimidating, but a shifter's eyes held something more—human intelligence. The other man broke eye contact first, stepping back. If his body language didn't spell out defeat, it was at least a momentary truce.

"I said *stop*. Good." There was a quaver in Frankie's voice that Grant had never heard before. He heard her shift her feet. "Come out here. Both of you."

Grant waited until the other man moved out into the light, and then shifted back into human form. He stood for a moment in the shadows at the edge of the cavern, then stepped half into the light.

"Frankie."

"Grant." Frankie's eyes were cold as ice, but Grant's attention was already elsewhere.

"Irina..."

He crossed the cavern in three long strides and knelt in front of his mate. She shivered in his arms. The damp wet of the cave had seeped through her dress, and her skin was cold.

She dropped her head onto his shoulder with a sigh, and he pressed his lips into her neck, drawing a desperate trail of kisses up to her jaw.

"Don't worry," he murmured, low enough that Frankie's shifter hearing wouldn't pick up his words. "I didn't come alone."

"Grant, what was that? In the—in the shadows? I thought I saw..." Irina's eyes widened as she took in his naked body. "What..."

"Stand up. Step away from her."

Grant glared up at his old friend. He didn't want to move, but then he saw the guns trained on him. Frankie's two accomplices were armed with more than just blunt instruments.

He moved away slowly, arms at his side. He couldn't risk Irina catching a stray bullet if things went wrong.

Frankie nodded, and Grant's eyebrows shot up as a third man appeared out of the shadows.

That shouldn't happen, he thought in shock as Frankie directed the man to pick up the fallen light and attach it to a temporary fixture. *I should have been able to smell that he was there. Hear him, at least. But...*

He inhaled experimentally. He could smell Irina, and Frankie, and himself—but the other three men might as well not have existed, for all his nose could tell.

The hairs on the back of his neck rose.

"Frankie, what the hell is going on here?" *Something very wrong*. He didn't need anyone to tell him that.

Frankie squared her shoulders. "I'll ask the questions here," she hissed. "*Where is my brother*?"

"I don't *know!*" shouted Grant, bewildered. "I've been trying to ask you the same question for the last week!"

"Liar!" Frankie spat. "I know exactly what you've been up to. Gloating over those paintings. Rubbing it in my face. My people tracked you down, you know. Found out exactly what you were doing all summer.

You knew my brother liked to fight, so you brought him out here, lured him out, where no one would be able to stop you."

"You've lost it," Grant said flatly. "I haven't seen Mathis since before I left. For Bolivia. Not the goddamn Adirondacks!"

Frankie was still speaking, her voice a dangerous monotone. "I had my doubts, at first. I honestly didn't believe that you, of all people, would betray my brother. His best friend. How could you? But then I saw those paintings..."

Her icy eyes turned on Irina, and Grant's whole body tensed. His knees bent automatically, ready to spring in front of Irina to protect her.

"My paintings?" Irina's face was pale, and her voice cracked with amazement. "What the hell do my stupid *paintings* have to do with anything?"

Frankie rounded on her, eyes blazing. "Don't you recognize where we are right now?" She didn't wait for Irina to reply. "The last time I heard from my brother, he was heading into these mountains. The same mountains you painted. The same trails, the same peaks, the same *caves!*"

Irina looked sick. "But—I told you! I didn't even *know* Grant then!" She turned pleading eyes on Grant. "Please, tell her!"

"She's telling the truth, Frankie," Grant said, fighting to keep his voice level. "Come on. *Listen* to me. *We had nothing to do with Mathis's disappearance. Am I lying to you?*"

He met Frankie's eyes, willing her to believe him.

Her shifter abilities should mean she could tell if he was lying. The smell of his sweat, his heart rate, the way he was breathing—all of them would paint a clear picture for a shifter with the intelligence to put it together.

So long as that shifter wasn't half crazy with fear and rage.

Grant spoke slowly, empty hands beseeching. "I swear, Frankie, I'm telling the truth. I only met Irina last weekend. I spent the summer in

Bolivia, not here. I haven't seen Mathis since before I left the country, and Irina's never even met him. You *know* I'm telling the truth."

Or he hoped so, at least. He'd never seen Frankie like this. If her lioness was as twisted up with anger and hatred as she was, it might override her ability to see sense.

Grant couldn't imagine how terrifying the last hours had been for Irina, strapped into that chair with no way to defend herself from the enraged lioness. His heart twisted with guilt.

It's your fault she's here. He couldn't stop the thought from searing across his mind, full of desperation and misery.

CHAPTER 19

IRINA

The harsh light of the spotlight burned into Irina's face, filling her eyes with tears. She could barely see through the glare, and what she could see was marred by her streaming eyes. Francine, her golden hair haloed in the light. Grant, standing half in the shadows. And somewhere beyond the light, the three soldier-like, masked men.

Her heart had leapt at the sight of Grant, and the knowledge that he had come after her. But her relief had been quickly swamped by more fear and confusion. She still had no idea what was going on, but a creeping feeling in her stomach told her there was far more below the surface here than she could ever have imagined.

She *couldn't* have imagined what happened to Francine's face: the lengthening teeth, the feral look in her eyes. And Grant's fight with the henchman in the darkness—she was sure some of the shadows on the cavern wall weren't human.

When Francine had stopped the fight and Grant had hurried over to her, his clothes ripped from his body, Irina's heart had almost stopped. What was left of his clothing was shredded. He didn't look injured, but... what had happened to him?

And what was going to happen to them both, if Grant couldn't convince psycho Francine that they had nothing to do with her brother's disappearance?

Irina twisted her wrists again their bindings. It would hurt, but if she could just get one hand free, maybe she could get out of this chair while Francine and her henchmen were distracted.

Francine's stance changed, and Irina froze. She couldn't make out her expression through the blinding light, but it was as though all her violent tension had vanished between one breath and the next.

"You... you're telling the truth," Francine said weakly. "But... how?"

Even through her streaming eyes, Irina saw what happened next. Francine stepped backward, in front of the spotlight. Irina blinked as the brutal glare of the spotlight was cut off. She watched as Francine raised a hand and pressed her fingertips to her forehead briefly, then looked around quickly.

"You," she said, but she wasn't looking at Grant. Someone moved in the shadows behind the spotlight—one of the soldiers? "Explain. You told me—"

Before anyone else could move, another shadow detached itself from the darkness and swung at her head. Francine cried out and fell to the ground.

Grant roared, and the lights went out.

Irina's skin crawled as the cavern was plunged into total darkness. Her sight filled with yellow and green blotches as her eyes failed to adjust. There were noises in front of her, thumps, cracks—and *snarls*. When she felt a touch on her shoulder, she screamed.

"Hey, shh. Stay calm, I'm here to get you out."

Irina relaxed as she recognized Lance's voice. "The lights?"

"All part of the plan." Lance sounded distracted, and Irina felt a slight tug around her wrists. A moment later, her arms were free.

She rolled her wrists, easing the joints. "Ow," she muttered. "My legs—"

"On it," came Lance's terse reply. She didn't hear him move, but she felt the straps on her ankles loosen. First the left, then—

Irina screamed again as something, some*one*, hurtled out of the darkness and slammed into her. She tried to leap out of the way, but she was still attached to the chair, and fell with it as it crashed onto its side.

The ground hit her like a fist. Irina gasped for air, rough rock scraping her knees and hands, and screamed as someone grabbed her hair and yanked her head back.

An animal roar ripped through the air, and something huge leapt over her, knocking her attacker to the ground. Irina flung herself sideways, landing in a trickle of icy water, but was pulled up short. Her right leg was still strapped to the chair. She wrenched at her leg, desperate to free it. It hurt, but she felt the strapping begin to give.

Irina bit back a sob. Where had Lance gone? And where was Grant?

A red point of light flickered on the ground in front of her, moving strangely over the water. Suddenly, something landed in front of her, pushing her out of the way at the same time an explosion sent chips of rock flying into her face.

Irina flung out one hand to steady herself, and felt warm, soft fur. An animal?

A *huge* animal. It moved under her hands, and she felt strong muscles flex under the plush fur, a massive shoulder that would have come up to her waist at least if she was standing. It was still standing between her and the shooter.

The red light appeared again, quickly followed by a yelp, and the thump of a body hitting the ground.

The soldiers, Irina thought, remembering the guns. *Was that Lance? Does taking out armed men come under his "PA" duties?*

Grant—Oh, God, I hope Grant is okay out there.

Hot breath rolled over her ankle, warm and damp and close, and then her ankle was free. Her foot splashed to the ground. She pulled her leg up quickly and winced.

The creature, whatever it was, was still there. She couldn't see it, but she could feel it. The cavern was cold, but the animal that had protected her from the gunman was so warm she could feel its heat from where she s at.

There was a scuffle farther into the cavern, and the creature turned and leapt away, leaving Irina with nothing but the darkness and a lingering, familiar scent.

Something spicy, and warm, and...

No, she thought. *No, that's... that's crazy.*

That spicy, warm scent? Of course it was familiar. It was Grant's scent.

She shook her head. *What? You're crazy. As crazy as Francine.*

Francine, with her teeth that lengthened into fangs.

The animal that had leapt to protect her...

That's impossible, she told herself. *You're tired, you're scared, you're—you're delusional.*

She clenched her fists, scraping her knuckles on the rocky ground. *I need to get out of here.*

Irina crawled onto her hands and knees. Every part of her body ached more now than it had when she was bound, but she ignored it.

How could she get out? She tried to remember what she had seen from the chair before the spotlight blinded her. The dark walls of the cavern—and a darker shadow. The same shadow Grant had emerged from.

There must be a way out there. All she needed to do was find a wall, and follow it around until it turned into the way out.

And hope that Grant follows me out.

The sounds of fighting were oddly muffled in the cavern, but clear enough to make Irina's muscles stiffen. Grunts. The thump of blows landing, and the scuffle of movement.

But mostly... silence. No more gunshots. No shouts, no yelled instructions. Just the quiet, careful noises of serious fighting.

Irina's voice caught in her throat. *Get out. I've got to get out.*

She crawled forward, through the shallow, icy stream, and straight into a still form. Her trembling fingers found cloth, skin— and hair. Long hair.

Francine.

She was lying in the water. Her skin was warm, but...

In a panic, Irina hooked her arms under the other woman's shoulders and heaved her into a sitting position. Francine was still unconscious, so she almost slipped out of Irina's grip, but Irina managed to lay her back down out of the water. She turned the unconscious woman on her side with her head resting on one arm, the other bent in front of her so she didn't roll forward onto her face.

Irina held her hand against the other woman's lips. She'd been knocked out, but she was still breathing. Irina was surprised at the relief she felt, even though the woman had been threatening her only minutes earlier.

"All right," she muttered to herself. "New plan. Get out—and get a goddamn ambulance."

Except there weren't ambulances, not if Francine was right and they were in the same mountain range where Irina had spent last summer. There were towns, sure. Small towns. Maybe one in five of them had a doctor's clinic.

She just had to hope they were close to that one in five.

Irina took a deep breath. She could do this. Get out. Doctor. *Police*, holy shit yes.

She raised her head, lifted her hands to find the closest wall, and stood up just as the lights went on again.

Irina froze, but this time, the spotlight wasn't on her.

The whole cave was illuminated in brilliant white light. Five figures stood like statues. Three men—and two massive animals.

Where's Grant? And Lance? Irina's breath caught in her throat. The three men were Francine's henchmen—or had been, before they betrayed her. There was no sign of either Grant or his friend.

Only the two animals.

Irina held her breath as she stared at the big cats. One had a thick, pale coat with dark spots, and a sturdy build. The other...

The other was a huge black panther, its sleek, midnight-colored coat the only shadow left in the cave. Irina's chest ached strangely as she stared at it, and it stared back at her with its gleaming green eyes.

CHAPTER 20

GRANT

Grant looked up, straight into Irina's shocked eyes. There was no hiding from her now. No hoping that the cover of darkness would keep his secret safe, and her safe from knowledge of it.

There he stood, a panther larger and more ferocious than any natural animal—and there she was, staring at him. Grant cringed. He knew what she was seeing: a huge, wild animal, crouched ready to attack. A *creature*, not a person; fierce and inhuman, with fangs long as her fingers and cold, gleaming eyes.

Before Grant could move, one of the mercenaries took advantage of his hesitation, stepping in close to Irina as though he was protecting her from the beast.

"Quick," the man said, "Get back into the tunnel, before that thing attacks you again!"

He held his hand out to Irina, as though urging her backwards, but Grant saw his other hand slip into a pocket. The knife he pulled out was made of some matte black metal that wouldn't catch the light.

Grant's heart almost stopped. He was too far away to get between Irina and the weapon, and the man knew it. He had Grant stuck as neatly as a rat in a trap. Make a move, and he risked Irina's life; stay where he was, and take a chance that he would do nothing more than watch the mercenary take Irina away to God knows where.

Gravel skittered under Irina's feet as she shifted her weight. She took a hesitant step backwards, and the mercenary smiled encouragingly. Or at least, he showed her his teeth.

"I—" she began, her eyes flicking from the man, to Grant, and back again. She walked sideways with her back to the cave wall, never once taking her eyes off Grant. The mercenary tracked her step by step, knife hidden at his side.

She stumbled into the spotlight cage and flinched as the light swung, sending shadows wheeling across the cave.

"Oh, God," she gasped, grabbing hold of the steel frame to steady it. The light rocked in its holding, and her fingers tightened around heavy bulb.

"Go on. I'll protect you from this monster," the mercenary urged her. He glanced back at Grant. His eyes were hidden by the mask, but his mouth twisted in a mocking sneer.

"Okay," Irina whispered, and as the man turned back to leer at Grant, she smashed the light over the back of his head.

There was a loud bang followed almost immediately by a flash, and the cave fell into darkness again. Grant heard Irina draw her breath in one long, ragged inhale. Behind him, the other mercenaries yelled. There was the sound of fighting, and then a satisfied *huff* from Lance.

That's them dealt with, Grant thought.

The next thing he heard made his heart sing.

"Grant?" Irina called out, her voice wavering. "That—that is you, isn't it?"

Grant heard a soft rumble, and it took him a moment to realize the noise was coming from him. He was purring.

She recognized me.

He heard Irina start to walk forward and rushed to meet her. He dodged around the fallen mercenary before Irina could stumble into him and stopped just in front of her.

Irina's fingers brushed his forehead. His *panther*'s forehead. He felt her hesitate and resisted the urge to close the gap between them.

"Oh, my God," Irina breathed, her fingers exploring Grant's ears and sliding down his neck. "Grant? Is this really you?"

Grant nodded slowly and concentrated.

This wasn't the right way to do things. He knew that. It wasn't how he had imagined revealing himself to Irina, if he had ever really imagined that would be possible.

But what else could he do? If he was ruining everything, at least he had kept her safe.

Grant found his human shape inside himself to focus on changing back. He surged upwards, front legs transforming into arms, paws shrinking into hands and feet, fingers and toes. His fur disappeared, leaving bare skin behind. His fangs and muzzle shrank away into a mouth that could form human words.

Irina's hands had stayed on him as he shifted. Through his transformation from animal to human, she hadn't moved an inch. She hadn't left him.

Grant shivered as Irina's fingertips found his face again, tracing the line of his jaw. At last, his control broke. He took his hand in hers, pressing her fingers to his lips and whispering her name along with his kisses.

"Irina—my darling—are you all right? Did they hurt you? Irina…"

"Grant, I…" Irina's voice cracked just before she threw herself at him, winding her hands around his neck and burying her face in his shoulder. "I'm fine. I—you—what happened…?"

She paused, shivering. Her dress was soaked through. Grant wrapped his arms around her waist, holding her so close he could feel her heartbeat against his own chest. She took a long, slow breath and rested her cheek against his shoulder.

"I'm not going crazy, am I? You turned into a—a panther."

Grant dropped his head onto hers, nestling into the wet mass of her hair. "Yes."

"I've never seen one before. Not even in a zoo." She laughed softly. "I mean—I've never seen anyone turn *into* one, either. Which is probably more relevant, here."

Grant froze. He couldn't help it. "Irina, I—"

"Shh."

Grant's muscles were tensed, but Irina was more relaxed that he could have imagined possible at this moment. She sank into him, trusting him more than he trusted himself.

Only when the unconscious mercenary twitched and groaned did Irina flinch. Grant wrapped his arms more tightly around her, putting his body between her and the other man. "We should get out of here."

"Wait," said Irina urgently. "Francine—we can't leave her here."

"She *brought* you here." Grant heard the growl in his own voice, and sighed. "I'm sorry. I mean—"

"She brought me here," Irina agreed. "But you saw what happened. Those men turned on her." Her voice grew cold. "Whatever is going on here, I get the feeling Francine isn't behind it all."

They left the cave with Frankie slung over Grant's shoulder and Irina at his side. As they emerged from the cave, Grant saw Lance, already back in human form and clothed, perched on a rock.

Grant ruefully thought of his own change of clothes, which was spread in tatters throughout the cavern behind them. But somehow, the cold didn't bother him as it usually did. Irina's presence at his side filled him with a warmth that was more powerful than any amount of snow and ice.

"Harley's on his way," Lance called, uncrossing his legs and bounding off the rock. "What happened to the other one?"

Grant jerked his head back towards the cave, and Lance loped toward the entrance. "I'll bring him out and add him to the pile."

Irina exclaimed, drawing Grant's attention to the other two mercenaries who were lying in a heap near the boulder Lance had been perched on. He drew Irina back, automatically putting himself between her and the men.

Lance paused as he passed their small group, holding something up to catch the light. "You didn't see if he had one of these on him, did you?"

Grant stared at the object, which glimmered in the winter sun. It was a black armband holding a thin oval, made of some flexible material.

"What is that?"

Lance's lips thinned. *Take a sniff,* he suggested grimly.

Grant bent to smell the object and frowned. He could smell Irina at his side, his own sweat, and even the unpleasant odor of the unconscious mercenaries. But nothing from the strange thing Lance had found.

And nothing from Lance.

"Shit," he breathed and sniffed again as if another breath would change the result. It was uncanny.

"What is it?" Irina's voice was uncertain, as though she wasn't sure this was something she should be asking.

Grant met Lance's eyes for a split second before he turned to her. "It's as though he isn't there," he explained. "Not to my nose, at least."

Irina shivered against him. "Creepy," she murmured. Grant told himself she was talking about the unnatural object, and not his shifter sense of smell, and held her close.

A moment later, the helicopter's engines cut through the air as it roared into sight, and by the time Lance came back, the chopper was hovering above them. The trees on either side of the small stream whipped back and forth in the wind from its blades.

"Time to go home," Grant said, relieved.

"Home," Irina agreed. She looked up at him, her eyebrows drawing together. "And you'll explain everything."

Grant's breath caught in his throat. *Explain everything?*

"Yes," he said. "I will. I promise." *Even if it means I lose you.*

Chapter 21

Irina

Irina didn't remember arriving back at the airfield. She fell asleep in the helicopter, cold and exhausted but safe in Grant's strong arms, and woke in bed.

For a moment, wrapped in soft, thick blankets, the kidnapping seemed like a bad dream. Then she stretched and felt her body complain. Bruises, strained muscles, grazed skin…

But I'm safe, she thought, suddenly very awake. *Where am I?*

She sat bolt upright and winced as her head throbbed. Her body did *not* like waking up this quickly. Even in a warm, soft bed, wearing a snuggly cotton T-shirt that smelled of…

"Grant?"

As soon as she spoke, Grant stepped through the bedroom door, damp curls stuck to his forehead, green eyes piercing.

So, that was where she was. She was home.

"You're awake," Grant said, stalking across to the bed and gathering Irina into his arms. She fought her way out of the blankets and wound her arms around him in return, inhaling his warm, spicy scent.

"It wasn't a dream, was it?" she murmured into his shoulder. "Being grabbed at the restaurant, the cave… and you."

She stared at Grant in wonder, running her hands over his face. His cut-glass cheekbones, Roman nose, the deliberate dusting of dark stubble along his jaw…

He had *transformed*. From a human, into—something else.

Something more. She'd been afraid to look too closely at him, to creep on his soul, but she never could have guessed what he was hiding.

"You turned into a panther," she said, awed. "You *saved* me."

A muscle twitched under Irina's hand on Grant's jaw, and he looked away.

"I promised I would explain," he said slowly. "I should. I *need* to. Before anything else."

"Yes, *please*, tell me how it is you can turn into a *panther*!" Irina said, excited. "And—can other people, too? Francine? I thought I saw—and Lance, he is too, right? The other cat?"

She clapped a hand over her mouth to stop herself from babbling. "Sorry."

Grant glanced up at her from lowered eyes, and a brief smile brightened his expression.

"Frankie, yes. And her twin. They're both lions from a local pride. And Lance is a snow leopard. It came in handy when we were tracking you." His smile, already tentative, disappeared completely. "But you wouldn't have been taken at all if it wasn't for me. Do you remember what happened?"

Irina pulled Grant down beside her on the bed and held him close so she could rest her head on his shoulder. He stiffened slightly and then buried his face in her tousled hair.

"I remember..."

Images of men in masks flashed through her mind, but she pushed them aside. She wanted to see the whole picture, not just focus on her own fearful memories.

Francine had been the only one of her abductors who showed her face. And she had seemed to be in charge, but the moment she began to doubt her conviction that Grant was behind her brother's disappearance, the guard had knocked her out.

"Frankie was being used," Grant explained, echoing Irina's thoughts. He lifted his hand to rest briefly against her cheek, and then started to stroke her hair as he talked. "She admitted everything. After she lost contact with Mathis a few weeks into his trip, she got a feeling something was wrong, and hired men to look into it. They came up with evidence that he'd last been seen in the Adirondacks, and that I'd been seen there, too."

"They planted the evidence?"

"Made it up, planted it—who knows." Grant sighed and knuckled his forehead. "Lance's theory is that they were behind Mathis's disappearance in the first place, and then used his sister as bait to capture more shifters. Poor Frankie. The first time she ever has a sisterly impulse, and it's used against her."

Irina thought of the expression on Francine's face. She had been desperate to make someone pay for hurting her brother. Her—lioness? Was that what she had seen behind her eyes? Her lioness had been mad with grief.

How must she feel now, knowing she was duped? Would she feel guilty for putting Irina and Grant through that same pain?

Irina shivered, and Grant's arms tightened around her. With him here looking after her, the cold, damp cave seemed like a distant memory. If it wasn't for her aching scrapes and bruises, she could almost believe she had imagined it.

How easy would it have been for Grant to pretend none of it had happened? To say that Irina had been drugged by the bad guys or drunk from dinner? To convince her that she'd hallucinated the whole thing? Instead, he was caring for her and offering to explain everything.

She sat up a little, so she could look him in the face.

"What was that you said? Shifters? Is that what you are?"

Grant sighed and dropped his head on to hers. "I'm not doing a very good job of explaining things."

"I don't know about that. I'm beginning to piece things together." She took his hand, winding her fingers around his. It seemed impossible that his long, slender fingers could transform into the powerful paws she remembered from the night before. "Shifters are people who can turn into animals?"

"Yes. But there's a bit more to it than that..."

Irina listened, fascinated, as Grant told her that there were people in the world who could turn into animals at will. Not just cats, either, but all sorts of animals. Lizards. Birds. Apparently the chef whose kitchen they'd bolted through on the night they met was a bison shifter.

But... she'd already known that, hadn't she? That some people were more than human. That magic lurked behind their eyes, making her fingers itch to put paint to canvas.

She watched Grant's face as he talked. His voice was smooth, as though he'd been rehearsing what to say all morning, but even when he was joking about being trampled by an upset chef, he didn't meet her eyes. She could tell something was still worrying him.

"Are you all right?" A thought struck her. "Does it hurt, transforming like that? Are you in pain still?"

Grant raised his eyebrows. "Does it—? No. It doesn't hurt. And we—shifters—heal quickly, anyway."

He stroked her neck with one finger, along the fading bruise. His hand drifted along her shoulder and down to her hand, where he traced a red line of scabs that marked where Irina's wrists had been bound together. A matching set of scratches on the palm of her hand showed how badly she'd landed on the cave floor. He was careful not to touch them.

"You're asking me whether I'm hurt, when I've been the cause of so much hurt to you," he said, his voice rough.

Irina flexed her hands. The grazes stung, but they were clean and already scabbing over. A fresh bandage covered the one deeper scrape. "Did you do that?"

"I did all of it." Grant paused, and then it was as though a dam had broken. Words tumbled out of him in a flood. "The biker who attacked you was one of Frankie's mercenaries. Lance found a tracking device in your handbag. That's how they knew where you were last night. And in the cave—you could have died, and it was all my fault."

"Don't," she protested, cutting him off. "That's not true. Besides," she added, feeling him draw breath to respond, "I meant, did you put this bandage on me?"

Grant sagged. "Yes."

"Thank you." She wound her non-bandaged hand around his neck. The muscles there were tight. Something was still bothering him. She leaned forward to kiss him, but he turned his face away.

"Wait. Please. There's more I haven't told you. And I can't keep it from you anymore. I thought I was keeping you safe, but I only put you in more danger."

Irina's eyebrows shot together. "Stop. Let's get one thing straight. The only person we are blaming for what happened is the person who kidnapped your friend and duped his sister into getting *you* captured, too."

"I should have told you that I was a shifter from the start." Grant sighed and knuckled his forehead, not meeting her eyes. "But you were so perfect, I wanted to spare you that, at least."

"Spare me—the knowledge that you can turn into a panther?"

His eyes shadowed. "There's more to shifters than just the ability to turn an animal. Every shifter has a mate—someone they're destined to be with. Their soulmate. Some shifters go their whole lives without meeting their mate, and I thought—I hoped—I would be the same. Until I met you."

Irina stared at him, stunned. *His mate? What does he mean?*

Something fluttered inside her. She remembered how she had felt from the moment she first met Grant. His attention had been so surprising, so flattering—but that wasn't all. She'd seen the power inside him, the *something more* that had mystified her all her life and which she now knew was her ability to see shifters' inner selves.

But it was more than that, as well. She'd seen other shifters' inner selves and never been as compelled by them. But Grant... She had felt an instant connection to him. She'd certainly let things move far faster than she would on a normal date.

But why was he talking like he was ashamed of it?

"I'm... your mate?" Irina asked uncertainly.

"Yes." Grant's mouth twisted. "I felt it the moment I met you. All my life, I've been afraid of what would happen if I found my mate—and then you appear, and my fears came to life."

Irina's heart sank. She didn't really understand what he meant by *mate*, but she understood the angry regret on his face.

"You don't want me?" She let her hands drop away from Grant and pulled back, but he grabbed her desperately.

"Of course I want you. More than anything else in the world. But I was so scared of hurting you. I should never have pursued you in the first place. If I were an honorable man I would never have drawn you into my life. But once I'd seen you..."

His eyes flared, his panther's emerald gaze wild and possessive. "I couldn't. You bewitched me, and I laid my trap for you."

"Your *trap*?" She shook her head. "You saved my *life*."

"You would never have been in danger if it wasn't for me."

She searched his eyes. His panther had retreated, leaving Grant's bitter shame with nothing to hide behind. "That's not true. Francine Delacourt had her eye on me from the moment she saw my paintings." Something shifted in her mind, like the pieces of a puzzle coming together. "If you hadn't come to my rescue then, you wouldn't have been able to save me from her yesterday. I would still be in that cave."

Dead. She didn't say it, but cold flooded through her in a wave. Francine had suspected from the start that Irina had something to do with her brother's disappearance. Hadn't she? Because she'd looked at her paintings...

The paintings that Irina had worked on all summer. The paintings she'd been too afraid to make portraits, because her portraits freaked people out, but which she'd infused with the memories of the people she'd seen on the trails that summer...

"You saved me," she whispered, and Grant's arms tightened around her.

"If I truly wanted to save you now, I would let you go." His voice was broken. "I didn't grow up in a shifter family. There's a reason for that. All shifters have soulmates, but panthers... My father abandoned my mother before I was even born, and he was a panther shifter, the same as me. What if I do the same? What if the same magical bond that drew us together shatters the moment my panther gets bored, or distracted, and I leave you, like he left my mother? I'm not your savior, Irina. I'm your curse."

Irina's mouth was dry. She licked her lips. "That's why you didn't tell me. You wanted to get to know me without me knowing about your panther, so there would be more between us than just the... magical bond?"

He nodded.

"And what does your panther think now that he—you—what do you think now?"

Grant drew a ragged breath. His Adam's apple stuttered. "I think that I love you, and I can't bear the thought of being without you. Not after last night. Not ever." He dropped his head. "And I think that I don't want to trap you, just because I put you into danger. If you want to leave, I understand."

"Leave?" Irina's head was spinning. "No," she said. "No, I'm not going to run off. Grant, you just *saved my life*. I'm not going to stay with you out of any sense of obligation. I'm going to stay with you because you're the most incredible man I've ever met."

Irina put one hand on either side of Grant's face, gently drawing him toward her. His stubble scratched against her grazed palms, but she ignored it.

She had to tell him. Maybe this was the real purpose of the strange, unnerving power she had always kept hidden.

To show her panther the truth of his own heart.

"There's something I've kept from you, too," she began haltingly. "My own... magic."

She'd never said it out loud before. She tensed, waiting for Grant to tell her she was wrong, humans weren't magic—but he said nothing. Just watched her, his gaze part human, part panther, and all for her.

"When I look at people, I see more than just their face. If I concentrate—or sometimes, if I'm not being careful enough to stop it—I can see something more behind their eyes. Something hidden. I used to think it was my imagination. That some people have this *something more* inside them, that only I could see."

She bit her lip. Understanding and wonderment dawned on Grant's face. "You can tell when people are shifters?"

"I didn't know that's what it was. When I tried to draw or paint what I saw, it made people... uncomfortable. I wasn't drawing anyone's inner animals. It wasn't that literal. I drew the feelings, the—the true sense of what they were. *Who* they were." She paused. "I've stayed away from portraits ever since, because of that. I'm sure there's a market for discomfortingly accurate portraits, but most people prefer to control what other people see when they look at them."

"What do you see when you look at me?" Grant's voice was little more than a whisper, worshipful and hoping.

She looked at him, letting herself sink into his warm green eyes, into all the love and longing waiting there for her, and let her power take hold.

Grant's aura was so brilliant that her vision blurred. The glimpses she'd let herself see before were nothing compared to his full, true self.

Beneath his guilt and bitter self-control, she saw Grant's heart: powerful and strong, possessive and protective. And vulnerable. A single swift attack would break him forever, and he was the one holding the blade, resting the sharp point against his own chest. He would destroy himself to keep her safe.

She couldn't let that happen.

The rest of the world fell away. There was only her, and Grant, and the magic that tied them together. Not a trap, or a cage. A lifeline holding them safe so they would never be alone.

When she was finally able to speak again, her voice was choked. "Until I met you, I never had anyone who made me feel special. Who didn't make me think I had to pretend to be someone I wasn't. And then, last night... I was so afraid. But you came for me." She stroked his cheek. "*You* did that. . And there is no universe in which you would ever let me be hurt. I see that every time I look into your eyes."

"My panther—"

"Your panther is *you*, Grant. Another part of you but still you."

"I can't believe that." His jaw tightened, but his eyes were pleading. "I've fought it all my life. Its instincts. Its wildness. Whatever you see in my eyes—"

"Then let me see it. Through its own eyes."

Wariness prickled over his skin. "You're sure?"

"Yes. Please, Grant."

He stood slowly. His lips moved, and she guessed his question before he spoke.

"Don't you dare ask me to pick up a weapon, or put space between us before you shift, as though you're dangerous to me. Don't you *dare*."

He firmed his lips and nodded his acquiescence. Irina sat cross-legged on the bed, anticipation crackling down her spine.

Then the air around him shimmered, and he transformed.

It took her breath away. It would never *stop* taking her breath away—she was sure of that. Standing where Grant had been a moment before was a massive panther, its inky coat like shadows brought to life. Emerald green eyes shone up at her, knowing and wary.

She'd told Grant that he and his panther were one. But that wasn't exactly true. They had the same heart, but their minds were different, man and beast like shoots from the same seed. The animal wariness in those brilliant eyes was his panther.

Did it believe what Grant thought about it, too? That it was fickle, cruel, and would betray her?

She let her power spill free.

Sensations rushed through her. The heavy heat of the jungle pressing in on her skin. The dark of night, the hunt—and the loneliness. Restless longing like no matter how far she roamed, how stealth-silent and powerful she was, she couldn't find what she was looking for. And then—

Her. She gasped. *She* was what the panther had been searching for, the answer to its restlessness. It wasn't fickle or careless. It wanted what its human wanted; in its own way it was as vulnerable as Grant, shipwrecked by emotions so huge it had no name for them.

It wanted to keep her safe. A home, a family. A world all their own. It didn't care whether they lived in the green living jungle or this place of concrete and ice, so long as they were together.

Irina blinked. The vision faded; she gasped for breath as though she'd surfaced from a long dive underwater.

She reached out and brushed her hand against the panther's cheek, just as she had touched Grant in the same way. "My love," she breathed. "I see you. I know you. Whatever your father was, you are loyal, and honorable, a nd *mine.*"

The panther shivered. Magic shimmered all around it and then it was Grant's face her palm was pressed against. She drew him close and kissed him.

He kissed her back, hesitant at first and then with passionate hunger. His hands found her waist. He pulled her to himself and lay on the bed, holding her on top of him. "That was... my panther?" he whispered, his voice unsteady. "I never knew..."

"Do you believe me now?" she breathed against his lips.

"I'm scared to. Still." It cost him to admit it, even now.

"Not as scared as I am of losing you." She stroked his hair off his forehead. "Grant, listen to your own heart. You were worried your panther's feelings for me were superficial. That it would betray me—us—when things got tough. But you were in your panther shape when you stood between me and gunfire last night. Both of you stayed with me. You *defended* me."

Grant's eyes widened. "I—you're right. All this time, I've been trying to repress my panther's instincts or ignore them because I was so terrified of what it might do. But we were like one in the cave. United. And what I just felt..." His brow cleared, and Irina's heart swelled. "I never had any reason to be afraid, did I? I was so sure about what I was, what my panther was, that I never stopped to ask whether it might not be true."

"You know now?"

"Oh, yes." His eyes narrowed, flaring emerald green. "And I'll never let you go."

"Good."

Irina gazed into Grant's eyes as her body pressed against his. Her breasts against his chest, her legs sliding apart over his hips.

"I love you," he whispered, and Irina's heart fluttered. "*All* of me. I want to spend the rest of my life with you."

"I love you, too," she whispered back, and Grant's hands tightened around her waist. His warm green eyes almost glowed as he gazed up at her, all the tension easing out of his face.

"I might not understand everything about shifters, but I want to learn," she said, brushing a curl off his forehead. "We'll figure it out together."

"Together," he repeated, his voice husky. "And your magic—if you like, we can find out more about it, too. I've never heard of anyone with powers like yours. They're incredible."

Incredible. Not weird. Not scary. Not her creepy little 'thing'. "Grant…"

"Yes, my own one?"

"Would you let me paint you?"

She hadn't painted anyone in so long. But her heart longed to use her brush and oils to give life to everything she'd seen in Grant's eyes. To create something he could look at and see his own true self in.

He seemed to understand. "I would be honored. Right now?"

"No… not right now."

She guided his hands to the hem of her T-shirt, and he pulled it off her, slowly, as though he was unwrapping a precious treasure. She wasn't wearing any panties, and by the time he dropped the T-shirt off the side of the bed, her naked skin was burning for his touch.

"God, you're so beautiful," he breathed, green eyes gazing hungrily at her.

Irina lowered herself down again, kissing him deeply. An electric hum of arousal was building inside her, sensitizing her skin. But she didn't want the fast, hectic lovemaking they had enjoyed their first time. "I want to take my time," she said, murmuring into his lips.

Irina moved her hands down Grant's chest, enjoying the solid curves of his muscles under her fingers. His nipple hardened as she brushed over it, and she stroked it again, amazed at how quickly Grant's body reacted to her touch.

Grant moaned as she bent down and licked his nipple. Her own body was responding, too, her pulse quickening as she explored Grant inch by inch. Grant swept her hair back off her face and she looked up at him. His eyes were heavy with lust.

Irina looked away and began to kiss her way down his torso. Her full breasts brushed against his abs, and she felt him tremble with desire.

At last, her lips met the velvet hardness of his cock.

He was already fully erect. She couldn't help but stroke it as she arranged herself over him. It was as thick and long as she remembered, and she licked her lips as she remembered how Grant had plunged into her the last time, pinning her to the bed.

She ran her fingers along the shaft, up to its heavy head. Grant moaned and she grinned up at him before sinking her lips over it.

"Oh, God," she heard him gasp. His hips bucked a little, pushing his cock deeper into her mouth.

Irina swirled her tongue over its head, slowly, savoring her mate's arousal. Her own pussy throbbed. She was wet and ready to be filled… but as she had told Grant, she wanted to take her time.

She hummed, taking him deeper into her mouth so he would feel the vibration. Grant clutched at her hair.

"Oh, God—Irina—I want you so much—" He brushed her face with one thumb, and she locked eyes with him, still holding his cock in her mouth. As he watched her, she licked her way down the shaft, listening to him moan, one hand gently holding her head, the other desperately clenching onto the bedsheets.

She gave his cock one last, lingering lick, and then pulled away. "I want you too," she breathed, pressing her body again his. Her whole skin felt as though it was on fire.

Irina nuzzled her way back up Grant's body, tangling his hair in her fingers as she pulled him into a deep kiss that left her panting. Grant stroked his hands down her back and waist, rounding the curve of her ass with a squeeze.

Grant groaned and gripped her around the waist, rolling on top of her and positioning himself between her open legs. The tip of his cock pressed against the wet folds of her pussy, tantalizingly close.

"I love you," Grant breathed as he sank home into her.

He was slow and controlled, but Irina still caught her breath as the thick girth of his cock stretched her. She could feel every inch of him, hard and thick, pushing her closer towards release.

She gasped as he buried himself completely inside her. Somehow, the slowness made him feel bigger, as though her body had more time to understand just how massive his cock was.

Irina rocked her hips gently, feeling Grant's cock press against every nerve inside her. Her fingers tightened instinctively around his waist as electric bursts of desire thrilled through her.

Above her, Grant moved with a cat's grace, pulling out with painful slowness and filling her again. Irina's whole body was focused in on the connection between them, her arousal so intense it was almost painful.

"Look at me," Grant whispered, and Irina opened her eyes, falling into Grant's forest-green gaze. His eyes, half shut, smoldered with lust, and Irina was lost inside them, tumbling headlong into an orgasm that shook her from head to toe.

She cried out as she heard Grant groan above her, his cock pulsing deep inside her as his own orgasm struck. They clung to each other, gasping as waves of pleasure rolled through them.

Irina was panting as though she'd been swimming and just breached the surface. Her nose was full of the scents of sweat, and sex, and *Grant*. Her Grant. Her mate.

"Oh, my darling," she murmured, knotting her fingers in his hair. "How was I so lucky as to find you?"

"I'm the lucky one," Grant murmured into her shoulder, his breath caressing her skin. Irina wriggled happily as he nuzzled along her collarbone and up her neck. "I'm the one who..."

The sound of a cellphone buzzing interrupted him. Grant groaned.

"...I'm the one who told Lance I'd go along to his debrief after you woke up," he admitted. "Dammit."

"Debrief?" Irina pushed herself into a sitting position. *Lance, the snow leopard. The so-called PA who took out a team of soldiers as easily as cutting flowers.* "Is Lance ex-military, or something? He really seemed to know what he was doing yesterday."

"Or something," Grant said. "That sounds about right. His aunt's high-up in the Army, and Lance..." He shrugged. "I don't know exactly what he did before he started his own business, but I'm sure he was as good at it as he is at spreadsheets and scheduling."

He pulled himself up beside Irina, offering his chest as an alternative to the headboard. Irina took up the offer without a second thought. Her mind was still deliciously hazy from their lovemaking, and really, she couldn't think of anything better than lazing here in Grant's arms.

She tipped her head back and gazed up at him. He stared back, a smile twitching at the corner of his lips. One of his hands drifted down her side to the curve of her hip.

"What are you thinking?" he asked softly.

"About Lance?" she teased.

Grant groaned, and she laughed.

"I was thinking... oh, it's silly, but I was thinking how safe I feel. How happy." She reached up to stroke Grant's cheek, feeling his stubble under her fingers. "And..."

Something went *click* in the back of her head. The puzzle pieces she'd all but forgotten about, coming together at last.

"Oh my God," she breathed, suddenly still.

Grant was instantly alert. "What is it?"

"I just realized—" Her hand flew to her mouth. "We need to see Lance, now. If I'm right..."

She met his concerned gaze, her eyes wide. "I know why Francine thought we killed her brother."

Chapter 22

Grant

Irina's revelation was still ringing in Grant's ears an hour later when they arrived at Lance's HQ.

MacInnis Investigations. The sign was subtle, barely visible from the busy street. The building looked no different from any of the other bland office buildings in the area. This was Grant's first visit to the place, and he'd expected… Well, something more exciting.

Maybe dull made sense, though. Lance had started his PI firm a few years back, certain there was a gap in the market for investigating crimes involving shifters.

Grant assumed business was slow, given Lance had seemed more interested in trailing around after him than running his company.

If Irina's right, all that is about to change.

Grant's panther senses went on high alert the moment he stepped through the door. He frowned and pulled Irina closer to his side, trying to figure out what his panther was telling him.

It was strange, working *with* his panther's instincts, rather than against them. But it felt good, too. It was *right*. Just like being with Irina was right, good, and the best thing that could possibly have happened to him.

He concentrated. *What is it? Something unusual…*

Grant had followed Lance's directions to this building to the letter. It was an unremarkable office block on an unremarkable street, and he and Irina had walked through the unremarkable front door into an unremarkable, beige-colored foyer. Two unremarkable receptionists sat behind the front desk; a matching pair of unremarkable security guards waved them, clearly advised in advance that they were expected.

Beside him, Irina sniffed. "Is it really dry in here, or is it just me?"

Grant tasted the air. "You're right. Dry and hot. There's something..."

Wait. Beige, hot, and dry? A light glinted at the edge of Grant's vision. He paused halfway through helping Irina out of the winter coat she had borrowed from him, which was completely wrong for the climate-controlled room. "What did Lance call this place, again?"

"The Manor," Irina replied at once. She narrowed her eyes. "You're right, there is something... I wonder..."

Her eyes went hazy as she looked around. A tremor went through her. "Grant, everyone in here is a shifter!" she whispered.

"And they would be terrified to learn you can tell that just by looking at them." Grant folded Irina's coat over one arm and reclaimed her waist with the other.

"No. Terrified? Of me?" She looked uneasy.

"You're a sort of magic nobody here has ever heard of. Wonderful and new." He lowered his lips to her ear. "Don't worry. I'll protect you."

She snorted. "So, I'm going to terrify them and you're going to threaten them? I can already tell this meeting is going to go well."

Another movement across the room caught Grant's attention. He winked at Irina and waved at the man who had just appeared through a door at the far end of the foyer.

"Mr. and Mrs. Diaz?"

The young man was neatly turned out in khakis, matching shirt and tie, and matching dusty-blond hair. He also clearly wasn't expecting his greeting to have the effect it did. He jumped backwards as Irina and Grant both tried to correct him at once.

Grant caught Irina's eye and shut his mouth.

"I'm *Ms.* Mathers," she explained to the man who looked like he could blend in with the desert so fast you wouldn't see him disappear. Her dark eyes flicked up to meet Grant's again. "At the moment, at least."

Grant's heart swelled as he looked down at her. *His* Irina. Was it too early to ask her...?

"My apologies. Mr. Diaz, Ms. Mathers. Your group is waiting upstairs."

Arm in arm with his mate, Grant followed the young man through a series of corridors and open-plan rooms. Everywhere they went, heads popped around doors or up over cubicles to check their progress.

Grant chuckled. The desert atmosphere, the agency's nickname—he knew what his panther had picked up on, now. And he was going to tease the hell out of Lance for it. Meerkat Manor? Really? And he thought snow leopards were meant to be cool.

"Here you are." The desert-colored man handed them through to a meeting room and then promptly disappeared. Grant blinked after him.

"Grant, Irina. I'm glad you could join us."

Lance was standing at the head of a large meeting table. Grant recognized most of the people gathered around it: Harley Ames, the cheetah shifter who had flown them out to the mountains to rescue Irina, was an old friend, one of the big cat shifters who had all grown up together in the city. Next to him was a thickset woman who couldn't have been more than mid-thirties, despite the graying threads in her dark hair. One of Lance's employees. Grant dug in his memory for a name. Yelich?

There was no forgetting the young woman standing at the back of the room. Carol Zhang was a shark shifter, and the only shifter Grant had ever met whose human form had animal characteristics. She had flat gray eyes with no whites and hidden behind her closed lips were double rows of sharp, pointy teeth. She paced along the back wall, slowly, making him think of the story about how sharks never stopped swimming.

He couldn't help the shiver that went down his spine. His panther was one thing, but what sort of uneasy alliance must she have with her inner creature, when she could never fully hide it?

At Lance's gesture, he and Irina took their seats at the table.

"Is this all of us?" Grant asked. Somehow, from Lance's communications, he'd expected more.

Lance pushed his glasses up his nose and smiled at them both. "I don't believe either of you have met my aunt."

He motioned to a screen on the wall, which Grant had assumed was turned off. When Lance stepped in front of it, though, a video feed appeared. *A privacy filter*, he thought.

The woman on the other end of the video call gave him a thin smile. She was in her early sixties, he guessed, and had Lance's dark skin and startling eyes.

Lance made the introductions. "Auntie, this is Grant Diaz, and his mate, Irina Mathers. Grant, Irina—my aunt, General MacInnis."

The General nodded at them both. "Thank you for joining us today. Miss Mathers, first let me extend my apologies for the situation you found yourself in yesterday. I hope it is some consolation that the discoveries made during the event may help us prevent such things in future."

"Discoveries?" Irina asked, straightening. She exchanged a look with Grant. He frowned, his panther on the alert. There was no way Lance and the others could know Irina's secret. What else were they about to discover?

"The shielding equipment used by your attackers," General MacInnis explained. "Lance?"

Lance held out the palm-sized object he'd shown Grant the day before: a shell-shaped, gleaming circle, encased in a plastic holder "We found these on all of Francine's 'hired help'. In these sheaths, they shield whoever's holding them from being scented or heard by shifters."

"Impossible." Harley frowned. "If there was a way to turn my nose off, I would have found it by now."

"Try it." Lance raised one eyebrow.

Harley closed his eyes. His nostrils flared and shock flashed across his face as he realized what Grant had already known. "It's like you're not even there!"

"All but invisible." Lance's voice was grim. "And that's only when I'm holding the case. When I touch the object itself..."

He placed his hand over the shimmering circle and vanished.

Grant leapt to his feet. Harley shouted, Yelich swore, and Carol stared. Only Irina seemed relatively unfazed. She exchanged a glance with him and raised her eyebrows.

"Is this new magic, too? Sorry, my weirdness scale is all out of balance. This is super weird?" *Does it make my magic more, or less, scary?* she seemed to be asking him silently.

He didn't know. He'd joked about terrifying the others. But this was something else.

"That's putting it lightly." Lance reappeared and placed the invisibility—thing? Spell? Magical charm?—on the table. He sighed and ran one hand over his head. "There are no records of anything like this existing. It's not technology. It's organic."

"It looks like a scale," Irina murmured. She reached across the table and Lance pushed the thing toward her. She picked it up and turned it this way and that. Light glinted oddly off it. Grant's panther growled as her scent vanished. "Don't you think? Like a fish-scale, or a reptile of some sort. Or—" Her eyes shone. "A dragon? Are *dragons* real?"

Silence answered her. Irina put her hands up. "Okay. Maybe that wasn't playing it cool. But—dragons? Is that possible? Someone please tell me it isn't before I lose my mind."

"There is no evidence of dragons, or dragon shifters, ever existing," Lance informed her woodenly.

All eyes went to the shimmering scale on the table.

"Shit," Lance muttered. "Grant, consider this my resignation as your bodyguard. If Irina's right..."

Grant nodded his understanding. He had suspected all along that Lance only bullied him into taking him on as a bodyguard because running a shifter PI agency wasn't as exciting as he'd hoped.

Well, it looked like it was going to be exciting now.

And as for his own reasons for keeping Lance around...

He glanced at Irina. His panther purred contentedly.

Grant was no longer afraid of who he was.

"We don't know where they come from, let alone what they are. Francine Delacourt is being very helpful," the General cut in. "Unfortunately, her own contacts appear to have been a smokescreen. Whoever is behind this didn't want to risk creating a witness who could easily identify them."

"Is she okay?" Irina said suddenly. Grant turned to her. Irina was frowning down at the table. "Was she badly hurt? That man knocked her out..."

Irina kept her eyes on the table, as though she was unwilling to look up and meet anyone else's gaze. Grant reached across and took her hand.

On the other side of the table, Lance cleared his throat. "Physically, she's fine. Her head injury was minor, and she's already recovered. But if that's a roundabout way of asking exactly how we're getting this information, then yes, we have her in custody. As my aunt said, now that Francine understands you had nothing to do with her brother's disappearance, she has been more than happy to help our investigation." He sighed. "And if I know Frankie, the fact that her apparent allies fooled her into targeting you both will make her even more fervent to see them cut down."

"But she was right," Irina blurted out.

Lance paused. Irina glanced up at Grant and he nodded. *Tell them.*

She drew a ragged breath, shoulders braced. "Francine became convinced that I had something to do with her brother's disappearance after she saw my paintings. I didn't think anything of it at the time, but now..."

She reached for Grant's hand under the table. He squeezed it reassuringly.

"I can see people's inner animals," she said plainly. "And when I paint—I've learned not to paint what I can see in people, but when I was working on the landscapes I exhibited at the gallery opening, I was thinking about the people I'd met in the mountains that summer. Some of them were shifters. I didn't know it at the time, I just thought there was something about them that made me want to paint them. One man in particular..."

Grant's panther stirred and he put his arm around his mate, holding her possessively. She snorted softly. "Not like *that*. Does anyone have a photo of Mathis Delacourt? If I can see him, I'll know for sure."

Lance pulled out his phone and passed it to her. She barely had to glance at it. "That's him."

The photo showed a young man with the same blond hair and aquiline features as Francine Delacourt. Mathis was built on harsher lines, but the same predatory power burned in his eyes as in his twin's.

"Wait." Harley ran his hands through his hair. "You can see our *inner animals*? How is that possible?"

"See them and paint them," Yelich remarked beside him. She raised her eyebrows at Irina. "And here I thought MacInnis was going to blow his top over the dragon thing. You're full of surprises."

"Okay, so. What am I? If you can tell what we are." Harley leaned forwards, elbows on the table, staring at Grant's mate. She stared evenly back at him, snugged in against Grant's side.

Grant glared at Harley. "You don't need to prove anything to him."

His mate shrugged. "I mean, it would be more convincing if I did, wouldn't it?" She leaned forward, echoing Harley's pose, and put her chin on her hands. Her gaze went distant as she locked eyes with Harley. "Cheetah."

Harley blinked. "Okay. Right. Yes."

Without moving any other muscle, Irina glanced at Yelich, next to him. "Rhino."

Yelich raised a hand in mock salute.

Irina's gaze flicked to the back of the room. Carol Zhang stared back, her expression fathomless. "Shark."

Carol's lips quirked. Grant couldn't tell whether it was a smile or a grimace. "You don't need magic to tell that." Even when she spoke, she took care to keep anything more than a flash of sharp teeth from showing.

"You're not a shifter?" Harley insisted. "Because we can usually tell another shifter. There's a scent, or a feeling of them being a big ol' predator asshole, or *something*."

"Something more than human," Irina mused, agreeing. "I'm not a shifter. Maybe my magic is related to yours, though. But that's not the important thing. I *did* see your friend in the mountains last summer, but..." She tapped the photo. "He wasn't like this. Smiling and confident and—is that a lion thing, how he looks like he owns the whole world? Francine is the same. *Was* the same." Her voice lowered. "No wonder she was so worried. When I saw him he was lost. Like your panther was."

She looked up at Grant. "You saw my painting, didn't you? The middle one in the triptych at the gallery. I painted him into it. It's not as strong as when I do a portrait, but... When you looked at it, did you feel...?"

Grant's mind went blank. Her painting? Fuck. He should remember it. He almost did. Maybe? The one she'd been standing in front of the night he'd first seen her, a voluptuous shadow in that black dress, her curls falling loose from her updo, her eyes dark and huge… Had there been a painting behind her? It was all a blur.

"Uh," he began, and Lance laughed at him.

"He didn't have eyes for anyone but you that night, Irina."

Irina flushed with pleasure. "Oh, well—and the rest of you weren't there anyway, so—"

"I remember it." Lance's voice was heavy. "I was surprised they gave it such a prominent position. It was—there was something wrong with it. Not with the painting, there was nothing wrong with the painting, but…"

"Looking at it made you feel like something was wrong," Irina murmured. "I was surprised Clare put it front and center, too."

"And it wasn't only the feeling of being lost. It was… loneliness. As though I was hunting for something that I was afraid didn't exist." Lance's gaze sharpened. "You're saying that's what you saw in Mathis? He's out there searching for some sort of meaning in life."

Irina swallowed and nodded.

Grant frowned. *Meaning* wasn't what his panther had been searching for. What he'd been after was sitting right beside him. The other half of his heart.

All the money in the world, and the poor bastard can't find what he really needs. His panther huffed its agreement.

"We have to find him." Grant's panther lent its weight to his words, and his voice came out a predator's growl.

"That can't be our first priority." General MacInnis's tone was clipped. "I'm sure your rich friend's emotional issues are very touching, but think of the bigger picture. We've just uncovered a technology, or possibly a type of weaponized shifter, that has never been seen before, being used by an anti-shifter ring. Everything else can wait."

"What if it's connected?" Irina steadied her shoulders as the General stared her down, and Grant was filled with pride for his mate. "Francine thought something awful happened to her brother. These people with the dragon-scale shields seemed happy to con her into looking in the wrong direction, and framing Grant and me. What if it's because they know where he really is?"

A shiver went around the table. Grant stood up. "That decides it. We find Mathis, and we find out who the hell these people are, and why they're walking around with bits of dragon on them."

EPILOGUE

IRINA

There was no sign of Mathis in Silverstream.

She was sure Grant would want to continue the search for his friend immediately, but he told her they could spare a few days. Lance and his agency were on the job. She pushed back—then saw how her mate's eyes kept returning to the scrapes on her hands and knees, and the remnants of the bruise on her neck. His panther's protective heart needed to know she was healed before they ventured out again.

Her Gran's cottage couldn't have been more different from Grant's high-rise apartment, and Silverstream was nothing like the city. But there was light, and silence, and a background of mountains that touched the sky. And Irina's fingers were itching.

She and Grant were lying in bed. The sun was high, but neither of them had found any good reason to get out up yet. Even the siren call of whatever they would scrounge together for breakfast wasn't enough to tempt Irina out of her mate's arms.

Not even coffee.

But... there was one thing that might change her mind.

"A portrait?" Grant's eyes danced. "I already agreed to this, didn't I? What sort of a portrait?"

"The sort that makes people uncomfortable to look at."

He grinned. "I shouldn't bother to get dressed, then?"

"Not *that* sort of uncomfortable." She bit the tips of his fingers, and he kissed her neck in return. "I haven't painted anyone's portrait in years. It's too easily to accidentally include... too much."

Understanding flared in his eyes. "And that's why you want to paint me."

"All of you."

"*All* of me..." His lips brushed her skin. "Yes. I think I would like to see myself as you see me."

The cottage was still packed up from last summer, but she hadn't taken all her painting gear back to the city. Irina spent the rest of the day warming herself in front of the cottage's cast-iron stove, sorting through canvases and frames and checking her oils. She remembered running out of some colors, and her stomach tightened with the memory of trying to think how she would afford to replace them.

Not something I need to worry about anymore, she thought wryly. Scraping together her pennies to pay for more paints wasn't an issue when you were a billionaire's soulmate.

Still, something stopped her from ordering more supplies. It felt *right*, to use these paints and these brushes and all the memories they brought with them, for her portrait of her mate. As the day wore on, she stretched a canvas out over a frame, arranged palettes until she was satisfied, and filled her head with imagined sketches of her composition.

"It's as though you forgot I was there," Grant complained light-heartedly over dinner—fresh-caught fish and pasta in a creamy sauce, courtesy of a recipe he had begged off Moss.

"You were the only thing on my mind all day," she told him truthfully. He poured wine into her glass with a teasing smirk.

"Did you even notice I left to pick up groceries?"

"...No?"

"How dreadful." Grant leaned back, his voice a purring drawl. "I go off, hunting through a barren wilderness to bring you sustenance, and you didn't even kiss me goodbye."

She narrowed her eyes. "You had it delivered, didn't you?" Silverstream's one small store didn't stock anything as exotic as paprika or fresh pasta, let alone the sprigs of microgreens Grant had decorated their plates with.

"You didn't even notice the *helicopter* that delivered it, yes."

"I was working!"

He laughed and leaned over the table to kiss her. "I know. And I loved watching every moment of it. You being lost in your work."

He kissed her again, more slowly. "I was happy to leave you to it today. But I can't promise to be as forbearing in future."

"Oh, really?" She grinned at him. "I don't think you appreciate just how single-minded my concentration can be, when I'm really in the zone."

*

She made Grant pose the next morning. The clear, bright light of the mountains wasn't quite right... but *he* was. Powerful and alluring, playful and warm. Her panther. Her mate.

"Stay right where you are," she ordered, and picked up her pencil to sketch out the composition.

The next time she looked up, he was gone.

Lips whispered against her neck. "Can I interest you in a distraction?"

*

"It's not that I was lying about liking to watch you work," he said, when she had finally managed to get some flat colors down. "It's just like I enjoy this perspective, as well," he added from between her legs.

She had to agree with that.

*

The problem with panthers, she decided after several days of achieving very little, was that they were *cats*.

"Do I need to tie you down?" she asked, exhausted and exasperated. "Or is it that you find the smell of turps so intoxicating you can't help yourself?"

"Something like that," he purred. "Though you can try tying me down, if you think it would help."

*

It didn't.

*

What felt like an eternity later, but which was probably only a week and a half, Irina's injuries had healed and her canvas was a riot of color and energy. She stepped back, trembling, Grant at her side.

There was no point looking for anything strange in her paintings before they were complete. It was only when she stepped back and took in the finished work as a whole that she could see what she had created.

The creep factor. Her *thing*, given life by brushstrokes and oils.

Her magic.

What lay on the canvas in front of her was... Grant.

The background was little more than a gesture in shadows. She'd been right about the light not being right, that first morning; Grant's soul required dusky half-light, the promise of secrets hidden in darkness. But those secrets weren't the fickle cruelty he'd once feared. They were his kindness, his loyalty and passion, and his warm heart.

As Irina stared at her painting, her flesh and blood mate put his arm around her. "Thank you," he whispered, his voice awed. "If I ever need to be reminded of what I am, I will only need to look at this. And thank you for putting yourself there, too."

What? "But I didn't—"

"Look closer," he told her, love roughening his voice. "Look into my soul."

Into his soul? She turned and searched his eyes, and he laughed.

"Not here." He gently turned her head back to the canvas. "There."

His eyes in the painting. The eyes she had painted, full of his love and laughter and...

And her.

She was there.

Not a painted reflection, not a concrete representation of her face or figure, but the magic that filled her canvas had taken its fill of her, as well, and poured it out into her work.

Irina stared. She had never painted herself before. She had never *seen* herself like this before.

"Oh," she whispered. The woman in Grant's eyes was happy and carefree and... fully, gloriously, herself. She owned her body, and her magic, and her fierce passion for the man who had made her his, with a confidence Irina never would have thought possible.

"My mate," Grant whispered, his voice the gentlest caress. "You showed me who I am. You saved me from myself. And you let me be the one to help you find yourself, too. You couldn't have given me a greater gift than that."

He kissed her, sweet and loving and then hot and passionate, and she fell into his embrace.

The world was more magical than she had ever dreamed, but this was the greatest magic of all.

EPILOGUE TWO

MATHIS

One wrong move, and Mathis Delacourt's mate would die.

The fighting ring where they were trapped was lit by a single bare light. Above, the windows that protected the spectator platforms were dark, but he wasn't fooled. Someone was there, waiting to see the bloodbath.

He'd been a fighter all his life. He'd fought humans in his human form, and it had felt like a game, testing his self-control against their strength. Fighting other shifters in his lion form had been a novelty at first—until he realized the sick truth about the game they were playing.

Behind him, Chloe pressed herself against the metal grill of the cage doors, fighting with the lock. His brave, beautiful mate. Trapped here because of him.

The polar bear shifter opposite him sniffed the air. Its tiny black eyes were bright with madness, or bloodlust, or both. Red dripped from its jaws. Mathis tried not to think about how much blood he'd already lost. How much longer he could stay standing, even in his powerful lion form.

Fighting for his own life he could handle. But if anything happened to Chloe?

It would destroy him.

And then he would destroy them all.

SAVED BY THE BILLIONAIRE LION SHIFTER

SHIFTER SUSPENSE BOOK 2

CHAPTER 1

MATHIS

One wrong move, and Mathis Delacourt's mate would die.

The fighting ring where they were trapped was lit by a single bare light. Above, the windows that protected the spectator platforms were dark, but he wasn't fooled. Someone was there, waiting to see the bloodbath.

He'd been a fighter all his life. He'd fought humans in his human form, and it had felt like a game, testing his self-control against their strength. Fighting other shifters in his lion form had been a novelty at first—until he realized the sick truth about the game they were playing.

Behind him, Chloe pressed herself against the metal grill of the cage doors, fighting with the lock. His brave, beautiful mate. Trapped here because of him.

The polar bear shifter opposite him sniffed the air. Its tiny black eyes were bright with madness, or bloodlust, or both. Red dripped from its jaws. Mathis tried not to think about how much blood he'd already lost. How much longer he could stay standing, even in his powerful lion form.

Fighting for his own life he could handle. But if anything happened to Chloe?

It would destroy him.

And then he would destroy them all.

A week earlier

The two men circled each other warily, each waiting for the other to leave an opening. Mathis narrowed his eyes against the harsh lights of the gym, staring down his opponent.

All it would take was one blink, and the other man would take his chance.

So Mathis blinked.

In the split-second his eyes were shut, he heard his opponent move. The soles of his shoes scraped against the hard floor, his breath sharpening as he launched himself forward. Mathis opened his eyes to see the man's right fist flying towards his face. He swayed out of the way, all feline grace and speed, and jabbed his own fist at his opponent's unprotected midsection.

His fist connected with the other man's flesh. Hard, but not too hard. Enough to make him twist into a defensive stance, protecting his injured side.

If Mathis had punched with his full strength, the man would have been nursing more than some bruised ribs. But Mathis wouldn't lose control like that. Not against a human.

His lion was close to the surface. It always was, during these fights. But although Mathis used its heightened senses to gauge his opponent's power, he kept the lion leashed.

Mathis circled around, his movements slow and deliberate. Inside him, his lion stalked with its eyes wide and its mouth open, tasting the air. Mathis grinned. He didn't need his lion's senses to tell him he was on the ropes.

He shook sweat out of his eyes, his gaze still fixed on the other man, a white guy in his early thirties. A seasoned fighter. Pale eyes, unwashed hair, and scars on his knuckles.

Mathis had seen him on the outside of the ring earlier in the night, watching Mathis fight. The guy must have been waiting for Mathis to tire himself out, so he could jump in the ring and finish him off.

No chance of that, Mathis thought, his skin prickling with adrenaline. This was his fifth match of the night, and he was just getting started.

Energy pumping through his veins, Mathis stepped forward. His opponent crouched defensively, and then surged up, taking Mathis by surprise.

Mathis raised his arms to take the blow, and the next one. The force of it jolted through his bones, but his shifter healing was already repairing his bruised muscles.

The crowd was cheering, their roar a faint ringing in Mathis' ears. He knew as soon as the bout was over it would flood through and over him, an ocean of sound buoying him up, but it was meaningless right now. He filtered it out.

The other man was still raining blows on Mathis' forearms, trying to beat him down, force him to drop his guard. Mathis lunged sideways, aiming another jab at his opponent's ribs while he was off-balance.

The man stumbled back and Mathis grinned. He waited for him to pull back into another defensive stance, protecting his ribs, which must be screaming by now.

He was so sure that he almost missed the flicker in the man's eyes.

The man twisted, but instead of protecting his injured side he spun sideways, hooking his arm around to plow towards Mathis' neck. Mathis dodged, but too late, and the man struck a glancing blow under his ear.

Mathis' vision went black, and then returned with crystal clarity. He growled, his lion rising within him as he turned on his opponent. The man was smirking, already anticipating his victory. If Mathis had been human, that blow would have left him dazed.

But Mathis' lion was roaring as loudly as the crowd. Mathis whipped around, taking his opponent off guard. His fist shot out—*Hold back, hold back, don't give it your all*—and caught the other man under the jaw.

Mathis stood still, his heart pounding in his ears, as his opponent fell senseless to the ground.

The referee counted *One! Two! Three! Out!* and then the rush of blood in Mathis' ears was joined by the roar of the crowd. He held up his hands, staring out into the audience, waiting for their applause to spark his own sense of triumph.

Waiting to feel anything at all.

Mathis upended a bucket of cold water over his head, shaking icy droplets from his hair. The facilities here weren't exactly top-notch, but state-of-the-art showers and gleaming changing rooms weren't what Mathis looked for these days.

He toweled off and stretched, flexing his arms and back. He'd won ten bouts that night, and could have gone for more. He would have, too, except he could feel himself losing focus. It was the same every night. The first few matches warmed him up, woke up his lion inside him, got the blood pumping. Then he could really challenge himself, setting himself personal handicaps: play weak on your left side, don't look for their next move in their eyes, stand so the spotlights blind you and fight that way.

For a while, that had been enough. But not anymore.

Mathis ran the towel over his head again, biting back a growl of frustration. *What the hell am I meant to do now?*

He'd thought fighting would fill the hollow space inside him, and for a while, it seemed like he was right. The exercise kept his lion sharp, and victory sated its animal instincts.

But now, every victory left him more hollow than before, yearning for something he couldn't recognize. There was no thrill in defeating human opponents. None of the men he'd fought in the last few months had been anything close to challenging, and his lion was getting edgy. It wanted more.

If only it would be a bit clearer about what it wanted more *of*.

One thing was certain. It didn't want to go back to the world Mathis had grown up in.

Last week he'd been in some podunk town in the desert. Tonight, a warehouse on the outskirts of Los Angeles. He didn't know where he'd go next. He'd keep his ear to the ground, follow the rumors of other under-the-table fights, operating outside the formal leagues and beneath official oversight.

He ran the towel over his hair again. *How long are you going to keep this up?*

The words appeared in his mind so suddenly he looked around, checking that he was still the only one in the changing rooms. The place was empty. He sniffed deeply: nothing but the smell of sweat and bleach. There was no one else here, let alone another shifter who could telepathically speak into his mind.

No. The voice had been his own. And so had the fear beneath the question: If he couldn't find satisfaction doing this... what else was there?

He could go home again, he supposed. He would have to eventually, anyway, go home and bury himself in the family business again. Just like everyone expected him to.

A knock on the door distracted Mathis from his thoughts.

"Come in," he said gruffly, hooking the towel over his shoulder and pulling on a pair of sweatpants.

The door swung open and Josh Lanyard, the gym's owner, walked in with his hands in his pockets.

Mathis turned to face him head-on, his own thumbs hooked into the waistband of his pants, posture open and unthreatening. Mathis had only known Lanyard a few days but he'd figured early on that the man was an old fighter, and not just inside the ring. Puffing up like a peacock or acting aggressive in front of the old man wasn't going to get him anywhere.

"Gidday, Matt," Lanyard said now, giving him a nod. "Good night, tonight."

"Not bad," Mathis agreed. He sat down on a bench, resting his back against the cool concrete wall. "What can I do for you, Mr. Lanyard?"

"Keep your face pretty and keep drawing in the crowds," Lanyard said dryly. He pulled his hand out of his pocket and threw something at Mathis. "Here's your share for the night. And there are three or four honeys lingering out the front, waiting for you to peek your little head out."

"Guess I'll be going out the back," Mathis muttered. He shoved the roll of bills into his pocket without looking at it. Lanyard didn't strike him as the type to short him on his cut, and besides, it wasn't like he needed the cash.

Lanyard snorted. "Your loss." He nodded back over his shoulder. "Fella here to see you, anyway. You gonna put a shirt on?"

Before Mathis could answer one way or the other the changing room door swung open again.

He didn't recognize the man who walked in. He was in his late forties. Trim, almost wiry, with leathery skin that fell in wrinkles under his eyes and jawline. As he walked into the room he rubbed his fingers together, as though wiping off the residue of the door.

He greeted Mathis with a curt nod, and turned his stone-grey eyes on Lanyard. "I'd prefer to speak to Mr. Dell alone."

Lanyard shrugged. "Well, I'm not his manager. See you tomorrow, Matt."

He sloped off, letting the door swing shut after him. Mathis wasn't surprised. If Lanyard *was* his manager, the old man would have kicked up a fuss at what appeared to be someone trying to home in on his talent. But he was the gym owner. He got his cut no matter who was in the ring.

"What can I help you with?" Mathis asked once Lanyard was gone.

"Matt Dell? My name is Gerald Harper." The man's voice was crisp and light, like paper rustling.

Mathis nodded, letting the issue of his name slide as he shook hands with the other man. His real name was Mathis Delacourt, but he'd been going by Matt Dell for the previous few months. The last thing he wanted was for someone to Google *Mathis Delacourt* and discover he was more than just some down-on-his-luck amateur fighter.

"So, what can I do for you, Mr. Harper?" he said again, and added inside his head: *No, Mr. Dell, it's what I can do for you...*

"Actually, Mr. Dell, it's more what I can do for you," Gerald Harper replied.

Mathis hid a grin. *Bingo.* "Is that right?"

"I own an exclusive resort on an island off the coast of Florida," Gerald Harper began, and Mathis felt suddenly very tired. He knew what was coming next. Either this guy was going to proposition him, or...

"...A private island, where I run a very discreet private club. I bring in fighters from around the world, on very competitive contracts, to entertain my few guests."

Mathis let his head fall back against the wall. "Your own private fight club, huh?"

"Precisely."

Mathis closed his eyes. It would be a change of scenery, but... no. Gerald Harper might have spent more time in the sun than was healthy for a human, but his clothes and the dull gleam of the watch on his left wrist screamed old money.

The same vintage of money that filled Mathis' own portfolio. Which meant that even if Mathis didn't know Gerald Harper from a pile of sticks, their social circles might overlap. If he showed up at this guy's club and one of his guests recognized Mathis as the oldest son of the New York Delacourts, the whole jig would be up.

"You're not convinced."

Mathis opened his eyes to see Gerald staring straight at him, his grey eyes amused. He raised his eyebrows.

"No offense, Mr. Harper, but you're not the first person to try to whisk me away to some discreet private island," he drawled. "And as for your line about this all being more what you can do for me..."

Gerald smiled thinly. "I imagine that's something you hear a lot in your line of work?"

"Sure. Hasn't been true yet, though. Besides, I prefer the freedom to pick my own fights. Being cooped up on some private island doesn't appeal."

"Well," Gerald said, holding out his hand for Mathis to shake, "Let me know if you change your mind."

Mathis grasped his hand. When they'd shaken before, he'd noted how dry Gerald's skin was. Now it seemed almost... scaly.

He looked down. Gerald's hand, still gripping his, was growing longer as the bones stretched under the skin. His skin mottled, then transformed, turning hard and grey. Fine, feathery hairs sprouted from his wrist and the back of his hand.

He's a shifter? Mathis' eyes flew to Gerald's face. The man's grey eyes glinted black for a split second, and then he was entirely human again.

"That's a convincing argument," Mathis said slowly.

"I thought it might be," Gerald replied, pulling his hand away.

Mathis' mind was racing. Gerald Harper was a shifter. That put a whole new light on his offer. It was risky, too—if the social circles of old wealth were small, those of shifters were even smaller.

Still. This might be just what he was looking for. A fight against a shifter. Someone he wouldn't have to hold back against.

Maybe this was what his lion had been searching for.

He stood up. "All right," he said. "Tell me more."

Chapter 2

Chloe

"Everything okay?"

Chloe looked up guiltily. Her roommate, Thandie, was looking across at her with concern. The bedroom Chloe shared with her new co-worker was set up college dorm-style, with two beds pushed up against opposite walls. And, college dorm-style, this meant she couldn't rely on anything she did going unnoticed.

"Sorry?" Chloe asked, her mind racing.

Thandie pointed at her forehead. "You were frowning at the lamp like you wanted to murder it, or something," she explained.

Chloe laughed. "Oh, sorry. I didn't even notice. I guess I'm getting more withdrawals from being without Wi-Fi than I thought!" she joked.

Thandie grimaced sympathetically. "Yeah, it sucks, huh? The pay's worth it, though."

"Pay for what, though? It's not like we have anything to spend it on out here. And I haven't even met the guy who's meant to be in charge here yet. Does he even exist?" Chloe pushed herself up on her elbows and sat up, resting her back against the wall. The whine in her voice made her wince, but it did the job.

She didn't want Thandie digging too deeply about what was actually bothering her. *Time to deploy the most reliable bitching technique: bitching about the boss.*

Thandie sat up too, obviously keen to talk. "I only started here a few weeks before you did," she said. "And no, I haven't seen anyone here except the other staff. Julian—um, Mr. Rouse—says the boss often only spends a few months a year here, but when he does come to stay he only gives a few hours' notice, so staff are kept on rotation all year around."

"He must be super rich," Chloe mused.

"Yeah well, he owns an island, doesn't he?" Thandie shrugged off the idea of their employer's vast wealth. "Anyway, apparently things really take off when he arrives. So you don't need to worry about having time to miss your Facebook updates."

"I can't wait," said Chloe, deadpan, and Thandie giggled.

Chloe kept picking Thandie's brains about the island and their mysterious employer, but her roommate didn't know much more than she did. In fact, possibly she knew less.

Which sucked, because until Gerald Harper turned up, Chloe's investigation had ground to a halt.

To Thandie and the others on the island, Chloe was one of the new housekeeping staff, taken on after a ridiculously lengthy and complex hiring process. Chloe had applied to work on Gerald Harper's island resort a dozen times under different aliases in the last year. Nothing had worked until she started pulling apart the social media profiles of other people she suspected of working for Harper. Little turns of phrase, strange references—she'd peppered a few of them through her own online presence, and abracadabra. Interview, tick. Job offer, tick. Investigation underway.

It had been a lucky break. And she hadn't had much to go on, really. The island was apparently one of those tech detox resorts, and not even the staff were allowed access to phones or the internet. All those social media profiles she'd combed through? Some of them hadn't been updated for years.

She didn't know why Thandie or anyone else would want to work here. A month without Facebook felt like hell, let alone a year-long contract. And that wasn't even counting the rumors that had brought Chloe here under false pretenses in the first place.

The tipoff had arrived six months into Chloe's internship at a local paper. She'd been the one who took the call, and even after her editor passed on it, saying it wasn't worth the paper's time, she kept following up. Their mysterious informant claimed that some rich asshole called Gerald Harper was running dogfights on his own private island down the coast. And not just dogfights. Other animals, too: exotics, endangered species—the works.

Chloe had imagined herself breaking the animal cruelty story of—well, not the century, but the year, at least. She'd worked her ass off lying her way into a housekeeping job, sure that this would be her big break.

And had discovered nothing at all.

Chloe had hoped that being in housekeeping would give her good access to everywhere on the island, but there hadn't been any time for exploring. Chloe's training had taken almost every waking minute of the last week, and by the time she finished each day she didn't have the energy to do anything but sleep. She couldn't believe there was so much to learn to work in housekeeping, but apparently the owner was *very particular*.

Not that the other staff seemed to have it any easier. Long-legged Thandie had been hired as a waitress, and Chloe had seen her the day before, balancing platters of champagne flutes *just so* for hours on end while Chloe dusted the room around her.

Very particular... or just sadistic? Chloe had her suspicions.

A week into the job, Chloe was beginning to think she was on a wild goose chase. Even if she had found something, she had no way to send notes or photos back to her old boss. Chloe still had her phone, but she hadn't found so much of a bar of signal anywhere on the island. If there was any Wi-Fi hanging around, she couldn't access it—and her data didn't work out here, either. The whole island was like some giant dead spot.

Definitely sadistic, Chloe decided. She hadn't been without internet for this long since she was fifteen. *This has got to be against some sort of human rights charter.*

"Anyway, I..." Thandie trailed off, her eyes widening. Her hand flew to her pocket. "Oh, sh—sugar! Are you getting this?"

Chloe frowned. "Getting what?"

She was starting to think Thandie had some sort of magic sixth sense. Sure enough, a second later, doors started slamming throughout the dormitory block.

"What's so urgent?" she wondered out loud.

Before Thandie could reply, there was a rap at the open bedroom door, and Julian Rouse poked his head around.

Julian was... Chloe had still not figured out what Julian was. Some sort of management, maybe? He seemed to have his finger in all the pies around the island, and from what Chloe could see, resented it immensely.

He was tall and pale-skinned, with black hair and piercing jade-green eyes. Not Chloe's type at all, but definitely the type of more than a few of the other women who worked on the island. Including Thandie, whose eyes brightened at the sight of him.

Julian didn't seem to notice. "Come on," he snapped. "Gerald's going to be here in thirty minutes, with a party of twelve."

"Thirty minutes!" Chloe jumped off her bed. "He couldn't give us any more notice?"

Julian fixed his dark eyes on her. "Are you going to complain, or prepare the rooms?" he said in his chilly voice. He looked past her to Thandie. "Thandie, Floss needs you in the kitchen to go over the plans for tonight's menu."

Thandie got up, blushing hot pink under her light brown skin. Chloe groaned and rubbed her face.

Thirty minutes to prep the guest wing? How was she meant to get any investigating done when she didn't even have enough time to do her cover job?

Chloe raced from the staff quarters to the main building, making sure to keep to the sunken paths behind the garden's decorative hedges. Julian had pointed these out to her on her first day. Anyone who kept to the paths was invisible to people looking out from the main residence. Julian had made it very clear that it was a requirement of employment that the staff not be seen littering the sculpted landscape of the island.

She was panting by the time she arrived in the guest wing. Nora, the head of housekeeping, grabbed her by the shoulders and spun her around. "You're on the third floor. Go."

The next half-hour was a flurry of dusting, fresh sheets and complimentary toiletries. The guest rooms were kept in good condition even when they were empty, but there were still so many finishing touches to be done that Chloe's head was spinning by the time she was finished.

Nora grabbed her again as she was heading out. "Where are you going?"

"Back to the staff building?" she suggested, puffing.

Nora gave her a pitying look. "Sorry, love. Julian just called. The boss brought back a surprise extra. He'll be staying in the entertainers' wing, with the rest of them."

"Can't he go here? There are still a few empty rooms, we can set him up in fifteen or sixteen—"

"Time wasted asking questions is time you're not spending getting the job done," Nora reminded her, and dropped a key into Chloe's hand. "Chop chop."

Chloe wrenched her trolley around and headed for the service elevator. The entertainers' wing was slightly separated from the main building, tucked away on the other side of the hill the resort sprawled over.

Damn it. If I wasn't in such a hurry...

This was her first time inside the entertainers' residence. She'd met a few of the "entertainers", most of whom were grim-faced gym bro types. What form of entertainment they provided, Chloe had no idea—unless they were secretly the dog-handlers for the fighting ring she'd come here to find.

She sighed. No chance to poke around now. She'd just have to find an excuse to come back.

Even with the clock ticking, she took mental notes on what she could see. The outside of the building was plainer than the primary residence, and the rooms were nowhere near as fancy as the guest suites she'd just prepped.

Whoever this extra guy is, I guess the boss doesn't like him very much, she thought.

She stretched her shoulders out and got to work, aware the clock was ticking. The surprise guest's room might be less incredibly opulent than the main guest quarters—polished tile in the bathroom instead of marble, no gold leaf on the walls—but that made no difference to Chloe's job. Fresh sheets, fresh towels, fresh smelly toiletries.

The door hissed and clunked locked behind her. Chloe was tired, sweaty, and knew she'd be fired if a guest caught even a glimpse of her at any time, let alone in that state.

But Gerald Harper was back on the island. And he'd brought guests. Guests who might, for example, have come to see animals fight in his illegal fighting ring.

It was time for her investigation to start in earnest.

Chapter 3
Mathis

Mathis leaned into the breeze as the boat made the final approach to the pier. The island was a few hours' journey from shore, a long, thin strip of land that barely seemed to reach out of the turquoise waters.

From the boat, Mathis could see a white sand beach leading up to rolling lawns spotted with lush palms. A large building made of some sort of pale yellow stone jutted up from the pleasant landscape, incongruous and unmissable. Mathis narrowed his eyes against the sea-spray, racking his memory.

Have I ever heard anyone talk about a shifter who lives out this way? One wealthy enough to have a place like this?

"Impressive, isn't it?"

Mathis was about the reply in the negative, but checked himself. So far as Gerald Harper and his friends knew, Mathis was just Matt Dell, not the heir to a wealthy New York pride. Mathis wanted to keep the charade up for as long as possible.

"It sure is something," he said instead, trying to look suitably impressed. The man who'd spoken was one of Harper's other guests, a middle-aged man with grey streaks in his dark blond hair. As he moved closer, Mathis got a whiff of lion from him. His own lion tensed inside him, on edge at the presence of a male lion from another pride.

Something must have shown in his eyes, because the other man stepped back, holding up his hands. "Hey, easy there. Save it for the ring, Simba."

Mathis smiled self-deprecatingly. "Sorry, sir. This is all a bit new to me."

"Haven't spent much time around your own kind, huh?"

"I guess not," Mathis lied reluctantly. *Not unless you count my pride, my friends, half the people I grew up around...*

But that was Mathis Delacourt. If this guy wanted to believe that Matt Dell was a loner who didn't know much about shifters, who was Mathis to argue?

"Well, you're in for a treat tonight, then," the man said, grinning. "So are we all! I don't think old Ger's managed to get a lion in rotation all the time I've known him."

"I'm looking forward to it. Never had the chance to fight other shifters before."

The man clapped him on the shoulder and Mathis bit back his lion's roar of injured pride. "Well, don't let the side down, huh? Us lions have got to stick together."

Mathis watched the other lion shifter wander back down the deck, hands in his pockets. It had taken the entire conversation, but he'd finally placed him. Grayson Masters, the uncle of the current alpha of the Masters pride.

Mathis had never met Grayson or his alpha before in person, but Grayson had done some business with his twin sister Francine a few years back. Mathis remembered him from the promotional photos.

And he'd heard of the pride. It was a tragic story. The previous alpha and his mate had been killed in a terrible accident when the current alpha—Leon, Mathis thought his name was—had been still in school. Grayson had taken the boy under his wing.

He must be in his twenties by now, Mathis thought. *No sign of him here, though. And Grayson didn't recognize me.*

Mathis frowned. What would he have done if Grayson had recognized him? His façade had worked in the underground bouts he'd been fighting in so far, but he was playing with fire coming here.

He shook his head. It wouldn't be a problem. If anyone did confront him, he could play it off as a joke. He was still young enough to pass the whole thing off as some sort of youthful acting-out, after all.

He couldn't tell them the truth. That there was a deep, ravenous emptiness inside him, a hunger for something he couldn't name. Falling into the deep focus that fighting required was the only thing that seemed to silence it. And even that only lasted until the fight was over.

Not when he was fighting humans, at least. If he was up against another shifter…

Mathis was still lost in his own thoughts when the boat nudged up against the wharf. A young man in a white uniform secured the boat and then helped the guests step out onto dry land.

Gerald Harper caught Mathis' attention while the luggage was being unloaded. He waved to the tall, black-haired man who had appeared at his side.

"Mathis, this is my assistant, Julian. He'll show you to your quarters, and let you know how things run here."

Mathis looked Julian up and down, his nostrils flaring. Julian was a shifter too, he was sure of it—just as sure as he was that the guy who'd handed him off the boat was some sort of wading bird. But he couldn't get a fix on what Julian's animal was.

He shook Julian's hand. There was something there, a sense of power, and lithe grace—and that was as far as Mathis got.

"Pleased to meet you," he said, trying not to let his frustration show on his face.

"Likewise," Julian replied in a cool voice. "If you'll follow me?"

Mathis did so, his rucksack slung over one shoulder. Julian led him up the white gravel path to the resort proper.

Closer to, Mathis could see that the yellow stone buildings were made of some sort of sandstone—a risky choice, for a building this exposed to the elements. Pits and crevices were already beginning to form where the sea and wind had attacked it.

"Looks like Harper's gone to a lot of expense for a house that'll be half eroded away in ten years' time," he mentioned, running his finger along a crack in the wall as they passed by the main building.

Julian shrugged, his green eyes flat, and said nothing. Mathis snorted. *Guess he doesn't want to badmouth his employer in front of the new guy.*

He dutifully tailed Julian up the shallow hill the resort butted up against. Over the ridge—if you could call it that—was another building, just as scarred and pitted as the first. Mathis' home for the next few months, he guessed.

He blinked in surprise as Julian led him inside. After months of concrete and lino floors, the wood and tile of the fighters' quarters was bafflingly opulent. His own rooms—*rooms,* not a cot in a dorm—were on the fourth floor.

"This suite will be yours during your stay here," Julian declared, waving one hand in a lazy arc that encompassed the room and doors leading off to a bathroom and walk-in closet. "The other fighters are on the lower levels, but you're the only one on this floor. We don't have a full house at the moment. Perhaps you'll enjoy the privacy; I know not all of Harper's contracts are here to make friends." His mouth snapped shut on that last bit, as though he had to stop himself from saying more.

Mathis heaved his bag onto the king-sized bed. "Other fighters, huh? Anything you can tell me about them?"

He only half-listened to Julian's reply. There was an unusual scent in the air, something warm and inviting. Not the floral air freshener, not the clean linen smell of the sheets—something else. Something enticing.

"...have all been with us for some time. A few wolf shifters, and one coyote. Mr. Harper's last star fighter was an orangutan shifter, but he is no longer... no longer with the establishment."

Julian's cool green eyes followed Mathis around the room. Mathis knew he was prowling. He couldn't help it. Where was the scent coming from? He had to know.

Julian coughed softly. "Dinner is served at seven. As you'll still be settling in, I'll send one of the staff around with your meal. Wash, change, and be ready for the first bout at nine. I'll return then to show you to the ring."

Mathis raised his eyebrows. "I don't get to see the ring before we start?" He waved it off before Julian could open his mouth to reply. "Nah, don't worry about it. One ring's much like another, right?"

"Right," Julian echoed, a hint of irony in his voice.

Mathis' lion grumbled inside him. He was chasing his tail—whatever or whoever had left the scent was long gone. Instead, he tried to remember what Julian had just said about his competitors. "Wolf shifters, you said? What, a pack of them, or something?"

"No, several independents. Mr. Harper isn't interested in melee fights, only one-on-one. At least, as long as I've known him."

"You've worked with him for a while?"

Julian smiled thinly and without humor. "You could say that. Though, I'm not the only one. Some of the shifters have been here for years."

"Mr. Harper must pay well." Mathis' attention was drifting again. That smell...

Out of the corner of his eye, Mathis saw Julian give that thin smile again. "We've all got something keeping us on the island," he said quietly. "I'll see you at nine."

CHAPTER 4

CHLOE

Chloe tugged on the hem of her dress. She'd raced back to her room for a lightning-fast shower, replacing her housekeeping outfit with a plain black dress. Her straight black hair was swept back off her face, which she'd made up in tasteful nude shades.

In short, she looked like any of the half-a-dozen waitresses employed at the resort. Now she just had to...

To do what? Lurk around dark corners, hoping Nora doesn't notice you and send you packing back to the mainland for stepping out of line?

Chloe shook herself. Okay, so she didn't have a plan, but she could make it up as she went along. She was good at that. *Look like you belong here, and most people won't even question it.*

And if they did, she could always baffle them into letting her run away. Her friends called it her "Jedi mind trick", which made it sound a lot fancier than what it was: babble at people to distract and annoy them, and then scram.

For something so stupid, it worked better than it should.

And even if it was all she had going for her, she had to do this. The need to act was a driving force inside her. She needed to *do* something.

It had always been like this. Like something inside her was fighting to get out. It made her heart pump and her muscles twitch, and once it started, she needed to direct it somewhere or she'd end up going stir-crazy.

Exercise helped. Playing sports helped. But nothing helped as much as setting her mind on one project and seeing it through. And the best projects were the ones that helped other people. Fundraising drives, coaching kids' teams... or investigating claims of animal cruelty.

Chloe had long ago given up trying to figure out what it was that made her fixate on things like this. One of her therapists had told her it was probably because of her parents dying, but the restless energy had been inside Chloe ever since she could remember. Long before she lost her family.

She clenched her fists, the need to *do something* thrumming inside her. *Patience. I'll get there. Just have to figure out the lay of the land first.*

She walked slowly down the hallway, trying to look as though wasn't meant to be hiding herself away in the staff quarters. Her heels clacked on the polished marble floor. She knew exactly where she was going: the tower at the far end of the building.

The resort had two towers, one on either end of the manor-house-like main building. Until now, they'd both been mysteries to Chloe. Like the "entertainers'" block, they'd been off-limits during her training. Tonight, though, she was determined to explore at least one of them.

The doors into the northernmost tower on every level had been locked firmly ever since Chloe arrived on the island but tonight they were open, welcoming in Gerald Harper's guests.

An itchy, prickling excitement made all the hairs on Chloe's arms stand on end. If Gerald Harper was hosting some sort of sick dogfighting ring for the wealthy, this must be where the fights were held.

A small group of people came into view as Chloe rounded a corner and she caught her breath, springing back out of sight. Scraps of conversation reached her and she froze, straining her ears to hear more. What she did hear was almost painfully bland. Compliments on the dinner and wine. Compliments on the décor. Quiet excitement for the entertainment ahead.

Thandie was flitting around the group like a little bird, offering flutes of champagne. Chloe crept up as the group moved through the tower door, trying to catch a glimpse of the room beyond.

The doors swung shut. *Damn it.*

Chloe lingered where she was for a few moments, then gathered her nerves and darted forward. The doors were heavy, solid wood, and although she could tell people were talking on the other side she couldn't make out any words.

She knelt in front of the door, pressing her ear to the keyhole. A deep male voice cut through the others, who fell silent. Chloe cursed under her breath. She *still* couldn't tell what anyone was saying.

She pressed one hand to the bodice of her dress, where she'd hidden a tiny micro-recorder. She'd felt stupid when she ordered it online, but if there *was* anything dodgy going on behind those doors, she needed to record it to have proof.

Unfortunately, it seemed like she'd lost her chance.

I could record this door, she thought glumly. *Real damning footage that would be.*

Irritation made her throat scratchy. Something was happening on the other side of the door. And not just canapés and champagne. Chloe was sure of it.

She just couldn't get to it.

She stood up. Kneeling with her ear against the door wasn't achieving anything. All she would gain by staying there was increasing the chance someone would walk by and see her. She sighed. Maybe if she checked out some of the entrances to the tower on other levels, she might have more luck finding an unlocked door...

She had only taken a handful of steps when the huge doors swung open again. Chloe spun around and saw Thandie sprinting out of the room, her eyes wide. She crashed into Chloe, sending them both to the floor.

Chloe rolled onto her knees and grabbed Thandie by the shoulders, steadying her. Thandie grabbed back, clinging to Chloe and almost pulling her over again. Her eyes were huge, the whites visible all the way around her dark irises. A hubbub of voices—and laughter—tumbled after her out of the room.

"Are you okay?" Chloe stammered, shocked.

Thandie caught her breath. "I—" She froze. Chloe looked up over her shoulder to see Julian stalking towards them, his expression severe.

"What are you doing out here?" he snapped, eyes flashing. Then he turned on Thandie. "Get up, and stop being so melodramatic. You're embarrassing yourself and your employer."

Thandie clambered to her feet, holding on to Chloe for balance. Chloe rose with her, wincing as her butt complained about being fallen on.

"You never told me they would *all* be—" she began, and then her mouth clamped shut. Her eyes swiveled around to Chloe.

The hairs on the back of Chloe's neck rose. Some understanding seemed to pass between Thandie and Julian, and then Thandie stepped away from Chloe, letting go of her arms.

"I'm *not* going back in there," she said sullenly, sticking out her jaw. "I don't care if you fire me. I'll do dinner service, sure, but I'm not going in there during the fights."

The fights? Chloe tried to keep her expression neutral as a thrill of excitement rushed through her. Her source had been right, after all. Harper was running some sort of animal fighting ring here.

"Fine. Go back to your quarters, and we'll discuss your continued employment in the morning," Julian snapped. His eyes flashed toward Chloe. "You—do you have any experience with bar work?"

"Sure," Chloe said quickly. "Three years behind the bar of a cocktail lounge during college." *Or at least, making cocktails in my living room. I'm sure that counts.*

Julian sighed. "That will have to do. Tidy yourself up and follow me."

To Chloe's surprise, Thandie helped her smooth back her hair and brush herself down.

"Do you... how much do you know about Harper and that lot?" Thandie muttered in an undertone to Chloe.

Chloe raised her eyebrows. "I..." Her mind raced, and the restless energy inside her surged. *Bluff. Always bluff.* "Like, enough, I'm pretty sure?"

Thandie nodded, but she still looked worried. "All right. I believe you. I'll stay up until you get off shift, okay? Because I'm guessing we will have a *lot* to talk about." She gave Chloe a quick hug and darted off down the corridor.

Chloe looked after her, blinking. *What was that all about?* she wondered. But she didn't have long to think. Julian grabbed her by the elbow and stalked back into the room.

Chloe fussed with the neckline of her dress as she scurried to keep up with his pace. The beaded collar was the perfect hiding place for her spy camera and she activated it as they slipped through the door.

"There. Drinks, glasses. Make sure everyone has one of the second, filled with their choice of the first."

Chloe pulled her elbow free of Julian's grip and fought the impulse to roll her eyes. "Aye aye, sir," she said, slapping a customer service smile on her face.

Julian just glared at her. "Don't mess this up," he muttered, and strode away.

"I'm not intending to," Chloe told his back. And she wasn't. This was the opportunity she'd been waiting for. There was no way she was going to mess it up.

She busied herself at the bar, her eyes flitting around the room. She didn't recognize any of Gerald Harper's guests; hell, she only recognized *him* because of the research she'd done before applying for the job.

The guests were about evenly split between men and women, none of them under forty and all of them clearly wealthy. Diamonds glittered at the women's ears and necks, and the men were all wearing tailored suits.

None of them paid her any attention at all.

Armed with a platter of fizzing champagne flutes, Chloe slipped into the crowd. She might as well have been invisible, although the visitors clearly thought her platter of drinks was worthy of attention. She made her way slowly around the room, turning so that her video could take panning shots of the whole space and its occupants.

Not that she knew what she was trying to record, yet. The room was smaller than she had expected given the diameter of the "tower". It was long and narrow, wrapped around the edge of the hexagonal space. The décor was the same extravagant not-quite-elegance Chloe was familiar with from the rest of the resort.

There were two things that really caught her attention. One was the window that ran the length of the inside wall. The glass was black, whatever it looked out on hidden in darkness.

The other was the smell.

Chloe tried to keep her sniffing discreet. Eventually she had to accept that the smell was coming from Harper's guests.

What is *it?* she wondered, half appalled, half intrigued. It was kind of... *musty.* Almost an animal smell, like a den or—she stopped herself from wrinkling her nose—like an old doghouse that hadn't been cleaned out in years.

It couldn't be the room. It had to be them. But... *Seriously?* Chloe thought. *This is the big secret? A weekend getaway for the stinky stinking rich?*

The woman next to her held out her empty glass, and Chloe raised her platter to take it. As she did so, a waft of the strange smell hit her nostrils. *It's not* that *unpleasant,* she thought. *Just... odd.*

The man she'd pegged as Gerald Harper walked to the darkened window and tapped his glass with one finger, calling everyone's attention. Chloe slipped to the back of the crowd. The hairs on the back of her neck were prickling. *Something* was going to happen, she knew it. But what?

"Friends old and new, thank you for joining me at my little home this weekend," he began, smiling beatifically around the room.

One of the other men replied with a joke, and the whole room tittered approvingly. Chloe couldn't help but notice how the guests' eyes kept sliding sideways, as though they were sizing each other up.

"I'm pleased to announce we have a new contender tonight, whom some of you met on the way over. I found Matt Dell in a little club outside of Los Angeles—far below his particular talents, of course." More tittering. This time, Chloe didn't get the joke.

Harper clapped his hands together. "Well, enough from me! You've all made your bets with Julian already? Excellent. Then, with no further ado..."

He motioned towards the darkened window. Lights flared on behind it, illuminating an open space that extended down below the floor of the room they were standing in.

Chloe craned her neck. She couldn't step forward without attracting attention, unless—yes, that woman was eyeing her up for a refill. Chloe swooped in, dutifully replacing the woman's empty glass and getting a glimpse at the room behind the window as she did so.

What she saw confirmed all her darkest suspicions. The floor, ten feet below the viewing room, was polished concrete to match the walls. There was a barred door on either side of the space, like the doors to a cage. Bright spotlights burned down on the arena.

Chloe's stomach twisted. She knew what she was getting herself into, following a tipoff about animal cruelty. But could she stand to watch it?

She had to. Or at least, she had to stand here, facing it. Her little spy-cam wouldn't be any good if she was bent over in the back corner, spewing her guts out.

Julian was watching her. She smiled blandly at him, and then retreated to the edge of the crowd, where she would be out of the way but still able to see down into the fighting arena. The guests were settling into plush white leather sofas arranged around the window. Some of them lolled back, feigning boredom, but most of them didn't bother hiding their excitement. The air was electric with anticipation.

Suddenly, the cage doors swung open. Chloe's eyes widened as she saw two men walk into the arena. She looked past them into the shadows beyond the open doors, wondering if they were leading the animals out to fight, but the doors swung shut, leaving only the two men in the ring.

Is all this just some actual Fight Club bullshit? she wondered, disgusted and disappointed.

The men looked like fighters, heavily muscled and with their hair clipped short. One of them had darker hair and three fierce scars running down his face like claw-marks. The other looked younger, maybe in his late twenties, and his close-cropped hair was blond. Even from this distance Chloe could see his eyes flash as he sized up his opponent. His irises were a strange, pale tawny color that intrigued her. Almost gold.

Something fluttered inside her that had nothing to do with nerves.

Harper spoke into a microphone at the side of the window, and both men looked up at their audience. The dark-haired one saluted; the blond one covered his eyes, staring up through the bright glare from the spotlights.

An alarm sounded, and the dark-haired man threw himself toward the blond. Halfway through the leap his body twisted, and changed.

Chloe blinked. Was she seeing what she thought she was seeing? The man wasn't just contorting his body—he was *transforming*.

Chloe didn't dare to even blink. *This can't be real.*

But she had to believe the evidence of her eyes. By the time the dark-haired fighter struck the other man, he had transformed into a giant grey wolf.

Chloe couldn't keep a gasp from escaping her lips. The blond man buckled under the weight of the wolf. The creature's fangs were white and sharp, and she wished she could tear her eyes away before the inevitable slaughter. She whimpered in empathy as the wolf tore a strip from the man's shoulder.

Then her eyes widened further as the blond man, too, began to transform. It happened in the space between one heartbeat and the next: one moment he was a man, falling to his knees and bleeding from his wound, and the next he was an enormous lion, flinging the wolf against the wall with one stroke of his massive paw.

Chloe became aware of a jingling, tinkling sound. She was shaking—and the trembling extended to the hand she was holding the drinks tray with. She took a deep breath and tried to still herself, but not before the noise had attracted attention from within the viewing room.

Gerald Harper spoke suddenly from just behind her shoulder and Chloe almost dropped the tray completely. She hadn't even seen him get out of his seat.

"You're one of the new girls, aren't you? Not what you were expecting?"

Chloe mind stuttered as her heart hammered in her chest. *Lie. Make something up. For God's sake don't let them know you had no idea what you were getting into.*

She started to speak, choked, and gulped. "I, er. I wasn't expecting it to be so—" Her brain stalled. *What the hell, Jedi mind trick? Don't fail me now!* "So... fast?"

Harper chuckled, a noise that sent shivers down Chloe's spine. "They have to be fast, sweetheart. I'm not paying them to make daisy-chains." His voice changed. "And I'm not paying *you* to stand around gawking."

Chloe flushed and returned to the bar. Harper ignored her, but she felt Julian's eyes on her as she pulled another bottle of champagne from the ice bucket. She moved as though she was in a dream. But, even dreaming, she made sure to direct her spy-cam at the action below when she returned to refresh the audience's drinks.

She'd come here expecting to find an illegal animal fighting ring. Instead, she'd stumbled on—what? The existence of magic? Werewolves? A whole hidden society of people who could turn into animals?

This was the scoop of a lifetime. And with no connection to the outside world, she had no way of getting it off the island.

Chapter 5

Mathis

The wolf came at him again. Mathis snarled, bracing to receive the force of its impact. The wolf was aiming for his throat but at the last moment Mathis twisted. The wolf missed its mark, leaving its own neck open for Mathis to clamp down on.

His mind was white fire, charged with adrenaline. The moment the other shifter had transformed—he couldn't explain what it felt like.

Finally, a worthy opponent.

He'd never fought like this before. With teeth and claws and the full weight of his lion behind each blow. It was exhilarating. Even the bite-wound in his shoulder only spurred him on to fight harder.

The wolf in his jaws yelped, claws scrabbling at the concrete floor as it tried to get purchase. Mathis shook it, and let it go. He wasn't going to tear out the man's throat, for God's sake.

He crouched in preparation as the wolf retreated to a safe distance, dark eyes assessing him.

None of his training in human bouts helped him here. With humans, he knew what tells to look for: weight shifting to one foot or the other, the flicker of tension before a strike. But a wolf? A wolf who was part man? Mathis had no experience with that.

He also didn't know how the fight was supposed to end.

There was no referee in the ring with them; Gerald had announced the start of the fight over loudspeaker, but would he do the same when he judged one or the other of them the winner?

Mathis narrowed his golden eyes. He should have paid more attention to Julian when he was explaining how the fights worked. But he had been so distracted by that scent...

Remembering it, he was distracted again, and almost missed the wolf's next attack. The wolf darted in and, too late, Mathis poised himself for a counter-attack. He calculated the wolf's leap and rose up, ready to meet his attack with a blow from his heavy front paw.

But the wolf's attack had been a feint, a trap Mathis fell straight into. Mathis was already raised up on his hind legs when the wolf, instead of leaping, dove down low and bit at Mathis' underbelly.

Mathis roared, as much with anger as from the pain. If they'd been human, he would have seen that coming. He had to stop thinking like a human, and fight like a beast.

The wolf was biting and clawing at Mathis' belly. He threw himself forward, trapping the wolf under his own great weight, regardless of the pain as the wolf's teeth and claws bit deeper into his flesh.

Mathis was about to hook one paw under to drag the wolf out when the alarm sounded again. Beneath him, the wolf stopped struggling.

The loudspeaker crackled. "Very good, Mr. Dell!"

Harper. Mathis shook his head. That must be it—the end of the bout.

He got up, releasing the wolf, and stood back panting. The wolf climbed to its feet, and gave Mathis an oddly human nod.

Good match.

Mathis blinked as the wolf's words echoed into his mind. It had been months since he spoke telepathically with anyone. He quickly nodded back.

The wolf stretched, bones clicking and creaking as he shifted back into his human form. Mathis followed, finding his human shape inside him and drawing it out.

He grinned at his opponent, adrenaline flooding his veins in the aftermath of the fight. The wounds in his shoulder and abdomen itched as they healed. By morning, there wouldn't even be a scar there. It was exhilarating. He hadn't felt so alive in months.

Fighting humans was an exercise in control and focus, but this—this was like the best workout session *ever*.

"Ladies and gentlemen, tonight's winner, Matt Dell!"

Mathis raised his hands to the viewing window halfway up the wall. He hadn't paid it much attention before the match. Now he picked out a dozen or so pale faces behind the glass. There was Grayson Masters, giving him a pleased nod. Gerald Harper, preening as a woman wearing ropes of pearls patted his arm. And right at the edge of the window...

Mathis' nostrils flared, as though he might be able to scent her through the inches-thick pane of glass. Her light eyes were startling against the pitch black of her hair. She was short and plump, and even the modest cut of her black dress couldn't hide her curves. Her eyes widened as she saw him staring at her, but not in fear. She looked... she was...

The wolf shifter clapped him on the shoulder, snapping Mathis out of his reverie.

"Come on, mate. Time for us to go."

Mathis couldn't help looking back over his shoulder as he followed the other shifter out of the ring. The woman was still staring at him, and as he watched, she lifted one hand to her chest.

The wolf shifter— he introduced himself as Sven—explained the situation to Mathis as they showered and dressed. They were to go up to the lounge and show off their muscles and scars to the guests for a bit, and then disappear quietly back to their own quarters.

Mathis had frowned. "That sounds..."

"A pain in the ass?" Sven snorted. "You've got that right. None of that lot have lifted a finger in their lives, but it gets them excited to see *other* shifters drawing blood."

Mathis shrugged. That wasn't much different to human fights.

The "gun parade", as Sven called it, was as dull and awkward as Mathis had expected. Grayson was the only one of the guests to exchange so much as a word with him; the others complimented Gerald on his "discovery", but ignored Mathis himself.

Worse, the woman in the black dress was nowhere to be seen. When he looked around for her, Sven explained telepathically that the house staff were excluded from the gun show.

Best not to get involved anyway, mate. Keep your head down and your mind on the game. And... Sven's mouth twisted. *I'll tell you more about that later. Harper gets... funny about some things.*

By the time Gerald waved the two fighters away, Mathis' good mood had completely evaporated.

Sven slapped him on the back as they headed back toward the north wing. "Buck up, Matty. It's not all bad. Sure, the bastards'll look right through you once you're out of the ring, but the pay isn't bad. You've just got to hold out through your contract."

Mathis bit back a bitter response. He might not have any need of the generous salary Gerald was offering, but Matt Dell did. And so must the other fighters here.

Unease struck him. The base salary was one thing, but Gerald was also offering a bonus for matches won. He hadn't considered before that his drive to win might go up against some other shifter's very real need for the prize money.

"Hey." Sven nudged him in the ribs. "That was a good fight tonight. Your first against another shifter?"

Mathis grunted. "Yeah."

"Bit different, eh?" Sven chortled. "How much do you weigh, four or five hundred pounds? Bloody oath. I've only been here the one season, but the other guys say there hasn't been anyone with that sort of mass since—well, for a fair while, anyway." He paused. "You want to come grab a drink with me'n some of the guys? It being your first night here, there's a few house rules we should get clear."

"Nah." Mathis rubbed his face. "Sorry. I'm feeling—I don't know. I need to clear my head."

"No worries. We'll be in Cap's rooms if you change your mind. Third door to the left, ground floor."

Mathis watched Sven until he disappeared around a corner. Any other day, he would have taken Sven up on his offer. But not tonight. Not with the dark-haired woman's scent still teasing his mind, and the memory of her eyes still taunting his heart.

Instead, he made his way outside. The night air was cool, a steady breeze coming off the water and making the palms shiver. Mathis inhaled deeply, taking in the smell of salt water... and something else.

The same smell he remembered from his room.

Her.

This woman, whoever she was, was out here somewhere.

Mathis closed his eyes, inhaling slowly, following the breezes. His feet began to move almost of their own accord. The gravel path at the front of the house gave way to close-cropped grass, then became wilder, deeper grass hiding clumps and divots in the earth. Mathis opened his eyes.

He was standing on top of a rocky outcrop. A few feet in front of him, the ground dropped away, fallen stones and hardy shrubs leading down to a sandy beach.

And a few feet to his left, a single, wind-warped pine tree clung to the edge of the bluff, spreading its twisted branches to the sky and holding the strangest bird Mathis had ever seen.

The woman from the viewing room was perched halfway up the tree. She'd exchanged her black dress for a sensible pair of sweatpants, and had her legs wrapped around the pine's trunk. One of her arms was gripping a branch, and the other was waving up above her head, holding something that glowed in the darkness.

He grinned. "Having a little trouble up there?"

The woman froze, and a moment later, Mathis heard the first words out of her mouth: "Oh, shit."

She twisted and glared down him; then, as she saw who he was, her face cleared. Mathis' heart leapt.

"Oh—it's *you*!" she said, her voice excited. "Wait there for me, all right?"

Mathis had no intention of moving. He planted his feet on the stony ground, enjoying the view as she wriggled back down the tree. She was curvier than the other women he'd seen on the island so far, guests and staff included, and her descending the tree was a beautiful sight.

She jumped the last few feet to the ground and turned around, dusting off her pants. Her face was alight with excitement as she looked at Mathis. Mathis' lion preened at the attention as she blatantly stared him up and down, her eyes pausing almost imperceptibly between his legs and on his muscular chest.

"So," he said, casually changing his stance to better show off his pecs, "Enjoying some stargazing?"

"Uhh..." The woman's fingers tightened around her phone, and she hastily shoved it in her pocket. "Stargazing? Yeah... something like that."

Her eyes were still locked on to Mathis. She was looking at him as though... as though he was something wonderful.

She smiled, and his heart sang. "Did you want to join me? There might not be room in the tree, but..." She gestured vaguely at the sky. The cloudy, starless sky.

"Nothing would make me happier," Mathis said bluntly. "Maybe... down on the beach?"

He watched her eyes flicker down the bluff to the sheltered, sandy beach. Private, secluded... out of sight of the house... He saw her make the decision even before she spoke.

"All right, then." She narrowed her eyes at him, a smile dancing at the corners of her mouth. She held out one hand. "I'm Chloe."

"Matt—Mathis," Mathis replied. He took her hand and a shock ran up his arm. Did she feel it, too?

Her grin grew wider. "Shall we?"

CHAPTER 6

CHLOE

Chloe couldn't believe her luck. She'd snuck out into the grounds after her shift was over to see if she could coax an internet signal from the far reaches of the island. Even climbing up the tree and wishing very hard for a satellite to cross overhead hadn't achieved anything, and she'd been almost ready to throw the whole thing in—until *he* arrived.

She couldn't describe the thrill that had run through her when she saw him looking up at her. At *her*.

Well, that was a lie. She absolutely, definitely could describe the thrill. She was a journalist, after all. Writing was her job.

It was just that it wouldn't be appropriate to accurately describe this particular thrill. Not if she was planning to use him as a source for her exposé. Journalists weren't supposed to have those sorts of thoughts about their sources.

She couldn't stop staring at him. And not just because her mind was still cartwheeling over the idea that she had seen him turn into a giant goddamn lion.

He was so... *big*. All over. Including—

Eyes up, Chloe, she reminded herself. *Including his... general physique. Yes.*

"Can I help you down?" Mathis offered her his hand, nodding at the rocky slope down the bluff to the beach.

"Yes, please." Chloe bit her tongue. She didn't need his help getting down the slope. Not really. She'd practically made a career out of climbing in and out of windows during various work-related and extracurricular escapades; a shingly hill wouldn't be any trouble.

But her white lie didn't need to sound so eager, either.

Chloe's cheeks blazed as she took Mathis' hand.

His skin was warmer than she'd expected, and his grip on her hand was firm, but surprisingly gentle. Working as a reporter, Chloe was used to men who thought the best way to impress their importance onto her was leaving a literal impression on her hand. She couldn't count the number of times she'd had to grin her way through some asshole trying to crush her fingers into paste.

Mathis didn't crush her hand or yank on her arm as they picked their way down to the sheltered beach. He let her take the lead. His touch was firm, and considerate; wherever she stepped, he was right behind her, moving with her as easily as if they on a dancefloor, not navigating a rough slope.

The level of attention Mathis must have been paying to her every movement made Chloe's blush deepen. She knew that if she did fall, he would be at her side in an instant.

It was almost enough to make her deliberately lose her footing.

Almost.

Mathis let her hand go as the slope leveled out. The loose stones and gravel made way for sand, and there was no point even pretending she needed his help on the flat. She tried not to feel disappointed.

The beach stretched out in front of them. The strip of sand was broader than it had looked from above, and the waves nibbling at the shore were ten or twenty feet away, glimmering in the thin moonlight.

Chloe took a deep breath, filling her lungs with the salty sea air. Down here, Harper's sprawling estate might as well not even exist. No sound from the buildings reached them, and the only noise was the soft shush of waves on the sand.

She tipped her head on one side. "Do you hear that?"

Mathis walked into her line of sight. His forehead creased. "Hear what?"

"No wildlife." Chloe filed the thought away for later, and let her mouth run on. "I wondered about it when I first got here. No seabirds, no manatees even though there's a colony just a short way up the coast, and hardly any creepy-crawlies even. I thought at first there might have been some sort of environmental disaster that wiped out local populations and was being hushed up, but now I'm thinking maybe Harper's guests got the munchies."

Mathis raised one eyebrow. "That lot? I doubt they've chased anything more lively than the bubbles at the bottom of their champagne."

"Of course," Chloe replied glibly. *When they're not scaring off poor kids like Thandie.*

She still hadn't decided what tactic to take while she was interviewing Mathis. Pretend to know all about people turning into crazy animals, or admit her mind was blown?

Admit nothing! she told herself firmly. *What if he tells Harper you came here under false pretenses? You'll be screwed.*

"Well, it's a relief to know you're all, uhh, were-animals, anyway," she continued. "There were some strange stories coming out of this place, I tell you. I almost didn't take the job. Back on the mainland people behave like this place is haunted, or cursed or something. Honestly, finding out it's just a bunch of rich... were-animals... is kind of a relief."

Mathis gave her a strange look. "Cursed? It's a better cover story than some I've heard. And better than risking people find out about the... were-animals."

Chloe winced. *Right. "Were-animals" is definitely not the right word. Shit.*

Mathis stepped closer to her, hands in his pockets and an amused smile on his face. "So... how much do you know about us 'were-animals', exactly?"

"Oh, loads," Chloe lied. "Like, uh, it's not just werewolves—some of you can turn into other animals. And, um..." Her gaze trailed over Mathis' face and arms. She was sure the wolf had bitten him on one arm—fore-leg?—but there was no sign of the wound there now. "And you heal quickly."

"Uh-huh." Laughter lines creased the corners of Mathis' eyes. "And how much do you know that you didn't figure out just now by looking at me?"

Chloe's blush crept down her neck. "Let's see," she said, playing for time. *Damn it.* She took a deep breath—and hesitated.

She could try the mind trick, bamboozle him long enough to get the impromptu interview back on track. But something stopped her.

Time to come clean. "Let's say that I knew... nothing at all?"

To her relief, Mathis laughed.

"Oh, hell," he croaked, wiping his eyes. "Don't let Harper hear you admit that! How did you manage to get the job, if you don't even know about shifters?"

Chloe thought back to all the social media profiles she'd pored over prior to making her own fake profile and applying to the job. Those weird phrases she'd included in the profile that had got her the job—they must have been some sort of code for them. For *shifters.*

"I... just slipped through the cracks, I guess. And honestly, I've been working here for a month now, and it's never come up."

Mathis stared at her, his eyes shining. "You're incredible."

This time, Chloe was the one who burst out laughing. "*I'm* incredible? You can turn into a lion! A—" She waved her hands around, searching for words. *You're a journalist! Words are your bread and butter! And the best you can come up with is...* "An actual lion!" she finished lamely.

Mathis' eyes softened. "And you're a human woman who's managed to crack open the secret my kind has been hiding for hundreds of years, without even trying. Right under the noses of what must be some of the most paranoid shifters in the country. You're incredible."

Chloe's skin felt hot. It wasn't a blush, this time. It was excitement sending heat prickling across her body as she met Mathis' eyes.

Mathis' eyes were a pale gold, the same startling hue as they had been when he was in his lion shape. As Chloe held his gaze, she thought they were going dark—then realized it was his pupils expanding.

"Chloe," he whispered, his voice husky. "You're the most amazing woman I've ever met."

Chloe wanted to scoff. He was clearly talking shit. Mathis didn't know anything about her. They'd only exchanged a handful of words, for God's sake!

But that didn't stop her breath catching in her throat as she stared into his eyes. It didn't stop her skin from thrilling at the memory of his touch, and the way his eyes had roamed over her body as she climbed out of the tree.

Or the way he was looking at her now, gold eyes black with desire.

Chloe's heart thudded in her throat. *Wow,* she thought. *Just... wow.*

She licked her lips. "So... what else is there to know about shifters?"

Mathis raised one eyebrow. He stepped closer again, so close Chloe could swear she felt heat pouring off his body. She swayed towards him, like a moth to a flame.

"For a start," Mathis murmured. "We're incredible in bed."

"Is that a fact?" Chloe replied, whip-fast, before her brain caught up with her ears. *Oh. Uh. Wow?*

"It is." Mathis leaned down, whispering into her ear. "Though since you've never met any shifters before, you should probably do some research."

Chloe's pulse started racing. Unfortunately, so did her mouth. "Well, that's not entirely true," she babbled. "If what you're saying is correct, then I've met *loads* of shifters already, actually. I'm even sharing a room with one."

"True." Mathis' breath tickled her ear. "Are any of them as interesting as I am, though?"

"N-no…" Chloe's voice caught in her throat, and she swallowed hard. Mathis was standing right up against her—but he wasn't touching her. Not yet. Just standing there, being really, really… *touchable*.

The hell with it, she thought, and before her brain could convince her it was a bad idea, she kissed him.

Mathis' lips were soft, and warm, and responded to hers with a tenderness that made Chloe's insides melt. His blond stubble scraped deliciously against her chin and she raised her hands, trailing her fingers across the sharp line of his jaw. The pulse in his neck thundered under her touch.

She gasped as he broke the kiss, but recovered quickly.

"Interesting, you said?" Chloe said slowly, getting her breath back. "Well, that's a good start, but *real* research will require—"

She didn't have a chance to finish the sentence. Mathis pulled her close, crushing her to his chest and covering her lips with his own. This kiss was deeper than the first, more passionate. Mathis' tongue flicked against her lips.

Chloe let herself fall against him, molding her body against his. Her breasts pressed against the hard lines of his chest. She didn't have to imagine what he looked like under his shirt… or his pants.

She'd seen everything back in the ring. He'd been sweaty and panting straight after his transformation, and Chloe had been thunderstruck by the sight of two men changing into giant animals, but…

She was a reporter. She might have been thunderstruck, but she'd still noticed certain details.

One of which was currently pressing into her stomach.

"Um," she mumbled into Mathis' lips. "So... how *deep* is this research going to go?"

Mathis hesitated. With an awkwardness that made Chloe bite her lip to stop herself giggling, he carefully re-adjusted his hips.

"Ah," he said. "Sorry about that."

"Don't be." The words were out before Chloe realized what she was saying—and the moment she spoke them, she knew they were true. She'd just been kissing him like he was the sexiest man on Earth. It was no surprise he'd had a physical reaction to it.

To *her*.

Just like she was having a physical reaction to him.

Warmth blossomed in her lower belly, growing into a heavy need. Chloe groaned.

She shouldn't do this. She *really* shouldn't do this. Sleeping with a source? It went against all her journalistic ethics.

Even just being this attracted to him was pushing up against the *hell-no-bad-wrong* line.

Of course... that only mattered if she was actually going to write the piece.

Mathis looked uncertain. "No, I am. Sorry. I shouldn't just jump on you—"

"Seriously?" Chloe grinned. *Screw it.* "Jump away."

She didn't expect him to take it literally.

Chloe squealed as Mathis leapt at her. For a moment, she was airborne, his arms closing around her. She braced herself to hit the ground but the impact, when it came, was surprisingly gentle, cocooned in Mathis' strong embrace. He lowered her to the sand, kissing her until her minds wam.

Chloe ran her hands up his chest, reveling in the hard curves of muscle under her palms. She slid her hands up to his jaw, feeling the scratch of stubble, and then around his head. His hair was too short for her to get a grip on and she grumbled wordlessly against his lips.

Mathis laughed. "I'll grow it long," he murmured, and bit teasingly at her lower lip.

"You—" Chloe broke off as Mathis slipped his hands down her sides, his fingertips sneaking under the hem of her shirt. He drew tantalizing circles on her skin, his touch just the safe side of ticklish. Chloe squirmed, and he hesitated.

"No, keep doing that," Chloe gasped. Her fingers grasped at his too-short hair as he resumed his teasing strokes, and she bit back a growl of frustration. She'd always been ticklish. And she'd always *hated* being tickled. But this was different.

She stretched out under Mathis, letting her hands drop back over her head. But as delicious as it was to let him tease her, she wanted more. She'd already seen what was under his clothes, and now she wanted to feel it.

Chloe grabbed the bottom of his shirt and pulled on it. Mathis got the message at once, sitting up and stripping off the thin t-shirt. Chloe's eyes roved over his bare chest. She knew he was tanned, but he looked pale in the darkness, the lines of his muscles etched sharply by the thin moonlight.

His muscles weren't the only thing the moonlight caught on. Chloe picked out dark lines on his abs, and bruised patches on his shoulder: all that remained of his wounds from the fight that evening. She touched the marks on his stomach hesitantly, not knowing if she should.

"Does it still hurt?"

Mathis covered her hand with his own. "Terribly," he said, grinning. "In fact, I think there's only one thing that could distract me from the pain…"

Chloe grimaced, but couldn't help laughing. "Oh, really?"

She sat up, grabbing Mathis' shoulder to balance herself. His eyes lit up and he pulled her up, lifting her so she could wrap her legs around his waist.

"Really," he said, deadpan.

"I should probably help you out then." Chloe smiled, playing along. Her hands crept along his sides—and then she struck.

Mathis yelped as she tickled the sensitive skin under his ribs. He retaliated immediately, pulling her shirt up and effectively trapping her arms above her head. Then he let it go and focused on her body, planting hot kisses along her breasts just above the cup of her bra.

Chloe fought her way out of her shirt-trap, half-amused, half-exasperated, and increasingly aroused. Fooling around with Mathis was one thing, but she was beginning to think it wouldn't be enough. Weeks of frustration, of carefully hiding her real identity and trying to investigate shadows, had built up in her until she was ready to blow.

And what better way to irresponsibly blow up than by sleeping with the hottest man she'd ever met?

She caught Mathis' eye, and the atmosphere between them changed. Before, they had been playing; this was serious.

Neither of them bothered with words. She was still straddling his lap, her legs wrapped around his waist and his cock pressing against her stomach.

Chloe rolled her hips forward. She was kissing him, her hands sliding from his chest up his throat, and she felt his moan of desire reverberate in her lips and fingertips.

Mathis slid his hands down under the waistband of Chloe's sweats, and her breath caught in her throat. Her hips rolled of their own accord as he fondled her ass, moving down to her upper thighs and pulling her pants down the further he explored.

I'm really doing this, Chloe thought, breathless. *Oh. Wow.*

I am definitely *not going to write that story now.*

Mathis' fingers brushed up against her slick entrance and Chloe gasped. There was no going back now. She was as ready as he was. And she wanted him so badly it almost hurt, a low, demanding ache inside her that only had one cure.

She kissed him again, long and hard, until her lips stung and she was almost vibrating with need. Her fingers tightened on his shoulders as he lifted himself just long enough to shuck off his own pants, and then they were skin to skin.

Mathis' cock slid against her folds. Chloe groaned. Her pants were still around her thighs, forcing her knees high against Mathis' sides. She wrapped her arms around his shoulders, pulling herself up. This was going to be awkward, but she couldn't wait. Didn't even want to think about changing position, about losing the heat of skin-to-skin for even one moment, about rearranging limbs and balance and—

Then Mathis' hands were on her hips, guiding her down, and his cock was at her entrance and pushing inside her and it wasn't awkward at all.

His cock was thick and hard and filled her like they were made to fit together. Chloe mewled, her head hanging on Mathis' shoulder as she took his cock all the way inside her in one smooth, perfect connection.

Her breath left her body in a single shuddering gasp. She was so wet that she hadn't noticed how big Mathis' cock was until it was inside her, but it didn't hurt. It felt amazing. Everything was...

"Perfect." Mathis' voice was a rough whisper, hoarse with desire. He stroked one hand up her back, cupping the back of her head as she collapsed against him. "You're perfect. You're the most perfect woman I've ever seen."

Chloe rolled her hips, clenching herself around his cock, and he groaned again. His breath tickled her neck. "And definitely the most perfect woman I've ever—*nggg*."

"I'm not sure I caught that last bit," Chloe taunted him, rocking her hips back and forth. Every movement deepened her desire and if their first kiss had swept Chloe away, now she was drowning with no land in sight.

She didn't care that she was naked on a beach with a man she'd only just met buried deep inside her. Or that she would probably—definitely—lose her job if anyone found out.

She didn't even care that this whole charade was for nothing, because there was no way in hell she could go back to the mainland and tell her editor she'd stumbled on a secret society of the super-rich who could turn into wild animals.

Nothing mattered except Mathis' bare skin against hers, slick with sweat, and his cock pushing deep and insistent inside her.

She mumbled something that wasn't quite words into Mathis shoulder and his hand shifted from the back of her head to under her jaw, tipping her head up. His pale gold eyes almost seemed to glow in the darkness. A thrill went down her spine.

Chloe pressed up against Mathis, sliding her breasts against his chest as she rocked back and forth on his cock. Mathis moaned, and then he was kissing her, one hand fondling her breast while the other gripped her ass, pulling her, pushing her, as greedy for her body as she was for his.

Mathis' clear desire for her body pushed Chloe closer to the brink. She ran her hands over his chest, down his waist, wanting more, wanting *everything*.

Pleasure was pulsing through her. Every nerve in her body sang with anticipation. Mathis surged beneath her, meeting her rhythm with his own need and she was close, too close—

Chloe cried out as she came. The last knots of frustration—*God dammit, that fast?*—burnt away in the white heat of orgasm, leaving her weak and panting with satisfied exhaustion.

Mathis rose up onto his knees, lifting Chloe with him. His fingers dug into her ass as his thrusts became more powerful, driving hard and deep into her until his whole body tensed and he came with a growl that shook Chloe's bones.

Breathing heavily, he slid to the ground, drawing Chloe to lie on top of him. He cupped her cheek in one strong hand and pulled her into a kiss that did nothing to bring her back to Earth.

Hot damn, she thought. *He really knows what to do with his... everything.*

Lying on top of Mathis was nice—but cold. A thin sheen of sweat made her skin gleam in the moonlight—and made her shiver, as a soft ocean breeze whispered across the beach. Chloe wriggled down to rest against Mathis' side, nestling herself into the curve of his shoulder.

Chloe stretched, which had the entirely unintentional effect of letting her slide her breasts against Mathis' chest as he rolled to face her. He slid one arm under her head and she let her head fall onto his firm bicep.

For a while they just lay together. Chloe waited for her heartbeat to settle back to its usual rhythm, but realized after a few minutes that that just wasn't going to happen. Everything about Mathis was just too, too much for things to go back to normal now.

He took one of her hands and started playing with her fingers, kissing her fingertips. "If you don't mind me asking... why are you here, if you're not a shifter?"

Chloe sighed, hoping it sounded genuine and not like a stalling tactic. "I guess I just... I don't know. Wanted to try something new. *Go* somewhere new. Of course I didn't realize just how far away from normal life this job would take me..."

Mathis brushed his lips against the pad of her thumb, making her shiver. "Running away from something?"

"Oh, no. Always running to. Actually..." The words spilled out of her before she could stop them. "It's not like I had a lot to run *away* from, anyway. I was brought up in the foster system. Lived with the same foster parents from eleven to eighteen, and they were great but there were so many of us, you know? They had a lot of love to go around but it wasn't really individuated as such..." She laughed. "What am I saying? Not running away from anything, that's it. Just trying to find my place in the world. Which I guess this *isn't*, after all, what with everyone here being magical..."

"You can have everything in the world and still be running to find something new," Mathis said softly.

Chloe wriggled closer to him. It was true, about her foster parents, but she hadn't meant to say it out loud. She'd never told anyone that before.

Maybe Mathis sensed her discomfort, because he changed the subject.

"So," he murmured, kissing the top of her head, "Do you think our research was a success?"

Shit.

A shaft of guilt lanced through Chloe. *Great change of subject, but...*

She had lied her way onto this island to write a story about illegal animal fighting. Instead, she'd found a scoop beyond anything she could have imagined.

And slept with him.

She groaned. Mathis' arm tightened around her.

"What's wrong?" he asked, concern in his voice.

"It's just..." Chloe bit her lip before the truth slipped out. *God, I'm such a piece of shit.* "You know, I'm pretty sure there's something in the employee handbook about... fraternization."

There was. She'd laughed at it when she read it—good luck to any boss trying to keep employees out of each other's beds on an island with no entertainment except the self-made sort.

Now she wondered if, like with everything else in this place, there was more to that line in the contract than met the eye.

The tiny journalist inside her head stirred. She couldn't help it. Even if she wasn't going to write that article, she needed to ask. Every atom of her body wanted to know more about him.

"So... Is that another shifter thing?"

Mathis frowned. "That what?"

"That... this..." Chloe gestured at their naked bodies, still half-entwined. "I mean, I wondered at first if the whole 'separate residences for male and female staff, immediately report any fraternization' thing was because Harper was some sort of mega-prude, but is there something else to it? Something shifter-y?"

She could almost see the cogs whirring behind Mathis' pale gold eyes. Her heart sank. *Whatever he's about to tell me, it's going to be fifty-per-cent lies, at least.*

Not that she deserved anything more than that. After all, the only true thing he knew about her was her name.

"It's... complicated," Mathis said at last, and Chloe had to fake an amused snort.

"Oh, really?"

"Mmm. Maybe it's our animal side, I don't know. Or maybe Harper is an old prude." He half-closed his eyes, a smile licking around his lips, but Chloe had been waiting and she saw it. The hesitation before he slapped on the easy smile and the bedroom eyes. He was hiding something.

Chloe ducked her head under his chin, just in case her own face betrayed the cold twist of emotion in her stomach. *Why are you reacting like this? It's not like you're being honest here. Who the fuck cares if a one-night stand wants to keep things back?*

Especially a one-night stand with the sort of secrets Mathis had. The sort of secrets they *all* had. How hard must it be, to keep something like this from the world?

She couldn't blame him for being private. She really, *really* wanted to know more—seriously, the urge was so strong it almost *hurt*—but she had to respect his privacy.

"It's all right, you don't need to tell me," she murmured into his collarbone. "This is only 101 research, not thesis-level."

He chuckled, for real this time, and his cock hardened against her belly. *Already? Geez, okay, this has* got *to be a shifter thing.*

His hand ghosted down her side, making her shiver against him.

He opened his mouth, but Chloe got in first.

"*Please* don't let the next words out of your mouth be something about 'extra credit'."

He winced. "Took the analogy too far, huh?"

Chloe laughed. *Maybe we're both lying. But that doesn't mean we can't both have fun, too.*

And then, since his mouth was right there, she kissed him.

CHAPTER 7
MATHIS

"Hey." Mathis' nose twitched as someone prodded his shoulder. He cracked one eye open, already bracing for the familiar tense restlessness to tighten its grip on his body.

But it never arrived.

Mathis opened both eyes wide. For the first time in years, he was utterly content. And the reason why was kneeling beside him with a shy smile on her face, gently but persistently poking him awake.

"Good morning," Chloe said, her smile widening.

Mathis smiled back. The morning sun bounced off Chloe's sparkling eyes—and her bare shoulders, and breasts, and bare everything else.

"That it is." Mathis reached up and cupped her cheek in one hand, drawing her down until he could kiss her. Chloe made a small, delighted noise, molding her body against his as she returned his kiss.

Mathis let his hand slip down over her shoulder. Chloe's skin was spotted with sand, and he brushed it off solicitously, his hand roaming further down her body. Everything about her was soft and warm. Even just touching her skin filled him with a sense of— wonder? Happiness? Fulfillment?

All of them at once, and more. Mathis had never felt it before, but he knew what it was. *Love.* The one thing he had been searching for all this time, without knowing it.

He wrapped both hands around Chloe's waist, abandoning the already flimsy pretense that he was just helpfully brushing sand off her. Chloe arched her back appreciatively and Mathis sat up, ready to pull her onto his lap.

"Aha!" Chloe cried out in triumph, reaching around behind him to grab something. She held up her shirt with an apologetic grin. "Sorry... that was all part of my nefarious plan."

Mathis sat back in defeat. Chloe's cheeks were pink, and her eyes were shining. "You sure don't look sorry," he accused her.

"Oh, all right. I'm sorry I have to get back to work, instead of spend the morning here with you," she admitted, standing up and brushing sand off her legs. "Thank God I've got the afternoon shift today. I think. Shit. It is Saturday, right?"

Mathis watched her pull the shirt on, and then wriggle into her pants. He was disappointed to see her body disappear under the sandy clothing... but the wiggling made up for that.

Chloe saw him watching her, and narrowed her eyes. "Oi," she said in mock warning, but the smug expression on her face gave her away. She finger-combed her hair and surveyed herself with a grimace. "Damn. I hope I can make it to the laundry before my shift."

Before her shift. Mathis' stomach went cold.

Finding Chloe was the best thing that had ever happened to him. And now what? He'd lied to her last night, shied back from the truth like a jumpy cat, and now she was shaking sand out of her hair and getting ready to walk out of his life.

His lion stirred inside him. *I can't let that happen.*

He stood up, and the satisfied ache of his muscles stirred something other than his lion. What he wouldn't give to have Chloe on him again. Under him.

For her just to be *there*, in his life. His everything.

"Chloe," he said, taking a step toward her.

"Yeah?" Chloe looked up from scouting the beach for her shoes. He didn't even remember her taking them off last night.

"I—"

He hesitated, watching her beat sand out of one of her socks. His mouth was dry.

What was he going to say? *I love you? You're my soulmate? I'm going to fall asleep dreaming of you every night for the rest of my life, and wake up with your name on my lips?*

And by the way, I thought I'd tell you now, the day after you've just had your whole world cracked open by the discovery that shifters exist, while you're stuck on an island in the middle of nowhere. Hope that's okay. Hope you're not going to freak out about that.

Also I'm a billionaire. Just so you know.

He coughed.

"What about you?" Chloe asked, pulling on her shoes. "Do you have another... er... shift today?"

"Not a clue." The thought of it made Mathis feel tired. "I'm a bit over it, to be honest."

"One-night wonder, huh?"

He didn't need enhanced shifter senses to catch the double meaning *there*.

"Maybe I've found something I like more than fighting," he said, and his heart flipped at the delighted surprise on her face.

"That so?" The corner of her mouth twitched as she tried to sound nonchalant.

"Yeah." Mathis rocked back on his heels, arms folded and a grin on his face that no power in the world could hide.

Chloe grinned back, and then groaned. "God. What am I thinking? I'm on week four of a twelve-month contract... and I bet you are, too."

Mathis shrugged. He didn't remember the details—but he was sure it wouldn't be that hard to get out of. While he was trying to think of a way to not say 'Well, if Harper kicks up a fuss, I'll call in a plane', Chloe's eyes started to sparkle.

"Mind you," she said, swaying her hips as she walked up to Mathis, "there *is* that fraternization clause…"

"Oh?" Mathis reached out as soon as she was close enough to touch, running his hands down her sides. *God, those curves*, he thought. "Reckon that would get us a quick trip back to the mainland?"

"Something like that." Chloe grinned, standing on tip-toes for a kiss. "Then you can tell me all about—oh, *shit*."

She stepped back, her face white. Mathis stepped with her, his chest going tight at her obvious distress. He slid his arms around her waist. "What's wrong?"

"It's—oh, hell. I told my roommate Thandie that I'd see her after my shift last night, but she wasn't in our room when I got changed and grabbed my—stuff—and… oh, shit. I'm such an asshole."

Running her fingers through her hair, Chloe pulled away from Mathis' embrace.

"I'm sorry, I've got to go. I have to find her—she was so upset—I can't believe I forgot."

She thumped the heel of her hand into her forehead, grimacing. Mathis grabbed her hand and kissed it while she groaned.

"You were distracted. Blame me. I'm very distracting." Mathis kept his tone light. Chloe just groaned again and, because her hand was unavailable, thumped her forehead against his chest.

"I don't know. She was super freaked out by all the predators in the viewing room. All the VIPs."

Mathis captured her head with his other hand and held it against his chest. Chloe grumbled, but didn't pull away.

"I'd better go," she said again, sounding more reluctant. "I don't know if Thandie is working this morning, but I really want to check on her."

She sighed and tipped her head up, resting her chin on Mathis' chest and looking up at him. "So. Walk of shame together, or solo?"

"I guess that depends on how fast you want to get fired."

Chloe squeezed her eyes shut. "Damn it. I want to talk to Thandie before we get chucked off the island. Can I sneak off now, and you follow in a few minutes?"

"Only if I get to come find you later." Mathis dipped his head to rest his forehead against Chloe's.

"Deal."

Mathis watched her make her way slowly back up the bluff. She was somehow even more attractive in her rumpled t-shirt and sweatpants than she had been in her fancy dress the night before. And he was sure she would have been able to move more quickly if she hadn't kept shooting glances back over her shoulder at him.

Even with her constant obviously-intentional micropauses, Chloe disappeared over the ridge too soon. Mathis' lion grumbled and huffed, treading in dissatisfied circles inside him.

Patience, grasshopper. He chuckled. His heart was lighter than it had been in years. *You heard her—she just wants to check on her friend. Like any of us would do for our pride. You've waited for her this long—what's a few more hours against your entire future?*

He stretched, reveling in the feel of the morning sun against his bare skin. His mate! And all he'd had to do to find her was...

...Pretend to be someone he wasn't, join a questionably-legal fighting ring on a private island owned by a man even his sister wouldn't do business with, and convince a beautiful woman to quit her job over a one-night stand.

Doubt started to gnaw at his insides. Meeting Chloe like this, with no plans, no expectations—it felt perfect. Nothing like the torturous matchmakers' dinners that Mathis knew Grayson's nephew Leon suffered through as the young alpha of his pride.

But once he got past how amazing he felt, and tried to look at the situation from the outside...

Shit. Is it really that bad?

Mathis shook himself. There was no point worrying. He had a plan, now he just needed to stick with it. And, God, did it feel good. Suddenly the future wasn't just night after night of chasing adrenaline in the ring. It was bright, and beautiful, and had a smile like the sunrise.

He picked up his shirt, which he and Chloe had slept on, and raised it to his face. He could still smell her on it, her delicate, womanly scent. It sent warmth flooding through his body... and to one spot in particular.

Mathis stretched again, flexing his leg muscles until his body calmed down.

Pulling his shirt back on wasn't nearly as good as having Chloe's arms around him again, but until he caught up with her, it would have to do. He inhaled deeply, then, judging he'd given her enough time, headed up the slope.

Her scent was still on the wind when he crested the rise, but there was no sign of her. She must have put on a turn of speed as soon as she was out of sight. Mathis didn't blame her—he was itching with anticipation, ready to get moving and get off the island.

He forced himself to walk, not sprint, over the manicured grounds back to the residential area. He was poking his way through the gardens when he caught sight of Julian.

The shifter—Mathis frowned as he realized he still didn't know what sort of shifter Julian was, then shrugged it away—was lying back on a bench, soaking in the sun.

"Slacking off?" Mathis was in a good mood; he couldn't help poking fun. Julian had seemed so tightly-wound the day before, and he still was—except he was also lying on his back on a stone bench, for all the world looking like a man sleeping off a night of hard partying.

Julian jerked as Mathis called out to him, and then slid smoothly into a sitting position.

"Ah. Mr.... Dell," he said, blinking slowly. His bottle-green eyes took in Mathis' sand-mussed hair and wrinkled clothes. Something that might have been a smirk lurked at the edge of his mouth. "Did you enjoy your first night under our benefactor's hospitality?"

"First and last night." Mathis ran his fingers through his hair, scattering sand over his shoulders. "I'm out."

"You..." Julian got to his feet. His eyes widened. "You can't be serious."

Mathis laughed. "Come on, man, what are you on about? Harper's great, but there's more to life than whaling on some other poor bastard while he and his friends gulp down champagne. Maybe I didn't realize that yesterday, but I do now."

"What's changed?" Julian was standing perfectly still.

Mathis' lion twitched its nose. That sort of stillness was unnatural. It was deliberate, wary—but was it the wariness of prey, or the watchfulness of a predator?

"I met someone," he said, narrowing his eyes as he waited for Julian's reaction.

To his surprise, the expression that passed like lightning over Julian's face looked something like fear.

"I see. Do you intend to tell Mr. Harper that you're leaving, or will you disappear like a thief in the night?" Julian asked, tight-lipped.

"In the night? Hell, that's a whole day away—I'm not waiting that long." Mathis flashed a wide grin. "Even if I have to swim."

The corner of Julian's mouth twitched downwards, so fast it had to be unintentional. All traces of any hidden smile were gone now. "I hope you will reconsider. Mr. Harper isn't—"

"Isn't what?" Harper's voice cut through the morning air like lightning.

The hairs on the back of Mathis' neck went up. *How did I not notice him coming over?* He checked in with his lion, who was as surprised as he was. Neither of them had sensed anything—not smelled or heard Harper approach, or sensed him through the shifter's animal sixth sense.

Harper gave a friendly smile as he walked over. "Not bothering the guests, are you, Rouse?" he called across to Julian.

"Not at all." Julian's face smoothed over. "If you'll both excuse me, I need to attend to my duties."

"Good man." Harper's eyes sparkled as he watched Julian head back to the house. "Now, Matt," he said, turning his pale eyes on Mathis. "What was that I overheard about you leaving us so soon?"

Mathis ruffled his hair. "Ah... something like that, yeah," he muttered. Except it wasn't *him*, was it? It was good old down-to-earth, down-on-his-luck Matt Dell.

Was now a good time to reveal his true identity? *Probably not*, Matt decided. *Don't want to drop that on the poor guy's head at the same time I tell him I'm skipping out on the rest of the season.*

Harper narrowed his eyes mockingly. "'Something like that'?" he echoed. "Come on, Matt, out with it! Why am I losing my best fighter after just one night?"

Mathis gave in. He explained about Chloe—but not that Matt Dell was really Mathis Delacourt, heir to one of the most powerful prides in the continental United States.

"This is a once-in-a-lifetime opportunity you've offered me, Harper, but Chloe? She's my mate. I might have gone my whole life without meeting her, but now that I have, I have to do right by her." Mathis' heart squeezed as he said the last bit. He laughed it off, adding, "And part of that is not getting my pretty face messed up, right?"

"You make a good point." Harper clapped him on the back. "Well, tell you what. You head back to your quarters now and get your stuff in order, and we'll get this sorted out by lunchtime."

Mathis grinned, relieved. After Julian's reaction, he'd expected push-back to his decision to leave, but Harper seemed to be taking it in his stride. "Great. Thanks, boss."

"Thank me later." Harper returned Mathis' grin, his teeth catching the morning sun.

Chapter 8

Chloe

Chloe kept finding new places sand had gotten wedged into as she hurried back to the staff quarters. Most of them she could brush off without too much trouble, but some of them were going to require a shower.

She had a quick sniff of one armpit as she came into sight of the main house and ducked behind a hedge. *Strike that. I'm going to need a shower even without the sand invasion.*

The sun was halfway up the sky by the time Chloe slunk into the staff quarters. Her hand automatically went to her pants pocket to check her phone, but it was out of power.

Dammit. Must have forgotten to put it on airplane mode. Which means it's been sucking up battery power searching for signal all night...

There was a clock in the kitchen. Ten fifteen. Time for a shower—and time to apologize to Thandie.

Chloe rolled her shoulders back and felt them click. A month of cleaning duties had made her back and arm muscles as tight as coiled springs. A shower would get her clean, but what she really needed was a long, hot soak to ease out all the knots.

She thought of her bathroom back home with a longing she wouldn't have thought possible a month ago. The tub in her apartment might be cramped, and have decades' worth of waterlines around the edges, but at least you could fill it with hot water and sit in it.

Chloe stretched her back and heard another crackling click. *Okay, ouch. I'm going to spend the next* week *in that shitty tub, I swear.*

She crept past the tightly shut doors of a few of her colleagues who she knew worked the night shift, and up the stairs to the room she shared with Thandie. She hadn't seen anyone yet, and more importantly, no one had seen her—or smelled her. All she needed to do now was grab a change of clothes and sneak back to the bathroom...

"Chloe!"

Chloe's spine slammed painfully into the doorframe as Thandie tackled her.

"Ow," she groaned. "Thandie, what—"

"Are you okay?" Thandie didn't seem to know whether she wanted to hug Chloe, or look her over. She grabbed Chloe's upper arms in a vice-like grip. "Oh God, Chloe, when you disappeared I thought—"

"You thought what?" Chloe started to shake Thandie off, but thought the better of it. Thandie's lower lip was trembling, and she had dark circles under her eyes. "Thandie, what's wrong?"

Thandie pulled her into a hug that made Chloe's back click. "I thought you were *dead*," she wailed.

"What?" Shock buzzed at the base of Chloe's skull. Back down the corridor, she heard a door bang. Moving on autopilot, she kicked the door closed, wrapped her arms around Thandie and half-guided, half-dragged her to the closest bed.

Thandie was sniffling as Chloe sat her down. Chloe slung one arm around her shaking shoulders.

"Can you tell me what's going on?" she asked gently.

Thandie drew in a ragged breath and wiped her eyes. "I thought—when you took over the drinks service for me last night, with all the apex shifters, and then you didn't come back to the room..."

Chloe winced. She'd felt guilty for forgetting about Thandie the night before, but she hadn't realized how much of a panic her midnight disappearance would put her friend into.

"You worried one of them had, what—hurt me?"

"Or *eaten* you," Thandie said hollowly. "When they sensed that I was just a hummingbird, they kept making all these jokes. But they were jokes that didn't feel like jokes, you know? And the way some of them were looking at me..." She sniffed and rubbed her nose. "God, I feel so stupid, now, but I was really freaked out. I mean, I knew we had a lot of shifters on staff, but I didn't know the big boss and his friends were like us, too."

"Shit. I'm so sorry, I didn't even think..." Chloe stopped, tongue-tied, as the events of the night before appeared to her in a new light. Thandie's frantic refusal to work the VIP lounge. The way that one guy had literally *sniffed* her.

Oh, shit. They must all think I'm a shifter, too.

"I'm sorry I didn't come back last night. After I watched the fight, I needed some air, you know? But I should have come back and checked on you." Chloe hugged Thandie awkwardly. "Sorry for being such a crappy friend."

Thandie gave a final-sounding sniff. "And I'm sorry for freaking out on you just now. I feel like such an idiot. I talked with Nora after I came back here and, you know, it's not just *most* of us who are shifters. It's *all* of us. The whole crew!" She sighed. "So, what are you, anyway? I can't figure it out, so you must be something with great camouflage skills, right? A chameleon or something?"

I wish. Chloe flicked her hair back over one shoulder. "What am I? I'm getting the hell off this island, is what I am. And you should, too."

"Well, I'm probably going to get fired, so..." Thandie's eyebrows knitted together. "Wait, how are you going to get off the island?"

"Um..." Chloe weighed up her options. Should she tell Thandie the truth about what she'd been doing last night, or gloss over the details?

She took in Thandie's expression. Her brown skin was still paler than Chloe had even seen it, and there were tensions lines at the corners of her mouth and eyes. Chloe made up her mind.

Time for her Jedi mind trick to do some good.

"I uhh... might have broken certain *fraternization* rules last night..." Chloe caught the glint of curiosity in Thandie's eyes, and privately pumped her fist. "Speaking of which, I really need a shower."

Chloe stood up and started rifling through her drawers for a fresh change of clothes, deliberately not meeting Thandie's interested gaze.

"Hang on..." Thandie's voice was suspicious. "Do you mean you met someone, or you—" Chloe could almost hear the inverted commas, "—'*met*' someone?"

"Um... the second?" Chloe grabbed a towel. "Save your questions for after I'm clean, okay?"

She made it to the door and turned back to see Thandie close on her heels. Chloe raised her eyebrows.

"You know, I'm really okay with going to shower by myself."

"Uh-uh. No way. I stayed up all night terrified you'd been eaten by a lion shifter or something, and now you're telling me you were with some guy? You *owe* me." Thandie jabbed her in the ribs.

Chloe groaned dramatically, and trudged down the hall to the bathrooms. "Ugh, *fine*. Well, he is a lion shifter, so you're right about that. As for him eating me..."

Chloe's spirits lifted as she teased Thandie out of her fears with salacious details about her night-time adventures—then sank again as the day went on with no news from Mathis. By the time her afternoon shift came around, she had to admit to herself that he'd probably forgotten about her.

If he'd ever meant what he said at all.

Chloe's stomach clenched as she thought about how stupid she had been. Had she really believed that Mathis would give up a sweet gig like this just to get to know her better? As if. It was far more likely that he'd seen the opportunity to jump into her pants, taken it, and then come up with a convincing story to make her leave in the morning.

She snorted. *Stay in your room until I come and find you?* What a great strategy for giving him time to GTFO before she figured out what his game was.

A soft snore from Thandie's bed echoed her snort. Chloe finished pinning her hair back and stared at Thandie's sleeping form in the mirror. She sighed.

Not only were her own plans to leave the island shattered, but now she would have to admit to Thandie that she'd been fooled, too, and that neither of them were leaving. She had suggested to Thandie that she take the chance to get off the island while she and Mathis were being given the book, but so much for that idea.

Her shift started in ten minutes. Chloe checked herself in the mirror one last time, pulled some apology-chocolate from her bag and put in on Thandie's bedside table for when she woke up, and headed for the door.

Someone knocked on the other side of it.

Chloe's heart thudded in her ears. *He wasn't lying. He really is here.*

She pulled the door open, heart leaping—and saw Julian Rouse standing on the other side, his hand still raised to knock again.

Chloe felt numb. "Oh—Julian, hi," she mumbled. "I was just heading over to start my shift..." *Which will probably include cleaning Mathis' room. God, how humiliating.*

Julian looked over her shoulder. His eyes narrowed as he took in the sleeping Thandie, and then snapped back to Chloe.

"I'll walk you over," he said, his voice clipped.

"All right, but I'm on guest room duties—"

"There's been a change of plans." Julian ushered her into the hall. "You'll be—" His eyes flicked back towards Chloe and Thandie's room. "—taking Thandie's shift again. She's been permanently moved off the service roster."

Julian's jaw set with an almost audible click. Chloe tried to keep her confusion off her face. Everything he was saying was perfectly ordinary—so why did he look so tense?

It's probably a shifter thing, she reasoned. *I wonder what he is?*

She stole sidelong glances at Julian as they walked. Whatever sixth sense it was that Thandie and the others had for figuring out what sort of animal people shifted into, Chloe definitely didn't have it. Julian was tall and slender, and moved gracefully—but to Chloe, he looked one hundred percent human, from his glossy black hair and green eyes to the nervous twitch in his fingers.

Who knows. He could be a chupacabra for all I know. Shit. I hope they don't actually exist, too.

Chloe's internal running commentary could only keep herself entertained for so long. She might not be planning to write an exposé about shifters, but that didn't mean she had to abandon the investigation altogether, did it? She was still curious, and since Mathis was making himself scarce, Julian would have to do.

"So... how about last night, huh? Maybe in future you should warn the wait staff before sending them into the lion's den like that."

Julian said nothing. Chloe barreled on.

"I mean, me, I would give the staff a heads-up before they have a chance to embarrass themselves in front of the big boss, you know what I'm saying? And I'm sure Mr. Harper wasn't happy about Thandie making a scene in front of his guests."

She waited. It was all she could do not to jab Julian in the ribs, just to get a reaction out of him.

"I mean, I get not bringing it up at job interviews, but what about at on-boarding? Once a new employee's already on the island?"

Julian's lips tightened. "Mr. Harper is, so far as I'm aware, perfectly happy with the current state of affairs."

Chloe grimaced. "Oh, wonderful. So he's the sort who gets his kicks out of freaking out his employees, is that it?"

She glanced at Julian, trying to judge what reaction he would have to her barb—if any.

His eyelid flickered, but that was all. And it could have just been a response to a change in the light as they stepped outside, anyway.

Frustration and disappointment were boiling in Chloe's stomach. She needed an outlet—and Julian was it.

She kept up the sniping as Julian led her to the main building. He was unfailingly stiff and polite, as though nothing she said penetrated his polished veneer. Which only made Chloe more aggravated.

She knew she wasn't being fair. Julian wasn't to blame for her gullibility. He was just a handy target for her bad mood.

Chloe gritted her teeth. "Dammit. Look, Julian, I'm sorry for being such a—"

Julian stopped her with one upraised hand. Something glinted in the dark green of his eyes. "Don't," he said through gritted teeth. A muscle twitched in his jaw. "I'm the one who should be sorry. For all of this."

Chloe blinked. They were still a floor below the VIP lounge, in a corridor she hadn't explored yet. She could guess where the service elevator to the lounge floor was, but they were nowhere near it. Instead, Julian had his hand on a heavy metal door.

He twisted the handle. Inside the door, a lock released with a heavy *thunk*.

"And I am sorry," Julian said in a grim undertone, before grabbing Chloe roughly by the shoulder and pushing her through the door.

Chloe fell clumsily to the floor. Pain shot through her knees and she rolled over just in time to see the door slam shut behind her.

"Hey—!" she yelled, rubbing her knees. "What the hell, Julian?"

There was no answer. The room he'd pushed her into was dark, and she blinked, willing her eyes to adjust. A moment later she hissed as bright lights flashed on.

Chloe stood up, shading her eyes. "Hello? What's going on?" *Is this some sort of—of solitary? Because of what Mathis and I did? No, that's crazy.*

Her stomach clenched. *Or maybe it's a lockup for non-shifters who put their nose in where it doesn't belong.*

She squinted around the brightly lit room. The floor was concrete, rough enough that it had torn holes in her stockings. The walls were the same, as far as she could tell. There was another sturdy-looking door on the opposite wall, and above them...

Chloe gulped. She knew where she was, now.

Ten or twelve feet above her, the concrete walls turned into thick transparent glass. She could just see the silhouetted shapes of people in the room on the other side. Were any of them looking down at her? She couldn't tell.

"Hey! Hey, you!" she yelled, banging her fists on the walls. "Hey, get me out of here! There's been some sort of mistake!"

This has to be a mistake, she thought, her heart thundering in her ears. Julian had just thrown her into the fighting ring where she'd watched shifters tear each other to pieces the night before. It had to be a mistake. It had to be.

"Hey! Hello? Anybody?"

The concrete walls seemed to swallow up the sound her fists made. Her shouts weren't having any effect on the people in the room above. *Can they even hear me?*

She kicked the wall. A metallic *thunk* filled the room, and she turned back to the door she'd come in by, hoping this was all a mistake—but it was still closed, and the metal grill cage-door had swung down like a portcullis in front of it.

Chloe turned on the spot, her body heavy with dread. The door on the opposite wall swung open.

For a second, she could only see the outline of the figure standing in the doorway. Then he stepped into the light. He was huge, muscles bulging under scars that crisscrossed his body like a fishing net. His chest was bare, and his pale skin was mottled with scars and bruises. Light blue eyes glinted from a face that held no mercy.

"I... I think there's been a mistake..." Chloe quavered, backing away.

The man grunted and spat to one side. Then, in one fluid movement, he transformed into a massive polar bear, as scarred and brutish as the man.

Chapter 9

Mathis

Mathis bundled up the last of his clothes and threw them into his bag. How had he managed to make such a mess in his room in one night? Less than one night, even—it wasn't as though he'd slept there, after all.

Just thrown everything I owned on every available surface. Mathis did a final sweep of the room. He didn't think he'd been that messy when he'd unpacked, but he'd already found his phone under the bed and his toothbrush on the dresser instead of the bathroom, so who knew what else he'd accidentally hidden?

Satisfied he'd found everything, Mathis squinted out the window to check the sun. It was low in the sky. Late afternoon.

His lion was itching to get moving. Harper hadn't offered any resistance to Mathis' plan to leave—but bureaucracy had. The moment Mathis had reached his room to start packing, Julian had turned up again with what felt to Mathis like a thousand unnecessary busywork forms for him to fill out and non-disclosure agreements to sign. But now, finally, it was almost time to go. To find Chloe, and begin his life with her.

He heaved his bag over one shoulder and pushed through the door. The fighters' quarters were quiet; Mathis guessed most of his soon-to-be-ex-colleagues were out exploring the island, or in the on-site gym. He hummed softly to himself as he walked outside. Part of him was sorry he'd never really gotten to know the other fighters, but most of him was happy to leave this part of his life behind.

The midday sun was bright, and pleasantly hot. A light wind played through the decorative shrubberies around the resort buildings. Mathis glanced up at the main building before turning toward the staff quarters.

He meant to go straight in and find Chloe, but something made him stop. The hairs on the back of his neck rose, and inside him, his lion's muscles tensed.

Something's wrong.

His eyes flicked back to the central building. Its two towers made it look like a fortress, crumbling in the elements. Its pale blond stonework looked like something from the Mediterranean. Sunlight glinted off its windows.

There was no one else around. Not staff, not guests—no one. Inside him, Mathis' lion's hackles rose.

He turned his back on the staff quarters and hurried towards the main building. Something was very, very wrong—and he intended to find out what it was.

His feet moved silently over the paved path, and he slipped inside without a noise. Without actively trying, he had moved into hunting mode, stealthy and precise.

Mathis' nostrils flared as he looked around the grand atrium. *Empty. Where is everyone?*

He thought of Chloe, waiting for him in her room. He hated to leave her hanging, but he couldn't shake the sensation that something was just... wrong. His lion wouldn't let him go and find her until he was sure everything was okay.

Mathis prowled across the foyer, ears pricked. The building was almost eerily silent. The only sounds he was picking up were his own heartbeat, the noise of the wind brushing through the trees outside, and—there! Voices.

He turned towards the distant murmur of human voices. No, *shifter* voices. They were up the stairs, and he followed the layout of the building in his mind: the lounge where he'd been shown off to the guests the night before, after his fight. He frowned and put one hand on the banister.

Stop. His hand clenched on the banister. *This is the wrong way.*

He couldn't explain how he knew it. The information was just there, embedded in his mind, as clear and true as the moment he'd met Chloe and known she was his mate.

Mathis turned and stalked back across the room. An unobtrusive door let him out of the guest area, and a few turns took him to the familiar concrete-walled corridors that led to the fighting ring. An unwashed, musky scent filled the dry air. Mathis' heart thundered in his chest. He still didn't know what was going on, but he knew he was meant to be here. It was important. Something deep inside him was certain of that.

His pace increased as he approached the northern tower. The fighting ring. Inside him, his lion was on its feet, eyes fixed intently on his target.

A heavy steel door appeared in front of him. He didn't hesitate. His shifter instinct was pushing him on, a constant, insistent urge that he couldn't resist even if he wanted to.

Mathis pulled the door open.

In the space between one heartbeat and the next, he stared at the scene in front of him. Chloe was backed up against the opposite wall, terror etched on every line of her face. Facing her, with his back to Mathis, was a hulking white man whose back and shoulders were crisscrossed with scars.

The secondary door, the cage-like grill, was still open. The man must have come through the door just moments before Mathis. He raised his fists and moved towards Chloe, his intentions clear.

Mathis' mind whited out with rage. He didn't know what was going on, or why Chloe was here—but there was no way he was letting anyone touch his mate.

Months of training in dodgy gyms and underground fights came to his aid. And one night of fighting as a lion. Mathis launched himself at the other man. He transformed mid-air, slamming into his opponent's shoulders just as they bulked out and became covered with thick white hair.

The rank smell of unwashed shifter filled Mathis' nose as he and the other man crashed to the floor. Any hesitations he had about attacking his opponent from behind vanished as the polar bear twisted under Mathis, roaring in fury.

Mathis got one glimpse of the bear's ice-pale eyes as it snarled and threw him off. He circled the scarred polar bear, putting himself between it and Chloe.

Every atom of his body was intensely aware of her. Chloe. His mate.

He could hear her breathing behind him, short sharp breaths that were just this side of hyperventilation. She was terrified, and her terror broke his heart in two.

But he had no time to reassure her, even if she could understand him in this state. The polar bear lowered his head, and thick muscles moved under the ragged fur on his shoulders.

He's about to charge. I can't let him get past me to Chloe.

Mathis moved before the bear had finished preparing for his charge. He feinted to the left, then as the bear's head swung around he leapt in at his opponent's neck.

The bear reared back. Mathis' jaws closed on air, and he struck out with his front paws instead, clawing at the polar bear's undefended belly.

This wasn't like any fight Mathis had been in before. He wasn't fighting for glory, or adrenaline, or as a test of skill. He was protecting his mate, and his mind was white-hot with rage.

Mathis' claws raked across a network of scars and grubby white fur. Then a piercing pain struck his shoulder, a dozen knifepoints cutting into his skin. Mathis roared. The bear crunched his jaws further closed, and shook his head, tearing at Mathis' shoulder.

Behind him, Chloe screamed.

The noise seemed to encourage the polar bear. He shook his head again, and threw Mathis against the wall. Mathis grunted as the impact forced air out of his lungs, but landed on his feet.

His eyes found Chloe's. The cage doors had slammed down and she was pressing herself against them as though she could force herself through it by will alone, and shelter in the space behind it. Her dark eyes were like black holes in her pale face.

The bear had turned away from Mathis the moment he dropped him, and was stalking closer to Chloe. Ignoring the hot trickle of blood running from his shoulder, Mathis growled and threw himself at the polar bear before it could reach her.

The fight seemed to take forever, and no time at all. Mathis' body ached with the force of the blows he exchanged with the polar bear, taunting him away from Chloe and trying to weaken him.

Mathis blinked. Sweat was trickling through the fur of his forehead, threatening to drip into his eyes and blind him, even temporarily. It was a risk he couldn't take. The fighting ring was so small, even losing concentration for a second could be too long. It would only take the polar bear a moment to leap past him and attack Chloe. He couldn't let that happen.

He shook the sweat off his face, and blinked again—the spots that fell on the concrete floor were red.

Not sweat, then, after all.

Mathis and the bear circled each other warily. Chloe kept behind Mathis, clinging to the wall. Her breath was more even, now, no longer panicked. But she must be thinking the same thing he was.

What happens next?

There were no lights in the viewing room above. No sign of anyone else who might let them out. He and his mate were trapped here with a violent shifter, and that could only end one way.

Mathis' stomach went cold. He was a fighter, not a killer. But he couldn't let his mate be hurt.

The polar bear was tiring, but still alert. He was protecting his stomach now more—and Mathis was limping from his injured shoulder. They were evenly matched, but one good bite or blow from either of them could turn the tide.

The cold in Mathis' stomach turned to ice. Could he kill, if it came down to it?

He glanced up at the dark viewing room. No way of knowing if anyone was up there or not. If not, then no one was coming to help them. And if there was someone up there—

His glance was one split-second too long. The bear rushed him, catching him on his injured shoulder with a blow that knocked him off his feet. Mathis roared in pain. He was dimly aware of Chloe running out of the way.

Red filled his vision as the bear crashed down on him. He pinned him, but not firmly enough. Mathis twisted, struggled, and sank his teeth into the other shifter's neck from below.

A pulse throbbed under his teeth. This was it. Mathis hesitated—

And brilliant floodlights slammed on, filling the room with cold white light.

Chloe gasped. The polar bear shifted his weight and Mathis released his neck, wriggling out from under him and taking guard in front of Chloe.

"Look," she whispered, her voice shaking. Mathis followed her gaze.

The viewing room wasn't empty.

Dozens of faces lined the windows. And they weren't all standing in the VIP lounge; part of the higher wall had slid back, revealing another window along the other side of the circular room.

Harper was looking down at them, his usually open face grim. Next to him, Mathis recognized Julian, and a few of the guests. Mathis noted briefly that he couldn't see Grayson among them. Behind them, black-clad members of the kitchen and housekeeping staff stood, horror clear on their faces.

Mathis only recognized a few of the men from the opposite window. There was the wolf shifter he'd fought the night before, and some others he vaguely recalled from the fighters' quarters.

Sven caught his eye. Mathis saw the corner of his mouth twitch down in—sympathy? Resignation? He was too far away to tell.

"That will do, Cane!"

Harper's voice rang through the room. The polar bear shuddered, and shifted back into his human form.

Mathis stayed lion, watching the other shifter warily. The polar bear shifter—Cane—turned his strangely flat, pale eyes on Mathis and Chloe, then trudged across to the door he had come in by, and stood there placidly as though waiting for the next thought—or order—to enter his head.

Behind Mathis, Chloe shivered. "Creepy bastard," she murmured under her breath. Mathis grunted in agreement.

He heard Chloe take a step forward, and hesitate. He swung his head around, and caught her gaze. Chloe's face was still pale, but her jaw was set in determination and her hands were fisted at her sides.

Mathis nodded at her. *Come here.* He knew she wouldn't be able to hear him, but hoped she would understand.

Chloe took another step forward. He watched her take a quick, deep breath, and then she buried one hand in his mane, her whole body trembling.

Mathis' heart twisted. He longed to hold Chloe in his arms, and, eyes closed, he reached inside himself, found that feeling and wrapped it all around himself.

Shifting while he was injured always hurt. It was as though the healing process resented being interrupted, and forced to start again in a differently-shaped body. But Mathis couldn't have cared less. He gathered Chloe into his arms.

Chloe grabbed him and didn't let go. "What the hell is going on?" she whispered into his chest.

Mathis couldn't answer. He raised his eyes to the VIP lounge window again, staring straight at Gerald Harper.

Harper met his gaze. His hand moved to the intercom button set into the window.

"Mr. Dell," he announced, his voice tainted with a smug superiority that made Mathis' insides crawl.

"What the hell do you think you're playing at, Harper?" Mathis yelled, sheltering Chloe in his arms.

Harper smiled. "I told you I'd get your request sorted by dinner, didn't I?" He made a show of checking the time on his watch. "Just on time. I'm so glad you weren't late."

Chloe wriggled in Mathis' arms, turning to face Harper and the silent figures standing behind him. "What is this—some sort of sick trust exercise?" she gasped.

"Ah. The interloper speaks at last," Harper sneered. "Did you really think I hadn't noticed what you were up to, Ms. Kent?"

Chloe's spine stiffened against Mathis. He squeezed her reassuringly, glaring up at Harper.

Harper grinned. The change in his appearance was striking. He looked as open and friendly as he had when Mathis first met him.

It was all fake, Mathis thought grimly.

"I'm so glad I left dealing with you until today, Ms. Kent. What luck that you and Matty here have such a special connection."

"What?" Chloe muttered.

Harper kept smiling, but his eyes were hard. "I hope you both understand what this little demonstration was in aid of. Sorry, Matt, but you're prime meat—I can't just let you leave! You'll stay here, and fight for me and my guests... or your mate will pay the price."

CHAPTER 10

CHLOE

Shit. Shit-fuck-shit. He knows why I'm here?

Chloe was so shocked by Harper's revelation that it took her a moment to understand the implications of what he had just said. When she did, it felt like someone had thumped her in the stomach.

She was a hostage.

If it wasn't for Mathis' arms around her, she would have collapsed. This wasn't meant to happen. She was meant to get some incriminating pics, fake sudden illness, and get shipped back to the mainland to work on her exposé from the comfort of her office-slash-bed.

Not discover a secret society of people who could turn into animals. Not have her world be turned upside down by a man whose lion shone through in his addictive smile.

Not be fucking *kidnapped,* and almost murdered by a *fucking polar bear.*

"Shit," she whispered.

"Don't worry," Mathis breathed in her ear. "I'm going to get us out of this."

Chloe wished she could believe him. Mathis seemed like a sweet guy, but he was as helpless here as she was. She gulped. Sure, he could turn into a lion—but was that really an advantage on an island where everyone else could transform into some huge animal, too?

Her mind was tripping over itself. Lions. Bears. Was there a tiger here somewhere, too?

Shit. A hostage? This is really happening? What am I going to do now?

She barely registered the sound of a door opening behind her. Only when Mathis tugged at her arm did she realize they were being escorted out.

I've got to figure out a way to get out of here. But her mind was fuzzy with shock. The restless, reckless energy that usually kept her going was weak, as though it was hiding deep inside her.

Mathis was holding her around the waist, and right now, he felt like the only solid thing in the world. She leaned her cheek against him, and it came away sticky.

Every muscle in her back clenched. She didn't need to wipe her face to know what it was. She could smell it. Blood.

Mathis' blood. From his fight. And he'd have to fight more, now, with her as collateral.

She had to get out of here. Had to get them *both* out of here. She just needed time to get her head straight—figure out what options she had…

Kidnapped. On an island. With a bunch of were…. Were-everythings.

And my phone isn't working.

Shit.

Whatever her options were, there weren't many of them. In fact, she couldn't think of any.

"Ah. Ms. Kent."

Chloe jumped as Gerald Harper seemed to dissolve out of the shadows. Mathis was in front of her at once, shielding her with his body.

Gerald tutted. "Now now, Mr. Dell. Don't be so rude. I was only going to invite your lovely mate to dinner. And yourself as well, of course."

Chloe found her voice. "We're not interested," she said, as evenly as she could manage. She needed to talk to Mathis alone. She wasn't sure whether he'd understood Harper's sly remark about her—but she needed to come clean with him all the same. She couldn't lie to him, especially not in these circumstances.

She felt sick. Especially not if Harper was expecting Mathis to fight for her safety. He deserved to know who he was fighting for.

Harper was still talking. "I'm afraid you'll be joining me regardless, Ms. Kent. Hostages don't get many options when it comes to meal arrangements. I'm sure you understand."

Harper was smiling benignly. He made a beckoning motion and walked off. For a split second, Chloe thought he was leaving them to their own devices—but of course he wasn't.

Mathis took her arm as the polar bear shifter loomed forward from where he had been standing behind Harper. The scarred man jerked his head towards Harper, and motioned for them to follow him.

Chloe glued herself to Mathis as they walked down the corridor, keeping so close she almost tripped over his feet.

"It's going to be all right," he murmured, planting a kiss on the top of her head.

She wished she could believe him.

Harper's mood improved even more when they reached the dining room. It was as gaudy as the rest of the residence, the far wall a floor-to-ceiling stained glass window that cast sickly patches of color onto the gold-and-marble finishings.

Julian was waiting for them, standing in front of the garish window. His face set in grim resignation as he saw Chloe and Mathis follow his boss in.

"Mr. Harper—" he began, and Harper cut him off with an impatient wave.

"No need to congratulate me, Julian. Thank yourself for being proof of concept."

Julian's expression went completely blank. Chloe glared at him, but she didn't have enough space in her mind to wonder what the hell his problem was. She had enough of her own.

Harper corralled her as she tried to sit down next to Mathis. "Uh-uh, Ms. Kent," he chided her, smiling happily. "Come, sit next to me."

Chloe's skin crawled as she took the seat next to Harper at the head of the table. Then she looked across at Mathis and her heart twisted.

He was trying to hide it, but the fight with the polar bear had been hard on him. Chloe winced in sympathy, watching the careful way he steadied himself with one hand on the table as he lowered himself onto the seat.

She wanted to reach out to him, support him and show him how grateful she was for his protection. More than that, she wanted to make sure he wasn't quietly bleeding to death on the other side of the table.

Her throat closed over. He healed quickly, she'd seen that last night—but the fight with the polar bear had been so vicious. What if he was more wounded than he was letting on?

"Mr. Harper," she said, as politely as she could manage. "Do you think Mathis and I could be excused for a few minutes? He needs some first aid, and—"

"Certainly not," said Harper promptly.

"But I—"

"Now, now, Ms. Kent. Look around! What an opportunity we all have now, to really get to know each other." He snapped his fingers and the doors opened, letting in a stream of stony-faced waitstaff. "Such as you, Ms. Kent. I am *very* interested to find out more about you. And I'm sure Matty here is, too."

Chloe's terror must have been clear on her face, because Harper laughed gleefully. "What an exciting day this is turning out to be for all of us. And now some drinks, I think. Julian?"

As Harper looked away, Mathis stretched out his hand across the table. Chloe took it without thinking.

"It's all right," Mathis told her, his eyes locked on to hers. "I'm going to get this sorted out."

How? Chloe didn't dare to say it aloud, but doubt must have been clear on her face. Mathis squeezed her hand. She tried not to notice the drying blood that flaked off onto the table.

Julian returned to the table with a bucket of champagne and glasses. He poured, and Harper raised his glass, beaming.

"A toast," he declared, and then paused. "Pick up your glasses. *Please.*"

His eyes landed on Chloe and Mathis' hands, clasped across the table. Chloe fought a sudden urge to pull her hand away and hide it behind her back.

She picked up her flute with her other hand, fingers trembling. Mathis did the same.

Harper sniffed. "How romantic. A toast, then—to the ties that bind us all together."

Mathis met Chloe's eyes as he raised his own glass. "To new connections."

Chloe mumbled something, incoherent even to herself, and took a too-large mouthful of champagne. She blinked furiously as the bubbles made her eyes water, almost missing Mathis turn towards Harper.

"All right, Gerald," Mathis said calmly, and it took Chloe another second to remember that Harper's first name was Gerald. "Not that this hasn't been fun, but Chloe and I are going to leave. Now."

Harper sat back, his eyes glittering. He took another sip of champagne, and Chloe's skin crawled. Excitement seemed to simmer under Harper's skin like the bubbles fizzing from their glasses.

"Is that so?" he said at last.

"Yeah." Mathis squeezed Chloe's hand and she looked back at him. He mouthed something: she thought he was saying, *I'm sorry.*

Chloe frowned. What did he have to be sorry about? If he had some way of getting them out of here, she would forgive him anything.

Chapter 11

Mathis

Mathis smiled reassuringly at Chloe, squeezing her fingers. When he turned his eyes back on Harper, he let his face settle into barely disguised disgust. Why bother hiding it now?

"You," Mathis growled. How could he ever have thought Harper's face was friendly and open? It was all a mask, hiding his rotten soul. "You've made a huge mistake, Gerald Harper."

"Really? From where I'm standing, everything seems to be going perfectly." Harper's smile became even brighter.

"You have no idea who you're dealing with."

This time, Harper laughed out loud. "What? Some drifter who gets his face bashed in on a nightly basis for a bit of under-the-table cash?"

Mathis gritted his teeth. He'd lived this lie for months—but it had outlived its usefulness. He'd have to explain to Chloe later. "I'm no drifter. And my name isn't Matt Dell. It's Mathis Delacourt. My pride owns half of New York City—"

"Sure you are, Matty." Harper's voice was condescending, but his eyes narrowed to slits.

"Ask Grayson Masters." It was all Mathis could do not to stand up and shake Harper until his teeth rattled. He took a deep breath. "My father was good friends with his brother, the old alpha of the Masters pride. If I can just talk to Grayson—"

"Grayson isn't here." Harper's voice was clipped. "He left earlier this morning on unexpected business. Probably more trouble with his nephew. Or..." He chuckled. "Who knows, maybe he did recognize you."

Mathis stomach felt hollow. *He can't mean...?* He shook himself. *He's just trying to unnerve you. Like in a fight—if he ever fought his own, instead of paying others to do it for his entertainment. He's lying. No lion would abandon another like that.*

But if Grayson isn't here to vouch for me...

"Call my pride," he said confidently. "Any one of them will confirm my identity."

Harper's eyes narrowed to slits. "Mathis... Delacourt," he murmured, barely audible. He rolled the name around in his mouth, like a piece of unwanted gristle. "Ah."

Mathis took a deep breath and squeezed Chloe's fingers. *Now he gets it.*

"Tell you what," Mathis said, grinning through the itch of blood drying on his face, "You throw me the keys to your boat and we'll say no more about it. How does that sound?"

Chloe was squeezing his hand so hard her knuckles were turning white. Mathis brushed his thumb over them, and Chloe winced apologetically.

It's all right, Mathis wanted to say, but he wouldn't say it out loud, not in front of Harper. *We'll get off this ridiculous island, and Harper will see what happens to shifters who prey on each other like this.*

Harper tutted quietly.

"That's a generous offer, Mr.... Delacourt," Harper said, drawing out Mathis' surname. "But I'm afraid I'm going to have to decline."

"What?"

Mathis couldn't believe his ears. He stood up, sending his chair clattering across the hardwood floor.

Out of the corner of his eye he saw Chloe pull her hand back, but his full attention was on Harper. The man sat back in his chair, regarding Mathis with a look of amused tolerance.

"I believe I was quite clear, Mr. Delacourt. If that is who you are. Your offer is appreciated, but not required. I am quite happy to continue according to our previous plans." His lips thinned in a smile that revealed only a sliver of grey-white teeth.

"You're joking." Mathis resisted the urge to shout out the cliché he'd always hated so much: *Don't you know who I am?* "My pride—"

"—Don't appear to realize you have even gone missing, let alone show any signs of wanting to find you," Harper continued smoothly. "Private as you lions tend to be, I'm sure I would have heard if an American pride had lost its golden boy. Would I be right in assuming you have, in fact, misled them about your activities the last few months, while you've been play-acting as Matt Dell? No need to answer—I can tell from the look on your face that I've hit the mark." He took another leisurely sip of champagne. "Really, what with the false identities and lying to your so-called loved ones, you and Ms. Kent are made for one another."

"What the hell are you talking about?" As soon as the words left his mouth, Mathis regretted them. Chloe's sharp intake of breath cut into him.

Harper chuckled. "Are you sure you're a Delacourt, Matty? No wonder your pride isn't bothered about bringing you back into the fold, if you're too blind to see the parasite you'll bring with you."

Mathis squared his shoulders. Protective rage was boiling through him, fizzing in his veins. "How dare you speak about her like that?"

"I'm only trying to open your eyes to the truth, Matty," Harper sneered. "You may think I'm a monster—but how long did it take you to spill our people's secrets to a human journalist?"

Mathis' heart constricted. He spun around to Chloe, ready to urge her to tell Harper he'd got it wrong, but the words died on his lips.

Chloe had gone so pale he worried she was about to faint. She opened her mouth and licked her lips, but couldn't speak. Her hand trembled so much her champagne flute chinked against the table.

She didn't meet his eye. "I wasn't going to tell anyone," she whispered through white lips.

"Of course not," Harper sneered. His lips peeled back from his teeth. "You were just going to keep it to yourself, weren't you? Your little secret. Well, it'll damned well stay a secret now."

Mathis' heart sank. Deep inside him, his lion growled, disbelieving. His mate would never betray him. Chloe couldn't have lied to him.

But she seemed very keen to leave the island as soon as you told her about shifters, a treacherous voice inside him said. His lion hissed at it.

Mathis stared at Chloe, willing her to look at him, to tell him Harper was lying. But she wouldn't meet his eye.

"Aha," said Harper happily as the doors behind them opened again, "Dinner is served. Be seated, please, Mr. Delacourt."

Mathis retrieved his chair from across the room and sat down heavily. His lion roared at him to fight back, that he should be ashamed of himself for capitulating so easily to Gerald Harper's demands—but his human mind was too dazed to think of fighting back.

Chloe lied to me.

His mind skittered back over every moment they'd spent together. Somehow, he was surprised to realize just how little time that was. He'd seen her in the viewing window—and had fallen head over heels, so hard he hadn't even questioned why she was trying to find a Wi-Fi signal so far away from the inhabited parts of the island.

Now he knew. She'd been trying to get the news out about shifters.

It was like taking a blow straight to the chest. Everything hurt, and his heart most of all.

His mouth went dry. *This isn't how it's meant to be.* Everyone knew that. When you found your mate, everything fell into place. Like it had last night, when everything seemed so simple.

Still not wanting to believe that what Harper was saying was true, he reached out to Chloe telepathically. He hadn't expected her to feel it, let alone respond—but her sudden flinch sent knives into his heart.

You should have known something would go wrong. The thought scraped at his insides, leaving him hollow. His skin itched as a hundred small wounds healed. He closed his eyes and waited for the hollow space inside him to crack open again. *You should have known it wouldn't last. Nothing lasts.*

For a moment, blackness overtook him. He was empty and hollow, and there was a gaping hole inside him where his lion should be.

Mathis fell into the void, scrambling at emptiness. There was nothing. No warm animal self, no answering roar to his silent cry for help.

Pain shafted through him, pulling him back into the world. Mathis opened his eyes and the first thing he saw was Chloe staring across the table at him, her eyes wide.

His arm hurt. He glanced sideways in time to see Julian pull his hand away from his wrist, sharp claws shimmering out of existence.

Julian reached out again a moment later, depositing cutlery in perfect alignment around Mathis' place setting. There was nothing but the sting in Mathis' wrist to suggest anything had happened.

And the empty space inside him, waiting for him to fall again.

Across the table, Chloe swallowed. Mathis watched her warily and tensed as she cleared her throat.

Chloe seemed to share his caution. Mathis saw her mouth work as she searched for words.

"Mr. Harper," she said at last, her voice shaking. "Thank you for having us for dinner, but how long is this going to take? Mathis doesn't look good." She swallowed again. "I'm sure you don't want him to keel over in the middle of the first course..."

"Oh, there's no danger of that, Ms. Kent. He may look a little under the weather now, but a good square meal will take care of that." Harper gestured with his fork, outlining Mathis' body. "Look at—*look* at him, Ms. Kent. I insist."

Mathis stared at Chloe. Her eyes were locked on the table between them.

Of course she doesn't want to look at me, he thought, feeling sick. *I'm just a story to her. She wanted to find out our secrets, and leave—not stick around to deal with the consequences.*

"Ms. Kent." Harper's voice was venomous.

Slowly, Chloe's gaze rose from the table. Under Harper's acid commands, she looked across at Mathis.

Her anguish struck him harder than any of the polar bear's blows.

"Now, pay attention, my dear. After all, you're still planning to escape, aren't you? You'll want to be specific when you report on our secrets, won't you."

"I..." Chloe's voice broke off and her eyes slid sideways, as though she couldn't bear to look at him. Mathis' insides twisted. Chloe's lips were tight, twisted down at the corners in what looked like disgust.

"Look at him, Ms. Kent. After all, he can't stop looking at you. Do you know why that is?"

Harper's voice hissed in Mathis' ear.

"Is this really necessary, Harper?" Mathis clenched his fists, fighting back an urge to shout at the other man to shut up.

Harper raised his eyebrows. "Of course! I want to make sure we're all on the same page, Matty. Just trying to *help out.* After all, if Ms. Kent here is going to be your good-behavior guarantee, she deserves to know why, doesn't she? What do you think, Ms. Kent?"

Mathis' mouth went dry. Chloe wouldn't meet his eyes; she looked at the table, and then stared at Harper, her eyes hard.

"Tell me," she said quietly, her lips a thin, tense line.

"Chloe, I—"

"Now now, Matty, she didn't ask *you*." Harper grinned toothily. "If you wanted to spill the beans, you had plenty of time last night." He sat back, carefully replacing his fork on the table. His grin turned Mathis' stomach.

"You and Matty here made a very special connection last night, didn't you, Ms. Kent? More special than you realized, I'm afraid. What were you after? A bit of rough? An exclusive scoop?"

Chloe didn't reply. Mathis' stomach turned.

Harper laughed. "Well, you've got more than that! Look at him: the hopeless expression, that hang-dog look in his eyes—he's in love."

Mathis' heart twisted. "How dare you—"

Harper raised one hand, and the polar bear shifter stepped closer to Chloe. Mathis shut his mouth, trembling with rage.

"You're right, Matty, that's not really accurate, is it? *Love.* Hah! Congratulations, Ms. Kent. You're Mathis Delacourt's mate. He would do anything for you—he can't help it. Fight for you. Die for you." Harper's eyes glinted. "Even now that he knows who you really are."

All the color drained out of Chloe's face. She stared across at Mathis.

"Is—is this true?"

Mathis looked away.

It was true. Everything Harper said was true.

Mathis would do anything for Chloe. He couldn't let her be hurt; it would destroy him more than any physical fight ever could. It would tear his soul apart.

Even if she had always meant to betray him.

"Aha," said Harper cheerily as the doors opened again. "Here's the food. I hope you're both hungry!"

CHAPTER 12

CHLOE

The door shut behind them. It didn't slam, or rattle in its hinges—just swung closed and clicked with quiet finality, shutting them both in Mathis' bedroom.

Chloe's breath hitched in her throat. She rubbed her face, not sure whether the empty quaking sensation inside her was going to turn into sobs or terrified laughter.

She could feel Mathis beside her, and then a cold feeling of absence as he moved away to the other side of the room.

He didn't say anything. He hadn't spoken to her since Harper told her she was his mate. And everything else.

Chloe gulped. Her mind was rattling like gravel in a tin can, crashing over and over the conversation from the dinner table.

Mathis had lied to her. She'd been right about that. Just not the extent of it.

And now he knew she'd lied, as well.

Shit.

She ran her fingers through her hair, shoulder muscles twanging. If they'd both lied—maybe that put them on an even footing.

Yeah, and I bet the stupidly rich guy who can turn into an apex predator will see it that way, too.

Chloe winced. The little voice inside her head could be an asshole, but this time, she had a sinking suspicion it was right.

She lowered her hands. Mathis was standing across the room, silhouetted against the window. He had his hands on the windowsill, his forehead resting wearily against the glass. He wasn't looking at her. He hadn't looked at her since they were finally allowed to leave the dining room.

Yeah, I really don't see this working out.

Chloe was surprised by the hollow ache that opened up inside her at the thought. Of all the terrifying things that had happened to her in the last few hours, *this* was the one that made her heart hurt? Not the fact that she was probably going to die out here, but the possibility that her one-night stand might not like her?

She must be in shock, because that was just ridiculous.

It was *all* ridiculous.

"So, what's the deal here, then?" she blurted out, nerves making her voice gritty and unpleasant. "Harper says all that shit to make us turn on each other, and still wants to use me as bait to keep you on good behavior? How good a hostage am I going to be if you hate my guts?"

"It doesn't matter." Mathis' voice was flat. Empty.

"What doesn't matter?" Chloe shot back before his emotionless tones could make her heart twist any more.

"Whether I actually like you, or not. Harper knows that. I would die for you, even if I hated you." Mathis raised his head, staring out into the afternoon sunlight. "Keeping us together will ensure that." He snorted. "Maybe you can add that to your tell-all."

"My *what*?"

"Isn't that why you're here? To do *research* on shifters, so you can reveal our secrets to the rest of the world?" His shoulders tightened. "That's why you were looking for phone signal last night, wasn't it? You were trying to report back. You must have thought you hit the jackpot when I turned up."

Chloe's stomach twisted. "Well, I'm a pretty shitty journalist if so, right? Looks like I targeted the one guy with enough money to make anything I tried to publish disappear!"

She clenched her fists and slammed one back into the wall, so angry she could hardly think straight. Angry and afraid. Either way, her blood was boiling.

"And so what if I was trying to get a message out? Maybe if more people knew about what was going on here, we both wouldn't be the prisoners of some *psycho* on his fucking *death island*!" She flung one arm out. "And what about all the other staff who were brought in to watch that bear guy rip me to pieces? You think they knew what they were getting into? And all the guests who come here to see people fight—what is *wrong* with you people?"

"We're not all like Harper." Mathis half-turned, but his profile was silhouetted by the fading light outside. "Most shifters are normal people, just trying to get on with their lives. You can't judge us all based on—"

"Based on what? Based on one bad apple? Because there were at least *twenty* bad apples watching you beat on that wolf guy last night—and scaring the shit out of Thandie when she was on duty." Another wave of rage poured through Chloe. "I talked to her this morning, by the way. She thought Harper and his guests had *killed* me. She was *terrified*."

And so am I! she wanted to scream. She gulped in breath, her heart hammering against her ribs. When she opened her mouth again, she couldn't keep her voice from wobbling.

"Last night, when you told me about shifters... I thought it sounded magical. But it's not, is it? It's a nightmare." *And I can't wake up.*

And I can't stop hurting, every minute you don't look at me.

Mathis stood like a statue at the window and she watched, transfixed, as a purple-grey bruise on his shoulder blade faded before her eyes. Last night, when she watched Mathis' scratches heal, it had been like watching a miracle. But this just made her feel ill. She couldn't forget how he'd got the wounds.

How many more will he get, while Harper uses me as bait? she thought, and swallowed hard.

Mathis looked up. For half a heartbeat, he looked lost—and then his eyes shuttered, locking away whatever it was he was feeling.

Chloe wiped the back of her hand over her mouth. For a moment, she'd felt so ill she thought she would throw up. But she could control it. She had to.

Just like she had to control this sad, pathetic crush on a man who clearly wanted nothing more to do with her, mate-bond or not.

"So what happens now?" she said weakly, all her rage burnt out.

"We escape."

Chloe turned her sob into a snort. "That easy, is it?"

"I'm not going to let Harper keep you here. The longer we spend together, the stronger the mate bond will become. And from where I'm standing, it sounds like that would be playing right into his hands."

There was steel in Mathis' voice, but it was tempered with resignation. His shoulders slumped, then he seemed to pull himself together. He glanced out the window.

"How long do you think we have until it's dark?"

Chloe leaned back against the wall. "A few hours, maybe. Twilight lingers on a bit here. It was—" She gulped, and hurried on, "It didn't get properly dark until quite late last night, remember."

"Yes." Mathis hesitated. Chloe wished he could see his face, but he had turned away again. "How much sneaking around the island did you do before I got here?"

Chloe pushed down an angry response. "Not a lot. But some."

She looked past Mathis, out the window. *How long until it gets dark...?*

Her mind caught onto that thought and followed it out of the rattling tin-can of terror she'd been trapped in. Mathis opened his mouth but she got in first, her voice low.

"There aren't any security guards, that's the first thing I noticed. There are floodlights and everything along the paths, but apart from that the whole island basically shuts down overnight." She brought up a picture of the schedule Nora had made them memorize in her mind, and ticked off each point on her fingers. "The final cleaning shift ends at one. Gardening crew gets up at four to make sure the paths and pools are clear before sunrise, before any guests get up. Kitchens at five." She bit her lip. "At least, according to our training. We've only had one night live, and I was… well. I wasn't there for most of it."

Mathis' gaze was like a flash-fire, leaving her breathless in the split second he looked at her. Then he turned away, again, his fists clenched at his sides.

"That gives us a window of a few hours, at least," he muttered.

He lifted his eyes to meet hers, and this time, his gaze didn't scald her. Mathis' pale gold eyes were intense, but the expression in them was grim determination.

"I swear I will get you off this island, Chloe. Tonight."

Looking into his eyes, Chloe couldn't help but believe him. He outlined his plan, and slowly she pulled herself away from the edge of panic.

They could do this. Escape. Get off this nightmare island. And after that…

Chloe waited until Mathis was in the shower to squeeze her eyes shut and grit her teeth. After that—God knows what would happen after that.

Mathis had said that the more time they spent together, the stronger the mate bond would become. Maybe that meant if they escaped tonight, and separated, it would—weaken? Dissolve?

Maybe she could leave *all* of this behind her, not just the island. Lock the door and throw away the key on this particular experience. Forget Mathis. Never see him again.

Maybe she could even convince herself that was what she wanted.

CHAPTER 13

MATHIS

Mathis rested his head against the cool tile of the shower wall. Steaming hot water poured over his back and shoulders, stinging on his newly healed skin.

You've really fucked up this time, Matts. The voice in his head sounded like his twin sister. He and Francine didn't get on well these days, and he no longer wondered why. Francine, with her razor-sharp business skills, was running her own mini-empire. Mathis had never had that sort of drive. Pretending to be Matt Dell had given him purpose for a while...

And see where that got you.

Adrenaline gripped his muscles. He grabbed a loofah and soap and scrubbed at his skin, scraping off dried blood and sweat. He wanted to get rid of Matt Dell, every trace of him. The shabby clothes. The close-cropped hair. He couldn't do anything about those, but this—the blood—the fights—

Who was he kidding? Matt Dell wasn't the problem. Mathis Delacourt was. The same as always.

He turned off the water and toweled off, avoiding his reflection in the bathroom mirror. No amount of water could wash away the bitter shame clinging to him.

Some future alpha you are. No drive. No direction. Even your mate is disgusted by you.

Mathis grimaced as he remembered the look on Chloe's face when he finally managed to control himself enough to look at her. She'd tried to hide it but hadn't been fast enough.

If he closed his eyes, he could see her now. That sickened look, as though she could barely stand the sight of him. And the anger that blazed out of her with every breath since they'd been herded back into his room.

Of course she hates you. You did this to her. If you hadn't slept with her last night, she would still be safe.

Barely looking where he was going, Mathis pushed his way through the door back into the bedroom and froze, his hand on the edge of the door.

When he'd left, Chloe was still standing by the wall, as though she was trying to keep as much space between the two of them as possible. Now she was sitting on the bed, her arms around her knees, her dark hair spilling down over her shoulders.

She looked exhausted. If she'd been blazing with anger before, then now the fire was gone, and he was seeing what it had hidden. Too late, Mathis saw through her vicious bluster to the fear she had been hiding beneath.

The empty space inside him twisted and suddenly his lion was there again, roaring protectively. Roaring at *him*.

"Chloe," he said, his voice rough. Something inside him died as he saw how she changed as she realized he was watching her. She pulled herself up, her eyes flashing indignantly—but her knuckles were still white where they gripped her knees.

Mathis' lion bared its teeth inside him, its protective rage burning inside his skin. His lion was protecting its mate.

Protecting her from *him*.

Shame crashed down on him, so heavy his bones shook under the weight of it. His lion rose up, ready to take advantage of his emotional turmoil to take form and protect Chloe in person.

Mathis pushed it down. They still had to carry out the plan. And for that, he needed to be human.

She was going to reveal shifters to the world, he reminded himself and his lion. *She's dangerous. If she'd managed to get her message out last night...*

But his lion wasn't listening. It hissed at him, lips drawn back over its teeth, and lay in wait inside him, ready to strike the moment his mate needed to be protected.

Mathis dropped his head. "Shower's free," he muttered. "And I—where did that come from?"

He stared at the dress hanging from the bedroom door. It reminded him of the sorts of dresses his sister would wear to charity events: sparkly and long. But little as Mathis knew about fashion, he knew Francine wouldn't be caught dead in a gown that shocking shade of scarlet.

Chloe was glaring at it like it was made of dead rats.

"Julian dropped it off," she explained, her voice flat. "They want you to fight again in an hour. A proper fight this time, he said. For the guests. To make it look like everything's business as normal."

"Shit."

"Yep."

Mathis flexed his wrists. He'd healed up from his fight with the polar bear shifter, but—

"This can't change our plans."

Chloe's eyes flicked over to him, then back to the dress. "I know." She pointed her chin at a battered suitcase beside the door. "He dropped off all my stuff, too, so at least I'll have something sensible to wear when we leave."

"Any idea who I'll be fighting?"

Mathis felt light-headed. A few weeks ago, he would have been asking these questions of Josh Lanyard, or any of the other small-time owners whose gyms he'd fought at. *Who'll I be fighting? What are their tactics? Strong points? Weaknesses? Anything else I should know?*

For the first time, he wondered what his human opponents asked about him—and how the owners and managers answered. What rumors had reached Harper's ears, and led him to find Matt Dell, the fighter who came out of nowhere and laid out everyone who went in the ring with him?

Chloe was shaking her head. "Sorry. He said Harper wanted it to be a surprise."

Which means she asked. She wanted me to know what to prepare for. Mathis pushed back the flare of warmth that burst inside him. *She just doesn't want you KO'd before you can get her off this island.*

Chloe stood up. Mathis swallowed as he saw her knees wobble, just a fraction, before she marched over to her bag. "He'll be back soon," she said, her voice clipped. "And I don't want to go back into that viewing room smelling like fear and blood, so if you're all done in the shower..."

She snatched the dress off its hanger and stalked past him into the bathroom. Mathis moved out of the way just as she grabbed the door from his hand and slammed it shut.

The shower started a moment later. Mathis groaned and forced himself to go to the other side of the room. He dressed slowly, every movement a fight against his instincts. His lion—his *soul*—was roaring at him to go to her, to put his arms around her and comfort her, despite everything.

He took a deep breath. *Just wait until we're off the island. Then—then...*

He couldn't let himself think past their escape. The possibilities hurt too much. Especially as the first thing he would have to do when they got off the island was ensure Chloe didn't reveal the shifters' secret to the world.

Against his better instincts, Mathis found himself listening intently to the noises coming from the bathroom. The rush of water, and the sputtering drip as Chloe turned off the shower. The soft splash of her feet on the wet floor, and of the towel rubbing against her skin.

Mathis wished he could turn off his ears.

Chloe took a long time finishing up in the bathroom. Mathis had convinced himself that she was staying in there to keep away from him, until the door swung open.

The dress fit Chloe like a glove, clinging to her generous curves and shimmering with every breath she took. Her hair hung loose over her shoulders, and in the dim light of the bedroom, Chloe's dark hair and eyes gave the tawdry dress grace and class.

"What do you think?" Chloe mumbled.

Mathis looked at her, hard. "I think you want to tear it off and stuff it down Harper's throat."

Chloe's mouth quirked, and that almost-smile made Mathis' heart ache. He finished tying his shoes and stood up.

"Chloe, I—"

A knock on the door interrupted him. A moment later, Julian stepped inside, his bottle-green eyes darting from Chloe to Mathis.

"Follow me, please."

Gritting his teeth, Mathis held the door for Chloe. As they walked down the corridor, she brushed against his arm. Mathis glanced down, and then lowered his head as she whispered:

"There's something else going on here, I know it."

Mathis nodded silently. He and Chloe couldn't be the only people Harper had trapped like this. It was too neat. The way Harper had put him off his guard, delayed him, and closed the trap. Like he'd done it before.

Chloe's footsteps faltered as they approached the tower. Just as Julian directed Mathis down the corridor to the ring, Chloe grabbed his elbow.

"Try not to hurt them any more than you have to," she begged him, her face tense. "We don't know how many of them are—are in the same position."

"I will," Mathis reassured her. *If I can.*

He knew without having to think about it that Harper would have some game around that, as well.

The fights went fast. Mathis faced off against the wolf shifter from the night before first, then a pair of coyotes. A caiman, for God's sake. Mathis would have laughed if it wasn't so obvious what Harper was doing.

He'd been too bold. Telling Harper about his family—that had been a mistake. And now Harper wanted to take him down a peg.

There hadn't exactly been time to chat during their bout, but Sven had muttered a few urgent messages while they exchanged blows. He warned Mathis to keep his distance from Chloe—already done. And he'd said something that had made Mathis' blood chill.

Sven told him he had hoped this wouldn't happen *again*. Mathis wasn't sure he wanted to know what that meant.

Mathis was bleeding from a dozen wounds by the time the gates opened again, releasing another shifter. If he'd been in human form, Mathis would have gone green.

The shifter was a young woman, in her mid-twenties at the most, with dark skin and close-cropped curly hair. Mathis could hear her teeth chattering from where he stood on the other side of the ring.

And that was all he could hear.

With the other fighters, he had been aware of a sort of psychic background hum, an overflow of the shifters' telepathic abilities. Not sentences, or even words, but a push of feeling: adrenaline, violence, steely determination. Not enough to tell Mathis whether they were here willingly or not, but enough that he knew they would fight to the best of their abilities.

But not this woman. All Mathis felt from her was a blank, and it disturbed him more than any amount of bloodlust.

Mathis shook his mane out, huffing uncomfortably. He prowled back and forth as the woman stood, panting, but not moving.

Chloe was right. There is something deeply *wrong here.*

He glanced up at the window. Chloe's scarlet dress was like an emergency flare, and a constant reminder of why he was here.

She was standing next to Harper.

Mathis snarled, fangs bared at the man who had imprisoned his mate, and the broken shifter woman struck.

He heard the slip of her bare feet against the concrete and turned just in time to see her shift mid-air, her body twisting and shrinking. Mathis reared back, ready to meet her attack.

When he saw what she was shifting into, he hesitated, horror filling him long enough for the ibex shifter to land, slice razor-sharp horns against the wound in his side, and leap away again.

Her hooves clattered on the concrete floor as Mathis sank down, bile filling his gut. An *ibex*. The creature was barely three feet tall at the shoulder, a fleet-footed, delicate herbivore.

A *prey* animal. No wonder her mind was whited out with fear.

Mathis padded sideways, feeling sick. Was this another of Harper's games? It had to be. Pitting him against a prey shifter.

Cold dread boiled in his stomach. *What does he expect me to do? Fight her?*

He sent out a tentative telepathic nudge to the ibex shifter, trying to reassure her that he didn't mean her any harm. It didn't get through. Her terror was so overwhelming it created a psychic barrier around her mind. Mathis' message glanced off it like oil off water.

Mathis huffed again. He knew he could only stall for so long. That was how Harper had set two coyotes against him earlier—he'd balked against fighting a shifter so much smaller than himself, and Harper had sent out a second to attack him in tandem.

What would he do if Mathis refused to fight now?

He could guess.

Hurt him—or hurt Chloe.

Mathis growled, lowering himself to pounce. *I'm sorry* he sent out to the ibex shifter, knowing it was useless. *I don't want to be here anymore than you do.*

He began to stalk the ibex around the ring, keeping low to the ground. He'd won all of the fights so far, but his healing abilities weren't keeping up with his injuries. The ibex had ripped open the bite wound in his side, and then there was his shoulder—*again*, damn it—scratches to his face, bites on his back and legs—

Mathis was caught off guard as the ibex lowered her head and charged. He crouched defensively, but the ibex was too fast. So graceful it was almost like a dance, she leapt around Mathis, targeting his wounds with her horns and surprisingly sharp hooves.

Confused, Mathis jumped back. Pain lanced through his side and he roared, which sent the ibex skittering back.

But only for a moment. A heartbeat later and she was back, single-minded with bloodlust.

Mathis dodged as much as he could, but wherever he moved she was there already, ready to slice at him and dart away again. He roared again, dread settling in his stomach. Was this what Harper wanted? For him to be driven to seriously hurt this unhinged shifter?

What did he do to you? he asked desperately. There was no response.

The next time the ibex rushed him, Mathis struck out. The ibex skittered away just in time and Mathis lunged heavily, overbalanced.

Inspiration struck.

He was bleeding. Injured. Exhausted. If Harper wanted to humiliate him by making him fight a deranged prey shifter—why not let her beat him?

But he couldn't make it seem like he was throwing the match. He couldn't risk Harper knowing it was a trick. God alone knew what he would do if he figured it out.

So the next time the ibex came near Mathis struck out again, and lost his footing; when he stumbled back, he held his head low, panting. He favored his un-injured side as he circled around the small deer. Blinked, and shook his head, as though his vision was blurring.

He let the ibex strike him, until his limping steps were only half-fake.

At last, and only when he thought Harper must be convinced it was real, Mathis stumbled and fell. The ibex was on him at once, dancing around and slicing at him. He flinched instinctively as she hit his side again, lashing out with a rear leg, then subsided, belly-up.

And the ibex attacked him again.

Mathis twisted, glancing up at Harper. This wasn't right. Every fight, every one, ended when one shifter showed their belly. The classic sign of submission.

He lay back and the ibex rushed at him again. This time he barely managed to roll to his feet to protect the delicate skin of his underside.

What are you doing? We can end this now!

No response. It was like shouting at a wall.

Mathis tried to get to his feet but this time his leg collapsed under him for real. He braced himself as the ibex charged him, ripping at his shoulder with her horns. He swung his head to bite her but she was gone, again, and then pain burst in his side, along his back, his rear leg—

Somewhere, metal clashed on metal. The smell of human-shaped shifters broke through the smell of blood and strong arms pulled the ibex off him. Mathis twisted around in time to see two burly men wrestling her into submission as a third injected her with something. He recognized one of them: Sven. His first opponent the night before, and tonight.

What the hell is going on? he shot at the wolf shifter, who just shook his head.

You should have joined us for that drink, Dell. Would have got you up to speed.

The men dragged the unconscious ibex out, leaving Mathis alone in the fighting ring.

He dragged himself around until he could look up at Harper again. He focused his gaze, refusing to look at Chloe even though she was still standing right next to the monster.

What must she think of me, after seeing that? The thought scraped at his insides, hollowing him out.

Harper was holding a glass of champagne. He sipped it, looking down at Mathis with unreadable flat eyes, and after what felt like an eternity stretched out one hand to press the intercom.

"Thank you, Mr.—aha—*Dell*. That will do for tonight." He paused. "Now, ladies and gentlemen, as the victor is indisposed, Mr. Dell will be joining us tonight to answer *any* of your questions…"

Mathis groaned, dropping his head. *This charade again.*

The fight had already gone on longer than he'd hoped. If they were going to leave tonight, they were running out of time.

Chapter 14

Chloe

Chloe was shaking. She couldn't help it. Every blow Mathis took was like a punch in her chest. When the ibex launched itself at his throat, she thought she would pass out.

And Harper knew it. Every gasp she tried to stifle, every time she swayed as Mathis stumbled or took another strike—every time, Harper laughed, as though it was the best joke he'd ever heard.

Even when the fight was over the nightmare didn't finish. The moment Harper called the match, Chloe spun away, only to be stopped by his iron grip on her elbow.

"Where do you think you're going?"

"Back to my quarters," Chloe hissed through gritted teeth. "You and the guests are going to have drinks in the gold lounge, aren't you? Like last night? So my shift is over."

"Oh, my dear Ms. Kent, you've quite misunderstood." Harper chuckled, guiding her back to the middle of the room. "You're not on duty. In fact, you won't have any staff duties for the rest of your time here. You're my guest, and you simply must stay until the night is over."

Chloe gulped. "I want to see Mathis—"

The words were out before she could stop them. Harper shook his head, a fatherly smile on his lying lips. "Of course you do. That's what makes this setup so exceptionally useful. Now, just follow me—and remember to smile for the other guests…"

Chloe let him lead her down the corridor to the gold lounge. She didn't need to smile at the other guests, because none of them looked at her.

Plausible deniability, she told herself, feeling ill. *If they don't see how upset I am, they can pretend they have no idea what's going on, when all this gets out. And they* must *assume it's going to get out someday. They're too rich not to be paranoid.*

Things were starting to click into place. The all-shifter staff, made up of small, weak shifters. The lack of security. The short-to-nonexistent advance notice of any visits. Harper's island was a fly-by-night operation on a grand scale—and just as easy to break down, if things got risky. Chloe had no doubt Harper would get rid of his staff with no hesitation, and what better way of hiding mass murder than having your victims be a group of birds and tiny creatures?

Chloe felt faint. *Thandie and the others. They're in so much more danger than they know.*

She almost stumbled, and Harper pulled her upright. He shoved her towards the window seat at the far end of the room.

"You look tired. Have a seat."

"I'm fine." She wasn't. But she wanted to see Mathis. If he was going to be here—

"I said, *sit.* And I wouldn't move if I were you, not until I say so." Harper's face split into a thin smile that had too many teeth in it, gray and narrow behind his lips.

Chloe sat, ice crackling up her spine.

She saw Mathis come in. He was human-shaped again, and someone had given him a change of clothes. Black sweats that outlined his thigh and butt, and a white muscle shirt that he was bleeding through.

Chloe could have sobbed. She didn't care if he thought she had come here to betray all of shifter-kind. She didn't care if he hated that she was his mate. She wanted nothing more than to run across the room and fling her arms around him, to breathe in his scent and check his wounds.

But she couldn't. She didn't know what Harper would do to her, or Mathis, or anyone else if she disobeyed him. So she stayed in the window seat like a bird in a cage as Harper showed off his prize fighter.

She was shaking with rage and exhaustion by the time the VIPs started to disperse. The moment Harper snapped his fingers at her and gestured for her to move, she was on her feet.

"My goodness, you two make a lovely pair," he said genially, eyes glinting. "Well done, both of you. Now, off to bed. Julian?"

Julian Rouse appeared so quickly Chloe jumped. She hadn't noticed him before, but he must have been around. He was always around, always just out of sight. She must have been so focused on Mathis that she didn't notice him.

He was paler this evening than Chloe had ever seen him, a tic twitching at the corner of one eye. *Good*, Chloe thought heartlessly. *I hope you feel bad. I hope this shit keeps you up at night.*

Neither she nor Mathis said anything as Julian took them back to his quarters, but Chloe grabbed hold of Mathis' hand. He didn't pull away, but to her horror, the further they walked the more he leant against her for support.

He's exhausted. Chloe's mouth went dry. *So much for our plans. He can hardly walk. Which Harper must be gambling on.*

No security team. No cameras. By forcing his victims to fight to exhaustion, Harper ensured their bodies were as much a prison as any cage.

Julian shut the door behind them without a word, and Mathis collapsed onto the bed almost in the same breath.

Chloe swore, panic gripping her. "You're hurt."

"It isn't that bad," Mathis said.

"Liar." Chloe gulped. "I'll get the first-aid kit."

"There's no time," Mathis protested. He braced his arms on the side of the bed and hissed in pain. "I'll be fine."

"Sure you will." Chloe's insides were churning. She grabbed the first-aid kit from the bathroom and hurried back into the bedroom, standing directly in front of Mathis so there was no space for him to get up. "You're fine. Everything's fine. And anyone tracking us will just have to follow the bloody footprints. Great plan."

Her voice was harsher than she intended, but to her relief, Mathis stopped trying to get up.

"Good point," he muttered.

He was shivering, just slightly, but his cheeks were flushed. Chloe frowned. "You're exhausted."

"I'm fine. We need to hurry." Mathis jerked his head away as Chloe put out her hand to test his temperature. "*Don't.*"

Chloe snatched her hand back. "But—"

Mathis' face had been stiff with pain and simmering anger, but just for a moment his eyes softened. "I'm sorry. It's safer if you don't touch me when I'm like this."

Chloe stared at him. "You need medical attention."

"I need you *not to touch me.*" Mathis spoke through gritted teeth, the words ripping out of his throat. Chloe stepped back, feeling as though she'd been punched in the stomach.

Mathis sagged. "I don't mean..." A muscle in his jaw moved and he raised his eyes to meet hers. "You didn't sign up to be my—for this thing between us. Harper is exploiting it to control you. I won't. I won't use you like that. But the more you touch me, the stronger the bond will become."

Chloe swallowed. Mathis' words just made her want to hold him more. Everything about him did.

But what he was saying made sense. The mate bond, or connection, or whatever the hell it was, gave Harper a hold over them both. What had Mathis said earlier? That being close to one another would make the bond stronger?

Making the bond stronger would make Harper's power over them stronger. That made sense. It was logical.

Even if not holding Mathis when he was in so much pain made Chloe's heart ache.

"Right," she muttered. "Well—here's the first-aid kit. Knock yourself out."

She bit her lip. *Oh, yeah. Snipe at him. That's going to help.*

I know what might help, though. Chloe darted across the room and rifled through her suitcase. "Here. Eat this. *All* of it. I can only imagine how much energy all that healing and transforming takes."

Mathis took the rest of her chocolate stash with shaking fingers. He ate it in a few bites and then cracked open the first-aid kit. Chloe's fingers twitched as he swiped antiseptic wipes over the wounds in his chest and side, where the bite and claw marks were already closing over.

Stop it. He doesn't want your help. You're a liability. She swallowed. *If it wasn't for you, he could probably have got away by himself by now. Instead of being torn apart for Harper's amusement.*

"This is insane," she murmured, watching his skin knit itself together. "And—oh, hell, your leg."

"It's not that bad." Mathis didn't look up.

"The hell it isn't. You're not even looking at it. It doesn't look like it's healed at all."

Mathis gritted his teeth. "Give it a few minutes. The chocolate will help."

It didn't. At least not visibly. In the end Mathis relented, packing gauze against the wound and wrapping a bandage around it.

He had stopped shaking, at least. He sat on the edge of the bed, and Chloe had to stalk over to the other side of the room to stop herself from sitting down beside him.

"What time is it?" His voice was like a magnet, pulling her back across the room.

Chloe closed her eyes. *Stop it.* "Are you sure you're well enough—"

"I have to be. What time is it?"

Chloe sighed and grabbed her phone from her bag. It didn't have any signal, but it could still tell the time at least. "Ten to one. We need to wait for the cleaning crews to be finished in the tower."

"You'd better get changed, then."

Chloe grabbed a bundle of clothes from her suitcase and hesitated. *He's seen it all already,* she berated herself. *Why are you suddenly so shy?*

She swallowed over a lump in her throat. Without even trying to find an answer for her own question, she hurried into the bathroom and shut the door after her.

Chloe practically tore her dress off. She'd stress-sweated so much during the fight that it was grimy already, and there was no way she was wearing it again. She left it in a crumpled heap on the bathroom floor and pulled on her sweats and a long-sleeved shirt. Her heels hit the wall as she kicked them off, before pulling on her trusty sneakers. She might not look glam, but she wouldn't be a shimmering blood-colored traffic light in the darkness.

Mathis was prowling around the bedroom. He'd turned off the main light, to make it look like they had gone to sleep, and Chloe blinked as her eyes adjusted.

"Have you seen anyone out there?"

"Not yet."

While Mathis' back was turned, Chloe went back to her suitcase and palmed the miniature camera she'd hidden in a secret pocket in the lining. Keeping a close eye on Mathis, she put it in a waterproof bag and tucked it into her bra.

It wasn't that she didn't trust that he wanted to get them both off this island. She just wanted her own security that once they were free, she would still have some evidence to make someone take notice of what was going on here. Not her editor—Thandie and the others deserved better than being pulled out of this cage into the media spotlight—but someone who could do something about it.

There must be shifter police, right? Someone who can do something about this. Stop Harper from hurting anyone else.

"People."

Mathis' whisper brought her over to the window. She recognized the figures traipsing out of the tower's staff entrance, shoulders slumped and heads hanging with exhaustion.

"That's the cleaning crew. There should be six of them. There, that's them all."

They both waited in silence until Chloe's six ex-colleagues disappeared around the corner, heading for their own quarters. Chloe took a deep breath, and felt Mathis tense beside her.

"Time to go?" she breathed.

Mathis nodded. "Time to go."

Chapter 15

Mathis

Exhaustion seeped into Mathis' bones, but he ignored it. Chloe had given the all-clear; it was time to put his plan into action.

He opened the window. It was configured to only open six inches before locking into place, but Mathis reached inside himself for his lion's strength and snapped the window out of its frame. He grabbed it before it could fall to the ground outside, and placed it carefully against the wall.

Mathis and Chloe exchanged a glance. They'd discussed this earlier. No talking while they were outside. Shifter senses were too powerful to risk it.

He crouched on the windowsill for a moment, scanned the outside, and dropped, landing on soft grass with barely a sound. He inhaled slowly, filtering out the scents of the resort and, beyond, the hints of wilderness. So far as he could tell the grounds around the building were empty.

Mathis motioned at Chloe to come down. She sat on the sill for a moment, and then dropped to the ground.

She should be dropping into your arms, his lion complained.

No. He gritted his teeth. *You can't think like that. Not now. After tonight—No. Think about it later. Concentrate.*

He led the way along the path, following the route Chloe had described to him. They had to make their way down along the side of the fighters' quarters, and then turn off perilously close to the main tower.

After that, there were thirty yards of open terrain, before they would reach the protection of a decorative stand of palms between them and the buildings.

And from there to the beach.

Simple. Except that Mathis was almost shaking from the effort of moving, and every sound in the darkness made his lion jerk inside him.

He was intensely aware of Chloe's presence, just feet behind him. Her breathing. Her almost silent footsteps.

Mathis turned his face to the sky and caught a glimpse of the stars. Something twisted inside him. It was too easy to remember how Chloe had fallen into his arms the night before, the press of her lips against his, the thunder of her heartbeat matching his...

It was happening. He knew it would. The longer they spent together, the stronger the mate bond would become. Even if they barely touched, and half the words they exchanged were angry or resentful.

He waited for his heart to sink, but it didn't.

Traitor, he muttered silently to his lion. It ignored him. He had a suspicion it knew his heart better than he did.

Chloe's breath hissed sharply, and he paused. They were about to turn in front of the tower; he felt the air move as Chloe almost touched his arm, and pulled back at the last second. She pointed up.

There was no light coming from the tower, but there was movement behind one window. Mathis stepped back, grateful for the design of the grounds which meant the staff pathways were all but hidden from the guest areas. A moment later he realized his mistake.

Light poured out the window, spilling out across the path. Mathis' stomach clenched. Hidden pathways or not, if he had been three feet further down the path, the light would have flooded across his head and shoulders.

Chloe touched his sleeve. Mathis stood like a statue as she crept past him, her feet silent on the sealed path. She kept close to the tower-side of the path, ducking down so she couldn't be seen through the windswept topiaries.

She kept the lead as they crept past the tower and across the empty lawn. Mathis' lion was almost crazy by the time they made it to the cover of the trees, but he couldn't let it out. His lion's scent was far stronger than his human smell. Someone out for a late night might smell two human-shaped shifters and think nothing of it, but if anyone sensed a lion in the grounds, the gig would be up.

They made it past the trees. They even got to the beach before everything went wrong.

The crunch of their footsteps on the pebbly sand was deafening compared to walking on the sealed paths and grass closer to the buildings. Mathis could just see the boat tied up to the jetty, looming like a white ghost in the darkness.

He motioned to Chloe, but she had already seen it. Her eyes caught the starlight as she glanced back at him. He could almost hear her question: *Are you sure this is going to work?*

Smiling, Mathis urged her forward, but he let the smile drop as soon as she looked away. He *hoped* it was going to work. And if he didn't, he'd come up with another plan. He had no other choice.

The jetty creaked as he stepped onto it. A few steps took him out to the boat, sea spray dampening his legs. He helped Chloe onto deck and then slipped into the cockpit, heart hammering in his chest.

What he found there made his shoulders sag in relief. He'd remembered correctly. The boat might not have the key conveniently left in the dash—but it had the same basic construction as the boats he and his friends had taken joy-rides in as kids on summer holidays. And those boats hadn't had keys, either.

He opened the control box and looked back over his shoulder, waiting for Chloe to cast off. She gave him the thumbs up and sat in the back of the cockpit.

Mathis took a deep breath. *This is it.* He glanced back at the beach one last time. It was abandoned. No one had followed them. Which was ideal, because once the roar of the boat's engine cut through the air, they'd be lucky if the whole island didn't wake up.

He turned back to the control box, ready to twist together the wires that would jump start the engine. The air behind him moved, and when he glanced back over his shoulder Chloe was gone.

He was on his feet before he realized he was moving. His chest clenched. *Chloe!*

There hadn't been a splash. She couldn't have fallen overboard. Mathis' jaw tensed so hard his teeth hurt.

Did he dare call out?

He took a deep breath, sifting through the smell of the coast for Chloe's scent. There was nothing. *Nothing.* It was as though she had never been there.

Wrongness jangled against his senses, and Mathis hissed out a sharp breath between his gritted teeth. Disappearing without a trace—no scent, no sound? There was one man on the island who fit that description.

"Rouse," he growled, and the ocean rose up around the boat.

Mathis blinked. For a moment, it had looked like the waves were billowing over the edges of the boat, blotting out the horizon—but that couldn't be right. Except now he couldn't see the horizon, or anything else either, just darkness and the sense of wrongness pressing against his mind again, and somewhere in the shadows the sound of scales sliding against one another.

The hairs on the back of his neck rose.

Wind swirled around Mathis, as though the air was rushing in to fill a sudden vacuum, and then Chloe and Julian Rouse were standing on the jetty.

Chloe was red-faced and panting and Mathis leapt onto the jetty before he realized what he was doing. He clenched his fists and advanced on Julian.

"Let her go!"

Julian had one hand firmly around Chloe's wrist. She twisted and stared at Mathis, eyes wide.

"He's a fucking dragon!" she hissed.

Mathis shifted his weight, moving into a fighting stance. His side ached, but he ignored it, just as he ignored the shock rocketing through his mind. *A dragon?*

He shook his head. "I don't care what you are, Rouse. Get your hands off my mate."

"I'm afraid I can't do that, Mr. Delacourt." Julian's always uptight voice was razor-sharp. "And I would recommend you take my other hand."

"What the hell are you talking about?"

A muscle twitched by Julian's left eye. "I can keep anyone else on the island from noticing you're out here, but only if you're touching me."

Mathis snorted. "You expect me to believe that? You might be a dragon, but everyone on this damned rock knows you're Harper's lap-dog."

Julian's nostrils flared. "If you don't believe me, try to start the engine."

Beside him, Chloe paled. "Shit."

"Your mate has figured it out, Mr. Delacourt. Have you?"

Eyeing the dragon shifter warily, Mathis jumped down into the boat and twisted together the wires that should have jump-started the boat. Nothing happened.

"It's a trap." His heart sank.

"And remarkably effective, it seems." He closed his eyes briefly. "Harper only sleeps for a few hours each night. If you go back to your quarters now, he'll already be awake. He will know you tried to escape and believe me, you do not want to find out the punishment for trying to leave the island."

"So help us." Chloe turned toward him. "If you don't want us to get caught, why not help us get away? You could fly us out, couldn't you?"

Julian held out his hand to Mathis, appearing to ignore Chloe's question. Mathis narrowed his eyes at him.

"You expect us to believe you're honestly here to help us?" he growled. "How do we know you're not going to march us in front of Harper and tell him you found us trying to escape?"

"Because I've seen what happens to people who try to escape," Julian barked, his smooth façade finally breaking. "And—" His face twisted.

"Something Harper said," Chloe whispered. "When he told us he was keeping me as a hostage for Mathis' good behavior. He said you were a proof of concept..."

"And so I am." Julian had his face back under control. "Now, please. Come with me so that Harper may continue to believe we are *all* on our best behavior."

"But—"

Horror dawned on Chloe's face the same moment Mathis' gut twisted. Julian's eyes flicked from one to the other.

"What is it?"

"We broke the window out of its frame."

Julian's face cleared. "Smash it in the morning, and make it look like it broke then. Harper is more forgiving of violent outbursts than premeditated disobedience."

"I guess I don't want to ask how you know that." Mathis' voice was harsh.

Julian raised one eyebrow. "No. You don't."

Mathis' whole body hurt as he trudged back to the fighters' block. He'd thought they were so close to freedom—but it had been a lie.

No wonder Harper's security was so lax. He had a goddamn *dragon* guarding his prisoners. And if Julian was Harper's 'proof of concept' for the bind he had Mathis and Chloe in—that must mean he had a hold of some sort on him. What the hell kind of leverage could anyone have over a dragon?

And how many people has Harper done this to before?

Bitterness rose in his throat. He'd been so certain this would work. Well, pride comes before a fall, and that's where he was now. Fallen. Failed.

He'd failed his mate. And now they would both pay the price.

Mathis pulled away from Julian the moment they were back in the bedroom. He didn't look at the dragon shifter as he left, the door clicking shut quietly behind him. And he couldn't look at Chloe. She—

His lion tensed. He couldn't *sense* Chloe. All the walk back, he'd been unable to ignore her angry, frightened presence only feet away from him, but now... nothing.

He spun around.

"God *dammit*!"

He blinked. Chloe was suddenly there, in the corner of his eye. He turned to face her like a man in the desert crawling towards an oasis.

She was hopping on one foot, wrestling her sneakers off and throwing them one by one at the opposite wall. Her face was white, with red spots of rage on her cheeks, and her eyes were shiny with tears.

Mathis' lion yearned to be close to her, to comfort her, and Mathis was halfway across the room before he got control of himself.

She turned to face him, and he saw her lean forwards, almost giving in to the same pull he felt. He saw her pull herself back, and his heart wrenched.

"Shit," she muttered, wiping the back of her hand over her nose. "I guess we still have to—*ugh*."

She turned away, fists clenched, and kicked the closed door. A second later and she'd spun around again. Mathis could almost feel the rage boiling off her.

"So," she hissed through gritted teeth. "Are you going to smash that window, or can I have a go at it first?"

Mathis sat down on the edge of the bed, facing her. His lion was snarling, telling him to take her in his arms—but he couldn't. Not now.

Chloe's next words knocked him out of his thoughts.

"I wasn't going to tell anyone, you know," she muttered. "Not about shifters. I only came here because I thought there was an illegal dog-fighting ring. That was the story I wanted to break. I wanted to stop animals from being hurt, not—not *this*."

Mathis let out a hard breath. Inside him, his lion stalked back and forth, whipping its tail. *I should have known she wouldn't betray me. I should have trusted her.*

What does it say about me that I believed Harper before even talking to her?

He stared at her, lion and man united in the desire to protect and comfort. But if the pain and fear on Chloe's face was enough to make him want to hold her, it also made him stay back.

She didn't ask for any of this.

Mathis' throat was dry, and his head was spinning from exhaustion and defeat. He shook himself, forcing his thoughts into line.

Chloe was his mate. If he had any purpose in life, it was to protect her. And that meant more than just getting her out of here.

She'd said it herself. She had thought the shifter world would be magical—but instead, for her, it was a nightmare. His world made her afraid.

So he had to do more than get her off the island. He could never force his mate to live in a world that frightened her; he had to let her go entirely.

"I believe you," he said, his voice gravely. "Harper's a monster, and I won't let him get away with this. But if we're going to make it out of here, we need some ground rules."

Chloe looked up at him, her dark eyes wary. Cold blossomed inside Mathis at the thought of what he was about to say, but he steeled himself.

"Like I said earlier. No touching. I can look after my own injuries, and I'll sleep in the chair. If I need help getting back here, one of the others can give me their shoulder to lean on. And after we're free..." He took a deep breath, and Chloe's gaze became sharper. "We'll go our separate ways. I promise."

Chloe's face went tight, and something flashed behind her eyes, too fast for Mathis to identify it. Pain? Sorrow?

He shook his head. *You're imagining things. Making it up because that's what you want to see.*

Chloe let out her breath in a ragged sigh. "Thank you."

"No problem," Mathis lied, and closed his eyes.

It was the right thing to do, he knew. But that didn't mean it didn't hurt.

By the time the sun rose the window was in pieces on the ground outside, only feet from where they'd jumped out hours before. Chloe was sitting in the armchair, glaring into space. She'd barely spoken while they broke the window, and now silence surrounded her like a wall.

Mathis had tried to tell her that they would find another way out of here, but his words sounded hollow even to himself. And the brighter the world outside got, the darker his thoughts became. Dread filled his stomach at the thought of what the next day would bring.

If Harper could control a dragon, what else could he do?

Mathis remembered the blank terror of the ibex shifter's mind. Harper must have had some hold over her once, and forced her to fight. Her obedience hadn't saved her sanity.

How many more fights could Mathis survive before he lost hold of who he was, too?

Chapter 16

Chloe

"You should get some sleep."

Mathis sounded exhausted. Chloe would have said so, but one look at him and the words died on her lips.

Three weeks. Even thinking the words made her want to curl up on the floor and never get up again. Three weeks since their failed escape attempt, and it felt like three months.

For a few days, Harper had ignored them. Chloe had been stupid enough to think that would continue.

Instead, the moment his guests left, Harper had turned the psychopathy up to eleven.

Every night, Harper forced Mathis to fight the other shifters. And every night he "treated" Chloe to a VIP spot in the viewing lounge, where she watched Mathis be hurt.

It wasn't just the physical wounds that hurt him. It was the choice Mathis made every time he had to hit or be hit. He'd told Chloe he didn't think the other fighters were here by choice, any more than the two of them were, and she knew that having to face off against other prisoners tortured him more than any injury.

Faking it wasn't an option. If Harper even suspected Mathis was throwing a fight, he would send in the polar bear shifter to, as he put it, "liven things up".

Chloe shivered. Harper's glee at seeing Mathis in the ring was unnerving—but the longer she was here, the more frightened she was by the thought of what might happen when he lost interest.

Mathis was killing himself out there, and he thought *she* needed sleep.

"You're the one who needs to sleep," she said, making sure her voice didn't wobble. "How's your shoulder?"

"It's fine."

It wasn't. Chloe could see that. A *child* could see that. An alien child from the Moon who didn't even know what a shoulder *was* could see that.

Chloe had spent three weeks listening to Gerald Harper gleefully tell her his plans for Mathis. Three weeks of none of her former colleagues so much as meeting her eye, even when Harper ordered them to pour her champagne or serve her dinner.

Three weeks of watching Mathis clean his own wounds while she sat on her hands, and then watching them heal, more slowly each time.

Chloe clenched her fists.

"Right. It's *fine*. Sure it is. And sleeping in that armchair again is going to help it heal faster, isn't it?"

Mathis turned away. "It'll be—"

"Bullshit." Chloe stabbed him in the chest with one finger. The touch sent a shock of electricity through her. She caught her breath and continued, hands clenched safely at her sides. "I saw you this evening. You could hardly lift your arm even before the fight started." She bit her lower lip as it started to tremble. "And you haven't stopped bleeding yet. Last week that bite on your cheek would have healed over in minutes, but it's been an hour and you're still, still—"

She swallowed hard. "It's getting worse, isn't it? Your healing ability can't deal with all of the injuries."

Mathis looked at her for a moment that stretched out too long. His pale gold eyes were tired, ringed with dark shadows and with deep lines at the corners that hadn't been there a week ago.

At last he looked away, leaving Chloe wondering what he'd been looking for.

"You're right," he admitted. "My healing powers can't keep up."

Chloe gulped. "How long—" She couldn't finish the sentence.

"I don't know. I've never known anyone this has happened to before, but from what Sven says…" He rubbed his hand over his mouth. "Eventually it will stop altogether. Burnout."

"Jesus." Chloe stepped forward automatically, ice running down her spine. "That means…"

Mathis' shoulders slumped. "If I stop fighting, he'll hurt you. You know that. You know I won't let that happen."

He placed one hand on the windowpane, over the faint reflection of Chloe. It was the closest he'd come to touching her in weeks. Chloe gulped, her mouth dry.

She saw how hard it was for Mathis to keep his distance. It was clear in the way his body turned to her, and the tension in his muscles as he forced himself to stay strong.

But she didn't know whether he saw how hard it was for her, too. It surprised her, how much she longed for his touch, as though her soul was reaching out for him. How much she *needed* him. Her, Chloe Kent, who'd never needed anyone. And never wanted anyone this badly, either.

Figures, she thought, bitterness rising in her throat. *You finally find a guy you* really *like, and touching him could mean signing your death warrant.*

"Did you get anywhere today?" Mathis' voice was barely a murmur. He was staring at her reflection, his fingers caressing the glass.

Touching the glass, Chloe corrected herself. *He's not—you're not—it's not worth even thinking about it.*

"Same as usual," she said, trying and failing to insert a bit of good humor into her voice. She just sounded resentful. "I must have been over every inch of this island, but there's nothing there." *Of course there isn't. If there was, Harper wouldn't let you wander around.*

Exploring the island might be a pointless exercise when it came to finding a way to escape Harper's clutches, but at least it kept her away from Mathis. Her walks gave them both a brief reprieve from fighting their attraction to one another—but only brief. Chloe couldn't stand to stay away too long.

She might not be able to touch Mathis, but at least she could be around him.

"No luck there," she said again. "But... I still haven't been able to get into the other tower."

Mathis' eyes met hers in the glass. "No."

Why won't he trust me that I can do this? Chloe waited for the spark of irritation to pass before she spoke.

"I know it will be dangerous. This whole *thing* is dangerous. You're out there risking your life every day—"

"That's different," Mathis cut in.

"How? Because Harper's relying on you wanting to keep me safe? His plan *relies* on me being alive, so he's not going to kill me for poking my nose in, right?"

Even as she said it she realized how weak her argument was.

"Just because he won't kill you, doesn't mean he can't hurt you." Mathis' voice was low. Defeated. "I know it makes you sick, not being able to do anything, but—"

He broke off, wincing. Chloe was rushing forward before she'd even thought of moving, her arms stretching out of their own accord. Mathis was clutching his ribs, his breath hissing between his teeth.

"It's nothing," he said. "It'll be fine in a minute."

"Liar," Chloe shot back. She was standing right next to him. Too close. There was less than a foot of space between them and the air between his body and hers was electric, waiting for one touch, one spark—

"If I can't find anything on the island..." Chloe stopped, her mouth dry.

They hadn't talked about this since the night of their failed escape attempt. It had hovered between them, looming large every time Mathis went into the ring and every night he spent sleeping in the chair by the window.

Every time he almost touched her, and didn't.

Chloe braced herself. Mathis was staring out the window, his whole body carefully, deliberately turned away from her. But she could feel his attention on her, like a ghostly caress.

They'd agreed not to do this. It was too much, too strange, and it would be playing straight into Harper's hands.

But she couldn't just sit around and watch Mathis kill himself in front of her, and not do anything.

She reached out and flattened her palm against Mathis' back. His tank-top was damp with sweat and under it, his muscles twitched with exhaustion. His breath hitched at her touch. But he didn't pull away.

"The whole... mate-bond thing." Her voice caught and she stopped. Swallowed. Tried again. "Could it help?"

Mathis' shoulders tensed but Chloe kept talking. Now that she had started she couldn't stop, as though she was caught in a current that was pulling her inevitably towards him.

"I can't keep watching you go into that ring every night and not do anything about it. I know you—you don't like me—but if strengthening the bond could make you stronger, if it could help you out there—"

"Don't, Chloe. Please." Mathis leaned against the windowsill, covering his face with one hand. When he pulled it away his eyes were full of anguish. He turned away again and dropped his voice. "If things were different… But it wouldn't be right. Not like this." He groaned and lowered his head. "Nothing about this is right."

"That doesn't answer my question." Chloe slid her hand up his back, to the tight muscles at the base of his neck. This wasn't a seduction; he was too exhausted, and she was too hollowed-out with weeks of stress to even think about that. But she longed for him all the same. To be close to him. To help him.

Mathis breathed in. Was it her imagination, or did he lean back slightly, pressing against her hand?

"It might help me heal," he said reluctantly. "But I can't ask that of you."

"God, I have had *enough* of this self-sacrificing *bullshit*, all right?" Chloe spun him around and planted her hands on his shoulders, pushing him back against the wall. "Harper is *killing* you and I *don't want you to die*."

Mathis' eyes softened, just for a moment. Then his face settled into a frown.

"And *don't* say that I'm only saying that because Harper will probably kill me if he can't use me as a hostage anymore. It's not true. I mean, he *will*, but that's not the point, the point is that—oh shit—"

Chloe's voice had been getting faster and higher and was perilously close to cracking when Mathis swore, took her face between his hands, and kissed her.

He kissed her hungrily, nibbling at her lower lip and teasing her with his tongue. Chloe melted against him, endless days of frustration flaring into bright desire. Mathis' touch was like fire tickling her skin: her cheeks, her neck, her waist and hips…

"Oh God," she whispered. She'd been wrong. She didn't just want to comfort Mathis. She wanted all of him. Now and forever.

Just like Harper intended.

"Chloe." Mathis' hands bunched in her hair. "I promised myself I wouldn't do this."

"Break your promise. *Please.*"

Mathis' hands stilled and Chloe bit back a curse. "Mathis, please. If we're going to be stuck here, however long that's going to be, I don't want to spend it alone. I can't stand it any longer."

Mathis moaned, rubbing his thumb across her cheekbone and winding his other arm around her waist. He kissed her again, weeks of frustrated passion burning against Chloe's lips.

CHAPTER 17
MATHIS

Mathis should have been strong. Even as he wrapped his arms around Chloe's deliciously soft body, guilt tore at his insides, warning him that he was about to ruin everything.

Then Chloe gasped against his lips, and the last traces of his self-control vanished.

Mathis was exhausted, but at Chloe's touch new energy surged through his body. His veins felt like they were on fire; heat burned into pure desire, and he kissed Chloe even more passionately, flicking his tongue between her lips.

He picked her up and carried her to the bed, groaning as she wrapped her legs around his waist. He was already painfully hard. He fell backward onto the bed, cradling Chloe against him. She molded her body to his, her curves soft and feminine against his hard muscles.

Mathis hissed as Chloe ran her hands down his chest. Her touch was like lightning, driving the need inside him to a tempest. He rolled sideways, pulling her shirt off as she rolled with him.

Her breasts were incredible. He ran his mouth over her skin, tasting her as his fingers found the hooks of her bra, pushed her pants down over her hips. She was all soft, beautiful curves, pale skin and tumbling dark hair and eyes that drew him in like magic.

He pulled his mouth away from her breasts and kissed her lips until they were red and puffy. A scar on his shoulder pulled as he positioned himself over her, but he ignored it.

Chloe stared up at him, her eyes huge and her lips slightly parted. "Please," she begged, and he drove into her.

She cried out as he entered her, her lips wide and her eyes closed. Mathis cradled her in his arms, a gasp escaping his own lips as he slid completely inside her. She was wet and hot and tight, and being inside her was the closest thing to paradise Mathis had ever known.

He dropped his head next to hers as they moved together, and every brush of her skin against his burned hot inside his heart, filling his veins. Chloe cried out again as he thrust into her, her body tensing. Her fingers scrambled over his shoulders, clutching at his too-short hair.

Mathis' heartbeat thundered in his ears, but there was another beat alongside it: hers. Her heart, her love, her pleasure building to a crescendo that he could feel coming with every ragged breath she took, every helpless scratch of fingernails against his scalp.

His cock throbbed as he thrust into her again. He was so close, and she was on the edge of ecstasy beneath him. He held her face in one hand and kissed her roughly, nipping at her lower lip while his other hand stroked down her side. He ran his fingertips along the delicious dip of her waist, sliding along her hips.

"Oh God," Chloe gasped, and Mathis almost came just from hearing her voice. "Oh God, Mathis, I—I—"

He reached between them to graze his thumb over the hard slick nub of her clit and she cried out, her whole body flexing under his as pleasure crashed through her body. Mathis drove into her one last time, groaning raggedly as he came. He found her lips again and kissed her, passionate and desperate, never wanting the moment to end.

Mathis held Chloe as her body trembled, the last shivers of pleasure making way for total satisfied relaxation.

He brushed a strand of hair off her cheek. Her mouth opened and he dipped his head to kiss her. Her lips were soft and she kissed him back slowly, every movement soft and languid. Mathis had never felt so at peace. Even if only for this moment, everything was perfect.

Propping himself up on one elbow, Mathis gazed down at his mate. She smiled back, her eyes hazy with pleasure. For the last three weeks he'd watched her face slowly close down, her lips becoming pinched and her eyes tense, but there was no sign of that now. Her face was clear and open. Relaxed. Happy.

Chloe raised one hand and traced her fingertips along his cheekbone. Mathis felt the tingle of her touch against newly healed skin, and the hairs on the back of his neck rose.

"It worked," she said sleepily, and Mathis' stomach went cold. "You've healed."

Guilt ripped through Mathis. He sat up, feeling sick.

You swore you wouldn't use her. What the hell do you call what you just did?

Chloe pushed herself up on her elbows. Her dark hair spilled over her bare shoulders. "What's wrong?" she asked, her eyebrows pulling together.

Mathis practically jumped off the bed. "We shouldn't have done that."

"But..." Chloe pulled her knees up to her chest. "I thought..."

Mathis couldn't let himself touch her, but he couldn't tear his eyes off her, either. She looked so small on the bed, delicate and vulnerable.

You were supposed to protect her.

Bitterness rose in Mathis' throat. He couldn't even keep that promise. Couldn't even keep his mate safe from himself.

He saw the moment Chloe realized what he'd done. Her shoulders slumped and her eyes went wide.

"Oh," she said in a small voice.

"I'm sorry. This was a mistake. This all—" He waved a hand at the bed, the room, unable to form the words he needed. *It's all a mistake. None of it should have happened. You shouldn't be here, you should be safe—but we are here, you're here and you're stuck because of me, and I can't even keep my vow to protect you.*

What would happen now? He felt stronger already, and the knowledge tasted sour in the back of his throat. He'd used her, reaching out for comfort he didn't deserve. Whatever Harper did now was his fault.

"You deserve better than this," he said under his breath. He didn't know if Chloe heard him, but he heard her sharp intake of breath.

"Shit," she muttered, and half-fell, half threw herself out of bed. Mathis jerked toward her as she scrambled to her feet, but forced himself to hold back. He curled his hands into fists at his sides. *Haven't you done enough damage already?*

Chloe was swearing, her voice shaking as she grabbed her clothes from the floor and pulled them back on.

"You don't need to—" Mathis stopped himself, cursing silently. "You take the bed. Same as before. Same deal."

"So, what? We just go back to—we keep pretending—"

Chloe's eyes were like pits in her face, and her skin was so pale it frightened him. If she got sick—he was under no illusions about Harper providing medical care.

Chloe gulped in a breath. "You can't tell me that what just happened—what we did—that wasn't..."

"It was a mistake," Mathis said again, but it didn't reassure her. Her shoulders slumped. He ran his fingernails through his short hair, hating himself. "Look—we can just pretend it didn't happen. Get some sleep. We'll figure something out in the morning—where are you going?"

"I need—" she leaned towards him and for a moment, he thought she was going to fall into his arms again. "I need some air," she muttered instead, and ran out of the room.

Mathis stared after her, an ache in his chest like someone tore his heart out.

Which is true. He had torn his own heart out, and now it was gone, fleeing from him with Chloe.

CHAPTER 18

CHLOE

Chloe got halfway across the courtyard before she started to run. It was pointless. She knew that. She wasn't going to escape by running. But that wasn't why she was doing it. Her chest was hollow and aching and her head felt strange, empty and light, as though if she put her hands up to feel it, the back of her skull would have disappeared.

She ran. She ran until the buildings were far behind her and her lungs were on fire and her head was throbbing and that was good, it was great, because if her head was throbbing then it must exist, and her body must be real and she wasn't falling apart and—

Chloe squeezed her eyes shut as the words *maybe everything will be all right* streaked through her mind like fire.

Her foot caught on something and twisted. She hit the ground and lay there, panting, as new pains shot through her. Her ankle was twisted, her hip and wrist jarred from impact. She rolled onto one side, breathing so hard she wasn't sure she wasn't sobbing, too.

And after a while her breathing calmed down. Her heartbeat slowed. And she didn't hurt anymore, not her ankle, not her wrist or hip or anything.

She smacked her fist into the ground and screamed. Of course she was fine. *Of course I am. I'm not the one being torn to pieces by wild animals every night. I'm not the one—*

Chloe groaned. The memory of Mathis' body against hers was so fresh she could almost feel it—and there it was, the pain she was looking for. She gasped as her heart twisted.

She squeezed her eyes shut but not fast enough to stop the first tears seeping out. It had felt so *right*. He'd wanted it as much as she had, she was sure of it, and he'd been so tender, gentle and loving and...

Stop it. Stop it! She pounded her fist on the ground again, hissing as gravel cut into her knuckles. *Stop being stupid. Forget that. Remember the look on his face afterwards.*

Chloe drew in a ragged breath. It was a mistake. She'd thought, just for a moment—but that had just been another mistake. She'd let the physical bond between the two of them take over, and played right into Harper's hands. And now Mathis wouldn't even look at her.

The emptiness came back, right on cue. Chloe lay still. Her body felt unmoored, like being lightheaded except everywhere, like she was falling apart...

I wish I could, she thought savagely. *If it wasn't for me, Mathis would be able to get out of here. I'm just holding him back. The only thing I could do, the only power I had, was* not *touching him... and I couldn't even do that.*

No wonder he can't even stand to look at me.

Something skittered on the path near her head. Chloe opened her eyes. For a moment, her vision was too wobbly with tears for her to see anything except shifting colors, green, yellow and blue. She blinked, and the world came into focus.

She'd run far out of the resort complex. What she'd taken for a gravel path under her was just gravel, loose stone scattered thickly on top of scraggly grass. She'd spent enough time exploring the island to know where she was: halfway along the ridge that ran the length of the island. The ground here was rough, and she was fairly sure the gravel was left over from the carefully manicured paths in the resort itself. No wonder she'd fallen.

Beyond, the grass grew thicker, a plush carpet that whispered in the breeze, and beyond that...

Chloe's vision wavered again as she stared out at the sea. Harper's island wasn't that far from the mainland, really. Too far for a normal human to swim, and she suspected too far for any of the shifters to make the journey as well, but with a boat or helicopter? It was a day trip.

She gritted her teeth. Harper must have chosen this island specifically for that. It fit his twisted mind. The mainland, and safety, were close enough to see... but too far to get to without risking drowning.

Whatever it was skittered again, and this time there was another noise too, a whirring or hum. Chloe sat up and looked around. The hum felt like it was buzzing straight into her brain.

She rubbed the back of her head and looking around. Something small, a bug or a bird, fluttered at the edge of her vision, but no one had followed her as she ran from the resort complex. The thought made her shoulders sag. *No need for security when the whole island is one big prison.*

What should she do now? The thought of going back to Mathis' rooms now made her stomach churn. She would have to go back eventually, but just...

Not yet. She closed her eyes. *I need to get myself under control first. I need to... do something.*

She held her breath, waiting for the restless energy inside her to take form. She'd take anything right now. Even the urge to do something impossible, like escape.

Nothing happened.

Chloe inhaled so fast it was almost a sob. There was nothing there. Just... emptiness.

This had never happened before. Even when it wasn't sending her hell-bent on some project or another, the energy had always been there. Biding its time. But now...

Chloe searched inside herself, her breath coming faster as she began to panic. What was happening to her?

The buzzing pressure in the back of her skull increased and then the air behind her popped. Chloe spun around and found herself face-to-face with Thandie.

"Th-thandie?" Chloe's mind whirred. *What is she doing here?*

She hadn't seen her old roommate in weeks. In fact, none of her old colleagues had exchanged so much as two words with her since Julian threw her in the fighting ring with the polar bear shifter. Which had stung... until Chloe realized they were just trying to protect themselves. All the island staff must be as terrified as she was.

And now Thandie had tracked her down, out of sight and hearing of the resort complex.

Part of Chloe was excited. Whatever Thandie had to say, it must be important.

And part of her was relieved, and guilty at feeling relieved. Because whatever this was about, at least it would be a distraction from the emptiness inside her.

"Quickly!" Thandie grabbed her arm and scrambled backwards into the shelter of two palms that had grown twisted together just below the ridgetop. Chloe's eyes flicked back towards the resort. *We're hidden back here. But why?*

Thandie grabbed Chloe's face between her hands. "I was trying to talk to you, but you didn't hear me, did you? You looked like—like it was hurting you." She bit her lip. "Is it... did Harper do something to you...?"

Chloe frowned. *Does she really not know...?* But, of course. Harper knew she was human, but it wasn't like he would see any need to share that knowledge around.

"I couldn't hear you because I'm not a shifter," she explained.

"What?" Thandie's forehead creased. "But... I thought..."

"I lied to get onto the island." Which was the truth—just not all of it.

Thandie settled back on her haunches, arms wrapped over her breasts. Crouched like that, she looked like a delicate bird perched on the rocky ground.

She was naked, of course, but by now Chloe was used to seeing naked shifters. At least Thandie wasn't covered in blood.

"Well, so much for my first question," Thandie muttered, frowning. "None of us could figure out what you were, but after Harper went off on Nora about the hiring process we thought you might have been something useful. Because of how he always only hires small shifters for house staff," she added quickly.

Chloe fought to control her expression. *Something useful.* Whatever she was, it wasn't that. "Sorry," she said, trying to keep her voice from trembling. "I'm only human."

Thandie squeezed her arm. "Well, okay, so I'm disappointed you're not a, a great white or something, but that's fine. I actually wanted to talk to you because—what was that?"

Her head whipped around and Chloe found herself scrambling to glance around the trees. There was no sign of anyone out there, but...

Thandie sighed. "I'm just imagining things."

"Or Julian is spying on us." Chloe kept staring at the grass-and-rock slope that led down to the complex. The grass was flattened where she'd fallen, and where she and Thandie had scrambled behind the palms, but everywhere else she could see it was swaying gently in the breeze. *If Julian was here, we would at least see his movements in the grass—wouldn't we?*

She turned back to Thandie to find her looking strangely at her. "You know he can do that, right? Go invisible?"

"What?" Thandie went so still, Chloe wasn't sure she was still breathing. Eventually she licked her lips. "You're not serious?"

"Dead serious." Chloe's skin prickled as she remembered the massive dragon picking her up.

She'd felt so helpless. She had screamed for Mathis to help her, to save her—and he hadn't so much as twitched. Whatever dragon magic Julian had, it was so powerful Mathis hadn't been able to sense her presence at all.

"Shit, well, okay." Thandie sucked her lips in and took a deep breath through her nose. "Fuck it. Louis didn't want me to even talk to you about this, but..." She gripped Chloe's shoulders and pulled her close, whispering into her ear. "We've got a plan to get off here on one of the cruise ships. The girls in the kitchen have it all planned out. You have to be ready to run as soon as it goes off—"

This time Chloe heard it, too. The soft crunch of someone walking on gravel.

Thandie froze, and then the air around her rushed in to fill the gap where she had been crouching. A shimmering hummingbird darted away, so fast Chloe blinked and the bird was already out of sight.

Chloe groaned. She could already guess who it was...

"Ms. Kent."

"Julian."

Chloe slumped back against the tree trunk, letting Julian see her blotchy face and tear-reddened eyes. His face went carefully blank.

Rage fizzed in Chloe's veins. She knew Julian was as much a prisoner here as she and Mathis were—but that didn't mean he had to play the part of Harper's pet so well.

"What do you want?" she growled.

Julian's jaw twitched. "Believe it or not, I'm here to check whether you're all right."

"Bullshit. You're only worried because Harper needs me alive." Chloe stared out at the distant waves, willing her eyes to stay dry. "Don't worry, I'm not going to do anything stupid."

Julian laughed bitterly. "I'd say you're only partially correct, but I expect you'd take it the wrong way. You know there's nothing I can do for either of you."

"Whatever Harper has on you must be fucking big."

"Yes." Julian paused, long enough that Chloe had to fight the urge to look at him. Eventually, he cleared his throat. "You and Mathis..."

"What about us?"

"Are you... getting along?"

Chloe's mouth twisted. "No."

She heard Julian inhale slowly. "Perhaps that is for the best."

"Like you care. It's not like it makes any difference to you, does it?" Chloe couldn't keep her anger out of her voice.

"True," Julian snapped back, losing his calm for the first time. "What's another few weeks here or there? Harper will get bored eventually, and then we'll have a new season of fresh meat."

Chloe's breath caught. If he was saying what she thought he was saying—then it was even more important that she and Mathis got off this island. Not just for themselves, but for all the other staff... and his next unsuspecting victims. She swallowed over a sudden lump in her throat.

She stood up, so quickly her vision swam. "How do I stop Harper getting *bored*, then?" she demanded, stomping up to Julian. He stared down at her, his own bitter rage dissolving.

"I wish I knew." His mouth quirked into a sardonic smile, and he gestured back down the ridge toward the resort. "After you."

***

Julian made his excuses the moment they were back on the resort grounds; Chloe supposed he had to report back to Harper.

Report back on what, she didn't know. And not knowing made her stomach churn. In retrospect, she should have at least tried to use the mind trick on him. But she'd been too frustrated, and scared, and she'd felt so empty... it probably wouldn't have worked.

It would have gone wrong. Like everything else you've tried to do.

Mathis was lying on the bed when Chloe slipped back into the room. He was staring at the ceiling. His chest rose and fell, but his eyes didn't even twitch as Chloe closed the door.

Fine. Be like that.

Chloe looked down at herself. Her feet were grimy from running across the grass and dirt, and her clothes weren't much better—but, frankly, fuck it.

Before she could change her mind, she strode across the room and lay down on the bed next to Mathis. His whole body stiffened and she could practically feel him trying to keep from touching her.

"Don't worry, I'm not going to jump you again," she muttered. "I just need to talk to you without anyone else listening in."

Mathis turned his head. His face was only a few inches from hers and for a moment, it was too easy to get lost in his golden eyes.

Chloe took a deep breath, ignoring the pain in her chest. It felt like something was trying to get out, a panicked fluttering of emotion—she pushed it down. There was no time for that. And Mathis wasn't interested, anyway. Even if he hadn't hated her before, she was sure he must hate her now that she had broken their agreement and strengthened the bond between them.

Speaking quickly, not meeting his eyes, she told him what Thandie had said.

"...They've got some sort of plan to escape. I just wish she'd given me more details. If Julian hadn't been so hot on my heels..." She swore. "Of all the times he could have followed me around the island, it had to be today."

Mathis was silent. *Too* silent. She bit her lip. "You don't think it could have anything to do with... us..."

Her voice trailed off. Mathis was so close she could feel the heat off his body. She wasn't touching him—God, she'd probably never touch him again—but even being this close…

Something roared to life inside her. She could have cried. Her restless energy was back, stronger than ever—and all it wanted was Mathis. The one thing she could never have.

"We have to get out of here," she muttered.

Mathis laughed weakly, and coughed. He lifted one hand, flexing his fingers as he stared at it. "Any bright ideas?"

Chloe ground her teeth. *Because my ideas are always so great?* "We can't just wait until Thandie's plan comes off, whatever it is." She took a deep breath. *Push down the anger. It's not useful now.* "You're… better, aren't you? So we have a bit more time." *Until you're too weak to fight anymore.* "If we need more time I could keep… healing you…"

"No." Mathis' voice was almost a bark. Chloe fought the urge to shrink back.

"Right, fine. No strengthening the bond to keep you alive." Chloe bunched her hands into fists, squeezing until her knuckles were white. "In that case… I've been thinking, and there *must* be a way to contact the outside world from here. If I can just—"

"No. Chloe, no, you can't put yourself in danger." Mathis' Adam's apple jerked. "I couldn't—if you were hurt—"

Chloe sat up. "Would you listen to yourself?" she snapped. "You're playing right into Harper's hands. He keeps you exhausted and hurt enough that you can't even think of escaping, which leaves me the only one who can actually *do* anything. And now you're telling me I can't, because of the mate bond you've spent the last three weeks ignoring?"

She couldn't lie still anymore. She jumped out of bed and paced back and forth in front of it. Her skin was itching, like something inside her was scratching to get out. She needed to *do* something. Her eyes fell on her sneakers, lying half-under the armchair.

They must have been there since the night she and Mathis tried to escape. She grabbed them, helpless angry tears making her vision shimmer.

"There's still one place on the island I haven't been. You can't tell me Harper doesn't have a phone in his private quarters. Or a computer. Or... anything, anything at all that we could use against him."

"And if he catches you?" Mathis' voice went throaty. "What am I meant to do? Just wait here until Julian swans up and tells me you're dead?"

Chloe snorted. "He's not going to kill me. I'm more valuable alive, remember? Alive and useless."

"You're not—" Mathis' voice cracked. He was sitting on the edge of the bed now, his hands gripping the mattress white-knuckled. "He doesn't have to kill you. He could just... hurt you. You're not a shifter, you can't heal like I can—"

Chloe wanted to scream at him. *Stop talking like you care!* Because he didn't. He was just worried because she was his mate—the mate he didn't even want. A real ball and chain.

She wrung the sneakers in her hands, wishing they were Harper's neck. Something fell out of them and Chloe knelt to grab it, keeping her face turned away from Mathis so he wouldn't see the tears in her eyes. The object was a flimsy black disc, slightly thicker at one end. Chloe turned it over in her hands, not really looking at it.

She took a deep breath as she stood up again.

"I *know* it would hurt you if I get hurt. But how do you think I feel, having to watch you in the ring every night?"

"Chloe—"

"Neither of us is getting out of this unharmed, Mathis. I just want us to get out of it alive."

"Chloe, what the hell?"

Chloe blinked. Mathis was lurching to his feet, an expression of utter bewilderment on his face. And not just confusion—pain. For a moment, his face was as pale as it was when he was most injured.

"I don't want us to *die*, Mathis. It's not that difficult a concept. And if I get—if something happens to me when I try to break into Harper's quarters—at least you'll still be out here. You might still have a chance."

Mathis' eyes were strangely unfocused. Chloe wasn't sure if he was looking at her, or through her. He stepped forward, hands outstretched.

"Mathis, are you even listening to me?"

Mathis froze. He rocked back on his feet, rubbing his hands over his face. "It's actually happening," he muttered, so quietly Chloe could hardly hear him. "I'm going mad. I'm losing it..."

"What are you talking about?" Chloe marched up and pulled Mathis' hands away from his face, dropping the black disc.

Mathis' eyes widened in shock. He grabbed Chloe's hands, pulling her close. "You—"

His pupils dilated as he cupped her cheek in one hand. He looked half out of his mind. Chloe frowned at him.

"Okay... what have I missed? Is this another shifter thing?"

"You *disappeared*."

Chloe stared at him. "Bullshit."

"No, I swear, one minute you were there, and the next..." He held Chloe's face in his hands and rested his forehead against hers. "You were gone. I thought I was going crazy."

"I didn't go anywhere," Chloe said, her hands sliding around Mathis' waist. Oh, God, she knew she shouldn't, she knew in a minute he would hate her again, but it felt good to hold him. So good she had to drag her mind back to what they were talking about. "I just picked up—*Oh my God*."

Chloe dropped to the floor, scrambling around for the black disc. "It's a *scale*," she gasped, looking up at Mathis. "It—you can't see me again, can you?"

A muscle was twitching at the edge of Mathis' mouth. Taking pity on him, Chloe reached up and took his hand.

His eyes widened. "Julian."

"It must be one of his scales. I kicked him up pretty bad when he grabbed me off the boat—well, I *tried*. It must have slipped into my sneaker..."

"His scales have the same shielding ability that he has." Mathis' voice was soft with wonder. "I'd heard that some dragons have powers, but this is something else."

Chloe's mouth twisted. "And it's been in my sneaker all this time. We could have..." Her mind was racing. "We still could. We could use it..."

A plan flashed into existence in her mind, bright and clear and full of hope. She explained it to Mathis, speaking so quickly she wasn't sure he would follow. But he did.

"...there must be *something*. Even just a phone line. Harper must have some way of communicating from the mainland to let the staff know he's visiting, and there's no way the rich assholes he brings over as his guests are here for some sort of device-free detox."

Mathis' hand tightened around hers and she sighed.

"You're going to tell me not to, aren't you? That I shouldn't put myself in danger."

Mathis knelt down. Chloe was suddenly aware that thanks to the magic in Julian's scale, the two of them were essentially in their own little world. No one could see them, or hear them, or—*I never would have even thought about this a month ago, but no one can* smell *us, either.*

It's just us. Together. Like that first night...

Mathis touched the scale. It was a dull, charcoal black, thicker and slightly ridged at one end, smooth and thin at the other. It didn't look magic.

Then he stared into Chloe's eyes. *That* was more like magic. Those pale gold eyes. *Lion's* eyes.

The eyes of a man she'd tried desperately not to fall in love with, and failed.

"Chloe..." Mathis closed his eyes briefly, and when he looked at her again his eyes were clear and determined. "I can't force you to do nothing. That would make me as bad as Harper. If you have a plan... I'll help. But on one condition. Whatever you find in Harper's tower, if you can get a message out or not, you keep that scale on you. Don't come back. Don't let anyone see you again. You have to disappear. And the next time Harper has guests come to the island, or heads back to the mainland himself, you stow away. Without me."

Chapter 19

Mathis

Another day. Another fight.

But today was different. Today, they had a plan.

Mathis just hoped it didn't end as badly as their last one.

He glanced up at the window to the viewing room, squinting through the spotlights. He couldn't see Chloe, but for the first time, he could *sense* her presence up there.

His skin prickled. *You're treading a fine line there. One step closer to a point you'll never come back from.*

Or maybe he'd already passed it.

He'd been so careful, resisting the mate bond's pull. One moment of weakness, and all that work was undone.

He felt stronger than before. Being close to Chloe without touching her had been a constant ache, but now that he'd touched her lips with his and held her soft body against his own again, felt her tremble as he claimed her—the mate bond burnt like wildfire through his veins. Chloe was his mate. He would do anything for her.

And it terrified him.

Harper was using his mate as bait for a reason, and that reason couldn't just be to keep him in line. The man was too sadistic for that. Mathis was just figuring out what he thought Harper's real game was, and it chilled him to the bone.

Focus.

The sound of metal grating on metal pulled him from his thoughts. Chloe's presence in the room above still tugged at his senses, but he moved his focus to the ring.

Mathis rolled his shoulders back as Sven, the wolf shifter, entered the ring through the opposite door. Something pulled in his left shoulder and he winced. The mate bond made him stronger, healing his surface wounds, but even it couldn't pull his healing abilities back from the brink.

Sven.

Mathis.

Sven cocked his head, his eyes narrowing as he looked Mathis up in down. *Shit. You broke, didn't you?*

Inside Mathis, his lion snarled, mane puffing out in defensive anger. *That's none of your business.*

A buzzer sounded. Mathis exchanged a look with Sven, and shifted.

His body protested. Shifting while he was injured always hurt, but with injury layered over injury it was excruciating. Mathis stood on all fours, panting as he waited for his head to stop spinning.

It's all of our business, Mathis. Sven's voice was grim. *I hope you haven't slept with her—*

Jesus, Sven!

Sven pulled his teeth back over his fangs, stalking around the ring with his belly close to the ground. Mathis set pace with him. Circling. Falling into the rhythm of the fight.

I'm serious, kid. I thought I made it clear. You need to stay away from that girl, for all of our sakes.

What the hell are you talking about?

You. Her. I've seen this happen before.

What aren't you telling me, Sven? Mathis growled. *You were cryptic enough last time. Same as everyone else on this bullshit island. Stop playing games!* He was half listening to Sven, and half paying attention to the window above them. He needed to be alert the moment Chloe made her move.

Fine. You want the truth? Sven's psychic voice was completely flat. **You remember the ibex shifter, Aisha, right? The crazy girl? Well, you and Chloe together, that's step one in Harper's game plan. And whoever's left afterwards, that's step two. Like Aisha.**

Mathis froze. **He's going to kill her.**

Or you. Probably her, though. A lion shifter who's lost his mind with grief is gonna provide more fun in the ring than a human, that's for sure.

No!

Mathis forgot Sven. He spun towards the window. He had to tell Chloe. She couldn't go ahead with the plan. It was too dangerous. She couldn't—

Sven hit him in the side, locking his jaws onto Mathis' injured shoulder. Mathis roared.

What the fuck, Sven?

The wolf shifter leapt back, circling around Mathis so quickly he almost stumbled over his own paws keeping up with him.

You think Harper wants to watch us stand here yapping? You want to hold off step two as much as I do, then we both need to give him a show. Same as every night.

Mathis' head was thudding in time with the pain throbbing in his shoulder, and Chloe's presence was a constant light in the back of his mind. But he caught on to Sven's words.

What do you mean, 'as much as you do'?

Sven didn't smile. Wolves couldn't. But his psychic voice was heavy with black, grim humor.

You think any of us want to face up to a crazy lion, kid?

Movement in the viewing room caught Mathis' eye. And he wasn't the only one. Sven leapt back and quirked his head, glancing up at the window.

Something's happening up there.

Even in Mathis' head, Sven's voice was cagy, and he moved quickly to the far end of the circular room. Mathis rolled his eyes to follow the wolf's path, and then focused on the window again.

He understood Sven's wariness. *He figures something's happened to Chloe, and doesn't want to be stuck in here with a lion enraged by seeing his mate in danger.*

I don't blame him.

From the ring, Mathis could just see what was happening in the viewing room. Chloe was bent over, supporting herself on the back of a sofa while Harper yelled out someone out of sight.

Chloe! Mathis let his psychic shout broadcast to all the shifters in "hearing" distance. He didn't need to fake the concern in his telepathic voice. His fur itched as Chloe retched again. He knew it was all an act, but that didn't matter to his instincts. *CHLOE!*

He paced up and down the center of the ring, eyes fixed on his mate. She looked sick. Surely she couldn't fake how pale her face was?

Mathis gritted his teeth. *You said you trusted her. So* trust *her.*

Chloe staggered as Harper grabbed her by the shoulder and spun her away, towards the door. He pointed and shouted something and she crept away, one hand over her mouth and the other clutching her stomach.

It's working. Mathis turned his sigh of relief into an angry snarl. Then his heart sank as Harper snapped his fingers and pointed after Chloe. One of the servers peeled away from their station at the edge of the room and trailed after her.

Shit. This isn't going to work if she has a babysitter.

Mathis braced himself, mind whirring. He had to cause a distraction. His eyes flickered sideways and met Sven's wary gaze.

Time for some of that mated shifter rage.

Mathis breathed deeply, gathering his energy, and sprang.

He hit the wall opposite the window three feet above Sven's head, ignoring the wolf's yelp as he darted out of the way. Muscles screaming, Mathis twisted as soon as his paws hit the wall, keeping momentum as he pushed off and hurled himself at the window.

He hit the window shoulder-first, whipping one fore-leg around to scratch at the glass with his claws. The window shuddered in its frame, and then gravity caught hold, dragging Mathis back down to the ground.

Blood thundering in his ears Mathis pounded across the concrete floor and leapt up again, smashing into the window with all his weight. Glass screamed against metal as the window shuddered in its frame. This time when he fell to the ground, flakes of concrete fell with him.

Harper wasn't interested in Chloe anymore. The server he'd ordered to tail her fled to the back of the room out of Mathis' sight—but not out the door. Not after Chloe.

It's up to her now.

Mathis crouched. The snarl that tore from his throat this time was pure fury. He didn't need to pretend he was enraged by his mate's distress. All the anger and frustration of the past month poured through him like liquid fire.

Distraction? He'd cause a distraction, all right. And if his distraction took out the window and Harper and his bastard dragon lap-dog at the same time, all the better.

CHAPTER 20

CHLOE

Chloe hustled back to the room as fast as she could while still pretending she was in the grip of a sudden vomiting bug. As soon as the bedroom door closed behind her she straightened up.

Twenty seconds to rinse her mouth and spit in the sink. Ten to pull the dragon scale from its hiding place in the lining of her bag. In less than a minute, she was out the door again, the scale tucked safely into her bra.

Less than a minute—but out of how many minutes total? On an island full of shifters, it couldn't be too long before someone noticed she was missing.

Chloe put her head down and marched toward the main building. She turned her back on the tower that housed the fighting ring, aiming for its counterpart at the other end of the building. The one place left that she had never managed to get into, even when she was on the housekeeping roster. The rooms there were off-limits to everyone except senior staff.

And one senior staff member in particular always finished her evening shift around now, while the boss was being entertained by his prisoners...

Chloe jogged up the steps to the veranda that looped around the second story. She felt incredibly exposed—until she looked down and saw nothing where her shadow should be. Chloe gulped. The world seemed to tilt.

She really was invisible.

This is nuts, she thought, and bit back a sudden gurgle of laughter. Seeing her feet move over the pale stone and no shadow following made her feel like a badly-rendered computer game character. Now all she needed to do was complete her fetch quest.

Chloe sped around a corner and had to throw herself sideways as she almost barreled straight into her old manager.

Nora was hurrying along the veranda with her head down, rubber gloves clenched in one hand and the other dragging her cart of cleaning equipment. She didn't look up as Chloe yelped and clattered out of the way, almost tripping over her cart.

She can't hear me. She has no idea I'm even here. Chloe's heart leapt. She'd imagined sneaking up on Nora while she worked and grabbing her keys. But this was going to be much easier.

Chloe kept pace with Nora inside and waited while she hit the button for the clanky, old-fashioned elevator. Her keys were on an elastic cord at her waist. She jingled them absently as she waited for the elevator.

And when it arrived, and she stepped forward, Chloe reached out and unhooked the ring of keys from her waist.

Simple as that, Chloe thought smugly, and fled.

She knew exactly where she was going. Back along the veranda, feet slapping on pale stone. Across the courtyard spotted with twisted trees in shallow pots. Right to the door set in the side of the second tower.

Chloe looked up at the stone tower, heart thudding in her ears. *This is it*. If her hunch was right, this was where she would be able to find a way out of here, for her and Mathis and everyone else trapped on this hellhole island.

And if it wasn't...

Her fist clenched around the keys. *It has to be.*

Even though Chloe knew no one could see her, the back of her neck was itching like crazy. This courtyard was visible from almost every window in the building. Unfortunately, the door here was the only way into the tower.

Which has got to be deliberate, Chloe thought. She slotted the key into the lock. *So I've just got to hope that no one is watching right now... Please, Mathis, make your distraction a good one...*

The key turned. The door swung open. Chloe darted inside and forced herself to ease it shut instead of slamming it. The scale only silenced her, not anything she crashed into.

She leaned back against the closed door, panting. Her whole body felt electrified. *No turning back now.*

The first room in the tower was dark, and it took Chloe's eyes a moment to adjust. *No windows*, she thought, and her eyes went immediately to the floating staircase that wound around the edges of the room. No light poured in from where it opened out onto the next floor. *So no windows there, either.*

Which was weird, cos it sure as hell had looked from the outside like there were windows in the tower.

Chloe stepped forward. The entrance-level room was furnished in the style she'd come to expect from Harper: gaudy bordering on tacky. Chloe hadn't even thought you could *get* sofas in gold leather. And then there was what looked like a fur-covered beanbag thrown carelessly under the staircase. The whole place was garish as hell... And perfectly clean. *Nora must have just finished up in here when I caught up with her.*

She slipped one hand into her pocket, feeling the reassuring smooth edge of her cellphone. *Right. Time to explore—*

Two things happened at the same time. First, her cellphone started beeping and buzzing like the Fourth of July was going off in her pocket.

Second, the fur-covered bean bag under the stairs surged up, and Chloe found herself staring into the eyes of the polar bear that had tried to tear her to pieces three weeks ago.

He can't see me, she told herself. The bear raised its muzzle and sniffed the air. *He can't see me and he can't smell me. Oh God.*

She had to get out. She was still leaning against the door. All she had to do was turn the handle and she'd be out. Lock the door behind her. That would stop him for a few minutes, at least. Enough time for her to run.

But she couldn't move. She couldn't even move her hand to the door handle.

She could barely breathe.

The bear shambled to its feet. It moved heavily, as though its limbs were weighted down. Chloe gulped. She remembered how those heavy paws had slammed into the wall only inches from her head. The bear's limbs weren't weighted down. They were just heavy as hell. Massive, claw-tipped mallets of flesh and bone.

It tipped its head on one side and Chloe had to remind herself, over and over, that it couldn't see her it couldn't smell her and it couldn't hear her. It couldn't. The scale kept her safe.

The bear huffed and lumbered towards her.

It can't see me it can't hear me it can't smell me.

Long, broken claws clacked on the floorboards as the bear shambled towards the door. Chloe's feet were glued to the floor.

Maybe it couldn't smell her but she could smell it. The thick, rotting smell that clung to the bear filled her nostrils, choking in her lungs. It was four feet away. Three. So close she could feel its foul breath.

Mathis—

Mathis couldn't help her. She was in this by herself.

Chloe threw herself sideways. The bear's paw just grazed her side and there was a table right in front of her, covered in glitzy ornaments. Delicate, shatterable, *noisy* ornaments.

She twisted in midair, landing on the floor inches away from the table. Inches away from making a noise that would have betrayed her presence.

If the bear's paw grazing her side hadn't done that already.

Chloe sprawled on the floor, too terrified to move. If the bear had noticed her—she didn't know what she would do. She didn't have any weapons. She was helpless, and afraid, and out of ideas.

The bear swung its heavy head around. It sniffed at its paw. It would have been almost funny if Chloe wasn't so terrified.

And then it turned away, fumbled at the latch with one massive paw, and left.

The door swung shut behind it, and Chloe collapsed like a puppet whose strings had all been cut.

It didn't see me. She gulped in a ragged breath. *And it was too stupid to figure out I was here. Thank God.*

And my phone...

Chloe's gasping breaths dissolved into desperate giggles. Her phone was still buzzing. In her terror, she hadn't even noticed it.

And neither had the polar bear shifter.

"Fucking hell, Harper," she choked out between giggles. "You run your own fucking death island, and you have an *unsecured Wi-Fi network* in your villain's lair?"

She pulled out her phone. It had automatically connected to the network the moment the door opened—there must be some sort of dampener in the outer walls of the tower. And now hundreds and hundreds of notifications were pouring in. Months' worth of them.

So many that Chloe could barely do anything on the phone without one popping up. She swiped them away, hissing with irritation and trying not to read them.

Friends. Family. Names flashed by but she couldn't let herself pause long enough to read them. She had to focus.

Then maybe she'd see them again one day.

She blinked until her eyes cleared enough for her to navigate to her email app. She typed in the address Mathis had given her—his sister's—and the short message they'd agreed on.

Coordinates. Names. A secret phrase that meant Francine would know just how serious things were.

Mathis had told her his sister must know something was wrong. They had a special connection, being twins and shifters. They could always tell when the other one was in danger.

Well, her Spidey-sense must have been going haywire for the last month, Chloe thought. *I hope she's ready and waiting to hit "go" on a rescue mission...*

Fingers crossed, Chloe hit Send.

Sending. Sending... gone.

Chloe was about to leave when her phone buzzed again. Another new email.

An out-of-office.

From Mathis' sister.

Chloe read it, hardly able to believe what her eyes were seeing. Francine Delacourt was on indefinite leave. Urgent messages to be sent to the acting CEO. *This email is being monitored but please allow forty-eight hours for...*

Chloe's fingers clenched around the phone. She didn't have forty-eight hours. Neither did Mathis. And they sure as hell didn't have forty-eight hours for some assistant to flick over the email and probably pass it off as spam or a phishing scam.

Why didn't I ask him for more addresses? Chloe's hand was shaking. Their plan had relied on workaholic Francine, whom Mathis had assured her was constantly glued to her phone, receiving the message. Email only. Apparently billionaire heiresses didn't do phone calls from unknown numbers.

And now it turned out she was on freaking *vacation.*

"What the hell am I meant to do now?" Chloe asked the empty room, her voice cracking.

Whatever you can.

Chloe blinked. The voice was hers, but also... not hers. She shivered, then steadied herself.

All right, voice inside my head. You have a good point.

Do whatever she could? She could only think of one thing. And it was sure as hell not going to make Mathis happy.

Chloe opened another app and started to upload the video of the fight between Mathis and the wolf shifter. It was slow. *Too* slow.

She checked the Wi-Fi connection. It had picked up the notifications okay, but it wasn't strong enough for the plan slowly taking form inside her head.

She needed to get closer to the source. The router.

It must be upstairs.

Chloe took the steps two at a time, balancing with one hand against the wall. She thought she would feel light-headed, but instead her head was clear as glass.

The upload bar sped up. She was getting closer. Time to start drafting. Mathis wasn't going to like it—hell, *she* didn't like it—but it was what she did best, after all.

She started typing. Hashtags. Keywords. Tagging in influencers. SEO, optimized for a very specific search engine, one she was certain must exist from everything Mathis had said about his shifter friends.

Five drafts. Ten. One of them must go viral. Especially with the footage she was attaching to them. She selected all the distribution channels she had accounts for, and paused with her finger over the send button.

Please don't hate me, Mathis, she prayed, and hit Send.

"*Shit.*" Of course. Nothing was instant, even on the internet. The *Pending* icon blinked, maddeningly slow.

She had to stay here until it was done. It could take minutes, and maybe she didn't have minutes. But she had to risk it.

And while she was here...

Chloe tore her eyes away from the blinking icon. *A watched Tweet never twits*, she thought, *and there's plenty else to look at here. Hell.* Heaps plenty.

She hadn't looked around when she sprinted up the stairs. Her eyes had been glued to the phone.

The upstairs room was an Aladdin's cave of *crazy shit*.

Chloe dropped her phone to her side as she stared around, and her mouth fell open. The entrance-level room had been glitzier than Glinda the Good Witch's underwear, but this was something else. It was still garish enough to make Chloe wince, but it was organized.

Like the world's trashiest museum, Chloe thought.

She'd expected, somewhat nauseously, that this would be the bedroom. Instead, a grid of glass-covered cabinets filled the floor. There wasn't a speck of dust on any of them; Nora had been very thorough.

As for what she'd been dusting...

Chloe frowned as she made her way down the aisle between two rows of display cases. It was just... *stuff*. Shoes. Some hair doodads. A few cellphones. Earrings, but not expensive looking.

Wallets. Photos. Chloe started to feel sick.

These weren't museum cases. They were trophy cabinets. And she thought she could guess what a man like Harper kept trophies of.

People like her and Mathis.

Chloe gulped and averted her eyes. Her gaze fell on a larger cabinet at the end of the room. There was something different about this one. It was set apart from the others, with a leather-cushioned sofa in front of it. As though Harper liked to lounge in front of it and look at his treasure.

She stepped closer. The case was different to the others. More complex. There were clear tubes running along the inside of the glass, filled with some sort of swirling black smoke. There was a strange lock on the clasp that held the glass lid on. Chloe leaned closer. It almost looked as though it was set up for the glass tubes to break if someone forced the case open—but what purpose would that serve? Covering the objects inside with glass shards and smoke?

The objects inside the case gleamed, lit from below by soft display lights. It was too dark for her to see them clearly from here. Chloe had an impression of swirling blues and purples, like the colors made by spilled gas on concrete. Smooth curves.

Chloe gasped. They looked like eggs—but not any sort of eggs she'd seen before. Each one was as big as her head, with a dimpled surface that made them seem to change color in the soft white light. Green. Blue. Purple. Black.

There was a sound behind her. Footsteps? Chloe ignored them. No one could see her, after all. And she had to wait until her messages were sent. She leaned over with her hands on her thighs, staring at the eggs.

What sort of creature laid eggs like that?

Take a photo. Chloe's fingers itched, but she didn't touch the camera app on her phone. Getting evidence of Harper's insanity out there was one thing, but these eggs must be one of Harper's pieces of leverage. And Chloe had a pretty good idea who he was using them to control.

"Feeling better, Ms. Kent?"

Julian Rouse. Speak of the devil.

Chloe's mouth went dry. She spun around, trying to slip her phone back into her pocket, but Julian's hand darted out and grabbed her wrist.

"How did you get in here?" Julian's eyes narrowed. "You've got one of my scales on you. Where?"

Chloe's hand flew automatically to where it was hidden. "Uh... basically, my cleavage..."

Julian snatched his hand away. "Ah," he said. His mouth made shapes, as though he was looking for more words and completely failing to find them.

"If you want it back..."

Julian stepped back, his face becoming absolutely expressionless. "That won't be necessary. Though you should be thankful Harper sent me to fetch you, instead of one of the staff. If anyone else had found your bedroom empty the whole island would be on high alert by now."

"Sent to fetch me? What are you talking about? And how did you find me here, anyway?"

Julian waved her question away. "I can tell when people are using pieces of my power. But that's not important right now. You need to come with me." His eyes went dark. "It's Mathis."

Chapter 21

Mathis

The world had disappeared. Mathis was only aware of himself, and that only barely. He didn't all seem to be there. Bits were missing. Floating away.

There was a constant low buzzing in the back of his mind, like a badly tuned television. White noise from a badly tuned brain. Food would help. Or Chloe, though he wished that wasn't true. Wished she'd never come here, that she was far away, safe from it all. Safe from Harper. Safe from him.

He had failed her. Chloe deserved better than to be tied to a fool who'd fallen so easily for Harper's trap.

At least it won't be for long.

The thought tasted bitter in his mind. He knew it was coming. Harper had forced him to fight to the end of his body's strength, and he'd pushed himself further. For the plan.

For Chloe.

At least he could be sure his body was going to give out before his mind. He wouldn't end up like that poor ibex shifter, her human mind lost and her animal self crazed with fear.

Mathis drifted for a while, his mind floating above the white noise, above the deep ache of wounds that weren't healing properly. That would never heal properly.

It didn't matter. Mathis felt like it should, somehow. The end of him. Shouldn't it hurt? Shouldn't he be afraid?

Nothing. He floated through endless gray fog, and nothing touched him.

Nothing from the outside, at least. No teeth. No claws. And he had one thought inside him, keeping his heart warm.

Chloe's safe. He can't hurt her now. She'll stay hidden...

"What happened to him? What did Harper do?"

Chloe's voice seemed to come from a long way away. Someone replied to her, their voice a muddy blur. Mathis didn't try to listen. He was focused on his mate, icy horror pouring through his body.

She didn't hide. She's here.

He won't keep her alive after you're gone.

"No," he cried out, except the word didn't go anywhere. It bounced inside his head. Had he even said anything?

No! he screamed, and felt someone throw up a telepathic barrier, the psychic equivalent of putting their hands over their ears. *Chloe!*

He struggled out of the fog, coming back into his body. Back into the world. Into pain.

He hurt. *Everything* hurt.

What did I do?

Chloe was somewhere out there, somewhere past the pain that lanced through him with every breath. He wanted to talk to her. He wanted to say, *You have to run.* Wanted to lie to her, tell her *Everything's fine, I'm fine—it was the polar bear shifter—Harper sent him in after I refused to calm down, but I beat him...*

Or had he? Mathis shook his head, trying to line up the snapshots of memory that had come up out of the fog with him. He remembered turning to fight the bear, but after that it got fuzzy.

"Mathis? Mathis, can you hear me?" Chloe's voice was like cool water on his thumping brain. He tried to reply, but his mouth wasn't working properly.

He felt small hands slide under his head, pulling it up to rest on a warm lap. *Chloe.* Her fingers brushed over his forehead and down his cheek. Soft skin against his sweat-matted fur.

Fur? Mathis' brain stirred. He was still in his lion shape. How could that be possible? He always shifted back after the fights. Even when he was hurt.

Chloe stroked his forehead again. "God, Mathis, what happened?"

This time he managed to make a noise, even if it wasn't words. He was lying on something cool and hard. The floor? But not the concrete of the gym—it was smoother than that...

"Give him this. He'll need food." A man. Julian? Mathis pulled up an image of the man in his mind. The dragon shifter. Harper's lapdog... who kept trying to keep him and Chloe alive.

Maybe Sven was right. Maybe the other prisoners here were as desperate to keep things from escalating as he was.

Too late for that.

"If he can even eat it in this condition..." *Chloe.* Something cool pressed against his lips, and then sweet liquid dripped into his mouth. Mathis swallowed. It was some sort of energy drink. Something to give his body the energy to heal enough to take in more nutrients...

So he could fight again.

He closed his mouth. He couldn't do it anymore. Maybe if he stayed weak, Harper would give him time to recover. The mate bond couldn't be strong enough yet for him to risk moving to step two, surely? He still had time. *Chloe* still had time. And even if he was like this, injured, more time with Chloe was sweeter than anything else he could think of.

"Mathis, drink it. Please." Chloe's springy hair brushed against his forehead. She whispered in his ear. "It's all done, Mathis. What we talked about. Please. You need to recover."

Mathis knew Julian could probably hear her whisper, but for this one moment he didn't care. Let him wonder what she meant and whether he should report it to the man who held his leash.

He was with his mate. Nothing else mattered.

He opened his eyes. Chloe's face was inches above his, and when she saw him looking up at her, a smile dawned on her lips.

"Hey," she whispered. Then she took a deep breath, and her smile faded away.

She looked up at a shadowy figure that must be Julian, and then back at Mathis, biting her bottom lip. "Just stay like this for now, okay? As a lion. I don't know how much you remember, but you were in a pretty bad way after—after the fight." Her voice dropped. "You still are. Julian carried you back here in his dragon shape."

Mathis raised his head, biting back a snarl as pain lanced through his skull. He couldn't speak to her in this form—maybe Julian could pass on his telepathic messages, but right now Mathis didn't want anything to do with the dragon shifter. He sighed heavily and, even though he knew it was useless, tried to whisper into Chloe's mind: *Harper? Is he bored yet? Does he know our bond is becoming stronger?*

Chloe didn't hear him, of course. She ran her fingers through his mane, over and over, her gaze becoming unfocused. Mathis ached with the need to communicate with her. To pull her out of whatever thoughts were darkening her expression—or at least be able to ask her to share them.

After a few minutes, Chloe gave a shaky laugh. "I have no idea what's going to happen now." Her voice was low, pitched for only him to hear. "Harper... Harper seemed entertained. I guess. He was glad I got back in time to watch the, the rest of the fight." She swallowed. "But you're okay. You're okay."

Mathis knew from the way she said it how close he'd been to not being okay.

After a while, the energy drinks started to take effect. He gathered enough strength to push himself up until he was sitting Sphinx-pose, if the Sphinx had to lean against a wall to stay upright. Chloe moved with him, keeping close against his side. Julian slipped out as Chloe buried her face in Mathis' mane and stifled a sniff.

Everything that Mathis was ached with longing.

She was miserable, and he couldn't help her. Not in this shape.

He was exhausted, and in more pain than he'd ever been in. The white noise was still there at the edges of his mind, a reminder of how damaged his body was.

But his mate needed him.

Mathis reached inside himself, gathering all the energy he had left, and shifted.

The world always looked different through human eyes than lion eyes, but it never looked this gray.

"Chloe," Mathis gasped. Where was she?

Shadows clustered at the edges of Mathis' vision as tried to stand up. The room spun and then Chloe was beside him, supporting his weight and pulling him toward the bed.

"You shouldn't have done that." Chloe's voice sounded somehow a long way off and very close at the same time. The world tilted, and the mattress gave against Mathis' back, the sheets soft and cool on his fevered skin. Her voice was tense as she muttered: "Julian said you're too badly injured to shift."

Julian was gone; even in this state, Mathis could tell that. Or maybe the dragon shifter was still here, but had shielded himself. No matter. Nothing mattered anymore.

Mathis took stock, wincing as new injuries multiplied the pain of old ones. Chloe was a dark blur in his vision, just out of reach. Mathis' heart twisted.

"You shouldn't be here."

His voice was too harsh, tight and raw with pain. Chloe's sharp intake of breath cut through the pulse thudding in his ears. He had to hold on to that. To *her*.

He raised one shaking hand and wiped his face. *What happened last night?*

"We had a plan," he said, and his voice rattled like gravel inside his skull. He winced, but kept going, kept trying to find his way back into his own memories. "You were meant to hide—"

Chloe had been pacing angrily, a dark blur against the white walls of the bedroom. Now she stalked over and stood beside the bed, arms crossed defensively.

"There was a change in plans. Apparently. Because I don't recall the plan being for you to almost *kill* yourself." Her voice grew quieter, but didn't soften. "That wasn't the deal. We were meant to get out of this together."

"If we could."

"That's not what you said. That's not what we *agreed*."

Chloe rubbed her face, and Mathis' eyesight must have been improving because now he could see how bloodshot her eyes were. Her cheeks were blotchy, puffy and red from being rubbed.

Mathis' insides wrenched. She might not be crying now but she clearly had been before he woke up. Because of *him*.

Memories began to surge up in his mind, bubbling from deep within where pain and exhaustion had crushed them down.

"You were leaving," he said slowly as images flashed in his mind. "Just like we'd planned. You pretended to be sick, and Harper sent you away. But he was going to send someone after you, and that would have ruined everything. I had to stop him..." He frowned. "But I don't remember what happened after that."

Chloe was staring at him, her face wracked with unhappiness. "You were... you weren't *you*."

Mathis' heart dropped. "Oh, God, Chloe, I—If I hurt you—"

Chloe was shaking her head. "No. No, nothing like that, don't be stupid. I know you'd never hurt me. But you were... far away." She wiped her hand over her eyes again. "I'm glad you're back. That's all."

"Jesus." Mathis dropped his head into his hands. "I'm so sorry."

"Uh," Chloe said, her voice under control again. "That's not all. When I was in Harper's tower..."

"What happened?"

She didn't answer right away. "I got the word out," she said at last. "Now we just have to wait and see what happens. Hope someone pays enough attention to come and stop Harper."

"Let's hope so."

She didn't say "Come and save us", he thought, his throat dry. *Just to stop him. She doesn't really think we're getting out of here.*

"We will get out of here," he murmured, trying to sound like he believed his own words. "I promise you. It'll be just like I said. You can leave all of this behind you. Forget it ever happened. Like a bad dream."

Wordlessly, he reached out to her. She fell into his arms, soft and warm and so right it made his heart hurt.

He was too bone-tired to do anything except this. Just lie together, here, skin to skin for however long they had left.

As he drifted into sleep, he half-thought that when he woke up—when he was feeling better, when he could think without his head aching—they would plan out their next steps. He thought there would still be time.

Instead, when he woke up, she was gone.

CHAPTER 22

CHLOE

The sun was so bright the whole island seemed to sizzle in its glare. Heavy ripples of heat filled the low gardens and made the sandstone walls of the estate shimmer like a mirage.

Walking beside Julian, Chloe was looking forward to getting back inside. Even the tacky décor of the Gold Lounge would be preferable to this blinding assault on her eyes.

How the hell is it this hot? It's not even summer yet. Chloe plucked at her collar.

"You'd think it was summer already," she complained. "Is this going to take long?"

Julian didn't seem affected by the heat at all. He was wearing his usual uniform of a crisp button-down and dark suit pants, as though he was walking down a city street instead of dodging sunbeams on a tropical island.

He was escorting Chloe to a surprise meeting with Harper. Chloe wondered what the hell he wanted, but she wasn't too worried. The opposite in fact.

Her success the night before had filled her with a kind of buzzing impatience. Stifled energy crackled along her bones. Maybe the message she'd sent out would work, and maybe it wouldn't. Either way she wasn't going to wait around and let chance decide her fate.

Mathis had almost died last night. She couldn't just sit tight and hope help was on its way. She *couldn't*.

They were halfway to the main residence when Chloe realized Julian had never answered her question.

"I said, is this going to take long?" she repeated, squinting as she tried to get a look at Julian through the glare of the sun.

A muscle twitched in his cheek.

"Oh, come on, you can tell me," said Chloe, laughing. Maybe it was the sleep deprivation, but she felt drunk. Reckless. She covered her mouth and muttered, "We both know you're not exactly on Harper's side, here."

Julian's face was entirely blank, apart from the panicked twitch of that one muscle. Not meeting Chloe's eye, he said coolly, "Keep walking, Ms. Kent."

Chloe's stomach went cold. "Why won't you answer my question?"

"Because I don't want to reassure you by saying 'Not long'."

"What are you talking about?"

Chloe stopped walking. The air around Julian shimmered, and Chloe blinked. *It's like he's fading in and out of sight, super fast. What the hell?*

"I'm going back to the room," she said, backing away. "Mathis should have woken up by now, and I want to see him before I see Harper. I don't want him to wake up and find me gone."

"Believe me, it's preferable to the alternative." Julian's voice was barely audible, a bitter hiss that filled Chloe with dread.

No way in hell I'm sticking around to find out what the alternative is. Chloe drove one foot into the gravel and spun around, ready to race back to Mathis' room.

Strong fingers closed around her arm, yanking her backwards.

"I'm sorry. Please believe that." Julian's face was a white mask as he pulled her along the path. Chloe tried to kick his legs, but it was no use. Her own feet made heavy divots in the gravel as she tried to brace herself.

"Sorry—like you were last time? When the polar bear almost gutted me? Mathis!" she screamed, painfully aware of the layers of glass and stone between her and her protector. "Help me!"

Something fluttered past her head and exploded with a *whoomph* of air behind her. Julian let her go so quickly she almost fell. Staggering, Chloe darted out of reach, and looked back to see Thandie, naked, crouching over Julian's prone body.

"Run!" Thandie cried. "Get to the beach—there's a—"

Her shouts were cut off as Julian groaned and pushed himself to his feet. There was a flash of black scales as he reached for her and Thandie jumped back, shifting mid-air. Air rushed in to fill the space as the human woman shrank and transformed into a glittering hummingbird.

Thandie-the-bird darted skyward, wings beating furiously.

She wasn't fast enough.

Julian didn't shift, but he moved supernaturally quickly, whipping out one arm and snatching Thandie from the air.

"Let her go!" Chloe screamed. "If you hurt her—"

She scanned the garden for something, anything she could use as a weapon. Thandie's hummingbird was tiny, its wings beating helplessly against Julian's fist.

There was nothing. Just gravel and spindly palms, and the hideous glare of the sun.

Chloe groaned. *Damn it, Thandie, why did you have to do this now? You should have left me and gotten yourself to safety—*

She could only hope that Julian hadn't heard Thandie mention the beach. Their plan must be underway. If he let her go now… at least one of them might escape.

"Please don't hurt her. Just let her go, Harper doesn't need to know anything about it."

"Oh, I wouldn't say that."

Harper strolled around a corner, smiling beatifically. Chloe gulped. She hadn't even heard him arrive.

"Mr. Harper, there's been a misunderstanding," she burst out. *Do it. Do it now. You have to try.* She gathered her scattered thoughts, clenching her fists tight as though she was holding herself in one piece. *Time for Ms. Jedi Mind Trick to come out and play.*

She reached inside herself, building up a vision of what she needed to be. Confident. Authoritative. The sort of person you couldn't say no to.

Walking up to Harper, she fixed him with a wide grin.

"There's been a misunderstanding," she repeated. She didn't sound angry; she burnt off the weakness of those emotions before the words reached her lips, distilling the gritted fear and rage into a smooth, soporific sing-song. Something inside her fluttered as fast as Thandie's wings. "Tell Julian to let Thandie go. You don't want her at all."

Harper's lazy grin began to slip off his face. "No, you're right."

Chloe took a deep breath. The words didn't matter so much as the tone. So she just let herself talk, focusing on drawing Harper in.

"I know, right? It just makes sense. She's not important. You've got so many other things on your plate right now, you don't want to bother with her. Tell Julian to let her go." *And I hope like hell she goes straight down to the beach and escapes, if that's what she was trying to tell me before.*

"Let her go..." Harper's eyes went hazy. Chloe felt victory begin to swell in her chest—and the familiar churn of her stomach. *Not right. Not right.*

"Let her go, yeah. It's for the best, right? It's all part of your plan. Everything's going fine."

"It is, isn't it?"

Chloe came back to Earth with a jolt. Harper's eyes were clear, and glittered in the sunlight as he narrowed them at her.

"Well, well," he drawled. "Now that *is* interesting. Julian, bring them both."

He spun around and walked off without another word, heading for the blinding white of the private wing of his estate.

Chloe sagged. Putting on the charm always drained her, but it not working made her feel like she'd just sprinted a marathon—and lost.

Julian grabbed her arm again and, with Thandie trapped in his other hand still, marched after Harper into the tower.

All the way up the steps to the tower door Chloe was desperately trying to think of a way to fix this. She glanced sideways, trying to get a glimpse of Thandie.

Why doesn't she shift again? Chloe thought she could guess. Thandie wasn't a fighter. Attacking Julian had probably taken every ounce of courage she had, and it had failed.

You might as well ask why you aren't trying to fight Julian off, too. Chloe bit back a groan. Every time she thought she'd found a hole in Harper's sadistic set-up, he'd gotten in there first.

The boat. Using her as collateral for Mathis' obedience.

She'd thought Julian was a chink in the fence, but now she was beginning to doubt it. Maybe the dragon shifter was another trap. Build enough trust so that Chloe and Mathis let their guard down around him, and then betray them.

Chloe's skin felt cold, even in the damp heat of the afternoon. She rifled through her memories. *Julian didn't see my message in the tower yesterday—but could he have overheard Mathis and me talking about it?*

All too soon they were at the tower door. Chloe didn't have any new plans.

The darkness as she stepped through the door was so sudden it made her eyes sting. She blinked, willing her eyes to adjust more quickly. Julian didn't give her time to get used to the darkness, firmly leading her forward.

Chloe mapped her steps against the image of the room in her head. Close to the hideous gold sofa—across to the staircase...

As they reached the staircase, Chloe's vision cleared enough for her to see the steps in front of her. Her foot froze on the first step.

The trophy room. *Oh God.*

"Tell me this isn't what I think it is," she muttered to Julian through gritted teeth.

She heard Julian swallow. "You're an intelligent young woman, Ms. Kent. I'm sure your predictions are accurate."

Harper was nowhere to be seen. *Already upstairs,* Chloe thought, her mouth dry. *Probably sitting down on that sofa. Waiting for us. Oh, hell.*

"Let Thandie go," she whispered desperately. "He only wanted to see me originally. Please let her go."

"I wish I could," Julian muttered back, and pulled her stumbling up the stairs.

Harper was waiting for them, as Chloe had guessed, on the sofa. He had one of the eggs cradled casually in his lap, and Chloe's last hope that Julian might turn on his employer faded.

"Ms. Kent." Harper's smile was as genuine as it always was, and for a fleeting moment Chloe felt her brain try to convince her that, hey, she must have got something wrong, because Harper was a nice guy, wasn't he?

She shook herself. It was a trick. With Harper, *everything* was a trick.

"Harper," she growled. "What do you want? Mathis is in a bad way, so if you want him to fight again tonight, you need to let me go back to him. That's how it works, isn't it? You need me to be around him so he can heal enough to be your *entertainment.*"

It was a dangerous tactic, she knew. She'd only ever used her charisma-whammy to charm people into things before, but that hadn't worked on Harper. Maybe going on the attack would.

Except all Harper did was grin wider. "My, Ms. Kent, what an *interesting* voice you have. I'm almost intrigued. It's a pity I've already decided to kill you—we might not be too different, you and I."

"Wow. Playboy billionaire to half-rate James Bond villain, and it only took you three weeks. What, you can't afford someone to write dialogue for you?" Chloe's mouth was flapping with no input from her brain. She frowned. *Hang on...*

"What do you mean, not too different? We're completely different! You're a monster, and I'm—"

"Also a monster, surely? What else would you call yourself?" Harper relaxed back on the sofa, slinging the egg like a football under one arm. Julian was still standing just behind Chloe; she heard him hiss in his breath.

"Uh, a *human*? Duh?" *Is this actually working? Is being a little shit a better distraction technique than begging for Mathis' life?* "I'm the only human on your little murder-island, I thought everyone knew that?"

"I thought you were, certainly. But this..." Harper leaned forward, elbows on his knees. The egg slipped to the cushion beside him, and Chloe knew she should be worried about how it spun towards the edge before it settled, but she was too distracted by Harper's grin. His bright, shiny teeth. And the rest of the room was so shiny, too, gleaming and glittering and why was she so worried, anyway? Harper wasn't a danger. He was—

"What the *hell* was that?" Chloe swayed. Her brain felt... fuzzy. Like it was full of moths. Flapping around, leaving dust everywhere. It...

Wait. Harper's still talking. And I'm still looking *at him. His teeth...*

"Wait," she said, dragging her eyes away from Harper's blinding smile. The rest of the room was just as blinding—*Wasn't it dark before?*—but at least it wasn't so, so toothy. "Everyone here is some sort of animal, right? So what the hell are you?"

"The question, Ms. Kent, is: what are *you?*"

Chloe's eyes flicked back to him. She couldn't help it. "Human," she said flatly. "Uh, like I already said."

"Are you so certain? I've never met a human with deflection skills like you just displayed. Perhaps dear Nora wasn't so lax with her hiring practices as I believed. *So* very interesting." He leaned back. "But not, unfortunately, as interesting as the possibilities offered by your mate."

Chloe tried to snort derisively, but it came out more like a scared wheeze. "But I thought—you need me alive..."

"Only so long as I wanted to control him," Harper replied lazily. His eyes hardened. "But you have both been so *uncooperative.* Honestly at this point I might as well kill you just to get a reaction out of him—anything at all!"

He reached out to the egg on the cushion beside him and spun it with his fingers. Chloe glanced sideways; Julian was staring fixedly at the egg, his face twisted with longing and fear. Thandie was still trapped in his hand.

Chloe's lungs felt like they were full of ice. "So—what?" she said, trying to sound like she wasn't about to cry with fear. "I'm the main event in tonight's entertainment, is that it?"

"Oh, not at all. We wouldn't want to disturb the other employees." Harper directed a toothy smile at Thandie—or Julian. "Julian, if you don't mind..."

Chloe whipped around to face the dragon shifter. "No—wait—"

Julian's jaw set as he stared back at her. In the corner of her eye, Chloe saw Harper lean back, a wide grin stretching across his face.

"Normally I'd ask Cane to do the honors, but... let's test your loyalty, Rouse." Harper tossed the egg from one hand to another and Julian jerked towards him. Harper hoisted the egg in one hand, laughing. "Uh-uh!"

He dug in his pocket and pulled out a small remote. Julian froze. Chloe backed away, trying to keep both men in her sights. Julian didn't want to hurt her, she was almost sure—but would he have a choice?

Harper flashed a grin at her, waving the remote carelessly in the direction of the dragon-egg case. "Sorry, sweetheart. Julian might try to save you if there was only this one baby lizard to worry about, but he knows that if he disobeys me, the two in the box are toast. Tell her, Julian."

Julian gritted his teeth. "The case is booby-trapped with aerosolized dragonbane. The eggs are in stasis now but if Harper activates the release, or if someone tries to interfere with the mechanism..." A shadow passed over his eyes. "An adult dragon might survive it. The eggs won't."

Chloe's heart beat like a trapped bird in her chest. *Like Thandie. Oh, God.* The edges of her vision were going dark, and she found herself looking at Thandie, still trapped in the cage of Julian's fingers.

He hadn't tightened his grip on her. He wouldn't hurt her—until Harper told him to.

Julian closed his eyes. "I'm sorry, Chloe," he whispered, and when he opened his eyes again they were focused intently on her.

Chloe stumbled backwards. "Hey—wait a minute—you can't—"

Her next words were drowned out by the roar of a massive explosion.

Chapter 23

Mathis

Mathis was halfway across the courtyard when the kitchen wing exploded.

Instinct made him squeeze his eyes shut, guarding his face with one hand. The boom echoed across the island.

He opened his eyes warily, blinking sun-spots from his vision. The bright lights danced and swam, but he'd covered his eyes in time. His ears were ringing, but the explosion hadn't blinded him.

What the hell just happened? His heart constricted. *Chloe—she can't have been in there...*

Chloe had made trips to the kitchen during their imprisonment, getting extra food for him to help him heal. Horror roared in his ears. She couldn't have—not now—

He lowered his head, breathing in slowly through his nose. The acrid stench of burning plastic filled the air, but beneath it he could just trace the soft warm scent of his mate. He'd tracked her path from the bedroom the moment he woke and realized she was gone, followed her trail from the dormitories out here to the garden courtyard...

Movement caught his eye, and he turned before his brain had filtered out whether it was real or another sunspot. The dark rectangle of the tower door was just visible from the courtyard and as Mathis squinted it opened, revealing deeper darkness within.

Mathis was already moving even before he recognized the pale face poking out as that of Julian Rouse. He might not be able to see what was in the room behind the dragon shifter, but the smell of Chloe's terror poured out of the open door like thick, black oil.

He ran. The kitchen wing—what was left of it—was still burning at the other end of the building, the fire so fierce it roared, but he ignored it and threw himself towards the black hole in the tower wall. Up the steps, six at a time. Across the raised patio. Julian squared off as he approached, a strange look on his face—was it relief, or fear?

Through the pounding of his pulse in his ears and his feet on the hot stone, Mathis heard shouting. Chloe's voice.

He drove his shoulder into Julian's midsection, smashing him out of the way. Julian's winded gasp transformed into a huge rush of air as he shifted. The dragon's bulk blocked out the sun from the door; Mathis paused just long enough to check that Julian's dragon form was stuck outside the tower, slammed the door shut and raced up the stairs.

He could hear Harper, his deeper voice drowning out Chloe's shouts. Light spilled down from the upper floor, glittering strangely on the steps. Mathis was halfway up the stairs when a trapdoor began to slide over the top of the staircase, blocking off the second floor.

He bunched his muscles and leapt, grabbing hold of the top step and throwing himself onto the floor moments before the room went into lockdown.

Mathis slammed into something. Dazzled by the glimmering lights, he barely covered his head in time to avoid the table crashing down on his skull. Glass shattered and fell around him, picking up the golden light and reflecting it in dizzying multitudes.

"You!" Harper snarled. Mathis could just see him, a dark shadow in the swirling lights. "That useless—Julian! I told you what would happen if you failed me!"

Harper was angrier than Mathis had ever seen him. All his fake friendliness melted off him, leaving nothing to hide his violent rage.

And Chloe was standing less than six feet from him.

Mathis' skin itched as his lion fought to take shape. He called out to Chloe, telling her to get behind him. Safe. He could only keep control so long as she was safe.

Chloe's eyes glittered with reflected light as she met his gaze. For one electric moment, he thought she was going to run to him. That everything would be okay.

Then the whole tower shook as something slammed into it from outside.

Chloe fell to her knees with a cry, and Harper's shouts turned into a screech. Mathis staggered as another blow made the floor jump. More of the glass-topped cabinets that filled the room collapsed, broken glass forming a glittering mosaic on the floor.

"Chloe!" Mathis yelled, and she glanced at him, her face tight. She yelled something he couldn't make out, pointing at Harper.

Or—not at Harper. At whatever it was he was holding.

Chloe yelled again. Her voice was lost under the crash of stone as the tower shook again, but Mathis followed her lips. *Distract him.*

Mathis' lion tore at his insides. *Distract him? This is no time for games. We need to get out of here. I need to get* her *out of here.*

Before he could shout back, a car-sized chunk of the wall behind Harper and Chloe disappeared.

One massive claw scrambled at the edge of the broken wall, and a roar of pure animal rage blasted into the room. Ears ringing, Mathis started forward.

Harper and Chloe stood frozen, silhouetted against the sunlight streaming in through the hole where the wall had been. Something huge moved in front of the gap, blocking out all the light. Mathis saw Harper burst into motion, darting to the far side of the room, but his attention was on Chloe.

Julian roared again. Each of his teeth was as long as Mathis' fore-arm, and the brilliant green eye that glared through the hole in the wall was bigger than a dinner plate. Its slit pupil blew out, and Mathis felt the moment the dragon locked its gaze on to Harper.

And then Chloe ran, not away from the dragon, but towards it.

Mathis leapt across the room, tackling Chloe to the ground just as Julian's head disappeared and was replaced by a groping, massive fore-leg. Pain sliced across his back as Julian's claws lanced through the air where Chloe had been standing a second before. He forced himself to roll as he hit the ground, protecting Chloe from the force of impact.

Chloe was swearing under him, cradling something against her chest. He gave her space to push herself up and look at whatever it was she'd picked up from the ground, but stayed crouched over her. If Julian reached for her again, he'd have to go through Mathis first.

But the dragon was ignoring the two of them. He was reaching for Harper, straining to snatch him out of the broken tower.

Even from the ground, Mathis could see it was no use. Julian's angle was too awkward, and he was too big—he would never reach Harper.

And Harper knew it. Mathis saw him realize he'd reached a position of safety. His charisma oozed up over his body again, and he lounged against the far wall, every inch of him radiating smug complacency.

"Mathis." Chloe's voice was urgent. "Mathis, Thandie was in here—can you sense her?"

Thandie. Another shifter? Mathis concentrated and felt a fluttery, feathery presence up in the rafters. He looked up. "She's safe."

"Oh thank God," Chloe gasped. She flinched as Julian thrust his arm into the tower room again, smashing several glass cases. "We have to stop Julian."

"Stop him?" Mathis growled. "I'm more inclined to *help* him." If the dragon had finally decided to stop being Harper's lapdog, it was no skin off Mathis' nose.

Just my back, he thought, wincing as a table leg bounced off his shoulder.

"No—don't you see—"

She broke off as Harper started speaking.

"Oh, Julian, my old friend. Is this the way you want it to end? You'll be so much less useful with no leash on your mind." Harper sounded pleasant. Cheerful.

Mathis' skin was crawling. As Harper lifted the object he was holding, he thought he was going to be sick. Pieces started to come together in his head.

"Shit," he muttered, lowering his mouth to Chloe's ear, "That's not—"

"That's the hold Harper has on him," Chloe whispered back. Her voice was tight with emotion. "And two more, but it's okay, I've got the remote—they're in the case beside the sofa—where the sofa was, I mean, now they're... shit."

Mathis followed her gaze. She was staring wide-eyed at another glass case. Miraculously, it was still intact, though it had been thrust against the wall.

What was left of the wall, at least. It was right next to the hole Julian had clawed in the tower.

"He must not be able to see it," Chloe muttered. "If he..."

Mathis closed his hand over hers. She didn't need to say it. If Julian accidentally knocked the eggs in the case out of the tower, and destroyed them... he would lose himself with them.

Harper was still talking. The egg he was holding caught the light and seemed to gather it up, glowing from within. Mathis licked his lips.

Egg? If the eggs were Harper's hold on Julian, then that meant they were alive. There were dragon children in there.

"Right," he said, mind spinning. "We—"

"Distraction," Chloe said firmly. "Do you trust me?"

"More than anyone else in this room."

Chloe's smile flashed in a sudden flicker of sunlight. "Same to you. All right. You make like you're going for Harper. I'll get the other two."

She didn't give him time to argue. Rolling from under him, Chloe ducked back against the wall. Julian's scaly head roared less than six feet from her tiny form.

Mathis' lion screamed at him, even louder than Julian's angry roar. He couldn't leave her there. His job, his *duty*, was to put himself between her and danger, to keep her from ever coming to harm.

He shook his head, steeling himself. *No.* He trusted her. Not just more than anyone else in the room, more than anyone else in the world. In all the time he'd known her, in all of this nightmare they'd shared together, she'd been quick, kind, and fiercely intelligent.

He trusted her. Hadn't last night shown him that? He trusted her to get herself into danger, and out of it again.

He trusted her with his life, and her own.

"Hey!" he shouted, interrupting Harper. Harper turned to him, eyes wide with innocent surprise. Even his pose called out, *Who, me?*

Mathis grinned and stepped forward, ignoring the pain from the cuts on his back. "What do you call this, Harper? Having some staffing issues? You should call my sister—I've never known a catastrophe she couldn't handle. Whereas you..." Mathis threw his head back and narrowed his eyes mockingly at Harper, ignoring the cries of rage from the dragon outside. "Things aren't looking too good for you, are they?"

Harper's lip curled back. He took a quick step sideways and slammed his fist down on a control panel set into the wall near the sealed staircase. "Cane!" he roared.

"What's the matter? Too scared to take me on myself?" Mathis didn't need to fake the growl in his voice. His lion wanted to attack, to permanently remove the danger Harper posed to every shifter on the island, but he held himself back.

Killing Harper would be satisfying, but it wasn't part of Chloe's plan. So instead, he crab-walked sideways, drawing Harper's line of sight away from Chloe. "You're pathetic, Harper. I'm injured and can barely see straight, and you're still looking for someone else to hide behind? Your pet polar bear?"

Harper's lips twitched as Mathis feinted closer. Mathis searched his eyes. Harper's gaze was full of hate and rage, but not—

"What *are* you?" The question burst out of him, but the answer was already there, in the shape of the puzzle-pieces coming together in his mind. "You're no hunter."

Harper's face twisted. "Aren't I? Aren't I? I caught you, didn't I? And you're not exactly—"

His face transformed, switching from rage to blank stillness so quickly Mathis' blood went cold.

"You're not attacking me," Harper said slowly. "Why might that be, I wonder?"

"Maybe I want to draw this out," Mathis shot back. "Enjoy it. Like you enjoy watching us tear each other to pieces every night."

Harper laughed, but his eyes narrowed. "No, that's not it." Harper's nostrils flared. He moved the egg from one hand to the other, and behind Mathis, Julian screamed with frustration. "I've watched you fight. You don't *get* it. The blood. The *power*. Last night you got close, but *enjoy* it? No. Not you. Not the *lion*." Harper spat out the last word. The edge of his mouth was twitching spasmodically and the egg shook in his hand.

This guy's crazier than I thought. Mathis fought to stop himself from glancing back at Chloe, to see how she was going. Harper's brain might be cracking into a thousand psychotic pieces, but at least he was focused on Mathis.

"All right, then, I'll bite. What should a lion be like?"

Harper's eyes blazed. "What should a lion be like? What should the *king of the beasts* be like? He should fight! He should *kill*! He should be worth defeating—Christ, even the ibex is more of a predator than you are!"

"And that's just what you're not, isn't it? You're not a predator." Mathis' mouth was dry with horror.

All shifters had something of their animal in them. Predators were more aggressive, true, but nothing like the bloodlust-crazed creatures Harper was making them out to be.

And prey animals—herbivores—had their own peculiarities. A tendency for herd behavior, or the ability to keep themselves hidden. Mathis had heard some herbivore shifters were wary of predator shifters, but never understood it until he was on the island.

And he still didn't understand Harper.

"You should have been perfect," Harper hissed. The twitch had gotten worse, twisting his mouth to one side. "The king of beasts! What a victory that would have been, to destroy you! But you wouldn't have even fought, if I hadn't forced you. Even now, you're stalling—"

His ranting cut off. "You're not acting like a lion at all. I know what you're doing. Tactics from the hunted's playbook..."

Harper's eyes slid sideways and widened, but he was too late. Even without looking, Mathis knew Chloe had succeeded. The bright warmth of her success flooded into his mind, bursting in via the mate bond.

He turned to see her with both of the other eggs cradled in her arms, the case lying open beside her. She held the eggs like they were treasures. Protecting them. Mathis' heart swelled with love and pride.

Harper rounded on Mathis, spitting with rage. "Deceiver! Traitor! You're a disgrace to your animal!"

Mathis moved with feline grace, putting himself between the madman and his mate. For the first time that he could remember, he was completely at one with himself. Lion and man united in mind and heart. "You're wrong, Harper. I'm exactly what I should be."

"And you're finished." Chloe's voice thrummed in Mathis' heart. "Hear that, Harper?"

Mathis tipped his head, concentrating. He heard it, too. The steady roar of a helicopter's engine. Outside, Julian raised his massive head to the sky and swiped at something out of sight.

"I guess someone heard the explosion before," Mathis joked, backing up until he could take Chloe's hand. She squeezed his, and he felt her wary joy rise like the tide across the mate bond.

"Or they got my distress call," she countered him. "Wanna take a bet on it, babe?"

"Give up, Harper," Mathis said quickly. They only had a few moments before Julian's attention was back on them, and he wasn't sure how much more the tower could take. "It's over."

Harper's eyes flicked outside, then he met Mathis' gaze with so much hatred that it felt like a physical blow. "Not yet!"

He raised the dragon's egg in the air. In a split-second, Mathis saw what he was planning. The trapdoor across the stairwell had retracted when Harper hit the security panel. He was going to try to escape.

Mathis had less than a heartbeat to decide what to do. But it wasn't any choice at all.

Harper threw the egg with vicious strength, and leapt for the stairwell. Mathis launched himself into the air. Time seemed to stop.

Mathis sprang, eyes fixed on his target. He twisted his body mid-air, ignoring the searing pain from the claw-marks on his back.

The egg was less than six inches from the floor when he reached it. Harper's feet slapped on the stairs as he raced away, but Mathis ignored them. He curled around the precious egg, cradling it against his chest as he hit the floor.

He hissed sharply and lay still for a moment until the pain in his back subsided. The egg was heavier than he expected, and strangely warm. *Alive.*

Mathis' heart constricted at the thought of what might have happened if he'd hesitated a moment longer.

"Did you get it?"

Mathis was lying with his back to the rest of the room. He sat up, turning to show Chloe the safe egg. Her whole body sagged with relief and she stepped forward into the light, the other two dragon's eggs safe in her own arms.

"Oh, thank God. Now we just need to—"

A low growl interrupted her. The sound was so deep it seemed to travel into Mathis' body through his bones, not his ears.

"Chloe, look out!" he shouted as the dragon's massive head filled the hole in the wall.

The light that had surrounded her was blotted out. Hidden by the wall, she might have been safe, but not there out in the open. She was too close, and the dragon had seen her.

Chapter 24

Chloe

Julian's breath was like a desert wind buffeting her back.

Chloe turned slowly. The look in Mathis' eye as the light was blotted out already told her what she would see.

When Julian had grabbed her that night she and Mathis had tried to steal the boat, she hadn't seen him. She'd felt his scales and the tight ropes of muscles beneath them, and the long, dark curve of his claws as he fastened them around her waist, but she hadn't *seen* anything. Whatever magic his scales held, it had kept his dragon out of sight, even when he was holding on to her.

He wasn't bothering to hide himself now.

Julian's scales were a smoky blue-black, absorbing light rather than reflecting it. His teeth glowed white in the darkness and his eyes gleamed like jade discs.

Chloe gulped. What if Harper had gone too far? What if the hold he'd kept over Julian had finally made the dragon shifter's mind snap?

Then we're all dead.

At least Thandie had made it out. She'd seen the fluorescent hummingbird dart down the stairwell after Harper.

"Julian?" she began, and then coughed as her throat closed up. Her mind was darting around like a fly trapped behind glass, but there was no way out of this but straight ahead. No distracting or dodging her way out of this encounter.

She took a deep breath. No tricks. Just the truth.

"Hey, Julian. Are you still in there?" She looked deep into the dragon's eyes. Was there anything human left behind those gleaming jade discs? How would she know?

She remembered Mathis' lion, and all the other shifters she'd seen in the ring. They'd been violent, intent on the fight—but always more than just animal. There had always been a spark of intelligence in their eyes. Some more-than-animal cunning in their tactics.

The dragon's eyes narrowed, its cat-like pupils slits of pure black in the gleaming green depths. Chloe's heartbeat thudded in her ears. Behind her, she heard Mathis grunt as he got to his feet. She didn't dare look back. She just hoped he wasn't going to do anything rash.

Of course he isn't. He already saved the egg instead of going after Harper. He's smart, and kind, and...

She groaned. *I can't think about this right now. I can't.*

Chloe stared in Julian's eyes. "Ok, so, you haven't eaten me yet, so I'm going to assume you *are* still in there."

The dragon blinked. She felt a strange pressure in her mind, and then Julian looked past her.

She heard Mathis catch his breath. "He's in there. Enough of him, at least. And his dragon won't let the eggs come to harm, anyway."

Chloe's first instinct was to grab the eggs and run. She pushed the thought away. Using the eggs—Julian's *children*, for all she knew—using them as collateral would make her as bad as Harper.

She shifted her grip on the eggs and held them out, one in each arm. Mathis came up beside her, his presence a welcome warmth at her side. He held out the third egg.

"Look, Julian, they're safe. And you can take them back, now. No one's going to keep them from you. Harper's gone off... wherever he's gone, so if you just wait for us to come down—"

The gravelly crack of stone grating on stone drowned out the rest of her sentence. Mathis' arms were around her in an instant, protecting her and the eggs. The floor tipped beneath them.

Chloe just had time to calculate exactly how screwed they would be when the tower collapsed under them, before Julian swept her and Mathis up in one massive claw.

Chloe was crushed against Mathis' chest as Julian pulled them out of the collapsing tower. The sunlight was so bright it hurt her eyes but she couldn't tear her gaze away as the tower crumbled.

A blast of heat surged from the other end of the building, followed by another echoing crash. Chloe twisted in Julian's claw, careful to keep the eggs safely cushioned, and saw flames licking at the roof tiles.

"What the hell is going on?" she breathed.

Mathis nuzzled the side of her head. "The kitchen wing exploded. I think Thandie had something to do with it. Shit—Thandie—"

"She ran after Harper," Chloe said quickly. "I mean, flew after him. While you went after the egg."

"That's something, at least," Mathis murmured into her hair. He saw something on the ground and his eyes flickered away, too fast. Chloe glanced where he'd been looking. The polar bear, Cane, was lying unconscious on the steps up to Harper's tower, a pile of rubble around his head.

Chloe's stomach lurched. He'd been so close. If he'd managed to make it to the tower—

But he didn't, she told herself before her imagination got any further. *He didn't. You're safe. We're all safe...*

"Look," Mathis murmured into her ear, and Chloe followed his gaze again—this time, down to the landing beach.

"Thandie's plan..."

The beach was crowded with Chloe's old colleagues. She saw Nora, and the girls she'd gone through training with clustered around her; the kitchen and grounds staff were there as well. Even some of the fighters.

Everyone was gathered in small groups but as Chloe watched they pulled together into a single group.

It didn't take a genius to figure out why.

The helicopter she'd heard earlier had landed on the path that led from the dock to the resort. It stood like a shining black bird of prey. In front of the crumbling sandstone building and windswept shrubberies, it looked like something from another world.

Mathis stiffened beside her. "What the hell is *he* doing here?"

Chloe had been focused on the crowd on the beach, but now she saw a man stepping down from the helicopter. He had dark skin and was wearing black fatigues. A moment later, an older woman followed him out of the chopper. He turned back, arm raised to urge her back, and Chloe didn't need to hear her response to know what it was. Whoever this guy was, the older woman was in charge.

"Do you know them?"

"Yeah..." Mathis still sounded confused. He glanced at Chloe. "But they're not exactly the people I would have expected my sister to send."

"Uhh," said Chloe, grimacing. "About that..."

Julian's growl reverberated through them both, making the eggs in Chloe's arms click together. She adjusted her grip on them hurriedly. "What—*Harper!*"

Her lips peeled back automatically. Harper was running down the path towards the helicopter, jerking from side to side as though he was trying to dodge something. As he got closer, Chloe saw what it was: a tiny, shining, fluttering hummingbird.

"Let us down, Julian," she said, her own voice almost a growl. "I don't want that asshole to put his charm offensive on those soldiers before we can explain what he's been doing."

Beside her, Mathis snorted. "Lance, taken in by anyone's charms? I'd like to see that."

Chloe felt that strange pressure against her mind again as Julian landed on the beach. Pebbles shifted under his massive weight, but no one else seemed to notice their arrival. Chloe exchanged a glance with Mathis, who shrugged.

"Beach full of frightened shifters, and a dragon turns up out of nowhere? That's a recipe for a bad day."

Chloe looked up into Julian's face. "So, you're just going to... hang out here, all invisible-like?"

The dragon stared back, impassive, and then the air around him shimmered. Julian, human-shaped, stared past Chloe's shoulder up the beach to where Harper was approaching their rescuers.

"Harper needs to be held accountable for his crimes." A muscle jumped in his jaw. "As do I." He hesitated. "Would you please..."

"Oh, of course." Chloe carefully handed the eggs she was holding to Julian, and watched carefully as Mathis did the same. She half expected him to fumble the three eggs, but instead he gathered them all safely into his arms. For a moment he leaned over them, and then his shoulders sagged as tension flowed out of his body.

Further up the beach, Thandie had given up dive-bombing Harper and had shifted back into human form to slap him down. By the hoots from the crowd, no one was likely to step in to stop her.

Chloe's heart thudded in her chest. Maybe she and Mathis would have a few moments to talk, before—

"Mathis? Mathis Delacourt?"

Or maybe not.

Mathis stared into her eyes. "Julian's right. It's time for Harper's house of cards to come down."

His eyes caught hers, and she couldn't look away. Pale, warm gold that she would be happy to lose herself forever in.

But that isn't going to happen, is it?

Chloe gulped. "Yeah," she said. "I guess this is it."

She was distantly aware of the male soldier hurrying towards them. They'd done it. The guy with the chopper clearly knew Mathis, so there weren't going to be any problems with Harper pulling the wool over their eyes.

Which meant they were done here.

Mathis' words echoed in her mind: *We'll beat Harper. And when we do—when we're done here—I promise, you'll never need to think about any of this again. You can pretend you never met me.*

Her throat went tight, and Mathis' eyebrows drew together. He stepped closer, one hand tentatively outstretched. "Chloe, are you all right?"

I'm fine. Everything's fine. She managed to hoist a smile onto her face, and couldn't remember when it had slipped off. "I—"

She hesitated. What was she going to say? What *could* she say? They'd had an agreement, and now it was over. Mathis had spent the last month being tortured. It wouldn't be fair of her to change the rules on him now.

"Delacourt!"

Mathis' hand was less than six inches from her face, but as the other man called to him he turned away.

"Lance MacInnis. Two questions: first, what the hell are you doing here? And second, what the hell took you so long?"

Chloe breathed out hard. She knew he didn't mean anything by it—the adrenaline from the fight must still be rushing through his veins, making him forget about their agreement—but if he had touched her, she didn't think she would have been able to hold firm. She would have told him how she really thought about him, despite all her promises.

She crossed her arms in front of herself. The soldier—Lance?—had stopped a few paces away, and was staring hard at Mathis.

"Christ, Delacourt. What the hell happened to you?"

Mathis glanced at Chloe with a frown on his face. "What do you mean? Didn't Frankie tell you?"

"Frankie?" Lance looked from Mathis to Chloe and back. "Frankie isn't telling anyone anything right now. I'm following up on a prank video that's had the shifter community all across the globe up in arms."

Oh, shit.

"Uhh..." Chloe hesitated as both men stared at her. *Shit.*

"What video?" Mathis frowned at Lance. "What the hell are you talking about? Didn't you get our SOS?"

"Is that what you call it? Because I call it a hell of a lot of paperwork I don't have time for. This isn't like that shit you used to pull when we were kids, Delacourt, these days you can't take a video of you shifting and expect it to stay under wraps."

"*What video?*"

"Um—I can explain about that." Chloe gulped. *No need to worry about breaking the agreement after this. He's going to hate me.*

"Please do." Lance's eyebrows drew together and Mathis stirred, placing himself between Chloe and the other man.

She stared at the sand between her feet as she explained. She could feel Mathis' golden eyes boring into her, but she couldn't look at him.

"I did it, all right? I took a video of you fighting Sven that first night. And last night, I tried to contact your sister when I broke into Harper's tower, but it bounced back. So I did the only thing I could think of." She took a deep breath. "I put the video online, geotagged for the island, and tagged in some people I knew would share it. I made it look like it was leaked footage for a new movie, so more people would see it. I know it's dangerous, but it was the only thing I could think of to do."

"You put our whole society at risk," Lance snapped, and Chloe threw up her arms.

"Well, we were *already* at risk. I'm sorry if I cared more about Mathis *dying* than some kids on the internet thinking there's a new Harry Potter Fight Club film out."

Lance's eyes flicked back to Mathis. She saw him take on the marks on his face: the cuts that hadn't healed, the mottled bruises lurking under his skin. His mouth worked.

"This isn't another prank, is it?" he said in an undertone.

"Wow, figured it out, have you?" Chloe snarled. He glared at her.

"It's not a prank." Mathis' voice was heavy, and Chloe's heart ached for him. "Gerald Harper has been keeping shifters captive on this island."

"Gerald *Harper*?" Lance looked over his shoulder. Chloe's stomach twisted. Harper had almost reached them; if he got there before they got MacInnis on-side, if he convinced their rescuers that it was all a mistake...

"You have to believe us," she burst out. "I know it sounds crazy, but everyone here will back us up. At least—"

She bit her lip and exchanged a look with Mathis. She hoped everyone else would tell the truth—but what if Harper still had some secret hold on the other fighters and employees?

Harper darted up behind Lance while her mind was still whirring. For a split second, she saw him as he was: sweating, panting, eyes wide and blood-shot with panic. Then he straightened up, swept his hair back, and became the suave, friendly Gerald Harper she knew and hated.

"Ah. Thank you for coming, Mr....?"

Lance looked down at Harper's outstretched hand, one eyebrow raised. "Mr. Harper, I presume?"

"The very same. And I'm so glad you were able to follow up on our call so quickly."

"*Your* call?" Chloe's cheeks flushed with anger. "You—"

"Nobody called, Mr. Harper," Lance cut in smoothly. "Try again."

Harper's smile became brittle. "The alarm from our little mishap in the kitchen wing..."

"Strike two."

Chloe stepped closer to Mathis. Not to touch, not to break their agreement. Just to feel his heat against her skin as Harper's empire crumbled around him.

Lance leaned toward Harper, a thin smile on his face. "We did receive an alert from a nearby cruise liner, though. You could try to work that into your story, if you like."

Harper's jaw worked. "I—you—*you*—"

His eyes landed on Chloe, and the force of his glare made her step back. He darted forward and then screeched as Thandie dive-bombed him. Somewhere between Chloe's arrival on the beach and Harper approaching them, she'd turned back into a bird.

Harper windmilled his arms, screaming, and then his body twisted and shimmered—and *shrank*.

Chloe blinked. For a moment, it looked like Harper had disappeared. His clothes were an empty pile on the sand.

Then something fluttered on the collar of his shirt.

"He's a *bug?*" she burst out.

Harper had shifted—into a moth, one of the ones with eye-shaped splodges on its wings. Chloe stifled a laugh.

"Look at his wings. I guess he was just playing by his animal's rules all along—pretending to be something he wasn't."

Thandie flew down and landed a few inches from the moth, puffing her feathers out as the world's smallest guard.

Julian stepped forward, the eggs cradled safely in his arms.

"If there is still any doubt about Gerald Harper's actions, I will swear under oath as to his activities for the last ten years," he said, his jaw set in determination.

Lance's eyebrow almost flew off his forehead. "Nothing's ever simple when it comes to you, is it Mathis?" he muttered out of the corner of his mouth.

Mathis laughed. "Like you're complaining."

Lance flashed a grin that included Chloe in the joke. For some reason, a lump formed in her throat.

She swallowed as Lance clapped his hands together. "Right!" he shouted, turning back to the gathered employees. "We need to get that fire under control. Who's in charge here?"

"Uh... you?" someone called out. Soft laughter rippled through the crowd.

Chloe meant to keep listening to what Lance was saying, but then Mathis leaned against her, his hand pressed against her lower back. She caught her breath.

"Good thinking with the video," he murmured, and she could feel his breath in her hair.

"You're not mad?"

Mathis laughed. "Mad? You're a genius. And don't worry about Lance. Scrubbing rumors about shifters from the internet is his idea of a fun weekend."

Chloe relaxed back into his hand. "So I'm not going to disappear into some mysterious government facility as soon as we're off this island?"

"I wouldn't let that happen. I told you. My job is to protect you."

Tears filled Chloe's eyes and she sniffed, blinking madly to keep them from spilling out. "Oh, God, I just want to go *home*," she cried, her voice cracking.

Mathis practically snatched his hand away and Chloe swayed, gulping back breaths that threatened to turn into sobs. *You idiot. You couldn't keep it together long enough to—*

To what? This isn't going anywhere. He was probably just holding you to feel better. To get his energy back, like... like when you broke the agreement...

Chloe sighed and straightened her shoulders. "Sorry, I didn't mean to freak out. This is all just so, so..." She dropped her head. "I'm glad it's over."

She felt Mathis move away. He cleared his throat and she turned around, careful to keep her distance.

"General MacInnis will get everything under control," he said, staring fixedly out to sea.

"Lance?"

"No, his aunt." He nodded at the woman who'd come off the chopper with Lance. "I swear, she's even more terrifying now than when we were kids."

Chloe bit her lip before she could say *I can't wait to get to know her better.* These were Mathis' friends, not hers. She was going home. It was what they both wanted. Wasn't it?

She took a deep breath. "Mathis—oh *shit*!"

Chapter 25

Mathis

Adrenaline flooded Mathis' veins as Chloe shouted in alarm. She was staring over his shoulder. He spun around and followed her pointing arm.

Half a dozen small motorboats were whirring unevenly towards the beach. Further out, a large cruise ship loomed on the horizon like a massive bird.

How did I not see them before? Mathis' mouth fell open. He swallowed hard as he answered his own question. *I wasn't looking at the ocean. Not really.*

He hadn't been looking *at* anything—he'd been looking *away* from Chloe. For a moment, feeling her lean against him, he'd managed to convince himself that they could make things work.

He was a fool. She'd been through hell. His duty was to get her safely home—and that was all, no matter how miserable it made him and his lion. His feelings didn't matter. Hers did.

"Shit, shit, shit," Chloe was muttering. "Are they—did they come off the cruise ship? What the hell are they doing here? Are they shifters?"

Mathis sniffed the sea breeze. "I don't think so."

"Then what are they—" Chloe smacked her forehead. "The explosion. And Lance said something about a tip-off from a cruise ship…"

"Looks like we've got our pick of rescue parties today," Mathis joked. Chloe was still frowning.

"Someone has to tell the others to stay human—no, I'll go!" she said quickly as Mathis made to run back up the beach. "You stay here and guard Harper!"

She sprinted off. Mathis glanced at Julian, but the dragon shifter was lost in his own world. He was sitting on the shingle, staring down at the eggs in his lap and whispering quietly to them.

Mathis shrugged and looked down at Thandie, who was still in hummingbird shape next to the moth Harper. "I guess it's just you and me—"

Thandie fluttered her incandescent wings and zipped off after Chloe. Mathis refocused.

Right. Just you and me, then, asshole. He glared down at Harper.

Harper had barely moved since he'd shifted. Sometimes shifters who spent a lot of time in one form had difficulty adjusting to their other shape, and Mathis hadn't seen any sign that Harper had shifted during the whole time they were on the island—but he didn't trust the man not to try something.

Go ahead. Harper's mental voice was a hiss that bit into Mathis' mind. *Do it. Kill me!*

Mathis snorted. "That would be too easy." Crouching, he pulled off one shoe. "I've got a much better idea."

He swatted the shoe at the moth—not squishing it, but trapping it inside. He covered the opening with his hand. "You're going to court, Harper. You'll pay for every one of your crimes. And it's going to take a long, long time." He heaved a dramatic sigh. "You're probably going to find it very, very boring. What a shame."

He stood up again and shaded his eyes with one hand. The first of the motorboats was almost to shore.

Chloe ran up beside him. She was panting, her cheeks red and her hair flying wildly around her face. "Okay, they're all sorted. No surprise shifting." Her eyes darted sideways and Mathis saw Thandie perched in her hair like a shiny earring. "...And Thandie is staying like this for now because naked, I guess, and *hiiiii*!"

It was like she'd flicked a switch inside herself. One moment her eyes were intent on his, her expression urgent—the next a brilliant smile flashed across her face. She looked like a different person.

Mathis didn't need to turn around to see who she was addressing. He could already sense the people behind him. The first boat had been pulled ashore, and as he'd thought, everyone aboard was human.

He turned around slowly, acutely aware of the grime and scrapes covering his body. *At least I'm the scariest-looking person here,* he thought. *Thanks to Chloe's quick thinking.*

Mathis held the shoe-prison loosely at his side as he sized up the humans walking up the beach. There was no way Harper would try to shift to escape—shifters needed enough space for their larger forms, and trying to bust out of the shoe as he shifted carried a risk of severe injury.

There were half a dozen humans walking towards them. They were all dressed in the casual shorts-and-brightly-colored shirt uniform of holidaymakers around the world. One woman was wearing a bum bag. And they were all staring up and him and Chloe with the same naked excitement fizzing on their faces.

"Howdy," one man said, tipping his cap back to reveal a sunburnt forehead. "You folks need some help here?"

Mathis relaxed. Tourists. Helpful, well-meaning tourists. This looked like a family group: mom, dad, grandparents and one preteen girl who, admittedly, looked less excited than the rest of them to be a part of their gung-ho rescue mission.

Chloe giggled. "I guess you saw our little fire, huh?"

"Little? Is that what you call it? What're you all doing out here, anyway?"

Mathis exchanged a glance with Chloe. On her shoulder, Thandie ruffled her feathers.

Right. We need a story...

"Dad! *Daaad!*" The girl who came ashore with the group tugged on Sunburn's arm. "It's *him!* From the clips I showed you!"

Mathis' heart sank. He glanced at Chloe again but to his surprise, her face lit up.

The man in front of them pulled his cap off entirely and ran his hand through his hair. "From the—damn it, honey, what did I tell you about how much the internet costs on that boat? How many times have you watched those videos?"

"Some amount of times," the girl whined, flicking her hair over her shoulder. She bounced on the spot, staring up at Mathis. "It's true though isn't it? You're him? With the—*rarrr!*"

"I'm..." Mathis stared helplessly at Chloe, who was biting her lip, her eyes bright with repressed laughter.

"He has signed a lot of important-looking documents telling him he is absolutely not allowed to answer that question," Chloe said solemnly, and then winked at the girl.

"Oh my God!" Still bouncing, the girl started to make a high-pitched squealing noise. "Dad, Mom, this is the best vacation ever!" She whipped out her phone and sped off down the beach, ignoring her father's hopeless cries of *Sweetie—remember the roaming charges!*

Chloe directed a good-natured grimace at the rest of the family. "Oh well—any publicity, right?"

Mathis sensed Lance jogging up to them. Speaking directly into the other shifter's mind, he quickly explained the situation—and their cover story.

Lance's long-suffering sigh was so loud, Mathis wasn't sure if he heard it through his ears or his mind. Mathis winked at him as he handed over Harper in his shoe prison. *You want to take custody of this?*

Thanks. Lance's hand closed over the shoe like a vice. *I get the movie cover, but how are you going to explain you handing over your shoe like this?*

Mathis grinned. *I'm a movie star. I don't need to explain anything I do.*

God save us all. Lance's mental voice was dry, but he was smiling.

"Thanks for stopping by," Lance said out loud, every inch the slightly-embarrassed professional. "I've just had your captain on the phone—he's very generously offered to give the crew a lift back to the mainland while the set is cleaned up." He winced and glared at Mathis. "This is why we leave special effects to the people with computers, not the—goddamn—gas *and* liquid fuel? And—"

It was meant to be just flour. Thandie poked her beak out of Chloe's hair. *Get a lot of flour in the air and it catches fire like crazy. Do you think we should tell him? But—oh no—the gas tanks are actually—*

Another explosion ripped through the air. Mathis felt it before he heard it, a tremendous pulse of force that made every tree on the island whip. Even the helicopter shook. Mathis wrapped his arms around Chloe and pulled her behind him, keeping his body between her and the flames.

Thank God everyone is down on the beach, he thought. Debris had been thrown through the air by the explosion, but none of it had made it to where everyone was gathered.

He kept one arm around Chloe as black clouds rose above the ruin of Harper's estate, and she didn't pull away. Inside him, his lion purred—but his human braced for the inevitable.

Around him, the tourists' faces had dropped. Responding to an explosion seen miles off was one thing, but seeing one this close up made things a bit too real. Mathis cleared his throat, trying to think of something to say to clear the air.

"Well," Chloe sighed, straightening her clothes. "There go our insurance premiums."

"Yes," Lance added, sharp as a whip. "I'd be surprised if the movie gets made at all, now." Relief flashed across his face and he glanced at Mathis. *Make sure your tiny fan-girl gets the news, will you? We need to nip this movie idea in the bud.*

Aye aye, captain.

Lance snorted. Out loud, he waved to the other resort employees to come closer. "Right. It's a five-hour trip back to the mainland according to the captain, so we'd better get moving before his generosity screws up his schedule even more."

Thandie's voice piped up in Mathis' mind again. *It's the first time the cruise liner has taken this route. Louis was working on-board last season and that's why he knew—usually ships don't come along this way, and if this one hadn't...* Her voice went silent. *Can you tell Chloe for me? She can't hear me.*

Because she's human. Mathis' arm tightened around Chloe. He wanted so much to be with her—but he'd made a promise. He couldn't betray her trust in him.

I'll make sure she knows, Mathis told Thandie. Chloe was going home, she wouldn't want to see him again—but Lance or someone else would debrief her. He'd make sure she got the full story then.

"Five hours by boat, but less than one by helicopter." Lance was looking at him and Chloe. "Sounds like a bit of a party boat, if that's your thing..."

"Helicopter. If that's okay," Chloe said quickly. Her spine stiffened and Mathis let her go, his heart sinking. "I've had enough of paradise island here to last me a lifetime. The faster I can get home the better."

Lance frowned. "We'll be stopping off at the branch—"

You'll take her home, Mathis growled.

"—But we can put you in a hire car from there," Lance finished smoothly. He raised one eyebrow at Mathis. *What about you? Are you and her—*

"I'll go on the boat." He kept his eyes off Chloe, but still heard her barely-concealed gasp. He forced a smile on his face, pushing down his lion as it fought to make him stop what he was doing. "Might as well get a head start on killing those rumors, right?"

Lance stared at him hard. "Right," he said, and for a moment Mathis was worried he was going to say something else—but he just shrugged and turned away to help his aunt gather up the crowd.

Chloe wrapped her arms around herself. "I guess this is it," she said quietly.

Mathis' mouth was suddenly dry. This was it—his last chance. He stepped towards Chloe involuntarily, his lion screaming at him to take her in his arms and never let her go.

Chloe looked up at him, a strange expression flashing across her face. It was gone too soon for Mathis to see it clearly, but what he did see sent ice stabbing into his heart.

She was afraid. And Harper was gone, which meant there was only one thing that could be causing her fear. Her connection to Mathis.

He clenched his fists at his side. She'd covered her emotions well, and there was no sign of fear on her face now—but he knew what he had to do.

"Goodbye, Chloe," he said, and joined the crowd walking down to the boats.

Chapter 26

Mathis

TWO WEEKS LATER

"You—she—*what?*"

Lance slammed his tablet down on the table. Mathis leaned back in his chair, trying to hide the tremor in his hand as he reached out for his water glass.

"It was the right thing to do." He still believed that. Didn't he?

"You..." Lance groaned, swore, and covered his face with his hands. "No wonder you still look like shit. Christ. I should set up as a bloody Agony Aunt at this rate. First Grant, now you..."

"What does Grant have to do with it?" Mathis frowned and shook his head. "We were talking about Harper."

"Fuck Harper. He's under control. But you're clearly not. What were you thinking, letting her go?" Lance gritted his teeth. "I should have seen something was up on that beach. Why didn't you say something? There was room in the chopper!"

Mathis closed his eyes. His lion growled a weak echo of Lance's question. *Why?*

Because he'd told her he would set her free. Because the mate bond had terrified her, and been used as a chain to control them both, right from the start.

Because he loved her, and he wanted her to be happy.

But he couldn't tell Lance that.

"We had an agreement," he muttered. "I promised her that once we were free, she could leave our world—shifters—behind her."

"I don't understand what's going on here, Mathis. Even without everything that's going on with Francine... This isn't like you."

Mathis knew what he was talking about. It was the main reason they'd never really gotten along. Lance had always had a stick the size of a redwood up his ass, and Mathis had never found a rule he didn't want to break. Until now.

"Maybe I've finally grown up," he growled, glaring at Lance.

Lance blinked lazily. In a human, the expression might not have meant anything; for a feline, it meant trust.

From Lance, it meant Mathis wasn't going to like whatever he said next. The cat equivalent of *Bro, you know I love you, but...*

"You really think the way you're behaving is *grown up*?"

Mathis set his jaw. "I made her a promise. She—"

His throat closed over the rest of the sentence. *She was so afraid. It was the only thing I could think of. Harper caged her, tormented her—I had to show her we weren't all like that. I had to set her free.*

It was the truth, but he would never say it out loud. Not to Lance. Not to anyone. His mate had trusted him with her fears, and he would never betray her to an outsider.

"Not all promises should be kept." Lance's voice was smoothly professional, the same smug asshole persona that had always made Mathis' hackles rise. "Take this."

Mathis stared at the slip of paper Lance handed him. An address. *Chloe's* address.

His heart stood still. *You made a promise,* he told himself, helpless in the flood of his lion's despair.

He'd done his best to work through the pain, these last few weeks. His personal doctor had looked after the physical side of things, putting together a training and diet regimen that would repair the stresses of Harper's blood fights. Mathis had focused on the regimen like it was a beacon.

And it hadn't helped. Every cell in his body longed for Chloe, and the stronger he became, the more everything hurt.

"Honestly, you're both as bad as each other. The trial starts in a week, and at this rate neither of you will have your statements ready."

Mathis tensed, his body going to high alert. "What do you mean, both of us? Is she all right?"

Lance stared at him, nonplussed. "She's as safe and healthy as you are," he said dryly.

A muscle twitched in Mathis' cheek. He rubbed it, frowning.

True, Lance didn't have his full statement yet. Mathis knew it was important, and he'd probably said enough that Lance or one of his assistants could piece the full story together, but...

Every time he'd started to talk about Chloe, his mouth had gone dry. He couldn't put what had happened to her into words. What he felt for her.

"I'm not going to make this decision for you." Lance's voice was low, but insistent. He re-settled his glasses on his nose and looked away. "Not least because you're not actually paying me for any of this."

Mathis frowned. "Why the hell would I pay you for this? It's your job."

"Not the investigation." Lance picked up his tablet and slid it into its protective shell. "The relationship counseling. You're worse than Grant was when he met his mate."

Mathis' lion rose up protectively. "I never said she was my mate."

"You think you need to say it?" Lance raised one eyebrow. "Sort yourself out, Delacourt. You're a lion—stop pussyfooting around."

He stalked out before Mathis could pull together a reply, leaving him alone in his apartment.

Mathis slammed his fist down on the table. *Damn it.* This was meant to be a routine catch-up, another attempt to get his statement straight before the trial started. Not an interrogation about his state of mind.

He frowned. Come to think of it, he'd been having plenty of these catch-ups recently. Almost daily. Lance, Grant, Harley and his folks... everyone had some sort of excuse to knock on his door.

Almost as if everyone in the goddamn city was keeping an eye on him.

Well, that was bullshit. He was perfectly capable of looking after himself. He'd managed so far, hadn't he? He'd spent his entire adult life controlling the restlessness inside him. He could do it again. He'd find a safer way to exhaust his lion, this time. No more lying about himself.

An image flashed through his mind, sharp as a knife. Chloe. Dark hair flopping across her face, hands hiding her cheeky smile. Laughter bubbling out between her fingers.

Chloe the way she'd been when he first saw her, her face glowing with wonder.

He looked at the slip of paper crumpled in his hand. He'd made a promise. A promise to keep her safe... to let her be happy again.

But she hadn't *been* happy when he left her. The smiling vision of Chloe in his mind dissolved, replaced by a memory of her the last time Mathis had seen her. She'd been smiling, but the smile hadn't reached her eyes.

His lion snarled unhappily, and Mathis made up his mind. He had to find her. He had to make this right.

It was a six-hour flight to Chloe's hometown, but in Harley's plane, the journey only took four. The cheetah shifter flew like he ran—scary fast.

He'd also been surprisingly easy to convince to give Mathis a ride with no advance warning.

Mathis glanced sideways at his speed-freak friend. "How many of you are in on this?"

"In on what?" Harley's eyes flickered as he taxied the plane off the runway.

"You know what." Mathis' lion growled through his human voice and Harley snorted. "This nursemaid bullshit you've all got going on."

"Hey, don't look at me. I'm just glad you finally got off your ass." Harley pulled off his headphones and flicked a final switch on the dash. "Speaking of which... no cabin service here, mate. You should just beat rush hour if you hoof it now."

Mathis leapt to the back of the cabin, then leaned back to punch Harley on the shoulder.

"Hey. Thanks."

Harley groaned and leaned his head back, eyes closed. "Don't stay up too late, Romeo."

Mathis grinned, and went in hunt of his mate.

An hour later, he was staring up at an old brick building. It was three storys of brown brick and rusting iron railings, garbage cans piled up beside the front step and music filtering through poorly fitted windows.

Chloe's home.

Throat suddenly dry, Mathis stepped up and hit the intercom for Chloe's apartment. 3B. Static crackled, then someone picked up.

"HIIIIIIIIIIIIIIIIIII!" a female voice shrieked down the intercom and then broke off. "Oh no *fuck* my drink—"

More static. Mathis frowned and leaned closer to the speaker. "Chloe?"

He could hear someone yelling in the background. Another woman—who wasn't Chloe. Neither of the voices was hers.

"Shit—give me that—hello?"

Mathis rubbed his forehead. This new woman might not be Chloe, but at least she didn't sound as totally wasted as the one who'd picked up. "I'm looking for Chloe Kent."

"Who is this? Fuck off Cindy, I'm on the phone."

"I'm—"

The line crackled again, a clanking noise suggesting that "Cindy" had taken possession of the intercom phone. "It's a booooooooy! Oh my god! Are you the stripper?" There was another clank as the phone hit the wall, and he heard Cindy's drunken whoop in the background: "GRADUATION STRIPPERRRRRR!"

Mathis groaned and covered his face. He had to have the wrong apartment. Walking back to the sidewalk, he pulled the slip of paper out of his pocket and stared up at the building.

No. This was it. 3B.

He might have assumed that Lance had given him the wrong address but, well it was *Lance* who'd given it to him. If Chloe had moved, Lance's creepy meerkat spy network would have told him about it before the landlord had even lodged her bond.

"Hey! Hey... guy!" The less-drunk woman called through the intercom. "You're not Mathis, are you? Oh, shit."

Mathis was back in front of the intercom in an instant. "I'm Mathis Delacourt."

"Mathis Delacourt who lives in New York?"

His heart sank. "...Yes?"

"Oh, *shit.*"

"What is it?" Mathis rested his palm on the wall next to the speaker. "Is Chloe there?"

"No, uh... Mathis... she's in New York City." There was a pause, and then a hiss of static that Mathis suspected was the drunker woman hollering 'Awkwaaaaaard'.

She's gone to NYC?

"When?" he asked out loud.

"Uh... just this morning... said she was going to go find... well..."

"Me." Mathis' heard thudded in his chest. *She went to find me.*

"Yyyyep." Chloe's roommate paused. "So, uh, you don't have her phone number, right?"

Five minutes later, Mathis had Chloe's number. Drunken shrieks still echoing in his ears, he made it to the airport to see Harley's Avanti still loitering off the runway.

He smacked the side of the plane, calling out telepathically. *Hope you refueled, Roadrunner.*

You know me, Simba. Never sleep on an empty tank.

Harley was still stretching when Mathis swung himself into the copilot seat. "Let's move."

The cheetah shifter shot a sly smile his way. "She throw you out already?"

Mathis grumbled under his breath, and then explained what had happened. Harley whooped with laughter. "So you—oh, hell, Mathis. Tell me you've actually called her."

His phone was burning a hole in his pocket. "I called the building manager. If she shows up at my apartment, he'll let her in."

"Jesus, Simba..."

Harley held up one hand as the radio crackled. He followed the flight controller's guidance out onto the runway, treating Mathis to his best selection of exasperated, mocking and condescending facial expressions.

They were in the air by the time he deigned to finish his sentence.

"...You *idiot.*"

Mathis sighed. "Not telling me anything I don't already know."

He pulled out the phone. Calling the building manager had been easy enough, but Chloe?

He wasn't sure he dared.

His chest went tight. What if she hadn't flown out to see him? Her friends had seemed convinced, but they'd also seemed, well, *really* drunk. How would she have even gotten his address?

She's your mate. And she's the best in the world at poking her nose into other people's business. She would have found a way.

He shook his head, but he couldn't ignore his lion's certainty. His beast was sure he would find his mate waiting for him back in his own territory.

But the human Mathis could barely dare to hope.

It was full night by the time they landed on the private airfield where Harley kept all his toys. Mathis waved off Harley's offer of a ride to his apartment building.

"Thanks, but I want to actually make it back home tonight, not end up wrapped around a power pole."

"You were happy enough having me fly you cross country," Harley sniffed, his cat offended.

"Sure," replied Mathis easily. "There aren't any power poles in the sky."

Now, standing in front of his own front door, he was all out of jokes. He licked his lips. On the other side of this door...

He closed his eyes. He'd snuck in the back way, avoiding the building staff. He didn't want anyone else to see the disappointment in his eyes when they told him no house guests had arrived.

But if she was there...

Mathis' lion growled low in his throat. This was ridiculous. He couldn't just stand here all night. He had to find out, one way or the other.

And if she wasn't there—he would cope. He'd have to.

Alone, in his apartment, as another black night faded into gray dawn. The same way he'd spent every night since they were evacuated from the island.

He braced himself, and pushed open the door.

The lights were on. Low, but on—and he knew he'd left them off. The apartment was quiet, but—

He sniffed the air, and his lion purred. She was here. Not just in his territory, she was in his *den*. His sanctuary.

And she'd made dinner.

Mathis' nose took him through to the kitchen, where the remains of a meal for one were stacked neatly in the dishwasher. Tenderness pricking at his heart, he checked the fridge, and found a second plate waiting for him. She must have poked through his fridge and all of his cupboards to find everything, and cooked dinner while she was waiting for him. Cooked dinner for *him*. The thought of anyone invading his privacy in this way would normally have made Mathis bristle, but the thought of *Chloe* doing it made his whole body warm up.

He prowled further. She'd left a dent in the largest of the sofas in his living room. He could imagine her stretching out, relaxing. Waiting for him.

And what had she done when he hadn't turned up?

Mathis' heart thudded in his ears. If she'd left...

He fell into a half-crouch, sniffing the air. Chloe's scent was warm. *Close.*

Mathis crept through his apartment, feeling strangely like an interloper in his own property. Chloe's scent was everywhere. After so long apart from her, even the hint of her presence made him drunk with pleasure.

He made his way through the apartment until there was only one room left. He paused with his hand on the door and his heart in his throat.

His bedroom. He hardly dared to hope...

He pushed gently on the door and it swung open with barely a whisper. His bedroom lay beyond, every inch of it familiar. The pale carpet and thick rugs. Huge windows, with heavy curtains now drawn against the night.

And his bed. He'd left it unmade, blankets piled in the middle of the supersized mattress. They were still crumpled and tangled, but now they were wrapped around the most precious treasure Mathis' home had even held.

His mate.

All the breath left his body in one sigh of pure relief. He was home.

And so was Chloe.

She was lying on her back, her head tilted to one side and one hand pushed up against her cheek. Her hair was a dark halo on the pillow, one sooty strand falling over her forehead.

Mathis' heart filled his chest. She'd never slept on her back on the island. She'd slept curled up on her side, defensive even in sleep. But no more. Here, in his den, she felt safe.

Chloe's breathing changed. Mathis sensed the moment she woke up—and the moment she realized he was watching her.

She grimaced, but not fast enough to hide the smile that tugged at her lips.

"God damn it," she muttered, still pretending to be annoyed. "I can't believe I fell asleep."

No hellos. No need to explain what she was doing here. A tight knot inside Mathis' chest, one that had been there so long he had forgotten it existed, suddenly unwound.

He padded further into the room, stalking towards Chloe.

"You can't believe you fell asleep? What are you doing in bed then?"

Chloe pushed herself up on the pillows, her sleepy eyes sparkling wickedly. "Waiting for you. What time do you call this?"

Mathis glanced at his watch. "I call it ten hours since I boarded a plane to surprise you at your apartment."

Chloe's mouth dropped open, but her eyes were shining. "No!"

"I'm afraid so." Mathis prowled closer. He wasn't in a hurry; he wanted to savor every moment of this. His mate, waiting for him in his bed.

Chloe hid behind a blanket. When she poked back up, she'd almost succeeded in hiding her laughter, but her eyes still sparkled. "Well, I took the bus, so if anyone's going to complain about being stood up, it's me."

Her lips quirked as Mathis closed the distance between them. He sat down on the edge of the bed, his movements fluid and feline. Chloe's eyes flicked over his body. She didn't move, or say anything—but her eyes went black with desire.

Mathis' lion purred.

"Stood up? I didn't realize I was meant to be sitting around waiting for you." He leaned forward until Chloe's soft lips were only a few tantalizing inches from his.

Chloe snorted. "From what I've been hearing, I expected to find you almost comatose with despair," she said with a wicked smile. "Though I was going to have to play Prince Charming to your Sleeping Beauty. And here I got all ready to kiss you better for nothing."

"Who told you what?" Mathis frowned.

"Oh... no one," Chloe teased, slipping down the bed until she was lying between Mathis' arms. She reached up and touched his cheek, and her expression changed. "Shit. Sorry. I had this whole speech prepared, but I just... you look so much better. I'm so glad you look better."

Mathis' heart twisted as Chloe pressed her palm against his face, covering the place that had been all scabbed, raw skin the last time she had seen him.

"Looks can be deceiving," he muttered. He brushed the pad of his thumb under one of Chloe's eyes, which were suddenly shiny with tears.

She sniffed and blinked, and Mathis dipped his head, nuzzling into her neck as she fought back tears. "Don't cry," he murmured into the soft skin under her ear, and heard her breath hitch.

"I'm not crying," she grumbled. Mathis heard her sniff, and then: "We've both been really stupid about this, haven't we?"

"I'm the one who was stupid," Mathis protested. He lowered himself onto Chloe, rolling so he could pull her protectively to his chest. She tugged at the neck of his t-shirt, pressing her face against his bared chest. "I thought I was being strong, but I was hurting us both."

Chloe sniffed, and it turned into a giggle. "Damn it. I thought *I* was being the strong one, following the stupid plan and not checking in with you. If Lance hadn't said anything, I'd still be sitting in my bath eating ice-cream and crying every night."

Mathis' fingers had been creeping up under Chloe's shirt. He stopped, frowning. "Wait—Lance? And I hope you're joking about the crying."

"Yeah, I've been seeing someone from his company about my statement and—well, one of the things that was going to be in my big speech to you, actually—and he kept popping into our meetings and glaring and making pointed remarks about me getting closure with any of the other people who'd been on the island, and..." She squirmed closer to him. "I wasn't lying about crying in the bathtub. Well, not about the ice-cream, at least. I must have put on half a ton."

"Is that an invitation?" Mathis nibble on the tip of Chloe's ear, and felt her shiver against him.

"God, let me check. I just spent a week torturing myself over the thought that you never liked me, or that I'd massively fucked everything up somehow, and—" She made a noise halfway between a sob and a growl of frustration that made every one of Mathis' protective instincts flare. "—So, yes, *please* take my shirt off, yes."

Mathis tipped her head back and kissed her, savoring the feminine softness of her lips. "Your wish is my command," he murmured, and moved down the bed.

Chloe was wearing a soft knit long-sleeve shirt. If she had been standing up, it would have hung loosely from her generous frame; but since she was lying down, it was twisted interestingly around her gorgeous curves. Mathis took a moment to admire the sight before slipping his fingers under the bottom hem.

Chloe's skin was hot, and she trembled at his touch. Mathis grinned. Inside him, his lion started to purr, a warm, insistent thrum of need. He brushed his lips against Chloe's belly where her skin disappeared under her pants. She gasped and pushed against him, her hands clenching at his sides.

Heat flooded through Mathis. This was so *right*. Being with Chloe, skin to skin, teasing her with promises of pleasure he had every intention of fulfilling.

Chloe's breaths became deeper, slower. Mathis slid one hand up under her shirt to rest against her breastbone, feeling her heartbeat speed up.

He kissed his way up her stomach, licking and nipping, reaching out the thumb of his hand on her chest to brush against her breast where it spilled out of her bra.

"Oh god." Chloe jerked beneath him, sucking in breath. Her hands fluttered to his head, fingers threading through his short hair. "This is—oh my god. How the hell did I stay away from you so long? I should never have gone back to freaking Nowheresville. God that was—uhh-h—that was so stupid."

Mathis slipped her shirt over her breasts. Her nipples were hard, pressing through the silky fabric of her bra.

"Shh," he murmured, and nipped one playfully. Chloe arched her back, crying out.

"That's not going to get me to be quiet," she shot back at him.

She sounded peevish, but Mathis could hear her grin. He nuzzled his way up her neck, feeling drunk with love and desire. Chloe was flushed, her lips slightly parted as she stared up at him and her eyes shining.

He nipped at her chin. "I promise you can talk as much as you like after."

Chloe snorted, but her eyes were dark with lust. "Oh, *after*. When you're asleep, I bet."

"That depends on how much you tire me out." Mathis covered her with his body, desire building to a storm inside him as Chloe pressed herself up against him. "Let's get rid of this."

He pulled her shirt over her head, and before he'd even tossed it aside she was in his arms, pushing him upright and wrapping herself around him.

"I think I should tell you one thing, though," she said quickly, and gasped as he grabbed her ass and pulled her onto his lap.

"Important, is it?" Mathis kissed the side of her neck.

"Mmmm." Chloe squirmed, but he wasn't letting her go. "Um, yes, I think it is... ooh..."

He unhooked her bra and slid the straps down her shoulders, moaning as her breasts were bared. *God, she's so perfect. So beautiful.*

Mathis brushed a thumb over one nipple, the same one he had bitten through the bra. It was rock-hard, red and tender looking. He circled his thumb over it, and Chloe gasped again through gritted teeth.

"You're so beautiful," he murmured, looking deep into her eyes. She stared back, eyes dark and shining.

He kissed her and her lips fit perfectly against hers, hungry and passionate as he claimed her. *Mine,* he thought, his lion growling in agreement. "Mine." The words slipped out, straight from his soul. "My perfect, sexy, wonderful mate—"

Chloe squeaked, and he was about to laugh and tease her for it, when she shimmered under his touch. The air around her seemed to dance, and then he was falling forward, his hands clutching nothing.

"Chloe!"

He sprang back off the bed, landing lightly on the balls of his feet. Chloe—it wasn't possible. She'd *vanished*.

Mathis' nostrils flared. He could still smell her. Except the scent was different, somehow. Wilder.

Something fluttered in the pile of bedclothes. Mathis watched in wide-eyed amazement as a brown-and-white banded wing fluttered free, and a small bird hopped unsteadily on top of the blankets.

Oh shit! cried Chloe-the-bird. *Oh shit! What do I do? Help!*

Mathis knelt down, resting his forearms on the bed for balance. All his feline grace seemed to have abandoned him. He couldn't believe what he was seeing.

"Chloe?" He shook himself, and repeated gently: *Chloe? Can you hear me?*

CHAPTER 27

CHLOE

Chloe felt... *small*. And she was pretty sure she didn't have arms anymore.

She tried to take a step forward, and tipped over on a duvet that seemed a hell of a lot bigger than it had been thirty seconds ago.

"Mathis, what the hell just happened?" she tried to shout, but all that came out was a... chirp?

Oh my fucking WHAT.

Chloe, try not to freak out. Can you hear me?

Mathis' voice appeared in her head, a warm, familiar murmur. In her *head*. Not through her ears.

She tried to shout again, but only managed a few chirps that even to her sounded panicked.

Looking at Mathis only helped a bit. The expression of concern on his face was gratifying, but not how *big* he was.

Oh god, Chloe thought, horrified. *I've shrunk? And I've got wings? Am I a bird?*

Mathis reached out one massive hand. It was the same size as *she* was. Flustered, Chloe pecked at it, then hopped back, embarrassed.

Shit. I should have known something like this would happen. But now?

If she'd had teeth, she would have grated them.

Mathis pulled his hand back. The look in his eyes was part concern, part—humor?

Well I'm glad you find this funny, she thought grumpily.

Mathis' eyes widened. *Chloe—do that again. Think at me. It's how we can communicate when you're—you're a shifter.* His mental voice was hushed with wonder. *Since when are you a shifter?*

Since... Chloe concentrated. *Since... now? I don't know! I told you I wanted to talk to you about... stuff, right?*

And this is "stuff"? The corner of Mathis' mouth quirked.

Stop teasing me and tell me how to change back!

Mathis reached out again, and this time Chloe managed not to peck him. He held his hand still at her side and she leaned into it, feeling her feathers—*feathers!*—rustling against the rough skin on his palm.

Her heartbeat slowed. Even in this form, Mathis' touch calmed her. Made her feel like everything was all right. She took a deep breath and looked across at him.

He was frowning. *It's been a while since I learned how to do this, but...* think human *thoughts.*

Human thoughts? Chloe chittered her beak in frustration. *I think I was thinking pretty* human *thoughts when this happened, actually!*

That made him laugh. Mathis covered his face with one hand, chuckling helplessly. Which Chloe could appreciate—God it was nice to see him smile again, and laugh—but, seriously. *Bird.*

All right. Mathis' mental voice was gentle, a telepathic caress. *It happened when I called you my mate, didn't it?*

A frisson went through Chloe. *Yes. And you kissed me.*

Maybe that's what woke up your shifter nature. Mathis' golden eyes glowed as he looked down at her. *Me claiming you as my mate.*

Chloe shivered as that strange feeling struck her again. *Mathis' mate.* The idea had been the source of so much pain for both of them, but now... it felt right.

More than that. Something inside Chloe seemed to settle into place, a feeling of wholeness she never knew she was missing.

She looked into Mathis' eyes, losing herself in their golden depths. Mathis' mate... Harper had tried to make their bond into something cruel, a chain, but it wasn't. It was beautiful, and strong, and she knew her mate would keep her safe forever.

She knew what to do. Looking deep inside herself, Chloe found her human form, waiting patiently for her. She slipped into it like a familiar shirt, and her body stretched and grew, wings transforming into arms, hard beak into soft lips. Lips that were *so* ready to be kissed.

Chloe crawled across the bed to where Mathis was kneeling. She ran her hands through his hair, and pulled him close.

"So, yeah," she said, feeling strangely awkward. "I guess I'm a shifter. I wasn't expecting it to happen so... quickly."

"But you knew you were?" Mathis' eyebrows furrowed. Chloe waited for the spark of uncertainty inside her, but it never came. She would never fear Mathis rejecting her again. She was his—and he was hers. Forever.

"I didn't *know*," she explained, stroking the back of his head. "I *suspected*. I mean, not at first, but after something Harper said that last day—in the tower—" Her voice shook slightly, and Mathis arms tightened around her. She let her head fall on her shoulder, feeling utterly safe and protected. Remembering how close she and Mathis had come to death that day made her throat close over with fear—but it hadn't happened. They had gotten out. *Everyone* had gotten out.

"Well, it made me start thinking about things," she said, drawing lazy circles on the back of Mathis' neck. "I've always had this... thing I do. Getting people to stop paying attention to something I don't want them to notice. And it works *really well*, like, so well that some of my friends call it my Jedi mind trick." She kissed Mathis where his neck met his shoulder. "You know. *These are not the shifters you're looking for.*"

Mathis rested his chin on her head. "You think that's how you got past Harper's hiring process in the first place?"

He understands. Chloe closed her eyes, a warm rush of love for Mathis—for her *mate*—filling her. Of course he understood. Mathis was smart; he only played dumb when he was being Matt Dell.

"Yeah. I used it a lot during the interviews. And after I figured out what Harper was doing with the lights—distraction techniques—and what he said... well, I asked Lance about it during the debrief, and he assigned one of his meerkat agents to check up on it. But I wasn't sure until, well..."

"Until right now?"

"You got it."

Mathis nuzzled her ear. "I'm glad I was here for your first time."

Chloe's heart melted. "I am, too," she said. "Even if it was *really* bad timing. Speaking of which..." All this stroking and nuzzling was reminding her of those very human thoughts she'd been having earlier. "Didn't you say something about the mate bond needing to be strengthened by... closeness?" she said, a wicked smile teasing at her lips.

Mathis purred. "That must have been from my very stupid period. Keeping you out of my bed hasn't so far been an effective way of keeping you out of my bed." He hesitated. "Or do I mean out of my head—or—"

Chloe groaned theatrically and flung herself backwards, pulling Mathis with her. He followed with catlike grace, covering her body with his own and claiming her lips with a passionate kiss.

Chloe froze, just for a second, but it was long enough for Mathis to figure out what was wrong. He chuckled. "Worried you'll turn into a bird again?"

She growled at him. "You're very funny for someone who's risking being cock-blocked by my magical voyage of self-discovery."

"Growling?" Mathis lowered his head to nip at her chin. "That's not very bird-like."

"Oh, should I peck out your eyes instead?" Chloe poked out her tongue. "Oh come *on*. You don't even have to take my clothes off this time, I'm already—mmmf..."

Chloe's words dissolved into a moan of pleasure as Mathis lowered himself onto her. The hard ridge of his erection pressed against her stomach, sending thrills of excitement down her spine to spark between her legs.

"Let's experiment," Mathis murmured into her ear. Her fingers found the hem of his shirt as though drawn there, and she slid her hands underneath, glorying in the hard planes of his abs and chest.

"Experiment?"

Mathis pulled away just long enough to whip his shirt off, and then he was on her again. The sensation of his chest pressing against her breasts was electric, sparks singing across her skin.

"We need to—" Mathis broke off, running his lips along her collar bone. "Mmm. I was saying, if you're going to go feathery without warning, we need to experiment to see what your triggers are..."

"Oh stop it." Chloe giggled, then hissed in pleasure as Mathis' hand ghosted up her side. "I'm not going to shift again. I'm—mmm—*definitely* too distracted for that."

"Huh. I bet you would have said the same thing ten minutes ago."

"Hey!" Chloe tried to jab him in the chest but he grabbed her finger and bit on it playfully. "You—"

She broke off, sensation flooding her mind as Mathis sucked on her nipple, swirling his tongue around the hardened nub.

"Hmm." Mathis glanced up at her, his golden eyes dancing. "Still human..."

Chloe let out a *tsk* and rolled her eyes—and then her whole body flexed as Mathis brushed his lips lower, kissing his way down the sensitive skin over her ribs to the hot cleft between her legs.

Toes curling, Chloe almost missed his next words, though she felt his hot breath on her most sensitive skin.

"Maybe this..."

Mathis closed his lips over Chloe's clit. Her whole body was already quivering with anticipation and this final touch was too much. The tip of his tongue lapped out and Chloe came with a scream, pleasure exploding through her.

She clutched at Mathis' hair and he raised his head, lips wet, eyes burning. When he dipped down again and ran his tongue across her sensitized skin, Chloe saw stars. Her body was still shaking with the force of her orgasm but every lap of Mathis' skillful tongue drew more pleasure from her until she thought her body would shake apart.

Mathis brushed his thumb along the inside of her thigh and she shouldn't have been able to feel it, not when his tongue was doing such amazing things only inches away, but she could. She could feel everything, every part of him that was touching her.

His tongue. His lips. His hands, the possessive grip of his fingertips in her soft flesh, the hard planes of his sides against her legs as she wrapped them around him.

A constellation of pleasure was building inside her, sharper and more powerful than anything she had ever felt before. Her core ached with need.

"Enough," she gasped. "Please—I need—"

Mathis rose above her with feline speed, cupping her face in one hand. "Say it."

"I want to feel you inside me." Chloe's voice was throaty with desire. "Please, Mathis, I've been waiting for so long—"

Her legs fell open beneath him and she could feel the hard ridge of his erection against her folds. *So close.* He slid one hand around her waist, still cupping her face with the other.

Chloe stared into his eyes. His pale gold irises were the thinnest ring around deep black pupils, heavy with lust. And more than that. Love. She felt an answering burst of emotion in her own heart.

"My mate," she whispered, and Mathis thrust into her.

Chloe gasped out a breath, eyes closing automatically as she gloried in the feeling of Mathis' cock inside her. He filled her perfectly, stretching her just enough that every nerve ending inside her flared white-hot.

Mathis' fingers curled against her cheek. "My mate. My perfect, beautiful, wonderful Chloe. I can't wait to spend my life with you."

She wound her fingers through his. "Me too."

To be honest, she hadn't even thought about it. Hadn't thought farther than seeing him again. But she knew it was the truth. It felt right. It felt *perfect.*

Just like him.

"I love you," she whispered, and Mathis crushed his lips against hers, claiming her with a passionate kiss.

"I love you too." The words went straight from his mouth to Chloe's heart.

He pulled out of her, slowly, and then filled her again. Deep need made Chloe breathless and she knew that no matter how slow he went, she wouldn't be able to keep control for long.

And this time, she promised herself, she would keep her eyes open.

Chloe pushed her fingers through Mathis' hair. He hadn't cut it; it was long enough for her to grab, long enough to hold onto. Just like he'd promised the first time.

Her breath grew ragged as Mathis plunged into her again and again. She met his rhythm, grinding her hips against him with every thrust.

Their bodies were completely in sync. Mathis thrust into her harder, faster, and she moved with him, drowning in his golden shifter eyes and lost in the pleasure of their bodies moving together. Mathis was so strong and powerful, and he looked down at Chloe with a fierce tenderness that sent her straight over the edge.

Chloe cried out as pleasure pulsed through her, legs clamped around Mathis' waist and fingers digging into his scalp. She felt Mathis tense above her and fixed her eyes on him. She wanted to see his pleasure.

He drove into her, his whole body clenched and trembling as he came. She found his lips, kissing and biting at them until he wrapped both arms around her and kissed her back, still buried deep inside her.

Chloe nipped him gently on the lower lip, looking up at him through her eyelashes. "What was that you said about spending the rest of our lives together?" she murmured.

Mathis stroked her hair back off her forehead, eyes glowing pale gold. "You must know I'm serious. I was stupid enough to let you go once, but not again. We're meant to be together. You're mine... and I'm yours. Forever."

Chloe trailed her fingertips over his cheekbones, across the light dusting of stubble on his jaw. "That sounds perfect." She kissed him again.

"You can feel it, can't you?" Mathis murmured against her lips. "The connection between us. The mate bond. Since you're a shifter—"

"I think I've felt it since the moment I first saw you," Chloe admitted. Her hands ghosted down his shoulders, along the muscles of his back. Even panting and sated, she couldn't stop touching him. "Even before I knew what I was. Which is... uhh... you know, I didn't exactly get a good look at myself..."

She didn't feel self-conscious; she didn't think she'd ever feel self-conscious again, not with the knowledge of Mathis' love lodged like a burning ember inside her heart. But that didn't make it any less strange that she was a shifter, and didn't even know what she shifted into.

Is that weird? she thought, and something inside her ruffled its feathers in a way that clearly meant: *Oh, hell yes it is.*

Mathis grimaced. "Honestly? I grew up here in the city. If it's not a pigeon, I don't know what it is. And you're not a pigeon." He rolled over, pulling her on top of him, and flashed her a very cat-like grin. "Why don't we take a photo next time you shift, and put it on your social media for the world to ID you?"

"Oh shut up." Chloe batted him gently on one ear, hiding her grin in his shoulder. Mathis combed his fingers through her hair.

"You know I've been fielding calls about that all week? Everyone wants in on this secret Harry Potter Fight Club movie I'm apparently starring in..."

"*Nooooo,*" Chloe moaned into his shoulder.

Mathis laughed out loud. "I'm not mad. And if anyone gets mad about what you did to get us off that island, they'll have to answer to me." He grabbed her chin and gently pulled her face to his. "You—" He kissed her. "—are—" Another kiss. "—beautiful, *and* smart, *and* the most amazing woman to ever walk on Earth. Or fly above it, when you figure out how to fly."

"Oh my God." A smile of pure wonder stretched across her face. "I'm going to *fly.*"

Mathis put his hands behind his head, smiling up at her with hooded eyes. "You know, it's going to take some getting used to, you being a shifter. What if I don't recognize you when you're in bird form?"

Chloe narrowed her eyes back at him, pushing herself up with her forearms on his muscular chest. *What is he getting at?*

"I'm going to need to get something to identify you by. Something like one of those ID bands rangers put on endangered birds. Something like... a ring."

Chloe's breath caught. "A—a ring?" she squeaked. "You mean—I thought—do shifters—?"

Mathis cupped her cheek in one hand. "Shifters will know you're mine because of the mate bond, but I want the *world* to know. I want everyone to know how much I love you, Chloe Kent. Humans, shifters, the whole world. Will you be my wife?"

For a moment, Chloe couldn't speak. Her heart felt like it was about to burst, she was so happy.

Then she realized she didn't need to speak. Not out loud, at least.

She focused, pouring all her feelings of love and happiness down the mate bond toward her beloved. *I love you. I love you so, so much. Of course I'll marry you.*

CHAPTER 28

MATHIS

Mathis was wide awake the moment the front door opened. Wide awake—and terrified.

There were only a few people who had a key to his apartment. And he knew immediately who had just come in.

"Oh, shit," he whispered into Chloe's hair. She wriggled against him and yawned, still half-asleep.

"Wassit?"

"My parents are here."

Chloe sat up so quickly Mathis had to jump back before she clocked his chin with the top of her head. "What? Here?"

She stared at him wide-eyed. Her hair was tangled from sleep and non-sleeping-activities, her cheeks pink and her lips soft and kissable. To him, she looked perfect. But he wasn't stupid enough to think she'd feel the same way.

"Oh God," Chloe gasped. "Now?" She winced as he nodded. "I need a shower—I need *clothes*..."

"Did you bring some?" It was a fair enough question, Mathis thought; it wasn't like he would know. She hadn't needed any since she arrived.

Chloe glared at him. "*Yes*. I brought a bag. I left it—in the entrance hall..."

She groaned and dropped her head into her hands as voices filtered through from the rest of the apartment.

"I don't know what will be worse. Going out there in *your* clothes, or sneaking out to grab my bag while they're not looking..." Chloe gave a tiny scream and the voices in the other room paused. Her eyes went wide. "*Oh shit...*"

Mathis laughed and pulled her into a kiss. She slapped playfully at his arms, but she couldn't even pretend to fight him for long. Her lips were soft and hot against his, but not gentle. She was as hungry for him as he was for her.

Chloe slammed her palms into his chest and pushed herself away. "Damn it! Parents—*shower...*"

"I'll get your clothes," Mathis reassured her, pulling one of her hands from his chest and kissing the palm. "Take as long as you want."

Chloe grumbled wordlessly. "You say that now. Wait until it's next week and I still haven't emerged."

Mathis kissed her fingertips. "If you want to hibernate in my en-suite, I'm sure Mom and Dad will understand."

"Oh, God. *Parents.*" Chloe's eyes flickered to his. "Mathis—you know I've never had the whole real-family thing, and..."

"They're going to love you." Mathis brushed a stray strand of hair off her forehead. "Every shifter parents' greatest wish for their children is that they find their mate. They're going to ask me what the hell took me so long to find you, and they're going to love you."

Chloe's tense expression melted into a smile. "Okay. But... shower."

Mathis watched her skip to the bathroom, enjoying the view. They'd shared a few showers since he came home to find her in his bed, and the temptation to join her now was strong, but...

"Mathis?" Mathis winced and rubbed his forehead.

"Out in a minute, Mom!" he called back.

He grabbed pants and a shirt and slipped them on, then sauntered casually out into the living room.

His mother was lounging on the sofa nearest the window; as usual, she'd nabbed the best sun-spot in the room. His father, just as typically, was rummaging through Mathis' fridge.

"Son!" he called out cheerfully as he spotted Mathis. "Thought I'd put on breakfast. You eaten?"

"Hi, Mom, Dad." He knew there was no point trying to wrestle control of his kitchen back from his father; Jacques Delacourt had very strong ideas about whose job it was to provide for his family, and if he had to break into one of his children's homes to make sure they were eating, he'd do it.

Which was one of the reasons he had a key for Mathis' place.

Mathis' mother, Donna, smiled languidly up at him. "Leave your father to it, dear," she murmured.

"I know better than to get between my alpha and a hot stove," Mathis joked back. "But—not that I'm not happy to see you—I thought we were meeting later..."

He'd always been close with his parents, but since coming back from the island he'd seen them so often he was beginning to think they wanted him to move back home. But they'd never met for anything earlier than lunch before. His mother hated early starts.

Mathis narrowed his eyes suspiciously at his parents just as the shower started in the en-suite.

Mathis' parents exchanged a look of pure glee.

"Now this *is* worth getting up early," his mother purred.

"Mom..." Mathis groaned. "Who've you been talking to?"

"That nice young Lance MacInnis," his mother drawled at the same time his father said, "Harley, you know, the Ames boy."

He stared at them both, and his mother cleared her throat delicately. "I believe I missed a call from your friend Grant this morning, too. Really, you boys are worse gossips than my shooting circle..."

"How did Grant know..." Mathis waved his own question away. From Lance or Harley, clearly. Damn it. When he saw them...

"You can bite their heads off at lunch, dear, but we did rather want to be the first to meet her."

"And breakfast!" Jacques waved a skillet for punctuation.

"And breakfast." Donna blinked slowly at her son. "And coffee!" she added, turning to her husband. "Remember, he keeps it in that little cupboard above the plates..."

Mathis took advantage of his parents being distracted by the possibility of coffee to dart by the entrance way and pick up Chloe's bag. He hadn't noticed it that first night because she'd tucked it under the coat rack.

He picked it up, and his stomach lurched. The bag was light—it couldn't have more than a few days' worth of clothes in it.

She wasn't sure whether I'd want her to stay. The thought hurt, and he tightened his grip on the bag's strap.

She knew now, though. She knew he would never leave her again.

And if he didn't get her bag to her in the next few minutes, he knew he was in trouble.

Mathis hurried back through the living area toward the bedroom. His father waved a spatula at him as he darted past. "Herbs?"

"Garden on the balcony!"

"Aha! Fancy!"

Mathis put his head down and barreled into the bedroom before either of his parents could interrupt him. He slipped into the en-suite just as Chloe was turning off the shower.

"Oh, good, you got—" The rest of her sentence dissolved into a hum of pleasure as he pulled her into a kiss. "You got yourself wet," she finished after a few minutes.

Mathis looked down at himself. She was right; her wet body had left some... *interesting*... wet marks on his clothes. "I'll change."

Chloe grabbed a towel and her bag, and then bit her lip. "The clothes I brought... they're not terrible, but they're not..."

Mathis glanced down again. His shirt was soaked—but it was also fine cotton, tailored for his body. "My family aren't snobs. But if you're worried about your wardrobe, we can go shopping. And if you're not, we can go shopping anyway, because you're going to need more clothes than there are in that bag."

"I do need to buy something for the trial..."

"I'm going to do the buying."

Chloe's eyes flashed at him, her lips curling into a delighted smile. "All right. If you insist. Just—no slinky red dresses."

Mathis grabbed her hand and kissed it. "I promise. Just yoga pants. *Lots* of yoga pants."

Chloe snorted and snatched her hand back. "Oh hush."

She was still smiling when they had both gotten dressed. Mathis folded his hand around hers. "Ready to meet my folks? Remember, hibernating in the linen closet is still an option..."

Chloe groaned. "Let's go."

Mathis couldn't help the protective urge that rushed through him as he led Chloe into the living room, and he didn't fight it. Chloe was his mate. She was *his*, and if his parents didn't accept her—

He shouldn't have worried. The moment his parents saw Chloe, they practically glowed with pride.

"Mom, Dad, this is Chloe." He slid one arm around her waist, his lion purring as she leaned against him. "If it wasn't for her, I wouldn't be alive today."

Chloe twisted to look up at him, her dark eyes questioning. "What? You saved *me*."

"I would never have made it off that island without you." He cupped her cheek in his free hand and kissed her. "You know that, right?"

Chloe grumbled, but her cheeks went pink. Mathis' lion purred.

"And, Chloe, these are my parents—Donna and Jacques Delacourt."

"Pleased to meet you."

"The pleasure is all ours, dear. It's so wonderful to see our Mathis happy again." Donna smiled and, to Mathis' amazement, actually got up out of her sun-spot to come and take Chloe's hand. "He probably hasn't figured it out yet, but he's been looking for you for a long, long time."

Mathis blinked. She was right. All those years of feeling like there was something missing, the need to find meaning in his life—it was Chloe he'd been looking for. His mate.

And now he had her, and everything was perfect.

"All right, Dad," he said, grinning. "How's that breakfast?"

Chloe slipped her hand into his as they headed for the table, and Mathis changed his mind.

Perfect made it sound like this was as good as things would get, and he knew that wasn't true. Every moment of every day that he loved his mate, every time he touched her or looked at her, his life got that much brighter. There was no limit to how wonderful their life together would be.

EPILOGUE

CHLOE

"I don't know why I thought you'd be more worried about this," Mathis muttered in Chloe's ear. She giggled and bumped her hip into him. They had just left Harper's sentencing, and despite the heavy traffic outside the courtroom, the air seemed that much sweeter knowing he was going to spend the next few decades behind bars.

Chloe grinned. "Worried? You should have been worried about me shifting and dive-bombing the asshole. Now I've missed my chance for good."

Mathis snorted. "Now I'm just relieved I didn't have to see you face-plant in the middle of the courtroom."

"Hey!" Chloe jabbed him in the ribs. "I'm getting better at flying—remember, I made it all the way down the block the other day!"

"And almost gave me a heart attack," Mathis grumbled. "The next time you want to somersault off the roof, give me a bit more notice. And some Xanax."

Chloe grinned and stretched her arms up above her head. "Six months ago, I rode a dragon off a collapsing tower. A week after that, I turned into a goddamn piping plover. Now I can *fly*, and Harper is locked up for *life*, and I'm never going to be afraid of anything, ever again."

Chloe snuggled into his side, glancing up at him through her eyelashes. Now that the trial was finally over, it felt like a huge weight had been lifted off her back. And looking at Mathis only made her feel more light-hearted.

His healing abilities had recovered once they left the island... and once they'd started living together. Now the only physical reminder of their captivity was a small scar on Mathis' cheek, so faint it could only be seen in certain lights.

Mathis had told Chloe he was worried it would hurt her to see his scar, but it didn't. The mark wasn't just a reminder of the island—it was a reminder that they'd escaped, and found each other.

And one of the best things about having found Mathis was being able to tease him.

Chloe threw her head back and cackled. "I've been talking to Harley..."

"About—oh, God, no. Please do not talk to Harley about flying. Anything but that. I—hey, Lance! Great job in there."

Lance nodded to Chloe. "Same to you. Harper's going to be inside for a long, long time."

"Good." Chloe's stomach clenched as she remembered the evidence that had come up during the trial. Harper had hurt so many people. He wouldn't be able to hurt anyone now, but that didn't fix the damage that had already been done.

Mathis squeezed her hand and Chloe looked up at him. His protectiveness made her heart swell in her chest, and the smooth band of the ring around her finger was a constant reminder of his love.

"I hope you can both join us for one last debrief," Lance said briskly. His eyebrow twitched. "Some other representatives from the defendants will be there—we're finalizing compensation packages this week. And there's something in particular I'd like to discuss with you, Chloe."

Chloe frowned, then glanced at Mathis. He nudged her encouragingly. "Sure," she said. "So long as we get to pop open some bubbly afterwards to celebrate this all being over."

"We've all got a lot to celebrate." Lance nodded again. "I'll see you both back at the Manor."

An hour later, Chloe stepped through the door Mathis held open for her. They were at Lance's workplace: the *Meerkat Manor*, as Mathis called it.

"They can't *all* be meerkats," Chloe whispered as they walked through to the meeting room.

"Well, Lance isn't," Mathis said, opening the door and ushering her through. "And I hear they have a hummingbird on board now, too..."

"Thandie!"

The hummingbird shifter looked better than Chloe had ever seen her. She grinned widely and waved across the table.

Chloe! I heard the good news—congrats!

Which news? The ring, or the fact that I am a shifter, like you thought?

Thandie rolled her eyes. "*Both*, silly!"

Lance cleared his throat and Thandie pinched her lips shut theatrically. *Whoops. Time to act professional. But we are* totally *hanging out later!*

You bet! There was no way Chloe was finishing this day without some celebratory champagne. And the more people she could celebrate with, the better.

She looked around the table as she and Mathis sat down. Apart from Lance and Thandie, she recognized Lance's aunt, General MacInnis, who greeted her with a stiff nod and a warm smile; Nora, her old manager, who kept sniffing and looking at her lap; and a few of the Manor's other staff. Like all the meerkat shifters Chloe had met so far, they were jumpy, with sandy-colored skin and hair.

She also knew the last two people at the table, a mated man and woman. The man was tall and broad-shouldered, with the languid grace and sense of power Chloe had come to associate with cat shifters. The woman with him was tall, too, with generous curves and curly dark hair that spilled over her shoulders. Chloe had met them at lunch the day she'd been introduced to Mathis' parents: Irina and Grant Diaz.

"Now that we're all here, let's get started." Lance was sitting at the end of the table, shuffling papers.

"Wait—what about Julian? He was the primary witness for the case, shouldn't he be here?" Chloe burst out.

Lance's mouth went into a thin line, and he stared at his papers. "Mr. Rouse has agreed to stay in custody until certain other matters have been attended to."

Chloe frowned. "But he was as much a victim as we were."

Lance sighed and rubbed his forehead. "True, there are extenuating circumstances—but there are many who don't see it that way. Mr. Rouse is being held as much for his safety, and that of his family, as anyone else's."

Chloe opened her mouth to say *But he's a dragon—who could hurt him?* and closed it again. Maybe that was the problem: Julian didn't want to be forced into another situation where he had to hurt someone. It was the suggestion that someone else might use the eggs as leverage that made her blood run cold.

"Where are his eggs now?"

Lance checked his files. "Ah, his sister's offspring. To keep them from being exploited, they've been placed in protective custody with another family until Mr. Rouse's sister and her husband are located." A shadow passed over his face. "More of Harper's victims. They're still alive, according to Harper's records, but where, we don't know. Mr. Rouse said they live full-time as dragons and that, along with their powers of invisibility, are going to make the mission somewhat... tricky."

"I guess that makes sense," she said softly. Mathis took hold of her hand under the table.

Julian will be fine, he said privately. *Lance has it under control.*

Lance pulled out his tablet and set it down with a *click*.

"The trial's over, but that doesn't mean we're done here. There's still the question of the repercussions on the lives of Harper's victims..."

Chloe held Mathis' hand as Lance detailed the support being offered to Harper's ex-employees... and captives. As Chloe had guessed, and the trial had proved, even his employees were captives of a sort, trapped by the same threat of violence that kept the fighters in line.

Harper was going to be in prison for a long, long time, and while he was there, his fortune was being put to good use. Along with the prison sentence, the shifter judge had forced Harper to pay into a fund that would provide ongoing assistance to everyone who had ever been hurt by him.

Lance pushed his glasses up his nose. "Harper's tentacles reached longer than we expected. We're still digging up buyers he sold the dragon's scales to, and as for his *guests*—" He snarled the word, and just for a moment, Chloe glimpsed the wild snow leopard behind the dapper man. "—They're continuing to protest their ignorance of Harper's activities, but we're working on them."

"You mean it's been half a year and you still haven't tidied this mess up?" Mathis grinned at Lance. "You're slipping."

Lance narrowed his eyes, but a predatory smile danced around his lips. "We'll get there. Don't you worry about that. I always thought there was more to the Diaz kidnapping case than we knew, and now we've got proof—and leads. And an office of agents to hunt this asshole's contacts from their hiding places."

Chloe squeezed Mathis' hand at the mention of the kidnapping case, sending love and support to him through their bond.

Mathis had been right back on the island, when he told her his sister Francine would sense he was in danger. His twin sister had noticed that something was wrong. But after Mathis had revealed his true identity to Harper, the bastard had sent people to put her on the wrong scent. Harper's minions had convinced her that Mathis had been murdered by one of his old friends—and had kidnapped and threatened to kill his friend's mate as revenge.

Mathis cleared his throat, looking away from where Grant and Irina were sitting. "Will this have any effect on my sister's situation?"

Lance shot him a sympathetic grimace, and Chloe remembered that Lance had been friends with Francine, too.

"That's up to her," Lance said in an undertone. He straightened his shoulders and checked his notes again.

"Speaking of the Diazes..." Lance nodded to the couple. "Grant and Irina are funding a research and development team to find out more about the effects of Mr. Rouse's scales. We don't know how many are out there, with outfits like the group that radicalized Francine. They'll also be looking into other shifter abilities, such as the ones displayed by Harper and by Chloe, here."

That got Chloe's attention. "I had a theory about that. Ever since I started shifting, I haven't used my... um, other ability. And Harper seemed to lose it as soon as he shifted that time on the beach, too. There might be a connection—is that what you're thinking?"

She stared down the table at Grant and Irina, who stared back. Irina grimaced. "Um, we'll... let you know? We're more on the 'providing money' end of things than the 'figuring stuff out' end..."

She blushed and Grant wound one arm around her shoulders, pulling her to him for a kiss. "Smooth, Lance." He winked at Chloe. "I'll put you in touch with our lead researcher. She'll be thrilled to hear from you."

"Sounds great," Chloe said.

"One final thing..." He paused, and an expression of something close to panic flashed across his face. "Apart from an unkillable rumor about a new Hollywood franchise that just. Won't. Die."

Mathis laughed out loud, and Chloe sketched out a mock bow. "You're welcome."

"Which brings me to our final action point this afternoon—Ms. Kent, can I interest you in a job?"

Chloe blinked. "What? I mean, excuse me?" She turned to Mathis. "Did you know about this?"

Mathis shrugged, one hundred per cent genuine artificial innocence.

"What sort of a job?" Chloe asked, looking back at Lance.

Lance settled back in his chair. "If there's one thing this matter with Harper has shown us, it's that shifters across the country are vulnerable to exploitation not by humans, but by our own kind. The Manor is opening a new division dealing with issues of communication between shifters—ways for us to communicate known dangers, and for civilians to alert us to problems—using modern comms channels."

Chloe couldn't believe what she was hearing, and Lance's serious frown wasn't helping.

"You... you want me to be your social media manager?" she choked out.

"Given your work experience, and quick thinking under pressure—yes, something along those lines. We'll work out the details once you're on board."

Chloe's cheeks went red. "Thanks," she blurted out. "I... really didn't expect that. It's very kind of you."

Lance snorted. "Kind? We're just snapping you up before anyone else does." He paused and rubbed his forehead. "And that includes shifter organizations *and* human ones."

"Everyone wants you on their team." Mathis' pride was clear in his voice as he slung one arm around her shoulders. "It's up to you. If you want to push me into a career as a Hollywood superstar..."

"I want to help people." A smile spread across Chloe's face. "Shifters like me, who don't have our own support networks. That's what you're saying, isn't it?" She turned to Lance. "We're going to stop anyone like Harper from being able to target vulnerable shifters again."

"That's the plan, yes."

"Then I'm in."

She barely heard what else was said as Lance closed the meeting. Her mind was flying over the possibilities of her new job. This was everything she'd ever wanted: her chance to make a real difference.

And with her mate at her side, she was ready to take on the world.

STEALING THE SNOW LEOPARD'S HEART

SHIFTER SUSPENSE BOOK 3

CHAPTER 1

KEELEY

"*Stupid, arrogant, asshole piece of shit.*" Keeley Smith ground her teeth as she stalked down the corridor. "Who the fuck does he think he is?"

Keeley wrenched her cleaning cart around a corner and almost bowled over a group of guests. She froze, and hauled a professional smile onto her face, hoping none of them noticed her white-knuckle grip on the cart handle.

She needn't have bothered.

None of the guests so much as glanced at her as they carried on down the corridor, laughing and joking. Dressed in her work uniform—white blouse, black skirt and apron—Keeley might as well have been invisible.

She stood with her head lowered as the guests passed her by. There were four of them: an older couple, a woman who looked like their daughter, and another man. A family get-together, Keeley guessed. From the way the younger woman kept flashing her left hand around, she could guess why they all looked so pleased with themselves.

The sparkly boulder on the woman's finger wasn't the only sign of how well-off the family was. Gold glittered on the women's ears and necks. Both men were wearing the sort of watch that was better for telling the wearer's annual income than the time, and their suits were tailored to effortlessly fit their bodies.

But that wasn't the reason her heart clenched as she watched them disappear around the corner. You didn't work at a hotel like this without getting used to rich people flashing their money around.

No. They were *happy*. That was the worst of it. The older two were holding hands with the easy familiarity of long-term love, and the younger couple kept bumping against each other, they were walking that close together. A happy family, celebrating together.

Keeley knew she'd never be rich. But it was the knowledge that she'd never have that sort of happiness that really hurt.

And these people have both? Come on, universe, that isn't fair, she grumbled silently, pushing her cleaning cart to the service elevator.

The doors opened, and Keeley's frozen smile softened into something approaching a genuine one as she saw who was already inside. "Dani!"

"Hey, girl! Didn't your shift end an hour ago?" Dani reached forward and pulled Keeley's cart into the elevator.

Keeley made sure the elevator doors had shut before she replied. "Meant to. Just had to finish one final call, no guesses who. Now I've gotta get out of here before he 'accidentally' spills another bottle of wine in his bed, and I get called in again."

"Oh, gross. Room 304?" Dani made a face as Keeley nodded. "How long is he staying this time? You know, we could swap blocks if it all gets too much for you…"

Keeley mock-glared at her. "Nuh-uh. You know he doesn't leave a tip until the last night. I'm not putting up with him for two weeks just for you to come in and snipe my tip at the last minute."

Dani laughed. "Well, just imagine you're punching him in the face every time you plump up the pillows on his bed. That's what I do."

"Yeah…" Keeley looked down at her hands, still resting on the cart handle. The scars that criss-crossed her knuckles had faded over the years, but she could still feel them as though they were fresh.

Keeley stuck her hands in her apron pocket. "That's probably not such a great idea."

"Well, you do you, babe."

Keeley couldn't get Dani's words out of her head as she pulled on her coat over her work uniform and hurried out the service exit. The cold night air smacked her in the face.

Imagining punching asshole guests in the face wasn't going to help her. But maybe there was something she *could* do to make work bearable.

It was the memory of the engagement ring on the woman's finger that did it. The Asshole of Room 304 brought expensive stuff with him on his trips, too. Not jewellery, but high-end electronics. Phone, laptop, smart watch, that sort of thing.

Keeley's fingers twitched. *It wouldn't be that hard to pocket something while he isn't looking,* she thought. *Or even when he is looking. Hah, imagine it. He's so busy staring at my ass he doesn't notice me picking up his wallet.*

She wouldn't need to actually *steal* them. Just pick them up and move them around to confuse him. Leave him a bit off-balance, and Keeley feeling a bit more in control.

Just a bit of fun.

She flinched, her fingers clenching in her coat pockets. Fun? No. Fun was a *stupid* idea. Even just thinking about it was stupid. Hadn't she learned anything ten years ago?

Have you forgotten why you're here, busting your ass in housekeeping? You're a good person now, remember?

Besides, who was she kidding? She couldn't mess with a guest's stuff and expect to get away with it. Even the suspicion of theft would be enough to get her fired, regardless of whether anything had actually gone missing or not. That was why she'd gone into housekeeping, after all. It was a job that forced her to keep to the straight and narrow.

Because getting fired was the best-case scenario, given how Keeley and this sort of "fun" tended to end up.

Keeley absently rubbed her fingers together, feeling the odd patches of numbness from her faded scars. She shivered, and it had nothing to do with the cold air.

Me having fun and being happy just screws everything up. Better to be good and miserable. Life is safer that way. I'm *safer that way.*

Anyway, work might be shit, but she had her own apartment now. With a shower that worked. And, she was pretty sure, at least half a leftover pizza in the fridge. She could soak away the feeling of the asshole guest ogling her legs, then wrap up in bed with some delicious pepperoni and cheese and watch the trashiest TV she could find. Then get up bright and early to do some laundry before her next shift.

She sighed, and tried to convince herself it was a satisfied sigh.

"Evening, kiddo."

Keeley jumped sideways as someone whispered in her ear. A wiry arm wrapped around her waist, pulling her back before she leapt into traffic.

"How's my favourite niece?"

Oh, shit no.

Blood drained from Keeley's face as she stared at the man who'd grabbed her. She would say "saved her from being flattened under a bus," but if it wasn't for him, she wouldn't have almost jumped into the street in the first place.

If it wasn't for him, she wouldn't have done a lot of things.

"S-Sean? What are you doing here?" She glared at the man, hating the way her voice stuttered. *It's just surprise,* she told herself. *You're just... surprised.*

Not terrified. Nuh-uh.

Oh, shit.

"Do I need a reason to catch up with my favorite niece?" Sean Bailey grinned at her.

Is this some sort of instant karma for thinking about stealing Asshole's things? Keeley thought wildly. Her pulse thudded in her ears.

She hadn't seen Sean in ten years. Ten boring, miserable, *good* years.

He hadn't changed much. Same too-toothy smile, same crinkly, friendly eyes. His face was thinner, and the cords in his neck stood out more than she remembered, but other than that he was the same old Sean. The same guy she'd tagged along behind ever since she could remember, convinced he was the coolest person in the world.

God, she'd been an idiot.

Sean made a mock-sad face and tapped her under the chin. "What's with the long face, kiddo? I thought you'd be happy to see your old uncle. And how was work?"

"You—" Keeley cleared her throat. Her mouth was so dry, it took her a couple of tries to speak again. "It was fine. Work was fine," she muttered.

Sean winked. "Sure it was, sure. You got a moment to talk, kiddo?"

"No, I really have to get going—"

"Don't want to miss the train, huh? I get it. Come on, I'll walk you to the station. You're still in that place in Queens, right?"

He found me. Keeley let Sean take her arm and lead her down the street. *He found me. How the hell did he find me? How does he know where I live?*

She'd been so careful. Kept her head down. No online presence, no social media, *nothing*.

And yet here he was. After all these years.

A shiver went down her back. If he'd found her—there had to be a reason. There had to be something he wanted.

Keeley wet her lips again. "What are you doing here? What's going on?" *Please don't say it, please don't...*

"I've got a job for you, haven't I?"

Oh, no. Keeley squeezed her eyes tight shut. "I've already got a job," she snarled.

"Oh, I know." Sean let the three words hang in the air. Keeley couldn't speak. At last the silence became too much.

"Sean, I—"

"Good job, is it? Pay you well? Treat you nice?" He plucked at the worn collar of her coat. "Can't pay you *that* well. Good thing I came along, really."

"Sean, please—"

"Won't take you long. I'd do it myself, but you know how things are. And I'll make it worth your while. Family rates."

"I'm not doing it." Keeley sucked in her breath. There. She'd said it. "I don't want your money. I've got a real job now. I've got my own life. I don't do... this sort of thing anymore."

Sean's grin got toothier, and he squeezed Keeley's arm, just enough to let her know how much harder he could squeeze it, if he wanted to. "Listen to yourself. 'This sort of thing'. You don't even know what the job is, yet."

"I don't need to. I'm n-not doing it." More stuttering. She was twenty-five, damn it, not some stuttering teenager. What was wrong with her?

"Really?" He yanked her around to face him, his face twisting into a snarl. "Think you're too good for us, huh? Think you can leave us all behind?"

He squeezed harder. Keeley gritted her teeth. She would *not* let him know he was hurting her.

"How about I go tell the people in that fancy hotel exactly who you are, Keeley 'Smith'? How would you like that?"

"You wouldn't!"

"Sure I would, kiddo. Because unlike some people, I understand what family means. It means you don't get to leave us behind."

Keeley wanted to scream. She should say no, tell him to take his "job" and shove it, but—the hotel. She'd worked so hard to build herself a life here. If he told the management there who she used to be...

And he knew where she lived.

Her whole body sagged.

"I knew you'd come around. Aw, don't look at me like that. It'll be fun. It's in your blood." Sean shrugged off his backpack and held it out.

Keeley took it, feeling numb.

"And now I owe you one, right? Like I said, I was going to do the drop myself, but I've got other things on. Go on, take it, you don't have all night. Good. Now, here's what you have to do…"

Keeley listened mutely. The lump in her throat was so big she wasn't sure she could speak, anyway. When Sean asked her if she understood, she nodded.

"I knew I could rely on you, kiddo. Get the job done, and I'll come around tomorrow and we can talk about your payment."

He sauntered off, and Keeley finally gathered the courage to ask:

"How did you find me?"

Sean stared at her over his shoulder. This time, when he grinned, it was genuine. Keeley's stomach went cold.

"Got a new business partner, don't I? Told me he could find anything, and I asked him to find you. Like a test run." He winked. "It's good, knowing who you can rely on."

He disappeared down the street, blending in with the late-night crowds. Keeley fought back tears as she looked down at the backpack.

Ten years. Ten damned years of trying to be a good person, and now she was back where she started. Trapped. Again.

The buildings either side of the road seemed to press in on her, dark and heavy and stifling. Keeley clutched the backpack and closed her eyes until her breathing settled.

There was something hard inside it with sharp corners and long edges. She swallowed. Whatever it was, it was her responsibility now. And if she failed…

My job. My apartment. Everything I've worked so hard for.

Ten minutes later, Keeley stumbled down the steps to the platform for the train that would take her to the rendezvous point. She couldn't tell whether the roaring in her ears was the noise of the train arriving or the sound of her own pulse thudding against her skull.

What did Sean say? The last car... Keeley found a seat at the very back, clutching the bag in her lap. The other passengers ignored her.

One stop. Two. A few more passengers got on and off, and eventually, Keeley was the only one left in the car.

Any other day, she would have switched cars. No way she wanted to risk the next person who got on deciding to harass the girl in the housekeeping uniform. But today...

"Fuck you, Sean," she muttered, gritting her teeth. And suddenly—probably because he was too far away to hear her—her fear transformed into blazing anger. How dare he? How dare he pull her back into his shit?

Well, screw him. He wanted her on board? Then she was going to find out exactly what it was he'd gotten her into.

Keeley unzipped the backpack, not sure what she expected to find. Its contents had felt bulky, and now she saw that there was only one item in the pack: a black case like a briefcase, but thicker. As she touched it, its sides seemed to hum, as though there was some sort of mechanism inside, but when she held it to her ear, it was silent. She must have imagined it.

What is it? Money? Jewelry? Drugs? Keeley scowled. Knowing Sean, it could be anything. He didn't exactly discriminate when it came to being a criminal piece of shit.

He was also a stupid piece of shit, because although the case looked expensive, it had the sort of push-lever combination lock that Keeley could break in less than a minute.

It'll be fun.

Fuck it. Her fingers were already itching. And it wasn't like her life could get any worse right now.

Keeley leaned over the case, her fingers moving automatically. She slid the unlock lever across, and then one by one pushed the combination numbers until she felt the slight change in pressure that told her she'd found the right number. One, two, three.

She let out a slow breath. *That felt... nice.* It was almost soothing, how easy some locks were to break. Child's play. Literally. Some kids grew up with teddy bears and toy trains. Keeley had learned how to crack a lock before she could spell her own name.

The case sprang open, and Keeley stared down at the thing her uncle had blackmailed her into transporting.

"What the hell?"

Chapter 2

Lance

Lance sat back and allowed himself a moment of smug pride.

At least, it should have been just a moment. Tonight was important, after all. The keystone that would make everything that had happened these last months worthwhile. The cherry on top. One contented sigh—perhaps the flicker of a smile—and then back on mission.

His snow leopard had different plans, which, in retrospect, Lance should have accounted for. Cats didn't do *moments* of smugness. They luxuriated in it. At length. And loudly.

Lance's vision fuzzed, a warning that his snow leopard was rising to the surface and taking over some of his senses. He clamped down on it hard.

I swear to God, if one of my staff come in here and find me purring... he warned the gleeful creature inside him.

His vision cleared and inside him, Lance's snow leopard stretched lazily, the very picture of innocence. Lance chuckled softly. His snow leopard might not be as disciplined as he was, but there was one foolproof way to keep it in line: appeal to its sense of dignity.

And a purring human was pretty much the opposite of dignified.

There was a knock on the door. A moment later, a sandy-haired man poked his head around.

"Sir?"

"Come in, Briers." Lance beckoned the sandy-haired man over. He paused at the door just long enough for it to be noticeable. Lance hid a smile. *Dignity.*

Sam Briers was one of several meerkat shifters Lance employed at his private investigator agency. At one stage, his staff had even been mostly meerkat shifters. They'd called it *Meerkat Manor*, after an old nature documentary.

That had been back when most of the work the agency did was basic PI stuff. Meerkat shifters were excellent at recon, able to stay alert for hours without losing focus. And they could hold their own in scraps.

Then there had been the Diaz affair, and Gerald Harper. The world had become a darker, more dangerous place; or maybe Lance had finally had the wool pulled from in front of his eyes, and faced up to reality. These days, the MacInnis Agency did more than hunt down small-time shifter conmen.

Lance realized he was clenching his fists. He relaxed them, forcing his fingers to unfurl one by one, as Briers darted from the door to in front of his desk.

"How's our latest recruit?" Lance asked. It wasn't the question Briers had been expecting; Lance saw his brain change gears behind his eyes before he replied.

"Zhang, sir?" Briers waited for Lance to nod. "I'm running another check on her background. Everything's clear so far, but—"

"Didn't you do that before her training started?" Lance frowned. Briers was the agency's technology specialist and was in charge of running background checks on all new employees. There was no way Briers would have let Carol Zhang begin her on-boarding without a clear security check.

"You can never be too careful, sir." Briers was practically trembling with righteousness. Lance sighed.

"I suppose you're right."

Inside him, Lance's snow leopard shivered.

He hadn't always been so careful, and God, did he regret it now. So much hurt could have been saved, if only he'd been more aware.

But that was in the past. This was now.

And now, they had something to celebrate.

Gerald Harper was locked up. His island of horrors was no more, and the survivors were rebuilding their lives in freedom. And over the last few months, Lance and his agents had tracked down every last thread in the web of criminals connected to Harper's evil.

Which meant the most vulnerable of all his victims were finally safe.

"I didn't come in here to talk about Zhang," Briers said, playing nervously with the cuffs of his shirt.

"Of course not." Lance stood up. "How's the transfer going?"

"Smoothly." Briers gave a brief nod. "Three separate vehicles, all due to arrive in the city in the next three hours. Rouse's handlers—sorry, sir, his assigned agents—have been alerted that something is happening tonight, but as you requested, we're keeping the details need-to-know."

"Good." Lance nodded slowly, though inside him, his snow leopard was bristling. *The dragon should know what we're planning,* it hissed. *They're his—*

Lance tuned his snow leopard out as it continued to grumble. This was a delicate operation. Briers, as his information security chief, had advised that even though they'd smoked out all of Harper's old associates, the transfer should be done as quietly as possible.

You can never be too careful. Only a select few agents, hand-picked by Lance and Briers, knew about tonight's mission. Even the dragon shifter Julian Rouse hadn't been told, despite his connection to the subjects.

Or maybe because of it. Briers had been insistent that Rouse not be involved, and Lance had to admit the meerkat shifter had a point. The dragon shifter wasn't exactly stable. Hell, the first time Lance had seen him, he'd been tearing chunks of solid stone out of a building.

No. Far better to surprise him with good news than to risk him becoming impatient if there were any delays to tonight's mission.

Once the mission was complete, Rouse would be far more stable. Lance's certainty about this should have surprised him, but it didn't: it was an instinctual shifter knowledge, lodged as deep in his soul as his own snow leopard.

And then all the darkness that had plagued Lance since the Diaz affair would be over.

He rolled his shoulders back, feeling as though a weight had been lifted off him. When Briers caught his eye, he didn't just smile, he grinned.

"Sir?"

"Just reflecting that this might be the first time in a year that I've felt happy about the world. It's a good feeling." Lance clapped the meerkat shifter on the shoulder as he headed for the door. "And I couldn't have done any of this without you."

"It's been an honor to work with you. Isn't that why we all joined up? Helping the great Lance MacInnis save the world?"

Lance chuckled. "Don't start with that crap again."

Saving the world. He didn't know who'd started it, but it had become a joke around the office these last few months. At least, he hoped it was a joke.

Because it sure as hell wasn't true.

After the Diaz affair and what happened on Harper's island people acted like Lance was a hero, but nothing could be further from the truth. All those two cases had shown him was how little he knew—and how easy it would be to take a wrong step, be too late, and see the people he loved get hurt.

He'd almost been too late to save Harper's captives. And although he and Grant Diaz had been able to save Grant's mate, Lance was too late to save the other woman who had been caught up in that web of lies.

Lance had spent the last year feeling like anything but a hero. Knowing that Harper's criminal network was out there, but not knowing where or who they were or what they might do next was like walking blindfolded along the edge of a cliff with the ground crumbling under his feet. He never knew if the next step would find him finally on solid ground—or send him and his allies tumbling into the void.

Not anymore. They'd won. Harper's network was in tatters. His victims were safe.

And no one needed to know how terrified Lance had been that everything would go wrong.

Briers fell into step beside Lance as they walked down the corridor. Lance slowed down automatically. At nearly seven feet, Lance was the tallest man at the agency. If he walked at his normal pace down the corridor, Briers would have to scuttle to keep up. Not the best look for a senior staff member.

Almost as undignified as a purring human, he thought to his snow leopard. It flicked its whiskers at him and didn't respond.

What's upset you? Lance shook his head as he walked into the main office. His snow leopard stayed silent.

The office was quiet this late at night, but not empty. Three meerkat shifters, gathered around a computer station at the far end of the room, immediately swiveled around to look at Lance as the door closed behind him. Lance nodded at them, and they bobbed back down.

Parker and Yelich, the two field agents he'd prepped for tonight's mission, were standing by the coffee machine, to all appearances deeply involved in a discussion about Parker's grandchildren. If Lance hadn't been looking for it, even he wouldn't have seen the hints of tension in their shoulders and the way their eyes flicked quickly to him as he walked into the office.

Parker was a lanky white man a few decades older than Lance. He had a calming effect on people, maybe because his face looked as gentle and slightly woebegone in human form as when he was in his bloodhound shape. Lance hoped that particular skill wouldn't need to come in handy on today's mission, but—dragons.

Yelich was heavy-set, with olive skin and hair cropped short. A bit less level-headed than Parker, but utterly reliable. The sort of person you wanted at your side in a tricky situation.

Not that anything like that's going to happen tonight.

Parker, Yelich. Lance sent a telepathic message to them both. *Corner meeting room, now.*

Briers hurried through to the meeting room, head already bent over his ever-present tablet. Lance hid a grin. Most of the time, he was the one with his face in a screen. Even now his own tablet was burning a hole in his pocket. If he wasn't careful, the briefing meeting would look more like the two of them playing mobile games while Yelich and Parker rolled their eyes.

We're really doing this? A grin flashed across Yelich's face. *Hot damn. I was sure this was another false alarm. Well, it's about time.*

Yelich's just excited because she heard the safe house has a pond, Parker added, downing the last of his coffee. Yelich elbowed him with a good-natured snort.

Both agents grabbed their coffees and headed for the corner meeting room. Lance followed them, and then paused and raised his eyebrows as he passed another desk.

"Still here, Zhang?"

Carol Zhang was in her early twenties, only a few years younger than Lance had been when he started the agency as a one-man circus. She had black hair cut in a neat shoulder-length bob, an athletic build, and gray eyes that had freaked the hell out of Lance when he first met her.

She was a shark shifter. Lance hadn't met many, and Carol was the only one he'd ever met who had this particular issue with her eyes. Lance's snow leopard sometimes jumped up and took over his eyes and ears or, God forbid, made him purr, but Carol's eyes were permanently shark-like: gray-black and flat-looking, with no distinction between the iris and pupil.

She didn't jump when Lance spoke to her, even though she hadn't looked up when he came in. That was unusual, even for predator shifters. Out in the wild, the best way to react to an unexpected presence was to jump the hell away from it, and the same tended to hold true for shifters even if they grew up in the city.

Instead, she looked up smoothly, her face and stance betraying not even the slightest hint of surprise. "Yes, boss. I'm reviewing some of the training materials, and—" She glanced over her shoulder at the other field agents. "Agent Yelich's still here, so I thought…"

"Yelich is on assignment tonight. You're free to head home for the weekend."

Zhang nodded and frowned. "Yes, boss. I didn't realize it had gotten so late. I'll just finish this reading first."

Lance nodded and kept walking, making a mental note to tell Yelich to tell Zhang about work-life balance. It would come better from her than from him; God knew he didn't make a good example.

He was halfway to the meeting room when there was a clatter behind him. He turned to see Zhang clutching at her half-overturned chair. She saw him watching her and flushed red.

A moment later, she was at his side. Lance blinked. Zhang usually held herself so still, he forgot about her strange turns of speed. When she did move, she was as quick and silent as—

Shark! his snow leopard snapped, puffing up defensively. *Danger!*

Stop that, Lance retorted. Out loud, he said, "Zhang? Was there something else?"

"Yes. Mr. MacInnis. Boss." Zhang's lips twisted, and her face flushed a vivid red that seemed at odds with her cool, flat eyes. "I wanted to tell you—I know I've only been here three months, and I'm still on my probation, but I…"

She twisted her fingers together. Lance had never seen her so animated. "Go on," he encouraged her.

"I wanted to thank you. For taking a chance on me." She shrugged, the movement a strange combination of shark-smoothness and jerky, entirely human awkwardness. "I know I'm not a full agent yet, but even bringing me on as a recruit—not many people would have done that. Not for a shark shifter."

A psychic nudge brushed up against the edge of Lance's mind. Briers, impatient as usual.

Lance held up a hand. "Their loss is our gain," he interjected as Zhang hesitated. "I mean it. From everything Yelich's told me about your work so far, you'll be an asset to the agency."

"Really?" She grinned in sudden delight, and Lance's snow leopard puffed up even more. He swallowed quickly. That was right. Zhang's eyes weren't the only perma-shark part of her appearance.

"Really," he said, hoping his voice was communicating the correct amount of reassurance and precisely zero of his snow leopard's freak-out. "In fact, I wanted to discuss your probationary period next week. I'll put it in your calendar. Right now, though, I have other matters to attend to."

"Of course. Thanks, boss. Sorry for interrupting." Zhang glided rapidly back to her desk and sat down, practically glowing.

"Anytime."

Lance hid a smile as walked into the meeting room. *Well, well, well.* Maybe Briers was still cautious of their latest recruit, but he'd see what Yelich had to say. If she thought Zhang was ready for it, maybe it was time to start sending her on missions.

Of course, after tonight, the missions would be boring. Because after tonight, everything was going back to normal. No more dragon exploitation. No more hidden criminal networks.

The door swung shut behind him, hissing slightly as it sealed. The sealing might seem like overkill, but overkill was the only way to keep meeting rooms properly soundproof in a company that employed sharp-eared shifters.

"Right," Lance said, re-settling his glasses as he stalked towards the gathered agents. "Parker, Yelich, we—"

He broke off as a wave of alarm battered against his mind. His snow leopard went on high alert.

Something was terribly wrong.

"What's happened?"

"Look at this." Briers pushed his hair off his forehead and held his tablet out to Lance. Lance took it, frowning. Meerkat shifters were notoriously edgy and highly strung, but Briers was actually sweating. And as he glanced around the room, he saw that even Parker and Yelich looked disturbed.

Lance looked at the tablet and swore. A red light blinked on a map: they'd lost contact with one of the transfer vans. "When did this come in?"

"Ten seconds before you walked in." Briers licked his lips. "It's Alpha transport. I've tapped the driver's comm, but he's not—"

Briers' phone buzzed, and he almost dropped it in his hurry to answer it. He listened, his expression intent, and when he ended the call his face was ashen. "That was him. Someone jacked the van and knocked him out." Briers swallowed, a tic twitching at the corner of one eye. "The payload's gone."

Dread settled on Lance's shoulders. "We've lost one of the eggs."

Briers nodded, droplets of sweat flying off his forehead.

Lance leapt into action. "Parker, Yelich, contact the other transports. They're still en route?" He paused for Briers to nod. "Then they're not in the city yet. Tell them to pull out, *now*. Someone knew we were making the transfer tonight. We can't risk losing the other eggs." He turned back to Briers. "Go."

Sam Briers had been on the agency's payroll since near the beginning. Lance didn't need to tell him what he needed; the meerkat shifter's fingers were already flying over his tablet's screen.

"It has to still be somewhere in the city." Briers frowned. "I'm putting everything I have on it. Tracking out from the last known sighting. If there's anything even—"

His eyes widened. Lance nodded at him to continue.

"There's... something. The light on these security camera feeds is wrong for the time of night." He pursed his lips. "Messy. They're looping footage from earlier in the evening."

Some sixth sense made the hairs on the back of Lance's neck prickle. Briers was good, but this seemed almost too easy. "You think it's a trap?"

Briers met his eyes. "I think it's the only lead we have."

And even if it is a trap... All of Lance's protective instincts surged. They had to get that egg back. If the people who'd taken it were anything like the groups he'd been hunting down these last few months...

None of the Rouse eggs had hatched while they were in protective custody, but according to Julian Rouse, the possibility was still there. Apparently the eggs were in a kind of stasis. When conditions were right, they would hatch.

Lance didn't want to think what might happen if the missing egg hatched while it was under the control of whoever had taken it.

He forced himself to stand straight, even as he felt like the ground was cracking under his feet.

I was so sure that we'd cut off every loose end. That the danger was over. But he'd been wrong. Something had slipped through the gaps. And now his sense of control was crumbling. Again.

"Right," he said. His voice was steady, not betraying the fear in his heart. "Here's the plan."

CHAPTER 3

KEELEY

For a moment, Keeley was confused. She stared down at the thing inside the case, nestled so carefully in a satin-covered cushion.

She'd expected drugs, or money, or some high-value item Sean was fencing for his new "business partner." Not this.

It's just... a rock.

A fancy, polished rock the size of her fists put together. But still... a rock.

Frowning, Keeley slipped the rock out of the case, cradling it against her stomach as she checked under the cushion it had lain on. There was nothing else in the case. Just the stone.

What the hell is going on here? Is this some sort of a joke?

Keeley's heart sank. *No. Not a joke. A test.*

Sean had tricked her, and she'd fallen for it. There was no job. He just wanted her to know he could still control her.

Her fingers tightened around the stone. She was about to throw it back in the case and slam the lid shut, but something made her pause.

It was just a fancy stone. The sort of thing Keeley had seen in New Age stores, the ones that sold crystals and herbs and stuff. It probably wasn't worth more than thirty or forty dollars, really.

But it was... pretty. Glimmers of purple, green and blue seemed to shift under its surface as the train rocked in its tracks.

Pretty, she thought again. And strange. The coloration made the rock look mysterious, valuable—

She shook her head. Whoever had carved it had done a half-assed job. It wasn't even properly round. Instead, it was tapered at one end, almost egg-shaped. And the surface wasn't finished, but had a dimpled texture, like a golf ball.

Still...

Keeley felt half-hypnotized. She ran her fingertips across the dimpled surface of the stone. She didn't have many pretty things these days. If this was a trick, a test, then she didn't need to leave it in the case, right? The stone was the right size to fit into her coat pocket. She could just—

Just steal it?

Keeley grimaced. *Wow. Doesn't take much to make you fall back into bad habits, huh?* Even her inner voice was bitter.

She sniffed and gritted her teeth, bracing herself to push down on the surge of rage and helplessness she knew was coming. Damn it, she'd tried *so hard.* For *years.*

All she wanted was to be someone else. Someone *better.* Someone who deserved even a taste of the love and happiness she'd seen in that family she'd almost bowled over back at the hotel. Was that too much to ask?

She closed her eyes, stretching her imagination as far as it would go. No point imagining herself as someone with a happy mom and dad. It was a bit late for that.

But this new, imaginary Keeley—the one she'd dreamt of when she left home ten years ago, the one she'd spent the last decade trying day after day to become... In her most secret dreams, she would have a man who looked at her like the guy with the fancy watch had looked at his new fiancée. As though she was the most wonderful, most important person in the world.

Someone that Keeley could look at like the woman had looked at him, smiling and giggly and pretend-tripping so he would catch her. Like she trusted him so much it wasn't even a question.

Like she couldn't wait to start their life together. Be a family. *Have* a family, have kids who would grow up surrounded by that much love...

Keeley shook her head. Well, it hadn't happened, had it? No chance of a boyfriend when she spent her evenings scrubbing floors and changing sheets instead of out clubbing. The most action she'd had in the last few years was dickheads like the guy tonight leering at her ass.

No. New Keeley, old Keeley, it didn't matter. She was stuck with the hand she'd been dealt. No way she would ever have anything like—

—Curiosity, warmth, hello?—

Keeley spluttered and blinked. That... wasn't her. It had been in her head, but it wasn't *her* that had thought it. Or felt it. It hadn't even been words, just a strong... feeling.

"Now I'm going crazy as well," she muttered. She wiped her eyes and checked the next stop. "Oh, shit."

The train had nearly arrived at the station where she was supposed to leave the backpack. She needed to put the rock away. Make it look like she hadn't tampered with it.

Keeley wrapped her fingers more tightly around the stone.

Her fingertips tingled and she stopped, eyes wide. A moment before, the stone had been cool to the touch. Well, it was rock, after all. But now it was warm. And growing warmer by the second.

Keeley looked at it more carefully. It was still just... well, a fancy rock. It sat heavily in her hand, its polished surface reflecting the light unevenly.

It shouldn't be this warm just from her holding it for a few seconds, should it? She turned it over in her hands, looking for a seal or join. Maybe it was some sort of electronic gadget?

Something moved inside the stone, and Keeley almost dropped it.

It felt *alive*.

Keeley held her breath. There it was again. The stone shook in her hands. A short, soft movement—like a heartbeat.

Thud. Thud.

"What *is* this?" she breathed, eyes fixed on the stone.

A bright, fluttery excitement burst against her mind. Not *her* excitement. She wasn't excited, she was freaking the hell out. *So what is—*

Crack!

A hairline crack appeared in the stone, so thin Keeley could barely see it. She ran her fingertips over it, just to make sure she wasn't imagining things.

"Oh, shit. Now it's breaking?"

The stone rocked at her touch.

Crack! Crack!

The hairline crack widened and another one appeared. And another. Keeley's pulse thudded in her ears. Was this part of the test? She opened the case, and the goods started breaking—was it some sort of failsafe?

A fragment of rock the size of her palm fractured and fell away, and Keeley gasped.

It wasn't a failsafe. Because this wasn't a stone. It was an egg.

A long, scaly nose poked out of the hole in the egg. Tiny eyes blinked, then peered up at Keeley, bright gold and shining with curiosity.

"Oh, my God," Keeley breathed.

The little creature poked its head up, staring straight at her with golden, cat-slitted eyes. Another piece of shell fell away, revealing—*No, that's impossible*—a pair of folded, gleaming-gold wings.

As Keeley watched, the hatchling flared its wings out, its eyes narrowing with pleasure as it stretched free of the confines of the egg for the first time in its life.

She knew it was pleasure the creature was feeling, because she could feel it too. In her head. A little sunburst of satisfaction.

The hatchling opened its eyes again and stared at her.

"Prrp?" it trilled.

Keeley stared back.

So this is what Sean wanted you to move. Not money, or drugs. Not a stone. A living creature.

"What *are* you?" she whispered, tentatively lifting her hand towards the hatchling. It sniffed politely at her fingertips and nibbled experimentally on her pinky finger.

The world seemed to whirl around her.

No, she thought, desperately clinging to reality, *that's not the world spinning. It's the train slowing down.*

Keeley licked her lips. Drop the case in the backpack in the last car and leave by the rear door. That was what she was supposed to do.

And fuck knows what Sean will do if you don't. No way he'll stop at getting you fired. Remember what happened last time.

The scars on her fingers ached.

The tiny winged lizard-thing blinked up at her with its huge, innocent golden eyes. Something shivered deep inside Keeley. A warm, gentle feeling she hardly recognized.

And this time, it wasn't from the hatchling. It was all her.

What sort of a person are you, really?

Chapter 4

Lance

"Are you sure this is the best route? Briers?"

"Best I can do, sir. Traffic's all backed up the other way. If you take the next left—"

Lance cursed. They were still a block away from the intercept site. If Briers' intel was correct, then this was their best shot at recovering the egg.

Or it was a trap. That was always an option.

Either way, if they didn't get there in time, they'd never know. And they'd lose their chance.

"There's no time," he barked. "We'll do it on foot."

"Sir, even with the re-route, it'll be faster in the car—"

"I know a shortcut."

Lance paused, his hand on the car door handle.

There were four agents in the van with him. Tori Bradford, one of the night-shift meerkat shifters from the office, was in the driver's seat. In the back with Lance were Parker, Yelich—and Zhang.

All of you, follow me.

Zhang might be a green recruit, but for this mission, he needed trackers. And no one tracked better than a shark. She'd be more useful on the front line than providing backup from the van.

Shields up!

The other agents obeyed his telepathic order immediately, flickering out of sight. Lance grinned and reached for the dragon-scale shield strapped to his upper arm. The scale pressed down onto his skin, and the world around Lance shimmered as he dropped out of sight.

So long as the scale was touching him, no one would be able to see, hear or smell him, unless they were shielded, too.

It was dragon magic. Julian Rouse's magic. The same magic that whoever had stolen the dragon egg wanted to exploit.

Lance jumped out of the van, signaling for the others to fall in behind him as he ran into the building the car had been stuck outside.

He knew this building. At least, he knew it ten or fifteen years ago, when it had been a burnt-out shell, and he'd been friends with the woman who bought and restored it into a glitzy hotel.

He'd thought he had known her, too. Francine Delacourt. But he hadn't, not in the end.

Lance shook his head, dislodging old hurt. He'd seen the blueprints for the new build, and now he navigated by them, slipping invisibly past guests and staff into a warren of employee-only corridors that eventually burst out in an alleyway near the station entrance.

He glanced at the station clock as he ran down the stairs to the nearest platform. The train should just be arriving. Motioning for Parker and Zhang to fall into position behind him, he raced down the final few steps.

The platform was almost empty. A dozen or so wilted late-night travelers were slumped at intervals along the platform, waiting disinterestedly for the train to stop.

Lance mentally filed the facts as he noticed them. Their arrival time. The rush of air that heralded the next train's approach.

The presence of civilians. If this all went wrong, they might be at risk.

He slowed, all senses on high alert, and six figures at the end of the platform caught his eye.

They were all wearing heavy dark fatigues, standing poised for action as they waited for the train to arrive.

Lance's snow leopard snarled as he took in the grim, impassive looks on their faces. They reminded him of his time in the military, but they didn't resemble soldiers. More like mercenaries, well-equipped and ready to jump for whoever was paying their fee.

None of the other passengers seemed to notice them. Which meant they must be shielded, same as Lance and his team.

Briers' lead had paid off. The enemy hadn't set a trap with those poorly forged video feeds; they just hadn't covered their tracks properly.

What the hell's this? They're here already? Yelich's psychic voice trumpeted in Lance's mind.

Lance shook his head. The black-clad figures were watching for the train with predatory intensity. *They're backup, or our thief's been double-crossed and we're dealing with more than one group. Either way, we need to get in there.*

Six enemy agents. Oh, and however many of the enemy were waiting on the train that this group was here to meet. And Lance had two agents, one green recruit, and Briers' eye-in-the-sky support once he reset the security cameras.

"Sir." Briers' voice crackled in his ear. "I've lost the feed for the station. I'll do my best to get it back online, but—"

Make that two agents and one green recruit.

Lance cut Briers' excuses short with a brief order, then sent a telepathic message to Zhang and Parker.

There. At the end of the platform. Move out.

Six to four? He'd faced worse odds, and with less hanging in the balance.

The train appeared at the end of the platform, and the other late-night commuters started to show some signs of life. The enemy agents didn't so much as glance their way.

They hadn't seen Lance or his agents yet. Which meant they had the element of surprise.

Lance unholstered his gun and led his small team down the platform as the train slowed to a stop. A hydraulic hiss told him the doors were about to open, and the six enemy agents' laser focus told him that his target was in that final car. If they could take out the platform team before whoever was on the train joined them—

He was expecting more mercenaries. A small, tactical team, who had taken out the driver and grabbed the egg and were now rejoining the larger group.

Instead, a woman appeared in the car door, directly in front of the enemy forces. She glanced up, her face tight as she checked the platform.

Even from twenty feet away Lance saw her eyes, stormy gray-blue and bright despite her clear exhaustion. She had dirty-blonde hair, pulled back into a strict bun, and was wearing a long coat that looked several sizes too big for her.

Head down, arms wrapped around herself, she stepped down onto the platform. Straight into the group of mercenaries.

Lance's snow leopard rose up so fast Lance felt claws burst from his fingers. He swore, corralling his snow leopard's form but keeping its heightened senses.

Danger! his snow leopard snarled.

Lance was already running. His snow leopard urged him on, faster, *faster*.

He was still ten feet away when one of the mercenaries shrugged, knelt, and tossed something under the car. As he stood up, the others closed in on the woman.

And the world turned to fire.

Lance's human brain put the pieces together as his snow leopard braced his body for the blast. The mercenary had thrown a grenade. In the middle of the goddamn city. If there had been any other passengers in that car—

Help her! his snow leopard snarled.

The far end of the car had exploded. The air was full of fire and shrapnel. Smoke billowed from the blaze in thick, noxious clouds that clawed at his lungs.

Lance plowed into the mercenaries, all his senses focused on the woman who'd stepped off the train a moment before the explosion. She'd been knocked to the ground by the blast and was kneeling with one hand on the ground, the other wrapped around herself. Alarms went off in Lance's head.

She's hurt. Get her out of here. Now!

He didn't know whether the voice in his head was his leopard screaming at him, or the other way around. Moving with feline grace, he knelt and pulled the woman into his arms.

Lance shouldered a mercenary out of his path as he rose and turned back towards the stairs. He could smell the man's scent even through the smoke, a rank combination of old meat and sweat that made his snow leopard puff up defensively. The mercenaries were shifters. Some sort of predators.

Lance didn't stick around to find out more. Under the smell of smoke and the shifter merc's stench, another scent was dancing across his senses, and his world shrank down to the warm body pressed against his chest.

Smoke choked Lance's lungs as he raced back up the platform. He was dimly aware of Parker and Yelich falling on the six mercenaries and Zhang leaping into the smoldering car, but the knowledge was distant, like some small part of his brain was taking notes for later.

The woman in his arms coughed, her whole body shaking. Lance swore. If the smoke was burning his shifter lungs, it would be all the worse for her.

He ran up the stairs six at a time, not slowing down until clean air hit his lungs.

Above ground, a crowd had gathered, half commuters still coughing up smoke, half interested onlookers. Every time a new figure emerged from the station entrance, which was still belching smoke, the crowd surged forward, gathering up the newcomer and pulling them back to safety.

The crowd stayed put as Lance carried the coughing woman out onto the sidewalk. He was still shielded and, since she was touching him, so was she.

The woman clutched white-knuckled at the front of his shirt.

"What the *fuck* just happened?" Her voice was serrated with shock. Stormy blue-gray eyes burned into his, bright with terror and—

Danger, his snow leopard had told him. Understanding struck Lance like a bolt of lightning. Danger was right. The woman in his arms was his mate.

Lance had spent every waking hour since the Diaz affair feeling like the ground was crumbling under his feet. Now the whole Earth seemed to tilt under him. *If I'd been there a second later...*

"It's all right," he said, his voice rough. "You're safe."

"Huh?" The woman shook her head. Her eyebrows shot together, making her eyes look even stormier. "I—the train—oh *shit*—"

She broke off and started to cough uncontrollably.

Lance carried her to an empty bit of sidewalk away from the crowd and set her gently on her feet, holding her until she stopped coughing and caught her breath.

"There was an explosion," he started to explain, and she glanced up at him, her eyebrows drawing together.

"What?" she asked sharply.

She was still holding onto the front of Lance's shirt with one hand. Lance's snow leopard preened. Either she was just steadying herself, or... was it possible she felt the connection between them, too?

A cool night breeze was whisking away the smell of burning metal and plastic from the station explosion. Under it, he could smell his mate's own scent, like sun and salt and the smell of cut grass.

"There was an explosion at the end of the platform," he repeated. "You were close to the blast. Are you hurt?"

"What?" She stared at him, and then released his shirt to rub the side of her face. "I can't hear a thing!"

Ah.

Lance closed his eyes briefly, feeling like an idiot. His shifter healing meant his ears were barely ringing any more, but she was human.

Boss! We need backup! We've found something, but—shit!

All at once, the rest of the world reappeared. Sirens blasted, and his mate's scent was joined by the gunpowder crackle of dragon.

He made a split-second decision. His mate was safe, and alive; and he had a mission to complete.

"I need to go," he said reluctantly. "There are ambulances coming. Get them to check you out. I'll..."

He trailed off. *I'll find you,* he wanted to say. But right now, he couldn't let himself think that far.

"Seriously, I still can't hear you!" his mate shouted back. She licked her lips nervously. "Look, I'm sure there are other people who need help, okay? I'm all good!"

And I need to go. Lance gave her a reassuring smile and, every atom of his being screaming at him to stop, turned and loped back down the stairs to meet up with his team.

I'll find her again. Later. When all this is finished. When the ground under my feet is solid again, he reassured himself.

The fight was over quickly. Lance's team had backed the mercenaries into a corner of the station, but there were too many of them. They broke through Yelich and Parker's defenses a moment before Lance joined the fray.

Heavy-duty sprinklers turned the smoke and flames into steam, and as the air cleared, the enemy disappeared like sea mist.

Lance bit back a curse and ordered his team back to the van.

"Tell me we've got good news," he barked as he slid into his seat. Zhang and Parker turned to him, while Yelich ground her teeth in the corner.

"I should have shifted," she muttered. "Like to see them get through my hippo."

"And I'm sure the humans would have liked to see a hippo suddenly appear in the subway," Lance replied. Yelich snorted, but the frustration on her face eased.

Lance turned to Zhang. "You found something?"

Carol had held back during the fight. At first, Lance had thought it was because of her lack of experience. It was only as they'd trudged back up to the street that he'd seen what she was carrying.

Now, she looked down at the black case on her lap, her eyes like pools of midnight.

"I found this under one of the seats at the near end of the car," she said. "There was nothing else there. No one else, either."

And that's strange. Lance felt another sixth-sense shiver of unease and made a mental note to follow it up later. The enemy had sent in a team to grab the egg, then left it on a subway car for another group to pick up at another station? Either that was the stupidest plan he'd ever heard, or he was missing something.

"It's locked," Zhang muttered, tugging at the lid, and Lance took the case from her.

"Allow me."

The fight might be over, but Lance's snow leopard was still alert and close to the surface. Like Yelich's hippo, it was champing at the bit to be let loose.

Lance concentrated. Heavy, sharp claws sprang out of his hands, and he removed the case's hinges with two sharp flicks.

"Let's see what we have here..."

His heart was already rising, anticipating success. He flicked the lid of the black case open.

Zhang gasped. "Oh, God, no," she whispered, and Lance wished he could do the same. His jaw set so hard he could feel the tendons in his neck stand out.

There was no life inside the case, no hope for Julian Rouse and his broken family. Just smashed fragments of shell.

"What happened?" Briers' voice crackled over the comm, startling after his long silence. "What's going on?"

"The egg's broken," Lance replied, his voice clipped. Professional. He stared blindly into the case.

He'd failed. He'd let one of the eggs, a potential life, be stolen—and now that potential was gone. Smashed.

He felt sick.

Parker leaned forward, his long face pensive. "Now, this doesn't seem right," he remarked, his nostrils flaring.

Lance's snow leopard sniffed, too, not wanting to be one-upped by the bloodhound. The sizzle of gunpowder filled his nostrils, overlaid with something like black pepper. He scratched his nose, resisting the urge to sneeze.

"That's just the shell, there. Now what's happened to the rest of it?" Parker sat back, frowning.

Lance stilled.

Inside him, his snow leopard's eyes gleamed as the memory of a scent filled his mind: sunlight and cut grass, with a hint of salt.

And the bright gunpowder spark of dragon.

"I know where it is," he said.

Chapter 5

Keeley

A thief. That's who I am. One hundred percent a thief. Oh, shit. I hope my ears stop ringing soon.

Keeley ran until the deafening nothingness in her ears popped, and the sounds of the world started to filter through again.

She wanted to run until she couldn't smell smoke anymore, but there was no escaping it. It clung to her hair, her coat, the inside of her throat.

At last her ragged steps slowed, and she looked around. She was a few neighborhoods away from the station. Far enough away that anyone who caught her eye quickly looked away again, instead of looking at her with concern, like they were asking her if she was alright. Disasters brought people together, but only to the edges of the blast zone.

Good. She didn't want anyone to find her. Not Sean. Not whoever he was working for. Not...

Gray-green eyes, startling against dark skin, appeared in her mind. The man who'd dragged her away from the explosion.

She had no idea where he'd come from. She'd checked the platform before she got off the train, and it had been practically empty. Definitely no giant, incredibly handsome black men who looked at her like—like—

Like you're some fancy New Keeley, and not a filthy thief?

She shook her head. She'd escaped the explosion at the station. Next step, get out of town. Away from Sean, and whoever was pulling on his leash, and incredibly fucking sexy guys who'd probably forgotten she existed by now, anyway.

Keeley walked until she began to recognize the storefronts around her. Somehow, in her panic, she'd run within a few blocks of her apartment.

She let herself slip into cruise control, her feet automatically setting in on the route to her apartment building. She was only a street away when Sean's words echoed in her mind. *You're still in that shit apartment in Queens?*

She stopped dead. *He knows where I live.*

Suddenly, the thought of going home to her apartment filled her with dread.

Heart pounding in her throat, Keeley found a quiet side-street and leaned against a wall. The brick was cold against her back, even through her coat. She dropped her head onto her chest, panting softly.

Okay. Think. I can still leave. What's in my apartment that's so important, anyway? I've got my wallet. Phone. That's all I need.

All we *need.*

Tiny claws prickled against her stomach through the cheap cloth of her uniform. Hidden under her coat, a tiny warm body lay curled in her apron pocket, its heart beating as fast as a hummingbird's wings.

Keeley swallowed as she remembered. A tiny body, lithe and snakelike. Four legs, each tipped with lizardy claws. A long, narrow head like a crocodile, with big cat-like eyes. And wings. *Wings.*

Lizard? Crocodile? Bullshit. There was only one thing the creature that had hatched from that egg could be. A dragon.

Holy shit, a dragon.

Keeley waited for her brain to tell her, *No, you must be imagining things.* But it didn't. It was crazy, but every part of her was totally on board with the fact that she'd just watched a baby dragon hatch out of an egg.

And stolen it.

Keeley swore under her breath. Sean was going to kill her. Sean's new business partner was going to kill her.

She was so fucking dead.

"Prrp?"

Keeley froze. The creature in her pocket—the *dragon*—was moving. She felt every wriggle as it unrolled itself, claws pricking through her uniform.

"Prrp?"

A long head nosed its way out of her pocket and up under her coat. Gold scales caught the light. Bright, cat-like eyes looked up, blinking, into Keeley's.

"Prr-rrp!"

The tiny dragon pulled itself up onto Keeley's chest, balancing with its tail whipping back and forth behind it and its wings spreading to either side. A feeling like "Aha! Found you!" bobbed against the edges of Keeley's mind.

"Hey, baby," Keeley whispered. "What's up?"

It chirped back at her, and flicked out its tongue to lick the tip of her nose.

Keeley closed her eyes. Opened them. The dragon was still there. It licked her nose again.

"Oh, f—fudge," she muttered. Her head was spinning. A dragon. Okay. So, dragons existed. The world had changed, without warning, and she was stuck in the middle of it.

She'd acted on instinct back on the subway, relocking the case and stashing it under a seat in the seconds before the train had stopped. But now that she had time to think, she had no idea what she was going to do next.

Sean was back. He was involved with people who were… smuggling dragons? Oh, God, she was in so far over her head.

"Prr-eep?"

Keeley took a deep, shaking breath. Maybe the world had gone mad, but she knew one thing for sure.

There was no way in hell she was letting Sean or his new friends get their hands on this baby dragon.

She drew another long breath. This time, it didn't shake.

"Okay, little... dragon," she said, staring the tiny creature straight in its burning-gold eyes. "We need a plan."

The baby dragon cheeped back at her, louder than before. Keeley quickly looked around, but the side-street was still empty.

"First bit of the plan," she murmured, easing the tiny dragon back into her apron pocket, "No one is allowed to see you, okay? We'll be in a shi—we'll be in a lot of trouble if they do."

To her relief, the baby dragon let her hide it back in her pocket. It rolled up against her stomach again, chirping happily.

"Okay. Okay. Good dragon. First bit, done. Second bit..." She paused. She knew what came next, but her mind jumped away from it like it burnt. "Second bit, you need a name," she relented, giving herself a few more breaths to build up her courage.

A name. A name for a dragon. What the hell do you call a creature that shouldn't even exist outside of stories?

Keeley peeked into her pocket. The baby dragon was the size of a kitten. With an extra-long tail, and extra wings. She rummaged through her memory. Weren't there dragons in *Harry Potter*? *Game of Thrones*? They had names, right?

This was supposed to be the easy bit to distract from the hard bit, she thought, swallowing. Her eyes felt hot. *How am I going to handle any of this if I can't even think of a name for it?*

She raised one hand to her neck, her fingers searching for the thin gold chain that was her only connection to her only good memories from growing up. There was nothing there.

Keeley's breath caught in her throat. Her gran's necklace. Had she lost it in the subway station? After the explosion—or when that handsome stranger had picked her up and carried her to safety?

No. No, it has to be here. Somewhere. It has to be... She scrambled at her coat collar and blouse, hoping against hope that the thin chain might have caught on a button. Nothing. And it wasn't caught on her apron shoulder-straps, either, or—

She paused and looked closer at the little golden bundle rolled up into a tight ball in her front pocket.

Gold scales. White-gold claws. Gold eyes with black slit pupils like a cat's, peering back up at her. And, wrapped around the baby dragon's neck and front legs...

"Oh, who's the thief now, huh?" Keeley breathed, relief washing through her. "Did you sneak that off me just now?" She hesitated, pursing her lips. *Thief.* Maybe she and the dragon had something in common.

She shook her head. The dragon needed a name, not an insult. What was something else that liked shiny things?

"Magpie. Well, dragons are supposed to like shiny things, aren't they? And it's better than nothing."

She reached into her pocket and scratched the baby dragon on the top of its head. "Hello, Magpie. Maggie."

"Prr-eep!"

Keeley giggled as the baby dragon nibbled the tip of her finger. After Maggie had thoroughly taste-tested Keeley's finger, she dove back into the depths of her pocket, hugging the thin gold chain as though it was a beloved teddy bear.

"Okay, Maggie. I think I'm ready now. Step three of the plan..." She took a deep breath to steady herself, and stood up. "Step three. We go to the bus station, pick a destination at random, and get the hell out of Dodge before Sean finds out what's happened here tonight."

Air moved against her face. Keeley didn't even have time to think, *That's odd, there isn't any wind tonight*, when Maggie shrieked and dug all four claws into her stomach.

Chapter 6

Lance

Lance ran around the corner. He'd followed the woman's scent through street after street, leaving the rest of his team far behind.

His mate had run aimlessly, as far as he could tell. As though all she wanted was to get as far from the danger as possible.

Which meant she must be an innocent in all this.

The thought eased something inside him. Something about the situation at the subway station still pinged him as wrong, but he put that aside for now.

Her scent was stronger here. Lance glanced along the street, letting his human eyes shift slightly so he was seeing with his snow leopard's more powerful senses.

There.

A short, stocky figure in a long coat, standing in a dark corner with her head bowed. There was exhaustion in every line of her body: the rounded shoulders, the hanging head. The shock of adrenaline from the explosion would be wearing off now, leaving her trembling and bone-weary.

She still had her hands wrapped around her front. Now that he knew what he was looking for, he saw the slight bulge under her coat.

Hope flared inside him. His hunch had been right. The hatchling had escaped—thanks to this stranger.

He could have laughed. How had he missed it earlier? The woman—his mate, God, this woman was his *mate*—had kept her hands in front of her stomach the whole time he was pulling her out of the burning station. She'd been protecting the hatchling under her jacket.

Lance lifted one hand to his shield. He'd kept it activated while he tracked her, but if she had the hatchling with her, a *dragon* hatchling, then she'd already seen enough weird shit for one day. A strange man appearing out of thin air right in front of her might just tip her over the edge.

His comm crackled.

"Briers here. I'm having trouble tracking the target, sir. And you, with the shield on. Can you let me know your location—"

Lance sighed. "I've got the target, Briers. Focus on tracking the shifter mercs from the station."

"You've found her? But—"

Resisting the urge to roll his eyes, Lance muted his comm. Briers was good at what he did—but he got in a hell of a mood when his cameras and computers let him down. Well, let him stew. Lance had work to do. He tapped his shield off.

As Lance strode purposefully down the street, his snow leopard raised its head. Lance's senses exploded as his animal tried to take in too much detail at once: the gas-dirt smell of the air, the million stale scents trodden into the sidewalk by passersby, the cold bite of the night air and the moving shadows on the street-front windows as cars passed by.

A million points of data, and not one of them explained his snow leopard's sudden sense of wrongness. Frowning, Lance tapped his shield again.

He saw the attacker a split second later. A split second too late.

A black-clad man loomed above Lance's mate, flicking an extendable baton. Lance broke into a run as he raised the weapon, aiming for the woman's head.

"Look out!"

Shit. He hadn't unshielded again. She wouldn't even hear him.

He sprinted. He was only twenty or thirty feet from the woman and her attacker, but it was like he wasn't moving at all. Time stretched out. The baton whistled towards the woman's head in slow motion, and he was still too far away.

At the last moment, she cried out, and ducked.

Lance didn't have time to stop or unshield, or thank his lucky stars that she'd moved in time. He barreled into the attacker, slamming him into the wall.

The man roared, dropping the baton and reaching for a gun. Lance grabbed his wrist and twisted, and the gun clattered to the ground.

Who are these people? he wondered as the man gave up on the idea of weapons altogether and tried to headbutt him. Lance stepped aside neatly and laid him out with one blow.

Lance knelt to make sure the attacker was out cold, and then looked up to see the barrel of a gun pointed directly at his face.

The woman had picked up the man's gun and was aiming it straight at him. Her grip was shaky, the barrel waving back and forth—but that wasn't exactly a good thing. Scared people did things they didn't mean to.

Always assuming she didn't actually mean to shoot him.

Lance considered his options. If he still had Briers on comms, he could have asked him to look up the woman's name, and any information he could use to get her on his side. But he'd muted him, and that would take time, anyway.

Time to do this the old-fashioned way.

Lance straightened up slowly, holding his hands palms-out at his sides. *Look, I'm unarmed,* his stance said.

"Hey," he said, keeping his voice low and even. "I hope you can hear me alright now, not like back at the station. My name's Lance MacInnis. I'm—"

And then he made the biggest mistake of the night so far. He looked into her eyes.

"I..." he tried again, but his throat was suddenly dry.

He'd heard of this happening. When shifters met their mates for the first time, the mate bond formed. It would remain weak until the shifter claimed their mate and the mate accepted them, but the creation of the bond was still—and Lance was quoting his friend Grant here—"like having a fucking house fall on your head, and then explode".

Lance thought the rush of adrenaline as he rescued her from the station had been his equivalent of that.

Oh, how wrong he'd been.

I tried to tell you, his snow leopard purred. *I knew we should have followed her from the start!*

He shushed it absently. The woman's scent danced on his palate, like sweetness and salt and the crackle of sun on a hot pavement. Like a day at the beach, and finally jumping into the surf. Like endless summer, and the burst of a cool drink against your lips.

She was... Lance couldn't put words to it. *Beautiful* wasn't enough. *Gorgeous* wasn't enough, even though she was. Her hair was pulled back severely, and she was pale with shock, but none of that stopped her beauty from shining through.

Lance's eyes lingered on her soft-looking skin and a body that promised soft curves under her enveloping coat. One loose curl of dirty-blonde hair hung across her forehead. Lance felt the seconds ticking by, knew he should say something, but he was trapped, helplessly soaking up every detail of her he could see.

The curve of her ears, each with two small gold studs. The tension in her neck and shoulders as she held the gun on him.

Oh, that's right, a voice said inside Lance, very far away. *The gun.* For some reason, that didn't seem important. Not when he could look at her lips, instead. At her rounded cheeks.

Her eyes, stormy blue-gray, fierce with determination.

And confusion.

"Okay, what the f—fudge?" his mate demanded. "Are you—what's going on? Are you alright? He just—you just..."

Her eyes dropped to the man crumpled at his feet and then shot to his face again, wide as saucers.

"You're—from the station!"

"I—" Lance began, but his mate was still talking. And glaring at him. And pointing a gun at him.

Two of those things, he could live with. The other one was somewhat worrying.

Her eyes narrowed, which was even more worrying. "You're after the dragon, as well!"

"Yes, but I—"

"You can't have her!" The words were almost a shout. She took a step backwards, as though surprised by her own vehemence, and a small golden head wriggled out from under her coat collar.

The hatchling blinked at Lance with bright, cat-like eyes. It couldn't be more than a few hours old, but Lance's skin prickled, like the small creature was doing more than just blinking at him. It was *assessing* him.

Its scent was like pepper mixed with fireworks, not the wild, fresh scent of a feline shifter, but Lance's snow leopard ignored that. It saw the cat-like eyes and small, wriggling shape, and greeted the infant shifter like it would any baby cat—with a playful psychic sniff and nudge.

The dragonling reared back, outrage in every line of its tiny body. Its eyes narrowed into suspicious slits, and it hissed before diving back under her collar.

"What did you just do to her—" the woman began, and then swore, her eyes flicking behind Lance. "Oh *shit*."

Lance's nostrils flared. A slight change in the air brought a familiar scent to his nose. The black-clad, shielded enemy agents from the station, their natural scents overlaid by the thick stench of smoke.

His snow leopard leapt to the fore, sharpening Lance's senses as he checked over his shoulder.

Three of them. Shifters. Predators of some sort, but that was as much as he could tell when they were in human form.

Lance turned back to his mate and stared into her eyes. His vision fuzzed at first—he was standing close enough to her that his snow leopard's farsightedness kicked in—but as he pushed his snow leopard's senses back, he saw her clearly.

"Did your *eyes* just change color?" she hissed, and then made a frustrated noise. "Not that that's the most important thing right now. They were at the station too, weren't they? Oh, shit."

Her pupils darkened as she stared back at him, and he wondered what she was seeing. The silver sheen of his snow leopard's eyes? His dual nature, the wild animal inside the man?

Did she feel what he felt?

"Do you trust me?" he asked, his voice hoarse.

She glared at him. "Is it a choice between you and those assholes at the end of the street?"

Her expression was fierce, but fear flashed behind her eyes, just for a moment. Lance's protective instincts surged as he realized how she could recognize the shifter mercs.

He'd picked her up while they were zeroing in on her. Before he touched her, she would have thought she was alone on that section of the platform. As soon as he put his arms around her, and she came under his shield, she would have seen the six black-clad soldiers suddenly surrounding her.

"I'll protect you from them," he promised her.

Her jaw clenched. "Fine. And..." Her eyes clouded with a confusion that was more vulnerable than the fear he'd seen in them a moment before. "I do. I do trust you. I don't know why, but I do."

Lance reached out. "Then come with me. I'll keep you both safe."

Shouts rang out behind him, but Lance didn't bother looking back. His professional, human side told him that the enemy shifters wouldn't dare shoot and risk hitting the valuable dragonling, and his snow leopard was too exultant to spare them a thought.

His mate's hand fit into his like he had been made to hold her. Her fingers were slender, but strong. She smelled like sunlight and the sea and was so close to him he had to force his snow leopard's eyes back, *again*, so he could see her clearly.

Lightning sparked where their skin touched. Lance grinned.

"Run!"

Chapter 7

Keeley

Do you trust me?

And fuck if she knew why, but she did. This strange man who'd knocked out her attacker without breaking a sweat. Who'd pulled her from the station after the explosion and made sure she was safe.

He towered over her, strength in every inch of his chiseled form, from his broad shoulders to the way his torso tapered to lean hips. He was just so... *huge*. With anyone else, she would have found his sheer size intimidating, but somehow with him, it made her feel safe.

She remembered how warm that chest had felt against her side as he held her. Every inch of it was pure muscle, powerful and masculine.

Keeley's life had turned upside down. She didn't know anything about this man, except that he made her skin fizz and her insides melt, and that was hardly enough to base a life-or-death decision on.

But he had saved her life. Twice. That had to count for something. And given a choice between a group of armed men dressed the same as the asshole who'd tried to crack her skull open, and a hot-as-fuck mysterious stranger who'd saved her life, she knew who she was going to pick.

Besides. The baby dragon liked him.

At least, she was pretty sure the dragon had hissed at the shadowy figures that had appeared at the end of the street, and not at him.

Mostly sure.

Too late to change your mind now, she reminded herself as they raced around a corner.

Lance's grip on her hand was strong and secure, but not crushing, even as they sprinted down the street. He pointed at an alleyway and pulled her into it a moment later.

Shivers of electricity raced up Keeley's arm from where they touched. Adrenaline, she told herself. This is definitely adrenaline, and not...

...I'm not going with this guy just because he's hot. Am I? Oh, God, I am. I am so going to die.

In her front pocket, tiny claws scratched at her stomach as the baby dragon clung to her through her apron. Keeley dropped the gun and flung her arm around her front, holding the scared creature tight.

Don't worry, she told it silently. *I'm not going to die. I have to look after you, don't I? Can't do that if I'm dead.*

"This way," said the man—had he said his name was Lance?—guiding her down a gap between two buildings, barely wide enough to be called an alley.

"Wait, what?" Keeley had to pause to suck in breath. She knew this street. "No, it's a dead end!"

Lance flashed her a reassuring grin. "I know this neighborhood like the back of my hand. Used to run around here as a kid."

Keeley yanked her hand out of his. "Well, I live here *now*, and I'm telling you, there's no way out!"

She turned just in time to see three men run into the alley.

"Great," Keeley muttered. "Now that way's blocked, too..."

Lance grabbed her hand, urging her further down. Brick walls loomed up either side of her, enclosing them. *Too close.*

Keeley felt a pressure on her chest. Too close. Too dark. No way out. Her fingertips tingled.

Her knees hit the ground with a crack. Someone shouted her name, and strong arms picked her up. Cold air blasted her face. They were running.

But there's nowhere to go, she wanted to scream through the dizziness enveloping her.

"See," Lance murmured in her ear, his breath still even despite running and carrying her. "Just around this corner, there's—oh, *damn.*"

"It's been there for weeks," Keeley mumbled, feeling hollow as she stared up at the shipping container that filled the other end of the alleyway, completely blocking off the exit to the street beyond. "Something to do with some construction next door's doing. My landlord won't shut up about it."

She cupped her hands around the tiny, warm lump in her coat where the baby dragon was huddled. "Can we hide her somewhere?"

"What?" Lance's green-gray eyes furrowed.

"They want the dragon, don't they? If we—I don't know, throw her, maybe she'll have a chance to get away, if we slow them down?"

Maybe she'll find someone better at keeping her safe.

Lance's frown deepened. "The hell with that," he growled, and the silver glint in his eyes was back. He shifted his grip on her. "Hold tight."

Keeley wrapped her arms more tightly around his shoulders. The dragonling peeped softly, cushioned between her stomach and Lance's chest.

Strong muscles moved under her fingers as Lance crouched. *He can't be about to jump,* she thought, her heartbeat pounding in her ears. *There's no way he'll make it!*

"Just lift me high enough to—" she began, and then Lance jumped.

Wind whipped Keeley's hair against her face. Before she could catch her breath, Lance had landed lightly on top of the shipping container.

The container was jammed up against the mouth of the alleyway. The street beyond beckoned, fully lit, people hurrying along the sidewalk. *The real world,* Keeley thought, *not this nightmare.*

"My team will be here soon," Lance whispered, striding to the other end of the container. "We need to get you shielded, and then—"

Lance grunted, the only warning before he staggered to his knees.

The container roof clanged as Lance collapsed. Keeley fell from his arms, landing on her hip on the hard metal.

"Lance—" she cried out, and saw the stain spreading across his chest. *Oh, God. He's been shot.*

She hadn't even heard it. Lance dropped onto his hands and knees, keeping his body between her and the attackers in the alleyway.

"Go," he urged her, fumbling at something on his right arm. "I'll stay here. Buy you time. Take this—find my team, they'll help you—"

"What? No." Keeley's fingers felt numb as she took the armband. This couldn't be happening. "No, you've got to come with me. I have no idea where I'm going, I can't just leave you here."

Lance's wry grin turned into a grimace of pain. "That's—ugh. I'm sorry. I wish this could have gone differently. But I'm only going to slow you down like this." He shifted his weight and hissed in a breath. "I don't even know your name."

"It's Keeley. Keeley B—Smith."

Shouted orders echoed out of the alleyway.

"Keeley." He said it like a prayer, gazing at her like she was the goddess he was praying to. "I'm sorry it had to end up like this, Keeley. I thought I'd have more time."

"More time? For what?" Keeley's heart hammered in her chest.

"This." Lance took her face in his hands and kissed her.

Keeley had been kissed before. Terrible teenaged crushes. Even worse early-twenties crushes. Nothing like this.

Lance's lips were soft. Gentle. If her name on his lips had been a prayer, then this kiss was a sort of worship. Longing shivered across her skin, awakening something inside Keeley she'd thought had died long ago.

She whimpered as he lifted his head.

"Now go," he whispered, his voice firm. Keeley blinked, and then the breath caught in her throat as she looked at him.

The stain on Lance's chest was spreading fast, too fast, and his face was going gray.

"They're almost here. I've told my team to watch for you. Take the hatchling. Be safe. *Go.*"

Brakes shrieked on the street beyond. The shipping container shook as something hit it from the side, the same way they'd come up.

Keeley looked past Lance and saw a hand appear on the edge of the container, only a few feet away. In her apron pocket, the little dragon screeched.

"You've got to get up," she told Lance. "I can't do this alone!"

He shook his head and pressed Keeley's fingers around the armband and tapped a button on its edge.

"This is your shield," he said, and the world around them shimmered.

Keeley gasped. The container, the walls, the street beyond—everything seemed thin and insubstantial, like they were made of tissue paper. Everything except her, and Lance with his hand on her back to push her away, and the tiny dragon forcing its way out from under her coat.

Lance's face was ashen. He frowned, staring at Keeley, then at his own hand.

"What in the world?" he murmured, and then the first of the attackers pulled themselves onto the container.

Keeley froze. The man was the size of a barn door. He pointed his gun at a red smear on the container roof—Lance's blood—and then looked up, straight at Keeley and the others.

And then he looked away.

"Where the fuck did they go?" he barked over his shoulder. "I thought you got him?"

"They're fucking shielded!" someone called from behind him. The container creaked as someone else began to climb.

"*I'm* fucking shielded," the first man snarled, and turned back around. His brow lowered as he stared at Keeley and Lance. Directly at them. And then past them. "So I'd be able to see them if they were too, fuckwit!"

The shipping container clanged again. Someone else was climbing up.

"You know what the contract says," grunted the man climbing up. "No payload, no pay. Stop wasting time!"

Keeley grabbed for Maggie as she tried to scramble out of her coat. Maggie swung her head towards the man with the gun and then started to scratch at the armband around Keeley's wrist, whining unhappily.

The world started to un-shimmer.

Oh, shit. "Don't do that," Keeley whispered urgently to the little dragon. "Don't do that, we need to stay hidden—"

"Wait," the man said, raising his gun. "There's something there—"

Keeley held the baby dragon tight, not daring to breathe. She was about to die. Lance was bleeding out at her feet.

Dragons weren't supposed to be real. None of this was supposed to happen. But it was, and oh, God, she wished she was anywhere but here right now. Except her whole body was frozen with fear, because of course it was, because she was as useless at being a thief as she was at being a good person.

"I shouldn't have let you go." Lance's voice was uneven, and she wasn't sure he even knew he was talking. His eyes were closed. "I should have stopped you back at the station. Taken you home. Safe... home..."

Safe. Keeley wasn't sure she remembered what that was.

As the gunman's face lit up and he shouted out that he'd found them, Keeley closed her eyes.

In her arms, the baby dragon sang.

CHAPTER 8

LANCE

"Prrp?"

Lance went from unconscious to wide awake in less than a second. His muscles bunched, ready to spring, as his eyes tried to focus on the thing moving in front of him.

"Prr-rrp?"

His eyes weren't following orders. The prrp-ing creature in front of him coalesced into a fuzzy gold-colored blob, but he couldn't focus any closer than that.

The blob jumped closer and batted him on the nose. "Prrp!"

Lance sniffed. His nose told him what his eyes hadn't managed. The hatchling. Of course. It was alive, and he was alive, which meant...

Mission accomplished.

Something deep inside Lance relaxed. *One more win. One more step away from the brink.*

He sank back, letting his senses continue their automatic check of his surroundings. His nose told him where he was at once: his own apartment. To be more precise, his bedroom.

Strange. He didn't remember coming home.

My team must have brought me here, he thought. *After...*

Lance shook his head. His skull felt like it had been stuffed with cotton wool and, now that he'd noticed that, the rest of his body chimed in, too. His bones were heavy as concrete blocks. Half his torso, from his collarbone in the front to his right shoulder blade, had the itchy, static tingle of fast healing.

Don't worry, his snow leopard said lazily. *I took care of everything. Since you were too slow to get out of the way of that bullet.*

Lance stretched carefully. His accelerated shifter healing had done the job. He ached all over, but he wasn't bleeding anymore.

But he was exhausted. Bone-tired and starving, thanks to the amount of healing his body had done while he was unconscious.

And something was still niggling at the back of his mind. Something about the lazy purr in his snow leopard's psychic voice, and where were Yelich and the others, anyway? And—

He frowned. *There's something I'm missing. Something about the feeling of* home…

"Prrp-eep-eep! Prrrreep!"

Lance shot upright. His weight felt strange, off-balance, but his senses were sure as he turned to find her.

Home. He was home. And it wasn't just the familiar scent of his apartment that told him that.

It was her. Keeley. His mate.

The reading light above his bed was on its lowest setting, barely filling the bedroom with a soft, warm glow. It lit up his comfortable bedroom furniture: the pale wooden headboard and dresser, and the plush comforter on his bed and thick rug on the floor. And his mate.

That explained why he couldn't sense the rest of his team anywhere nearby. Once they saw that he was healing safely, they must have quietly withdrawn to give him and Keeley some privacy.

She was standing at the end of the bed. Her coat was gone, and for the first time Lance saw what she was wearing under it. Some sort of uniform, he guessed: a black apron over a white blouse and black trousers.

She must have just left work when everything went down, Lance thought. His heart went out to her. There was no way she could have expected her night to end up the way it had. *Thank God the others were here to explain things to her while I was asleep.*

He raised his eyes to her face and frowned. Whatever the others had explained to her, she was still afraid and exhausted. Deep shadows haunted her eyes, and thick hanks of her dirty blonde hair were hanging around her face.

"You're awake, then," Keeley said, her voice harsh in the way that voices get when it's either that or start to cry, and Lance's protective instincts went into overdrive. The hatchling bounded off the bed and jumped up into her arms.

Lance didn't know how long he'd been out, but it was clear Keeley hadn't had a moment's rest. Her hand shook as she pushed hair off her face.

He cursed himself silently. She had been attacked, discovered the existence of a world that must have sent everything she thought she knew upside-down—and he was lying around in bed. What sort of a protector was he?

Keeley cleared her throat. "Can you hear me?"

Does she think the bullet deafened me, or something? Lance thought. He nodded and swung his legs off the side of the bed with military precision.

And found himself on the floor in a pile of blankets, limbs, and... a tail?

Oh, shit. He was in his snow leopard shape. But—when had he shifted?

I told you I took care of everything, his snow leopard said smugly.

When? he thought, rifling desperately through his memories as he fought his way out of the blankets.

When you were too busy making eyes at our mate to notice you were bleeding out. Idiot human.

Lance shook his head. His legs wobbled a little as he escaped the tangle of blankets, but if he ignored his aching bones and ravening hunger, he was fine. And his snow leopard seemed content to sit back and radiate smug superiority while Lance tried to get its body under control.

Lance swung his head around to find Keeley again. The deep shadows under her eyes had been joined by a small tic at the corner of her mouth.

Time to explain everything, he decided, and concentrated. His body protested, but he focused on his human shape and in a few moments, was standing on two feet.

Keeley gasped, her eyes traveling the length of him. Lance straightened his shoulders. First, to check his human body was healed, too. Second, because of the way his mate's cheeks went pinker the lower her gaze dropped.

"Keeley?"

Her name came instantly to his lips. The rest of the minutes before he'd lost consciousness might be a blur, but not that.

Keeley. His mate's name washed over him like a cool breeze, soothing his aching body.

"Yes," she said, her voice like sandpaper. "And you're—? Lance—?"

"That's correct." *Oh, fuck.* Lance's cock twitched at the sound of his name dancing on his mate's tongue.

He cleared his throat. He was supposed to be a professional, damn it.

"Lance," Keeley repeated, all the harshness gone from her voice.

Lance bit back a moan. Once had been bad enough, her voice sandpaper-rough and halting. But the second time, his name slid over her lips like softest silk, promising…

Gray shadows gathered at the edges of his vision. Lance was unconscious before he hit the floor.

*

The next time he woke, it was to the sound of whispered voices. Or rather, one whispering voice and one ear-splitting chirping and trilling.

"No, you can't jump on his head again. It didn't work the first time, did it? Leave him alone."

Chirp, chirp, screech, chirp.

"Oh, for—here, play with this. And no more biting!"

A pleased prrp-prrp, followed by a low, happy growl.

Lance opened his eyes. He was lying on the thick sheepskin rug next to his bed. His mate, Keeley, was sitting a few feet away from him, staring down at the dragon hatchling in her lap with an expression that was half fond, half frustrated. She dangled something shiny in front of the hatchling's face and laughed softly as it grabbed it.

Lance must have made some sort of noise, because Keeley looked up. A strange expression flashed across her face, and then she smiled uncertainly.

"You're awake? Again?"

Lance smiled back at her. "Tentatively." He looked at her carefully. She was still clearly exhausted, but her voice wasn't cracking with stress anymore.

And she was smiling. That had to be a good sign, right?

"You're not gonna pass out again?" she asked warily.

"I'm not planning on it, no."

"Were you planning on it the first time?" she quipped.

Lance groaned and carefully pushed himself upright. He was relieved that his tongue had worked, and that the hands he pushed himself up with were his large, dark-skinned human ones, and not his snow leopard's heavy paws. He hadn't shifted again.

"A lot of things have happened tonight that I wasn't planning on," he murmured.

"Tell me about it." Keeley's voice was hollow, but there was a hint of wonder in it. Lance looked up to find her staring at him.

She quickly looked at the hatchling instead, but that wonder in her voice had definitely been when she'd been looking at *him*.

Lance's snow leopard preened.

"I mean. Dragons. That's a new one for me." Keeley's eyes were laser-focused on the hatchling, and her cheeks were going pink. "Never been almost blown up before, either, and I gotta say, it wasn't exactly on my bucket list."

"What about meeting a man who can turn into a snow leopard?" Lance's voice rumbled, a hair's breadth from being a purr.

Keeley's eyes shot up. "Yeah. I guess I'm more used to people dying when they get shot, not turning into giant cats."

Her gaze hardened, as though walls were going up behind her eyes.

"Prr-rrp?"

The hatchling looked back and forth between Lance and Keeley, confusion pouring from her psychic aura.

"Prrp!"

The hatchling darted forward, faster than Lance could react, and bit him on one hand before racing back to perch in Keeley lap. "Prrp!"

"Ow," Lance said, shaking his hand. The hatchling's teeth were soft and nubbly, but she'd bitten him hard enough to leave dents in his skin.

"Sorry. She's a bit bitey," Keeley said as the hatchling grabbed one of her fingers. Lance couldn't help but notice that the hatchling was gnawing on her finger a lot more gently than she'd bitten him.

"I think I deserved it," he said. "She's very protective of you."

"Prr-eep!" the hatchling agreed.

Lance leaned back against the bed.

"And very alert. I wouldn't have guessed she's less than a day old. Then again, they've been in their eggs for a long time. Perhaps dragons' personalities start to develop before they hatch. That would explain…"

He stopped talking. Keeley's face had gone frozen, with a side of frazzled. Lance groaned and rubbed the bridge of his nose, noting that his glasses were missing.

That wouldn't be an issue, so long as his snow leopard behaved and kept its short-sighted eyes out of his face. What was an issue, however, was him and his apparently endless ability to ignore what was important.

"Sorry," he continued. "I don't imagine you're in the mood for a lecture on shifter biology. Why don't we get out of my bedroom, and I'll find us something to eat?"

"Your—?" Keeley's eyes widened, and then she sighed and pushed her hair back off her face. "Well, that answers one of my questions. One out of several thousand," she said at last, staring down at the baby dragon in her lap.

"You must have a lot of questions," Lance said, and Keeley nodded slowly, her eyes still fixed on the dragonling.

"Oh, yeah. You could say that." Keeley's voice was soft with wonder. Lance reached out and brushed the back of his hand along her wrist.

She leaned into his touch so naturally he wasn't sure she even knew she was doing it.

"Then I have a suggestion. Let's go downstairs. I'll make you breakfast, and you can ask me anything you want."

Keeley turned to him. Her scent danced in Lance's senses, sweet and salty and infinitely alluring.

She bit her lip. "Okay. But one more thing."

"Anything."

Her cheeks darkened. "Put on some pants, first?"

Chapter 9

Keeley

Lance did better than put some pants on. He wrapped a blanket around his waist and stood up with easy grace. Every movement he made was strangely compelling.

At least it's relatively dark, she thought, a second before he reached out and did something to the light switch above the bed. Keeley's stomach flipped over.

It had taken her what felt like hours of terrified groping around the room to even find the light switch, let alone turn it on. And even then she'd only been able to turn it onto its lowest setting. Just enough that she could see the walls closing in around her.

Her heart started beating faster. *Stop that,* she ordered herself. *Stop it, stop it, calm down—you've had all night to get over this, just* stop—

She looked around the bedroom, hoping that seeing it properly as a *room* and not as a shadowy box would help fend off her impending panic attack.

And knowing it was Lance's, too. For some reason, the thought helped her heart calm down.

The room was gorgeous. Even nicer than the penthouse suites at the hotel. One wall was all gray stone, like the side of a mountain; the others were a cool black and... non-existent?

Keeley gaped at the empty space, which appeared to open out onto a staircase leading out to an even larger room. *Damn it! I've spent the entire night freaking out about being boxed in an unfamiliar room, and there was all this space only a few feet away this whole time?*

"Excuse me." Keeley almost jumped out of her skin at the sound of Lance's low, deep voice. "I'll just wash up before we go down."

"Um. Sure." Keeley froze her train of thought in its tracks before it could follow those two words—*go down*—into the gutter.

She stifled a sigh of relief as he pushed through a door in the stone wall. A moment later, she heard a shower turn on.

Wait. Was that better than having to force her eyes to keep off him, or worse?

He'd left the door open behind him. *Worse. Definitely worse.*

Keeley turned deliberately away from the bathroom door, with its calming sound of rushing water and the less-calming promise of all that water running over Lance's naked body.

What the fuck is wrong with you? Last night you were almost killed, you spent the night trying desperately not to have a panic attack, and now you can't stop thinking about hooking up with some guy you only just met?

Keeley picked Maggie up. The little dragon had gotten herself entirely tangled up in Keeley's gran's necklace, and Keeley absently started untangling her limbs as she focused on keeping her back to the bathroom door.

Hooking up. God, she sounded like a teenager. Except teenagers probably didn't call it that these days, not that she would know. Hell, she didn't even know what people her own age called it.

She just knew what she wanted to do, regardless of what name you stuck on it. Run her hands over those muscles. Taste his lips, and feel his strong hands on her, wanting her as much as she wanted him. Wrap her legs around—

"*Stop,*" she burst out, and groaned. "Oh, *fuck*. What is wrong with me?"

Keeley winced and covered the little dragon's ears. Or where she thought its ears might be, anyway.

"Sorry, baby," she muttered.

A soap bubble of happiness burst against the side of her mind and she blinked.

"Shit, that feels weird. Um. Sorry again. And... it's good-weird, anyway." She paused. "Definitely a better weird than most of the other sh—stuff that's been happening to me lately."

She shivered. Dragons, guys turning into giant cats—that, she could deal with.

It was the sight of the shiny new scar on Lance's chest that made her soul quake. And the memory of sitting over his unconscious cat-body all night, watching his chest rise and fall and wondering each time if this would be when it stopped moving.

When are you going to learn? You ruin anything you get involved in. And this time, Lance is the one who got hurt.

Her fingers itched with the memory of splinters and broken skin. She rubbed them together absently. Now that she could see the size of the bedroom, and how it was a sort of mezzanine or loft over another enormous room, her chest felt less tight and she could breathe more easily. One less thing to worry about, which frankly, she needed right now.

Yeah, especially when you're expecting Lance out of the shower any minute. Clean and glistening.

She gritted her teeth and slammed one open palm against the nearest wall. It was cool and smooth, as she discovered as she ran her hand across it.

This feels more like glass than wallpaper or paint, she thought. *Maybe it's some sort of rock, like the other wall?*

"Looking for the switch?" Lance's voice did terrible, terrible things to Keeley's insides.

She'd been so focused on not listening to the sound of the shower, she hadn't noticed it turn off.

Oh, God, she thought. *What's gonna be worse—turning around and seeing him fresh from the shower, or staying here staring at the wall and imagining it?*

"Uh?" she muttered, because "Isn't the light already on?" was too many words for her brain to handle, apparently.

"Here."

Damn it, she could *feel* how close he was, even if she was still staring at the wall. His voice felt like the softest touch on her skin, making her shiver. Out of the corner of her eye, she saw him press his hand against the wall a few feet away.

Light shone from the walls. Keeley jerked back, blinking, and then gasped. The light wasn't coming from the walls—it was coming from *outside.* The walls were actually windows, looking out over the city.

Sunlight glittered off a hundred thousand windows and, in the distance, the water.

Keeley whirled around, Maggie chirruping delightedly in her arms. The windows ran the whole length of the walls and up to the ceiling, making the room feel like it was out in the open air. The larger room down the stairs lit up too, as its wall-windows turned transparent. Light filled everywhere that Keeley could see.

She turned back to the window, staring at the city stretched out below.

"It's like standing on the top of a mountain or something," she whispered.

"That's the idea."

Lance's voice was warm, and touched with just a hint of smugness. Keeley turned to face him and swallowed hard.

He'd toweled off and pulled on a shirt and pants, but his arms still glistened with a few stray drops of water.

Muscly *and* glistening. Oh, hell. She was so fucked.

Running off with him last night was one thing. People had been trying to kill her and Maggie, and he was helping her get away. Simple. Mostly because it had all happened so quickly, she hadn't had time to worry about what happened next.

But then he'd kissed her. He was dying, and he'd kissed her, and then everything had gone white and she'd found herself in a dark room and his whole body had shivered and she'd thought he was about to actually die right in front of her, and instead he'd turned into a *fucking giant cat*.

And instead of taking the opportunity to run the fuck away and get out of the city before Sean figured out she'd betrayed him, she'd sat next to him. Paralyzed. Unable to tear her eyes away from him as the bleeding stopped and his heartbeat became stronger.

She had no idea what was going on. But two things were for sure. The world was a hell of a lot more complicated than she'd ever thought possible.

And she still couldn't stop thinking about that kiss.

Well, that stopped right now. She might have been too paralyzed with terror before to think about her situation, but her brain was finally starting to unfreeze. And she had far too much shit to deal with right now without adding a pathetic crush into the mix. She needed to tell him, now, that she was leaving. Whatever was happening here with dragons and cats and whatever else, she wanted no part of it.

Lance smiled at her, one eyebrow raised. "Are you ready to go down?"

Keeley swallowed, hard.

I am so fucked.

"Sure," she croaked.

*

Keeley didn't watch Lance walk down the stairs from the mezzanine bedroom, because even the thought of seeing how his ass fit those pants made her skin fizz embarrassingly. She looked at her own feet and Maggie snuggling in her pocket, and nervously rubbed at her fingertips.

Which meant that when Lance suddenly stopped, she walked straight into him.

She jumped back immediately, her cheeks blazing. Lance smiled at her, apparently not noticing that her entire head might as well have just caught fire, and Keeley looked away quickly. His smile was just as mind-melting as his ass.

"Sorry," he said. "I should probably grab my phone—you know what? Never mind."

His green-gray eyes were so warm, it made her feel dizzy. She looked away, gravitating towards the massive windows. It was so light already. She must have been here longer than she'd thought. Hours and hours, watching Lance slowly come back to life.

The space below the bedroom felt like a living room, with a huge leather-covered sofa, rugs, and a drinks cabinet. A row of bookshelves either lined one wall, or *was* the wall. It was all light and airy, and Keeley couldn't even imagine how much it cost.

My whole apartment could fit inside the space that sofa takes up, she thought.

"How high up are we here?" she asked out loud.

"Almost high enough." From the way Lance said it, it was an old joke. Just not one she understood the punchline for.

"Cats like to be up high, huh?" *Yeah. Just act casual about all the craziness. Be cool.*

She tapped the window, feeling herself relax as she took in the view. *I like to be up high, too. Far away from Sean and all his bullshit.* She bit her lip, threads of unease winding through her gut.

Poking her head out of Keeley's pocket, Maggie copied her, her claws scraping at the glass.

Behind her, Lance coughed. "Snow leopards do."

"What?"

"I'm a snow leopard. Not a giant cat."

She turned to him, eyebrows raised. "Isn't a leopard just a sort of giant cat?"

Bad Keeley. Don't tease the nice man who saved your life.

But she'd already decided she was going to leave as soon as she could. A little flirting couldn't hurt. Could it?

Bad, Keeley. Very bad.

Lance narrowed his eyes—*Bad*—and a smile danced around his lips. *Double bad.* A thrill went up Keeley's spine.

"Actually, if you'd like a closer—" Lance staggered, his face going gray. He staggered backward, barely managing to support himself against the wall, and Keeley was at his side in an instant, jamming her shoulder under his arm.

His head fell onto her other shoulder, his breath hard and hot on her collarbone. Another shiver went through Keeley, but this one had nothing to do with lust. All the warmth and life had gone out of his face in an instant.

Just like the night before.

"Sorry," Lance grunted. Keeley had flung her arms around him and felt his back muscles spasm as he tried to stand upright. "Might be—more exhausted than I thought. Healing—"

"So that's a no on you making breakfast, then?" Keeley's voice blared in her own ears, so loud and sharp that she winced. Her heart was pounding like she was the one about to pass out, not him, and something inside her—

She shook her head. She was being stupid, panicking and imagining things that weren't there.

Lance laughed weakly into her shoulder. "Not today. Sorry."

"Well, then." Keeley anchored herself under his shoulder. "I hope you like sandwiches."

*

Fanciest fucking sandwiches I ever made, Keeley thought five minutes later.

She'd helped Lance to the kitchen. He'd made it—barely. Keeley's legs were shaking by the time she dropped him into a chair at the kitchen table.

At least seeing him almost pass out had made her libido calm down. And the cool blast of air from the fridge when she opened it helped on that front, too.

Lance had more food in his fridge and pantry than Keeley had seen outside of a grocery store. She grabbed a loaf of bread—the fancy stuff that didn't come pre-sliced—and an armful of cheese and deli meats, and began blindly slapping sandwiches together.

"You really don't need to do this," Lance protested as she dropped a plate of sandwiches in front of him. "I—is this salmon and pastrami?"

He sniffed the top sandwich warily, and Keeley winced as he bit into it.

"Mf's del'cious," Lance murmured through a mouthful of mixed fish and meat.

Keeley picked at a hunk of bread as he demolished the sandwiches. She knew that if she thought about it, she would realize she was actually hungry, but her brain was busy. Without Lance's hot bod to obsess over, it had moved onto more serious things.

Like the fact that she'd almost been murdered. Twice. Or three times, maybe. *It depends on how you look at it.*

Anyway, as it was, if she did eat anything, she'd probably throw it up.

"Talk to me, Keeley."

Keeley jumped in her seat, making Maggie cheep in alarm. She reached into her pocket to calm the baby dragon while she tried desperately to haul her thoughts into order. "About what?"

"You've been glaring at me the whole time I've been eating. Something's got to be on your mind."

Keeley pinched her eyes shut. "Sorry. I was just—staring into space." *Or staring at you like a creep. Take your pick.* "How are you feeling?"

"Better. Thank you." Lance smiled.

He's looking better, too—oh, for fuck's sake. Whatever protective home-maker urge Lance's weakness had awoken inside her was shoved aside by another entirely different urge. Keeley gritted her teeth.

"Sorry about the weird sandwiches. There's a reason I'm a maid, not a cook," she said, glaring at the top of the table.

"They were just what I needed." As if to prove the point, Lance bit into what she was pretty sure was a slab of salmon-and-some sort of goopy white cheese. "Now. I told you I'd answer any questions you had, and I will."

"Okay," she began slowly. *Where to start? Dragons? Giant cats? Getting shot at and blown up?*

Keeley took a deep breath. "You can turn into a… giant cat. Snow leopard. Let's start with that."

She tipped her head back in time to see Lance set down his sandwich. Just for a second, his eyes gleamed silver, the pupils flaring out into cat-like slits.

A moment later, his eyes were normal, and Keeley's heart was racing.

"That's as good a place to start as any," Lance said, and began to explain.

Ten minutes later, the whirlpool in Keeley's brain was no calmer, and she felt as though the top of her head was about to fall off.

"Wait," she said, holding up a hand. "Just—let me see if I've got everything straight?"

Lance nodded, and Keeley swallowed, looking down at Maggie curled up in her pocket.

"You're a shifter. Is that what you called it? Which means you can turn into a snow leopard. Which I saw earlier, thanks for the surprise demonstration, by the way."

Lance's eyes crinkled. "It's not just snow leopards. Other shifters have other animals. Meerkats, panthers, lions—even sharks."

"Sharks." Keeley stared flatly at him as she waited for her brain to process the new information. "Okay, no. Giant cats, yes, tiny dragons, yes, but sharks—no, thank you."

"Oh, come on. Zhang's great. You might not have realized she's a shifter, of course. It's not like she would have had the opportunity to shift here in the city."

"Who's Zhang?" Keeley stared at him, running the last few minutes of conversation over in her head. Had she missed something?

Lance sat back, frowning. "I'll admit I don't remember much after we shielded on top of the shipping container, but I do remember feeling Zhang and the others approaching. I assumed they brought you here."

"N-no..." Maggie wriggled around in Keeley's pocket, and she automatically wrapped a hand around the tiny dragon.

"Then how did we get here?"

Keeley stared at Lance, and he stared back, honest confusion radiating from his face. She took a deep breath as Maggie poked her head out of her pocket.

"You really don't remember?"

Maggie cheeped, and Lance's eyes flicked from Keeley's, to the baby dragon, and back. Keeley took a deep breath.

"Okay. Well, that was actually going to be my second question, anyway. Do we need to be worried about Maggie randomly teleporting us places?"

Lance stared. His stare turned into a frown, and his frown deepened into confusion.

"What?" He sat back in his chair like all the breath had been knocked out of him. "Teleporting?"

Chapter 10

Lance

Dragons. Lance groaned internally. Every time he thought he had them pinned down...

Lance had expected his explanation of shifters to blow Keeley's mind. He hadn't expected to have the rug pulled out from under his feet, too.

"The hatchling teleported us here? To my apartment?"

"Maggie, yeah. Um. Which is short for Magpie, because she... likes shiny things?" Keeley's voice trailed off uncertainly. In her lap, the hatchling—Maggie—cheeped happily. The gold chain was wrapped in a triple loop around her long, scaly neck.

Lance ran his fingers over his head, digging his fingertips into his short, curly hair. *Teleportation. The hatchling can teleport.*

"You're sure?"

Keeley threw her hands up. "Oh, yeah, sorry, I forgot. Actually I carried you here, while you were bleeding to death and also a *giant cat*, to this apartment I didn't even know was yours. I remember now." She put her elbows on the table, her gaze tense. "Lance, I've got a baby dragon making a nest in my work uniform, and you've just told me that there are people all over the world who can turn into wild animals. Is teleporting really that much of a stretch?"

Lance sighed. "It's only been a few months since we discovered some dragon shifters could make themselves invisible. Teleportation is...

something else." *Something else I didn't know. Something else I wasn't prepared for.*

His stomach went cold. *How many other surprises are out there, waiting for someone to use them for evil?*

"Invisible—you mean the shield thing you gave me, right? That's a dragon thing?" Keeley absently scratched Maggie under the chin, and then froze. "Wait—so that was a *part* of a dragon?"

Lance nodded. "Yes, a scale. It—"

"Oh, God. Oh, *fuck* no." Keeley gathered Maggie up in her arms, squeezing her tight despite the baby dragon's indignant squawks. "They wanted to—to—oh, *God*."

She went so pale that Lance was afraid she was about to pass out. He reached across the small kitchen table and held her shoulders, staring into her eyes.

"Hey. Easy. They didn't get her. She's safe. Because you saved her."

"Because I..." Keeley's eyes settled on Lance's. "Because I got her out of the subway station. I didn't leave her in the car."

"She's lucky you were there."

"Lucky..." Keeley squeezed her eyes shut and shook her head. Maggie took advantage of her distraction to wriggle free and jump onto the kitchen table.

"Yes. Lucky. I don't want to think about what might have happened if you hadn't been there." Lance sent out a tentative psychic greeting to the hatchling as she sniffed around the table. Maggie's psychic pepper-and-fireworks signature was stronger than it had been the night before.

Lance rubbed his nose. His snow leopard was intent on the baby dragon; it was almost as enraptured by Maggie as it was by his mate. *To the extent that I'm trying not to sneeze from sniffing psychic pepper*, Lance thought wryly.

"But everything that happened..." Keeley's voice was tight with worry. Lance smiled reassuringly at her as his snow leopard gave the hatchling a psychic nudge.

Maggie reared up, cheeping indignantly, and Lance laughed.

"She isn't suffering any ill effects from last night. Of all of us, I'd say she got off the lightest." Lance smiled at Keeley, and she grimaced back.

"Not shot, not getting her head almost bashed in... yeah, I'd say so." Keeley frowned. "She can't remember almost getting blown up, though, can she?"

"I can't read minds," Lance explained, letting Maggie sniff his fingers. "But infant shifters are a bit freer with their feelings than adults. I can see enough to know she's fine. She feels safe here, and happy." His snow leopard nudged him, and he corrected himself. "Safe here with you, I should say."

"Safe with me?" Keeley pushed herself back in her chair. "Are you sure about that?"

Lance raised one eyebrow. "As sure as I am that she's about to steal one of the delicious sandwiches you made for me."

He nodded down to where Maggie was creeping inch by inch across the table, as though, if she moved slowly enough, no one would notice a shining, gold-scaled baby dragon on her way to steal breakfast.

The kitten is already an excellent hunter, his snow leopard commentated. *Look at that focus!*

It's a sandwich, Lance replied, amused. *It's not like it's going to run away.*

His snow leopard flicked its tail derisively. *That is not the point. The point is—she got it! Yes! The mightiest hunter!*

The mightiest hunter's butt wiggled madly as she raced back to dive into Keeley's lap.

"Oh, you—" Keeley giggled helplessly. It was the most beautiful sound Lance had ever heard. "Is it okay for her to eat that?"

Lance shrugged. "If she was in human form, no, but dragon? I guess we'll find out."

I should call Julian. Ask him. He filed the thought under "Things to do later". Right now, he was sitting in his kitchen with his mate and a baby dragon his snow leopard insisted on referring to as a kitten, and nothing else seemed important.

"Human form." Keeley stopped giggling, her eyes shooting to Lance's. "You mean she's—there's a baby in there?"

Her voice rose into a squeak at the end. Lance nodded, trying not to grin at how shocked she looked. "Same as me. Same as any shifter."

Keeley sat completely still as Maggie wriggled back into her apron pocket. "Oh," she said at last. "A baby. You know... I think I've reached my brain's reached its limit for crazy new things, now."

"Most shifters are born in human form, but from what I understand about this particular family, they're more dragon than human to begin with." Lance set his elbows on the table.

Keeley raised her hands. "Really. Brain completely full. Unless you want me to freak out and collapse in your arms again like at the station..."

She stopped, her eyes meeting his like they were being dragged by magnets. Slowly, very slowly, her cheeks went pink.

Lance's snow leopard whipped its tail back and forth. *Yes!*

No, Lance told it.

She wants to! Look at her face! You should tell her everything now. She—

Lance gritted his teeth. *No. I saw her face. I saw how terrified she was last night. How lost she feels now. I will not burden her with this now, on top of everything else. Besides. You heard her. Her brain's reached its limit. We're not going to make her feel safer by pushing more world-changing information on her.*

He forced a light smile on his face, pushing back his snow leopard's insistence that he openly pledge himself to his mate and her "kitten".

"I meant to reassure you. Most shifter kids don't actually shift until around puberty, so she'll probably stay in her dragon form for a few years, at least."

"Oh." Keeley broke eye contact, her cheeks still pink. "Thanks. Yeah. Freaking out a bit less, now, actually."

She wrapped her arms around her stomach, where Maggie made a wriggling lump in her apron pocket. A surge of warmth flooded through Lance. Through everything that had happened, all the violence and fear, she had never once stopped protecting the hatchling.

My mate, he thought, the warmth sharpening to a longing that went deeper than lust. *I wish I could tell you how much that means to me. How much you mean, with your kindness and your courage.*

He frowned. Kindness and courage, yes—and shadows under her eyes, and hands that shook with exhaustion. "Have you slept at all since we got here?"

"Me?" Keeley blinked at him. "No. Too busy watching you not die, remember?"

"You must be exhausted. And you haven't eaten anything." Lance stood up. "I'll show you to—" *Your bed,* his snow leopard urged him, *OUR bed,* and he just managed to catch the words before they leapt onto his tongue "—the guest bedroom."

"What? No, you don't need to..." Keeley smothered a yawn as her body betrayed her words. She grimaced. "Okay. Maybe I am a bit tired. I feel like my brain's going to fall out the back of my head."

Lance showed her to the guest room, and left her to shower and change while he made her a cup of hot cocoa. By the time he knocked on the door again, she was fast asleep.

He put the hot cocoa on the bedside table—it would still be chocolatey when she woke up, even if it was no longer hot—and looked around for Maggie. The hatchling was snoozing on the dresser, curled up in a nest made of pillows from the bed and Keeley's apron. Her psychic aura was calm and happy. No lingering ill effects from the people who had tried to capture her.

Or the salmon and brie sandwich, Lance thought, smiling fondly.

He stopped at the door, and his gaze caught on Keeley's sleeping face. She was so expressive when she was awake that, relaxed in sleep, her face looked strangely vulnerable.

A protective urge rose up in Lance. He couldn't let anything like last night happen again. Keeley might not know she was his mate, but that didn't matter. Her safety, her happiness, were his one priority. So long as he was alive, he swore, he would never let any harm come to her.

With one last lingering look at her sleeping face, Lance turned off the light and headed for his own room. The mezzanine mountaintop-style bed seemed colder and emptier than usual, but he was too exhausted to let it bother him. Still exhausted from the healing, he was asleep before his head hit the pillow.

A few hours later, the sound of Keeley's screams jerked him awake.

CHAPTER 11

KEELEY

The darkness pressed in on her, dense and suffocating.

No. No, this isn't happening, Keeley thought desperately. The taste of dust in her throat, the splinters under her fingernails—*It's not real. It's a dream. Just a dream. You're not back there. You just need to open your eyes, and—*

Fighting against the nightmare, Keeley dragged her eyes open.

Oh God, no.

The endless pitch black of her dream was still there. Pressing against her eyes. Squeezing the breath from her lungs.

Keeley tried to sit up, but something yanked at her limbs, trapping her in place.

It was too dark. Too close, walls on every side, ceiling so low her knees barely fit, muscles screaming to stretch out.

No room, too dark to see, no space to move, no way out NO WAY OUT—

"Keeley!"

Strong hands grabbed her shoulders. Suddenly there was light, not outside, but inside her. The barest glimmer, like a candle flame behind foggy glass. Keeley grabbed hold of it with all her heart and heard a hoarse gasp.

Lance's voice cut through her panic.

"Keeley. Keeley, I'm here. Tell me what's wrong. Tell me what you need."

Keeley's tongue felt thick. There was too much dust, too much—*No. There's no dust. No trap. It was just a dream. It was just a—*

Another wave of panic crashed over her.

"Light," she croaked. Her legs kicked out automatically, and even though she knew now that she was tangled up in her blankets, not trapped, her heart started hammering even harder. *Can't escape.* "Get this off me!"

Lance tore the blanket away with one arm. Keeley sucked in a breath—*Which is stupid, because you* could *breathe before, it's all in your head, it's not real*—and then choked on it as Lance lifted her up.

She didn't feel trapped in his arms. She felt weightless. And... precious. The flickering candlelight inside her flared higher.

"One moment," Lance murmured in her ear, and whisked her out of the guest room.

Keeley was limp in his arms, barely believing what was happening. Part of her still thought she was trapped in the dark. That *this* was the trick, and she would wake up and find herself back there again.

Lance's hand curved around her thigh as he carried her, his grip so firm she could feel every individual finger on her bare skin. That was right. She'd gotten changed before she fell into bed. Stripped off her uniform and pulled on a soft t-shirt from the guest room dresser, and nothing else.

Borrowed t-shirt. Panties. Bare legs. Heart still hammering, Keeley managed to pull herself together enough to take stock.

This was real. *This*, the crazy mountain-top apartment and the baby dragon and the man who could turn into a snow leopard. Not the nightmare. Not the suffocating darkness.

Although she'd only seen the rooms once, Keeley recognized where Lance was taking her. The room lined with bookshelves... with the staircase that led up to his bed.

Her heart was still racing from her nightmare, but suddenly the beat of her pulse changed. Her skin heated up. Her thighs tingled.

And then Lance stopped, still on the lower level, and put her down.

"Here," he said, and before Keeley had the chance to segue from *more-than-slightly-turned-on* to *wait-what-now?*, he placed his hands gently on her shoulders and turned her around to face the window.

Keeley gasped. One hand holding on to Lance's arm, she leaned forward, marveling at the sight of the city spread out below her. It was nighttime, but this was New York. It wasn't dark, it was…

"Enough light for you?" Lance murmured in her ear.

"It's beautiful," Keeley whispered. "I've never seen the city like this before, it's… it's like a sea of stars." Shaking her head, she added, "All I can see from my apartment is the wall of the next building along. Three feet from my window."

Lance cleared his throat. "It's not as good as a real mountaintop—but it's close. I thought, if you needed not to feel enclosed…"

Keeley stepped forward, not aware that she was dragging Lance with her, and pressed her palm against the glass. "Thank you." She grimaced. "Back at my place, I have to pretty much fall out the window to get a bit of fresh air."

"You have these nightmares often?"

Keeley bit the inside of her cheek. Lance must have seen something in her face, reflected in the window.

"I'm sorry. It's none of my business."

"No, it's fine." Keeley shrugged, but her hand resting on the window turned into a fist. "I used to, but not so much anymore. Which is good, since the neighbors tend to complain…"

What the hell are you saying? He doesn't need to know that! Keeley looked up at Lance, and her heart sank. She didn't want him to *know* any of it, either. All those pathetic details about her life.

The nightmare had made her feel helpless. And Lance knowing about it, that was even worse. She didn't want him to think she was some pathetic, weak little girl, weeping over bad dreams.

She wanted...

Keeley turned until she was facing Lance. She was surprised to find she was already touching him—his hands were on her shoulders, and, at some point while she was marveling at the city lights, her own hand had drifted up to touch his. The realization sent a thrill through her, but at the same time, it left her feeling unbalanced.

She didn't touch anyone. Not ever. Especially not when she was freaking out after a nightmare, and touch just felt like another thing weighing her body down. But with Lance, it felt... natural. Him holding her hand in the kitchen. Picking her up. Her resting her hand on his arm as they stood here, looking out over the blazing city lights.

It felt... right. But it didn't feel normal. It made Keeley feel like she was walking on a tightrope, unsteady and vulnerable.

But it was better than the nightmare.

Keeley let her fingers ghost over Lance's bicep. He was wearing a short-sleeved shirt, and his skin goosebumped at her touch. A thrill went through her.

"You know," she said, her voice slow and lazy, "when you picked me up and carried me up here, this wasn't what I thought you had in mind."

"Oh?" Lance's eyes gleamed silver, as though they were somehow reflecting the streetlights from outside. He put his index finger to the bridge of his nose as though he meant to push up his glasses, but he wasn't wearing them. "What were you expecting?"

I was expecting to wake up trapped in a—no. No. Keeley thrust the thought away. She had to focus on what was real. What was right in front of her.

Which right now was this amazing, handsome man, who'd saved her life twice and made her skin hum with excitement.

She leaned closer to him. "For a start, I didn't expect you to put me down before we got to the bed."

Lance's eyebrows shot up. The silver sheen on his eyes disappeared, leaving them a pure green that reminded her of new leaves in the spring, and a surprised smile lit up his face.

"Is that so?"

His voice was so low, it was practically a purr.

Keeley licked her lips. Lance's voice vibrated deep inside her, filling her with delicious shivers of anticipation. He leaned closer, his spring-green eyes filling her world, and she couldn't wait any longer.

Keeley grabbed his collar with both hands and stood on tip-toe to crush her lips against his. He kissed her back, immediate and passionate. His lips were as soft as she remembered, but warmer. Hotter. *Hers.*

Lance cupped the back of her head in one hand, the other wrapping firmly around her waist. Heat shot through her.

"Oh, God, Keeley." Lance murmured something wordless and pulled her against him. His cock jutted against her belly, and Keeley wound her arms around his neck, need spiking through her as his tongue flicked out to brush her lips. "I don't have a—"

"Don't stop." Keeley felt him hesitate and grabbed his hand, pushing it under her t-shirt. Her skin sizzled where he touched it. "Please. I need you to touch me."

Lance moaned and spread his fingers wide over her belly and waist. She urged him on, pressing herself against him and unbuttoning his shirt. The thin fabric fell open, revealing his magnificent chest. And the scar.

Keeley ripped Lance's shirt off. He'd almost died, and the reminder made her desire even more urgent. She threw herself at him, kissing his chest. Lance swore as she scraped her teeth over one nipple.

"I thought you said you needed *me* to touch *you*?" he groaned, his voice ragged.

In answer, Keeley straightened and stripped off her t-shirt. Panting slightly, she stood in front of Lance in nothing but her panties.

He stared at her, his eyes heavy with lust but his gaze reverent. For about half a second.

Keeley gasped as Lance put his hands around her waist and pushed her gently backwards until her back was against the window. He kissed her neck, her collarbone, making his way down to her breasts. She groaned and arched her back as he sucked one nipple into his mouth and bit it, just hard enough to make her cry out.

"Don't stop," she begged him. Every part of her was aching for his touch. It was like she'd been starving all her life without knowing what she was missing.

Lance ran his hands over her waist and hips as he dropped to his knees. He tugged at the waistband of her panties, a question in his desire-hooded eyes.

Keeley nodded, afraid that if she opened her mouth, she'd scream.

Lance tugged her panties down and slid one hand between her legs. His fingertips brushed against her folds. Keeley moaned, leaning back against the window and parting her legs for him.

She was already hot and wet, every nerve ending thrilling to be touched. Lance lowered his head between her legs, and Keeley almost cried out as his tongue flicked out.

He started slow, almost methodical, and then his tongue hit Keeley's clit. She moaned, her whole body shuddering, and something seemed to break loose inside him. He pressed one finger up inside her, then two, curling them to brush against her g-spot as he sucked on her clit.

It was too much. Keeley's whole body clenched as her orgasm shuddered through her, pleasure and release so powerful her knees almost gave out. Panting, she grabbed for his shoulders, and he let her pull him up—slowly, kissing her thighs, her belly, under her breasts, along her shoulders.

"I want to taste every inch of you," he murmured, running his lips along her jawline. His eyes burned into hers.

Keeley was still trembling with pleasure, but the look in his eyes sent a sharp shock of desire straight to her core. "What else do you want?" she teased, reaching down his pants to wrap her hand around his cock.

Oh, wow. Fuck.

She'd seen him naked before. Obviously. Of course she'd looked, even though she'd tried, or pretended, not to. And she'd felt his cock pressing into her stomach when he kissed her.

But. *Wow.* Seeing wasn't believing. *Feeling* was believing.

"Keeley." Lance's voice was rough with need. "I hadn't planned on—If we're going too fast—"

His whole body trembled, as though it was taking all his self-control to hold himself back. To be the self-possessed, disciplined soldier Keeley had seen earlier, not the man, wild and passionate and hot with desire.

"Lance," Keeley whispered. She changed her grip on his cock, pumping it until Lance groaned. "I don't care how fast we're going. I don't want to slow down."

He kissed her, pushing her up against the window as he fumbled with his pants. Keeley helped, or hindered; at this point, she couldn't tell.

Lance grunted as he kicked his pants off. His cock pressed against Keeley's stomach. Need blazed inside her, rougher and more primal than her earlier desire.

"Take me," she gasped, and Lance picked her up and thrust into her in one smooth movement.

Keeley cried out, her body tensing as she adjusted to Lance's size inside her. He rested his forehead against hers, his expression half concern, half fiery lust.

"Are you all right?"

She wrapped her legs around his waist and kissed him. The stretch inside her was easing—and she wanted more. The flicker of candlelight inside her was burning as hot and bright as a blowtorch.

"I see," Lance murmured wickedly, and kissed her back.

His fingertips dug into her ass, and he thrust into her again, fast and hard. Keeley gasped against his lips. With every thrust, pleasure built inside her, sharp-edged and desperate, until she came, burying her scream in Lance's shoulder. Lance buried himself fully inside her, filling her more than she'd ever thought possible, and groaned deep in his throat as he came.

Keeley rested her head on his shoulder as her breathing slowed and her pulse stopped pounding in her ears. She felt... peaceful. Like something twisted up inside her had finally been released.

God, when was the last time she'd had sex?

Sex like this? Literally never.

"Feel better?" Lance lowered Keeley to the ground but didn't let her go. Which was good, because she was pretty sure if he had, she would have melted into a pile of goo on the floor.

"God, yes," she said, resting her cheek against his chest. She could feel his heartbeat, strong and steady. Just like him. Her knight in shining armor.

She felt more relaxed than she had since— *ever*. Like she'd been on edge so long she'd forgotten what it was like not to have every muscle in her body knotted up with tension.

"I'm sorry," Lance murmured into her hair, and Keeley frowned.

"For what?" *Giving me the best orgasm of my life? Orgasms, plural?*

"I turned the lights off when I saw you were asleep." He grimaced. "Then you woke up, terrified, saying you needed light—I fucked up. I'm sorry."

"What, because you didn't read my mind and know I would freak out?" Keeley's throat felt tight. Her happy-goo feelings were rapidly melting away, leaving a prickly, cold feeling inside her.

Lance grumbled deep in his throat. "I should have sensed something was wrong."

Well, thank fuck you didn't. A cold, gristly lump lodged in Keeley's throat. She forced herself to smile flirtatiously up at him, fluttering her eyelashes.

"I think you've more than made up for it. Really."

Lance smiled, with more than a hint of smugness. "Is that so?"

"Mmm..."

"In that case..." Lance's eyes unfocused slightly. "Maggie's still sleeping. It's the middle of the night. Will you give me another chance to get you to bed?"

Taking her playful snort of laughter as assent, he picked her up again. Keeley wrapped her arms around his neck as he walked up the stairs to his perch-like bedroom.

He must have stripped the bed while she was sleeping. It was made with military precision, and there was no sign of the grime left from when he'd collapsed there to recover from his wounds. Just crisp sheets, plump pillows, and a comforter as smooth and white as fresh snow.

Lance gently laid Keeley down on the bed and climbed in after her. He was so heavy on the mattress, she couldn't help sliding closer to him. Or so she told herself.

Take control. That's what she'd wanted to do. Drive away the nightmare and the cold, empty terror of everything that had happened the night before. Well, she'd succeeded. None of that scared her now.

No, what scared her now was the thought of what was going to happen next.

Keeley lay in Lance's arms, feeling his chest rise and fall as he fell asleep. Her knight in shining armor.

Except he didn't know who she really was.

What have I done? she thought, dread settling like a lump of ice in her stomach.

Chapter 12

Lance

*H*ungry!
The wordless command battered its way into Lance's sleeping mind, ripping through his mental defenses like tissue paper. He blinked, immediately awake.

Hungry hungry hungry!

In his arms, Keeley stirred and murmured something under her breath. Her eyebrows drew together. "Wazzat?"

"It's—" Lance shook his head. Keeley was human; she wouldn't be able to hear the hatchling's plaintive psychic cries. His snow leopard, on the other hand, was pressing against his skin in its urgency to follow the wail of hunger. "It's nothing."

"Hnergh," Keeley replied, and sat up. "M'm go—"

Her eyes were still shut. Lance kissed her forehead, smoothing away the crease between her eyebrows. "Go back to sleep. I'll look after it."

He pulled on a pair of navy sweatpants and turned just in time to see Keeley staggering toward the steps that led down to the mezzanine lounge. He grabbed her before she could fall head-first down the staircase.

"What are you—" he began, then looked harder at her. "Are you still asleep?"

Keeley's eyes were still shut, but her intention was clear. She was following the same psychic wail that was pulling him downstairs.

Maggie's psychic powers are better developed for her age than should be possible. Lance frowned as he led Keeley down to the apartment's floor level. *Or this is a dragon thing.*

Dragons. He rubbed his temples. Everything that had happened the last few years seemed to lead back to dragons.

Maggie's psychic cries were so loud, he couldn't tell where they were coming from. He hurried to the guest room, but the nest-bed Keeley had put together for the baby dragon was empty.

Hungryyyyyy!

Keeley had slipped out of his arms. Lance wheeled around, following her to—the kitchen?

I'm an idiot, he thought, smacking himself on the forehead.

Hungry hungry hungry HUNGRY!

Lance followed Keeley into the kitchen and found a scene of utter chaos. Everything that had been on any flat surface had been flung to the floor. The culprit was clear. In the middle of the floor, in a pile of smashed crockery and fruit, Maggie was wrestling with the fruit bowl.

Has she grown since last night? Lance thought. *Or does she just look bigger surrounded by chaos?*

Maggie looked up at him and Keeley. She had an apple clutched in her front paws, which she nibbled experimentally and then tossed away with a hiss. The apple rolled to join a pile of nibbled, chewed, and gnawed-on fruit and cutlery under the table.

Hungry! she demanded, and then the ridges on the top of her head stood up as she caught sight of another piece of fruit. The dragonling's whole being, physical and psychic, radiated wonder and excitement as she leapt for the wondrous yellow foodstuff.

The look on her face as she bit into the lemon could only be described as utter betrayal.

Lance laughed, and Maggie turned the look of betrayal on him. Confusion and sadness broadcast from her mind. How could the fruit be so nasty? It was the same color as she was!

He blinked. The dragonling hadn't used words, but he knew exactly what it was trying to tell him. He rubbed his forehead. Maggie's psychic abilities, while still juvenile, were already so much more refined and powerful than they had been the day before. The battering-ram of hunger in his head was evidence of that.

She's going to be more of a handful than I thought. Lance pinched the bridge of his nose as his snow leopard perked up, delighted.

What a smart kitten we have!

She's a dragon, not a kitten, Lance reminded it. His snow leopard flicked its tail derisively. It knew what it was talking about, even if Lance insisted on being a dull, slow-witted *human*.

Now, feed the kitten so it falls asleep again, and then take our mate back to bed, his snow leopard went on. Another psychic wail slammed into Lance's mind, and his snow leopard flinched. *Feed the kitten QUICKLY,* it added.

Lance hurried across to the fridge. He got there just as Keeley, still apparently sleep-walking, pulled the door open and almost slammed it straight into her own forehead.

"O-kay," Lance said, grabbing the fridge door and whisking Keeley out of the way. "That's enough of that, Maggie."

The little dragonling chittered at him, and a feeling that was the psychic equivalent of *Who, me?* floated into his mind. Lance frowned. *Leave her alone.*

Maggie whipped her tail. *Hungryyyyy!*

Lance sighed. *She's only, what, twenty-four hours old? A baby. She doesn't know what she's doing.* He looked at Keeley, who was shaking her head and blinking.

"Sorry about this," he muttered. "Another thing I should have seen coming."

"Wha...?" Keeley blinked hard. "Hang on, how the fuck did I get down here?" Her eyes fell on Maggie, peeping piteously in the ruins of the fruit bowl. "I mean... fudge..."

She frowned, raising one hand to her forehead. "Wait. Am I hungry, or is she—? Shit, I feel strange. I mean. Sugar. *Fu*...hngh."

Lance laughed and kissed her on the forehead.

"Maggie's throwing her weight around. Sit down, I'll make you both breakfast."

Groaning, Keeley flopped into a chair, resting her head in her folded arms on the kitchen table. "God, I feel like I—wait." She straightened up and looked down at herself. "Am I *completely* naked?"

Naked enough that my snow leopard won't shut up about getting you back into bed, Lance thought. Out loud, he tried to reassure her. "Shifters are a little less prudish about that sort of thing than humans."

"Well, last time I checked, I was still human." Keeley stood up. "Back in a minute."

She rubbed her chest as she walked past him, murmuring, "I feel so *strange...*"

Lance paused in the middle of rifling through his fridge.

Last night had been—he shook his head. Not a mistake, but not how he would have planned things.

But he felt something, too. Something *strange,* something that hummed like a plucked string in his heart, audible even through Maggie's hungry complaints.

He reached inside himself, barely daring to think what he would find there.

"Hey-y-y, *nope!*" Keeley yelped, coming back into the kitchen and diving at Maggie. The dragonling had been about to leap into the fridge.

Keeley wrinkled her nose. "I think that's her telling you to hurry up," she said as Maggie wound herself around her neck.

Keeley had changed into a long-sleeved shirt that Lance recognized. Part of him was disappointed that she'd dressed at all, but he couldn't help but be pleased that she was wearing his clothes. The shirt was tight on him but fit her like a tunic, draping down over her thighs.

And he was sure it had been in *his* dresser, not the one in the guest room. A smug smile lifted the corners of his mouth.

"How do you feel about pancakes?" Lance grabbed a carton of eggs from the fridge. "I—hey!"

Using his arm as a bridge, Maggie scampered off Keeley's shoulders and into the fridge. Containers and vegetables went flying. Maggie found what she was looking for at the very back of the fridge and turned around with the package grasped in her front claws, her eyes imploring.

"I think that's a no to pancakes," Keeley said, laughing. "Smoked salmon?"

"Bagels. I can do bagels." Lance beckoned to the baby dragon. "If she doesn't break into the package before—what's she doing now?"

Maggie let him take the smoked salmon. Her eyes were narrowed with concentration as she sniffed the air. She leapt—Lance winced as she used his bare chest as a springboard—and crashed into the inside of the fridge door.

"Oh, baby, no," Keeley laughed. "You're a bit young for that! Here, I'll—oops, no."

Glass rattled against glass as Maggie scrambled to get her footing. She was winding herself protectively around—Lance's heart sank—around the beer bottles he kept in the fridge door.

The beer bottles Mathis and Chloe had given him to celebrate putting Harper away. The ones with the gold-colored trim on the labels.

He sighed. "That's not real gold, Maggie."

From the way she hissed when he tried to pick her up again, either she didn't agree, or she didn't care.

He grabbed the package of smoked salmon, throwing it from hand to hand, and cocked one eyebrow at Keeley. "Let's see if breakfast can tear her away from her treasures."

Five minutes later, the air was rich with the scent of hot coffee and toasted bagels, and Maggie hadn't moved from her spot guarding the beer bottles. Every time the fridge beeped for someone to close the door, she growled as if she was worried it was going to steal her prize.

Lance plated the smoked salmon and managed to dodge Maggie's whipping tail (and sharp claws) to pull cream cheese and jam out of the fridge.

He sat down opposite Keeley and slid a mug of steaming coffee in front of her. "Milk?"

"Just sugar, thanks."

"Jam or salmon on your bagel?"

"Mmm, salmon, please." Her eyes gleamed as she glanced over to where Maggie was still sitting in the fridge door, jealously guarding her beer bottles. "Ooh, yum." She took a bite from the bagel. "Mmm. So deliciously salmon-y."

Lance knew she was teasing the hatchling, but he still had to bite back a groan as Keeley played up her enjoyment of the breakfast he'd made for her. His snow leopard purred as she closed her eyes.

"God. You know what. I don't think that was all Maggie mind-walloping me with her hunger pangs. I'm *starving*." She opened her eyes again, mischief dancing in their stormy depths. Lance cleared his throat, glad he was sitting at the table, as he went hard as a rock.

Keeley leaned forward conspiratorially. "I'm not imagining it. She can definitely tell what we're saying, right?" she whispered.

"I expect so." Lance cleared his throat again. *Damn it.*

Keeley leaned back again and sighed extravagantly. "In fact, I'm so-o-o-o starving, I think I'm going to eat *all* of this salmon by myself..."

"Preep!"

Maggie stretched her neck out as far as it could go, her cat-like eyes fixed on the platter of salmon. "Preep!" she repeated, as though ordering the salmon to come to her.

Lance chuckled and speared a piece for himself. His snow leopard was silently urging the baby dragon on. *Be the hunter! Strike down your prey!*

Maggie looked from the salmon to her row of beer bottles and back. She hissed disgruntledly. Then, to Lance's amusement, she grabbed a beer bottle, wrestled it out of the shelf, and flapped to the ground with it clutched in her front claws.

"Fleh!" she announced. "Prr-*eep!*"

Lance turned a burst of laughter into a cough as the tiny dragonling wrestled the bottle over to the kitchen table, then ran back and transported the others over in the same way. When she'd moved all six bottles over, she carefully arranged them on their sides and sat on them, muttering grumpily.

Lance's heart ached as Keeley, serious-faced, held out a sliver of salmon to the tiny dragon. Maggie stretched out her neck as far as it would go, chittering possessively as Keeley's hand got closer to her hoarded beer bottles.

"Oh, come on, baby," Keeley exclaimed. "I'm trying to feed you—there you go." Maggie snatched the salmon from her fingers and retreated to her pile, chewing madly. Keeley raised one eyebrow at Lance. "What is she *doing*?"

"Building her hoard, I think." Lance picked up another piece of salmon and held it out to Maggie. "I don't know much about it, but my understanding is that dragons thrive according to the size of their hoard."

"Which is made of gold, or... things that look like gold?" Keeley winced. "I guess this means I'm not getting my Gran's necklace back."

Lance followed her gaze to the thin gold chain wrapped around Maggie's neck and forelegs. He hadn't noticed it before. It wasn't just that the gold blended in with the tiny dragon's scales, it was that it seemed like it belonged there.

Just like Keeley belonged with him and—at least, so his snow leopard kept telling him—the tiny dragon belonged with them both.

With Julian, he reminded his snow leopard solemnly. *The dragonling belongs with her family. And God knows Julian deserves to see his niece grow up alive and happy after everything he's been through.*

"How did you find her?" he asked, keeping his tone casual. Panic flashed across Keeley's face, and he added, "If you feel up to telling the whole story. It can wait."

Keeley ran her fingers through her tangled hair. Her expression darkened, and Lance regretted ever bringing it up, but before he could say anything she shook her head.

"Might as well get it over with, right?" She sighed and placed her hands on the table. Her stance was determined, but her eyes were still uneasy.

It was all Lance could do not to take her in his arms and pull her against his chest, offering her comfort in the most primal way. He clenched his fists behind his back. "I'll need to take your statement back at our HQ, but if it would help for you to talk about it now..."

"HQ?" Keeley looked wary.

Right. I never actually explained about... anything, did I?

"I work as a private investigator for shifters. We help shifters who can't go to the human police or other services for help. Mostly small stuff—thefts that they can't report because no one's going to believe a parakeet broke into a safe, big predator shifters using their animals to intimidate people into paying protection money, that sort of thing. But recently we've uncovered a dangerous ring of shifter criminals who've been involved in everything from kidnapping to murder."

He paused. Keeley had gone pale, and he reached out to take her hand. "That's why I was at the station when the explosion went off. Maggie's uncle was involved in one of our recent investigations. We were in the middle of transferring her egg from foster care back to HQ, before reuniting her with her uncle when she was taken. The station was our one lead." He rubbed his face. *If that lead hadn't paid off—if we'd been there even a minute later...*

He pushed the thought away. Keeley was still white.

"So you're a sort of shifter police?" she asked uncertainly.

"Nothing so formalized. We have connections with shifters in the force and the legal system, but we work independently."

"Oh." Keeley squeezed his hand tight. "I guess that makes sense. It's not like there are any laws about dragon-smuggling. So... you do lock people up, if you catch them? They go to jail?"

She bit her lip, and Lance tried his damnedest to not think about how much that made *him* want to bite her lip, too. *Down, boy*, he ordered himself.

"We wouldn't be doing a good job of keeping innocents safe if we let the criminals go free, would we?" he reassured her.

"I..." Keeley hesitated, her eyes darting across his face. Then she took a deep breath. When she continued, she spoke slowly, as though she was testing the words. "Okay. My statement, huh? Well, I, I work as a maid. In a hotel. It's good work," she added quickly, "it's a really good job, and my manager is a lovely person."

She made a face. Lance grinned back at her. *So the job's a dump and her manager's a prick*, he thought.

Keeley took a deep breath and kept going, her voice more confident. "So I got off my shift, and headed home on the subway. I guess I wasn't paying attention. I don't like being the only person in a car, you know? But when I looked up, there was no one else there, except..." Keeley ran her fingertips across the fine ridges on Maggie's spine. "I don't know where she came from. I looked up, and there she was, looking back, and she just jumped on my lap.

"I thought she was someone's escaped pet lizard at first, but then I saw the wings, and then—then there was the explosion..." She covered her face, and Lance tensed, ready to leap to her side. With a sigh, she lowered her hands and rested her chin on her fists, staring at Maggie. "And—well, I guess you can fill in the bit after that, and I've already told you about the teleporting, and now... here we are."

"Here we are," Lance echoed. His heart was pounding, and his fingers itched to get hold of his tablet and start on his report, as though typing out the story would make it less terrifying. "We came so close to losing her. But instead she's fine, thanks to you.

"Better than fine," he continued. "She's already growing—doesn't she seem bigger than she was last night?" He pushed another piece of salmon towards Maggie. "She won't be this helpless forever. Her uncle's the size of a Greyhound bus and twice as frightening. The first time I met him, he was tearing chunks off a building. And she has the beginnings of a hoard, which I understand is very important. Her uncle will be happy to see her."

Have I ever seen Julian wearing gold? Lance frowned, sifting through his memories. The dragon shifter's style was spare, ascetic—and he had been a captive for so long. He owned little more than the clothes on his back. *If he does have a hoard somewhere, none of us know about it.*

And whatever it is, it's probably more classy than a pile of beer bottles. He frowned and cleared his throat. "Perhaps we will be able to convince her to swap out the beer bottles for something more appropriate before we return her into her uncle's care."

"That's the same uncle who tore chunks off a building?"

Lance flashed Keeley a smile, only noticing too late that it hadn't been a light-hearted question. Keeley was twisting her fingers together, and her mouth was pinched and thin.

"Lance..." Her voice crackled with uncertainty. Lance's snow leopard was instantly alert.

"Yes?" He reached out, capturing her twisting fingers under his.

Keeley bit her lip. "I just—I keep thinking, okay, I'm handling it, this is fine. And then there'll be something new, and I'm back to freaking out again." She stared at him, her stormy eyes troubled. "I don't belong in this world, do I?"

Lance tightened his grip on her hand. "Of course you do."

Keeley snorted and raised one eyebrow, but her eyes were still unhappy. "Really? Based on what? Getting shot at?" She took a deep breath. "I—I've been thinking. I should leave, right? Like, right away. I mean, it's not like I stand any chance against a bunch of guys who can turn into God knows what. If anything else happens, I'm just a liability."

Lance caught the word *No!* before it escaped.

Not freaking her out, he reminded himself. "I think Maggie would disagree," he said out loud. He reached partway across the table and rested his hand there, an invitation for her to take it. "You saved her life. And she's not Greyhound-sized yet. She still needs you." *I still need you,* he added silently.

Keeley searched his eyes. "I... but she has you to look after her," she said weakly. "I'd just be... in the way."

Her eyes flicked down to his hand, and a conflicted look passed over her face. For a moment, he thought she would take his hand. Instead she placed both of hers on the edge of the table and pushed herself upright. "And the sooner I leave the better, right? I—"

She stopped and looked down. Maggie had crawled away from her hoard. *Entirely* away. She hadn't even kept her tail wrapped around it.

Instead she had both front claws clamped onto Keeley's hand and was staring up at her with her big, golden eyes.

"Prrp?" she cheeped softly.

Keeley gasped. Relief unfurled inside Lance.

"I think Maggie disagrees with your plan," he remarked, and lightning sizzled across his skin as Keeley's eyes jumped to his. "Stay. Look after her. She's only a baby, and you're fifty percent of all the people she's ever known. Stay and look after her, and I promise I'll protect you."

Forever. With my life.

Keeley's eyes turned pleading. Lance raised his hand, and this time she took it, so she was standing with one hand in his, one held down by the dragonling. Keeley's lips parted.

She groaned and closed her eyes. "Lance, I—last night." She swallowed, her mouth working as though she was trying to find the right words. "I can't— It was—I don't *do* that sort of thing. I don't know if it's just because I was scared, or..."

Lance's heart sank. He'd hoped that their shared passion the night before had been a sign that she had, somehow, understood the connection between them. And this morning, her automatic response to Maggie's cries of hunger; he'd filed that under the same category, of her slipping easily into the world of shifters.

Now it was clear that had been wishful thinking. He'd let his own selfish desires blind him to the facts: that she was terrified, and lost, and overwhelmed.

He loosened his fingers so he was holding her hand gently, not gripping it, and stared deep into her eyes. The golden mate bond connecting his heart to hers glowed, and warmth rose up inside him, but he couldn't see any response in her gaze.

He could feel the connection, but she couldn't.

"There's a lot about the shifter world that even I've forgotten is strange to those who don't know us," he said, his voice soft. "I'm sorry for throwing you in the deep end."

The corner of her mouth jerked down. "You're not the one who threw me in the deep end," she muttered, glancing at Maggie. "More like you're the one keeping me afloat. But..."

The hope that had flared in Lance's heart died down at that last word. *But.*

"But you're still in over your head," he said, the words falling like rocks from his lips.

Keeley's fingers twitched under his. Her eyes were stuck to the table. "Yeah."

"Let me help." Lance kept an iron grip on his snow leopard as Keeley's eyes met his. "I want you to stay, but I don't want you to feel trapped here, and I don't want you to feel like you're floundering without the knowledge you need to feel safe. We'll take it in small steps, I promise."

"Small steps." Keeley nodded. "I think I can handle small steps."

She took a deep breath. "Okay. I'll stick around. For now. For Maggie. Just until she's back with her family."

She smiled, and Lance smiled back, longing crashing through his veins. He swallowed hard.

He'd apologized for throwing her in the deep end, but there was another metaphor he could have used. Everything she thought she knew about the world was turning upside down. The ground was crumbling under her feet, just like it was under his.

Small steps. Small steps until they were both back on solid ground. And then, once they were both safe, he would tell her the whole truth about what she meant to him.

CHAPTER 13

KEELEY

I think he bought it. Keeley felt sick. Lance had saved her life, *twice*, and she was lying to him.

But what other choice did she have? She couldn't tell him the truth about how she'd come across Maggie.

If he knew who I really was, and how I was really involved, he'd hate me.

She wasn't leaving. So much for that plan. Maggie still hadn't let go of her hand; it was equally clear that the tiny dragon understood what they'd been talking about, and that she didn't want Keeley to leave. Despite everything, Keeley couldn't bring herself to break the baby dragon's heart.

But if Lance found out the truth... He'd take the baby dragon away from her. And stop looking at her with that strange expression, like she was worth something.

And he'd probably never fuck her again, either.

She shook her head. *No. Bad.* That was *not* going to happen again. Once was bad enough. At least she'd made that clear, during their awkward kitchen-table talk.

Keeley touched her lips. They still tingled where Lance had kissed her. And the rest of her... Well. Other places tingled, too. Her whole body did.

He was so big, and strong, pure masculinity and power—and kindness. He'd been gentle with her, even when they were running for their lives. Not like the men at her work, who used their power to make her feel small and weak.

And now she was in his home. And she'd fallen asleep in his arms.

And she was a terrible, terrible person, because despite everything that had happened, despite the fact that she'd almost died several times, and lied to Lance about who she was, and had stolen the baby dragon—all she could think about was how much she wanted him to touch her again.

Maybe he will, a small, treacherous voice said inside her head. Lance had explained that shifters were less prudish about nudity than humans, due to the fact that most shifters couldn't take their clothes with them when they shifted.

Maybe they're less prudish about other things, too. So last night could just be—

No. She was being a good person now, God damn it. She was lying enough about other things, she had to draw a line in the sand somewhere. This was it.

Okay, a bit late, but last night had been a one-time only thing. Lance knew that. She knew that.

She just needed to stick to it.

Her stomach churned. *Lance isn't the only one I'm trying to fool.*

"How are you feeling?" Lance asked, his velvety voice doing very bad things to Keeley's insides.

Oh, I am so not answering that question. She turned around, her heart catching in her throat at the sight of Lance dressed in casual pants and a button-up shirt with all but the top button fastened. His eyes shone leaf-green behind a pair of gold-rimmed glasses that looked strangely old-fashioned and nerdy compared to his powerful body.

Keeley swallowed. "I, uh. Fine. Did you call in at your office?"

It was a few hours since she'd told him the big lie about how she had gotten hold of Maggie. Afterwards, Keeley had helped Maggie finish her food and then settled her for a post-binge nap before she had a shower and got dressed. The whole time, her stomach had been churning with guilt.

She needed to do something. She just didn't know what.

Tell him.

Keeley forced the thought away. That was the one thing she *couldn't* do.

Lance smiled ruefully. "You know, I did mean to check in, but somehow it slipped my mind while I was busy finding every single item in my kitchen than Maggie had smashed or chewed on. How about you? Do you need to borrow a phone?"

Keeley hesitated. She'd had her phone the night before—before the nightmare. But she hadn't checked it.

"No, there's no one I need to call." Not work. She hadn't turned up for her shift. Twenty-four hours ago, that would have made her panic, but now? She wasn't planning on sticking around the city long enough for them to fire her, once Maggie was safe back with her uncle.

The uncle who could tear apart a building with his bare hands. Or claws. Oh, God. If *he* found out what she had done...

Another reason to leave as soon as she could.

Once Maggie was safe.

Keeley rubbed her chest. When she thought about leaving, something inside her ached, like a muscle she hadn't known existed. But she had to. She didn't belong in this world, regardless of what Lance said. Not when Sean was the one who had dumped her into it and left her to drown.

Or be blown up. Her stomach went cold. Lance was right, she was in well over her head. If she was going to get out safely, she needed to know what she was running away from. She needed to know as much as she could about shifters.

"Lance..." she began. Her thoughts ran ahead of her mouth, and she hesitated, surprised by her own reaction to what she was about to ask. "Will you shift for me?"

Lance had been reaching into a pocket for his phone. He dropped it, and his eyes flew to meet hers. "Of course."

Silver flickered in the depths of his eyes. Keeley swallowed, rubbing her chest again as he pushed his glasses further up his nose. *Ow*, she thought. *Why does that hurt?*

"That isn't too weird a thing to ask, is it?" The words came out too fast. Keeley licked her lips. This was supposed to be about gathering information to keep herself safe, so why did it feel so... intimate? "You can tell me if it's something I shouldn't be asking, or..."

"It's not a problem." Lance's eyes smouldered. "You're sure about this? The last time you saw me shift, I wasn't exactly in good shape."

"I want to know more about shifters," Keeley said, which was the truth. The way Lance's face lit up as she said it made her wish it was the *whole* truth.

Terrible person. The worst.

What made you think you could be anything better?

A lonely cry from the guest room distracted her from her grim thoughts. "I'll just grab Maggie," she said quickly.

Maggie refused to go anywhere without her bottle hoard, so Keeley dragged on her work apron. The bottles all fit in the front pocket—just. Maggie checked each individual bottle and then climbed up Keeley's arm and wrapped herself proprietorially around her neck.

"Silly creature," Keeley murmured to her as she rejoined Lance in the living room. "You'd better not be thinking of making me part of your hoard."

Lance frowned. "I don't believe people can be part of a dragon's hoard. At least..." He rubbed his forehead. "Who am I kidding? I'm hardly the world expert on dragon shifters." He caught Keeley's eye. "Don't tell anyone from the agency I said that."

Keeley raised her eyebrows. "Uh, sure." *He's got work issues too? Well, at least I'm not the only one.*

"Do you want to..." Lance gestured to the sofa.

Maggie rearranged herself around Keeley's shoulders as she settled back against the plush leather cushions. She dropped her tail down so the tip of it just tapped against the tops of the bottles in Keeley's pocket.

Keeley sighed. "I'm not part of the hoard, I'm just the pack-mule," she joked. Maggie cheeped and nibbled her earlobe. "*Ow*," Keeley said, and raised her eyebrows at Lance. "Do you think that was her agreeing with me?"

"I think she's looking for more gold," Lance said, smiling. "Your earrings."

Keeley felt the studs in her ears. "These are about as gold as the labels on those bottles, baby," she told Maggie.

"Here." Lance knelt down in front of her. "I need to take it off to shift anyway."

He slid a heavy-looking watch off his wrist. Gold glinted in the early afternoon light coming in through the living room windows.

Maggie's eyes widened as he held it out to her. "Prrrp-rp?" she asked, stretching out her neck.

"Go on. If Keeley has to give up her gran's necklace, the least I can do is add to your treasure pile." Lance was talking to Maggie, but his eyes burned into Keeley's. Her mouth went dry.

"Prrp!" Maggie snatched the watch and darted back around Keeley's shoulders. Keeley steadied her with both hands, feeling her cheeks blaze as she broke eye contact with Lance.

"You realize you're not getting that back, right?"

"Oh, well." Lance shrugged it off. "I'll find something else to trade your necklace back for."

"You don't need to..." Keeley's voice drained away as he stood up and began to unbutton his shirt.

"Hmm?" Lance's fingers stilled. He looked at her, and a smug smile lifted the corners of his lips. "Ah."

"Ah" what? I'm not even blushing anymore. Keeley touched the back of her hand to her cheek to check. *Oh. Or, maybe I'm blushing so much I can't even tell it's happening.*

"This is supposed to be educational, you know." He undid another button, one eyebrow raised.

Keeley snorted. "Oh? And kid-friendly?"

She made a show of covering Maggie's eyes. Maggie squeaked indignantly and clambered up over her hands so she could see again—and then immediately scampered down Keeley's front to check on her bottle-hoard.

Lance's eyes danced. "While she's distracted?"

Keeley laughed and sat back. Maggie was head-down in her apron pocket, and her tail was whipping back and forth in front of Keeley's face. Lance grinned.

"Then let the lesson begin."

He dropped his glasses into his shirt pocket and undid the rest of the buttons. Then, with a careful efficiency that made Keeley groan, he began to fold his shirt up.

"Lance, I work in housekeeping. I know how to fold clothes."

Lance raised one eyebrow. She focused on that, not the fact that he was now standing shirtless in front of her.

I already know what he looks like naked, she told herself. *I don't need to... ooh.*

"Ahem," Lance said, his eyes crinkling with amusement. "Now, the next part of the lesson..."

Keeley covered her eyes as he reached for his belt buckle. The next thing she knew, Lance was gently pulling her hands away from her face.

"I want you to see this," he told her, his voice gentle and somehow vulnerable. "I want you to see me shift the way it's meant to happen, not because I'm injured and bleeding. I don't want that to be your strongest memory of my snow leopard."

Keeley was about to reassure him that it wasn't, but the words died on her lips. It would be a lie. And it wasn't just that she'd already lied to him too much.

She wanted a different memory of him shifting, too. Something to overwrite the image of him bleeding and helpless.

"Okay," she said, staring directly into his eyes. "I'm ready."

Her eyes didn't drop, even when she could sort-of tell in her peripheral vision that he was undoing his pants. And dropping them. And—

Keeley gasped. Lance's whole body shimmered. His eyes gleamed silver, the pupils stretching long and cat-like, and fine silver and black hairs sprouted over his dark skin. Then everything seemed to speed up and a moment later an enormous cat was standing on all fours in front of Keeley.

No, she thought. *Not a cat. A snow leopard.*

"Lance," she said, stunned. The snow leopard nodded.

Heart racing, Keeley slipped off the sofa and knelt on the floor in front of him. In his cat form—*snow leopard,* she corrected himself—he came up to just below where her waist would be if she was standing. His fur was thick and plush, his eyes a pale silver surrounded by rings of dark fur like heavy eyeliner.

Her eyes dropped to the snow leopard's chest, and she gulped. "The first time I saw you like this..."

She reached out, her hand stopping just before she touched Lance's fur. He stepped forward, and she buried her fingers in the thick fur over his chest. His heart beat like a drum against the palm of her hand.

"You were bleeding so much, and you said something I didn't catch. Then you collapsed, and... changed." She dug her fingers in deeper until she found what she was looking for. A hard ridge of scar, hidden under his soft white fur. Her breath caught in her throat. "And you were still bleeding. I thought you were going to die. I thought I'd gone *crazy* and hallucinated you turning into a giant cat, and you were going to die."

The snow-leopard-Lance dropped his head and nudged it under her hand. She stroked his forehead, marvelling. "I don't know why I thought you turning into a giant cat was any stranger than me meeting a baby dragon. Probably the shock."

Lance blinked his huge, pale silver eyes at her, and she laughed. "Sorry. Snow leopard, not giant cat."

A glint of leaf green appeared in the depths of his eyes. Keeley stared. "Are you... switching back and forth? Just a bit?" Her hand lingered on his fur of its own accord. "I thought I was imagining it before, when your eyes changed color."

Lance-the-snow-leopard looked at her for a moment, and then rolled his shoulders back in a gesture that was close to a shrug. Keeley laughed. "This conversation is a bit one-sided, isn't it?"

Her front pocket clanked, and Maggie poked her head out the top. "PRRP!" she announced, staring at Lance. "Prr-eep rrp?"

Lance blinked at her too, and then moved a few feet away. He swung his head to point at his shirt and pants, neatly folded and in a pile on the edge of the sofa, and back to Keeley.

"Oh, you're going to—" *Shift,* she was about to say, but then he was doing it. His fur moved in a non-existent breeze, and then Lance was sitting on the floor opposite her. Human-shaped.

Human-shaped, and naked, and...

"Ow!" Keeley winced as Maggie's pinprick claws dug into her stomach. The tiny dragon was wriggling out of her bottle-hoard pocket. All the spines on the top of her head were standing on end. "Baby, what are you—*oh, God.*"

Maggie's scales started to glitter more than usual. Then they shimmered. Then her whole body shimmered, from the tip of her nose to the end of her tail, and then...

"Oh, no. Oh no, no, no. Lance, what do I do?"

Keeley grabbed Maggie before she could roll off her lap. Tiny, wriggling, *human baby* Maggie.

"Damn." Lance leapt up and grabbed his pants. "Just hold her like that—"

"Like what? Like this?" The baby's head lolled backward, and Keeley quickly slipped one hand under to support it. She cradled Maggie against her, ignoring the beer bottles jabbing into her stomach. "I don't know anything about babies!"

Lance pulled his pants and shirt on, leaving his shirt unbuttoned, and sat down next to her. "You're doing fine," he reassured her. "You've got her head. Good. Hold on to her gently, but tight enough she won't wriggle out of your arms."

"Okay..." Keeley stare wide-eyed at the baby in her arms. Maggie. "This is way freakier than when she was a dragon," she whispered to Lance.

He laughed and put an arm around her waist. "You're incredible, you know that? Most people would have it the other way around."

"She's so... small." Keeley carefully maneuvered Maggie until she was cradling her in one arm. Her eyes were a striking ice-blue, and she had the tiniest fluff of black hair on the top of her head. Keeley stroked it softly. "She looks so much more vulnerable."

Lance's arm tightened around her waist. "I wish I could say that if the people who were trying to kidnap her saw her like this they would've had second thoughts, but those mercenaries were shifters, too. They knew what she was."

Keeley's stomach lurched. *Sean. Did Sean know?*

Would you really be surprised if he did, and still wanted to do the job?

Maggie kicked out with her legs and waved her arms. Her tiny face screwed up, and Lance grunted.

"Ow," he muttered, rubbing his forehead. Keeley was about to ask him what was the matter when it hit her, too.

Want want want want want! Want—kick, air-punch—*want go—-scowl, kick—want go move NOW!*

Maggie's face screwed up even more, and she began to scream.

"I don't think she likes being a human baby," Keeley said faintly. Lance groaned and dropped his head on her shoulder.

"Human infants are a lot less able to do... well, anything at all compared to dragons, it seems." His voice was muffled by Keeley's shirt, and she could feel his breath, hot through the thin fabric. She leaned into him.

"I don't know about that. She never screamed this good as a dragon." Keeley had to raise her voice to be heard over Maggie's outraged howls.

Lance chuckled, holding her closer. She let her head drop down against him. "Can you talk her back into being a dragon? With your psychic powers?"

Lance sighed and sat up straight. Keeley's whole body felt colder as he let go of her waist.

"I can try. Most shifters don't shift for the first time until they're a few years old at least. Old enough to reason with. Here, let me take her."

Keeley was in the middle of maneuvering the screaming, punching, and kicking baby into Lance's arms when a thunderous knocking echoed through the house.

CHAPTER 14

LANCE

Lance sprang up at once, shielding Keeley and the kitten.
Bang! Bang!

The noise echoed through the apartment, the open-plan layout making it difficult to track where the sound was coming from. Lance let his snow leopard take over his senses long enough to determine it was coming from the front door.

He relaxed his guarded posture. Well. There were two possibilities here. One, they were under attack, and their attackers had decided to abandon the element of surprise in favor of trying to beat down a fortified, armored door.

Two...

Lance gritted his teeth. Only a select few people had access to this level of the building. And one psychic sweep of the apartment told him exactly who was banging on his door.

He turned around and held out a hand to Keeley, who was still sitting frozen on the floor. "It's all right," he reassured her, and sighed. "I apologize in advance for this, but—"

The banging stopped. Lance resisted the urge to roll his eyes. *That makes it, what, almost a minute for them to remember they have front-door keys?*

His snow leopard flicked its tail, half-dismissive, half-territorial. *The panther should have reminded him.*

"They're my friends," Lance reassured her as the front door burst open and slammed against the wall. "Or they were, until this very minute."

Heavy footsteps thudded through the apartment, and then Mathis Delacourt's broad-shouldered form appeared from behind the bookcase partition.

"You're alive," he remarked in his gravely voice, and then called over his shoulder: "It's alright, everyone! He's not dead!"

"Clearly not," Lance snapped. Another man appeared behind Mathis: Grant Diaz. Lance nodded greetings to the panther shifter and returned his attention to Mathis. "Should I be?"

Mathis grinned. "Depends on who you ask. I thought going straight to the source would be the best bet."

Mathis hop-skipped sideways as his mate, Chloe, pushed past him. "Idiot cats. If he's fine, then get out of the way... Hi, Lance." She grinned at him, but her eyes were darkly shadowed. "You've caused a lot of people a lot of overtime, you know that?"

Lance frowned. Chloe worked in comms at the agency, but—"The mission was meant to be need-to-know only."

"That was *two days ago*, Lance! The last anyone saw or heard from you, you'd just been shot!"

What? "That can't be right," Lance said, taking in Chloe's angry glare and the two men's quiet relief. "I'm sure I checked in after I woke up this morning. No, yesterday morning. Or... I meant to, at least." He patted his pockets.

Grant feigned shock, leaning back against the bookshelves. "My God. He doesn't even know where his phone is. Are you sure you're really Lance? Or should we add bodysnatchers to Irina's X-Files investigation?"

"No, just teleportation," Lance muttered, giving up on his pockets. When had he last seen his phone, or his tablet, for that matter?

"I heard my name." Irina Diaz walked slowly in past the others, one hand resting on her round belly. "I'm assuming that means it's safe to come in, and—ooh. Sofa."

Grant had sprung upright the moment his mate walked into the room, but Irina dodged his arms and moved towards the couch. She turned lovingly teasing eyes on him.

"I see a sofa, love. Have you checked it for traps? Germs? Unpasteurized cheeses? Too late, I'm going for it."

She grabbed his hand and pulled him with her as she eased herself onto the sofa with a sigh of relief. Grant sat beside her, wrapping his arms around her possessively.

Chloe, meanwhile, had stopped glaring at Lance and was looking behind him with open interest. Lance's snow leopard snapped defensively, which only made Chloe raise an eyebrow at him. He could sense her plover regarding him coolly from behind her eyes.

"Well, well, well," Chloe drawled, eyeing up Keeley. "*Someone's* been busy... I guess the reports of you being shot through the chest were exaggerated, after all."

"Not exactly." Lance rubbed his chest, where the fresh scar was a constant ache.

The room fell silent. Chloe looked at him in shock, and Mathis' face fell into grim lines. Grant pulled Irina closer to him.

"What?" Mathis surged forward and for a moment, Lance thought he was going to tear his shirt off. "When were you going to tell us about that?"

"When—" Lance began, and was interrupted by an unhappy howl.

"Okay!" Keeley started to stand up, struggling slightly as Maggie wriggled in her arms. Lance helped her up, and she flashed him a quick, only slightly panicked look before turning to face the others. "If any of you want to know what Lance meant by that—yeah, you too, lady hiding behind the bookcase there—then you're going to help us get this baby to shift back into dragon shape." She added, under her breath, "Because holy *fudge* no one is going to be able to hear anyone else speak while she's like this."

Lady hiding behind the bookshelves? Lance sniffed the air, filtering out Keeley, Maggie, and his friends. "Zhang, is that you?"

Carol Zhang edged around the side of the bookshelves. "Sorry, boss."

Lance just shook his head. "What are you doing here?"

"We provided her with a key, and she provided our break-in with legitimacy," Grant drawled, massaging Irina's shoulders.

Carol opened her mouth, then winced and closed it. Although she was technically no longer standing *behind* the bookshelf walls, she was clinging to them like a limpet.

Sorry, boss. Briers told us there was no sign of anyone going in or out of your apartment, but I didn't feel right not checking. And then your friends all found me downstairs and insisted on joining in. She winced again as Maggie let off another round of wails. *But you don't need me here now...*

Stick around. You can tell me what the hell's been going on while I've been... in recovery. This time, Lance was the one who winced. He hoped that last bit didn't sound as weak an excuse to Zhang as it did to him.

Two days without checking in, after the last his team heard of him he was under fire. What was wrong with him?

Keeley brushed against him and caught his eye. The touch of her arm against his burned like fire. *There's your answer.*

"Hang on... dragon shape?" Chloe's eyes widened as she stared at the red-faced, screaming baby in Keeley's arms.

"Yes, she's a, a dragon," Keeley raised her voice over Maggie's yells. "And we need to get her *back* to being a dragon, before we all go *deaf*!"

If we all shift— Lance began, and then switched to speaking out loud so that Keeley and Irina could hear. "If we all shift, she might get the idea. I think that's how she went into human form in the first place."

"Uh-huh," said Chloe, sounding unimpressed. She gave Lance a meaningful look, her eyes flicking from her, to Keeley, and back. "And...?"

First I forget to check in at work, and now I forget to introduce my mate. Lance could have punched himself. Instead, he put one arm around Keeley's waist.

"Everyone, this is Keeley Smith. She rescued—" He paused as Maggie shrieked with rage again. "She rescued Julian Rouse's niece from the kidnappers when our retrieval mission went south." Tenderness softened his gaze as he looked down at her, tucked into the curve of his arm.

"Julian's niece? Hang on—is that? Is she...?" A wondering smile broke out across Chloe's face. "Oh, do you think she remembers me?"

"She's a newborn?" Irina asked from the sofa, her voice weak. She looked up at Grant. "I thought newborns were supposed to be sleepy and adorable?"

Grant gave her a reassuring kiss and then turned away with a look that suggested he needed reassuring himself.

Lance hid a chuckle and took Maggie from Keeley. She handed the baby over, looking relieved, and Lance immediately realized why. Holding Maggie in human form wasn't like holding her in dragon from. Dragon-shaped Maggie was sleek and nimble and used her tail to keep her balance; human-shaped Maggie didn't even seem to know what her arms and legs were, let alone how to use them.

Lance sent psychic feelings of calm and reassurance to the baby dragon shifter. They bounced off her mind like oil off a hot pan.

He pushed his glasses up his nose. "Maggie hatched in dragon form, and this is the first time she's shifted. She's not, er, exactly taking it well." *No shit,* six pairs of eyes replied. "She shifted after watching me do it, but watching me shift back wasn't enough to pull her back into her dragon form. Maybe if you all show her, too..."

Mathis and Grant exchanged a look. "It's worth a try," Grant said.

Mathis frowned, and Chloe touched him gently on the cheek, just below the knotted scar that crawled from his forehead to below his eye. He smiled at her.

"I'll be okay," he murmured, so softly Lance could barely hear him over Maggie's shrieks. He looked up and caught Lance's eye, straightening his shoulders. "Let's do this."

He stepped forward, one hand outstretched to shake Keeley's. She took it, smiling nervously.

"Mathis Delacourt. Lion shifter," he introduced himself as he shook her hand. "It's a pleasure to meet you, Keeley."

He moved into a spot of open floor in the middle of the room and, with only a moment's hesitation, pulled off his shirt. Long scars ran down his back, souvenirs from his time as Gerald Harper's prisoner. He grinned over his shoulder, dropped his trousers, and began to shift.

Lance's spine stiffened as he saw how much effort it took Mathis to shift. He glanced sideways, meeting Chloe's hard-eyed glare. She was fiercely protective of her mate, and with good reason. Mathis had almost died on that island, and none of them knew how long it would be before he was fully recovered.

When Lance looked back at Mathis, he was in lion form, his golden mane warm in the afternoon sun pouring through the windows. He shook his heavy head, looking up at Maggie in Lance's arms.

Maggie stared back. She'd frozen mid-scream, her face still screwed up, but utterly silent. And still human-shaped.

Lance sighed. "Try changing back?"

The buzz of private telepathic conversation reverberated against the edges of Lance's mind. Was Mathis talking to Maggie, he wondered, or was Chloe talking to him?

Mathis shook his mane, and the air around him shimmered. A moment later, he was kneeling, human-shaped, on the floor. Chloe hurried to his side, and Lance felt the buzz of private communication as she checked on him.

"Sweetheart, I'm fine," Mathis complained, though the shining pride in his eyes at his mate's attention made his complaint ring false.

Lance jiggled Maggie in his arms as she began to grizzle quietly. She'd been enraptured by the sight of Mathis shifting—but was still human-shaped.

"Me next?" Grant rose from the sofa, his movements preternaturally smooth and feline. He introduced himself to Keeley—Grant Diaz, panther shifter—and held an arm out to his mate.

Irina smiled. "Irina Diaz. Human. And…" She patted her stomach. "Mystery Diaz. I guess we will find out in a few months what his or her story is."

With a feline smile, Grant shifted, as smoothly as every other movement he made. Green eyes stared up from his panther's pitch-black face as he looked across at Lance and Maggie, who was once again intent on the shifter but, still, human-shaped.

She's very alert for a newborn, isn't she? And shifting, after only two days. Grant's psychic voice was rueful. *Honestly, after last week's prenatal class, this is the last thing we need. The other parents terrified Irina enough with all their stories of what shifter children get up to.*

Grant shifted back, and as soon as he was dressed, slipped back onto the sofa beside his mate.

"My turn." Chloe cracked her knuckles, then turned back to Carol. "Unless—no, you probably don't…"

"Not unless there's a private swimming pool around here," Carol mumbled.

"It's all down to me then. Boys, watch how it's done."

Chloe shot a dazzling smile at Keeley as she walked over. "Chloe Kent. I work for Lance, as you might have picked up. Mathis is my mate, same as Irina over there is Grant's." Her eyes gleamed mischievously. "It really is *lovely* to meet you, Keeley. Now, let's get this baby back her wings, shall we?"

She knelt down in front of Maggie, her eyes going soft. "Hello, sweetheart," she crooned. "Do you remember me? I bet you do, somewhere deep inside. And you remember how to be a dragon, too. You just don't remember that you remember." She crinkled her nose. "Wow, that's getting confusing. Let's just stick to the basics, huh?"

Chloe shrugged off her dress—Lance stopped looking at this point—and there was a soft whoosh of air as she shifted.

Maggie gurgled with excitement, punching the air with her arms and legs.

Lance knelt down so the little dragon shifter was closer to Chloe. Chloe, a plover shifter, was barely a foot high in her bird form, but Maggie's eyes went wide and gold as she stared at her.

Gold. Her dragon was peering through her eyes, and Lance thought he knew why. As Chloe hopped back and forth in front of them, he became sure.

It was simple, really. Chloe had wings.

She spread them, flapping them slowly while Maggie watched, entranced. Maggie's pupils lengthened, becoming cat-like slits.

Chloe hopped up closer. *Aw, hey, cutey. Do you remember me? I didn't even know I could shift, back when I first saw you. I'm still not very good at it. And all the others are probably laughing at me right now because I can't stop them from listening in on me talking to you. What can I say, I used to be a reporter. And now I work in comms. Why even bother talking if everyone can't hear you?* She waved her wings slowly. *But being a bird shifter is great. Because it means I have wings, and with wings, I can* fly.*

Lance felt Chloe gather her psychic energy, and the image she sent to Maggie exploded into his mind. An image, and feelings, too. Wings stretched out either side, balancing on the changing breeze as the world unrolled miles below. Freedom and excitement and the promise of adventure.

Maggie stilled, sneezed, and a moment later Lance was holding a wriggling baby dragon. He set her down, and she pranced up to Chloe.

Oh, she's gorgeous, Chloe gushed, hopping on the spot. *Hello sweetheart!* She spread her wings as Maggie trotted towards her and let the tiny dragon carefully sniff at her. *You're a million times cuter than your uncle, no mistake. I'll tell him so next time I see him. Wait...*

Her bird face couldn't frown, but Lance *felt* the suspicious glare in her psychic voice.

Lance... he does know about her, right?

Lance pinched the bridge of his nose. *I'll add that to the list of things I absolutely intended to do in the last 48 hours.*

Better put a note in your calendar. If you even remember where your phone is, Chloe said, mockingly. *Ooh, cutey, do you want to learn how to fly?*

Keeley sighed with relief and grimaced as Lance caught her eye. "Is it bad that I'm handling her being a baby dragon better than her being a baby, er, baby?"

"Not at all. I think Maggie prefers being like this, too." *Though I hope Chloe isn't serious about teaching her how to fly,* Lance added silently. *She's enough of a handful as it is.*

"Boss..." Carol looked on the edge of putting her hand up like she was in class. "I've let the team know you're okay. Do you want that report now?"

"I think we all do." Mathis rubbed the scar on his cheek. "And Lance's, too."

*

Knowing that the dragonling's first shift would have taken a lot of energy, Lance suggested they convene in the kitchen.

"Is anyone else hungry?" he asked, after Maggie started digging in to what was left of the salmon.

"Only for information," Chloe retorted at once. "Come on, Lance. What the hell happened?"

Lance sighed, made sure Maggie was settled with her meal, and sat down next to Keeley. She leaned in close to him.

My mate, he thought, his heart glowing. His snow leopard was practically purring with the chance to tell them all how brave she was.

"I separated from the rest of the team at the station, when it became clear the egg had hatched," he began.

He told them a version of the truth that excluded Keeley being his mate and watched their reactions. Mathis, Grant, and Chloe all glared at him as though they knew he'd left something out. Carol Zhang frowned to herself, her flat black eyes lost in thought. And Irina looked pale.

"The dragon scales," she whispered. "Before Francine kidnapped me, none of you even knew shifters could go completely untraceable like that, but now it seems like they're turning up everywhere."

"Not everywhere," Lance said. Mathis' eyes flew up. "Remember, we traced them back to the source."

"You think this has something to do with Harper?" The lion shifter automatically pulled his mate to his side. Chloe grumbled, but pressed the side of her face against his chest, giving him the comfort he needed.

"How can it be? He's locked up, and we've investigated all of his business associates." Lance rubbed his face wearily. "But the people who took the egg had scale shields. Which means there's either another, separate group out there that not only knows about the Rouse dragon powers, and already has access to scales, or..."

"Or Harper wasn't the head of this particular snake." Mathis' face settled into tired lines. "You hunted down everyone who ever visited the island, but if he's only one branch of a wider organization, then... Christ. How deep does this all go?"

Lance felt the ground crumble under his feet. *Good question.* He gritted his teeth. "That's what we need to find out."

"Who's Harper?" Keeley asked.

And while you're standing on the edge of a cliff top, wondering how far the drop is, Keeley's already in over her head. Lance brushed the backs of his fingers along her arm.

"Gerald Harper is a shifter criminal," he began, and Chloe snorted.

"A shifter piece of shit, more like," she muttered.

Lance nodded. "Yes, that, too. He owned a private island off the east coast, further south, where he imprisoned other shifters and forced them to fight gladiator-style for his amusement."

Keeley swallowed. "I'm guessing you don't mean in the giant-rubber-weapons, *American Gladiator* sense."

"No." Mathis' voice was heavy. "Harper is a sadistic psychopath. If it wasn't for my mate, I wouldn't have survived." He pulled Chloe close, his face uncharacteristically serious. Then he flashed a teasing grin at Lance. "I guess you know how that feels now, Lance. Shot through the chest. Jesus. Good thing you'd already dragged Keeley into your problems."

Lance's skin prickled. Beside him, Keeley frowned.

"No, Maggie's the one who teleported us out of there," she said, sounding confused. "I'm just here to make sandwiches and carry the beer. Right, Maggie?"

Lance cleared his throat. "As I was saying, it may be that we missed some connection between Harper and another criminal group—"

No one was paying attention to him. Chloe sat forward with her elbows on the table, grinning at Keeley.

"Should have known Lance would be as organized and efficient about finding his mate as everything else. Get all the drama and shooting over with first, then literally *teleport* back to his place. Talk about not wasting time!"

Lance groaned silently. Keeley was staring around the table. Her eyes were wide, but her lips were pinched thin, as though she was trying not to let on how confused she was.

So much for small steps.

Chloe winked at him and opened her mouth. Lance knew he had to stop her before she said anything more. He had to take back control of the conversation.

STOP, he bellowed telepathically. Every shifter around the table jumped, including Maggie. Lance sighed and steadied himself.

Take back control of the situation. Not bawl them out like you're a drill sergeant. As quickly as he could, Lance explained the situation. From the looks on the faces of his shifter friends, his explanation didn't impress them.

You're shitting me, Chloe said flatly. *You know how dangerous it can be to ignore your mate bond!*

It's only been two days, he said helplessly. Mathis glared at him.

Grant shook his head. *It's easier to hand out life advice than to take it, isn't it?* he remarked. *Who was it who scolded me for keeping Irina in the dark for so long?*

It's not like that—

Lance was about to explain that they'd agreed to take small steps, rather than launch Keeley head-first into all the intricacies of shifter culture, when Irina leaned forward, smiling shyly.

"I know I should just be glad that Lance has found his mate at last, but honestly? I'm *so* happy that I'm not going to be the only human in the group anymore. If you have any questions about being a big cat shifter's mate—well, I'm still figuring it out myself, but I'll help where I can." Her smile became impish. "Mostly it's scratching their chins and telling them how pretty they are, anyway."

"Hey…" Grant objected, not even half-heartedly.

Keeley stared at them both, her eyebrows furrowing. "Wait. You all think I'm Lance's... mate? What even is that?" She looked at Lance, and he hoped he was imagining the way her eyes hardened as she turned to him, as though she was preparing herself for the worst. "Lance, what are they talking about?"

Lance opened his mouth to explain—and no words came out. Shame crashed down on him, tying his tongue into knots. Chloe was right. They all were. He should have been honest with her from the beginning.

He cleared his throat, but it was too late. The wary hardness in Keeley's eyes crystallized into solid rock, and she looked away.

"Mates are an essential part of shifter social culture," he heard himself saying as though from a very long way away. Inside him, his snow leopard rolled up tight, hiding its head under its paws in shame. "Each shifter has one person, human or another shifter, who is indelibly connected to their soul. Being with them... is the one thing that can make a shifter truly complete."

His voice broke on the last word as he realized just what he was saying. *This is what I wanted to leave until later,* he thought, his mouth dry. *I thought I could put it off. Schedule it, like a meeting, or paperwork. Save the big reveal for an appropriate moment.*

God, he was an idiot.

"Keeley, I—"

"Well, it's a good thing I'm not, isn't it?" Keeley tried to smile, and then just looked down at her hands. "Seriously, that's..."

She went so pale so fast that for a moment Lance was afraid she was about to pass out. Instead, she grimaced and shook her head, muttering, "Things are complicated enough as it is."

Silence fell around the table. Even Maggie was quiet, frozen in the middle of chewing a mouthful of salmon. Lance sent her a psychic hug of reassurance and rubbed the tense spot between his eyebrows.

Mathis was glaring at him. Grant's look of mocking fondness was transforming into a frown. Carol just looked confused, but Chloe was straight-up grimacing at him, making sharp movements of her head toward Keeley. Even sweet, shy Irina was looking at him with something perilously close to disapproval.

Lance took a deep breath. "I'm sure you all have... things to do today..."

"No, can't you all stay?" Keeley's voice was brittle-bright. She reached out and gathered Maggie to her chest, kissing the tiny dragon on the top of her head as she screeched indignantly. "Really, it's so nice to meet shifters who aren't trying to shoot me or blow me up—not counting you and Maggie, of course, L-Lance..."

Her cheeks were blazing, the blush spreading down to her neck and the sliver of cleavage visible above the borrowed t-shirt she was wearing. Lance's heart ached, and deeper inside him, the golden bond connecting him to her twisted and pulled.

"Of course we'll stay." Chloe looked from her to Lance, her expression worried. "The boys will all want to do some cat male bonding rubbish since Lance got shot, and we want to get to know Maggie better, don't we? Irina? Carol? Say yes, Carol, we can put this on your Professional Development timesheet."

Carol and Irina nodded quickly.

"If that's all right with you, Lance?" Chloe raised both eyebrows at Lance in a way that told him he'd better answer right.

"Of course." Lance rubbed his face. "Stay as long as you like." There was no way he would counteract his mate's request—even if she had clearly invited everyone to stay to prevent herself from having to be alone with him.

"Boss, when would be a good time to give my report?"

Lance looked to the end of the table where Zhang was sitting. She actually had raised her hand, this time, but quickly stuck it under the table when she saw him looking.

He took a deep breath.

"Go on, Zhang. Now's fine." She looked as if she was about to say something, her eyes darting around the table, and he held up a hand. "I trust everyone at this table. And if this latest attack on the Rouse dragons is another extension of Harper's influence, then they're all involved, anyway."

"Right, boss." Carol pulled out her phone and cleared her throat. "I'll send you the written version, too."

Lance nodded absently, his attention on Keeley. She still looked uncomfortable. Maybe even more uncomfortable now than she had done before he'd said he trusted everyone in the room.

His heart sank further, meeting the growing pit in his stomach.

Carol cleared her throat again and began her report. She moved quickly through the main items: the six enemy agents had gotten away, including the one Lance had knocked out. Harley Ames, their Beta transport driver, had taken custody of the remaining two eggs and whisked them away to a safe location.

"Where is Ames now?" he asked Zhang.

Her flat eyes flicked around the table again, and she referred to her phone. "Er. With your aunt, boss."

Lance sighed. "Well. They're safe there, at least." He rubbed his forehead. "But I'd still prefer to have them under my own nose."

His fingers automatically twitched for the tablet that he hadn't used in days. Ruefully, he made a mental note and asked Zhang to add a memo to his calendar. She did so while Chloe smirked.

If I contact him today, he can bring them in tomorrow. To the agency, which will be even safer than here.

"Apart from that, there's... not a lot, boss. Your report matches up with some of our blanks, but there's still a lot we're missing. We don't know who's behind the kidnapping. We don't even have footage from the station where the explosion happened. The whole system's been wiped. Briers almost had a fit."

Lance leaned back in his chair. "Our first priority has to be to keep Maggie and her siblings safe. Once that's achieved, we can focus on finding out who is behind this."

"You make it sound so easy." Mathis grinned at him. "I say, bring Rouse in. Next time these assholes come for the babies, set him on them. Happy families and no more bad guys. Problem solved."

"I'll keep that in mind for Plan B," Lance replied dryly. "Either way, tomorrow is going to be a big day. Zhang, you're off duty, you can go. Chloe—"

"Why, yes, Lance, I would be *happy* to stay for dinner, as your friend and not an employee, and spend more time with your delightful dragon baby." Chloe's grin was anything but innocent. "And so would the others."

Keeley's quiet sigh of relief sent another wave of shame crashing over Lance.

"You don't get to leave us thinking you're dead for a day and get away with it," Grant drawled. *Besides. We need to talk about you and Keeley. Don't make the same mistake I did and almost leave it too late.*

Or me, Mathis added. *You know where that ends. Nowhere good.*

As though I don't already know what an ass I've been, Lance thought.

He deserved to be grilled. And tonight, he would tell Keeley everything. She was his mate, and it wasn't fair to keep that hidden from her.

CHAPTER 15

KEELEY

Thank God I'm not Lance's mate.

After the initial shock—well, who wouldn't be shocked, to discover that something like soulmates actually existed?—Keeley had felt sick with relief.

Of everything she'd found out about the shifter world so far, this whole "mate" idea was the most terrifying. Sure, it had been awkward when Lance's friends had gotten the wrong end of the stick, but that was better than the alternative.

Because seriously—her, Lance's mate? This gorgeous, brave, kind, and incredibly sexy man, chained to someone like *her*?

No. The universe wouldn't let something like that happen. Not to someone as good as him.

Night was falling by the time Lance's friends left. Keeley wrapped Maggie around her shoulders and helped everyone gather up coats and bags.

Maggie had been awake all day and was getting crotchety. She snapped and grizzled until Chloe had the bright idea of swaddling her in her scarf, with the necklace, Lance's watch, and—after some more grizzling—Keeley's gold-ish studs wrapped up in the fabric with her. Maggie's grizzles softened to the occasional hiss, and by the time their guests had left, she was fast asleep.

Keeley leaned against the wall as Lance reset the security system, pretending to coo over the sleeping dragonling. In reality, she was memorizing the code on the door lock.

Her shoulders slumped. Today had been... nice. But she had to get real. The longer she was here, the higher the risk that someone would find her out.

She'd followed all of Lance's plans as he talked them over with his friends. Tomorrow, the other two eggs would be brought back to the agency and then flown direct to the safehouse where Maggie's uncle was staying.

And as soon as Maggie was back with her family, Keeley would quietly slip away, and Lance and his friends would carry on with their lives as though she'd never existed. Irina and Grant would have their maybe-shifter baby. Chloe would... well, Chloe would probably set up camp wherever Maggie was, because it was obvious she was besotted with the tiny dragonling. And Mathis would follow her, because it was equally obvious that he'd go to the ends of the Earth for her, let alone be neighbors with a family of dragon shifters.

And Lance would—would...

Find his real mate, and settle down with her, and have a thousand adorable snow leopard shifter babies, probably.

She winced as something pulled in her chest. "Ow."

"Is everything all right?" Lance was suddenly at her side, steadying her with a hand at her waist.

"Just a cramp," Keeley replied quickly, stepping away from Lance's comforting embrace.

Lance stilled and pulled his hand back. She had to be imagining the look of disappointment that flashed behind his eyes, didn't she?

"Maggie's asleep," she said, keeping her gaze on the snoozing bundle. "I think she enjoyed meeting your friends, though. Or she enjoyed getting more loot off them."

Lance chuckled. "Grant barely got away with his wedding ring intact. I'll have to issue a warning to the office tomorrow for everyone to leave their jewelry at home."

"Tomorrow's gonna be a big day." Keeley couldn't keep a hint of sadness from her voice. "I should get her to bed."

Lance resettled his glasses. "Yes," he said, but his voice was a bit more serious than she'd expected. "When she's settled... there's something I'd like to talk with you about."

Well, that doesn't sound foreboding, Keeley thought. "Uh-huh?"

"I'll clean up the kitchen and meet you in the library?"

In the library... does he mean the den under his bedroom? Right *under his bedroom?* "Um, sure," she muttered, trying desperately to keep her thoughts G-rated. Damn it, she'd been doing *so well.*

After she'd settled Maggie in the guest bedroom, Keeley followed the sound of clinking glass, a shiver of anticipation going through her as she walked into the library.

Lance turned his head as she entered the room. Damn it, even the sight of him standing over the drinks cabinet made a thrill go through her.

"Whiskey?"

Keeley sat down on the sofa as Lance handed her a glass and immediately sank down into the plush cushions. Lance hesitated, then sat down on the opposite end.

She pulled her legs up and twisted around so she was facing him, her back against the arm of the sofa. Lance sat, staring into his glass, and the silence lengthened.

Keeley's stomach twisted. Whatever Lance wanted to say, he was clearly having difficulty putting it into words.

She needed to fill the silence. Luckily, she had a great topic of conversation literally in her hand. The amber liquid in her glass gleamed as she held it up to the light.

"I haven't drunk whiskey since I left home," she said. "I remember distinct overtones of car fumes and a delicate aftertaste of old puddles."

She took a sip, and her eyes widened. "Wow. Either I've grown up enough that my tastes have actually matured, or this stuff is... nice." She sipped again, just enough so the flavor burst across her tongue. "I mean. Two mouthfuls, and my throat isn't even on fire. Are you sure this is whiskey?"

Lance's pensive mask slipped, and he laughed. "I'm glad you like it. My aunt brings it over from Scotland, when she goes over to visit that side of the family. It makes this apartment feel like more of a home."

"Come on. Really? It takes beer goggles to make *this place* feel like a home?" Keeley gestured, her arms taking in everything around them. The lush furniture. The polished floorboards. The floor-to-ceiling windows and the *view*. God, the view.

God, the things they'd done together, in front of that view...

Keeley quickly looked away from the windows, her cheeks burning.

"It's a very nice house," Lance said, staring hard at the glass of whiskey in his hand. "But it's only a house. It doesn't have what's needed to really make it a home."

He met Keeley's eyes, and her heart sank. There was no mistaking the longing in his gaze. She wasn't stupid; she knew what he was talking about. What really made a home?

Those thousand adorable babies, she thought, a heavy lump lodging in the back of her throat.

She felt irrationally, stupidly angry.

Lance pulled off his glasses and set them aside. "I've always worked on the assumption that even the most complex mission can be broken down into small pieces. And that makes them simple. Controllable. Understandable. But recently, I've seen just how complicated the world is." He sighed. "And how limited my ability to understand or control it is."

"You seem pretty in control from where I am," Keeley said. "You have those invisibility things, and this place, and—"

And friends, and a family who loves you if your aunt is any example, and, and... *And so many other things that I'll never have, even if I do manage to escape from Sean again.*

"And an enemy I can't even name, attacking the people I'm supposed to protect. Even my friends."

"But you saved them," she said, and remembered another of the stories his friends had told around the kitchen table. "The same as you helped Grant save Chloe, when that woman—Francine—kidnapped her."

Lance shook his head. "And I was almost too late. Both times. I didn't see how Francine was hurting, and now she's gone, because someone else saw how they could exploit that hurt before I could help her. And Mathis..." He took another gulp of whiskey and grimaced. "He sent a final, desperate call for help, and I thought it was a prank. Another of his stupid jokes. I was that close to ignoring it altogether..."

He looked away, his face twisting with guilt.

"This whole time, I've been one step behind. Racing to catch up, only to discover how far ahead of me the enemy has already reached. Francine. Harper. And now, whoever is behind the attempt to take Maggie." He dropped his head into his hand, massaging his forehead. "And now you're here, and I don't know how to manage that, either."

"I didn't realize I was something to be managed," she said, wishing the butterflies in her stomach would go away.

A sort of panic flashed across his face. "I didn't mean—" He groaned. "I'm doing this all wrong."

He emptied his glass in one gulp and set it down on the floor.

"My agents call me a hero. I thought they were wrong because I could see how close we came to disaster each time we encountered the enemy. I was right about not being a hero, but wrong about the reason." He turned his eyes on her. Silver mingled with gray-green as the man and the snow leopard both stared at her. "There's nothing heroic about the way I've been ignoring my feelings for you."

Keeley's heart flipped over. "But this afternoon you said—"

That I'm not his mate. Her heart soared. *But that doesn't mean he isn't attracted to me.*

"I know what I said." Lance's gaze turned pleading. "Tell me I'm an idiot. I already know I am. Everything else in my life is so complicated, I thought this had to be, too."

"But it doesn't," Keeley breathed.

It doesn't have to be complicated. It can be simple. Because I'm not his mate. We're just two people. And...

Warning bells started going off in her head, but she ignored them. She knew who she was, now. She knew there was no escaping her past.

But this time tomorrow, she'd be gone. Out of Lance's life forever.

What had he said, when she'd come down for breakfast ass-naked? *Shifters are less prudish about this sort of thing.*

"Let's keep things simple," she whispered, so softly she could barely hear her own voice.

I'm a terrible person. Guilt gnawed at her gut, but the painful longing in her heart was stronger.

She stared into his eyes and held her breath. Even her heartbeat seemed to slow as she waited for—God, she didn't even know what.

Lance made a small noise low in his throat as his eyes went dark with desire. "You mean that?"

"I wouldn't say it if I didn't." Keeley leaned forward. Gleaming silver flickered in the depths of Lance's eyes, like the first hints of fall leaves in the green, and she was so lost in them that his kiss took her by surprise.

Lance pulled her to him. He held her against his muscular chest as his lips closed over hers, passionate and demanding.

The warmth already building inside Keeley burst like fireworks, sending desire spilling through her veins. She kissed him back, flicking her tongue out to tease against his lips.

Lance groaned, and the sound went straight to her core. Keeley flung one leg over his so she was sitting astride him. His hands dropped to her waist, pulling her closer, and the hard ridge of his erection jutted between her legs.

She gasped out loud, the need inside her flaring hot and sharp. And something else, as well. Something bright and taut in her chest, like a shining guitar string ready to be plucked.

"You feel it, too?" Lance's voice was gravely with desire. He caught her face in one hand, resting his forehead against hers.

"Yes," Keeley whispered, and the tightness in her chest thrummed. She felt—she didn't know what. Safety. Desire. More longing than she'd ever felt in her life before. *If I didn't have to leave after all of this—*

She cut the thought off before it could get any further. If she stayed, she would only be staying until Lance found out the truth about her. Or found his mate. Two bad options, no good ones. Better that she get out soon.

Lance breathed out hard. "I want to take you to bed."

A delighted giggle bubbled out of Keeley, making the golden string inside her dance. "Isn't that what we're already doing?"

In reply, Lance stood up. Keeley squealed and wrapped her legs around his waist. Not that she was in any danger of falling; she was safe in Lance's arms.

Keeley snuggled against Lance's chest as he carried her up the stairs to his bedroom. The star-like cityscape visible out the windows spun as he turned, and then she was lying on her back on the bed, and he was leaning over her.

She reached for him, pulling him down to kiss his lips, his neck, the curve of his collarbone. When he groaned, she felt the rumble against her mouth.

"Oh, God, Keeley," he murmured, and the sound of her name on his lips made Keeley's insides melt. "After last time—I want to take it slow. I want to explore every inch of you." He pushed himself up on his elbows. His eyes were dark with lust, the bright green of his irises barely visible around the heavy darkness of his pupils. "Tell me what you want."

Keeley grabbed fistfuls of Lance's shirt. "You." She pulled the shirt over his head, fabric tearing. "Simple." She ran her hands over his chest, glorying in the heat of his bare skin. "Straightforward." She dropped her hands to the button of his pants. "Now."

Lance's eyes glittered. "Is that so?" He kissed her, biting down on her bottom lip just hard enough to make her gasp. "I think I can manage that."

She gasped as he pushed her shirt up over her breasts, one hand reaching around to undo her bra. Keeley fumbled to drag her shirt and bra off over her head, and Lance took advantage of her distraction, sliding his hands down her sides and hooking his thumbs under the band of her underwear.

"Yes," she cried out as he brushed one thumb against her clit. Her legs bucked automatically. Lance laughed, burying his face in her shoulder as he kicked his pants off and climbed on top of her.

Keeley moaned as his teeth raked across her skin. More than a kiss, less than a bite. It was strangely, compellingly intimate.

So she did the same to him, nibbling, nipping, until every touch between her and Lance blazed with sensation.

Need throbbed between her legs. She stared up into Lance's eyes, seeing the same need reflected there.

He kissed her again, his teeth grazing her lips. Keeley wrapped her legs around his waist, straining upwards, and he bore down on her at the same time.

He filled her in one thrust. Keeley's back arched, and a soft cry escaped her lips as her body adjusted to his size. He thrust again, and the stretch was a delicious ache, bright and pure.

Lance pressed his forehead against hers. His eyes burned into hers, the green of spring. Of new life.

Second chances.

Keeley's breath caught in her throat. The thought *hurt*. Like running her fingers across the blade of a knife.

She pulled away from it. Back into the blaze of desire, the burn and thrill of sensation that danced across her skin whenever she and Lance touched. Whenever she looked at him. Hell, whenever she *thought* about him.

Her thoughts hurt. Her memories hurt. Who she was, *hurt*. But not when she was with Lance. Not now. Right now, right here, she was free and flying in the center of a burning sun of joy, drunk on her own desire and Lance's desire for her.

Keeley dug her fingertips into Lance's shoulders, desperate for every scrap of touch, every inch of closeness.

Lance groaned. He swept one hand to the small of her back, adjusting the angle of her body. Keeley was already burning with sensation. The next time he thrust inside her, she exploded.

Pleasure raced through her veins, a flash of light that shorted out every thought in her brain. She clutched at Lance, her breath coming in ragged gasps as she rode out the crashing waves of her orgasm, and the light grew stronger. She wasn't flying in the center of the sun anymore, the sun was inside *her*.

Lance tensed, his arms tightening around her. He claimed her lips with his, their breath mingling as he cried out with his release.

The bright light filling Keeley shrank down until it was a gleaming jewel in her heart.

And Lance's, too.

Keeley's eyes widened. *What—?*

"Simple enough for you?" Lance's voice was practically a purr, warm and heavy with satisfaction.

Keeley nudged him to roll off her, then snuggled against his side. She felt like purring, too. Her skin was still tingling. "Very straightforward."

Lance wrapped one arm around her and stared up at the ceiling. He looked thunderstruck by happiness, and Keeley couldn't help the stupid grin that spread across her face at the simple, open joy in his expression.

She rolled on top of him and kissed him, losing herself in another wave of bliss. Lance held her close, his arms strong and comforting.

"I don't deserve you," he breathed into her hair.

Keeley giggled. She felt as though she was floating on golden clouds of pleasure. "Don't deserve what? Simple?"

"Nothing in my life is simple." He touched her face gently, his eyes full of tenderness. "Not recently. Why would finding my mate be?"

The fire and light in Keeley's veins turned to ice. "Your mate?"

His gentle touch turned into a caress as he traced the line of her jaw, following his fingertips with a line of kisses. She felt like her whole body had gone stiff as a board, but he didn't seem to notice.

"Keeley. My mate. The one good thing to come into my life out of all this madness."

He buried his face in her hair, sighing contentedly.

Keeley forced herself to breathe normally. Her fingers were knotted in the bedsheets. She loosened them, one by one.

His mate. I'm his mate. Oh, fuck me. Her heart began to race. *What have I done?*

Thoughts tumbled over each other, a flood that, this time, didn't short out. *I thought simple meant casual. I thought we were just a casual shifter thing, like everyone getting naked in front of each other and it not even being a thing.*

I didn't think simple meant serious.

But it did. More serious than anything else in her life.

Lance was stuck with her. With *her*. The thief. The liar. The person who'd almost put Maggie in the hands of monsters.

Her chest cramped. She rubbed it slowly, her mind racing. What the hell was she going to do now?

Lance was stuck with her. Which meant she couldn't run away, not anymore. She had to stay.

And she had to make things right.

CHAPTER 16

LANCE

For the first time in months, Lance felt like his old self as he looked up at the nondescript building that housed the MacInnis Agency. The lingering dread that had dogged his thoughts since Irina was kidnapped was, if not gone, then reduced. Manageable.

No, he thought as he drove up to the carport. *Not my old self. Better. Because now, I have her.*

Keeley fit. It was as simple as that. All his life, there had been Lance, and his snow leopard. And now there was Keeley, too, filling a gap in his soul he hadn't even known was there. Steadying the ground under his feet.

And her kitten, too, his snow leopard insisted.

Lance shook his head. *The dragonling isn't her... You know what, I don't have time for this.*

He pulled to a stop and looked across at Keeley in the passenger seat. Warmth flooded through his body as he reached for her hand, an electric thrill of anticipation already whipping across his skin—

Chomp!

"Ow," Lance muttered, shaking his finger as Keeley exclaimed, "Maggie! No biting!"

"Prr-eep-eep!" Maggie argued back, her head-spines bristling. She glared at Keeley and Lance in turn, hissed, and burrowed back into the box Lance had found and filled with her ever-growing hoard.

"What is up with her this morning?" Keeley pushed her hair off her face. Her stormy eyes were troubled. "She's been tetchy ever since she woke up. And she hardly ate anything for breakfast. I hope she isn't getting sick."

Lance reached out psychically to the tiny grumpy dragon. Her response was the telepathic equivalent of another bite. He sighed.

"I think she's jealous."

"Jealous?" Keeley frowned at him, and then her expression cleared. "Oh," she said, going pink.

Lance smiled and took her hand. "I told you her psychic powers are ridiculously well developed for her age, didn't I? She can probably sense the bond between us."

"Poor baby," Keeley murmured. She stuck her free hand into the hoard box to pet Maggie. "Don't be sad. You'll be back with your family soon. You won't even notice we're gone."

"PREEP?"

Maggie stuck her head out the top of the box, outrage radiating from every golden scale.

"She didn't like that," Lance remarked out the side of his mouth.

He sent Maggie a burst of reassurance and scratched her under the chin. Maggie accepted the scratches, but still looked suspicious. She gently gnawed on his thumb, and then on Keeley's pinky finger, before burrowing back into her hoard.

Lance exchanged a puzzled look with Keeley. He squeezed her hand.

"How are you feeling?"

She took a moment to reply. "About...?"

"You know." Lance kissed her fingertips. "This isn't exactly small steps."

"No kidding." For a moment, Keeley's light-hearted expression slipped, and she looked lost. She took her hand out of Maggie's hoard box and brushed it against her pocket.

She wasn't wearing Lance's t-shirt today. He'd made several calls the night before while she was putting Maggie to bed, and one of them had been for a full new wardrobe. Keeley had chosen a soft, knee-length knit dress in a navy blue that made her eyes seem even more storm-tossed, with a light cardigan thrown over the top. He'd seen her slip her phone into the cardigan's pocket back at his apartment.

"Do you need a charger for that? You can take my office if you need a quiet place to make any calls."

Keeley saw him looking and grimaced. "There are some things I have to check in on." She paused, and Lance couldn't read the expression on her face. "Stuff from—well, it's my old life now, I guess."

"That doesn't mean you have to leave it behind," Lance reassured her.

"Oh, trust me, this is sh—stuff I want to leave behind."

"Your cleaning job?" Lance guessed, running the pad of his thumb over her fingers. He frowned. He hadn't noticed it before—how was that possible?—but there was a fine, pale scar running along two of her knuckles.

"My job, yeah," Keeley mumbled.

Lance lifted her hand into the light. The scar on her knuckles wasn't the only one.

"Um." Keeley pulled her hand away. "Should we get moving?"

Lance darted around the car to open her door and help her with the hoard box, questions whirling in his mind.

He took Maggie's box and led Keeley through to the foyer with his hand on the small of her back. His snow leopard purred with satisfaction as she automatically leaned into him.

"Welcome to my workplace," he said. "If you'd been here five years ago, it would have been just me and a desk. Today..." He balanced Maggie's hoard-box against his hip and flashed his security card to open the door. "Four floors of office and training spaces, a rooftop terrace, and more paperwork than you can possibly imagine."

Did he sound too smug about that last part? Probably.

Keeley blinked, and he hid a smile. He had to admit, the foyer wasn't exactly impressive. He was proud of that. Any stray door-to-door marketers or time-wasters would find themselves faced with an elevator that didn't work, a reception desk that wasn't staffed, and a reception bell that would ring exactly four times before falling silent with a dispiriting *whonk-whonk* sound.

And then there was the smell. Damp, with a hint of desperation.

It also had a fully integrated defense and shutdown system, bullet-proof windows, and rhinoceros-proof internal walls—but those were a bit harder for the average onlooker to spot.

"It's... nice," Keeley managed, and Lance laughed.

"It's a deliberate amalgamation of the worst aspects of the worst office buildings in the city," he explained. "From the front end, at least. A friend and I spent months researching just what makes office buildings so depressing—ah, never mind."

A muscle in his jaw twitched. Francine had been the one who handled the interior design—a fun distraction from her high-class hotel projects, she'd called it.

Back when they'd been friends. Before he failed her.

Lance pressed his thumb against the elevator button. It looked like your standard elevator button, complete with suspicious greasy smear, but it was calibrated to only respond to the thumbprint of employees of the agency.

"Come on. My first meeting for the day should be arriving soon."

He checked his phone as the elevator doors closed and found a message from Briers. Dissatisfaction prickled from every word.

Lance chuckled softly. "Make that now." He turned to Keeley. "Time for you to meet another of the old crowd."

"Preep?" Maggie poked her snout over the edge of her box. She flicked her tongue out at Keeley, then turned her shining eyes on Lance. "Prr-eeep?"

"We're going to the roof?" Keeley asked as he pressed the button for the top floor. "Is that safe for Maggie?"

"Preep?"

"Don't you give me that look, Maggie. I saw you jumping off the kitchen table last night. I don't want you jumping off the side of a building, too." Keeley frowned and bit her bottom lip. "And—what if someone sees her?"

"You'd better hold her." Lance grinned as Keeley bundled the wriggling dragonling into her arms. "She's going to be a handful when she's bigger."

"She's an entire *armful* now," Keeley shot back. "Ow. *Claws*, Maggie. I hope your uncle has tougher skin than I do."

Her words made Lance's snow leopard prickle. It stalked inside him, unhappy but not letting Lance know why. Lance frowned, but whatever had upset it, it refused to explain.

If you can't figure it out yourself, I'm not telling you, it sniffed, whiskers bristling.

Suit yourself. Lance pushed his snow leopard's moodiness to the back of his mind as the elevator doors opened. The elevator opened out into a window-lined room with a view of the roof.

The agency didn't have a helipad. Wrong zone, too many restrictions. None of which apparently meant anything to the pilot gently easing a shiny black chopper down on the roof.

Lance sighed and rubbed the bridge of his nose. *Damn it, Harley.*

Well, he'd told him the risks. The people who'd tried to take Maggie were still at large. Clearly, Harley thought the best solution was not letting his feet or the eggs touch the ground between Lance's aunt's place and the agency.

Briers was already there, watching the helicopter land with his hands clasped behind his back.

Lance greeted him with a nod. "Everything ready to go today?"

Briers' mouth went pinched as he looked back out the window. "I would prefer it if you'd let me use my contacts for this part of the mission. Is this Harley Ames even licensed?"

Lance brushed aside the meerkat shifter's question. "Until someone reports him landing on our roof, I expect. Briers, meet Keeley. She's—"

His heart glowed as he introduced Briers to his mate. Even his snow leopard unwound from its huff, purring smugly as he showed off the wonderful woman he was going to share his life with.

Briers' pinched expression actually relaxed slightly as he shook Keeley's hand.

"A pleasure to meet you—Keeley Smith, was it?" Lance swore the meerkat shifter almost smiled as he turned back to him. "I want to double-check the arrangements for your call later this morning. We can't afford any more mishaps."

"Agreed." Lance hugged Keeley closer to his side as Briers scampered to the elevator. "You're wonderful," he whispered into her hair.

"For managing to shake his hand without letting Maggie jump out of my arms and run off the side of the roof? That's pretty wonderful, I guess."

"No, you're—" Lance gazed into her eyes. "You're incredible, and I want everyone to know."

Keeley looked away, biting down on her lower lip.

Something's wrong. Lance was about to ask if there was anything he could do for her, when the *thwop-thwop-thwop* of the helicopter blades outside finally slowed. Light glinted off the helicopter's door as it swung open.

"Ow!" Keeley yelped. "Maggie!"

The tiny dragonling was struggling out of her arms, wings flapping madly. Keeley hissed as she clawed her way up onto her shoulders, and Lance grabbed the dragonling before she started clawing her way up Keeley's head as well.

Maggie chirped urgently. Emotions battered Lance's mind, a frenzied, half-happy, half-worried storm.

He glanced across to the helicopter. *Of course.*

It's okay, he whispered into Maggie's mind, his psychic voice overlaid with as much soothing emotion as he could manage. **They're here. You can see them soon.**

NOW NOW NOW, Maggie thundered back, her tail whipping back and forth.

Lance chuckled and tucked the little dragon under one arm. "She's excited to see the other eggs," he explained to Keeley.

"She couldn't be excited with less claws?" she replied, wincing as she checked her shoulders for scratch marks.

He gave her one last squeeze and waved to Harley, who was stalking across the roof with a sturdy carryall in one hand and a winning smile on his face. Lance hit the button to open the foyer doors as he approached.

"Harley!" he called as the cheetah shifter stepped inside. "You know this isn't a helipad, right?"

"Really? Shit, my bad." Harley swept his light hair out of his eyes and grinned. "Good thing I know a nice old lady who can make any complaints go away, eh?"

"One day, I'm going to not regret introducing you to my aunt," Lance groaned. "Regret it more, I mean."

"Your aunt?" Keeley asked, and Lance rubbed his forehead.

"Ex-military, like me. *Unlike* me..." He tried to find a way to describe his aunt that wouldn't take all day. "Most people see retirement as a chance to catch up with their family and gardening. My aunt saw it as a way to start playing with all the toys she'd missed in her years behind a desk. And sharing them with friends, apparently."

Keeley went pale as she looked out at the helicopter. "That's army issue?"

"Retired, same as General MacInnis," Harley said.

"Oh." A line formed between Keeley's eyebrows. "Police, army—sounds like your agency has contacts everywhere," she said quietly. Her hand slipped into her cardigan pocket.

He took her hand gently. "Is everything alright?"

"Yeah, it's all good." Keeley smiled unconvincingly, and the golden light that stretched between his heart and hers wobbled. "It's—nice to meet more of your friends."

Lance's heart dropped. Of course. He was introducing her to his people—friends, family, colleagues—but what did he know about her social circle? Only that she had a workplace that treated her like crap, and no one who would even notice she'd disappeared for two days.

And a network of old scars on her fingers.

He squeezed her hand. "They're your friends now, too."

"Speaking of..." Harley cleared his throat. "Is this who I think it is?"

Right. His friends might be her friends, but he still had to, for example, make sure she knew all of their names.

"Keeley, meet Harley Ames. Ten years ago, I made the mistake of bringing him home for the holidays. He's stuck to my family like hot tar ever since. Harley, this is—"

"Keeley Smith. Beautiful. Charming. Your mate. Yes, Grant filled me in. Your aunt's going to be thrilled. Hey, do you mind if I'm the one to break the news? It might sweeten the whole 'airspace violation' issue." Harley flashed Keeley a grin, but otherwise stood completely frozen. "Lance, I was talking about *her*. Wings. Scales. Biting my hand off at the wrist."

Our kitten, Lance's snow leopard said, and its smugness must have reached Harley's cheetah as well, because the other man's eyes went wide.

"What?" he spluttered, his eyes flicking between Lance and Keeley. *She's not—you're not—what?*

Lance disentangled Maggie from Harley's hand but couldn't convince her to let go of the bag.

"Let's get them all settled in my office," he said, "And then I'll explain everything."

Chapter 17

Keeley

Harley was nice, Keeley decided. Still a bit freaked out by the way Maggie had decided his hand was all that stood between her and her siblings' eggs, but... nice. Just like Lance's other friends were nice, and his colleagues. His aunt was probably nice, too.

She felt sick.

Lance kept asking her how she was. She couldn't tell him, so she just kept lying, and now the hairs on her neck prickled every time she felt him looking at her.

She looked across Lance's desk to where she'd plugged her phone in to charge. Suddenly anxious, she checked it.

Still dead. Useless piece of crap. As soon as it was charged, she was going to get in touch with Sean and make sure that he got the hell out of whatever shifter cartel he'd gotten involved with.

She gritted her teeth. Ten years ago, she wouldn't have had a clue how to convince Sean of anything. But that last job they'd done together was good for something, after all.

He's in over his head. He just doesn't know it yet.

And if there was anything that Sean liked better than money, it was keeping his own skin safe.

Keeley double-checked that her phone was still plugged in and forced herself to stop staring at it. At least it had progressed from the lifeless brick stage to showing the little flashing battery symbol on the screen. Maybe, by lunchtime, it would have enough power for her to make a call.

She clenched her fist in her pocket, then forced herself to relax. She would fix this. God damnit, for once in her life, she was going to *fix* things, not run away.

It was the least she could do for Lance.

She turned away from her phone to see Harley leaning over Lance's desk. Maggie was perched right in the center of the desk, visibly and loudly enjoying being the center of attention.

"It's Maggie, right?"

He seemed entranced by the dragonling—entranced, but keeping his distance. He flexed his scratched-up hand as Lance placed the carryall on his desk.

"Short for Magpie," Keeley explained, and blushed. The more she had to explain that, the stupider it seemed. "Um, except her uncle's probably going to give her a better name."

"Magpie, huh? Can't think of a better name for a flying menace who likes shiny stuff." He took a tentative step closer to the desk, and then apparently decided that the far wall was a safer location.

He flashed Keeley a smile from the other side of the room. "How are you holding up?"

"What?"

Harley shrugged. All of his movements were small and quick: his smiles, his shrugs, even the way he glanced at Lance before focusing his hazel eyes on Keeley again.

"I had the whole story from Grant last night. Explosions. Shootings. He said you seemed fine, but honestly? The guy can't see past his mate right now."

"I..." Keeley broke off as her phone buzzed on the desk. The usual lie died on the tip of her tongue. *I'm fine.*

One buzz. Two. Finally, her phone was charged enough to turn back on.

Except now that the moment was finally here, why was her stomach filling with dread?

Harley moved his weight from foot to foot. "Well. There's something I should say while Lance is in earshot."

Lance lifted his head at the sound of his name, and Harley laughed softly and raised his voice.

"We're all damn happy you've turned up. Can't tell you how long we've been waiting for someone to help Lance pull the stick out of his ass."

"I haven't noticed any sticks," Keeley retorted absently, and Harley snickered.

Lance glared at them both. "Come over and help me with this, will you, Harley?"

"Aye aye, cap'n."

Keeley watched as the two men unlocked the carryall. Maggie was almost beside herself, alternately chirping and hissing with impatience. Her claws left tiny chips in the desk's polished surface as she jumped back and forth.

"Looking forward to seeing them again, huh?" Keeley reached out one hand, and Maggie snuggled her head against her palm. Then she grabbed one of Keeley's fingers with her stubby teeth and pulled her hand closer to the carryall.

"You want me to open it?" Keeley exchanged a look with Lance. Maggie looked at him, too, cheeping what sounded like an order. Lance raised his eyebrows.

"Both of us," he said. "If you don't mind, Harley?"

Harley raised his hands. "Whatever the tiny monster says."

They'd already unlocked the carryall; all Keeley had to do was pull it open and lift out the rectangular case inside, with Lance's help. Maggie watched them, her golden eyes intent.

Harley made a noise that was half-amused, half-annoyed. "Your aunt's going to be pissed. This case is meant to be water-proof, airtight, basically a portable, shifter-proof controlled environment. But Maggie saw through it before she even *saw* it."

Lance shrugged. "Dragons. The more I find out about them, the more I think they just don't play by the same rules as the rest of us."

Keeley's stomach clenched as she and Lance took hold of the case's lid. It was so similar to the one she'd found Maggie's egg in.

The one she'd almost left her in.

She swallowed hard and pulled open the lid. There was a moment's resistance, and then the case opened with a soft hiss of air.

A lump lodged in Keeley's throat. The inside of the case was *exactly* like the box she'd freed Maggie from. It was lined with a black velvety fabric that was warm to the touch and split into three sections, each with an indented part for a dragon's egg to nestle. Two were full, the eggs gleaming softly in the light streaming through the office windows. One was empty.

Maggie climbed into the case, cheeping and pr-eeping as she sniffed the two eggs. Once she'd checked each of them over, she shot her neck out and chirped an order to Lance.

"Yes, ma'am," he said, pushing her hoard box over from where he'd placed it on the edge of the desk.

He caught Keeley's eye, and her heart flipped. He looked so... happy. Not that she hadn't seen him happy before—certain window- and bed-related activities came to mind—but this was something more.

He wasn't just happy. He was confident, assured, utterly in his element. In power, and using that power to help people.

Her heart ached. Lance was so... *good*. She had to live up to that.

Her phone buzzed again, and again, and *again*. She grabbed at it and jabbed the volume button until it was on mute.

"Sorry," she muttered. "Must be work, telling me how fired I am." She shoved the phone back in her pocket, where it sat like a burning coal.

Lance leaned over and pressed his forehead against hers in a feline gesture that was, to her surprise, strangely comforting.

"I have to call Maggie's uncle and tell him the good news," he murmured. "Will you look after Maggie and the eggs?"

"Sure."

"And Harley—make sure no one's going to bust down our front doors over that helicopter on the roof?"

Harley gave a mock salute. "On it!"

Keeley caught Lance's arm as he turned to leave. She waited until Harley was out the door, and then tugged him closer.

He pulled her into a hug, which hadn't been her plan—and then kissed her. Which was, again, definitely not part of the plan.

But still really, really nice.

Lance's lips were soft and gentle. He teased her lips with his tongue until she deepened the kiss, relaxing into his arms with a moan of surrender.

"Prr-eep?"

"Damn it," Lance murmured into Keeley's mouth. She giggled.

"Not in front of the baby?"

"The baby who's got her claws in my—*aargh*."

Lance reached behind himself and unhooked Maggie from the seat of his pants. She chittered at him and then scurried back to the other eggs.

Keeley snorted. "Someone doesn't like not being the center of attention." Her stomach went tight. If she was going to stick around, she had to do things right. Especially if she could convince Sean to double-cross his new business partner. "Lance—can we talk? Maybe after your call with Maggie's uncle?"

Oh, good one, Keeley. Put it off. Like an extra few minutes is going to make him hate you less when you tell him who you really are.

She drew a shaky breath. "There's—there's a lot of things I think we should discuss."

"I know." Lance grimaced, his eyes soft. "These last few days have been crazy. I promise you, as soon as Maggie is back with her uncle and we know who's behind the kidnapping, we'll have all the time in the world together to get to know each other properly."

He pulled her close again, nestling her head on his chest. His heartbeat thrummed against her cheek, a steady tattoo that made some of the worry ease from her own chest. "How would you like to go away somewhere together? Just us. We can get to know each other properly. Talk about all of the things that we would have been able to cover if we'd met under any other circumstances. I know this great place in the mountains. My snow leopard can't wait to show it to you."

"I'd really like that." Which was so true, it made Keeley's heart ache. "But can we talk this morning, first?"

"Of course." Lance kissed her again and left for his meeting.

Keeley waited until the door closed behind him, then collapsed into his desk chair. "Holy f—fudge," she groaned, burying her face in her hands.

Right. She'd done it. Step one. Or Step one-half, maybe. Tell Lance the truth, contact Sean, and... fix things. Fix all the shit she'd gotten wrong.

Her hand went to her pocket. Her phone must be charged now, what with how much it had been buzzing as all the messages she'd missed while it was dead came through. Some of those must have been from work. She could only imagine the messages her manager would have left for her when she didn't show for two shifts in a row.

But—it had buzzed a *lot*. Even the hotel wouldn't have called her that many times, would they?

Her fingers twitched. What else? Notifications for the podcasts she subscribed to, sure. Maybe some app updates.

Something in her gut told her that wasn't all.

Sean had found her workplace. He knew where she lived. How hard would it have been to find out her phone number?

Keeley was about to pull her phone out of her pocket when someone knocked on the door. She snatched her hand away from her pocket like it was burning.

"Um, hello?"

A familiar face poked around the edge of the door. Carol Zhang, the shark shifter with the strange, flat-looking eyes. Her lips curved oddly, and it took Keeley a moment to figure out that she was smiling.

"Do you mind if I join you?"

"No, sure, come in." Keeley put her hands on the table, like she'd never even thought of pulling out her phone. Christ. If there *was* a message on it from Sean—well, it would have to wait. No way she was risking one of Lance's agents seeing it.

"How is the dragonling? Oh—the eggs are here, too?" Carol hesitated at the door, then seemed to flow into the room, stopping again a few feet from the desk. And when she stopped, she *stopped*. "They're beautiful."

Maggie popped her head up and cheeped in protest. Carol quickly corrected herself. "But not as beautiful as you."

Maggie poked her tongue out at Carol and dove into her hoard box. When she emerged, she was trailing the sparkly scarf. Keeley and Carol watched as she dragged the scarf up to the closest of the eggs, dangled it in front of it, then yanked it away.

"What is she doing?" Keeley wondered out loud as Maggie narrowed her eyes at the egg and chittered to herself. "Can you, um, understand her?"

Carol shook her head. "She's too young to mindspeak."

"Oh." Keeley thought about the strange brushes of emotion that seemed to press against her mind sometimes when she was around the baby dragon.

I must have been imagining it, she thought. *Except—didn't Lance feel them, too? And talk to her?* She shook her head. She had far too much else to worry about without adding more questions.

Carol stood as still as a store mannequin, her eyes fixed on Keeley. "I wanted to check some details about the night you and Lance rescued the dragonling," she said, holding a tablet in front of herself like a shield. "Do you have a minute?"

Keeley's stomach turned over. "Sure."

Carol slid into a seat on the opposite side of the desk. "It says here you didn't see any of the attackers at the station."

"No, like I said last night. Just—Maggie, and then the explosion, and then Lance grabbed me and took me outside." *That is what I said last night, isn't it? Oh, shit. Why is she checking my story?*

"But you saw them when they were chasing you later?" Carol looked down at her tablet and scowled. "Mr. MacInnis' report isn't... clear."

"I..." Keeley met the shark shifter's eyes and froze. "The first guy? Who tried to smash my skull in? I saw him after Lance tackled him?"

Why am I saying everything like it's a question?

"And you saw Mr. MacInnis then, too?"

"Yes?"

Keeley licked her lips. Carol's eyes were so dark and still—*all* of her was so still—it was unnerving. Weren't sharks supposed to have to be on the move constantly or they couldn't breathe, or something? Hadn't she seen that on TV sometime?

Carol's eyebrows drew closer together. "So you saw Mr. MacInnis then, too."

"Yes?" How could she forget? He'd charged in and saved her.

"But he was shielded, and you weren't. That should be impossible."

"Uhh?" *Oh, shit fuck shit.*

Carol leveled her flat eyes at Keeley. "Unless..."

She's figured it out. I'm fucked.

Keeley's throat was dry. How could she be so stupid? She had known all it would take was one person figuring out how many holes her story had in it. And now—

Hang on. What were the holes in *this* bit of the story? Shielding? She didn't know enough about how the shields worked to lie about it.

Carol's face went smooth. "Unless the hatchling is already able to shield."

"Oh, yeah." Relief crashed down on Keeley. "Yeah, I'm pretty sure? And the teleporting too, that's... pretty crazy..."

"Just hatched, and she can already shield. And teleport."

"It's pretty nuts, yeah."

Keeley relaxed. She was being way too jumpy. Carol wasn't trying to interrogate her. She just wanted...

What does she want? Keeley frowned. Carol was still tapping at her tablet. Her movements were creepily fluid, but Keeley got the feeling she wasn't really concentrating on the written report.

"Anything else you wanted to ask?"

Carol's eyes flickered. "No. The hatchling's abilities are all I was missing." A strange, dark look flashed across Carol's face, and Keeley felt suddenly uneasy.

Because that was wrong. Maggie's powers weren't the only missing piece in the report. Hell, not even Keeley's half-assed lies filled in all the gaps.

From what Lance had let slip over the last three days, the theft—the *kidnapping*—had been slick. Professional. They'd known exactly where the egg would be. And while the subway transfer might confuse Lance and his agents, Keeley knew exactly what that part of the plan had been. A handy way to get rid of the human link in the chain.

And all the other kidnappers had been shifters. Shifters who'd known exactly when to grab Maggie's egg.

It was too much of a coincidence.

Everyone's been talking about this Harper guy and his associates, she thought, dread curdling in her stomach. *But what if it was an inside job?*

Maggie chirruped happily as she flipped Lance's watch from her hoard-box to dangle off the tip of her nose. Keeley didn't miss how Carol's eyes immediately focused on the baby dragon.

"Hey, cutey, what are you up to?" Keeley picked Maggie up and cuddled her, trying to quell the suspicions rising in her gut. "So, uh, was that all, Carol?" she asked, trying to keep her voice light.

What the hell is taking Lance so long?

"Almost. There was one other thing."

"Oh, yeah?" Keeley leaned back, keeping her arms wrapped around Maggie. "What?"

She's between me and the door, she thought. *Shit.*

In her arms, Maggie went still. "Prrp?"

"I'm sure you've guessed already," Carol said, her eyes still fixed on Maggie. "After I barged in yesterday. God, I really screwed everything up, didn't I? I've been so *stupid*."

You and me both, lady. Keeley glanced around the room. Shifters could move fast, right? But maybe if she got the jump on Carol, she could throw something at her and get away.

Yeah, and then all she needs to do is shift and suddenly you're facing a giant angry shark. I don't care what Lance said about her not shifting out of the water.

"What'd you screw up?" she said out loud. "Didn't you say you were tracking Lance? You did that. Mission accomplished, right?"

Carol's lips went thin. "I wasn't expecting to find him. Not alive, at least." She reached into her blazer pocket and pulled out something that glinted in the light.

Keeley tried to get a better look at it, but Carol dropped her hand into her lap. "I was looking for the egg, not him."

"You were looking for Maggie?" As if attracted by her name, Maggie started to wriggle free of Keeley's grip. *No—damn it, stay here, I don't trust* her...

Carol's lips were white-rimmed with tension. "Well, we didn't know she'd hatched at that point. Though we should have guessed. The whole site where Lance disappeared smelled like dragon." Her eyes reflected the light coming in the windows. "That, and blood."

"Yeah, thanks, I remember the blood. You don't need to bring it up." Keeley's voice was scratchy. What was that in Carol's hand? She kept turning it over and over, and it looked... sharp.

She tensed, scrambling to keep hold of Maggie.

"I thought he was *dead*." Carol's fingers tightened around the object in her hand. "And so did everyone else! And, and—"

Maggie gave one last giant wiggle and flapped onto the desk, in between Keeley and Carol.

The shark shifter's mouth moved, but Keeley couldn't hear what she was saying through the adrenaline buzz in her ears. Carol started forward, and Keeley leapt into action. She darted around the desk, sending papers flying.

Keeley jumped in between Carol and Maggie, ready to protect the helpless dragonling. Light reflected in a flash from the object in Carol's hand as she flung her arms around her—and dropped her head onto Keeley's shoulder with a sob.

"What sort of a tracker am I? Sharks are supposed to *know* when people are dead or not! Aren't we?" she wailed. "Maggie isn't even a week old and she can already shield people, and I can't even smell if someone's still *alive*?"

Keeley stood motionless as her shoulder became increasingly damp. Carol's whole body shook with heaving sobs. "Um... is that a bad thing?"

"I have to be good for *something*! Lance is the first person to let me keep a job after I told him that I'm a shark shifter! And I just gave up on him!"

Keeley relaxed. *God, I'm such a dumbass.* Carol wasn't some crazy person, here to kidnap Maggie. She was just regular fucked up, same as everyone else. With a special shifter twist.

"Hey," she said softly, easing Carol off her shoulder. The shark shifter sniffled. Her face was blotchy and red, and her flat black eyes were swimming with tears. "Look, it all turned out okay, all right? I'm sure you'll have another chance to show Lance how much the job means to you." Her mind raced. "Maybe your next mission will be underwater?"

Carol sniffed. "I hope not. I hate being in my shark form." She wiped her eyes and blinked blearily.

"Well, that's something you and Maggie have in common, then. She hates being in her human form."

On a sudden instinct, Keeley reached out and gave Carol a quick hug. "You okay?"

Carol hiccupped. "Yeah." She hunched her shoulders. "Sorry for freaking out on you. I just—yesterday, and thinking the boss was dead and now he's *not*, and not being a good shark and now the rest of the eggs are here, and you know what people say about sharks and babies..."

"I really don't." Keeley shrugged as Carol stared at her. "Seriously. I only found out about shifters a few days ago. Whatever they say about shark shifters and babies, it's news to me."

"Oh." Carol pulled a tissue out of her pocket, blew her nose, and then settled back into her usual stillness. "It's just nonsense, really. You know, in the wild, sharks eat their siblings in the womb before they're born? Some people think it's the same with shifters. Except, bonus, we also eat other people's babies, too." Her face darkened. "If *any* of that were true, maybe I wouldn't have *seven* brothers."

"Is that why it means so much to you that Lance gave you a job?" A golden warmth fluttered in Keeley's chest. Of course Lance would do something like this. He was just so... good.

Not like you, a nasty voice in the back of her head added. The golden light inside her flickered.

Carol grimaced. "It's not like I have a lot of other options, with my face." She indicated her eyes and mouth. "I used to work for my family business—Dad does fishing charters—but I always wanted *more*. And Lance offered me that."

Keeley swallowed. If Lance was willing to offer a chance to a shifter that everyone else distrusted, then maybe—

She forced the thought back. *Nuh-uh. The difference between you and Carol is that she hasn't* actually *done anything wrong.*

"Prr-eep?"

"Ow..." Keeley held back a hiss of pain as Maggie clambered up her back onto her shoulders, but part of her—a *big* part—was glad of the distraction. "Hello, you. Did we stop paying attention to you for a whole minute? That was so mean of us. I *definitely* deserve to be—ow—climbed up."

"She probably smelled this." Carol held out her hand. Something gleamed bright and sharp, and Keeley flinched back before she saw what it was: a fancy gilt pen. "I thought, you know, she's a dragon, so maybe she'd like it..."

"I think she'd definitely like it," Keeley deadpanned. Maggie was wrapped around her shoulders, her long neck stretched out as far as it would go towards the shiny pen.

"Oh, do you?" Carol's eyes gleamed. She reached into her bag again and rummaged around. "It's a calligraphy pen. I brought some ink, too. *Gold* ink."

She held the squat inkbottle in front of Maggie and shook it so the ink swirled around. Maggie's eyes glowed like it was the most amazing thing he'd ever seen.

"Pr-eep!"

CHAPTER 18

LANCE

Lance tried to relax as he waited for the call to the safehouse to go through. His skin felt itchy, like he was wearing a suit that didn't fit.

We'll go back and see her in a few minutes, he reassured his snow leopard. *Come on. We can't stay at her side every minute of the day.*

His snow leopard grumbled, but calmed down. Slightly. Lance groaned. *She's looking after Maggie. They're both safe here.*

The videocall rang—and rang—and rang. Lance frowned. *What's taking them so long?*

This was hardly the first time he had called in to check on Julian. The dragon shifter had recovered from his time on the island, at least physically. His mental state was a different matter. Julian kept his emotions close to his chest, but even through the video link Lance had been able to tell he was still hurting over what had happened to his family.

Lance didn't blame him. Gerald Harper had killed Julian's sister and her mate and stolen their eggs to use as collateral to keep the dragon shifter in line. The eggs were all Julian had left. It must have broken his heart to part from them, even if it was for their own safety.

Well, no longer. Frankly, if any off the assholes who'd tried to kidnap Maggie wanted to go after her or her siblings, they could face an angry full-grown dragon.

Lance pushed his glasses up. Two minutes, and no reply. This was more than unusual. It was *worrying*. Ignoring the screen on the wall, he put through a call on his cell phone.

The head guard from the safehouse picked up at once. He was panting. "What?" he barked into the phone.

Lance explained that he was waiting on their call, as previously arranged. He could practically hear the guard glare down the phone.

"Another one? Wasn't the last one—ah, fuck. Look. He'll be at the phone in a minute. It's taken us this long to talk him down, though, so good news only this time, eh?"

Lance ended the call. *Talk him down?*

The hair on the back of his neck prickled. Something was wrong.

A soft chime told him that his video call had been picked up.

Lance looked up, automatically straightening his jacket and his glasses. His snow leopard bristled as Julian appeared on the screen in front of him.

Julian inclined his head. "MacInnis." His normally brilliant eyes were shuttered and wary.

"Rouse. I hope I'm not disturbing you."

"What could I possibly be doing that being hauled away by my guards twice in one day could disturb?" A tendon in his neck flexed, or maybe it was just the video bugging.

Lance frowned. Julian's voice had a bitter edge to it, but he was used to that—this was something different. A deeper, blanker misery that his bitten-out words barely masked.

He leaned forward, wishing the video connection could conduct his feelings as well as a face-to-face conversation would. "Rouse. Julian. I've got good news."

"Better than the news that the man who made me a monster is imprisoned?" Black glass glinted behind the dragon shifter's eyes. "Better than the knowledge that I lost my sister and her children, but at least the creature who took them from me has faced justice, paltry though it is?"

"Julian, your sister's children aren't gone. One of the eggs has hatched. The plan's changed. Hiding eggs is one thing, but a living dragonling? Keeping you apart isn't going to keep them safe. They need a real family." Lance smiled. "You'd better tell the guards to clean out a spare room, Julian. It's time you met your niece."

Julian stared at him, his face completely expressionless. There was no noise except the low hum of the audio connection.

Then Julian's face twisted. "How dare you?" he snarled. "Is this some sort of trick? What could you possibly want from me now?" His eyes narrowed to black-gleaming slits. "More scales for your shields? Was this your plan all along?"

Lance sat back in his seat, winded. Julian's rage crackled through the speakers, hitting him like a blunt force even through the hundreds of miles that separated them.

"It isn't a trick. I'm not lying to you. One of the eggs hatched, and—"

"Impossible." Julian's lip curled, as though the word hurt to say. "None of them will ever hatch. Not now that their parents are dead. Not without…"

The video blurred, and Lance had barely opened his mouth when the screen went blank. *Shit,* he thought, scrambling for his phone. His call to the safe house guards rang—and rang—

"What's your status?" he barked when someone picked up, thirty excruciating seconds later.

A weary laugh crackled into his ear. "We're not hip-deep in angry dragon, if that's what you mean."

Lance sighed, dropping his forehead to rest on one fist. "Carter. How's Rouse?"

"Catatonic." On the other end of the line, Carter sucked in breath through his teeth. "It's not good, boss. I'm no shrink, but this guy needs help. It's like he's fading away here."

"He doesn't have anything to live for." Lance swallowed as bile rose in his throat. "At least, he doesn't think he does."

He shivered, the memory of Julian's rage like acid on his skin. He told Carter to expect them in the next ten hours and hung up. His snow leopard paced inside him, feeding off Lance's new sense of urgency.

Keeley would want to come. She wasn't cleared to see the safehouse, but what the hell did that matter anymore? All the careful strategies he'd put in place to make the MacInnis Agency feel legitimate, and not a fly-by-night operation—what were they worth, when Julian was slowly killing himself with misery?

What were they worth when Francine betrayed you? Or Mathis disappeared?

Lance sighed and rubbed his forehead.

Whatever I'm doing here, it led me to her. You can't knock that.

Heart lightening at the thought of his mate, Lance strode towards his office. Maggie's psychic aura permeated the air around his office door like a golden mist. Lance smiled to himself. If anything could pull Julian out of his depression, it was that child.

"Sir, if I could have a word?"

Briers' office was three down from Lance's. He popped out of it like the world's least wanted jack-in-the-box.

Lance bit back a sigh. His soul was scratching to get back to his mate's side. "What is it, Briers?"

"I've got an update on the camera feeds from the subway," Briers replied, his voice somber. "You're going to want to see this, sir."

CHAPTER 19

KEELEY

"What is she *doing*?"

Carol was crouching beside the desk, heedless of her crisp gray pantsuit. She was eye-level with Maggie, watching her with open enthusiasm. And confusion.

"I think she's trying to tease them?" Keeley put her head on one side. "Baby, I don't think you can tease people who are still in eggs. They can't even *see* you."

Maggie blinked at her. She was holding Lance's gold watch between her front teeth like a pacifier. "Prrp?" she asked, and then turned back to the nearest egg, waving the watch tauntingly back and forth.

When that didn't get the response she wanted—or, indeed, any response—she snorted and dropped the watch back in the pile she'd pulled out of her hoard box. After nosing around briefly, she re-emerged, this time with Keeley's necklace clutched gently in her jaws.

"Prrp!" she declared, and stalked back to the egg. This time, she dropped the necklace in front of the egg for a few seconds before snatching it away.

"Is she trying to make them jealous?" Carol wondered aloud. "Look at all my cool stuff, nyah nyah?"

"I don't think so." Keeley frowned. "It's like she wants them to come and play with her."

She was only half paying attention. Lance had been gone longer than she'd hoped, and her phone felt like it was burning a hole in her pants. Why couldn't he hurry up and get back here, so she could come clean and they could...

A cold lump formed in her stomach. *Fix this. Somehow.*

"Huh. Like... make them hatch?" Carol looked thoughtful. "If only we knew how she hatched. All three eggs were in foster care for months without any sign of life, then all of a sudden, here Maggie is. I wish I knew *how.*"

"Yeah..." Keeley said weakly as Maggie stretched out her neck and tapped the gold pendant against one of the eggs. *Tap, tap, tap*—on the third tap, she darted away and hid the pendant jealously under her belly.

Keeley laughed, and then paused, frowning.

Was it her imagination, or had the egg moved?

It must be because Maggie bumped it, she told herself. *Or you're imagining it.*

Or... another dragon is about to hatch.

"Oh, sh—sugar," she murmured. "She's using the gold to hurry them up? Is that how dragons work?"

Keeley touched her collarbone, where her gran's pendant used to rest. Where it *had* been resting, when Maggie hatched. She swallowed.

"Um, Maggie, can I have that pendant back now? Maybe you should try using something else..."

She resisted the urge to reach out and snatch the pendant off Maggie. One baby dragon was enough of a handful.

Even if another one would mean a brother or sister for Maggie to play with...

Raised voices came from the corridor outside. Keeley looked up, recognizing Lance's deep tones, and Carol quickly jumped up and tidied her clothes.

The door swung open.

"Lance! You'll never guess what Maggie's trying to do..." Keeley's voice faded. Lance's jaw was set, and his eyes skated away from hers. The knot in Keeley's stomach twisted. "What's happened?"

"Get her away from the eggs!"

Keeley hadn't even noticed Briers come in. The mousy-haired man stormed in front of Lance, pointing at—her?

For a moment, she wondered what he was doing. Then she saw the look in his eyes. Pure, unvarnished hatred and disgust.

What the—? Oh, no. Oh, no, no, no. Not now.

The bottom fell out of her stomach.

Carol looked from Keeley to Briers and back, confusion in her flat black eyes. "Boss?"

"Lance, what's going on?" Keeley stood up. At a nod from Briers, Carol grabbed her arms behind her back and pulled her away from the desk. "What the hell?"

She tried to pull away, but Carol was surprisingly strong. Or not surprisingly, maybe. On the desk, Maggie rose up on her hind legs, looking from Maggie, to Lance, and back. "Preep?" Confusion buffeted against Keeley's mind.

Lance swore under his breath and gripped his forehead, then waved his hand calmingly at the baby dragon. Maggie stared at him, eyes wide, and kept cheeping in distress.

Keeley gritted her teeth. Maggie's confusion was like the start of a migraine, wearing against her brain. "You're scaring her, Lance. What the hell is going on?"

Lance's throat moved like he was biting back words. For one long breath, he didn't meet Keeley's eyes, and when he did, his gaze was dark and troubled.

"Some new information has come to light about the night Maggie was taken." Lance's voice was clipped. Professional. Keeley shivered. "Keeley, I—"

Something behind his eyes broke. He ran the back of his hand over his mouth, and before he could say anything more, Briers strode forward.

"The dragon *should* be scared. But MacInnis isn't the one she should be scared of. Isn't that right, Keeley Bailey?"

Keeley's stomach dropped. "I d-don't know what you're talking about," she stammered. "That's not my name. I'm K-Keeley Smith."

The lie was out before she could stop it, and she knew the moment it left her lips that it had been a mistake. She swallowed hard and tried again.

"I mean, I—"

Without thinking, she glanced toward the door. Her mind made the calculation without prompting: there was no way she could make it out without one of them catching her, even if she managed to slip out of Carol's grasp.

It was less than a second before she looked back at Lance, but even that was enough. He'd seen her eyes flick to the exit, and the broken shards of pain in his eyes turned sharp as splintered glass.

He held out a tablet. Keeley forced herself to look at the images flashing across its screen.

"Briers recovered the footage from the station. It shows you arriving. *With* the case containing Maggie's egg." Lance swiped the screen, and another clip began to play. "He was able to track your movements back to when you received the case from your associate."

Keeley's throat was dry. "It's not like that," she protested. "Please, I was going to tell you, you have t-to understand—"

"You thought you were safe after I told you the CCTV footage was lost, didn't you?" Lance's voice was hollow. "You were planning to leave before then. You only changed your mind after you heard Carol's report. Why?"

Keeley's voice caught in her throat. It was true. When she'd heard the footage was gone—she'd felt safe. But that wasn't what had made her decide to stay.

"I—"

Briers cut in. "Get her phone," he barked.

Keeley automatically grabbed at her pocket, but Carol was too quick for her. The shark shifter muttered a quick apology before she threw the phone to Briers.

An ugly sneer twisted his face as he activated the screen.

"Just as I thought," he hissed. "You said she wanted to check in with her work, MacInnis? It wasn't the hotel she was worried about. Arrangements for the drop point, payment details—it's all here." He scrolled down. "Interesting. It looks like our thief dropped off the radar without checking in with her associates. What happened, Bailey? Did the plan fall apart after Lance caught you running off?" His eyes narrowed. "Or were you waiting until there was a bigger payload to sweeten the deal?"

He looked meaningfully at the eggs on the desk and slipped Keeley's phone into his pocket. "Thank God we got to her in time."

"That's *bullshit*," Keeley spat. "You're lying! There's no way he has my number, he can't have messaged me on—"

"He?" Lance's voice was glacier-cold.

Keeley choked. Lance's expression was sterner than she'd ever seen him.

No, that wasn't true. He'd looked like this when he talked about tracking down the people who'd tried to take Maggie. Who'd hurt his friends.

And now he thought she was one of them. Because she *was* one of them.

"You've got it all wrong," she said desperately, struggling to pull away from Carol's iron grip. "I'm—that's not *me*. You have to let me explain—"

"Not you?" Briers cut in again, his voice dripping with acid. Keeley's heart sank as Lance let him talk. "Let's talk about who *you* are, Keeley Bailey. You've got quite the history, don't you? Breaking and entering. Burglary. Assault. No wonder you're living under an assumed name."

"I never—" The words died on Keeley's tongue as Lance stared at her, hurt in every line of his face.

"You lied to me. Everything—" Lance groaned and clutched his chest. Pain twisted his face. "No," he muttered bitterly. "Not everything was a lie."

The mate bond. It's hurting him. Keeley's chest ached, as though in sympathy for Lance's pain. "Lance, please. I can explain. I know I've fucked up, but—"

What could she say? Her ribs cramped. Explain? More like confess.

Bitterness filled her mouth. Most of what Briers had said about her was true. How could Lance believe anything she said now, knowing her history?

"I never meant to hurt you," she burst out. "And you know I would never hurt Maggie. *Never.*"

Lance searched her face, his eyes so intent she found it difficult to hold his gaze. All her instincts were telling her to run and hide, but it was too late for that. All she could do was hope he would give her a chance.

A chance she knew she didn't deserve.

Lance's eyes, usually so bright in contrast to his dark skin, looked faded and dull. For the first time since Keeley hard known him, he looked defeated.

No, she thought desperately. *It wasn't meant to be like this. I was going to tell you everything. I didn't want you to be hurt like this.*

Lance looked like he was about to say something when Briers spoke up.

"We don't have time for this, sir," Briers muttered, loud enough that his voice carried through the pounding in Keeley's ears. "I can use her phone to pin down her associates' locations. You need to go, now, before the trail goes cold again."

Pain twisted like a knife in Keeley's heart as Lance straightened, grim determination replacing the torn anguish in his eyes.

"Take her to the holding cell."

Chapter 20

Keeley

Keeley felt faint. Her feet skidded and stumbled under her as Carol and another agent marched her to the basement level. She barely noticed where they were taking her.

The only thing she could see was the look on Lance's face when he realized who she was. *What* she was.

Her guards stopped outside a heavy-looking door that opened to reveal a windowless cell. Four plain walls, concrete floor. The only furniture was a steel-framed bench welded to one wall.

Keeley stumbled in, feeling light-headed, and the door slammed behind her.

She fell to her knees, her head swimming.

I should have told him earlier, she thought vaguely. *I should have told him everything. Who I really am. Who Sean is. He could have tracked Sean down, found out whoever was behind the kidnapping...*

Keeley shook her head. Cold was creeping through her limbs, bone-deep and icy enough to make her shiver.

Telling Lance the truth wouldn't have helped. What was she supposed to do, tell Lance she'd lied about everything else, but she was totally telling the truth this time, honest?

He wouldn't have believed her.

And now... it was too late. It was all too late. Even if Lance did hear her out now, what could she say? That she used to be a criminal, but that was all behind her now?

Because it wasn't. Sean had made sure of that. No matter how far she ran, she would never escape him.

She slumped on the ground. There was a low bench along one wall, but right now, she couldn't see any point in moving to it. Nothing mattered. Lance knew who she was, and...

In some ways, it was a relief.

She didn't need to lie to Lance anymore. Or worry about how he'd react when he found out the truth. The worst had already happened, after all. Lance hated her.

... And he was going to take down the other bad guys. And Maggie would be safe. She was back with the other eggs now, and soon, they would all be reunited with their uncle.

Keeley blinked. That sounded suspiciously like a happy ending. For everyone except her, but... it wasn't like she deserved a happy ending, after all.

Maybe she hadn't wanted to get involved with the kidnapping, but she had, hadn't she? And she'd known who was behind it—one of the people, at least—and hadn't told Lance. She could have helped with the investigation, but she'd chosen to protect herself.

Everything that Briers had said was true. She deserved this. She was a thief. And a liar. She'd even—

Wait.

The concrete floor was like a block of ice under her legs. She rested her palms on it, willing the chill to snap her out of the fog that filled her mind. What had Briers said?

She closed her eyes, pulling up the memory of Briers' twisted smirk. *Breaking and entering. Burglary. Assault.*

Keeley's eyes snapped open. How the hell did Briers know about the assault charge?

Because there *wasn't* an assault charge. Nothing on the books, nothing official. That had been the deal.

Keeley swallowed, her tongue scraping dry against the top of her mouth. Only four people knew about the assault. Her. Gran. The guy she'd attacked. And Sean.

Keeley's gran was dead. The guy she'd attacked wouldn't talk—that was the deal, that they would keep quiet or they'd go public with what *he'd* done, too.

Keeley sure as shit hadn't told anyone.

Which left...

Keeley jumped to her feet so quickly her head spun. She stumbled, scraping her palms on the floor as she caught her balance, and threw herself at the door.

An inside job. She'd been wrong to suspect Carol, but not wrong about someone in Lance's agency being involved.

She pounded on the door as hard as she could, ignoring the stinging pain in her hands.

"It's a trap," she yelled, hoping at least one of the agents sent to guard her was still on the other side of the door. "It's a trap, you have to stop them, it's a trick—"

The door opened under her fists, and she fell forward, cracking her knees on the ground. Someone was standing behind the door; they'd stepped back as she fell, keeping their shiny black brogues out of her path.

"Tell Lance," Keeley gasped, winded. "Tell Lance—he's in danger. Whatever lead he's chasing, I think it's a trap. The people who tried to take Maggie have someone in the agency. They're feeding you information. They—"

She looked up, and all the blood drained from her face.

"A trap?" Briers said. "Well, well. Aren't you clever."

Chapter 21

Lance

The city flashed by outside the van windows. Lance clenched his fists. This was it; they were zeroing in on the enemy's hideout. He had one chance to finish this. He needed to concentrate. Every breath he took, every beat of his heart, had to be focused on the mission ahead.

But inside, he was being torn apart.

His snow leopard raged against him, demanding that he turn back. It didn't understand what Keeley had done. It only knew that she was his mate, and he'd abandoned her.

No. Worse than that. He hadn't just abandoned her, he'd left her locked up, imprisoned in one of the agency's shifter-proof holding cells. And when he returned...

He gritted his teeth. When he returned, he would hand her over to the police. Briers had shown him the outstanding warrants for Keeley Bailey's arrest. She was a criminal, and she'd tried to hurt Maggie, and she would pay for what she'd—

Pain shot through his chest. Lance doubled over, gritting his teeth to keep from crying out. The shimmering, golden bond that connected him to Keeley was stretched tight, pulling on his heart. His snow leopard howled in pain as the bond twisted and frayed.

No.

Lance knew he should let it happen. Let the bond fray and break. Turn his back on his mate the same way she had betrayed him, and put an end to the connection between them.

I can't.

Lance clutched at the delicate bond, not relaxing until the pain in his heart and soul eased.

He didn't know for sure what would happen when the bond broke, but right now, he told himself, he couldn't risk it. Even the pain of it almost breaking was enough to unsettle him, and for this mission, he needed to be in total control.

The bond stayed. For now.

We're here. Parker's voice in his mind sounded like an echo, and it took Lance a moment to realize why. Of course. Hadn't the night he'd recovered Maggie started like this? A lead appearing like a miracle from heaven, Bradford driving like a madman to the location—

And him, tearing himself to pieces with guilt and fear.

Not this time. Lance steeled himself. He'd been caught on the back foot for too long. Always one step behind, always scrambling to keep up. No more.

He nodded to the Parker and Yelich. All three of them slipped out of the van, moving as one, and approached the target.

Briers' lead had brought them to an empty warehouse along the water's edge. Barbed wire topped the fence around the building, and what lay beyond it didn't seem worth guarding. Boards covered the door and windows of the office at the front of the warehouse, and piles of trash blocked the large main doors. Flies buzzed in the late morning sun.

Abandoned, according to Briers' intelligence. Or it had been, until the people after the dragon eggs had moved in.

Lance checked the ground at his feet. No shadow; the shield scale strapped to his arm was holding.

Not that that will help us if the enemy agents are shielded, too. Like they were at the station.

He frowned. *Another thing to worry about. We thought we had secured all the shields—all the ones Julian remembered, anyway. If we were wrong about that, then how many other criminal groups might have access to dragon scale shielding?*

Lance paused and took a deep breath. *Focus*, he told himself. *You can't afford to be distracted right now. Not after Keeley.*

Everything she did was a distraction. All she wanted was to get her hands on the eggs.

His hand went to his comm, and he realized almost too late than he'd been about to ping Briers and ask for an update on their prisoner. He gritted his teeth. *Focus.*

Briers' voice buzzed in his ear, passing on information about the target. There was a second small door around the side, but no other exits. Lance gestured to the other agents, directing them to pincer in on the building.

The midday air was completely still. The smell from the piles of trash grew stronger as he approached the warehouse, the stench so rank it seemed almost solid. Lance grimaced and held his breath.

Yelich was already at the front door. She dropped her head as Lance approached. *Can't smell shit through all this... shit.*

Parker? Lance fell into position beside Yelich and waited for the bloodhound shifter's assessment.

Not shit. Parker had gone around the side of the building. *Just rotten. Old trash.* He grumbled a bit, and then added: *Can't smell anything past it, but can't tell if that's because it's so rank, or there's nothing there to smell. Should've brought Zhang.*

Lance shook his head. Carol had been too shaken by what happened with Keeley to come on this mission.

Lance focused all his senses. He couldn't hear anything from beyond the door, but according to Briers, Keeley's associates had entered the warehouse several hours ago and not yet emerged. They were in there somewhere, and Lance would find them, shielded or not.

He nodded to Yelich. *Break down that door.*

Yelich grinned.

If they needed any more reasons to carry out this mission under shield—this was it. Lance's snow leopard strained to take form as Yelich rolled back her shoulders and began to shift. Her hippo was a tank made of pure muscle. The door disintegrated as she charged it.

More crashes came from the other side of the building, as Parker broke in the side door. Lance fell into position behind Yelich, quickly scanning the room.

Lance spun around, searching every corner of the huge shed. Light filtered through gaps around the edge of the main warehouse door, barely illuminating towers of crates and rusty machinery. His nostrils flared.

What the hell? Yelich stamped one foot and huffed. *There's nothing here!*

Her voice disappeared in the gloom. A door opened halfway down the side wall, and Patel appeared, shaking his head. *Empty.*

Parker followed him, his bloodhound's heavy feet padding silently on the concrete floor. He swung his head back and forth, sniffing the ground. And the air.

Lance cursed and lowered his gun. If there had been anyone hiding here, Parker would know.

"What the hell is going on?" he muttered, and activated his comm. "Briers, your lead's a bust. There's no one here."

He turned around, not wanting the others to see the frustration on his face.

There was no response on the comm. Lance tapped his ear. "Briers?"

Behind him, Parker huffed out a breath. *That smell—*

Lance's nostrils flared. His snow leopard surged, sharpening all his senses until his ears and nose started to go cat-shaped to match his silver eyes.

The inside of the warehouse smelled as bad as the outside. The stink wasn't hiding enemy shifters, though.

Lance's eyes widened as he sifted through the garbage stench to the chemical tang beneath. "Everybody out!"

He flung himself at the door. The floor shook as Yelich started a one-woman stampede, and Parker—

Lance paused, scanning the room. Parker had been over there—and now—

I've got him, you ass! Yelich roared into his mind, and Lance started moving again. An instant too late.

A *whoof* of air hit him less than a second before the heat of the explosion.

Chapter 22

Keeley

"You fucking *asshole*. You won't get away with this—Lance will—"

Keeley gasped and doubled over as pain ripped through her chest. Her vision went gray at the edges. When it cleared, she was on her knees on the basement's concrete floor, shaking.

And the strange new thing inside her, the golden light that she had been so certain she was imagining—was gone.

She hadn't even been sure it was real. Now that it was gone, she knew it had been.

The world spun. Somewhere above her, Briers laughed.

"Well, isn't that convenient? Forget coming to your rescue. It looks like Lance isn't going to be doing anything, ever again."

What is he talking about? Keeley felt sick. Every breath hurt, and the empty space inside her chest stung like a raw wound. Her nausea turned into panic.

Something's wrong. Something's wrong and I don't know what it is, I don't understand enough about this whole crazy magical world, but this—this shouldn't be happening...

Briers said something else, but Keeley didn't hear him. She dived into the black empty space in her chest, searching for—something. She didn't know what. Just that she had to find it.

There! The barest hint of light. Not a candle flame, not even a spark, but still there. Still alive.

Keeley clutched at it, willing it to stay alight, and bit back a cry.

Pain and exhaustion washed over her, along with a jolt of adrenaline that made her vision blur. Her breath rasped.

The pain she was feeling—she shuddered as her senses blurred, as though she was in two places at once. As though she was two *people* at once.

It wasn't *her* back that stung with searing pain, or her ears that were ringing so loud she couldn't hear anything. Grazed knees and palms, that was *her* pain, her body. This was...

Briers kicked her in the ribs. "Get up!" he barked, his top lip twitching. "You've still got work to do."

The strange blurring between her own body and... whatever it was she was experiencing faded away, leaving nothing but the tiny spark of light lodged in her chest.

Still there. Still alive. Whatever it was.

Keeley glared up at Briers.

"And what the fuck makes you think I'm going to do anything you say?" she snarled.

She rose to a crouch, one hand pressed against her chest as though she could physically hold the strange, barely there spark of light in place. Her fingers trembled.

Briers sneered. "Because you work for me." He snapped his fingers. "Come out, Bailey."

Oh, no.

Keeley's blood ran cold even before Sean flickered into sight behind Briers. He had one of the scale shields strapped to his arm and was wearing dark fatigues.

Just like the men from the station, Keeley thought, her skin prickling cold.

Briers sniffed and addressed Sean over his shoulder. "Control her, will you?" He turned back to Keeley and added, his lip curling, "You've been a valuable investment so far, Miss Bailey. Don't make me change my mind about your usefulness."

Sean strode up and grabbed Keeley, pulling her roughly upright.

"You'd better listen to him, kiddo. Way we've planned it, there's two ways out of here for you. Either you come with us and share in the cash and glory—well, some of it, maybe—or you cause trouble and, *whoops*, someone got in front of a bullet while the baddies were making their getaway."

He squeezed Keeley's arm, hard enough that she had to grit her teeth to stop herself wincing.

"You're planning to kill me?" Bile rose at the back of Keeley's throat. It shouldn't be a surprise, not after everything else... "What happened to the importance of *family*?"

Sean shrugged. "Hey, *I'm* not going to shoot you. We'll leave that to the pros. All the agents upstairs? What do you think they'll do if they see an escaped, dangerous prisoner suddenly appear in front of them?"

"I'm not dangerous," Keeley protested, and Briers snorted.

"You ensnared MacInnis, gained the affections of an infant dragon, and made sure you were on the ground when the other eggs were brought into the office." Keeley opened her mouth, and Briers cut her off with a gesture. "And in case that wasn't enough, haha, everyone upstairs is about to discover that their colleagues on the mission all got blown into tiny pieces. Trust me, they won't be in a mood to hear your excuses."

"W-what do you mean, blown up?" Keeley's hand went to her chest, and she remembered the strange feeling that had washed over her.

The burning sensation on her back. Fire. Another explosion?

"Oh dear, Miss Bailey. Your uncle told me you would be useful, but he didn't warn me you'd be this dim. Haven't you figured it out yet?" Briers' smirk made Keeley's skin crawl. "That little fit of dramatics you treated us to before? That was you feeling Lance MacInnis' death."

Keeley took a step backwards. "No. You're lying."

Briers shrugged. "Suit yourself. You're the one who experienced it. And if fooling yourself that Lance is still alive means you put up less of a fuss, who am I to argue?" The corner of his mouth curled up. "My colleagues upstairs, on the other hand... well, they might not be as patient as I am. In fact, seeing as they think you're part of the conspiracy that just got their boss and three of their coworkers killed, I imagine they'll shoot you on sight."

"No. No, he can't be—he can't..."

Keeley's voice trailed off. Briers was looking at her, not with a sneer of victory, or pity, but a vague, neutral expression as though he was waiting for her to calm down so that they could all get to work. Somehow that, more than any villainous crowing over his success, convinced her he was telling the truth.

Lance was dead.

Lance was dead... and it was her fault.

The last remnant of light inside her died.

Her vision blurred. Briers' voice barely made it through the sudden roaring in her ears.

"Shield her. We need to get moving."

Sean pulled a second scale shield from his pocket and pushed up Keeley's sleeve so that when he strapped it on her arm, the scale pressed directly on to her skin.

Keeley felt light-headed as the world shimmered slightly—except that wasn't right, was it? The world wasn't doing anything. She was the one flickering out of sight.

Just like she'd wanted to do all these years. Disappear, so no one could find her. And now she finally had the ability to do so, by using a piece of dragon magic.

The raw wound in her heart opened up again, searing with pain and black as pitch. She could disappear. Wasn't that what she'd wanted, a way to disappear from Sean and her old life forever? Except Lance was dead, and nothing else mattered anymore.

He was dead, and he'd died thinking she'd betrayed him.

Keeley bit back a sob as what was left of her heart broke.

Lance was dead, and Briers and Sean were going to destroy everything, and she was… nothing. Worse than nothing. If she'd been *nothing*, if she'd never gotten involved, then Lance would still be alive.

The edges of her vision went gray again, and she barely felt Sean grab her arm and drag her along the corridor after Briers. He led them to the elevator, then stepped in and pressed the button as though completely unaware of the two people invisibly tailing him.

Sean shoved Keeley in just as the doors started to close. She tripped and fell against the back wall, and Briers made an irritated noise.

"The shields mute the noises *you* make," he muttered under his breath. "Not environmental effects."

Sean grinned at Keeley, then reached forward and tapped the back of Briers' hand twice. Briers nodded, almost imperceptibly, and Sean leaned back against the elevator wall beside Keeley.

"What's wrong, kiddo? Still sad about the boyfriend? Seriously, that was a piece of luck, you catching him. Especially after you fucked up the drop at the station." He shook his head slowly, his eyes fixed on Briers' back. "Mind you, it's not like Briers' pickup team was any better. Have to figure a way to get them out of the picture. Bunch of amateurs."

"And what does that make you?" Keeley snapped automatically. Her voice sounded a long way away.

The hollow, broken feeling in her chest was spreading to fill her entire body. She couldn't even feel the golden spark anymore, and now, she was too scared to even look for it. Whatever it was, it was connected to shifter magic. She was scared that if she looked for it too hard, she would destroy it. Just like everything else she touched was destroyed.

Sean was right. She had fucked up the drop at the station. If she'd known what she was doing, she could have...

Gotten myself blown up.

Keeley raised her head and glared at Sean.

"You were supposed to do the drop. If I'd followed your instructions I wouldn't be here right now, I'd be *dead.* And that would have been you! Are you shitting me with this right now, Sean? You're calling the other guys a bunch of amateurs, saying you need to get rid of them, but Briers wanted to *kill you.*" She clenched her fists, just managing to hold herself back from punching the wall. "And you're still working with him? How fucking stupid are you?"

Sean slung an arm around her shoulders. In a less fucked-up family, it might have seemed friendly. "I know Briers was trying to cut off loose ends, kiddo. He just hasn't noticed that I figured it out yet." He pulled her closer as the elevator slowed down. "Remember how I said there were two ways this could end? It's actually three."

Sean made a gun with his fingers and mimed shooting Briers in the back of the head. He grinned at Keeley.

"We'll show him who's a loose end, huh, kiddo?"

The elevator doors opened, and Sean dragged Keeley forward before she could respond. Her stomach sank.

"We'll" *show him?* Sean might be acting buddy-buddy with her now, but Keeley knew him too well for that. If it came down to it, he'd throw her to the wolves to save his own skin.

Just like he'd done ten years ago.

Keeley drew a ragged breath.

She'd spent the last few days letting herself be pulled around by events. She'd gotten involved because she was too stupid to get out right at the start. Stayed with Lance because it was easier than leaving.

And see what that had done. People were dead. *Lance* was dead, all because she'd just waited to see what would happen next instead of taking action herself.

Keeley took another breath. This one was less ragged, and although she still felt hollow inside, there was a new strength growing inside her.

Briers had a plan. Sean had a plan. She needed a plan, too.

Because Maggie still needed her.

CHAPTER 23

KEELEY

A plan was starting to form in Keeley's mind. Even before she had hatched, Maggie had been able to shoot feelings into Keeley's mind. What if she could do the same, in reverse? She could tell her to hide. Make it seem like a game—hide-and-seek—just long enough for Keeley to make a bigger distraction somewhere safely away from the tiny dragon and force Briers to reveal himself.

She concentrated. *Hey, Maggie, baby. If you can hear me, and I'm not just thinking to myself here...*

A cotton-candy puff of curiosity fluttered against the edge of her mind. *Maggie? Is that you? Is this actually working?*

Keeley was trying to build a mental image of how exciting hide and seek was when the elevator stopped. Briers stepped out promptly, and Keeley was surprised to see they were on the ground floor.

She followed Briers out into the foyer. Not that she had any choice, with Sean's hand like a vise around her arm.

Okay. Ground floor. But Maggie and the eggs were in Lance's office, so why does she feel so close?

"Mr. Briers?"

"What's she doing here?" Keeley burst out as Carol stood up from behind the reception desk. Her heart sank as she saw the egg carrying-case on the desk. Carol kept one hand protectively on it as she stepped around the desk to greet Briers.

"Prrp?" A feeling of joy buffeted against Keeley's mind as Maggie appeared over Carol's shoulder. She stared directly at Keeley, as though she could see her even through the shielding.

The joy was definitely Maggie's, because Keeley was feeling sick.

Hey, baby, she thought desperately. *Remember being up high on the roof? Why don't you run back up there now? I'll race you!*

"Prr-eep!"

Carol winced as Maggie dug her claws into her shoulder and flapped her wings excitedly. "I brought them down like you asked, Mr. Briers. I don't understand, though. Are we moving them now? Mr. Ames is still out, and he said he'd need to refuel the helicopter before the flight to the safe house. And, obviously, the helicopter is on the roof, not down her e..."

"Don't worry about that," Briers said sharply. "Give me the case."

The air around Carol and Maggie shimmered as she reached for the case. *Maggie's shielding her,* Keeley thought.

"Don't do it!" Keeley yelled. "Don't let him touch them!"

Carol heard her. And saw her. Her eyes went wide, and she reached for her belt. "What the hell?"

Maggie screeched and launched herself off Carol's shoulder, towards Keeley. Keeley grabbed her out of the air and clutched her to her chest.

You're safe, she thought as Carol drew her weapon.

And pointed it at her.

"Mr. Briers, get behind me," Carol barked. "Keeley Bailey and one other unknown behind you. They must be after the eggs." She frowned, and her gun wavered, pointing a few feet to Keeley's right.

Keeley's heart thudded against her ribs. *She can't see me. Without Maggie on her shoulder, she fell out of the shield-zone again.*

Briers sighed. "Bailey?"

Carol looked at him, confused. "Yes, she's—"

She never finished the sentence. Sean let go of Keeley's arm, reached under his jacket, and shot something at her.

"No!" Keeley yelled as Carol's whole body jerked and she slumped to the floor. She raced around the desk and fell to her knees beside the shark shifter. "What did you do?"

She pulled Carol's limp body face-up. There was no blood, but Carol didn't so much as whimper. Keeley's fingers shook as she searched for a pulse. Clinging to her chest, Maggie whined in panic.

She found Carol's pulse and, a second later, saw the glimmer of wires running from her shoulder back towards Sean. She glared at him as he tossed the taser next to Carol's limp body.

"The taser?" Briers' voice was tight with frustration. He slid another scale shield from his pocket and slipped it onto his wrist. "Just kill her, you idiot. I don't want her putting two and two together when she wakes up."

Sean shrugged and reached for the holster on his belt. "Thought you said the tasers were shifter-grade?"

"To stun. Not to finish the job. Now hurry up. Our ride will be here in less than a minute." Briers tapped something on his phone and placed it back in his pocket with a satisfied smirk. "And my dim-witted colleagues upstairs are about to hear what happened to Lance's team. What with that and the other surprise I have planned, I don't think they'll be in any state to follow us."

"What do you mean, other surprise?" Keeley stood up slowly, keeping herself between Carol and the two men.

Briers smirked at her. "Let's just say the agency's safe house is about to become a lot less safe. These things will happen when you try to cage an unstable dragon. I don't envy my former colleagues the clean-up job that will be required."

Oh, shit. The uncle?

Keeley put her arms around Maggie, who was still clinging to her chest. *Don't look scared. Look angry.* Be *angry.*

She glared at Sean.

"What the fuck have you gotten us in for, Sean? Seriously, did you hear what he just said? These shifters aren't going to stop at anything to find out who killed their—" She broke off, forcing back a sob. "—who killed their friends. And they're not going to go after him. They're going to go after *us.*" She drew a deep breath. "And on top of that, Briers is setting up a *full-grown dragon* to cause shit? I hope you're fireproof, Sean, cos I'm sure as shit not."

She spat out the last few words. It was either that or break down. *Lance. Oh, God, Lance, I'm so sorry. I've failed you completely.*

Briers smirked at her, but his eyes were shooting daggers. "You were right about her being a pain in the ass to deal with," he said to Sean, not taking his eyes off Keeley. "But it's worth it if she hatches the other eggs for us."

So that's what he wants me for. Keeley swallowed back a wave of nausea. "I don't know what you're talking about."

Briers raised his eyebrows at her. "Oh, for—you can stop lying now, you realize that? Lance may not have noticed the gaping holes in your story, but something made the egg hatch." He nodded at Maggie, clutched tight in Keeley's arms. "You've managed what neither Harper nor the foster family nor—haha—the dragon's *actual* family managed in months of trying. And I want you to do the same for the other two eggs. They'll be far more valuable that way."

Keeley took an involuntary step back. She felt light-headed as the full implications of what Briers was saying crashed down on her.

Valuable? He didn't just want to kidnap the clutch, he wanted to enslave them.

Maggie shivered in Keeley's arms, and her nausea was replaced by rage. How *dare* he. Maggie was only a baby. She shouldn't even know there were people this evil in the world, let alone be threatened by them.

"No." She'd stolen Maggie, fair and square. The dragonling was *hers*. She wouldn't let anything bad happen to her.

"No, what?" Briers *tsk*'ed. "You really are more trouble than you're worth."

"No, I'm not going to do shit for you," Keeley spat. "Right, Sean?"

Sean's eyes narrowed. "Damn it, Keeley—"

"What? Isn't it time to let Briers know about *our* little plan? You know, the one where you double-cross him and make off with the eggs yourself?"

"What is she talking about?"

Brakes squealed outside. *What did Briers say? Forty seconds until their getaway car arrives?*

Keeley licked her lips. "Come on, Sean. Getaway car's almost here. You told the driver about the change of plan already, right? What are you waiting for?"

Keeley felt like she was standing on a knife's edge. For a moment, nobody moved. Then Sean laughed and holstered his gun, and all her hope faded away.

"Seriously, kiddo? That's your plan?" He stepped closer to Briers and slapped the meerkat shifter on the shoulder. "Briers knows he can trust me. Right, bud?"

Briers relaxed and nodded, and in one swift movement Sean kicked his legs from under him and slammed his head against the edge of the desk as he fell.

Keeley didn't even have time to cover Maggie's eyes; the tiny dragon chirped in terror, clutching tightly to the front of her dress.

"Okay," she said unsteadily. "Sean, we've got to hurry, but there's still time to make this right. We're shielded. We can take the eggs and Maggie back upstairs and they'll be safe."

"Funny joke, kiddo."

Sean grinned at her, but the expression didn't even have his usual pretense of good feeling in it. "You always told me I was shit at making plans, didn't you, kiddo? Well, how about this. I don't need to make up my own plan this time. I'm going to use his." He aimed another vicious kick at the unconscious Briers and then nodded in the direction of the door. "Come on. Like you said, our ride's here."

"You actually think I'm going to come with you?" Keeley marched forward, putting herself between Sean and the bag that held the eggs. "Didn't you hear me? You want to end up burnt to a crisp? We don't belong in this world, Sean. We need to get out. Now."

Sean shook his head, his eyes locked on to the egg case on the desk. "This is my chance to make it into the big leagues, Kee."

"Oh, where have I heard that before?" Keeley didn't even bother trying to keep the bitterness out of her voice.

Sean pointed at her, his face twisting with rage. "You're not going to ruin this for me, kiddo. Not this time."

Keeley's throat went dry. "Ruin it for you? Is that what you call it? I've spent the last ten years trying to keep away from you because the last time I followed you, you almost got me killed."

Sean snorted. "Aw, come on, kiddo. That was all a misunderstanding. You know I would have come back for you…"

"When? After I'd suffocated to death?"

Keeley clenched her fists. She'd meant to distract Sean by making him angry, but some things ran in the family. And now her own temper was driving her on. Ten years of anger poured out of her.

"You left me there for *five days.* Alone, in the dark, trapped in that chest. Don't lie to me. You were never coming back for me. If Gran hadn't forced you to tell her where I was—"

Memories surged up inside her. She'd been so proud that her uncle had chosen *her,* out of all the kids, to come in on the job with him. She'd been so eager to prove herself to him.

She hadn't realized what part he'd decided she would play in his plans.

Keeley gulped, rage and fear boiling in her stomach. "You keep pretending you're some sort of big crime boss, but you're always doing someone else's dirty work. And whenever you try to be something more, you fuck up. You really think this is going to be any different?" She bared her teeth. "The only good thing you've done here is get me involved. But I'm not going to let you get away with it. If anyone's taking these dragons, it's going to be me!"

Even though she was shielded, her voice seemed to echo around the foyer.

Something moved in the corner of her vision. She turned her head and gasped.

Lance was standing at the front door. She hadn't even heard the door open, but there he was, one hand braced against the doorframe. His eyes were shadowed with pain and exhaustion, but he was *alive,* Briers had been wrong, he was alive and—

Some instinct made Keeley search inside herself for that golden spark of light. Too late, she remembered it had gone out.

Her chest felt scraped and hollowed out. Somewhere in the distance, she thought she heard Sean talking. Words filtered through her ears, but she wasn't paying enough attention to make sense of them. *Shielded—Can't see us—Slip past him—*

"I don't think so," Lance said. His voice was low, but as compelling as ever; and despite his clear exhaustion, there was a feline grace to the way he stood in the door, as though he was poised for action.

He could see her. He could see her, here, standing over the fallen bodies of two of his colleagues, and he'd heard her yell that she was going to take the eggs for herself.

CHAPTER 24

LANCE

It's gone.

Lance's heart clenched as he searched Keeley's eyes. Inside him, his snow leopard whined. It had been all but silent ever since he and the others escaped the explosion. He'd thought it had been bunkering down, saving its strength for the fight to come, but now he realized it had been focusing all its energy on hiding the truth from him. In his urgency to get back to the agency he hadn't noticed, but now there was no hiding it.

His mate bond with Keeley was gone.

Across the room, Keeley's eyes widened, and something like pain flashed in their stormy depths.

"Lance?" Her voice was little more than a whisper.

The strange man she'd been yelling at glanced at Lance and swore. "Fuck's sake. Briers said—"

"That I was meant to die in the warehouse explosion?" Lance's voice was gravelly, a result of the smoke he'd inhaled as he escaped the blaze. Keeley stiffened, and Lance cleared his throat in a useless attempt to gentle his voice. "I'm surprised. His intel is usually much more reliable."

"But I *felt*..." Keeley's voice faded away, and her eyes went hard. "It doesn't matter now."

Lance's jaw tightened. *It doesn't matter? Christ. What have I done?*

He nodded to the strange man standing next to her, wincing as pain shot through his head. "Are you going to introduce me to your friend?"

The stranger was the last piece of the puzzle that had begun to take shape in Lance's mind as he raced back to the agency. And now he thought he was starting to understand.

When Keeley grudgingly introduced the man as her uncle—the words almost choking her—the picture became clearer. Lance's gut crawled with self-disgust.

An inside job. His suspicious had been aroused when Briers had dropped off comms just as they were entering the warehouse. Then, the fact that his intel had led Lance straight into a trap had cast off all doubt. Briers had laid his plans carefully—including rounding up human scapegoats to take the fall for him.

Lance had been a fool, and Keeley had been the one to pay the price.

He flicked a glance at the meerkat shifter, lying unconscious on the floor. Whatever had happened here... he shook his head. He'd ask Keeley later.

If she forgave him and ever wanted to speak to him again. His heart ached. He'd never felt the emptiness inside him where his mate bond would be before it was there; now that it was gone, he couldn't feel anything else.

"I know Briers is the one behind everything," he said slowly, looking from Keeley to her uncle and silently alerting the agents elsewhere in the building. The rush of relief that surged back to him from his colleagues almost knocked him off his feet.

He turned his attention to Sean Bailey. "I don't know how you're involved, but if you give up now, I'm willing to be lenient—"

"Preep?"

Maggie's gold-scaled snout poked over the top of Keeley's shoulder. Seeing Lance, she jumped to the ground and flapped her wings at him.

A ribbon of questioning and uncertainty wound around Lance's mind. He broke off, his attention momentarily distracted as he reassured the baby dragon, and Sean struck.

Keeley yelled, her voice cutting off as Sean wrapped an arm around her neck. He dragged her backward around the side of the desk, reaching out his other arm to grab the egg carrying bag.

"I've got another idea," Sean said, baring his teeth in an expression that couldn't be called a grin. He reached under his jacket and pulled out a gun, which he pressed against Keeley's jaw. "I leave, with the dragon eggs, and maybe your girlfriend here doesn't get hurt."

Lance's snow leopard bristled. "She's your niece. You're not going to—"

Keeley shook her head, just slightly. One look at the expression in her eyes, and his heart broke a little more. She was deathly afraid.

Lance raised his hands placatingly. "Okay. Okay. We can work this out. You don't need to threaten her."

"I do if I want you to do as I say. Don't I? Briers said that she's your mate, and that means you'll do anything to protect her." Sean squeezed his arm tighter around Keeley's neck. "Shit, you're growing more useful by the second, aren't you, kiddo? Hatching eggs, playing the pretty little hostage... Told you that you were wasted at that hotel job."

Keeley went white, and Lance was struck by a desperate need to comfort her. He reached for the golden cord that had connected them, that should have still connected them, and found only emptiness.

No. Lance's shoulders slumped. Of all his failures, this was the worst.

A psychic nudge brought his attention to the street behind him. The others had finished dealing with the carload of Briers' associates and were falling into position.

But he couldn't risk them moving in while Keeley was in danger.

Suddenly, Keeley gasped and jerked her head. "No, don't!"

Lance's eyes flew to her. *If he's hurting her—*

But Sean hadn't moved. Keeley was staring at the floor, her eyes wide with panic. "Maggie, *no*! Stay away!"

The little dragon was crawling towards her. When Keeley yelled at her to stay back, her neck drooped in confusion.

"Aw, come on, kiddo. Give the monster a cuddle. We'll bring it with us, anyway." Greed shone in Sean's eyes, and any sympathy Lance might have had for a human caught in shifter crime evaporated.

Come here, Maggie. Lance imbued his psychic voice with as much love and warmth as he could manage with the empty space in his heart dragging at his emotions.

Maggie's head swung around, and she ran towards his psychic feelings-burst like a moth towards a flame.

Lance grabbed her as she leapt up and cradled her safely in one arm, her chest resting in his palm. Her tiny heartbeat thrummed against his hand, and this close, he was enveloped by her psychic aura.

She was scared, and confused and angry about why Keeley didn't like her anymore, and her emotions buzzed in the air around her like heavy black flies.

Lance's throat felt tight. He sent more reassurance to the tiny dragon—and then felt something else in the scared, confused storm of her emotions. A strange shimmer of movement in the fabric of the air.

Suddenly, he knew how he was going to get Keeley safely away from her asshole of an uncle.

She does love you, he said to Maggie, and he filled the message with everything he had thought he knew about Keeley. No. Everything he *did* know.

How brave she was, and kind, even in the face of all the terrifying things that had happened. How quickly she'd fallen for Maggie, and learned how to keep the baby dragon safe and happy.

He sent that memory of Keeley to Maggie, and with it, all his longing to be with her.

Home. That's what he'd been thinking of the moment before he lost consciousness in that alleyway, when Maggie teleported them. He'd thought of home with all his heart, and Maggie had taken them there.

It wasn't his apartment he thought of now. Now, home was warm skin, shining storm-bright eyes, and the soft tickle of dirty blonde hair on his face as Keeley turned her face towards his—

Take me home. Longing was an ache in his heart, sharp and brittle as ice.

Air moved against Lance's skin, fluttering like a mountaintop breeze. The room shimmered around him as Maggie began to trill, her voice like tiny bells.

His snow leopard surged forward, lending him its enhanced senses. Lance tensed. Every second was vital. If he was off by even a fraction of a second—

His eyes were useless. The shimmer around him was so strong he couldn't see a thing. He closed his eyes, concentrating.

Take me home.

Home.

There—

Keeley's scent filled his senses, sweet and salt and sunlight. And beside her, the rank, fear-sweat smell of Sean Bailey.

Maggie's trilling song faded, and the world around Lance began to solidify. He turned, pushing between Keeley and the thick fog of fear-sweat.

Eyes still closed, he lifted his arm. Cold metal whispered against his palm, and then the world snapped back into focus, and he grabbed the gun and wrenched it away.

The sharp retort of the gun going off bit at Lance's ears, but the shot went into the floor. Lance wrapped his free arm around Keeley, putting his body between her and the man who'd threatened her life.

Sean's face twisted as he turned on his heel and ran for the door. Lance sent out a quick psychic order to Parker and Yelich outside. Sean wouldn't make it another ten feet.

She's safe. All the tension drained out of him, and he let his head drop down onto Keeley's. Maggie wriggled up onto his shoulder and draped her tail around Keeley's neck, tying them all together.

Keeley was shaking. Lance held her closer, and then realized he was shaking, too.

That had been close. *Too* close.

"It's okay," he whispered into Keeley's hair. "You're safe now. I won't let them hurt you."

Something that was half-laughter, half-sob burst out of Keeley. "Briers said—" She drew a ragged breath and shivered in his arms. "He said you were dead, he said…"

"Briers has said a lot of things. It's taken me too long to figure out that most of it was lies."

Lance tipped Keeley's head back so he could press his forehead against hers. He wished he could send her emotions like he did to Maggie—all his regret, his guilt, and his love, in one tidy package.

"Not all of it. What he said about me—" Keeley's shoulders went up. "I was involved. Sean grabbed me when I was coming off work and gave me the bag w-with Maggie's egg in it. I was just too afraid to tell you—but that's no excuse, is it? I should have been braver, I should have—"

"I should have trusted you," Lance said simply. He nuzzled her cheek, still feeling slightly off-balance, like something was still wrong.

Guilt stung like a knife in his gut. Of course something was wrong. Everything was wrong.

"Regardless of what Briers said. I already knew your heart, and I'd seen how you were with Maggie. You're kind and loving. There's nothing evil about you. I should have known you'd never be willingly involved in anything that would hurt Maggie."

He cupped her cheek in one hand. "I should have trusted you. Instead, I almost lost you. I don't think I can ever forgive myself for that."

"I though I'd lost you," Keeley said quietly. "After you left, I felt..."

Her eyelashes fluttered against Lance's face. He lifted his head, gazing down at her.

It took his eyes a moment to adjust. His snow leopard was still near the surface, searching for—something—and he had to push it back and focus his human eyes.

Keeley was staring up at him, her stormy eyes troubled. A heavy line formed between her eyebrows, and her hand flew to her chest. "I felt—"

Her voice cracked, and she swayed on her feet. Lance steadied her.

"I thought I felt you dying," she whispered. "But it wasn't that, was it? It was—whatever was between us—it's gone."

Lance and his snow leopard watched the blood drain from her face. Just when he thought his heart couldn't break any more, she smiled brokenly.

"It's gone. That means you're free."

Chapter 25

Keeley

Keeley wrapped her arms around herself.

Lance had brought her to this meeting room and left her. It felt like hours ago, but the clock on the wall told her it was only a few minutes. She supposed there was a lot to do, right after you discover that one of your high-level employees is actually a psychopath who'd tried to kill off half his colleagues. Lots of paperwork, probably. Lots of hushed conversations.

At least one thing was going right. She wasn't his mate anymore. *And that must be such a fucking relief for him, now that he knows...*

Keeley sank down in the chair and buried her face in her hands. She couldn't gather the vitriol to be angry, even inside her own head. Everything hurt too much.

But it shouldn't. Maggie is safe. Carol's going to be fine, and no one got blown up at the warehouse anyway and they've caught Briers and Sean, and... this doesn't have anything to do with me, not anymore.

Lance is free.

And if it hurt, deep in her heart like someone had taken a hacksaw to her chest, well, she should stop being so fucking selfish. He was better off without her.

Everyone was.

They'd left her in a meeting room, not the cell again, which she supposed meant Lance had been telling the truth about trusting her. Then again, from the number of whispered conversations she'd heard through the door, it sounded like there was a guard outside. So maybe it was just that the cell was otherwise occupied.

There was a knock on the door.

Keeley's head snapped up. The room wobbled in front of her, and when she blinked, she felt wetness on her cheeks. "Oh, shit."

She dragged her sleeve across her eyes, grimacing. By the time she looked up again, eyes clear, Lance was standing in front of her.

Keeley fought the impulse to jump out of her chair. Her hands made fists on the desktop, and she quickly put them in her lap.

"Um. Hi."

"I brought you something to eat." Lance placed a tray on the desk in front of her. His movements were stiff.

"Thanks." If Lance's movements were stiff, Keeley's voice could have been used for scaffolding. He'd brought her food? Why? "How's C-Carol?"

She winced. Great. Her voice could either be stiff or crumble completely. What a great couple of options.

"She'll be fine. Chloe's looking after her."

He fell silent, his face getting the distracted look Keeley was beginning to recognize as the tell that he was using telepathic speech.

She dragged her eyes away from him. She didn't know why she bothered noticing stuff like that. It wasn't like she was going to be around him long enough to do anything with the information.

Her stomach twisted as she looked at the tray of food Lance had brought her. Pastries, savory rolls, cookies...

Not that she had any appetite. She grabbed the paper cup of coffee from the side of the tray and cradled it in her hands.

"Sorry about that." Lance straightened his jacket and sat down opposite her. "That was Chloe. Carol's just woken up. She was asking after you."

"I'm surprised anyone wants to talk to the human who almost got everyone killed."

"Keeley, no one believes that. We know Briers lied about your involvement." Lance swore under his breath. "Along with other things. He's been selling scale shields on the black market for months, apparently. Not to mention…" His voice softened. "Sorry. You don't need to know any of that."

"Yeah, need-to-know, right? And I'm the last person who needs to know." The paper cup began to buckle between Keeley's hands, and she quickly put it back on the table. "So what happens next? When do I get to leave? Or are you keeping me here?"

Her voice grated against her ears. She sounded like a sulky teenager, and she still couldn't make herself even look at Lance. She glared at her hands.

"No, I thought… we need to talk."

"What about?" Keeley shot back. "You know the whole story now, and you've got Briers—that's everything, isn't it?"

The memory of Lance teleporting across the room struck her like a train. His arms around her, his lips pressing against her forehead—

She untwisted her fingers and ran them through her hair, scraping at her scalp with her fingernails. "Unless you want another official statement from me, I mean, a real one, not just me lying like last time."

"I meant we need to talk about us."

Keeley froze. "What us? There isn't—" She swallowed and rubbed her chest. "There isn't any us. Is there. It was just the mate bond, and now it's gone."

Her voice was flat. Lance was silent, long enough that her eyes started to wander towards him of their own accord.

She wrenched them back to her hands.

Lance cleared his throat. There was another short pause and a movement at the edge of Keeley's vision. She guessed he was repositioning his glasses. God, he was so adorable when he did that.

"You thought I was dead," he said, his voice painfully slow. "And I thought—"

Keeley flinched, and he didn't finish the sentence.

He doesn't need to. I already know what he was going to say.

He thought I betrayed him.

Lance kept talking. "It can happen. The mate bond breaking. Not... frequently, and it isn't something shifters like to talk about." He cleared his throat again. "Finding your mate is meant to be like finding the other half of your soul, and to lose that—"

"Could be pretty good luck, if the other half of your soul turns out to be a piece of shit?" Keeley muttered under her breath.

Lance hissed in a sharp breath.

"You can't think that." His voice was incredulous. "Keeley, you're not—you're everything I could have hoped for. More."

"Bullshit!"

This time, she was too slow to stop herself looking at Lance. Their eyes met, and there was no sizzle, no heart-yanking pull of connection. Just pain in Lance's eyes, and a hollowness that wrenched at Keeley's insides.

She caught her breath, and with it, the rush of emotion that had made her interrupt him.

"Bullshit. You don't even *know* me. I've lied to you since the moment I met you. You don't know anything about me, you don't know who I used to be, who I really am."

"So tell me."

No. No, no, no, I can't.

The words died on Keeley's lips. What did it matter, now? It wasn't like it would make any difference. Lance wasn't tied to her anymore, so what she was shouldn't hurt him.

Maybe it would even help. If he knew what sort of a bullet he'd dodged. Keeley swallowed hard.

"Look, Sean, all of this—it's just the way my family is, you know? Criminals, but *shitty* criminals. Someone says 'jump' and the Baileys say 'how high', and then act all confused when it turns out they wanted us to jump in front of bullets, or the cops, or whatever. We're bad, but we're *bad* at being bad. And ever since I can remember, Sean always wanted more."

She tried to shrug, but her shoulders were already up around her ears. She rolled them back, trying to ease the tension that was crackling through her whole body.

"Sorry. I've never... talked to anyone about this before. Not even after..." She bit her lip. "Well. That part's coming up." *What better way to convince him he's better off without me than to tell the whole story?*

"I'm glad you're telling me." Lance's voice was gentle. And it was a good thing he was sitting between her and the door, because if he hadn't been, she would have bolted.

Instead, she had to keep going, and wait for that gentle voice to harden up again.

"Anyway, when my uncles weren't all signing up to get shot at, we did basic jobs. Burglary, mostly. Nothing big, because big meant security systems, instead of just normal people's houses."

She risked a glimpse at Lance. He was sitting completely still, his expression neutral.

"So basically, I spent my childhood fucking up other people's lives because they could afford a big TV but not a security camera," she continued, her fists clenching as she waited for Lance's reaction.

His eyelids flickered. Nothing else.

"Don't you have anything to say about that?" Her fingernails were digging into her palms. "I was *good* at it. It was *fun*. Like solving a puzzle and hide-and-seek rolled into one."

Lance lowered his head. What was he going to do, feed her some line about it not being her fault? She'd gone along with all of it.

"Everything that's gone wrong these last few days has happened because I jumped in without knowing the full story," Lance said quietly. He rubbed his forehead, a line forming between his eyebrows.

And then, to Keeley's surprise, a smile flashed across his face. "Besides. I'm convinced that if I tell you it's okay, you were only a kid, you'd throw it back in my face."

"Well. Yeah." Keeley's hands relaxed. "I mean, even a kid knows that stealing's wrong. I spent enough time in school to know *that*."

"But if it's what you grew up with—sorry." Lance held out his hands in surrender. "The whole story. Go on. Convince me that you're really a terrible person."

Keeley glared at him. That was—no. Too close to flirting.

Stop kidding yourself, she thought, rubbing her chest. *You're imagining things.*

"Anyway. So, Sean was always looking for his next big shot, and one day he thought he'd found it. And he wanted me on the job with him, because I was good at being small and breaking into places, basically."

Keeley hesitated. This was the hard bit. She wasn't sure she'd even gone over all of it in her own head, before.

She'd just run away and never looked back.

"I thought it was just another burglary. The house was fancier than we usually hit, but Sean told me he had everything under control. We got in easy enough, and then the plan changed…" She licked her lips and shrugged to cover the shiver that went through her. "Turns out it was another case where someone said 'jump' and Sean said 'how high?' Only I didn't know it until we were there."

"What happened?"

Keeley sucked down a mouthful of coffee before she returned to the story. Her mouth was dry, and it got dryer as she kept talking.

"We got in all right. Almost freakily easily, really, so I should have figured something was up." Keeley ran her fingers through her hair agitatedly, pulling at the knots as though untangling her hair would help her straighten out her thoughts. Why was it so hard to tell this story? "It was a nice house. Nice neighbourhood. But as soon as we were in, Sean let slip that this wasn't just a normal job. One of the local gang bosses had told him to shake down a competitor, and that's what we were there to do." Her fingers caught on another knot, and she jerked at it so hard the coffee in her other hand almost spilled. "I was so mad. I should have left, but…"

She swallowed. *But I knew what Sean would be like if I ditched him.*

Keeley glanced at Lance, and the concern in his eyes made her throat close up for a moment. She coughed and made sure she wasn't looking at him as she continued.

"Anyway. I wasted time arguing with Sean, and getting angrier, and then I did what he wanted anyway. His boss wanted stuff smashed, well, I was already mad enough for that. I went crazy, and I was so wound up already that it was *fun*. Like breaking in had been fun. He had this living room full of display cases with fancy plates and stuff, and big sea chests full of other really smashable valuables, and I just—lost it. I didn't even hear the front door open."

She paused and rubbed her eyes. "Sean was upstairs. It was a really big house, so I don't know, he probably didn't hear…" Another gulp of coffee. The cup was shaking.

"Keeley—"

"So the guy came home. I was in the living room, just… smashing shit. Then I turn around and he's there, and—I ran, and I don't even know if I hit him first or he just hit me back, and I tripped and fell over one of the chests I'd been pulling stuff out of…"

Her throat closed over as the memory flew to the top of her mind. Everything had hurt and the world was still spinning from when the man punched her, and then—

"Your nightmare." Lance's voice was heavy. "You said everything was dark, and you couldn't move."

"Something like that." Keeley's voice shook. "Anyway, I was there for—I don't know, a few days? Eventually I guess my Gran got the story out of Sean and came and found me. He'd taken off as soon as the guy came home, of course."

She grinned, because the sight of her old Gran coming into the house like a knight in shining armour probably would have been funny, if she'd been conscious enough to remember it. Then she made the mistake of looking up at Lance.

His face was ashen.

Keeley looked away quickly. Her fingers were twisting together in her lap. "And... that was that, basically. Gran sorted it out with the guy whose house it was. He wouldn't report the break-in, she wouldn't report him for not calling an ambulance or whatever." Her voice dropped. "And Sean got paid. His boss was happy enough with how things went, I guess."

"Jesus." Chair legs scraped across the floor as Lance stood up. He moved towards Keeley, and then paced away, one hand to his mouth. "Your uncle set you up."

She tried to laugh it off. "You catch on fast! It took me until Gran came and rescued me to figure it out." Her hand went to her neck. Nothing there. Of course, Maggie still had her necklace.

Good. She should keep it.

"That was it, for me. I couldn't hack it anymore. It wasn't just that Sean left me there, no one else even—anyway. Gran gave me some money and her old locket, and I got out. I haven't looked back since. Or, not until Sean found me..."

"And blackmailed you into transferring the egg for him."

Keeley nodded. Her forehead itched, and when she scratched it, she felt dampness. She'd been sweating? *But I don't feel warm. I feel cold...*

Lance swore and charged across the room. The next thing Keeley knew, he was kneeling in front of her, folding her in his arms like she was the most precious thing he'd ever touched.

She put her hands on his chest to push him away. "You don't need to—I know I'm not your mate anymore—"

"The hell with that." Lance pushed his fingers through her hair, cradling her head against his shoulder. "God, Keeley. Everything you've been through... How could you think I'd hold that against you?"

"What?" Keeley pulled away, just far enough so she could look into his face. "I just told you! I hurt people. I didn't even care that I was doing it. I stole things and made people feel like they weren't safe in their own homes, and..."

"When was the last time you felt safe?"

Keeley just stared at him. Lance shook his head slightly, his eyes troubled.

"Not living there, I'll bet. And since then?"

Once. Keeley tried to fight the thought back, but it escaped her. *Just once, when you carried me out of my nightmare. Just for a moment.*

She kept her mouth shut tight. What would be the point of telling him? It was stupid, anyway, to feel safe in the middle of all of her lies. She was still the same as she had been then. Still lying. Still out for herself. Still hurting people.

But just for that moment...

Something stirred in her chest, like the remains of a fire shifting to reveal one last ember, already cooling to dull, dead gray.

"Keeley, look at me." Lance's voice was suddenly urgent. "Did you feel that?"

CHAPTER 26

LANCE

A flicker. Barely even that. A sudden glimpse of light, like a sunbeam hitting a single mote of dust.

Lance's snow leopard was faster than he was. While he was still staring into Keeley's eyes, hoping against hope for some glimmer of recognition, it leapt.

Lance didn't wait to see whether it caught the lone spark of light, or what would happen if it did. Or didn't. He grabbed Keeley's hand.

"Tell me you can feel that."

She bit her lip, her gaze going hazy. "I did feel it. Before. Like being filled with light. But that stopped after—" Her eyes sharpened again, and Lance almost groaned with frustration. "It *hurt*. But it wasn't me who was hurting."

The frustration disappeared in an instant, replaced by horror. "The explosion. You felt that?"

Keeley shrugged tightly. A hole opened in the bottom of Lance's stomach.

He'd felt it too. Not the hurt. The moment of connection, of calm, in the middle of the chaos.

"It was like touching a live wire, and afterwards—boom. No more light." Keeley grimaced. "Sorry. 'Boom' probably isn't the best word. But maybe we, I don't know, overloaded it. Like plugging too many things in, and the fuse box blows. I mean, it makes sense, doesn't it? I'm not a shifter. I don't have any of these powers, and I'm not as strong as you, so... it just didn't hold up."

Lance shook his head. "No. You are strong, Keeley, even if you can't see it." Guilt burned at the back of his throat. Everything Keeley had said about her childhood—how had he not seen that she was hiding so much pain?

She'd been so full of love and hope all the time they'd been together—and Briers had destroyed that.

No. Lance had destroyed it.

"I gave up on you. That must be what did it. I gave up, and when you thought I was dead, the bond needed my faith in you to survive. Instead, it broke. All because I believed Briers' lies. Of all the mistakes I've made, that's the worst."

He took a deep breath, slowly, as though any sudden movement would disturb the hunt going on inside his soul.

"But it isn't the end. If you can feel the same spark of potential inside yourself that I felt just now, there's hope."

Please. Please let there be hope. Let me be able to fix this.

"I feel—" Keeley shook her head, her gaze skittering away from his. "I thought there was something, still. Afterwards. But I must have been imagining it."

"Please. Try. For me."

Keeley's eyes shot to his as she heard the tremble in his voice. Her throat bobbed as she swallowed. "Okay."

Her voice was barely even a whisper, but it made all the hairs on Lance's arms stand on end.

He knelt, frozen, barely daring to breathe as she closed her eyes. A line formed between her eyebrows. The corners of her mouth turned down in concentration.

Lance had one hand on the small of her back, the other holding hers. Physical touch.

Every atom of his being longed for more.

Keeley's breath stuttered. "I see it—but I can't—"

Inside Lance, his snow leopard raised its head. The faintest hint of light spilled from under its front paws.

Let it out, Lance urged it. His snow leopard raised its paws, one by one, and the tiny spark of hope floated up in the dark not-space of Lance's soul.

He reached out psychically until he could almost feel the tiniest flicker of heat, and then focused his sight on the outside world again.

Her face was screwed up. Lance didn't need the mate bond to see the frustration and fear rolling off her. Her fingers tightened around his.

Inside him, his snow leopard leaned forward, eyes fixed on the spark of light. Together, they pushed it toward Keeley, forging a new path where the old bond had broken.

Keeley's eyes flew open. Her lips parted, and as Lance's eyes locked with hers, he finally sensed the spark of light inside her soul.

Hope shivered down his spine.

"See? I knew you would find it," he whispered.

"But it's tiny." As she said it, the light inside her flickered. "And—what are we even doing? Why do you want to fix it? Everything's fine, we caught the bad guys... you don't need to be stuck with me anymore."

Lance pulled her closer, until their foreheads were touching. He breathed in her scent.

"I can't lose you, Keeley. Fate has given us another chance to make this work. I know there's no one in the world who could make me as happy as you do." He brushed his thumb across the palm of her hand. "Will you give me a chance to make you happy, too?"

Keeley hesitated. Her eyes darkened, and she licked her lips.

Lance waited. He knew how hard it had been for her to tell him her story—and it broke his heart, how she'd spat the things she'd suffered at him as though she expected him to reject her.

"Before," she began, and paused again. "When you asked me if there was anywhere I've ever felt safe. I could only think of one place. One time."

She drew a ragged breath. Lance was barely able to breathe himself. He felt frozen in time.

He had pushed the spark from his own soul out towards Keeley, and cold was pricking his heart now that it was gone.

The mate-bond was a one-time thing. Either Keeley accepted him now, or...

"The last time I felt safe was the first time we fell asleep together." Keeley's voice was barely a whisper, but her words brushed against Lance's skin like the warm caress of a flame. "Being in your arms..."

Heat shivered across Lance's skin, like he was sitting too close to a fire. He leaned forward.

"Don't let go of that thought."

He nudged the bright spark from his own soul towards the flickering ember in Keeley's heart. She gasped as the two sparks almost touched.

"What now?" Keeley breathed.

The two sparks moved slowly around each other, like dust motes caught in a soft breeze. Dancing, spinning—but still separate.

Lance gritted his teeth. "I'm... not sure. I'm kind of making this up as I go along."

A muscle in his jaw hopped. *Why isn't this working?* Keeley was relying on him. If he failed now—*oh, God.*

She meant so much to him, even without the mate bond. And now that he'd seen under the tough face she showed the world, he knew how vulnerable she was.

If this didn't work, Keeley would blame herself. She would lock the pain away inside and let it eat away at her, like she had with everything else.

That was worse than all the pain he would feel from losing her.

"You're making it up as you go along?" To his surprise, Keeley laughed.

Lance frowned as she lifted her hands to his shoulders, then his face. She smoothed her fingertips down the strong line of his jaw, and Lance opened his eyes to find himself already caught in her gaze.

Keeley's stormy eyes were half-laughing, half-sad. With his eyes open, Lance couldn't track the sparks of the mate bond, but suddenly, it didn't matter.

"We screwed this up together," Keeley said, her voice hitching. "I think we have to fix it together, too."

Before Lance could respond, she kissed him, and it didn't matter that his eyes were open, because the world filled with golden light. And when Lance closed his eyes, sinking into the kiss, his mind's eye found the mate bond blazing into life, joining him to Keeley heart and soul.

When they broke apart at last, he and Keeley were both kneeling on the ground. Keeley's chair was overturned behind her. Lance's hands were around her waist, holding her close against him, and she was cupping his face in both hands.

"Oh," Keeley breathed. "I think... that worked?"

Her smile was tentative. Lance's protective instincts surged; even now, she was still afraid that none of this was real. That she would lose him.

It was time to kill that fear once and for all.

"It worked," he said, and kissed her.

Inside him, Lance's snow leopard rumbled with a happiness deeper than he'd ever known. The mate bond between him and Keeley was shining and new, like the first sunrise after a night of storms.

"Let's get you home," Lance murmured to his mate.

CHAPTER 27

KEELEY

Keeley tumbled out of the car the moment Lance opened the door for her. She half-stumbled, half-threw herself into his arms, laughter bubbling out of her.

Lance kissed her long enough that if it wasn't for his arms around her she really would have fallen down. Then he raised his head, and the expression on his face made her legs go liquid.

"You know what I've just realized?" he asked her, his eyes dancing. "This is the first time I've brought you home."

The low rumble of his voice sent delicious shivers up Keeley's spine. "It's not like I haven't seen your place before."

"Hmm." *Oh, God. More shivers.* "Teleporting in while I was passed out from a gunshot wound wasn't exactly the most romantic introduction. This time, I'd like to—"

He interrupted himself with a kiss that made Keeley's knees go weak and left her with no doubts about what he wanted to do.

"I thought this was supposed to be a quick stop?" she murmured. "Grabbing overnight bags before we get on the helicopter?"

They'd left Maggie under the safe eyes of Parker, Yelich, and a half-dozen watchful meerkat shifters. She'd been cheerfully smearing gold ink over her sibling eggs, none the worse for wear for her latest adventure. Lance had murmured something about him and Keeley needing to pick up their toothbrushes from his apartment while Harley got the chopper ready, and...

... and *every single other adult in the room* had given them a Look that said they knew *exactly* what they were actually heading home for.

Well, fuck it. Lance was the best thing to ever happen to her, and she didn't care who knew how much she loved him.

Lance chuckled and began kissing her neck. Keeley let her head fall back.

"Just—a quick—hey!" she giggled as he caught her dress in his teeth and began to pull it over her shoulder.

"I'm sure we could be very efficient about it," Lance rumbled. His eyes flashed as he looked up at her, his breath hot against her skin. "But I don't want to be. I want to take my time."

"Hngh." Keeley groaned and tried again. "Take your time, huh? Is that code for ripping my clothes off in the parking lot?"

Lance's eyes narrowed. "Hmm," he said, straightening. With an expression of extreme solemnity on his face undermined only by his sparkling eyes, he offered her his arm.

Keeley took it, feeling like she was walking on clouds. Lance walked her formally to the elevator.

She managed to wait until the doors closed before the urge to kiss him became too strong to resist. Lance pressed the button for his floor, and the moment his attention was distracted, Keeley struck.

Lance murmured in surprise as she dragged his head down. His lips were soft, and his surprise melted away as she slipped her tongue between his lips, replaced by urgent passion.

"Oh, God," he muttered when they finally broke apart. "That's really not fair."

Keeley stepped back, smirking. Lance was hard up against the elevator wall. His pupils were blown wide with desire, the cool green of his eyes a thin circle around pools of red-hot darkness.

"What are you going to do about it?" she challenged him.

Behind her, the elevator bell dinged. Keeley thought about taking another step back, dropping her hands from his shoulders and slipping out the door, but her heart thudded *no.*

She leaned forward instead, trailing her fingertips up his chest. Now that she'd let herself really feel how much she wanted him—needed him, desired him, *loved* him—she couldn't stop touching him.

Not even to tease him.

Lance's eyes were hooded as he gazed down at her. "I'm going to do what I should have done the moment I met you. Take you home, and begin our life together."

His eyes flared silver, and this time, Keeley was the one taken by surprise as he swept her up in his arms.

"Hey!" she squealed as Lance strode out of the elevator. "What are you—?"

Lance crossed the corridor to the door to his apartment in a few long strides.

"Just what I said. This is what I should have done all along." He unlocked the apartment door without putting Keeley down. "Welcome home."

Our home, she thought.

Lance's eyes flicked up to meet hers, as though she'd spoken aloud and not kept her happy thoughts locked up in her own heart. He smiled gently, and a rush of affection buffeted against her.

Oh. Of course. The mate-bond. She must have sent her feelings through it, and he'd replied in kind.

"That's right," he said, the barest hint of a purr in his voice. "This is our home, now. Everything that's mine is yours."

The pure flood of love Lance sent her through the mate bond as he stepped over the threshold made her breath catch.

He kissed her, slow and deep, and she thought: *If I could send a feeling by accident...*

She concentrated. It was like using a muscle she hadn't exercised, *ever*. Not just the sending part, but letting her guard down. Letting herself really feel what she was feeling, and not be afraid of her own desires.

Lance's breath stuttered against her lips. "God, Keeley—"

He leaned his forehead against hers, breathing heavily. Keeley kissed him again and whispered, "Did that work?"

"Did it—? Christ." Lance groaned deep in his throat, and Keeley giggled, feeling light-headed.

She'd sent him everything he made her feel. Loving and loved. Protected and protective. The sheer joy of the knowledge that she was no longer on her own. From now on, it wasn't just her against the world. It was her and Lance, together.

Everything that had happened that day felt like part of an intricate lock that she'd worked through stage by stage and had finally clicked open. Instead of a constant ache of stress and worry inside her, there was peace.

Peace... and the desperate urge to screw Lance's brains out.

Keeley knew what she wanted, and she wasn't afraid of wanting it anymore.

Lance had lifted her bridal-style, but as he carried her towards his bedroom she wriggled around in his grasp until she could wrap her legs around his waist. This gave her access to his chest. She pulled his shirt up, unbuttoning it and glorying in the feeling of his strong muscles under her hands.

"God, Keeley." Lance's voice was thick with lust. She looked up from his chest and almost drowned in the liquid heat of his eyes.

Need pierced her. She let herself drop down lower on his hips, until the hard rod of Lance's cock rubbed between her legs.

Lance swore, and the sensation that burned down the mate bond made Keeley's blood catch fire.

They were on the steps up to Lance's room. Keeley dragged Lance's face to hers, kissing him and biting his lips until she thought she would explode. He groaned against her mouth. In a rare moment of un-catlike clumsiness, his foot slipped.

With feline grace, Lance caught them both before they could fall. The edge of a step pressed into Keeley's back. Lance changed his grip to pick her up again, and she pushed back, laying him back against the stairs.

"The bed is literally less than six feet away," Lance reminded her, his eyes dancing.

"I know." Keeley slid one hand between his legs. "I don't think I can wait that long. What about you?"

Lance groaned. His eyes rolled back in his head as Keeley squeezed his cock through his pants.

"You make a convincing argument," he admitted.

Keeley half-stood to mount him and didn't realize he'd dragged her panties down until they tangled around her knees. Giggling, she let herself fall onto him, kicking her underwear the rest of the way off as he removed her dress and bra just as quickly.

Her nipples tightened as they brushed against his chest. Urgency gripped her, need pounding like a drum between her legs.

Lance's belt buckle gave way under her light fingers, then his fly, and then she was wrapping her hands around his cock.

"I want you so much," she gasped as she ran her fingers along his thick length.

Lance's fingertips dug into her hips. His eyes burned with the same need that blazed through Keeley's veins.

Biting her lip, she lowered herself onto him.

Keeley cried out. She wanted him too much to wait for her body to adjust; she pushed down, driving herself deeper and deeper, every movement stoking the fire burning inside her.

Lance grabbed her face in his hands, drawing her down to claim her mouth as he surged beneath her. He was as frenzied as she was.

"I won't lose you again," he said, his voice ragged with desire. "Oh God—Keeley—"

He was losing control. Keeley could hear it in the hitch of his breath, the gravel rasp of his voice. She pressed her body against his. Every touch set off new flames of need inside her.

He needed her. He *wanted* her. And she wanted him. Nothing in her life had ever been as right as this.

Keeley thrust her hips forward one last time. Fireworks went off behind her eyes as she came in an explosion more visceral and intense than ever before. Lance wrapped his arms around her and roared as he spilled himself inside her.

Keeley lay limp on top of Lance for a few breaths. She rested her hand on his chest, feeling his heartbeat become calmer. Lance ran his hands down her back in long, slow strokes.

He chuckled. Keeley raised her head.

"What?"

Lance's gaze was hazy with sated lust, but there was no hiding the pure love in his eyes as he looked at her. "I think I'm going to need to move the bed closer to the front door, if this keeps up," he said.

Keeley crossed her arms on his chest and rested her chin on them. "I don't know. This feels fine to me," she said, and wriggled her hips. Lance's cock was still buried deep inside her, and the movement set off a new surge of warm, lazy desire. "Feels *very* fine."

"Perhaps for you. I'm worried my spine is going to become permanently stair-shaped." He brushed a stray strand of hair off her face. "But for some reason I don't want to move."

Keeley sighed. The lazy desire coiling inside her was sharpening up. But this was only supposed to be a quick stop...

Except. There was one thing they *definitely* needed to do before they headed away again.

"What are you thinking?" Lance murmured. "I can tell it's making you happy."

Keeley smiled.

"I was remembering how attracted to you I was that first morning here," she said, tracing patterns on Lance's collarbone. "I thought I was going crazy. I'd never felt like that about anyone before. So... sudden, and intense."

"That's because—"

Keeley put her finger on Lance's lips and rolled her eyes. "Well, I know that *now*, don't I? But at the time, I thought I was losing it. And... it was all I could do not to follow you into the shower."

"Really?" Lance's smile promised to fulfill all of Keeley's wildest dreams. "I suppose we do need to clean up before we return to the agency."

*

"Um, holy *shit*."

Keeley's legs were still wobbly from the stairs. Her mouth hung open as she looked around Lance's en-suite.

She'd thought his guest-room bathroom was fancy. This was something else.

There was a shower, sure. Or at least that's what Keeley thought it must be. There were at least a dozen shower heads arrayed along the ceiling at the far end of the room. Some of them were above the bath. The *enormous* bath. Everything was warm marble and granite, and Keeley had never seen stone look so cozy and inviting before. Even the long marble block running alongside the bath looked comfy. For a block of rock.

"Okay, I *definitely* should have snuck in here with you the other day. What was I thinking?"

Lance swept her hair off her shoulder and kissed the back of her neck. "At a guess, something along the lines of 'Who is this freak who can turn into a giant cat, why am I playing mommy to a baby dragon, and who just tried to kill us all?'"

"Watch it, or I'll start to think you really can read my mind." Keeley leaned back against Lance's chest. "I can't believe it was only three days ago."

"Shifter relationships tend to move quickly." Lance nuzzled the top of her head. "Are you okay with that? This is your home too, now, but if you'd prefer to take things at a more human speed..."

"No." Keeley's certainty surprised her. She turned to face him. "I spent the last ten years hating myself for who I thought I was. Now..."

She bit her lip, but the faith and love in Lance's eyes gave her the strength to go on. To say out loud words that a day ago she wouldn't have even dared to say inside her own mind.

"I have ten years of life to catch up on. And I don't want to waste a minute of it without you."

Relief flashed in Lance's eyes. Keeley knew he would have given her all the space she needed, no matter how much it hurt him. Well, frankly, she'd had enough of his self-sacrifice the moment he put himself between her and a bullet.

Lance's hands slipped down her sides. "Let me show you what you're not missing out on, then."

He drew her over to the shower and adjusted the controls until they were both drenched under a waterfall-like cascade of hot water. Keeley hadn't thought she could possibly be more relaxed, until Lance directed her to lie down on the raised marble block beside the bath.

"It's warm!" she exclaimed.

"My snow leopard likes the heat," Lance explained. "And it's good for relaxing after a long day. Not as good as a sun-heated rock by a mountain pool... but close enough."

"Mmm." Keeley lay down on her front. Warmth seeped up from the stone, easing her muscles as hot water pattered down from above. "Are you going to lie down, too?"

"Not yet." Lance's voice moved away.

Keeley closed her eyes, letting herself sink into the heat. This was luxury beyond anything she'd ever imagined. She was warm, and satiated, and safe with her mate. Things couldn't get better.

Lance came back and sat next to her. She heard him handling something and then felt the brush of a soapy loofah on her back.

Things had just gotten better.

"What's this?" she murmured, her voice blurring with pleasure.

Lance coughed softly. "I told you, we're doing this properly. You're my mate." He lowered his mouth to her ear, so close she could feel the tickle of his breath. "I'm grooming you."

He hesitated, and she could imagine his eyebrows drawing together. "Of course, if you don't want me to…"

Keeley reached out and grabbed the nearest part of him she could reach, which turned out to be his knee. "I want everything about you," she said firmly.

She stretched luxuriously across the marble as Lance washed her. He started at her shoulders and moved down, gently soaping every inch of her and scrubbing in soft, slow circles with the loofah.

Keeley's breathing slowed.

It wasn't just a shower—this was intimate, a slow, careful worshiping of her body that left her head spinning with wonder.

Her skin was tingling by the time he set down the loofah. And then he started using his hands.

"Is this good?" he asked, digging his fingertips into the knotted muscles around her shoulder blades.

"Yes," Keeley breathed. The heat from the marble suffused her entire body, but now it was joined by a new warmth from inside her. Not a blazing fire this time, but a liquid, languid heat.

Lance continued his massage, his gentle fingers finding every ache and knot in her body. He turned her over and she lay on her back, gazing up at him while he made long strokes up her thighs.

"Lance..." Even her voice sounded liquid. Keeley couldn't remember ever being so relaxed.

Because she'd never felt as safe as this before. Not with anyone.

He made her happy. He made her feel *safe* to be happy. She wanted him to be happy, too. He had to know how much she cared for him. All of him. Everything that he was.

"Lance, I want to groom you, too."

Lance's hand stopped. Keeley sat up.

"Please?"

Lance made a strange, strangled noise in the back of his throat. Keeley swept her legs around and took his hand.

"I'm going to take that as a yes," she decided, and the sudden delighted light in his eyes assured her she'd made the right choice.

Keeley gently pushed Lance down onto the warm marble, then grabbed a fresh loofah and began to soap him up.

Lance had groomed her in worshipful silence. Keeley didn't find herself able to do the same.

"Your back!" she exclaimed as Lance rolled onto his front. "You're all bruised!"

"Only bruised?" Lance remarked under his breath.

Keeley ran her hand across the marks that mottled his dark skin. "I thought you weren't hurt at the warehouse," she accused him.

"Not badly."

"You should have said something when we were on the staircase."

"I was distracted."

Keeley hissed in her breath as she carefully scrubbed at Lance's back, but he was right; it was only bruises, no broken skin. Still. "Don't scare me like that. It's only a few days since you got shot."

"Mmm."

"If I'm going to be living with you, you need to start telling me when you're hurt *before* I get your shirt off."

Lance's back had been going up and down as he breathed; now it stopped. In one fluid movement he sat up and swung around, grabbing Keeley's hand. His eyes blazed silver and green at the same time.

"I will," he said, his voice rough.

Keeley's heart melted. Lance had lost control on the staircase, the same as she had, but this was a different loss of control. The way he looked now, the snow leopard staring out at her at the same time as his human half, was more vulnerable than she had ever seen him.

"If this is going to work," she began, and regretted it immediately as worry flashed across Lance's face. "No, I mean, it *is* going to work, but it has to be more than just incredible sex and you looking after me. I know I'm the more broken one out of the two of us, but you have to let me look after you, too."

A smile fluttered tentatively at the corners of her lips. "I don't have a lot of experience looking after someone else, but that's one of the things I've got to catch up on, right?"

Lance's expression relaxed. "Deal."

"Good." Keeley put her hand in the middle of his chest. "Now, lie back down. I haven't finished grooming you yet."

Lance made a happy rumbling noise as he settled back down on the warm marble. Keeley frowned, and then laughed silently to herself.

Is he purring? Actually purring?

Oh, my God.

She finished washing him, as slowly and carefully as he had groomed her, and then laid the loofah aside. The shower was still cascading over their heads, sluicing off Keeley's shoulders and the edges of the marble.

She leaned over Lance, spreading her fingers across his pecs. Her body made a shelter from the rain-like shower, and he smiled up at her.

"Now I've looked after you, and you've looked after me," he said, his voice curling around Keeley's heart. "What was the third thing you said, about what we need to make this work?"

Keeley laughed. "Seems like you remember. Why don't you remind me?"

This time, their lovemaking was slow, as gentle and intimate as the shared grooming had been. Lance kissed her from her neck down between her breasts to her upper thighs, his lips teasingly soft and never touching her most sensitive spots.

The bath had filled while they washed. Lance slipped off the marble bench and gently pulled Keeley into the water after him. Keeley's breath was already hitching with pleasure. As they both sank into the water, she thought it would only take one touch for her to unravel entirely.

The new scar on Lance's chest gleamed as the water hit it. Keeley covered it with her hand, and then took her hand away and kissed it.

She met Lance's eyes, and he picked up her hand and kissed the fine scars on her fingers and the slight grazes from the holding cell.

Life has hurt both of us, his gaze seemed to say. *But we're together now. Stronger. I won't let you get hurt again.*

And I won't let you get hurt, Keeley thought.

She wrapped her legs around Lance, her movements slow and almost dreamy in the warm water. When he entered her, every nerve in her body lit up with the sensation of pure pleasure.

Lance groaned into her shoulder as he filled her, slow and deep and perfect, and Keeley cried out. Her fingertips bit into Lance's shoulders as she came, holding him close against her until the crash of pleasure faded into perfect, peaceful joy.

Afterwards, Keeley rested her head on Lance's shoulder. The golden light inside her was fixed now, and she knew nothing would destroy it again. She and Lance were bonded for good.

He was hers. And she was his. And if he looked after her, and she looked after him, it would all work out.

Especially if the sex stayed that incredible.

EPILOGUE

LANCE

"No! Maggie, *no*! Leave the pilot alone!"

Lance chuckled as Maggie finally paid attention to Keeley's exasperated tone. The tiny dragon swiveled her head around on her long neck, an injured 'Who, me?' expression on her face.

Keeley sighed. "Don't give me that look, baby. I'm not the one trying to blind our pilot as he flies us a million miles above the ground." She tapped Maggie on the tip of her snout. "Some of us need this helicopter to stay in the air, okay? We don't all have wings."

She flicked a grin at Lance, and his heart turned over.

"Ready to meet your first full-grown dragon?" he asked out loud.

Keeley grimaced. "Sure. I'll just hide behind Maggie if he gets too scary." She wrestled the baby dragon into her lap and re-secured the makeshift dragon-seatbelt around her.

Lance sighed quietly and rubbed his forehead. He gave it ten minutes, max, before Maggie got tired of being cuddled and broke out of the restraints again.

Don't sweat it. Harley's psychic voice was all grin. *I've flown with a half-dozen of my nieces and nephews in the back. I can handle one miniature dragon.*

Even with her wings over your eyes?

In the pilot's seat, Harley shrugged. *I've been looking for a new handicap. Might mention it at the next race meet.*

Lance sat back in his seat, grinning. A nudge from his snow leopard made him reflect that, yes, a few days ago Harley's comment might have made him groan. Maybe he was a little less uptight now.

He glanced at Keeley again. *I wonder why that might be.*

The unsteady feeling that had plagued him since they first discovered the scale shields was gone, too. Lance no longer felt as though he was walking on the edge of a crumbling cliff, afraid that every next step might be the one to plunge him into the abyss.

Again, no surprises why. Keeley's presence—her bravery, her protectiveness, hell, the way she gritted her teeth when she was angry—everything about her grounded him.

The world still held its mysteries. There was still crime in the world, shifter as well as human. Briers had been dealt with, but Lance wasn't convinced that he was the final piece in the puzzle. Something was still missing.

But it didn't frighten him anymore. Even if his next steps did send him tumbling into the unknown, he wouldn't be alone—because, as Keeley put it, he was no longer being a dumbass who thought he had to deal with everything on his own.

He had his gorgeous mate by his side. Loyal friends who he trusted. They'd been there all along, he'd just been too boneheaded to realize he could rely on them. Grant and Irina, Mathis and Chloe. He'd been a fool to leave them out of the loop about his investigations.

Julian, too. He'd kept the dragon shifter separate to protect him... on Briers' recommendation. No more. Julian Rouse had more reason than most of them to smoke out the last traces of whoever was involved with the attack on his family.

And Frankie. Lance straightened his shoulders. Frankie Delacourt, his old friend who he'd lost before he even knew any of this was going on. She was another victim of the criminals' web of lies. She deserved better than the self-imposed exile that was her current existence.

He'd bring them all together. And together, they'd deal with the situation once and for all.

His comm crackled, and Chloe's voice burst into his headphone. "Hey, helicopter! Found you!"

Lance laughed and un-muted his mic. "You mean we caught up with you," he said.

Keeley leaned over Lance to look out the window. "I didn't realize this was a race," she muttered.

"Did someone say race?" Harley called from the front of the helicopter.

This time, Lance did groan. But—he had to give himself credit—he laughed, too.

The helicopter swung around, heading for distant mountains. Nestled in a small town in the foothills was the safehouse where Julian Rouse had been living for the last six months. Alone, except for his guards.

Well, he wasn't going to be alone anymore. Soon he'd have his niece with him—and two more eggs, which were probably as ready to hatch as Maggie had been.

Keeley wrapped her fingers around his. "Hey," she said, bending her head towards him even though thanks to the helicopter's engine noise, they were speaking through the headsets. "How big is this safehouse, anyway?"

"Two stories, a yard. Why?"

Keeley nodded to where the two dragon eggs were safely stowed behind them. "They're going to come out dragon-shaped too, aren't they?"

"Ah." Lance thought about this.

He glanced at Maggie, who stared innocently back. One of the reasons the makeshift seatbelt was so unsuccessful was that the tiny dragon was rapidly becoming less tiny. Eating twice her body weight in fish and red meat for every meal was having results.

We're going to need a bigger safehouse, Lance thought, looking sideways at Maggie.

And if her behaviour here in the chopper was anything to go by, she was ready to start flying. At less than a week old. With two more dragonlings on the way...

A bigger safehouse. In a more remote location. A very remote location.

"I'll sort it out," he said automatically, and Keeley elbowed him with a grin on her face. "Sorry. *We'll* sort it out."

The mountains rose up in front of them, and Lance's heart lifted as he glimpsed snow in their highest peaks.

Maybe he didn't have all the answers. But he had something better. A mate who loved him, and friends he could trust with his life.

"We should arrive in time for dinner," he broadcast to the rest of the helicopter and the others driving on the road below. "And after that—who wants to help me save the world?"

The resounding cheer from everyone on his comms was so loud he had to tear his headset off before his snow leopard came out and ripped it off for him. He kissed Keeley's hand, staring into her laughing eyes as the helicopter headed for the mountains.

Who knew? Maybe, once Maggie was settled with her uncle, they might even have time for a mountain vacation.

MAGGIE

Maggie liked the helicopter. It was fast, and went high, and the *fwoom-fwoom-fwoom* of its spinny wings was so loud it made her entire body rumble.

Best of all, under the hot makes-things-go smell and the familiar smells of Keeley and Lance and the new but also friendly smell of the other man, it had *gold* in it.

Maggie climbed up Keeley's front and peered over her shoulder to where her hoard was. It was still there. Good.

But the box was too small to put the helicopter in.

Bad.

Maggie chirped sadly to herself, then nibbled on her gold chain to make herself feel better. Above her head, Keeley and Lance and the cat man were talking. It was too much work to listen to their voices through the *fwoom-fwoom-fwoom*, so Maggie snuggled herself down in Keeley's lap and listened to their feelings instead.

The other cat-man was full of *fly-fast-fly-fast* feelings. Maggie liked him immediately. Lance and Keeley were mostly soft fluffy feelings, especially when they looked at each other.

But there was something else, too. They weren't all fluffy *all* the time, which was good, because that would be very boring.

Keeley was a little bit scared of being up high and going fast. That made sense. She didn't have another being inside her who she could send out to be tougher. All she had was her human body. Maggie shivered. Being a human was *terrible*. Poor Keeley. No wonder she was scared.

Maggie draped a bit of her necklace over Keeley's hand to make her feel better.

Just a little bit of it, though. It was her necklace, after all.

Lance was different. He was excited, with sharp edges. And his excitement reached out in front of them, up where the ground came even bigger than buildings.

Maggie stretched her neck out. What was Lance so excited about out there? Her wings fluttered, and Keeley made an *oh-no* noise and held onto her more tightly. Maggie didn't mind. She didn't actually *need* to flap her wings to sniff over by the mountains. She just liked doing it. Having wings was *the best.*

She didn't need to actually sniff either, but she did, anyway, poking her snout this way and that while she stretched out her mind to see what Lance was so excited about.

When she found it, she shrieked and flew up to the helicopter's ceiling.

Keeley and Lance were both making *oh-no* noises now, but Maggie ignored them. She dug her claws into a bit of soft stuff in the ceiling and trilled excitedly.

There was *another dragon.*

A *big* dragon.

He was too far away for Maggie to talk to him, but that didn't matter. She already knew the shape of his mind. He'd been around... before. When she was still in her egg.

He'd been sad then. And he was sad now, too, which made Maggie's claws itchy.

But they were going to see him. Maggie perked up.

She knew he'd feel better when he saw her. *Everyone* felt better when they saw her. And then they gave her things! She'd be able to show the big dragon *all* of the things in her hoard. Like the bottles. And the scarf. And her necklace and her watch and the sparkly paper, and Keeley and Lance.

Maggie snuggled down in Keeley's lap, matching her chirrups to Keeley's human heartbeat. Keeley and Lance were absolutely the best bits of her hoard. Even better than the necklace. They gave her food, and cuddles, and also they carried the rest of her hoard around. The *best.*

She couldn't wait to show them off to the big dragon. He would be *so* jealous.

Printed in Great Britain
by Amazon